SEAL OF PROTECTION COLLECTION 2

PROTECTING SUMMER / PROTECTING CHEYENNE / PROTECTING JESSYKA/PROTECTING JULIE

SUSAN STOKER

Cover Design by Chris Mackey, AURA Design Group
Manufactured in the United States

PROTECTING SUMMER

SEAL OF PROTECTION, BOOK 4

Sam "Mozart" Reed's life changed the day his little sister was found abused and murdered when he was fifteen. He's spent the past nineteen years looking for the serial killer who took his sister from him and ruined his family. Using his connections, and SEAL training, Mozart believes he's finally tracked the killer to the town of Big Bear, California.

Summer Pack is working in a crappy motel up at Big Bear Lake until she can find something better, more meaningful, more real. Living in an unhealthy situation, she meets a man who is everything she's ever dreamed about and who helps her see that there are some people in the world who will actually do what they say they will.

But somewhere in Big Bear a killer is waiting to strike again. Watching for the perfect victim.

**Protecting Summer is the 4th book in the SEAL of Protection Series. It can be read as a stand-alone, but it's recommended you read the books in order to get maximum enjoyment out of the series.

CHAPTER 1

Sam "Mozart" Reed fingered his scarred cheek as he drove his old battered truck toward Big Bear Lake. He'd only told his friend and Navy SEAL teammate, Cookie, where he was going. It wasn't as if he was keeping it a secret from the rest of the team, but he'd been on so many of these "leads" in the past, he'd learned to keep them close to his chest in case it turned out to be nothing.

The good part about being on such a close-knit team was that Mozart knew if he asked for help, all five of his friends would drop whatever it was they were doing to come and assist him. Hell, they probably already had a very good idea of where he was.

And this could very well be a wild-goose-chase, just as most of the other leads Mozart had recently followed up on, but he couldn't blow it off. He'd spend every spare minute he had on any lead, no matter how crazy, because it might, just might, lead him to Ben Hurst.

Mozart had been fifteen years old when his little sister, Avery, was kidnapped. His entire neighborhood in their small town in California had acted quickly and search parties were set up. It'd been an excruciating long seventeen days. Every day had been full of searches and television appearances. His parents had begged and pleaded with whomever had taken Avery to bring her back.

In the end, it'd been a couple hiking in the woods two hundred miles away that found Avery's body. They'd been on a scavenger hunt and had almost tripped over her remains, naked and dumped in the dense forest as if she was trash.

Mozart would never forget the day his parents had heard the news. He'd never seen his dad cry before, but that day he'd bawled. His little baby girl had been violated and murdered. It wasn't something a fifteen-year-old boy could ever forget. His parents were never the same after that and divorced, as many parents of missing and murdered children did, because of the strain. Mozart's dad had passed away a few years later and his mom remarried a man with a ton of money. He didn't see her much anymore, she was too busy gallivanting around the world, trying to forget she ever had a daughter, and definitely not caring her only son was still alive.

The cops had never found the person who'd killed his sister. They were pretty sure they knew who'd done it though. A drifter named Ben Hurst had been traced to their area at the same time Avery had been nabbed. Hurst was a survivalist-type guy who was just as comfortable living off the land as he was living in the middle of a big city. He was big, about six feet tall and weighed about two hundred and fifty pounds. It would've been easy for him to overpower Avery, hell, any child. Hurst was a nasty man who'd spent time in jail for molesting children and for assaulting several different people, and showed no signs of rehabilitation after each of his stints behind bars. It wasn't a stretch to believe Hurst had seen Avery walking home from school and snatched her right off the street. The problem was, the cops couldn't prove it.

Hurst never cooperated with the investigation, of course, and as the years went by, other cases took precedence for the police department. Mozart would never stop searching, however. He'd taken one look at the face on the booking photo he'd seen and memorized it. Mozart vowed to avenge Avery one way or another and he'd made it his goal in life to catch Ben Hurst and make him pay.

Mozart had joined the Navy right out of high school with the specific goal of becoming a Navy SEAL. All his life he'd watched movies and TV shows about the SEALs. They were the best of the best, and the toughest men he'd ever seen. Mozart knew that was what he needed to become if he was going to catch Hurst and make him pay for what he'd done to his baby sister.

His dad might not be alive to see justice served, and Mozart had no idea if his mom would even care anymore, but he couldn't let it go. Mozart had stood next to his sister's tiny little coffin and swore to her that he'd never rest until her killer was behind bars or dead. Even as a teenager, Mozart hadn't backed away from the thought of being the one to kill whomever had murdered Avery. He'd spent the past nineteen years trying to fulfill that promise. It was hard-wired into him now. Nothing and no one would prevent him from following through.

Mozart thought back to the last Christmas he had with his little sister. Avery had been so excited. She'd woken him up way too early and they'd gone downstairs and sat in front of the Christmas tree, presents piled up around it. She'd insisted on "sorting" the presents, even though Mozart had warned her their mom would be pissed.

Mom *had* been mad, but Mozart talked her down and he'd watched with pleasure as Avery exclaimed over her presents. She was the type of kid who appreciated every single thing she'd been given. The cheesy stuffed bear that Mozart had given her had received the same praise as a cheap bracelet set given to her by their neighbor. Mozart had loved Avery with every fiber of his being. She was innocent and precious. Losing her had nearly killed him. He'd barely graduated from high school; his grades had fallen drastically after her death. Life had no meaning, until he'd graduated from BUD/S and made it his mission in life to find Ben Hurst.

Mozart would use his leave to follow up on any lead he'd get to try to track Hurst down. Tex, their computer hacker friend in Virginia, had been monitoring the internet and his computer network for any mention of the man. It was pure chance that Hurst had possibly been seen in Big Bear Lake in California. Big Bear wasn't that far from Riverton, down by San Diego, and Mozart had a week of leave coming to him. They'd been on some intense missions recently. Not to mention, Caroline and Wolf had just gotten married and were on their honeymoon. Commander Hurt had given the whole team the week off, and they'd all been thrilled. Some *real* time off, with no chance of being called in for a mission at a moment's notice. Mozart knew, however, that if the CO knew exactly what he was doing on his time off, he most likely wouldn't be thrilled, so Mozart had kept his mission of revenge to himself.

Mozart thought about his SEAL team buddies as he continued his drive up to Big Bear. He smiled when he thought about Wolf and Ice. Ice, also known as Caroline, was a tough as nails chemist who'd almost single-handedly foiled a terrorist attack on the plane that he, Wolf, and Abe had been traveling in. If it hadn't been for her, they all would've been dead. That alone made her precious to Mozart.

Mozart was pleased as he could be that Wolf had finally stepped up to the plate and had asked Caroline to marry him. The wedding had gone as wrong as a wedding could go when the limo the men were traveling in to the church was sideswiped by a car that had run a red light. Caroline never faltered though. After hearing that Cookie had been hurt, she, Fiona, and Alabama showed up at the hospital in all their wedding frippery. After making sure Cookie was going to be all right, and the rest of the team was as well, Caroline revealed that she'd offered the pastor a sizeable donation if she'd come to the hospital to marry her and Wolf.

And that's what they'd done. Wolf and Ice stood by Cookie's hospital bed, surrounded by their friends and pledged to love each other for the rest of their lives. Mozart would never admit it, even if tortured, but it was one of the most beautiful things he'd ever seen. Ice was a hell of a woman, and he was thrilled Wolf had found someone to complete him.

Mozart didn't think he'd ever settle down with one woman though. He was the flirt of the team. Mozart couldn't remember most of the women's names he'd hooked up with over the years. Time and time again he'd gone home with some woman from a bar, then left as soon as they'd had sex. That was all it was to him. Sex. Mozart never bothered to "date" a woman, he didn't need to.

Unfortunately, the terrorists that kidnapped Caroline in Virginia carved up Mozart's face pretty good. Knowing it made him sound like an asshole, but not caring, Mozart figured if a woman didn't want to have sex with him because of his face, he frankly didn't care. At least five more women were behind that one that would love to suck him off or spend a night in his bed. Being a SEAL was good for his sex life, nasty facial scars or not. His scars didn't bother Mozart. He'd been through a lot worse in his life; scars on his face were the least of his worries. Losing his sister to a psychopath was bad. Scars on his face? He didn't care.

Mozart was aware women found him good-looking. When he was younger he'd taken advantage of that, but now it was what it was. He was muscular, as was everyone on his team. He had dark hair that was just a shade too long to be considered appropriate for the military. A woman once told him he had high cheekbones and dark eyes that seemed to be able to look right into a woman's soul and pull out her deepest desires. It was all bullshit to Mozart, but since his looks helped him get laid, he'd cultivated it.

Now, with his once rugged face split by three deep scars on the right side, he had to rely more on his personality to find a woman who would sleep with him. Mozart knew on some level Ice felt guilty about what had happened to his face. He'd told her every time she brought it up that it hadn't been her fault, and at last, she'd stopped apologizing to him. Mozart was honest when he told Ice he was okay with his face, because he was. He was old enough now, thirty-four, to know he'd escaped death too many times to take life for granted.

He was tall, about six four, and he generally towered over most people. That, coupled with his dark intense look, had been good for intimidating bad guys and for making women feel small and cherished, even if it was only for a night. And it was *always* only for a night.

Thinking back to his team, Mozart recalled how Abe had been the next team member to find a woman after Wolf claimed Ice. Abe and Alabama had been together for a while now. Abe had almost screwed it up with her though. Alabama tried to project a tough image, but Mozart, and Abe, had seen right through it. She was currently taking classes at the local community college to see what it was she wanted to do with her life, but for now, she and Abe were disgustingly happy.

Cookie and Fiona were also pretty darn happy, but for Fiona it'd been a long hard road. They'd all met Fiona in Mexico where they'd saved her from a sex-slave ring. She'd been violated and the kidnappers had hooked her on some serious drugs. The women in Mozart's teammates' lives certainly had the market on strength. They'd all been through some horrific things, but somehow, with the help of their SEAL men, and some professional help, had come through all right.

Mozart smiled, thinking about how close all the women were. When the team was called away on a mission they all spent time together supporting each other. Nothing made their men feel better than to know their women had a support system while they were off fighting for their country. Mozart might pretend to be annoyed at the guys for being so attached to their women, but if he was honest, deep down, a part of him was jealous.

Mozart had always looked out for others. He'd always been the guy people called when they needed help. He was the flirt, the laid back good-time guy. The guy to take home for a night then left in search of another conquest. Mozart had never known what it was to be wanted for who you were, not for what you could do for someone, or what job you had.

Mozart shook his head in disgust. Whatever. In the end, it didn't matter. He just had to get up to the lake and see if he could find the person that may or may not be Hurst. Once he found him, and either killed him or turned him over to the authorities, he'd see what he could do about possibly getting a long-term girlfriend. Being around Ice, Alabama, and Fiona had made Mozart see, for the first time, that having someone to love might not be the horrible thing he'd always thought it was. Of course, he'd have to find someone as perfect as his teammates' women, and that would be a pretty tough task.

Mozart pulled into the parking lot of *Big Bear Lake Cabins* and cut off his ignition. Looking at the place, he could only shake his head. He'd made the reservation online. It was cheap and looked clean enough on the few pictures that had been showcased on the travel site. In reality, it was pretty run down and the cabins looked like they'd fall down with one hard storm.

There were twelve separate small buildings, each within about five feet of each other. Some had small porches and others just had an overhang over the door. The paint was peeling off most of the buildings, and Mozart could see that most of the roofs on the buildings needed some sort of repair.

Mozart noticed a maid's cart in front of one of the cabins on the far side. He had the mean thought that the maid was probably as run-down as the cabins themselves, but dismissed even thinking about the person that cleaned the crappy motel for a living. There was a small building with a sign that read "Office" off to his right, and next to that what looked like an outhouse. The only reason Mozart knew it wasn't a restroom was because of the sign on the door that announced it was for storage.

Mozart absently fingered the scar on the right side of his face again, he'd noticed he'd started doing that when he was deep in thought, and turned his mind to what his first steps were in trying to track Hurst down. Mozart didn't care where he slept; he'd certainly slept in worse conditions on most of the team's missions. Mozart would have moved on and found a different place, but justified staying because he just needed a place to keep his stuff and to sleep each night. If it was clean, it was only a bonus.

Mozart exited his truck and headed toward the office. It was time to hunt down a child-molesting killer.

CHAPTER 2

Summer, kneeling by the cleaning cart, stood up slowly and heard her knees creak in protest. She ignored the sound, grabbed a stack of towels, and headed into the little cabin she was currently cleaning. The job was monotonous and boring as hell, but it was a job and it allowed her the freedom to just...be. She'd needed it after the hellacious year she'd had. Cleaning hotel rooms wasn't what she'd envisioned for her life, but for now, she didn't want to be anywhere else. It was easy and comfortable and she could be anonymous. She couldn't handle anything else right now.

Summer thought back on her life. She used to *be* somebody. She had her Master's Degree in Human Resources and worked at a Fortune 500 company in Phoenix, Arizona. She was married and had a good salary, lived in a nice house, and had a perfect life. That life came crumbling down like a house of cards and Summer still wasn't sure how it happened. She'd come home from work one day and her husband was gone. Just gone. All his stuff in the house moved out. There was a note on the kitchen counter that explained he wasn't happy and had met another woman. He didn't want to hurt Summer, but he didn't love her anymore and he thought their life was a sham. Summer had been blindsided. Sure, she knew there wasn't much passion in their relationship, but they were comfortable. Maybe that was the problem. They were too comfortable. Summer signed the divorce papers without contesting them when they'd arrived in the mail later that year. There was no point in protesting.

It wasn't too long after she'd been officially divorced, that she learned her company was downsizing and she lost her job. She'd tried to find another position, with no luck. It seemed as if no one wanted to hire a thirty-six year old woman with only HR experience. They wanted to hire new graduates with no master's degree so they could pay them less than her experience and education would warrant. Summer soon couldn't pay her mortgage and lost the house.

Summer knew she was an introvert. Sure, she could socialize with anyone, but she had a hard time making lifelong friends. All her life she'd met people, but not one took the extra effort to keep in touch once she moved away. Not high school friends, not college friends, not friends from work. Summer wasn't sure what it was about her that made people not want to form close attachments that would survive a long-distance relationship. Losing her job was no different. All of her coworkers were very sympathetic and made all sorts of offers to get together for lunch and nights out, but not one of them followed through. Summer was used to it.

She made friends easily enough, but they weren't the kind of friends Summer saw on television and read about in books. They weren't life-long friends who she could call up for a girls-night-out or crash at one of their houses temporarily.

One day she'd had enough. She'd been living in a crappy apartment where she didn't feel safe and didn't have any job prospects on the horizon. Summer packed up what was important to her, and just left. She drove her piece of crap car until it too died on her. She used the last of her money to get a bus ticket to the little town of Big Bear in the mountains of California.

Summer had seen the little motel called *Big Bear Lake Cabins* one day, and miraculously there was a "Help Wanted" sign in the office window. The owner wasn't very friendly, but apparently, he was desperate, because he told her she had the job.

So here she was. No car. No money. All of her belongings fit into one suitcase. She was pathetic, but she was also free. No mortgage, no expectations. She had nothing, she was nobody. And for now it was heaven.

When she'd arrived with her suitcase in hand, Henry, the owner of the cabins, had been blunt with her.

"I don't have any open cabins you can live in, but if you really need a place to stay, you can sleep in the building next to the office."

"The storage building?" Summer had asked incredulously, looking askance at the tiny building that looked like it could hold a maid's cart, and little else.

"Yup. There's no kitchen or bathroom, but there's a small shower and toilet in the back of the office that you can use."

Summer had taken a deep breath and almost told Henry where he could shove his pathetic motel and his not-so-generous housing offer, but she bit her lip and meekly nodded. She really didn't have a choice.

When Summer opened the storage building she saw that it did have a small sink, she was vastly relieved to know there was at least some running water in her new "home." The sink was used mostly to fill the mop bucket, but it didn't matter. Water was water. The building had no heat or no air conditioning, which in the summer months wasn't a huge deal because it rarely got sweltering hot up in the mountains. Winter would be a bit dicier, but Summer figured she'd worry about that when the time came. Maybe by then she'd have earned enough money to move into a real apartment and it'd be a moot point. The little storage shack wasn't very sturdy, but Summer knew that beggars couldn't be choosers.

Her bed was a cot up against the wall. Henry had dug the thing out of some closet somewhere when she'd asked where she was supposed to sleep. It was missing one foot so it sat lop-sided and swayed precariously when she sat or lay down on it. Luckily, it was one of the back feet that was gone, so her head wasn't hanging lower than her feet all night.

Mops, brooms, and shelves that held various cleaning implements and liquids surrounded Summer. It smelled like ammonia and other funky cleaning supplies, but she was thankful for it. She supposed some people would look at her and at her life and turn up their nose or even feel sorry or pity for her, but after living a so-called "perfect" life, and still being miserable, at least now Summer only had to rely on herself. It was liberating.

The only issue had with her new life was that she was always hungry. She wasn't making enough money to be able to buy huge meals, and besides that, she had nowhere to put anything. She had no refrigerator and no stove to cook anything. Henry grudgingly provided breakfast for her, of course subtracting it from her already meager pay, but Summer was on her own for lunch and dinner.

Henry had explained why he served a continental breakfast to the people staying at the motel. "I sure as hell don't want to, it's wasted money if you ask me, but because of all those fancy-ass hotels and things now, people expect it. They're cheapskates and want more and more for less and less money," he'd complained to her.

Summer had just shook her head. She didn't dare say aloud what she was thinking, namely that Henry himself was the cheapskate.

"Now I have to go shopping every damn week and buy fruit and shit. It's expensive and I hate it. I get granola bars and cereal as well. The guests usually don't stay and chat, they just grab the free breakfast I provide for them and head out to the slopes or to the lake." Henry finally got to the heart of the matter, at least what was important to Summer. "I suppose it'd be okay if you grabbed something each morning as well, but don't go crazy. If I catch you taking more than you can eat and taking advantage of me, I'll change my mind."

"Thank you, Henry. That's very generous of you. I'll just take something small each morning. I won't take advantage."

Henry had just grunted and said in a low voice, "Hope it stays that way."

Even though Summer had promised to only take something small, she usually managed to grab an extra piece of fruit or bread at breakfast that she could snack on during the day. Dinner was usually out of the question. Summer couldn't afford to actually pay to eat at any of the nearby lodges, and she had no transportation, or money, to eat at any of the fast food restaurants in town. So, after cleaning all the cabins, Summer either took a hike around the nearby lake, or she went back to her little cubby hole and tried to ignore her rumbling stomach.

Luckily, it hadn't been too cold, or hadn't been so far, but the warm weather was coming to a close. It was getting colder in the mountains. Henry had told Summer she could keep her job over the winter, but he warned her that she'd make even less money than she did now. They weren't as busy in the winter and he couldn't afford to pay her the full salary he was paying her now. Summer knew it was absurd. He wasn't paying her very much as it was, but she agreed anyway. She figured it'd be a place to stay over the winter if she needed it, and if she felt like leaving, she would. Nothing was tying her here.

For the most part, Summer was satisfied. She was just tired. Tired of merely existing, but she didn't know what to do. This was it for her. This was her life. Yes, she had a master's degree, but it hadn't helped keep her marriage intact, and hadn't helped her keep her job. So be it.

Summer turned away from her cart with an armful of clean towels and turned, without looking, toward the door to the cabin. She bounced off a hard chest and would have fallen if the man she'd just plowed into hadn't grabbed her elbows and steadied her. Summer looked up and gulped. She was looking at the best looking man she'd ever seen in her life. No lie. The best looking *and* scariest looking. The man was huge. At least a head taller than her five-eight. His arms were big. His hands were big. But the scariest thing about him, was the look on his face. He had a five o'clock shadow that didn't hide the scars that covered the right side of his face. The scars pulled at his mouth and made it look like he was grimacing at her. His hair was dark and a little wild around his head. He was dressed head to toe in black. Each thing, taken separately, wouldn't have worried her, but when Summer took in all of it at once, it was intimidating and actually scared her. But when the man didn't actually do or say anything, just stood there, looking down at her with an incomprehensible look on his face, she got a little pissed. After a few seconds, when he *still* didn't say anything, just continued to keep hold of her elbows and stare down at her, Summer knew she had to do something.

"Uh, sorry, sir," she stammered out. Summer would've backed away from him if she could, but he was still holding on to her elbows where he'd grabbed her to steady her.

Summer expected him to apologize back, or at least respond verbally to her words, but he merely held on to her for a beat more, then let go and took a step back. He nodded at her, then stepped around her and headed toward another cabin that was nearby.

Summer watched him go. She wished she could've heard his voice. She bet it was low and rumbly. His butt was tight and....shit. What was she thinking? Summer whipped around and headed into the cabin she was cleaning. He wasn't for her. No one was anymore. It wasn't easy, but she put the big man out of her head and went back to the monotonous job of straightening up the cabin. If her thoughts strayed back to the man and his delectable ass every now and then, she figured no one would blame her. He was a fine specimen of the male species.

Mozart walked into his cabin and chuckled under his breath at the maid's actions. She'd startled him as she ran right into him as he'd walked past her, but luckily he hadn't knocked her over. He didn't think he'd been walking quietly, and had thought for sure she knew he was there, but obviously he'd been wrong.

Mozart had been surprised at how well the woman fit in his arms. If he'd pulled her into him, her head would've fit right in the crook of his shoulder. Mozart couldn't tell what kind of hair she had, as it was pulled back into a severe looking knot at the back of her head. Her hair seemed to be a mixture of light colors, but he could also tell she wasn't young. Mozart was surprised to see that she wasn't a college kid earning money while taking classes, but she also wasn't elderly, working because she was bored. If he had to guess, Mozart would say she was probably around his age. Mid-thirties most likely. The *Big Bear Lake Cabins* was the last place he'd have expected to find someone like her.

She was attractive. Mozart admitted it, but didn't like it. He was busy. But she smelled clean, she had laugh lines at the sides of her eyes, of course she'd probably call them crow's feet. The complete package looked good.

Mozart laughed at himself. His thoughts were ridiculous. He'd had seen the look of interest in the woman's eyes, before it'd turned to consternation. He'd seen it time and time again. Women would first think he was good looking, and then once they'd see his scars, they'd be turned off. But now that Mozart thought about it a bit more, the maid hadn't seemed turned off, just startled. Once she'd had a chance to gain her equilibrium, she'd looked him straight in the eyes and even looked as if she was getting pissed at him. It'd been a long time since a woman had bothered to show him any *real* emotion. Mozart was too used to women being fake and doing anything they could to get him into bed. And that pissed look on her face was kinda cute.

Mozart shook his head and tried to put the maid out of his mind. He had to focus on Hurst and on where he might be. As good looking as she'd been, he didn't have time for a roll in the hay. He thought about the information Tex had sent to him before he'd left Riverton. The man believed to be Hurst, was apparently camping out somewhere in the forest surrounding the lake. There'd been reports of petty thefts of small items that Mozart would bet his life had been Hurst. He pulled out the terrain maps of Big Bear and tried to narrow down where the son-of-a-bitch could be holed up. The forest surrounding the area was huge, but Mozart would find him if he was there. Mozart had been trained by the best. Hurst would have no idea he was being stalked until it was too late.

CHAPTER 3

Summer tried not to be aware of the big man in cabin three, but it was hard not to notice him. Every time she cleaned his cabin, she was aware of how good he smelled. She only allowed herself to bury her face into one of his towels once, and felt ashamed after she did it. He didn't know she existed, and that was par for the course. First of all, she was a damn maid, and second he was beautiful, even with his scars. She wasn't. She wasn't putting herself down; she just knew what she was and what she wasn't. In her former life she knew she needed to lose some weight, but that was hard to do with a desk job. But now that she really only ate one meal a day, she'd lost a lot of weight, too much. She figured it wasn't helping her looks any.

The man was extremely neat. All of his clothes were put away in the drawers in the room. His shoes were lined up next to the wall. Any towels that he used were hung up over the shower rod. He'd made his bed every morning. There really wasn't much to clean in his room, but Summer always vacuumed and changed his towels out. She saw him twice at the office. The first time he was eating breakfast and was dressed to go hiking. She saw his backpack against a wall and he was wearing boots, a flannel shirt, and khakis. The second time she saw him was when she knocked on his door to clean his room and he opened the door, nodded at her, and left. She wondered what he was doing here and how long he was staying.

Most of the time when people came to the cabins they were there for a long weekend and almost always with someone else. It was unusual for someone to stay as long as this man had and be by himself. Summer had noticed he went hiking most days, so maybe he just needed the time off of work and wanted to be alone. She mentally shrugged. She had another long day ahead of her. She ignored her rumbling tummy and forced herself to close and lock the cabin door and head for the next room.

* * *

MOZART BLEW OUT A BREATH. It'd been a long day, but a productive one. He'd found evidence that a person had been in the mountains nearby. Mozart figured it had to be Hurst. He was careful not to disturb the primitive campsite so Hurst wouldn't know someone was onto him. This was as close as Mozart had ever been to catching him. He considered calling Cookie and seeing if he'd come up and help him, but decided against it. Cookie and Fiona were still working through Fiona's issues, and he didn't want to disturb them when they had a rare week off.

Mozart eased himself into the chair on the front porch of the small office building. He'd noticed that each night the people staying in the cabins generally gathered around the office to chat. He wasn't one to crave the attention of others, but he wasn't ready to go back into his cabin yet. The evening was beautiful.

Mozart held a beer loosely in his hand and watched as a SUV pulled into the parking lot. Three women climbed out. They were the kind of beautiful that came from hours spent at the spa and in the bathroom before stepping a foot outside. They were all wearing skin-tight dresses and high heels. They looked like they'd just spent a night out celebrating something. The cabins weren't exactly the Hilton, so Mozart wondered briefly what had brought them there. Being a man, he also admired the way their dresses showed off their bodies. It'd been a while since he'd been with a woman, and these were some fine looking specimens.

"Oh shit, Cindy," the woman in the blue dress said a bit too loud, "he looked hot from the car, but you can have him, I wouldn't be able to look at him while fucking him." All three of the women giggled drunkenly.

"But you could always have him do you doggy style then you wouldn't have to look at his face," the woman, who was apparently Cindy, said. "I'd do him, look at his muscles!"

Unfortunately, Mozart had gotten used to those kinds of harsh comments from women since he'd been injured. He chugged the rest of his beer and shifted to stand up and leave. He didn't care what they thought, but he wasn't going to sit there and listen to it. The shallow comments from the women didn't deserve a response.

Before he could move, he felt a hand slide over his chest from behind in a tender caress and felt a woman lean over him.

Before Mozart could say or do anything, he heard a husky voice say from right behind his right ear, loudly enough for the three bitches to hear, "Come on, honey, those three orgasms you gave me before dinner weren't enough. I can't believe you can stay hard that long. Before you call for the jet can we have one more round in the shower?" The mystery woman nuzzled the side of his face, his scarred side, as she playfully ran both hands up and down his chest.

Mozart's body locked tight. His teeth clenched and he could feel his jaw clench. Even not knowing exactly what the woman's game was, her tone, and words, made his cock stand up and take notice. He brought up a hand up and wrapped it around one of her forearms as she continued to caress him with her other hand. Mozart didn't know if he wanted to wrench it away from his body, or force it down lower into his lap. He did neither, just held on as her hand moved up and down his chest and he watched as the bitches' mouths dropped open and they stared as they walked past him on their way into the small office.

The woman who had her hands all over him apparently wasn't quite done. As the trio passed by, he felt her head turn toward them as she sneered in their direction, proving she knew they could hear her the entire time, "He's *all* man, and he's *all* mine. If you're stupid enough to not be able to look past his face, then you don't deserve to have a man spend all night pleasuring you. And *believe* me, he knows how to use every *inch* of his body for *my* satisfaction."

The woman then stood up, grabbed Mozart's hand, and pulled him off the porch toward his small cabin. Mozart didn't even look back to see what the other women did, he only had eyes for the dynamo who was towing him to his room.

Summer's heart was beating at what felt like a million miles an hour. What this man must think of her. But she couldn't stand there and let those bitches say those things about him. While Summer didn't really know him, she felt as if she has a small connection to him. After all, she'd been cleaning his room and handling his linens… linens that had been up against his body. No one deserved to be treated that way.

Summer had no idea what happened to him and how he'd gotten the scars on his face, but she had a feeling he was probably military of some sort. He had that look about him and maybe he had some sort of PTSD and that's why he went on the long walks in the woods. Those women being rude to him felt wrong on so many levels. He was always polite to the employees at the motel. He was neat. He was quiet. But if Summer had stopped to actually think about what she was about to do, she never would've done it. She was pretty embarrassed, but she had to keep going until the women were gone.

When they reached the door to his cabin, Summer stopped, took a deep breath, and turned around to face the big man who was still holding her hand.

Mozart watched as the woman in front of him took a deep breath before she turned around. He grinned. Now that he could see her face, he knew exactly who she was. She was the maid for the cabins. He waited for her to speak.

Summer tugged at her hand, but the man wouldn't let it go. She looked up at him a bit nervously and watched a crooked smile take over his face, and all the words in her brain fizzled away.

"Do you think I could know the name of the woman to whom I gave three orgasms and apparently pleasured all night long?

Summer nearly choked. God, she was embarrassed. "I'm so sorry about that back there," she quickly said. "Those women were such bitches; I just wanted them to be jealous as hell and to realize what they were missing. I didn't mean to embarrass you or anything. I really am sorry." She trailed off when she saw he was still smiling.

"Your name?" Mozart demanded in a low voice.

"What?"

"What is your name?" he repeated easily, seemingly not upset in the least.

"Summer," she told him without thinking. Shit, maybe she shouldn't be blurting things out without thinking first. It had always gotten her into embarrassing situations in the past, seemed like she hadn't learned her lesson after all these years.

"Summer," Mozart told her, "I'm not embarrassed. I think that was one of the nicest things anyone has done for me in a long time. Don't be sorry. Shit, don't be sorry. I'll never forget the looks on their faces when you said jet. I just wish I had it all on film to show my buddies."

Summer chuckled a little, still feeling embarrassed and very aware he still held her hand. It felt awkward, but at the same time it didn't. "I don't know what came over me. I'm not usually like that. Anyway, well, I'll be going..." she trailed off and attempted to once more remove her hand from his, but he still wasn't letting go. She looked up at the man questioningly again.

"Come to dinner with me." It wasn't exactly a question; it came out more like a statement.

"What?" Summer couldn't have heard him right. She knew she sounded silly asking him to repeat everything, but she was confused.

"Come to dinner with me, Summer," the man said again.

"But you don't even know me," Summer said in bewilderment.

Mozart laughed a little. "But Summer, I gave you three orgasms before dinner."

Summer blushed and looked down. "Jesus, I'm never going to live that down am I?"

Seeing Summer's embarrassment, Mozart got serious. He put his finger under her chin and lifted it so she was looking at him, noticing she didn't fight him. "You're too easy to tease, but please, let me take you to dinner to thank you. You didn't have to step in there for me. It honestly doesn't bother me what people say about me, but you didn't know that. You went out on a limb for me. Please let me treat you to dinner in return."

Summer looked at the man again. He was serious, she could tell. She *was* hungry. It didn't matter where they went, she hadn't had a good meal in forever. She tried one more time to dissuade him.

"But I don't even know your name."

He finally let go of her hand, only to immediately hold it out to her again. "I'm Mozart, nice to meet you, Summer."

"Mozart? Can you play piano?"

Mozart laughed and continued to stand there with his hand out. He'd stand there all night if he had to. He'd forgotten how fun it was to pursue a woman. He hadn't had to do it very often and it made him feel ten feet tall. If Summer knew how cute she looked and how her actions only made him more determined, he knew she'd be mortified. "Go out to dinner with me and I'll tell you how I got my nickname."

Summer smiled and shook her head in exasperation. He was crazy, but she was finding she liked his brand of crazy. Finally, she put her hand in his and shook it. "I think that's blackmail, but you have a deal."

Apparently, they were going to dinner.

* * *

MOZART ENDED up taking Summer to a local steak place. It wasn't fancy, but the food was good. He'd already been there a few times and had enjoyed everything he'd eaten. Maybe even more important, the restaurant was quiet and Mozart felt like he could get to know Summer a bit better. The hostess had sat them at a booth in the back and asked what they wanted to drink when they'd arrived.

"Get whatever you want," Mozart told her when he saw her hesitate.

"I guess I'll just take a water." At Mozart's raised eyebrows, Summer hurried to defend her selection. "It's fine. I'm hungry and don't want to fill up on soda or alcohol."

Mozart nodded and ordered a beer. After the waitress had left to collect their drinks, he turned back toward Summer and just watched her as she read over the menu.

"You aren't going to even look at the menu?" she asked Mozart nervously.

"Nah, I've been here a couple of times and know what I want."

The way he said he knew what he wanted made Summer nervous for some reason, but she didn't call him on it. Maybe it was how he looked into her eyes as he'd said it instead of looking at the menu itself. Summer looked down at the menu as if it held the answer to world peace and tried to ignore Mozart's presence and steely gaze.

When the waitress came back with their drinks, Mozart ordered an appetizer of cactus dip with chips and a Rib Eye steak with potatoes and spinach. Summer asked for a sirloin, medium rare, with a baked potato and fire-roasted green beans.

After the waitress left, Mozart leaned his elbows on the table and asked, "So, how long have you worked at the motel?" As a get-to-know-you question, it was pretty tame, but Summer was embarrassed anyway. She'd grown very adept at handing out vague answers that sounded like she answered the question, but never really gave much away.

"I've been there for a while now. It's okay, but not something I want to do the rest of my life. You've been there a while, what are you doing up here in Big Bear?"

"Oh you know, just enjoying some time off and hiking in the woods."

Summer nodded, she'd figured that was what he was doing there. Something didn't ring true about his answer, but it wasn't as if she could call him on it when she was trying to avoid answering any deep questions about herself either.

"Have you seen any animals when you've been out there?"

"Yeah, quite a few deer, but no bears."

Summer laughed. "I guess that's good then."

Mozart just nodded and watched the woman across from him. She never stayed still. She fiddled with her water glass, then put her napkin in her lap. Mozart could see her leg moving up and down with nervous energy. On the outside, Summer seemed composed and calm, but he could tell she was nervous just being with him. He liked it. Not that she was nervous, but that she *cared* enough to be nervous.

"Tell me something about yourself, Summer."

"Oh, um..." she shrugged, "there's not much to tell really."

"Bullshit. Come on, give me something here." Mozart really wanted to know this woman. Not the superficial crap, but something about her he wouldn't find out unless he pushed.

"My middle name is James." At his look of incredulity, Summer put her head in her hand in embarrassment.

"James?" When she didn't immediately explain, Mozart leaned across the table and smoothed a piece of hair behind her ear. "Summer James. I like it."

Summer raised her head and looked at the gorgeous man across from her. She honestly had no idea what had possessed her to come to his defense back at the motel. He was obviously a man who could take care of himself. He didn't need her jumping in trying to make those women jealous. Mozart was easily the buffest man she'd ever seen. He probably could've flattened them with only a look. But she just *had* to be a hero. She sighed, knowing since she'd blurted out her embarrassing middle name she'd have to explain.

"My parents wanted a boy. They convinced themselves I *was* a boy. They didn't want the doctor to tell them the gender of their baby, convinced they already knew because of old wives tales or something. So they had my name all picked out already. James. It was a disappointment when they found out I was actually a girl. They didn't have time to really think of a good name, so they chose Summer since it was July when I was born. They kept James because they'd become so attached to it."

"Summer is a good name."

Summer whipped her eyes up to Mozart's and looked at him in confusion. That wasn't what she expected him to say.

Mozart expounded on his statement. "You said they didn't have time to think of a good name. I disagree. Summer is a great name. It fits you. Your hair is blonde, you have the bluest eyes I've ever seen, the blue of a beautiful summer day. Your skin is tan…I don't think I've ever met a woman whose name fits her better than Summer fits you."

Oh. My. God. Summer thought she was going to melt into a puddle right there in the booth. Mozart was looking at her in that intense way he had again. Summer felt goose bumps break down her arms. She hadn't been fishing for compliments, but he'd given her a doozy of one. "Uh, thanks," was all she could squeak out. Summer was saved from having to say anything else because the waiter arrived with their food.

Summer ate as slowly as she could, but her steak was so good. It'd been forever since she'd eaten such a good meal. It was if she could actually feel her body soaking in the nutrients from the meal as she ate.

Mozart watched Summer eat. It was obvious she was enjoying the food, but as he paid more attention, she enjoyed it a little too much. They weren't talking a whole lot, which was fine, but Mozart could tell Summer was purposely trying to slow herself down, to not eat too fast. She'd take a bite to eat, then put her fork down against her plate, and rest her hands in her lap as she chewed. It was methodical and purposeful. Mozart pressed his lips together in consternation. He'd been there a time or two in his life. Almost the entire team had been captured during a mission and they'd been half starved. For almost a month after they'd been rescued he'd had to force himself not to gorge himself every time he'd sat down to eat.

His body had told him to eat as fast as he could, but his mind fought and tried to tell him there was plenty of food and he didn't have to hoard it or scarf it down. Mozart hated seeing that same dilemma in Summer's actions. He knew he wouldn't say anything about it though, it would embarrass her, and the last thing he wanted was for her to be embarrassed.

"So, what's your last name Summer James?" Mozart wanted to soak up every scrap of information he could about this fascinating woman.

"Pack."

"Summer James Pack. I like it."

Summer merely shrugged. It wasn't as if he had to approve of her name, although she supposed she was glad he didn't hate it. "So, you told me you'd tell me the story about your nickname if I came to dinner with you."

Mozart put his fork down and pushed his plate back. He leaned toward Summer and put his arms on the table. He was pleased to note she continued to eat as he started his explanation. "I'm a Navy SEAL," he began, satisfied when she merely nodded instead of fawning all over him as many women did after hearing what he did for a living. "It's commonplace for men in the military to be given a nickname. Typically the names are tongue-in-cheek jokes or modifications of a person's name, or even an out-and-out reminder of some dumb-ass thing the person did."

"Which category does Mozart fit into?" Summer asked with a smile on her face.

Laughing Mozart said, "Unfortunately, the last one." He continued with his story, loving the smile that crept across Summer's face. "One night, after we'd made it through Boot Camp, me and a bunch of the other seamen went out and got completely hammered. We'd been working our butts off for a few weeks and we were all young kids. We ended up at a karaoke bar." Mozart paused, enjoying the hell out of the wide smile on Summer's face. When she smiled a real smile, it lit up her whole face.

"Yeah, we thought we were all that and a bag of chips, and apparently I refused to leave the stage after singing three songs. The patrons were noticeably pissed and one guy yelled, 'Hey Mozart, get off the stage and let someone else slaughter a song for a while.' That was it. That's all it took. The name stuck. So my one foray into the land of music ended up marking me for life."

"I'm sure there's a karaoke bar somewhere in Big Bear. We could always find it after dinner."

"Oh, hell no, Sunshine. I'm pretty sure if you heard me sing, your ears would bleed."

Summer put her fork down and sighed. She could probably eat more, but she knew she'd regret it if she stuffed anything else down. Mozart was funny. She'd never have guessed he had such a good sense of humor when she'd first seen him. It just reminded her that everyone had more depth than could be seen on the surface. "So what's your real name?"

"I'll tell you only if you swear you won't use it."

Summer looked taken aback. "What? Why?"

Mozart smiled to take the sting out of his words. He was serious, but he didn't want her to feel as if he was mad or anything. "I have five friends on my SEAL team. We all have nicknames. Three of them have women. For the most part, the girls refuse to use our nicknames. Wolf, Abe, and Cookie don't care, but it's been so long since I've been called anything other than Mozart, it makes me feel as if their women are talking to someone else when they insist on calling me by my given name."

Summer decided to tease him. She didn't really care what she called him, but wanted to give him crap. "What is it? Fred? Winston? Oh no, I have it. Sherman?"

Mozart reached across the table and grabbed her hand and playfully pretended to bend her index finger back in retribution. Summer giggled and tried to pry her hand out of Mozart's grip with no luck.

"No, smartass. It's Sam. Sam Reed."

"Sam." Summer loved the feel of her hand wrapped up in his. He made her feel…safe. "It's so normal."

Mozart let go of her hand reluctantly and sat back and crossed his arms across his chest.

"Normal?"

"Yeah. You don't look like a 'Sam' to me. You look like you'd have some bad ass name."

"Like what?" Mozart was enjoying the hell out of the conversation.

"Um...maybe Jameson...or Chase or Blake." Getting into it, Summer continued, "I know, what about Tucker or Trace?"

"Jesus, Summer. Seriously? I look like a *Jameson*?" Mozart said through his laughter.

"Okay, maybe not, but I'm not sure I can call you Sam either, it's just so...plain."

"Well then, it's a good thing you *don't* have to call me Sam. You promised."

"Actually, I didn't. You assumed." When Mozart opened his mouth to rebut her, Summer reassured him. "Kidding! I'll call you Mozart. No worries."

"Thanks, Sunshine, I appreciate it."

Summer smiled at the big man sitting across from her. Sunshine. Her ex had never called her by any nicknames. He'd always just called her Summer. She didn't realize how much she liked hearing a pet name until Mozart had said it to her...twice.

"Come on, you about ready to go?" Mozart asked, putting his used napkin on the table.

"Yeah, thank you so much for dinner. I appreciate it, even though it wasn't necessary."

"Of course it was. You stood up for me. It doesn't happen much. Usually people go out of their way to steer around me. You waded right in and put yourself between me and those women. Although, it must be said, you shouldn't make a habit of it. You have no idea what someone will do. They could've turned against you, or I could've been a dick about it and dragged you in my room to make you put your money where your mouth was."

"I can read people pretty well; I didn't think that would happen."

"Want to take the leftover rolls back?" Mozart changed the subject, knowing she believed every word she said about him and that she'd probably do the same thing over again. He didn't think she'd ask to take the extra food home, but somehow he knew she both needed and wanted them.

"Sure, if you don't mind." Summer tried to shrug nonchalantly, knowing the bread would be her lunch, and probably dinner, the next day.

When the waiter put the check on the table, Summer made an effort to reach for it so she could pay for her own dinner, not that she really had the money, but she felt like she should at least let Mozart know she wasn't expecting him to pay for her food.

"Seriously?" Mozart asked with a raised eyebrow, reaching out and snagging the bill before Summer could open the folder to look at it.

Summer just looked at Mozart and said, "Yeah, You don't know me, there's no reason for you to pay for my meal."

Mozart pulled out his credit card and put it in the folder and laid it on the end of the table. "I asked you to dinner, I'll pay. Believe me, I appreciate you even offering. I can't remember a time when a woman even made the suggestion, but it still irritates me that you'd think for a second I'd *let* you pay."

Summer just looked at Mozart for a second, then, not knowing what else to say, she whispered, "Thank you."

"You're welcome. You should always expect a man to pay when he takes you out, Sunshine."

"That's not the way of the world today, Mozart."

"Well, it's the way of *my* world."

Summer could believe it. Mozart was intense in a "take charge, Alpha man" kind of way. She wanted to hate it, but couldn't. She'd never had anyone treat her that way before and it was almost scary how much she enjoyed it. Summer didn't say anything when the waiter returned with the credit card slip and Mozart signed it. He stood up and held out his hand for her as she scooted out of the booth.

Summer took hold of Mozart's hand and he didn't let it go as he walked them out of the restaurant and back to his truck. He waited until she stepped up and into the passenger seat and got settled before closing her door and walking around to the driver's side.

They drove back to the motel in a comfortable silence.

They pulled up in front of his cabin back at the hotel. Mozart watched as Summer got out of the car and self-consciously smoothed her hair over her right ear.

"Thanks for the dinner, Mozart, I appreciate it."

"You're welcome. How are you getting home?"

"Oh, I stay here on the premises."

"You do?" Mozart looked around in confusion. He couldn't see where she might be staying, unless she was living in one of the cabins or if there was a room in the office area, which he hadn't seen when he'd been in there eating breakfast.

"Yeah. Thanks again for tonight...have a good rest of your vacation. Be careful out there hiking. Don't piss off any bears, okay?" Summer smiled nervously up at Mozart, hoping he'd let the matter of where she lived drop.

"I will, Sunshine. Thank *you* for sticking up for me with those bitches tonight."

"I see now you didn't need me to do anything, but seriously, I hope you don't see yourself as flawed in any way. Believe me, you are *not* flawed."

"Are you flirting with me, Summer?" Mozart teased, thrilled at the blush that crossed her face.

"Uh, no, I..."

"I'm teasing you, Sunshine. I don't really think about it anymore and it honestly doesn't bother me when people look at me weirdly because of it. With that being said, anytime you want to throw down with bitches who look at me the wrong way, I won't object."

Summer just shook her head at him and smiled. "Have a good night, Mozart."

"You too, Sunshine." Mozart watched as Summer walked toward the office and disappeared around the side of the building. Was she related to the owner? Where exactly was her home? What made someone as pretty and intelligent as Summer seemed to be, work at a run-down motel such as this one? Mozart had a ton of questions, and not enough answers.

Mozart went into his cabin. He had enough on his plate at the moment, too much to really even have the time to think about

Summer's mysteries, but he couldn't help it. She'd gone out on a limb tonight for him. He'd been honest with her when he'd told her that he couldn't remember the last time someone did something like that for him without wanting anything in return, other than his teammates of course.

He lay back on his bed and thought back over the night. There were little things bothering him about Summer. She didn't wear a coat, even though it was a bit chilly. She wasn't wearing any makeup, not that was a big deal, but most women he knew would at least make an attempt to put something on. Summer's clothes seemed a bit big on her, like they were the wrong size. She tried not to show it, but she was hungry tonight.

Mozart also hadn't seen her around at night before, so how had she just popped up tonight? And while he hadn't really *seen* her before tonight, her actions had now put her in his crosshairs. There was something about her. Something that made him want to be the man that would give her three orgasms and would pleasure her all night long. Mozart knew it was crazy. He wasn't the type of man to pursue women; at least he wasn't before his accident. He hadn't had to. They always came to him. But he was curious about *this* woman, and wanted to solve the mystery. He *would* solve it before he left.

If Summer knew what Mozart was thinking, she probably would've found a way to leave that night. But she figured it was the last time she'd see him. He was most likely leaving soon and that would be that. Summer was forgettable. She knew it. It'd been proven to her time and time again in her life. He'd be no different. She *knew* it.

She snuggled down into the sleeping bag she'd bought at the thrift store. It smelled slightly musty, as if it'd been sitting in the store for a while, but it was warm, and at the moment that was all that mattered to her. She fell asleep thinking about Mozart and ended up dreaming about him as well.

CHAPTER 4

The next day Mozart was up early, as was his usual, and he was on the trail before the sun rose. If he wanted to catch Hurst, he knew he had to sneak up on him unaware. The man was lethal and Mozart couldn't underestimate him.

As he hiked silently, Mozart thought more about Summer. He was heading back to Riverton tomorrow. His leave was up, and as much as he hated to leave his search for Hurst, he was equally loathe to leave before really getting to know Summer. It was crazy, he'd lived the past nineteen years wanting revenge for Avery and nothing had ever stood in the way of that. But one encounter with Summer was all it took for his interest to be piqued and for his intense drive for revenge to slip a bit.

She was an enigma. She was well spoken and smart, yet she was working at a run-down motel as a maid. Mozart shook his head. He didn't understand, but he would. He wanted to talk to her before he left. He wanted to reassure her he'd be back. Mozart knew he'd be coming back to continue trailing Hurst, but if he was honest with himself, he knew it was also because of Summer.

Mozart wanted to introduce Summer to his friends, and *that* was unusual for him. He kept the line straight and narrow between his real life and his sex life. The women he slept with knew the score, they knew their encounter was one night. Sometimes he kept one around for longer than that, but he told them upfront that he wasn't relationship material and if they wanted to stick around and sleep with him for a while, he wouldn't be opposed, but he always told them they'd never get more than that out of him.

Surprisingly, as much of an asshole it made him sound, most women were okay with the arrangement.

Mozart shook his head and brought himself back to his present surroundings. He had a feeling his days of sleeping around were gone, all because of a too-thin mysterious woman who had no idea how beautiful she was. He'd track her down when he got back to the motel and let her know his plans. His plans to come back and get to know her better.

* * *

MOZART STEPPED out of his truck into the dirt parking area at the motel. He sighed and ran his hand through his hair. He'd found Hurst's campsite for a second time, but the man had cleared out before Mozart could get there. Mozart had been so close, but once again, he was too late. He'd already called Tex and updated him on what he'd found. Tex had reassured him he was on his trail and they'd get him, but Mozart just shook his head and didn't agree or disagree.

He'd heard it time after time and he was no closer today than the cops were all those years ago. Mozart wondered for the first time in his life if the bastard would ever be caught. He thought again about his teammates and their women. Could he one day be as happy as they were? Would finding the woman meant to be his, somehow make up for not avenging Avery? Mozart had no idea, and he wouldn't figure it out today, but it was something to think about. For the first time, he allowed himself to admit that he was tired. Mozart's life was passing him by, but he didn't really know how to stop it.

Mozart looked around at the cabins to see if he could find Summer. He saw her cleaning cart parked at the last cabin. He started toward where he hoped she was. Mozart hadn't seen anyone else cleaning the rooms since he'd been there, so hopefully the cart meant Summer was inside the room.

He wished he didn't smell so...funky...but he'd been hiking all day and couldn't help it. Since he'd checked out that morning, he wouldn't have a chance to shower before he headed back down to Riverton.

Mozart peered into the cabin and smiled at what he saw. Summer was making the bed and swearing at it under her breath.

"Stupid sheets. Why do the beds have to be so damn heavy? Jesus, most normal people wouldn't demand their entire sheet set be cleaned every day, but *this* guy? Of *course* he did. Dammit!"

"Need some help?" Mozart said laughing.

Summer spun around with a screech, and seeing Mozart, scolded him with a hand on her chest, "God, you scared me! Don't *do* that!"

Mozart smiled. When was the last time any woman had spoken to him in that tone of voice? He couldn't say. Most women, and men for that matter, were scared of him. The women would always simper and do whatever they thought he wanted them to do while men typically just went out of their way to avoid him.

"Sorry, Sunshine. Didn't mean to frighten you," Mozart told Summer softly, still leaning nonchalantly against the doorjamb. "I just wanted to let you know I checked out today and will be gone for a while."

When Summer simply looked at him he continued, "I didn't want leave without letting you know."

Mozart was nonplused when she responded with, "I knew you checked out when I went to clean your room and saw everything gone. Why would you come back to tell me?"

Summer was honestly confused. Usually when people checked out, she never saw them again. Every now and then someone would come back because they left something in their room and they'd seek her out to see if she'd found it, but never had someone come back to tell her they were leaving. "You left your keycard in the room, you don't have to turn those in. It's not a big deal." When Mozart didn't respond,

Summer continued hesitantly, "Is that why you came back? To give me your keycard?"

Mozart took a step into the room and came toward Summer. He noticed she took a small step back, but then caught herself and stood her ground.

"I came back because I like you. Because I wanted to see you again. Because I think I want to be the one who gives you three orgasms before dinner for real. That's why." Without waiting for Summer's response, Mozart took two steps until he was right up against her and reached a hand out to tag her behind her neck. He pulled her close so their lips were almost touching.

"I couldn't leave without tasting you at least once." Mozart's lips were over Summer's before she could say anything. Summer was mid-gasp so it made it easy for him to slide his tongue over her lips and into her mouth.

Summer groaned, her situation and where they were fell away instantly. She couldn't think about anything other than how good Mozart felt. Her arms came up hesitantly and flattened on his chest before she ran them up and clasped them together behind his neck.

Mozart was about to pull back when he felt Summer's tongue come out and shyly slide over his. There was no way he could stop now. He groaned and pulled her closer to him. Mozart tightened his hand around her neck and pressed his other hand into the small of her back, forcing her into his body until they were touching from head to hips. He deepened the kiss and felt Summer shift against him restlessly.

Mozart felt satisfaction curl through him. Summer apparently wanted him as much as he wanted her. He couldn't hide his erection from her, but her squirming told him she was just as turned on as he was. Running his tongue over hers one more time, Mozart slowly pulled back, not letting go of her waist or neck, but separating their mouths.

"I'll be back, Summer. I want you. I want to see where this can lead us, and for once in my life, I'm not talking about a one-night stand."

Summer slowly opened her eyes and looked up at the man whose arms she was engulfed in. She took one hand from behind his neck and put it on his scarred face. She rubbed her thumb over the worst of the scars. She was flattered beyond reason, no, she was thrilled this gorgeous, virile man wanted *her*.

"Okay," she whispered with a shy smile.

Mozart finally removed his hand from her back and took her face in both of his and rested his forehead against hers. "Stay safe until I can get back to you."

Summer just nodded.

Mozart leaned down and took her lips in one last hard kiss before letting her go and backing up. They kept eye contact with each other until he reached the door of the room and disappeared into the parking lot.

Summer sat down hard on the un-made bed. "Holy Hell," she said softly aloud to the empty room, "that man is lethal!"

CHAPTER 5

Summer waited. Mozart said he'd be back. The weather got colder and he didn't return. She didn't know what happened, but she wasn't completely surprised. A part of her wanted to believe Mozart. He'd seemed so sincere, but Summer should've known. All her life people seemed sincere when they'd told her things like, "I'll call you," or, "we'll go out for lunch," but more times than not, they didn't call and they didn't ask her out for lunch. So Summer wasn't entirely surprised, but found herself depressed about Mozart's absence all the same.

She knew it was time to move on anyway. The weather up on the mountain was cold, even for southern California. Many people assumed since it was in California that it'd be warm all year, but in actuality, this area had some of the best skiing in the state in the winter months. Starting in November, Henry had cut her salary in half, which was ridiculous because it wasn't as if she was making that much to begin with, but Summer was pretty much stuck until the spring because she had no transportation and the cold weather made it that much harder to up and leave. Nevertheless, she'd already decided she'd be going.

But for now, today, Summer felt like crap. She knew she was sick, who wouldn't be after living in the kind of situation she was? She wasn't eating enough, and the storage building was freaking freezing. Summer had stuffed paper towels into the cracks trying to keep the cold air out, but it wasn't doing much good. Henry had given her an old space heater and let her run an extension cord from the office into the storage building, but she didn't use it a lot. It didn't seem safe. However, there were times at night when she was just so damn cold that she had no choice.

Summer didn't have any friends in the small town because she was kept busy cleaning the cabins, and even when she wasn't working, it wasn't as if she had transportation to get anywhere to meet people. She was stuck, and it was definitely time to go. As soon as it got warmer and she could save up enough money for a bus ticket, she was getting out of there. What had seemed like such a great idea a few months ago, now just seemed stupid. Summer was an intelligent woman, and if she knew of anyone else in her situation she'd just shake her head at them and call them an idiot.

She lay on her cot and snuggled down deeper into her sleeping bag. She closed her eyes and re-lived the kiss Mozart had given her the day he'd left for the thousandth time. She'd never been so attracted to anyone before in her life. Even her ex-husband had never made her feel like that in all the years they'd been married.

Summer had made good money and they'd been equals in their relationship, almost *too* equal. Summer sighed, remembering how she'd felt when Mozart had hauled her into him and not given her a choice about whether or not she wanted him to kiss her. She wasn't an idiot, she'd read plenty of romance books where the woman was submissive to the man...and she'd scoffed at each one. But now, remembering how she'd felt in Mozart's big arms, she was rethinking her beliefs. Just remembering him telling her to "be safe" as he left her standing in the cabin, was enough to make her insides quiver. No one had ever cared if she was safe before, and it felt good. Too bad he hadn't meant it.

Summer fell asleep once again thinking about the man who'd

turned her nice plain life upside down, and then left without looking back.

* * *

MOZART SAT at the table at *Aces Bar and Grill* with his friends and sighed. He wasn't really in the mood to hang with his teammates, but he'd promised he'd be here, so here he was. Caroline and Wolf had come back from their honeymoon looking relaxed and happy. Fiona and Cookie had also settled into married life. Fiona seemed a lot more relaxed while out in public, so obviously her sessions with the therapist had done her a world of good.

Mozart thoughts turned back to Caroline. He remembered how she'd trusted him to sew up her wound when she'd been injured on the plane that had been taken over by terrorists. Mozart hadn't ever experienced that sort of trust again...until Summer. It wasn't as if he'd had to sew up a knife wound or anything, but she'd taken his hand and let him bring her to dinner. She'd let him kiss the hell out of her, and she'd melted in his arms. Summer wasn't scared of him, and had stood up for him when she hadn't even known who he was.

Mozart gritted his teeth. Fucking hell. He'd told Summer he'd return to Big Bear to see her, and he hadn't been back. He argued with himself over it daily, but he hadn't had the time. No, that was a lie, he hadn't *made* the time. Yes, he and the team had been sent on a few missions since he'd been up to the lake, but that honestly wasn't an excuse. It wasn't that far to drive and Mozart could've honestly made it up there in a few hours on his downtime.

He'd convinced himself that whatever connection they had was all in his head. Mozart had only taken one woman home since he'd met Summer, and it was a complete disaster. All he could think of was Summer and how she'd lit into those women for him. Recently, when he'd caught the woman he'd been about to bring to his bed looking at the scars on his face in disgust, Mozart lost his erection and any desire to get naked with the woman immediately. He'd told her to get out and he'd lain on his bed thinking about what a mess his sex life had become since meeting Summer.

"What the hell has you thinking so hard over here, Mozart?" Benny asked, sitting down next to him with two beers. He handed one to Mozart and took a drink out of the one still in his hand, waiting for his friend to answer.

"You wouldn't believe me if I told you, Benny."

"Try me."

"I met a woman…"

Benny burst into laughter, interrupting Mozart's explanation. "When don't you meet women?" When Mozart didn't say anything Benny looked at him incredulously. "Shit, seriously? You too? I'm gonna be the last one of us left the way you all are falling so hard."

"I didn't say I was gonna marry her, jackass," Mozart mumbled throwing back the beer and almost finishing it off in one gulp.

"Yeah, but you're *you,* Mozart. You're the flirt. You're the one who takes care of the ladies when we're on missions. If you've got one woman on your mind above all the others, you're screwed. You've already tagged and branded her in your mind. You just have to catch up and do something about it."

Mozart put the mostly-empty beer bottle on the table and stared at Benny thoughtfully. Was he right?

"Let me put it this way," Benny continued, unconcerned about the turmoil going on in his friend's head. "When did you see her last?"

"About two months ago."

"And when was the last time you got laid?"

Mozart didn't answer, thinking back. Jesus. Yeah, he'd taken that one woman home, but he hadn't been able to follow through. It'd been about two and a half months since he'd actually had sex.

"About two months, right?" Benny pushed.

"You are one scary guy, Benny," Mozart commented, pushing his chair back and crossing his arms over his chest.

"Look, just because I have this ridiculous nickname doesn't mean I don't see stuff. Mozart, you're my friend. As much as I make fun of the other guys for being tied down to their women, I think it's great.

I'd give anything to be where they are. I see how content and happy they are and I can't help but want that for myself. Stop fighting yourself. If you've found someone who makes you reconsider pulling your dick out for any woman that wants it, I say you need to explore that."

"That was certainly a crude way of putting it, but I get it." Mozart felt the pit in his stomach swell to an almost unbearable size. He lowered his voice and fingered his scarred cheek. "I told her I'd be back, and I haven't been. I hurt her. I know I did."

"Then make it right, Mozart." Benny stated matter-of-factly. "Look at Alabama and Abe. She forgave him for the asshole thing he did to her. If this woman is meant to be yours, she'll forgive you too, but you have to go to her. If you don't give her a chance, you'll never know."

"Jesus, Benny, I feel like you're Doctor Phil or something."

Benny just laughed and slapped Mozart on the back. "Yeah, well, I don't want to hear all the mushy details, just go and talk to her. See if she's feeling half of what you are. If she is, you can see about making it work. If not, you're no worse off than you are now. But at least you can move on if you know."

Mozart nodded. "I'll see if the Commander will give me the weekend. I'll head up to Big Bear and talk to her. "

"Big Bear? Isn't that where you went up to look for Hurst?" All of the team knew about Hurst and Mozart's mission to make him pay for what he'd allegedly done to his sister. Mozart had told them where he'd been during their week off when they'd all gotten back. There were no secrets from the team. "Do you think he's still up there?"

"Yeah, I found evidence of a campsite, but he'd left by the time I had to get back here. Tex has been working on leads and says he's not sure he's left the area, but he doesn't have a lock on him yet. He could be a thousand miles away, or he could be wintering up there at the lake."

Benny's face turned serious as he put his beer on the table next to Mozart's empty one. "If you need us up there to help track him, all you have to do is ask."

"I know, and I appreciate it. I think this time I'll just head up here to see if Summer is still there. I wouldn't blame her if she ditched that crappy motel and left for warmer weather."

"All I'm saying is if you need it, we have your back."

"I appreciate it, Benny, seriously."

They nodded at each other and Mozart stood up to head over to Wolf and Ice to let them know he was headed out. He congratulated both of them once again, and when Caroline stood up to hug him goodbye, Mozart bent her over his arm just to irritate Wolf. Laughing when Wolf snatched Caroline back into his arms as soon as Mozart stood her up, Mozart told them he was on his way out.

"I talked to the Commander and he's thinking we'll be headed out next week," Wolf warned.

"Got it, I'm only going up for the weekend; I'm not tracking…this time. I'll keep you up to date and I should be back on Monday."

"Is everything all right?" Caroline asked with worry in her voice.

Mozart picked up her hand and kissed the back of it. "Everything's fine, Ice. And just because I know you're nosy, I'm going up to see a woman."

Caroline rolled her eyes. "I'm sorry I asked. You aren't satisfied with all the bitches throwing themselves at you down here? You have to drive into the mountains now?"

Mozart simply smiled. He loved how Caroline wasn't afraid to speak her mind around him or the other SEALs. "What fun would that be?" He wasn't about to tell her the real reason he was headed up to Big Bear.

Ice rolled her eyes, as he expected. Mozart gave a chin lift to Wolf and said his goodbyes to the rest of the team and Alabama and Fiona. As he headed out the door, he wondered what kind of reception he'd get from Summer. Lord knew he didn't deserve for her to be glad to see him, Mozart just hoped she would be anyway.

CHAPTER 6

It was late Friday night by the time Mozart arrived at the cabins up in Big Bear. He pulled into the familiar parking lot and noticed only a couple of cabins had lights on in them. The office also had a light shining dimly through the grimy window.

Mozart pulled his jacket around him and zipped it up as he stepped out of his truck. It was cold, the wind was blowing, making it seem at least twenty degrees colder than it actually was. There was no snow on the ground, but it was probably only a matter of time. Once the snow fell, the cabins would most likely become a bit busier because of ski season, but generally people who came up to this area to ski would choose a more well-known and popular hotel to stay at, rather than the run down, locally-owned motel.

Mozart strode up to the office door and tried the door. It opened and a bell tinkled above his head as he entered. The space was empty, but it wasn't too long before someone came out of a room in the back of the small building. Mozart recognized the man as the owner of the motel. He'd chatted with him briefly the last time he'd been up here.

"Hey, I remember you. Need a room?"

Mozart refrained from rolling his eyes at the desperate sounding man. Of course he remembered him. He was big and mean looking and had a huge scar on his face. Mozart wasn't the kind of man that anyone would forget. "Maybe. I'm looking for Summer. She was the maid the last time I was here. Does she still work here?"

Henry looked upset. "Why? What did she do? Did she take something?"

"Jesus, no. Why would you automatically think that?" Mozart was pissed. He didn't really know Summer, but he didn't think there was a chance in hell she was a thief, and he was mad that it was the first thing this guy thought of. After what had happened to Alabama he was hyper-sensitive about people being accused of stealing with no provocation.

"Sorry, man, I just didn't know why else you'd want to know if she was still here."

"*Is* she still here?" Mozart growled with barely concealed impatience, wanting to reach across the scarred counter and shake the man.

"Yeah, she's still here. You want me to get her?" Henry placated, as if he knew Mozart was on the edge of losing his temper.

"No. Just tell me where she is."

Without even thinking that it might not be a good idea to tell a large pissed off stranger where a woman was living, Henry jabbed a thumb toward the building next door. "She stays in the storage building."

Mozart took a step back as if the man had hit him. "What? What building?"

"You know, the little storage building. She gets to stay there as a part of her salary. Free of charge. You know, room and board without the board."

"Are you kidding?"

"Uh…no?"

Mozart just shook his head and turned on his heel toward the door.

"Will you need a room tonight?" Henry called out behind Mozart.

Mozart stopped. He wanted to give this man money like he wanted a hole in the head, but he also wanted to be near Summer. If

Summer was staying on the property, he wanted to as well. He spun back to the short man standing behind the counter. "Yeah, one night. If I'm going to stay another, I'll let you know."

Henry turned to the ancient computer and punched a bunch of buttons. "Credit card?"

Mozart pulled some twenties out of his wallet and threw them down on the counter. "Cash."

"Oh, okay. Uh, I'll put you in number seven, there's no one on either side of you, so it should be quiet." When Mozart didn't say anything Henry looked down and hurriedly swiped the keycard to program it. He held out the paper for Mozart to sign, and sighed in relief as he pocketed the key card and turned to head out of the office. "Breakfast is from seven to nine, winter hours," Henry called as the door shut behind the large man.

Mozart clenched his teeth together and looked to his right as he exited the small office. He took a hard look at the small storage building set back from the office a bit. He'd never really looked at it before, because he had no reason to. Why would he? It was a fucking storage building, not a place where anyone should be living. Mozart didn't like what he saw.

He took in the ramshackle building at a glance. It was probably about a hundred square feet, at most, and had one door with no windows. There was an old fashioned lock on the door. As he walked up to the building, Mozart couldn't believe anyone was actually *living* inside it. The owner had to be wrong.

There were no electricity lines leading into the roof of the shack, but looking closer, Mozart could see an orange extension cord snaking from the office into a crack in the back of the building.

Mozart held on to his temper by the skin of his teeth. There was no damn way this was safe, or even legal. He hoped like hell he wasn't going to find Summer in this hovel, but he was afraid he was going to be disappointed.

* * *

SUMMER SHIVERED inside her sleeping bag. She couldn't get warm. The wind felt like it was whipping through her little building as if she had the door open. She'd given up on the space heater because it had started making such horrible rattling noises she was afraid if she fell asleep with it on, it would burn down the building she was sleeping in.

Her head spun. She'd been dizzy for a while, but tonight it seemed worse. She wasn't sure what was wrong with her, but there wasn't any way to find out either. Henry expected the cabins to be cleaned, and it wasn't as if she could call in sick. She had no money or transportation to get to a doctor anyway.

Summer nearly jumped out of her skin when she heard a brisk knock at the door. No one ever knocked on the door. The guests just assumed it was a simple storage building, and if Henry needed her, he typically just yelled out the back door of the office for her.

"Who is it?" Summer asked tremulously.

"Mozart. Open the door, Summer."

"Oh. My. God," Summer whispered. Shit could he really be here? *Why* was he here? She couldn't see him now. Raising her voice so he'd hear her she asked, "Why, what are you doing here? Do you need something?"

"Yes, I need something, Sunshine. Open the fucking door." Mozart tried not to lose patience with Summer. He could hear the surprise and yes, even a little fear in her voice.

"I don't think..."

"Don't think. Just open the door." Pausing a beat, he tried to tone down his impatience and pleaded with her. "Please? I want to talk to you. I *need* to talk to you."

"Can't it wait until morning?"

"No."

"I'll be right there, we can talk outside." Summer sat up on the cot and unzipped the sleeping bag. Shit, it was freezing. There was no way she was letting Mozart in her little space to talk. She'd go and meet him outside and maybe they could go into the office, or into his truck, or somewhere else to talk. She didn't care where it was, as long as it was warm.

Summer swung her legs out of the warm haven she'd been cocooned in and leaned over to the flashlight sitting on the corner of the sink. She clicked it on and the beam shone upward, illuminating the small space. Summer stood up and stuffed her feet into her sneakers. She still had her clothes and socks on, so she was as ready for this late night visit as she'd ever be. She shuffled over to the door and fumbled with the latch. Summer opened the door and went to step out, but was pushed back by a large body stepping into her space.

Mozart knew Summer wouldn't want him inside. He had no idea how he knew that, but he did. That made him all the more determined to *get* inside. As soon as the door opened a crack, he was there, pulling the door open gently and stepping into Summer's space.

"Step back, Sunshine. I'm coming in."

"Oh, um..." Summer didn't have a chance to say anything else before Mozart was there, inside the little building, making it seem twice as small as it actually was. She watched as his eyes roamed around, taking everything in at a glance, before settling in on her. She shivered, as much at the look in his eyes as with the cold.

Seeing Summer shiver shook Mozart out of his stupor. He immediately unbuttoned his jacket and eased it off his body. He took hold of Summer's shoulders and turned her so her back was to him. "Arm," he told her gruffly. When she held an arm up, he steered it into one sleeve and did the same to the other as she lifted that one too. He wrapped the coat around her and pulled her back into his arms.

She felt even skinnier than when he'd held her in his arms a few short months ago. Summer was shivering lightly and Mozart could feel her swaying where she stood. Mozart wrapped his arms around her a bit more tightly, holding her snugly against him, willing his body heat to sink into her skin.

"I'm sorry, Sunshine." It wasn't what he'd planned to say. Mozart had an entire speech planned about how busy he'd been, how many missions he'd been on and how he'd wanted to come back and see her, but couldn't. But seeing how she was living and the condition she was in, only made him want to kick his own ass. The apology was for so many things, the least of which was for not coming back up the mountain as he'd said he would.

Summer, being Summer, didn't ask why, didn't make him grovel, but simply nodded and said, "Okay."

Mozart turned her around to face him and put one hand on her shoulder and tipped her chin up with the other. "I'm really sorry, Sunshine. I said I'd be back and I wasn't before tonight."

Summer merely shrugged, "It's okay, Mozart. I didn't think you meant it."

Mozart's hands tightened on her. "What do you mean you didn't think I meant it? I said it didn't I?"

"People say stuff all the time. I've found most of the time they don't follow through."

"Well, when *I* say something I follow through. I should've been here before now though. I let you down."

"Mozart…"

Knowing she was going to let him off the hook again, he interrupted her. "No. Tell me you believe me. Tell me you know that when I say something, I do it."

At the stubborn look in her eyes, and her lips pressing together Mozart could only laugh. "Okay, that sounded conceited I know, but I hate having you think that nobody does what they say they will." Mozart wrapped her up in his arms again and picked her up as he sat down gingerly on the rickety cot. He put Summer in his lap and kept his arms locked around her. Without saying anything else he took a second look around the small room.

The space heater sat forlornly in the corner, silent and turned off. The orange extension cord was plugged into it as it snaked under the edge of the boards that made up the wall. There was a sink, but it was old and cracked. There were shelves lining the back and sidewall over the sink, filled with bottles of cleaning materials and cloths of some sort. There was a suitcase sitting against the back wall as well. It was closed, but not zipped.

Mozart closed his eyes and leaned his head against the side of

Summer's. She'd lain her head against his chest and sat on his lap awkwardly with her hands in between them, clutching his jacket around her.

Standing up suddenly with Summer in his arms, he gripped her tightly as she startled. "Shhh, I've got you, Sunshine. Do you need anything for the night?"

"Uh...no?"

At her answer, Mozart took a step to the door and leaned over so Summer could reach it. "Open the door for me, please." Summer did as he asked and Mozart walked out into the cold night with Summer held tight against his chest. He shut the door behind him with a kick of his boot and took long strides toward cabin seven. He dropped Summer's feet to the ground when he got to the door, but didn't let go of her waist. Keeping her body close to his, Mozart took the keycard out of his pocket and slid it into the slot on the door. It clicked and Mozart pushed it open.

Summer didn't say a word as Mozart carried her across the parking lot and opened one of the cabin doors. He put his hand on the small of her back and guided her into the room once he'd opened the door. He kept walking until he got to the small bathroom.

"Take a hot shower, Sunshine. I'll get you something to wear when you're done. Get warm. I'll be back. I'm going to make a short trip into town. Don't open the door to anyone. I mean it. If your boss knocks, ignore him. Take your time in the shower. Got it?"

Summer could only nod at Mozart. She was bemused and a bit in shock. She hadn't expected to see Mozart again, but here he was. She knew he wasn't really *asking* her to do anything, he was telling her. At the moment, she had no issues with his demands though. She felt like crap and was cold down to her bones. A hot shower sounded heavenly.

She watched as Mozart leaned down and brushed his lips over her forehead. "In you go. I'll be right back with something for you to wear. I'll put it right outside the door here. Then I'm going into town."

"Okay, Mozart. Thank you." Summer knew she should be protesting his Alpha tendencies, but she couldn't.

"Don't thank me, Sunshine. This is all on me."

"What is?" Summer was confused. "What are you talking about?"

"Go on, get in the shower. We'll talk when I get back."

"God, you're annoying," Summer huffed, finally showing some backbone, as she tried to pull out of his arms to do as he'd demanded.

Mozart laughed and whispered, "I'm sure I'll annoy you more as we get to know each other, but just remember I always have your best interests in mind."

"Whatever," was all Summer could come up with as a comeback. It was lame, but the shower was calling her name and she really was freezing.

Mozart let go of Summer and watched as she walked into the little bathroom and shut the door behind her. He blew out a breath and put both hands up into his hair and raked his hands over his head. Jesus, all this time she'd been living in a hovel and he'd been making excuses as to why he shouldn't come back up here. Mozart should've thought more about her situation that night when he'd taken her to dinner. All the signs had been there, but he'd ignored them. Some observant Navy SEAL he was. God, he was a fucking idiot.

He was here now and he'd fix this. Mozart would make sure she wasn't hungry or cold again. He wasn't sure she was going to like his solution, but he didn't give a damn. She was *his*, dammit. She was vulnerable, yet spicy at the same time. She wasn't a young naïve woman in her early twenties, she was like him. Seasoned. The combination was intriguing to Mozart. He hadn't thought twice about her being his. She just was. As soon as he'd seen her trying to act as if nothing was out of the ordinary with her living in a shack and telling him she had no expectation for his return, he'd known.

Mozart walked out to his truck and grabbed his bag along with a bottle of soda he'd forgotten to drink on his way up to the lake. He reentered the cabin and remembered to crank up the heat in the room before he did anything else. The overly warm room might make him uncomfortable, but he'd bet Summer would appreciate the added warmth. Mozart smiled at hearing the shower running. He could imagine Summer standing under the spray of water naked as the day she was born. He willed his erection to go down as he pulled a T-shirt out of his bag. Usually he didn't wear any underwear so he didn't have a pair of boxers she could wear, not that they'd have fit her anyway.

He dug some more and came up with a pair of shorts that he usually ran in. He knew they'd be huge on her, but he also didn't want her to feel vulnerable without something covering her lower half. Mozart went over to the bathroom door and eased it open. Steam rolled out the door and he couldn't help but smile again. He knew he'd told Summer he'd leave the clothes outside the door, but he couldn't resist going into the bathroom if his life depended on it.

"Sunshine? I'm leaving a shirt and stuff on the sink. I brought in a soda as well. Drink it. The sugar will do you good." When she didn't immediately answer, he called out, "You okay?"

He heard a muffled shriek and watched as she stuck her head around the shower curtain. She obviously hadn't heard him when he'd opened the door to talk to her.

"Mozart? Get out of here!"

"Okay, I'm going. I just wanted to make sure you were all right before I headed out. There's clothes on the sink, and drink the soda I left for you."

"All right. Just go!"

Summer heard Mozart laugh as he shut the bathroom door. She should've been more upset at him, but she couldn't be. She hadn't been able to take a lazy shower in what seemed like forever, and it felt heavenly. Summer grabbed the cheap little shampoo she'd left in the room earlier that day, and washed her hair twice, using the bubbles from the lather to scrub her skin as best she could. She conditioned her hair and rinsed that out as well.

Then, cranking the knob so the water was even hotter, Summer sat down and let the stream beat on her back as she huddled in the bottom of the tub. She moaned as the water hit her shoulder blades and massaged her muscles.

Not knowing how much time had passed, Summer finally reached behind her and turned off the water, but sat still for a moment or two. The bathroom was completely filled with steam, she could barely see an inch in front of her face. She'd been cold for so long the heat felt heavenly. Finally, she stood up, wobbling from both the heat and hunger, and peered out the shower curtain, making sure she was alone.

Seeing the door was still shut, she pulled back the curtain and reached for one of the towels. It was small and scratchy, but Summer didn't care. Once she was dry, she pulled Mozart's T-shirt over her head and laughed as it fell mid-thigh on her. She tried putting the shorts on, but knew immediately there would be no way they'd work. They were miles too big and she had no way to keep them up. She left them sitting on the counter and prayed Mozart was as much of a gentleman as he'd been so far. Summer didn't want to be completely naked under the shirt, so she pulled her panties back on.

Seeing the soft drink sitting on the counter, her mouth immediately started watering. She wasn't much of a soda drinker, but at that moment, she thought she'd die if she didn't drink it right that second. She twisted the top off, enjoying the hiss of the carbonation as it rushed out of the bottle. Summer tipped it up and guzzled the fizzy drink down. It was slightly warm, but it tasted so good. She finished the bottle and sighed happily. Her sigh was immediately followed by a gigantic burp. She blushed, hoping like hell Mozart wasn't sitting out in the room laughing.

Summer cracked open the bathroom door, watching how the steam rushed out of the bathroom as she pushed it all the way open, and walked into the small motel room. Mozart wasn't back from wherever he'd gone yet, so, avoiding the bed, she wandered over to the easy chair in the corner and pulled her knees up to her chest as she stretched the huge T-shirt over her knees so she was covered from neck to toes.

She knew Mozart had questions and wasn't happy with how he'd found her. Summer hadn't done anything wrong, but knew he'd want to talk to her about it. She just had to figure out how much she was going to tell him. Summer didn't usually blurt out her entire sad life history to just anyone. She wanted to trust Mozart, but she also remembered how much he'd hurt her by promising to be back, and then not showing up until now.

Summer cocked her head to the side as she thought about Mozart. He *had* come back. He'd never said how long it'd be before he returned; only that he would. So technically, he hadn't broken any promises to her. Summer sighed. She'd play it by ear and see what he wanted when he got back. Maybe Mozart just wanted her to be warm for the night. He was a SEAL after all; it was ingrained in him to rescue people. Maybe he wasn't back for anything, other than to fulfill his promise or to go hiking some more.

She hated waiting. Mozart would return soon enough. Lying her head against the side of the chair, she quickly drifted off to sleep, secure in the knowledge that, for the moment at least, she was safe and warm.

CHAPTER 7

Mozart juggled the bags in his hands as he opened the door to his motel room. He'd driven into town to find some food. He knew Summer would never admit it, but she had to be hungry. He hadn't seen any food in the damn storage building she'd been living in, and of course, he remembered how she'd enjoyed the steak when they'd gone out two months ago.

The room was dark, except for the light coming from the open bathroom door. Mozart looked around and found Summer curled up in the chair in the corner of the room. He silently put the bags of food down and went over to where she slept. Mozart kneeled down in front of the chair and put one hand on her knee, still covered by his shirt, and the other on the arm of the chair. He rubbed her knee softly, trying to bring her out of sleep slowly so she wouldn't be scared.

"Summer? Wake up, Sunshine." Mozart grinned as she grunted in her sleep, and turned her face deeper into the side of the chair. "Come on, wake up."

Summer squinted at Mozart, then closed her eyes again. "Do I have to?" she sighed, sounding much whinier than she wanted to.

Mozart grinned. God, she was cute. "No, not really, but I did go and find a twenty four hour grocery store, and I brought back food."

Summer's eyes popped open comically. "Food? What kind of food?"

Mozart ran his hand down the side of her cheek. He wanted to find her actions funny, but he couldn't. Most women he knew would've been perfectly happy to fall back asleep, but he knew first-hand when your body was craving calories, food always came before sleep.

"Sit up and see for yourself, Sunshine."

Summer shifted upward and straightened her knees. The shirt rose up and off her knees, but luckily still covered her adequately. Mozart hadn't moved from her side and his hand was now resting on her bare knee. They stared at each other for a moment.

"Your scar looks better," she said quietly as she brought her hand up and fingered the worst of the scars on his face.

Mozart grunted. "Yeah, Ice insisted on me rubbing some crappy cream on it every night. I keep telling her it doesn't matter, but she won't give it up. I do it just to shut her up."

"Well, it seems like she knows what she's talking about. It really does look better, Mozart." Suddenly thinking he might think it mattered to her, Summer quickly backpedaled. "Not that it looked bad…"

"Shhhh, it's fine." Mozart put his fingers across her lips stopping her from saying anything else that might make her feel she was digging herself into a hole. "I know what you meant. I give Ice crap, but the cream does actually make it feel better." At the look of relief on Summer's face Mozart continued, "Now, come on, get up and see what I got for us. I didn't stop on my way up here, so I got a bit of everything." Summer would never know he was lying about not stopping to eat, but he didn't want her to feel bad about all the stuff he'd bought.

Summer stood up and would have fallen over if Mozart hadn't been there to steady her. "Whoa, take your time. I'm sure the heat of the shower made you woozy. Let me help."

Summer was too embarrassed to say anything else, and if she was honest with herself, she was just too damn hungry to care too much. She let Mozart lead her over to the bed.

"Here, sit, while I go through the bags."

Summer sat and watched Mozart bend over and grab the bags with one hand. He sat sideways next to her on the bed with one knee bent and the other foot propping himself up on the floor. He reached into the bags and pulled out a loaf of bread, a small jar of peanut butter, a six pack of V8 juice, a jar of dill pickles, two cans of corn, green beans, and carrots, two boxes of granola bars, a package of provolone cheese, sliced turkey, a salad in a bag, a small bottle of ranch dressing, and a bag of green apples and oranges.

Mozart looked up sheepishly at all the food scattered around them on the bed. Summer threw back her head and laughed. "Jesus, Mozart, I thought you just went out to get a snack?"

Summer wasn't ready for Mozart to lean over and put his hands next to her hips. He kept coming forward until Summer had no choice but to lean back and put her weight on her hands behind her, or let him run right into her. Mozart had a serious look on his face. She thought he'd laugh with her about the food, but apparently she'd read him wrong.

"You aren't eating enough. You're even thinner than you were when I held you in my arms a couple of months ago. I don't like it. I bought what I thought would last without being refrigerated. Except for the salad and the cheese and turkey, everything will keep in that damn hut you're living in. You need more protein. I don't like that you get dizzy when you stand up, and I certainly don't like that your only bed is a broken cot with a sleeping bag in a building that has holes in it. And I *really* don't like the fact that your only source of heat is a scary looking heater that's this far from burning down the entire structure." Mozart held his thumb and index finger about an inch apart in order to punctuate his last thought, then leaned forward again. "I don't know why I care so much, but I do. I can't explain it any more than I think you can, Sunshine. I made a mistake in not coming for you sooner, but I'm here now, and you can bet I *see* you now. I don't mean to freak you out, but I'm not going anywhere."

Summer could only watch with wide eyes. She *should've* been freaking out at his words. She was an independent woman who could take care of herself, but she wasn't doing a very good job of it lately, and she was tired. She wanted nothing more than to let this man take care of her. If that meant she was weak, so be it. Summer was hungry, tired, and cold. At the moment, Mozart was offering to lighten all three of those burdens. She'd take what she could get and hope for the best. Summer said the only thing she could at the moment. The only thing she was thinking. "Okay."

"Okay?" Mozart looked confused.

"Okay."

A smile slowly came over Mozart's face and he shook his head as he leaned back, allowing her some space. "You're gonna keep me on my toes aren't you, Sunshine?" He didn't give her time to answer. "Now, what do you want to eat?"

Summer sat up looked down at all the food surrounding them. "The salad." She'd eaten so much crap over the last few months and her body was craving the vegetables. "And a can of green beans. Then an orange for dessert."

"You got it. Sit still, I'll get it ready for you." Mozart moved off the bed, but not before running his large hand over her head and pushing a strand of her blonde hair behind her ear. He then turned his attention to the food and used some tool he'd pulled from his belt to open the can of green beans. He handed it to Summer with a plastic fork, before opening the bag of lettuce. Mozart watched out of the corner of his eye as Summer dug into the can. Once again, he saw how she tried to control herself and not inhale the food, but she had a little less control tonight than she'd had when they'd gone out to eat.

Mozart dumped the lettuce in a big plastic bowl he'd also picked up at the store and opened the cheese and turkey as well. He tore off pieces of the meat and cheese and included it in with the lettuce. He stirred in more dressing than she'd probably normally use, but she needed the calories.

Mozart handed her the doctored lettuce and another plastic fork and sat down on the bed next to her, peeling an orange as she ate.

They didn't say anything, just enjoyed each other's company in silence. Mozart couldn't help but feel a little cavemanish. He'd gone out and gotten food for his woman. He was providing her with food, warmth, and a safe place to sleep, everything psychologists said was vital for a person's wellbeing.

Summer put aside the bowl of salad she'd practically inhaled and sighed. She was full, but she still craved the sweetness of the orange, its smell now permeating the air around them. She reached for the fruit only to have Mozart hold it out of her reach.

"Open," he demanded in a low harsh voice.

Summer looked up only to see a look of determination and desire on his face. "I can do it, Mozart."

"I know you can, but I want to. Now open."

Summer looked in Mozart's eyes and saw he wasn't going to budge on this. She opened her mouth and moaned as she bit into the first slice of the orange Mozart put into her mouth. She opened her eyes and blushed. Mozart's erection couldn't have been more obvious, but he wasn't hiding it from her in any way. His legs were spread, and he was sitting sideways on the bed again.

Seeing where Summer's eyes had strayed, Mozart smiled at her. "I can't help it, Sunshine. The noises that come out of your mouth are sexy as hell. But I'm a patient man. I'll wait as long as it takes you to be comfortable with me. But be forewarned, that doesn't mean I won't be pushing you and trying to make you comfortable with me sooner rather than later."

He held out another piece of orange to her. Instead of answering his conceited remarks, Summer leaned forward and grabbed Mozart's wrist. She held on to it without breaking eye contact with him and took the piece of orange into her mouth. She shifted it to the side and suckled his finger into her mouth at the same time. She licked around his knuckle and nipped at the tip before drawing backward and letting go of his wrist. "I'm not sure why you think it's going to take a while for me to be comfortable with you, Mozart. I feel more at ease with you than I did with my ex, who I'd been married to for ten years."

Summer watched fascinated as a muscle ticked in Mozart's jaw.

One hand was clenched in a fist so tight his knuckles were white. She watched as he brought the finger she'd just had in her mouth up to his lips and sucked it into his own mouth. Without breaking eye contact with her he unclenched his other fist and brought it up to the back of her neck, drawing her closer to him. Summer loved when Mozart did that, granted he'd only done it once before, but she hadn't forgotten the feeling. It was controlling as hell, but it comforted her, without a doubt.

"Are you finished eating, Sunshine?"

Summer nodded in the confines of his pseudo-embrace.

"Here's what's going to happen. I'm going to put the food away and you're going to climb under the covers. I'll get changed and come back to you. We aren't going to make love tonight, but you'll sleep in my arms. We'll get to know each other better and when we both know it's right, I'm going to take you so hard you won't remember anyone else and you'll certainly never think of having anyone else. Got it?"

Summer shivered in delight and answered him in a whisper, "Got it."

"Jesus, Sunshine. I gotta know before I let you go. You wearing anything under my shirt?"

Summer giggled and shook her head. "The shorts were too big, but yeah, I put my undies back on."

"God. Okay, I'm getting up now, scoot yourself up and climb in. I get the right side; it's closer to the door."

Summer did as Mozart directed, not taking her eyes off him the entire time. She watched as he gathered up the food and put it on the dresser. He went into the bathroom and she heard the toilet flush and him brushing his teeth. Finally, Mozart cut the light off and the room went dark. She felt Mozart climb into the bed beside her. Summer hadn't thought about his statement about taking the side of the bed closer to the door when he'd made it, but now, lying in the dark, knowing he was between her and anyone that might try to get in, made goose bumps break out all over her body. No one had ever done that sort of thing before. Her ex wasn't into protecting her in any way, figuring she could do it herself.

Summer lay stiff in the bed, wondering what Mozart's next move was going to be, but she didn't have to wait very long. He rolled over and gathered her into his arms. He didn't turn her so her back was to him, he just pulled her right into his embrace.

Her arms were between them and she could feel he'd taken his shirt off. Summer flattened her hands on his chest and snuggled her head into the indentation between his neck and shoulder. She sucked in a breath, loving how he smelled. "You're so warm."

Summer felt him nod and kiss her head before putting his head back on the pillow. "Shhhh, go to sleep, Sunshine."

"I have to get up by eight so I can get some breakfast," Summer sleepily murmured.

"I said, shush. Don't worry about tomorrow. I'll take care of it."

"Okay...Mozart?"

He sighed a disgruntled sigh. "You aren't sleeping."

"I just wanted to say...thank you for coming back. People usually don't."

Mozart held Summer closer to him and couldn't find the right words to say, so he stayed silent until Summer fell asleep in his arms. Only then did he whisper into the silent room, "I'm sorry it took me so long. I'll always come for you, Sunshine."

CHAPTER 8

Summer woke up the next morning slowly. The room was lit up with the light of the sun. She immediately knew it was way later than it should've been. She was going to miss breakfast if she didn't hurry. If she missed the food that Henry put out for the guests, she knew she wouldn't get a chance to eat. She rolled over, remembering suddenly that she wasn't in the little storage room.

Summer felt better than she had in a long time. Her belly wasn't trying to eat itself and she was warm. Not only that, but for the first time in months, her back didn't hurt. The mattresses in the cabins might not be top-of-the-line, but they were damn sure better than the cot she usually slept on. Summer snuggled deeper into the covers, not even caring, for once, that she was probably going to miss breakfast.

Mozart wasn't in the room. Summer remembered waking up a few times in the night and rolling over, only to have him crowd her and wrap his arms around her again. She thought she even remembered him whispering soothing words to her, but she couldn't remember anything he might have said. She rolled over and smelled the pillow where his head had been resting. God, she had it bad.

Summer sat up and scooted so her butt rested up next to the headboard and looked around. The bags of food were sitting on the small dresser against the wall. The TV was old, but still worked just fine. She could see Mozart's bag on the floor next to the dresser, the sight of it comforting her, because it meant he hadn't left.

She was surprised to see her own suitcase sitting next to his duffle though. Mozart had obviously gone out to the storage building and retrieved it for her. At least she could put on some of her own clothes now. As much as Summer wanted to continue to wear Mozart's T-shirt, she knew she'd have to put her own clothes on sooner rather than later.

She threw back the covers, for once not shivering in the cold morning air, and padded to the bathroom. It was amazing how nice it was not to have to go outside and into a different building just to pee.

Summer had just exited the bathroom to go and grab her stuff out of her suitcase so she could get ready, when the door opened. She froze in place, then sighed in relief when she saw it was Mozart.

"Hey," she said and then took a step back as Mozart came toward her. He had a serious look on his face and he didn't stop until she'd backed up into the wall.

He came up against her and put his forearms on the wall on either side of her head. This brought his mouth so close to hers, if either of them moved an inch, they'd be touching. "Good morning, Sunshine. Sleep well?"

Summer could only swallow hard and nod silently.

"Good. You like this room?"

Not knowing where he was going with his questions, she answered, "Uh, yeah, it's fine."

Mozart smiled and took one arm off the wall and brushed her hair back from her face and smoothed it behind her ear. "Good. You'll be staying here for the winter."

She tipped her head to the side. "What?"

"You heard me, you're staying in here instead of that damn shack."

"No, I'm not," Summer argued, getting pissed.

"Yeah, you are. I had a little talk with Henry this morning, we came to an agreement."

"That's just it. *You* came to an agreement. I didn't. I can't afford to stay here." Summer didn't like that Mozart was in her space now. At first she'd loved how protective he seemed to be, but she was seeing the drawbacks of that now.

"I know you think I'm being controlling, but listen to me for a second. Please?"

Jesus, if Mozart had demanded and yelled she could've resisted him. But pleading with her to listen? Shit. "Go on."

Summer watched as Mozart suppressed a smile, but before she could blast him for it, he continued. "I talked with Henry about the unsanitary conditions you've been living in. I don't think he was surprised by anything I told him, but I did get his attention when I said I'd already talked to the Better Business Bureau."

Summer gasped. "You didn't!"

"Of course I didn't, but *he* didn't know that. All I told him was that because all the rooms weren't being rented out every night in the winter, it was the least he could do to allow you to stay in one of them. You'll be responsible for cleaning it, of course, and he still isn't budging on the meal thing, but at least you'll have a warm and safe place to sleep." Mozart stopped. He'd wanted to wring the old man's neck. He hadn't given a shit that Summer was freezing to death and practically starving. If Mozart had his way, he'd take Summer back down to Riverton tonight, but he knew in his gut she wouldn't agree. She was prickly and independent.

"I can sleep here?"

The incredulous way she'd asked made Mozart's blood boil. No one should ever think that living in a crappy motel like this one was an answer to their prayers. "Yeah, Sunshine. You can sleep here. And you can put your stuff here. You'll be living here until the spring, or until you find something else." He had to tack that that part on, because he hoped against all hope she'd want to find something else… down the mountain in Riverton.

"I don't know what to say."

Mozart leaned in close to her again. "Say, 'Thank you, Mozart,' then kiss me to thank me properly."

Summer grinned. "Thank you, Mozart." She leaned toward him and at the last minute shifted until her lips met his scarred cheek.

Mozart laughed and grabbed her around the waist and took two steps backward and fell on the bed on his back, still clutching Summer in his arms. She shrieked and laughed as they fell. He bounced once and clasped her hips to his.

Summer sat up and gazed down at the man beneath her. She could feel Mozart's muscles tense under her. He'd manhandled her as if she were a child, and a part of her loved it. She could tell he'd moved so he didn't hurt her, but he was definitely in control. Even now as he was holding her to him. She couldn't move if he didn't let her, but she wasn't worried. Summer knew if she made the slightest move or in any way gave him an indication she didn't want to be right where she was, he'd let her go.

The T-shirt she was wearing had ridden up her thighs as she straddled him. She was still decent, barely. Mozart's hands spanned her waist and his thumbs were rubbing back and forth on her stomach. She shifted and felt him grow hard under her. The only thing keeping them separate were his jeans, whatever he was wearing under them and the small piece of cotton covering her womanly parts.

"I promised myself I'd take things slow with you, Sunshine, but you're making it hard."

"I can tell." Summer grinned and shifted in his lap again, feeling how "hard" she was making it.

Mozart's head went back and thunked on the bed. "I knew you'd be a wildcat in bed. I didn't mean to bring us here yet, but I'm not sorry we're here." He lifted his head back up and looked at her. "You have no idea how difficult it was for me to leave you in bed this morning. You were lying next to me, curled into my arms. One leg thrown over mine and I could feel your heat against my leg, just as I can now. If I hadn't promised both of us that we'd take it slow, I'd be buried so deeply inside you, you wouldn't know where you ended and I began."

"Mozart," Summer whispered, more turned on than she'd ever been in her life. She ran her hands over his chest, rubbing against him as he continued to speak.

"I'm not proud of my history, Summer. You'll hear about it sooner or later, and I'd rather you heard it from me. I've slept with way more than my share of women, but none of them meant anything. I've never thought twice about sleeping with them and leaving in the morning. I've never looked back. Not once. Until you. I'm sure when you meet my friends they'll delight in letting you know what a man-whore I've been, and they won't be lying. But I swear to you, right here, right now, that's all behind me. I haven't been with anyone since I met you two months ago. Since losing my virginity, I've never gone for two months without sex. I know how that makes me sound, but please believe me. You've crawled inside me and won't leave. I don't want you to leave."

"I..."

"No, let me finish." Mozart moved one hand from her waist up to the back of her neck. It seemed to be his favorite place to grab hold of her. "I want to have sex with you more than I want anything in my life. But, it's not happening this weekend. I have to leave on Sunday. I have to go back to work. I want to prove to you, and to myself, that I'm a different man. That you've made me a different man. I want to be with you because of who you are, not to use you for sexual release. Don't get me wrong, I want that too, but I want to get to know you more."

Mozart brought Summer's head down close to his face using his grip on the back of her neck. She braced herself on his chest. "I want you, Summer. I want all of you. I want you in my bed. I want you in my house. I want you to get to know my friends until they're your friends too. I want to wake up to you hogging the covers every morning. No matter what it takes to get there, I'm willing to do it. If I thought you'd do it, I'd haul your ass down to Riverton before you knew what was going on. But I think I know you enough to know you don't want that. What I'm not willing to do is rush this, to make you think I'm here for a quick fuck and that's it. I'm not willing to leave you up here in some damn run-down fire-trap of a shack knowing you're shivering and hungry every night. I need you to let me help you. Please, God, let me do this so I can sleep at night knowing you're all right up here."

Summer melted against Mozart's chest. Breaking eye contact, she rested her forehead against his chest and took a deep breath. Mozart didn't move his hand from her neck and his other hand was now sweeping up and down her spine in a soothing motion.

"Thank you, Mozart," Summer said, repeating her thanks from earlier. "I don't doubt you're popular with the ladies. I have no idea what you see in me and why I'm any different from any of them." When she felt him take a breath as if to answer her unasked question, she brought her head up and put one finger over his lips to shush him. "Will you do me a favor?" At Mozart's immediate nod, Summer continued, "I'm willing to try this, whatever this is, but if at any time you find someone else who you want to hook up with, please let me go. I won't be able to stand it if you change your mind and don't tell me. I'm a big girl. Just tell me and I'll leave you alone."

"I'm not going to change my mind, but if for some reason we aren't working out, I'll tell you." They looked at each other for a long moment. "But this is exclusive. You're mine for as long as this lasts, Sunshine. It goes both ways."

Summer could only nod. She felt as if she were in an alternate world. A world where she was a femme fatale and men threw themselves at her feet begging her to choose them. It was ridiculous; no one had ever been passionate about her, until now. "If I'm yours, then you're mine too."

"Damn straight," Mozart answered. "Now, thank me properly, woman." Loving the smile that crept across Summer's face at his words, he brought her lips to his. Mozart devoured her. He kissed her as he'd never kissed a woman before. In the past, he'd only tolerated kissing as a stepping stone to getting to the good stuff. Now, with Summer, kissing *was* the good stuff. He tasted her, loving it when her tongue came out to play with his. He nipped and licked and ultimately controlled the kiss. He was playful one moment, and forceful and demanding the next. Finally, he pulled back a fraction. "Jesus, Sunshine, I could eat you alive. You're my match in every way."

He felt Summer smile and he turned them over until she was under him. Seeing her hair spread out on the mussed covers turned Mozart on even more. He was so hard, he literally hurt. He couldn't remember ever being this turned on, and it'd happened with just a kiss. Mozart felt Summer's hands running over and squeezing his ass. He clenched his teeth and warned, "Watch it, Sunshine, you're playing with fire."

"I haven't been burned yet," she cheekily shot back.

Mozart took one hand and shoved it under her, and taking a risk, under her panties as well. Her skin was warm and smooth as he smoothed his thumb over her cheek. Mozart wanted to do so much more, wanted to delve his hand lower between her thighs and see for himself if she was as turned on as he was, but he behaved himself... barely. "We need to get out of this room before I do something I swore I wouldn't."

Summer just smiled up at him. "I have to work, Mozart," she reminded him gently.

Mozart didn't frown or act disappointed in any way. "I know, Sunshine. I'll help you get the rooms clean, then we can play." When she froze under him Mozart cocked his head and queried, "What?"

"You're going to help me? I thought you might go and do...something. Hike, something, while I worked."

Mozart shook his head. "Nope, I came up here for you. You're stuck with me until Sunday night."

"Seriously?"

Not understanding why she was so surprised, Mozart answered gruffly, "Yes, Summer. Is it so hard to believe that I'd want to help you clean the rooms?"

"Actually, yeah. It's just...I thought you came up here to do...whatever...and you were glad to see me while you were here."

Mozart clenched her ass harder and shoved her into his erection. "No, I'm here for you. No other reason. There'll come a time when you won't doubt my feelings for you. I see you and get hard. I smell you and get hard. Hell, I *think* about you and get hard. No, I'm here for *you,* Sunshine. And the sooner we stop talking about it and get our butts out of bed and clean the damn rooms, we can get to know each other better and I can get you back in bed and not let you up for air until we're both so exhausted we don't know our own names."

Giggling, Summer told him, "That was a long, run-on sentence, Mozart."

Mozart rolled his eyes and murmured, "That's what I get for having the hots for a smart woman." Then louder, he told her as he slowly got to his feet, "Get up. Shower. We have time to run and grab some breakfast at this kick ass little hole-in-the-wall café I found before we have to start cleaning."

He pulled Summer to her feet and playfully shoved her toward the bathroom. "Go on, I'll wait outside for you. If I stay in here while you're naked in the shower, I'll definitely break my promise." Mozart kissed Summer once more hard, then headed for the door. As he opened it, he looked back and said, "You've got fifteen minutes, Sunshine. Better hurry." He winked at her once more before shutting the door behind him softly.

Summer collapsed against the wall. She had no idea what Mozart saw in her or why he'd decided he wanted her, but she'd ride the ride for as long as she could. She'd be crazy not to. Shaking her head, she hurried to her suitcase on the floor and pulled out a pair of jeans, a long sleeved henley and undies, and headed back to the bathroom. Summer had no doubt that if she took longer than Mozart's allotted fifteen minutes he'd be back in the room just as he'd warned.

She smiled. Keeping him on his toes would be fun.

CHAPTER 9

Summer sat back in the booth and sighed. She'd just stuffed herself with the best omelet she'd ever eaten. Cheese, green peppers, bacon, fajita chicken, onions, tomatoes, and sausage, all smothered in more cheese, sour cream, and salsa. Mozart had ordered the special, which came with two eggs, bacon, sausage, and a small stack of pancakes.

"I don't think I can move."

"You can move. We've got rooms to clean, then shopping."

"Shopping? For what?"

Mozart looked at Summer, knowing what he was going to say would piss her off, so he kept it as vague as he could. "Stuff you need."

Summer crossed her arms over her chest, not buying his vague response. "Stuff I need? What kind of stuff?"

"Give me your hand." Mozart put his hand on the table palm up.

"What?"

"Give me your hand, Sunshine."

Without thinking, Summer took one hand and reached across the table toward Mozart. When his voice got low like that and he ordered her around, something inside made her cave every time.

Mozart grabbed her hand tightly and put his other over hers. He learned forward as he spoke. "Stuff you need. A microwave. A hot plate, food. A warm jacket. Stuff. You. Need." When Summer tried to pull her hand out of his, Mozart tightened his hold. "I know you don't want to accept it. I know you feel bad and are embarrassed. But that's not going to stop me. If I'm going to leave you up here, I have to know you're eating. That you're warm. That you're okay."

"Mozart, you got me a room to stay in. I'll be fine."

"You should've had that fucking room all along. I can't go home, can't go on my missions knowing you're not eating. I can't believe you lived in that fire-trap of a storage shed for as long as you did."

Summer took a deep breath. Mozart was right. She was embarrassed as he'd said. She tried one more time. "Mozart, Henry hired a new handy-man, he's working on making the building safer. He's helped me out a lot. I'll be fine."

"I don't see *him* living in a run-down shack with no bathroom or electricity. Where's this handyman living? Where's Henry living?"

"Well, I don't know."

Without giving Summer a chance to say anything else, Mozart said, "Exactly. They're not living in that piece of shit. They're eating three meals a day. They have warm clothes. They're not you."

They stared at each other for a long moment.

"I don't like not being able to get those things for myself." Summer finally said quietly.

Mozart sighed in relief. "Jesus, you think I don't know that, Sunshine? You have 'independent woman' written all over you. But you don't get that I want to do this for you. I need to do it. I wouldn't care if you had a million dollars in the bank, I'd still want to give this to you."

"If I had a million dollars in the bank we would've never met."

Mozart just brought Summer's hand up to his lips and kissed the back of it. Then he turned it over and nipped the fleshy part of her palm. "Come on, Sunshine, we've got some rooms to clean."

* * *

"You're really good at this," Summer told Mozart honestly when they were working on the last room for the day.

"I don't mean to be a dick, but it's really not that hard, Sunshine."

Summer laughed. "Sorry, you're right."

"Besides, I'm single. I have to clean my own apartment and the Navy made sure I could make a bed so tight, a quarter would bounce off the sheets."

Summer laughed again. "Obviously a good life-skill to have." She smiled at Mozart. He'd made the job of cleaning the rooms fun. They'd talked while they'd cleaned and she'd gotten to know him a bit better. Summer learned he had a wicked sense of humor. Mozart could laugh at himself as well as make her see humor in situations that she might not have seen otherwise. Overall she really enjoyed spending time with him.

Summer stopped and stood still for a moment and looked at him. "Thank you, Mozart."

Mozart heard the seriousness of Summer's tone and turned to her. "For what?"

"For helping me today. For not freaking out about having to clean toilets or make beds or vacuum floors. For everything. Just...thank you."

Mozart dropped the bundle of dirty towels he'd been carrying to the cart, and took Summer's head in his hands and rested his forehead against hers. "You're welcome."

They looked into each other's eyes for a beat, until Summer pulled away and looked away feeling awkward.

"Look at me, Sunshine," Mozart ordered.

Summer immediately looked up into his eyes, not even questioning why she'd immediately done what he'd asked.

"Don't ever feel embarrassed for telling me what's on your mind. If you're pissed, tell me. If you're happy, I want to know. If you're embarrassed, tired, hungry, sad...I want to know. Got me?"

Without breaking eye contact, Summer simply nodded.

"Okay then. Let's finish cleaning this shithole and grab something to eat then get to the store. I'm in the mood to spoil you."

"Okay."

Cleaning the rest of the room took no time at all and soon they were stashing the cart in the back of the office building and the cleaning supplies in the storage room.

"Come on, Sunshine, let's go. We have crap to buy."

"I hope you know I'm not going to let you go overboard."

"Yeah, yeah, let's go."

* * *

SUMMER SAT on the edge of the bed and looked around in bemusement. Mozart had gone overboard. Nothing she'd said made any difference. He'd just ignored her protests and bought whatever he wanted to. There was a small microwave now sitting beside the television set. A dorm-room size refrigerator now stood, motor running, against the wall and there was food everywhere. Mozart had bought so much food, it was stacked around the room haphazardly. The small fridge was overflowing with enough food to keep her fed for at least two weeks.

Summer could tell Mozart was in a weird mood while they were shopping, so she hadn't protested what he'd thrown in to the cart after the first time she'd tried. He'd turned to her and said gruffly, "Let me do this, Sunshine. I *need* to do this." So she'd let Mozart do what it was he felt he needed to.

He'd sent her to the clothes section of the store and ordered her to find long sleeved shirts and pants, a jacket, and even underwear in her size. Mozart had threatened if she didn't come back with what he thought was enough, *he'd* then go and find clothes for her. Summer took him at his word and brought back what she'd thought was way too many clothes. Mozart had only sighed and let it go with a, "that'll do for now."

Now they were in the room, and Summer felt awkward. She wasn't used to anyone buying her things, well buying her things because she couldn't afford it. She didn't like the feeling. Mozart sat next to her on the edge of the bed and she saw him staring at the food they'd brought in.

"I don't know if that'll be enough," he said morosely.

"Are you kidding?"

"No," Mozart said in a flat voice, turning to her. "We're headed out on a mission on Monday. I have no idea how long I'll be gone, and I don't know when I'll be able to get back up here again. I know you don't have a car so you can't just run to the store to get anything if you run out."

Summer put her hand on Mozart's leg, then snatched it back when he flinched. Before she could say or do anything, he grabbed her hand and put it back on his leg. Mozart tilted his head in an invitation for her to say what it was she obviously wanted to say.

"I'm not saying this to make you feel guilty, or mad, or anything, okay?" When Mozart nodded, Summer continued. "Mozart, for the last few months I've been eating one meal a day. When Henry opens the office I head over there and eat a yogurt and a bagel. I typically snatch another bagel and a piece of fruit for later. Sometimes a guest will leave something in their room that I feel is safe to take for myself to eat. Trust me, all of this food..." She gestured around them, "...will last me a good long time."

Summer watched as Mozart's left hand curled into a fist and the muscle in his jaw clenched. Not wanting him to torture himself, she brought the hand not resting on his leg, up to his face and turned it toward her. Whispering, Summer said, "I'm okay, Mozart. You have no idea how much what you've done for me in the last two days means to me. If I was okay before, now I'm *more* than okay."

Mozart took a deep breath and turned his head and kissed the palm of Summer's hand. "You'll never have to eat the fucking trash that someone leaves behind again. Just the thought..." he shuddered and closed his eyes for a moment.

Summer could tell when he'd gotten himself back under control. He opened his eyes and told her, "I'll be back up here as soon as I can, Sunshine."

"I know."

"I know you don't have a cell phone, but I'm going to leave you my number so you can call me whenever you want. I'll call you here at the motel to let you know when I'll be back up, but in the meantime, when I'm out of the country, if I give you a friend's number will you call it if you need anything...and I mean anything?"

Summer stayed silent and just looked at Mozart.

"Shit. You won't will you? I knew you were going to be a pain." Mozart smiled when he said it, so Summer wasn't offended. "Will you take the number for my peace of mind then? I'll feel better if you have it."

"Whose number is it?"

"His name is Tex. He's a friend who lives in Virginia. He used to be a SEAL, but was medically retired after having his leg partially amputated. He's a computer genius and I'd trust him with my life...or yours."

"Leave me his number, Mozart. I can't promise to call if I get a splinter or something, but if something goes seriously wrong I'll call." At the look of relief in Mozart's eyes, Summer knew she'd said the right thing, even if it made her uncomfortable.

Mozart stood up and held his hand out to Summer. "Come on, Sunshine. Let's climb in bed, there has to be a movie or something on television we can watch."

Summer took Mozart's hand and he led her to the bed. He didn't pull back the covers, but helped her onto the bed and climbed in behind her. He pointed the remote at the TV and flipped through the channels until he came upon *True Lies*.

"I've always loved this movie. This okay?"

"Yeah, Jamie Lee Curtis kicks butt."

Mozart laughed and settled back against the pillows and drew Summer into his side. She snuggled down against him and put her head against his chest. Mozart took a deep breath and inhaled her scent.

"You smell good." He couldn't have stopped the words to save his life.

"It's just shampoo."

"No, it's not. It's shampoo, and the orange you ate tonight as a snack when we got back to the room. It's a hint of salt from your perspiration, it's *you* Sunshine."

Summer squirmed. She'd never had anyone talk to her like Mozart did. "You're crazy."

"Take the compliment, Summer. Say thank you."

"Thank you."

Mozart smiled at her and pulled her even closer. "Now, shhhh. Watch the movie."

Summer tried to lose herself in the movie, but couldn't. Her mind was jumping around and she couldn't turn it off. Finally, she tipped her head up to ask Mozart a question, only to find him staring down at her, instead of at the TV.

"You're going on a mission on Monday?"

"Yeah."

"Can you tell me anything about it?" Summer didn't think he could, but asked anyway.

"No." After a minute or two of silence Mozart told her regretfully, "It's what I do, Sunshine."

Summer nodded immediately and tried to reassure him. "Oh, I know, Mozart. I don't know much...okay, I don't know anything about the military, but I know enough to know what you do is kept hush hush and that you can't talk about it. I just...I just will worry about you." She rushed to continue, "I know, it's silly, I don't really even know you, but I don't like thinking about you heading off to some foreign country doing something dangerous and not knowing anything about where you are, what you're doing, or when you'll be back."

Mozart sighed and turned to Summer. He leaned over until she was lying sideways on the bed and he was leaning over her. "I don't like keeping things from you, but you have to know I can never tell you. It's the hardest part of being with a SEAL. I wish I had time to introduce you to Ice, Alabama, and Fiona. They're my teammates' women. They've learned to deal with our missions by getting together and doing girl stuff. We know us leaving drives them crazy, but they support each other and help each other get through it. And you should know, the team knows what we're doing. Yes, what we do is dangerous and there's always the chance we'll be hurt…" Mozart drew a finger over his scarred cheek, then continued, "but you have to believe in us. We've trained for this. We're good, Sunshine. The fact that Wolf, Abe, and Cookie have their women waiting at home for them makes them even more determined that we all come home." He stopped talking and stared down at the amazing woman under him.

"I get it, Mozart. I know you're good. I know you're a professional. But I'll still worry." Summer said the last in a small, unsure voice. "I don't even know why you're here really. I mean, you don't know me…"

"Come here, Sunshine, and listen to me." Mozart lay back on his side and pulled her toward him. They were face to face on the bed, not touching, but close enough to feel each other's breaths as they exhaled in and out.

"You're right in that we haven't spent a lot of time together. If one of my buddies was in this same situation I'd probably be warning him to slow down. I'd tell him that there was no way he could have feelings for you after knowing you two damn days. But, I know my own mind. I see *you*. You're smart. You're compassionate. You're tough. You're selfless. You're hardworking. You're shy. You're passionate. You're beautiful. You're everything I've ever dreamed about in a woman. If you think I'm walking away from you, you're out of your mind. I'm not proposing. I'm not saying we'll be together for the rest of our lives. What I *am* saying that I want to see where this can go. I want to get to know you better. I want to protect you. I want to taste you so badly, I'm practically salivating. So, yeah, I get what you're saying when you say you'll worry, 'cos I'll worry too. I worry about you up here with that asshole, Henry. I worry about you eating enough. I worry about you being cold. I worry about you working too hard. I worry about you not having any transportation. I know we haven't known each other very long, but that worry is there. So while I don't like that you'll worry about me, at the same time, I like it."

"Mozart…" Summer couldn't get anything else out. She wished she could've taped what he'd just said so she could play it back over and over again.

"Any other concerns about us not knowing each other or why I'm here?"

Summer could only shake her head.

Mozart smiled. "Then can we finish watching Arnold kick the bad guys' butts?"

"Yeah, we can do that."

"A pain in my ass." Mozart leaned toward Summer and kissed her. He didn't touch her with any other part of his body, only his lips.

After a long intense kiss that left them both breathless, Mozart sat up against the headboard again and pulled Summer back into his arms. They watched the movie until the credits rolled across the screen.

Mozart kissed the top of Summer's head and said, "Ready for bed?"

"Yeah," she sleepily muttered.

"Up you go, Sunshine. Go and do your thing." Mozart helped Summer up and gently pushed her toward the bathroom. "I'll change and switch places with you after you're done."

Summer nodded and shuffled into the bathroom. By the time she finished brushing her teeth, washing her face, and using the restroom, Mozart had changed into a T-shirt and was wearing a pair of black boxers. She swallowed hard. "Your turn."

Mozart walked toward her and leaned down and kissed her hard before scooting by. "Mint toothpaste. I've dreamed about that taste on your lips as well," and he disappeared into the bathroom.

Summer hurried into the new pajamas he'd bought for her. Not being the nightgown type, she'd chosen a shorts and mini-tee set. They were loose and pink with little white flowers. She didn't think it was too revealing, but everything seemed very intimate with Mozart.

She was still standing by the bed when he came out of the bathroom. Mozart stopped in his tracks and just stared at her.

Not able to stand the silence and the weird look on his face another moment Summer asked, "What?"

"Get in bed, Sunshine. Now."

Confused, and feeling vulnerable, Summer scurried to the bed and got in. She watched as Mozart came around the side of the bed that she was lying on and said, "Scoot over, I'm on this side."

She'd forgotten. She'd crawled into the side of the bed closest to the door without thinking. Summer scooted over and watched as Mozart leaned over and turned off the light next to the bed. The room was plunged into darkness. She felt Mozart settle onto the mattress. Summer waited, but he didn't turn toward her. It felt like he was lying as stiff as a board.

"Mozart?"

"Don't." Mozart cut her off.

Summer was so confused. She had no idea what had happened between when he kissed her and commented on the taste of her toothpaste and when he'd come out of the bathroom. She rolled over so her back was to him and tried to keep her tears from falling.

After a moment, Summer felt Mozart finally move. He turned into her and curled himself around her back. One arm went under her neck, and the other curled over her side and he laid his forearm along her breastbone. She felt protected and safe in his arms. She was so confused.

"Don't cry, Sunshine. Fuck. I'm sorry. You are so gorgeous. Seeing you standing there in that cute little sleep set almost made me lose control. It took everything I had to let you climb in here by yourself. I still want nothing more than to turn you over and bury myself so far inside you that you'll never forget the feel of me. But I promised. It's too soon. Jesus, Sunshine, don't ever doubt that I want to be here with you. I just needed a moment to control myself."

Summer could feel Mozart's hard length against her. She didn't doubt him, but he'd hurt her. "Don't do that again," she sniffed once, hard. "I thought you'd changed your mind. I can't take up and down emotions directed at me. I need you to be one person. If you're mad, tell me. If you're stressed, tell me. If you're losing control, tell me. I know with what you do you'll probably have some moments where you're dealing with some heavy stuff. I'll give you the space you need, but if you don't tell me, I'll think it's about me." She shrugged as best she could in his embrace. It was easier to talk to him since she wasn't looking at him. "I'm a woman. We tend to think *everything's* about us."

"I will. I'm sorry."

There it was. He laid it out straight. He didn't make excuses or try to blow off what she'd said. She sighed and snuggled into his arms.

"Thank you."

"Sleep, Sunshine. Tomorrow we'll go back to the diner and have another way too big breakfast, we'll drive to the overlook and do the touristy thing downtown. We'll clean the damn rooms and then we'll go out for dinner. I have to leave after we eat, but I want to spend every moment I can with you before I go."

"I want that too."

"Sleep."

"I'm glad you're here, Mozart."

"Me too. There's nowhere I'd rather be. I just wish I'd gotten here sooner."

"Don't. You're here now."

"Yes, I'm here now. Now...sleep woman."

Summer giggled. He was so demanding, but she loved it. She couldn't resist trying to get the last word in. "I'd sleep if someone stopped talking to me."

Mozart growled. "Don't make me turn you over my knee, Sunshine."

"You wouldn't!"

"Try me."

Summer giggled again and wiggled in Mozart's arms until she'd turned over and was now facing him. She could feel his erection pressed up against her. She squirmed closer to him and buried her head in his neck.

Whispering, she told him, "I'll try anything you want to do, Mozart."

"Good God, woman. You're pushing me. Now hush. Have some pity on your SEAL. Go. To. Sleep."

Summer fell asleep feeling safe and warm for only the second time in months, the first being the night before. She didn't know that Mozart stayed awake for hours watching her sleep and counting his lucky stars he'd come back up the mountain for her when he did.

CHAPTER 10

After another huge breakfast, they made their way back to the motel to clean the rooms. Summer was amazed how quickly the job went with two people doing it. Mozart was right, it wasn't hard, but it was tedious. Not all of the guests were slobs, but enough were that it made the job annoying and, at times, disgusting.

Mozart made the job, if not fun, bearable. He took over the making of the beds and cleaning the toilets, while she was in charge of the dirty linen, the cleaning and vacuuming. The first time she'd bent over to tuck in a sheet, Mozart had made a noise in the back of his throat that sounded a lot like a growl and had pulled her upright.

"I'll do that. There's no way I can watch you bend over bed after bed and not throw you down on one of them, Sunshine."

Just the memory of the way he'd growled the words at her in his low rumbly voice, made goose bumps break out over Summer's body.

She'd just smiled at him and agreed.

Now the cleaning was done and they were sitting on a bench overlooking the lake. It was chilly, and Mozart had one arm wrapped around Summer's shoulders. The area was quiet. Winter wasn't the most popular time for people to hang out at the lake. They were usually up in the mountains skiing.

"Penny for your thoughts," Summer said, breaking the comfortable silence.

"I'm thinking about how if I didn't get my head out of my ass and get up here when I did, you'd be sleeping basically outside all winter."

Summer turned and kissed Mozart's jaw then rested her head on his shoulder with her face turned toward his neck. "If it got too bad, I would've said something."

"Would you?"

Summer sat up and sighed. "Yes, Mozart. I might be down on my luck, but I'm not a complete idiot. Henry's an ass, but even he wouldn't have made me sleep in that thing if there was a foot of snow on the ground. Besides, Joseph was working on making it more like a guest room than a storage room."

"Joseph? Who the hell is that?"

"He's the new handyman. I told you about him."

Mozart snorted. "I can't believe someone else knew you were living in that shithole and didn't say anything."

The silence stretched between them. Mozart finally broke it.

"I want to have Ice or one of the other women call you while we're gone. Will you talk to them?"

"Why?"

"We talked about this a little bit yesterday. They're each other's support while we're gone. I want you to have that."

"But they don't know me, Mozart. They aren't going to want to talk to me about that stuff."

"They will."

Summer just shook her head. She knew better. "Okay, whatever you want, Mozart."

Mozart turned on the bench and put his hands on Summer's shoulders. His thumbs rubbed against her collarbone. He knew she wouldn't be able to feel it through her clothes and jacket, but the motion soothed him. Hell, anytime he touched her soothed him. "I've been told that when a woman says 'whatever,' they usually mean anything but. What's wrong, Sunshine?"

Summer sighed and avoided Mozart's eyes. She looked past him to the trail that meandered around the lake. "It just won't work, Mozart. You can't go to your friends and tell them you've met a woman and would they please call, make friends, and talk about their feelings of worry about their men. It doesn't work that way. Hell, I had people I knew for *years* not bother to call me to see how I was doing after my divorce and losing my job. For all your catting around, you don't know much about women."

"Look at me."

Summer sighed and brought her eyes back to Mozart's. She could see he was concerned and frustrated. His eyebrows were drawn down and his forehead was wrinkled in stress lines. Even the scar on his face seemed to be redder than normal.

"I want you to get to know them. I want them to get to know you. I don't want you up here alone. Everything in me is rebelling against it."

"I've been alone a long time. This isn't anything I haven't been through before."

"But you're not alone anymore. You have me."

Summer's eyes teared up and she bit her lip.

Mozart tugged her lip out of her teeth and leaned forward. "Let me try, please? If one of them does call, will you talk to her? Will you give their friendship a try?"

"Of course I will. I miss having someone to talk to, but I don't want you to go back home and browbeat them into calling me. If you're as much as a flirt as you've told me you were, if you've slept with as many women as your reputation warrants, they're going to think I'm just another woman in your long line of conquests."

"They won't."

"They *will,* Mozart. Jeez, we've been through this. I'm a woman. I know these things. You'll go down there and say, 'Hey, I met a woman up at Big Bear, while we're gone will you please call her and include her in your tight clique of friends?' and they're going to agree, because they like you and you're their friend, but when push comes to shove, I'm a stranger. To them, I'm just another woman you've picked up."

"You're wrong."

Pulling away, Summer stood up and stalked two steps away from the bench and Mozart and faced the lake with her arms around her stomach. "Shit, Mozart. I'm not wrong."

Summer felt his arms come around her chest from behind.

Mozart put his head on Summer's shoulder and squeezed her tight. His lips went to her ear and he spoke low and earnestly.

"I have never asked Ice or the others to talk to any of the women I 'picked up.' Those women were gone from my life the second I left their bed. I've never seen any of them more than once. I know this is hard for you to understand, but Ice is just like you. She's loyal to a fault. She was there when those assholes carved into my face. She *knows* me. I'm not going to go to her and tell her I met a woman. I'm going to go to her and tell her I met *my* woman. As soon as the words leave my mouth, she'll be hounding me to give her your phone number. Trust me, Sunshine. I won't leave you hanging again. If I tell you she'll call, she'll call."

Summer felt herself being turned and she buried her face in Mozart's chest. She felt his arm go around and rest in the small of her back. His other hand went to the back of her neck and he held her to him. She clutched his jacket in her hands that were wedged between their bodies.

"I need this, Sunshine. I need to know you have my friends at your back. I swear after talking to them once, they'll be your friends too. They won't leave you hanging. They'll follow up on the friendship. I swear it."

"Okay, Mozart. I trust you. I'll talk to her if she calls."

"*When* she calls."

Summer smiled, despite her emotional state. "When she calls."

"Jesus, you're a pain in my ass." Mozart pulled away and looked down at Summer. Her nose and the tips of her ears were red with the cold and she had no make-up on, but she was the most beautiful woman he'd ever seen. She wasn't afraid to argue with him. She wasn't afraid to tell him exactly what she was thinking, and she wanted him to tell her what he was thinking. She was perfect. "You're mine, Sunshine. I'll be back up here as soon as I can. Just please remember that my friends are your friends now. Okay?"

"Okay."

"Let's get out of the cold and go grab something to eat."

Summer let Mozart lead them back toward his truck. The day was going by too fast. He'd be leaving soon. Way too soon.

* * *

DINNER WENT BY QUICKLY. No matter how much Summer tried to ignore the elephant in the room, she couldn't. Mozart was leaving. He'd done so much for her in the short time he'd been back, it almost felt like it was happening to someone else. Summer wasn't naïve. She knew Mozart was controlling and her situation was as out of control as it could get. She hoped he'd feel the same way about her when he got back from wherever it was he was going, but she couldn't be sure. She'd have to play it by ear.

They left the restaurant and made their way back to the motel. Mozart grabbed her hand and led her into room seven without a word. When they were back inside the room he finally dropped her hand and went over the little desk. He tore a piece of paper off the pad of paper there and wrote on it. Then he went over to the phone sitting next to the bed and wrote the phone number listed there on another piece of paper, which he shoved into his pocket.

Mozart came back over to where Summer was standing, and took her hand again. He led her to the end of the bed and they sat down. He sat sideways, as he had only two short nights ago, and kept her hand in his.

"Okay, Sunshine. Here are the numbers I told you about. Tex is my friend in Virginia. I've also written down my cell, home, and work number. Ice's number is here as well. I would've given you Fiona and Alabama's too, but I know you well enough to know it will be a stretch for you to call any of the numbers I've given you. Just please, promise me you'll call me or Tex or Ice if you need anything."

"I'm not going to need anything, Mozart."

"You don't know that. Anything can happen at the drop of a hat."

"It won't."

"Seriously, listen to me. I'm going to tell you something that only my fellow SEALs know. I'm not sure if they've even told their women."

Summer could only nod. He was drop dead serious. She'd never seen Mozart look so anxious and concerned.

"I thought the same way you do once. I was a teenager, living my life. We were happy, we were normal. Then my little sister was kidnapped. She was gone for over two weeks. We had no idea where she was. A couple found her beaten body in the woods. She'd been sexually assaulted and strangled. She didn't deserve it. We didn't think anything bad would ever happen either. I *know* bad things can happen, Summer. I've lived through it. Please…for me. Promise, if anything happens you'll call. If I can't be in the country to help you, I need to know you'll reach out. Tex can help you."

"I promise." Summer didn't even pause. It was obvious Mozart needed this from her. She couldn't imagine how he and his family had made it through something like that, but it explained a lot about him.

Mozart let out a breath he wasn't aware he'd been holding.

"I promise, Mozart," Summer said again, putting her hand on his scarred cheek.

"Thank you." Mozart pulled Summer into his arms and they sat on the bed holding each other for a long moment.

"This sucks."

Summer had to laugh. It did suck, but Mozart sounded like a petulant little boy. She pulled back. "Don't be such a baby. You'll be back before you know it. I'll be here doing the same thing day after day. I have the gazillion phone numbers you gave me. People have long-distance relationships all the time."

"I don't."

"Well, I'm not sure you count. Have you ever even had a relationship before?"

"Well, no. But it still sucks."

Summer smiled. "I don't know how this happened so fast. It's crazy. But I'm going to miss you."

"You better."

They smiled at each other.

"I have to get going. We have to meet at the base early in the morning." Mozart said the words, but didn't move.

"Will you kiss me before you go?"

"As if you have to ask. Come here." Mozart pulled Summer back into his arms and fell sideways on the bed clutching her to him. He put his hand on the back of her head and pulled her to him. There was no tenderness in his kiss. He controlled her, he inhaled her. He devoured her.

Mozart's other hand caressed her back, then her side, then went down to the hem of her T-shirt. As he kissed her, Mozart pulled up her shirt until he was touching her warm skin and slowly ran his hand up her side until he'd reached her breast.

He re-angled his head and rolled until Summer was underneath him. He put one of his legs in between hers and held her in place. He felt her other leg pull up until her foot rested on the bed and she pushed her knee against his hip. Mozart knew the entire situation was getting out of control, quickly, but he couldn't help himself. He needed to feel her at least once before he left.

He brought his hand to Summer's chest under her shirt and encased her bra covered breast with his hand. Mozart felt her inhale at the same time he felt her nipple go taut under his palm. Wanting to see her eyes when he touched her for the first time, he drew back. Summer's eyes were closed and she arched her back into his touch.

"Open your eyes, Sunshine," Mozart ordered gruffly.

Summer's eyes popped open, they were dilated and she was panting against him.

"Touch me," she begged softly, not breaking eye contact.

Mozart shifted and brought himself closer to her. He could feel her heat through both their clothes, against his hard length. Not looking away from her face, he slowly brought the edge of her bra down until it caught under the curve of her breast. He wished like hell he could see her, but this was almost more erotic. Her T-shirt covered her, but he knew if he looked down he'd see her nipple straining against the fabric.

Finally, he curled his hand over her bare breast. They both inhaled at the same time. Not satisfied, Mozart explored. He ran his fingertips in circles around Summer's areola, not touching her hardening nipple. He pushed and caressed, all the while staring into her eyes.

After a moment, not being able to stand not touching her fully anymore, he asked, "Ready, Sunshine?"

"Oh God, yes. Please. Touch me."

Not making her beg anymore, Mozart took his thumb and index finger and squeezed her nipple. Summer arched her back and groaned, closing her eyes for the first time since he'd touched her bare skin.

Mozart continued to roll her nipple with his fingertips. "Jesus, you're magnificent. You're perfect. I can't wait to see these beauties. You're so responsive. When I finally get you naked underneath me I don't think we're going to come up for air for days."

"Yes, oh God, *yes*."

Mozart leaned down and took her nipple in his mouth through her T-shirt. This was further than he was planning on taking this, but he couldn't help himself. Summer was so sexy and so open. He sucked as hard as he could through the cotton of her shirt and was rewarded with another agonized moan from her. Mozart could feel her squirming under him.

Knowing they were both almost too far gone to stop, Mozart took her nipple in his teeth and lightly tugged. Finally, he brought his head up to look at Summer's face and saw she was watching him.

"That is sexy as hell," she told him honestly, once again laying it out for him with no artifice.

"No, you're sexy as hell," he responded, all the while still rolling her nipple in his hand.

After a long moment, Mozart stilled and covered her breast with his large hand regretfully. He laid his forehead on her shoulder. He felt one of her hands come up and rest on the back of his head. He vaguely remembered her nails digging into his back while he'd been feasting on her nipple, but couldn't be sure.

"The second we land, I'm on my way up here. I'm done giving you time." It wasn't a question.

"Okay."

Mozart raised his head and told Summer seriously. "You're mine. I've never almost come from sucking a woman's tits through her shirt before. I have no idea what it is about you, but all I know is that you're mine."

"Uh...that wasn't the most romantic thing I've ever heard, but..."

"I'm not usually a romantic guy, Summer, but with you, I want to be. I can feel how hot you are through our clothes. If you think I'm going to spend another night lying beside you and not feeling that heat on my skin, you're crazy. You're fucking mine." Mozart wanted so badly to order her to come to Riverton with him, but knew he couldn't.

"I've never come just from...that...before either."

Mozart did a double take. "You..."

"Yeah."

"Jesus. A pain in my ass." Mozart smiled when he said it, but felt ten feet tall. "If that's all it takes, we're going to have a hell of a good time when I get back."

"It's you. Your smell. The growly sounds you make. The way you take charge. The way your hands feel against my skin. The way you look into my eyes. It's just *you*."

Mozart's hand still rested again her skin and Summer could feel it clench in reaction to her words. Her nipple immediately peaked again.

Reluctantly, Mozart took his hand from her breast and pulled her bra up to cover her again. He ran his hand sensuously down her stomach and over until it rested on her hipbone. "You're too skinny. The next time I see you I want some meat on your bones."

"Okay."

"And if you run out of food, you call Tex, he'll take care of it."

"Okay."

"And I want you to call me every day while I'm gone. Leave me a message so I know you're all right."

"I don't have any money to make long distance calls." Summer was honest with him.

"I'll leave a calling card for you."

"But, you won't even get the messages if you're out of the country."

"Sunshine…"

"Okay, okay. Bossy. I will."

"And please, God, lock this door and stay safe."

"Okay."

"I gotta go."

"I know."

"I'll be back."

"Okay."

"I'll be back."

"I *know*."

"Kiss me one more time before I go."

* * *

"WOLF? This is Mozart. Can I talk to Ice?" The second Mozart pulled out of the parking lot of the *Big Bear Cabins* and away from Summer, he picked up his cell and called Wolf. He needed to talk to Ice now.

"Everything all right?"

Mozart knew Wolf would protect Caroline from any danger, emotional or physical. He didn't get pissed. Mozart knew Wolf was just protecting his woman. For the first time in his life he got it. He felt the same way about Summer. Mozart didn't even give Wolf any crap about it, just answered, "Yeah, everything is okay. I just need a favor."

"Hang on."

Mozart waiting impatiently, drumming his fingers on the steering wheel as he headed down out of the mountains. He had no idea how much it would hurt to leave Summer. Everything was so up in the air and he hated it. Hell, he hadn't even slept with her and he couldn't imagine not seeing her every day. He had it bad.

"Hey, Sam, what's up?"

Mozart didn't think he'd ever get used to be calling Sam, but for Ice, he didn't complain.

"I need you to expand your posse during this mission."

"My posse?"

"Yeah, your group. You know, you girls get together and support each other while we're gone."

"I don't understand."

"I met someone. I'd like for you to call her while we're gone. Make sure she's okay. You know...include her. She'll worry like you guys will, and I'd like for her to have a support system."

"You met someone?"

"Yeah."

"You *met* someone?"

"Yeah, Ice. What the hell?"

"Hold on."

Mozart actually took the phone away from his ear and looked at the screen in confusion for a second. He knew this would be weird, but Ice was acting even stranger than he thought she would. He smiled a second later when he heard Ice let out a muffled screech in the background then exclaim, "It's about time!" She sounded completely calm and composed when she came back on the phone. "What's her name?"

Mozart chuckled. "I told Summer you'd act like this."

"Summer? That's her name?"

"Yeah."

"And you told her you'd be calling me and I'd be excited that you'd met someone?"

"Not exactly in those words, but yeah."

"I like her already."

"You'll like her. But, Ice, she's got some hang-ups..." Before he could continue Caroline interrupted him.

"Who doesn't?"

"I just mean, I told her you'd call her. If you don't...it'll destroy her."

"Don't worry, Sam, I'll call her."

Not able to keep the relief out of his voice Mozart said, "Thank you."

"Now tell me everything."

"Everything?"

"Yeah, how you met, where she works, what's going on…you know…everything."

Mozart chuckled. When Ice got her mind set on something, there was no shaking her. At least it'd make the drive back to Riverton interesting.

By the time Mozart pulled into the parking lot at his apartment complex he felt a lot better about leaving Summer. He still wasn't happy about it, but he knew Ice and the other women would take care of her for him until he could get back. He'd have to live with it until he could convince her to move down and to live with him. The thought of her living with him didn't even freak him out. She was his. Period. *But,* the thought of her needing him when he wasn't there, *did* freak him out. He knew it stemmed from Avery's kidnapping and feeling helpless in the aftermath, but it was what it was.

He'd been honest with Summer that the thought of her being cold or hungry made him crazy. He knew all the times he'd made fun of Wolf or Abe or Cookie while they'd been on a mission would come back to haunt him. He knew now why they felt so anxious when they were away from their women. He felt it now. They were protectors at heart and being in a position where they *couldn't* protect their women, was not a good feeling.

CHAPTER 11

Hey, Mozart, it's me. For the record, again, I think it's silly that you ordered me to leave you a message every day. What if your message space gets used up and someone important needs to leave you a message? Anyway, nothing is going on here. The guest load has still been light, so that's good for me. Henry is as ornery as ever. Not sure what's up his butt, but he's leaving me alone. I still have ten tons of food to eat, so that's all good. Joseph has been working on upgrading the rooms a bit. Apparently the fridge and microwave in the room thing that you did for me made Henry think, and he's putting one in every room. Not sure it'll help bring people in, but it's something. Joseph has also been trying to spruce up the grounds to make them look better. Today he started painting some of the unused rooms. He's been a great help around here. Anyway, I hope you're all right and your...thing...is going okay. I miss you. Bye.

SUMMER HUNG UP THE PHONE. It really was ridiculous that Mozart wanted her to leave a message every day, but she couldn't deny it gave her goose bumps to think of him listening to all of them when he got back. It was like she was leaving a diary of her days and it was intimate. Even if it was only a message.

She didn't really have anything interesting to tell him though, and Summer worried about that. Her life was pretty boring. She didn't have a car, so she just hung around the motel all the time. But at least now she was warm and wasn't constantly hungry.

She hadn't heard from Mozart's friend though. She didn't really expect it, no matter what he'd told her, but it still hurt. It reminded her of how she felt when she'd first met Mozart. He'd said he'd come back and hadn't. Even though Summer didn't think he was serious, a part of her, deep down, believed him. He'd been so earnest when he'd told her that this Ice person would call, he'd made her believe. Now, four days had gone by and her phone hadn't rung once.

Summer loved being able to skip breakfast in the office. She'd always hated how Henry glared at her when she'd taken extra food to eat later. Now that Mozart had set her up, she didn't have to worry about it. She was able to sleep in and get ready leisurely in her room. This morning she didn't have as much time as usual, however, because Henry told her they had a few more people than usual checking in that day. Check-in was typically three o'clock, but this group had requested an earlier arrival time. It wouldn't have been a big deal, but because Joseph was painting some of the rooms, they didn't have as many to rent out. Summer had to start work earlier than usual in order to get the rooms ready. It wasn't a big group, only three rooms, but Henry was desperate for whatever business he could get, so he was acting as if they were about to entertain the queen of England or something.

Summer had just closed the door to the last room she had to clean for the day when she heard a car drive into the small parking lot. She glanced over as she headed toward the storage building to put away her cleaning supplies and to stow the cart, and saw three women climb out of a big-ass SUV. The vehicle looked new and it was huge. Summer knew she'd never be comfortable driving something like that around. She just shrugged and continued on her way. She couldn't wait to crash in her room. She was tired and a bit depressed. She missed Mozart more than she thought she would and she just wanted to watch TV and veg for a bit.

As she was walking back to her room, the three ladies came out of the office. Summer looked over at them and was shocked when one called out her name. Summer stopped and turned to look at them. They were now walking toward her. Summer clasped her jacket more firmly around her. When guests talked to her, it always made her nervous. She was adamant about turning in anything that was left in the rooms, but it was inevitable that one would eventually accuse her of stealing something they'd misplaced themselves. Summer didn't recognize these women, but that didn't mean they didn't remember what she looked like. She *was* the only maid at the motel.

"Yes?" The word came out a bit harsher than Summer intended, but it was too late to take it back.

"You are Summer right? Sam's Summer?"

"Sam?"

One of the other women laughed. "Mozart. Caroline means Mozart."

Summer could only stare at the women in confusion. "Uh, I know Mozart if that's what you're getting at." Were these some of Mozart's previous conquests? She felt completely in the dark.

"Shit, you guys, you're scaring her. Summer, I'm Fiona. That's Caroline and Alabama. Did Sam tell you about us?"

Summer was floored. She thought Caroline was going to *call* her. Not show up here, and not with anyone else in tow. She nervously smoothed a strand of hair behind her ear. "He said you'd call me." She said bluntly, looking at the woman called Caroline.

"I know. He phoned the minute he left here on Sunday and asked if I'd call you. But I talked with Fee and Alabama and we decided we should take a road trip. We wanted to meet the woman who brought Sam to heel, and we also wanted to do what he wanted us to—reassure you about our men. That they know what they're doing and that they'll be back in one piece."

Summer still didn't know what to say. She felt completely awkward. "O-kaaaay."

Caroline laughed and took a step forward and linked her arm with Summer's as if she'd known her for years, rather than minutes. "I know, I sound like a crazy lady. But I swear I'm not." She looked at Summer with a seriousness she hadn't shown before. "You've caught Sam's eye. That doesn't happen. Ever. So when he told me he was worried about you and he wanted me to give you a call, I knew we'd be coming up here. You're one of us. Being with a SEAL isn't an easy thing. In fact there are times when it down-right sucks. So we wanted to come up here and show you our support. We have to stick together. So how about it?"

"Are you staying *here*?"

Alabama spoke up for the first time, "It's not exactly the Ritz is it?"

"Uh. No. I'm sure you guys could find a better place than this."

"Yeah, but this is where *you* are. So here we are." Fiona said bluntly. "Come on, Summer. What do you have to lose to spend some time with us? Are we so bad?"

Horrified these women might think for a second that she didn't want to spend time with them, that she wasn't excited to have them here, Summer quickly sputtered, "Oh no. God. No, I'm thrilled you guys are here. I just don't really understand why, but I'm still thrilled. Anyone that is Mozart's friend, I hope is my friend too."

"Are you done for the day?" Caroline asked.

Summer nodded.

"Good. Let us get settled then we'll go and see what trouble we can get into. We're hungry."

"Okay. Meet back here in fifteen minutes? Is that enough time for you guys?" Fiona asked the group in general. Everyone agreed and scattered to their rooms. Summer stood in the parking lot for a moment before shaking her head and heading toward her room. She wasn't sure what was in store for her tonight, but whatever it was would be interesting.

* * *

SUMMER THREW her head back and laughed hysterically. These women were hilarious. She couldn't remember a time when she'd had this much fun. They'd met back in the parking lot and all crawled into the monstrous SUV. Caroline had laughed and said that Matthew had bought it for her because he wanted her to be safe. It sounded very familiar to Summer.

They'd eaten dinner at the same steak place Mozart had taken her to when he'd first met her, then they'd moved their little party to a run-down little shack of a bar. Fiona wasn't drinking, but the rest of them proceeded to down drink after drink. It was fun to be able to let loose for the first time in a long time. Summer wasn't sure she'd feel comfortable enough with these women to let down her inhibitions, but she quickly decided she trusted them enough to get a bit tipsy.

"Do you guys remember when we all went out that one night and the guys followed us and sat in the corner glaring at every man who even *looked* at us? The manager was so glad when we finally decided to call it a night. I think he was afraid our SEALs would unleash hell on the other patrons and he'd never be able to recoup his losses." The women recounted story after story of their men being protective and bad ass, and they'd done it with a laugh. None of them minded their men's actions.

Seeing Summer's confusion with their stories, Fiona tried to explain, "Summer, being with a SEAL is a balancing act. They're taught from the first time they set foot in boot camp that they are there to protect others. Their teammates, women, other countries, the abused and neglected...it's a part of who they are. While you and I both know we can navigate this world without someone constantly looking over us, they can't get it through their thick skulls. We just have to learn to manage it. We allow them to follow us around when we go out because the rewards outweigh the irritation tenfold."

"What do you mean?"

"Hunter will do anything for me. All I have to do is ask. He will make sure no one harasses me. He'll put aside anything and everything, and *has*, just to see to me. When you're sad, they'll want to make you happy. When you're happy, they want to know what's causing it so they can make it happen over and over again. And the sex. Whew. I'm assuming you know this, but the sex is out of this world. I never thought in a million years that I'd ever be able to enjoy sex again after what happened to me, but having Hunter focus completely on my satisfaction in bed is something I'll protect and nurture with everything in me."

Feeling the effects of the alcohol, Summer didn't filter her words as she normally would. She could sense something was different about Fiona but didn't know what. "After what happened to you?"

Fiona put one of her hands over Summer's. "Yeah, I'll tell you the whole story someday, but quick version is that I was kidnapped and taken to Mexico to be a part of a sex slave ring. Hunter and the team came down to save someone else, and found me too."

Summer was appalled. She'd read about those sorts of things happening, but had never dreamed she'd meet someone who'd actually survived it. "What?" she shrieked, standing up suddenly, knocking her stool to the floor with a clatter. "Are you shitting me? Did they get them?"

Fiona didn't even look alarmed at her reaction. "Sit back down, Summer, I'm okay. See? I'm here, I'm talking to you. I'm fine. They didn't catch them, but I don't care. Hunter saved me. That's what I'm trying to tell you. I love that he watches over me. I love that he's concerned about me. I'll take his overprotectiveness any day of the week over living through what I did again."

Summer sat down, tears in her eyes. She looked at the other women suddenly, noticing finally that they had been quiet. "What about you guys?" she demanded urgently. "Did that happen to you too?"

"Sam didn't tell you anything about us? Really?" Caroline asked curiously, not answering her question.

"No, now tell me. I can't stand this." Summer rubbed her chest.

"I saved Matthew's life, then he saved mine back after I was kidnapped by terrorists," Caroline said simply.

"I met Christopher when we were at a party and the building caught fire," Alabama said quietly.

"Are you guys serious? Really?" At their nods she continued. "Oh man, I'm so screwed. I'm so boring compared to you guys. I can't save anyone. I haven't done anything. I'm so normal it isn't even funny."

Fiona leaned toward Summer again. "But don't you see? It doesn't matter. You caught his eye. I think you know that Sam doesn't 'do' relationships. Ever. The fact that he wanted Caroline to call you and bring you into our circle says everything. You obviously don't have to do anything. You being you is what caught his eye."

Slurping the last of her sugary drink out of the bottom of her glass, Summer looked up and muttered, "What if Mozart thinks I'm boring in bed?"

Caroline was the first to react. "Are you saying that you haven't slept with him yet?"

"No, we've slept. But he didn't want to...you know. He said he wanted to wait. I don't know why. Maybe because he doesn't like me that way?" Summer didn't really believe what she was saying. She'd known Mozart was aroused when they'd messed around on the bed before he'd left. It was obvious he wanted her, but he hadn't taken the opportunity. She needed another woman's opinion.

"That proves it, Summer," Caroline said earnestly, sounding much more sober than she was. "If Sam hasn't made love to you yet, he's yours. You don't get it, and I'm sure you probably don't want to hear this, but he's slept with a lot of women. A *lot*. And they all meant nothing to him. Hell, he probably couldn't tell you any of their names." At the look of disappointment on Summer's face, she hurried to make her point. "He's never held back, not once. If he's with you, it means you mean something to him. Hell, it means you mean everything to him. He's not a man that goes out of his way to spare the feelings of the women he sleeps with. Don't you get it? It's because he *hasn't* slept with you that shows how much he cares."

Feeling much more vulnerable than she wanted to, Summer asked quietly, "Are you sure?"

"Oh yeah. I'm sure," Caroline said vehemently.

A smile came over Summer's face. "I like him too."

The other women whooped and laughed. Summer was so happy they'd come up to see her. She felt so much better about Mozart being away. She wasn't going to be happy to see the women leave, but hopefully they'd stay in touch. For the first time in a long time, Summer thought they just might.

After another hour of laughing, drinking, and talking, they decided to call it a night. The four women stumbled their way out of the bar, holding on to Fiona, who was the only sober one, as tight as they could so they wouldn't fall. Giggling and laughing they crawled into the huge SUV and told racy stories all the way back to the motel.

After pulling into an empty spot in front of their rooms, Fiona helped the others out of the huge car. She walked each woman to her room and admonished each one to lock the door. They made plans to get together the next day for lunch, knowing they wouldn't be up for breakfast. Summer knew she'd have to get up and work, but at the moment she didn't care. Fiona came to Summer's door last.

Summer stood in the doorway waiting for Fiona to come and say good night. While waiting she looked over and saw Joseph standing at the end of the row of rooms. Summer had no idea where he'd been staying, but assumed Henry had let him stay in one of the motel rooms just like she was. She half raised her hand to wave at the handyman and watched as he smiled at her and lifted his chin in greeting. Joseph continued to stand there watching, as Fiona secured her friends in their rooms for the night.

"Who's that?"

Summer turned at Fiona's question. "It's just Joseph. He's the handyman around here. He's done a lot of work to make this place look better."

"He's creepy."

Summer looked back to where Joseph had been standing, he wasn't there anymore. She shrugged. "Nah, he's harmless. He's just a loner." Changing the subject she said, "Thank you for coming up here, Fiona. I appreciate it. I know you guys didn't know me and I could've been a bitch."

"We knew you weren't."

"How?" Summer's buzz was wearing off. She wasn't completely sober, but she earnestly wanted to hear what Fiona had to say.

"We heard the story of what you did for Sam when he stayed up here the first time."

"What? How?"

"When he was asking Caroline to call you, he told her the story. He wanted us to know who you were, and it worked. You not caring about Sam's scars was the one sure-fire way to get Caroline to champion you, and Sam knew it. Caroline still feels a lot of guilt for how it happened, even though Sam has told her time and time again that it wasn't her fault. So for you to stand up for him in front of those other women when you didn't even know him? Yeah, that guaranteed she'd be up here. You're one of us now, Summer. We hate it when our men are gone, lying in bed at night worrying about them. We're scared shitless they won't come home. But we never, and I mean *never*, put that worry on them. We will never tell them how we suffer. They suffer enough in their own way. So we get together and get drunk. We talk to each other about our worries. We need each other, and you need us too. We're a part of a unique club. None of us asked to belong, but here we are. I'm sure you're wondering if it's worth the worry and the dread and the not knowing where they are or what they're doing. I'm telling you it is. It's one hundred percent worth it. These men will do anything for us. For most of us that have been through hell, they're our rocks." Fiona took a breath and leaned toward Summer.

"If you're thinking that you can't handle it, now is the time to break it off. Don't wait. They might act all badass and tough, but deep down they aren't. They're probably more vulnerable than regular men because of what they do. If you need to talk to someone about it, you can always call one of us. We'll be honest with you. But please, don't string Sam along. Don't use him."

Summer relaxed, glad that this was finally coming out. She'd been wondering when it would. She thought it would've come from Caroline though, not Fiona. "I'm glad Mozart has you to look after him. I'm not going to hurt him. I still don't know why he's with me, but I want him." Her words were simple and heartfelt.

Fiona nodded. "Good. Now, get some sleep. We'll see you tomorrow."

"Good night, Fiona. Thanks again."

Summer watched as Fiona went to her room and shut the door behind her. She took one more look around the dark, empty parking lot and saw no one. She shut and locked the door and peeled her clothes off, letting them fall to the ground where she stood and not caring. She hurriedly used the bathroom and brushed her teeth.

Summer pulled a T-shirt over her head and crawled into bed. She reached for the phone. She couldn't resist calling Mozart. She wanted to talk to him so badly she hurt. Leaving a message would have to do.

Hey, it's me. Caroline, Alabama, and Fiona drove up here today. We went out for dinner and had drinks afterwards. Don't worry, Fiona was our sober driver. I like them. I like your friends. I'm so glad you have friends that will look out for you. And just so you know, I like you. I can handle what you do. I can handle your job. If you really want to be with me. I'm here. I can't make it through an hour without remembering everything you've done for me. You've taken care of me without making me feel stifled or weird about it. I like being yours...Shit. I've had too much to drink, so that probably came out wrong, but I just wanted to make sure you knew that I'm not fucking with you. I'm old enough to know what I want, and I'm pretty sure that's you. So, I like your friends. They're funny. I'm not sure they like staying here at the motel, but they did it anyway. Fiona thought Joseph was creepy but I tried to tell her he wasn't, he's just a loner, like I was. But I'm not anymore. I have you. I think I do at least. Okay, now I'm rambling. I have to get up in about five hours but I didn't want to wait to say thank you for calling Caroline. I can't wait to see you again. Bye.

Summer hung up the phone, knowing she sounded like a complete idiot, but hopefully Mozart would figure out what she'd been trying to say. She rolled over and shut her eyes. She was asleep within minutes.

CHAPTER 12

Summer waved as the SUV pulled out of the parking lot. She'd spent the last three days with Caroline, Alabama, and Fiona, and was genuinely sad to see them go. They'd certainly opened her eyes about what it was like to be with a man who was a SEAL. She vaguely knew much of what they'd told her, but having them spell it out was eye opening for her.

But nothing they'd said made her want to end it with Mozart. If anything, it made her more determined to be the kind of woman he needed. He worked hard, he risked his life for others, and she wanted to be there when he got home. She wanted to make Mozart's life easier.

Meeting Fiona and knowing she was one of the people Mozart and his team had helped, really brought everything full circle for her. The SEALS went out there, helped other people, and no one knew about it. It was all kept hush-hush. Summer wasn't naïve, she knew they were also sent on missions to kill people. Terrorists, dictators, drug dealers…it didn't matter. She'd put up with Mozart's protective tendencies because she knew for a fact it was how he was made.

The women had one conversation where Summer had wondered out loud if it was her circumstances that made Mozart interested in her. Interested in rescuing her. She'd been quickly disabused of that notion.

Caroline had bluntly told her, "Summer, if that's all it was, don't you think he'd be with someone by now? He's seen hundreds of people like you. Down on their luck, hungry, cold, whatever. He hasn't claimed *them*. He hasn't called us up wanting us to check on *them*. What he's done in the past is contact the authorities, or give that person a business card of a shelter or whatever. So don't think this is that. He saw *you*. Being able to help you is just a bonus."

Summer had believed her.

They'd all made plans to keep in contact. Alabama, who was definitely the quietest of the bunch had bitched about the fact Summer didn't have a cell phone. She'd wanted to be able to text her and communicate with her that way. It made Summer feel good, but she stood her ground when they'd started talking about putting her on one of their family plans. It was one thing for Mozart to spend some money buying her some food. It was another to allow his *friends* to spend money on something so frivolous and unnecessary in her life.

So they'd agreed to communicate via the land-line phone that Summer had in her room. They'd promised to call when they got back to Riverton to let her know they'd arrived all right.

Summer pulled Fiona aside to thank her for her honest words the first night they'd been there. Fiona had blown it off, but Summer could tell it meant a lot to her.

Summer sighed heavily. She had the rooms to clean and another boring week ahead of her. It was amazing how uninteresting her life seemed now that she'd met both Mozart and his friends. Summer was nervous to meet the rest of his team, but the women had reassured her that they'd love her. Summer wasn't so sure, but it wasn't like she could do anything about it now. She was too practical. She had to get through this day first. Then the next. Then the next.

Summer was cleaning one of the rooms and day-dreaming about seeing Mozart again, when she heard a throat being cleared behind her. She jumped, knowing she needed to pay more attention when she was alone in the rooms. It'd be easy for someone to sneak up on her and close the door and assault her. She turned to see Joseph standing in the doorway.

"Jesus, Joseph, you scared me. What's up?"

"You should pay more attention to your surroundings, Summer," he told her with a weird look in his eyes.

"I know, I was just thinking that," Summer laughed nervously. Joseph had never made her nervous before, but he was certainly acting weird enough to make the hair on the back of her neck stand up. She couldn't help but remember how Fiona had thought Joseph was "creepy" as well. "Can I help you with something?"

"Yeah, I just wanted to tell you that I'm done with room two. It should be ready for guests again. Henry wanted me to tell you to go ahead and clean it and get it prepared."

"Okay, thanks for letting me know. I'll put it back on my rotation and get to it after I'm done with the other rooms." Summer watched as Joseph just stood there. "Was there anything else?"

"Are you seeing anyone?"

"What?"

"Are you seeing anyone?" he repeated in a flat tone of voice.

"Uh, actually I am." Summer wasn't going to apologize for it, but she wasn't sure what else to say. She hoped like hell Joseph wasn't going to ask her out. He was way too old for her, and she felt nothing toward him but a general kinship because they both worked at the motel.

"I haven't seen anyone around. Just those women who left today."

"Yeah, well, I am. Okay? He's in the military and he's currently on a mission." As soon as the words left Summer's mouth she wished she could take them back. Why had she told Joseph Mozart wasn't around?

"I see. Well, it can't be too serious as I've only seen him once."

When he didn't say anything else, Summer stammered, "Well, it is."

"Hmm. Okay. Well, maybe you'll introduce me to your 'military man' the next time he's here."

"Yeah, sure. No problem, Joseph."

"Have a good day, Summer."

"You too." Summer let out a relieved sigh when Joseph left the doorway and headed toward the office, most likely to tell Henry he was done with whatever task he'd been assigned.

Summer cleaned the rest of the rooms with one eye constantly on the door to the room. She'd even closed the door all the way when she had to clean the bathrooms. She felt vulnerable after her weird conversation with Joseph, and didn't want anyone surprising her again.

Summer went to her room as soon as she was done for the day and closed and locked her door. She put on the chain as well as flipping the deadbolt. She shivered a bit, even though she wasn't really cold. The day had been weird, and it was all because of Joseph. She hadn't really even talked to the man before. She'd been introduced to him by Henry when he'd been hired, but after that they'd only exchanged waves and the typical "hi's" and "hellos" in passing.

For him to suddenly want to have a conversation about who she was dating was odd. She thought back to earlier that weekend. Alabama had seen him watching them and thought he was weird. *Was* he weird? Summer didn't know.

She made herself a salad and nuked a microwave meal for dinner. Knowing she needed to put some weight on she forced herself to eat a candy bar for dessert. Normally she relished the chocolate treat, not having been able to splurge on something as little as a candy bar in so long, but tonight it wasn't cutting it. She desperately wanted to talk to Mozart. To see him. To have him hold her and tell her it'd be fine. Summer leaned over and picked up the phone.

HEY, Mozart. It's me. For some reason it's not weird anymore for me to call you every day and leave you a message. It makes me feel closer to you. I find myself thinking of stuff I want to tell you during the day and I can't wait to pick up the phone and tell you. I'm looking forward to when you can actually talk back *to me when I tell you about my day. The girls left today. I was sad to see them go. You were right. It's nice to talk to someone who understands about you being gone. They're going through the same thing as I am and it's good to be able to talk to them. They said they'd keep in touch. So thank you for that. I should've trusted you to know what you were talking about...and no you can't throw that back in my face when you get back. Something weird happened today with Joseph. I don't think I can really explain it over the phone though. It's probably nothing, but it was just out of the ordinary. He asked me if I was dating anyone. Which is weird because we haven't really talked before. Don't get upset, of course I told him I was. He backed off after that. Anyway, other than that, things are the same here. I ate the last candy bar you bought me today. I'll have to see about getting more of those, you got me addicted to them. I miss you, Mozart. I hope you're okay. I can't wait until you get back. Bye.*

SUMMER PUT the phone back on its cradle on the little table and snuggled down into the covers on the bed. Her mind raced with all the things she wanted to say to Mozart. He hadn't even been gone a week yet, but she hoped like hell this mission would be one of the shorter ones. She'd feel better if he was back in California instead of who-knew-where. It wouldn't change their circumstances, she was here and he was in Riverton, but at least he'd be in the country and she could talk to him.

CHAPTER 13

Summer groaned when the phone rang the next morning. She rolled over and saw it was only six thirty. She didn't even think about ignoring it though, because the only people that would be calling her were Mozart or his, and now her, friends.

"Hello?" Summer tried to sound more awake than she was. She had no idea why people did that, pretended to be awake when they weren't, but it seemed the polite thing to do.

"Sorry I woke you up, Summer. How are you?"

"Uh…who is this?" Summer knew it wasn't Mozart, she'd recognize his voice in an instant. She'd never heard this person before.

Chuckling, the person on the other end of the line said, "Sorry. I'm Tex. I think Mozart told you about me?"

"Yeah. What's wrong? Is Mozart okay?"

"Shit. Yeah. He's fine. Sorry, didn't mean to startle you. I just wanted to call and introduce myself. I know he told you to call me if you needed anything, but if you're anything like most women I know, you won't do it because you don't know me. So I'm calling so you can *get* to know me and you'll call if you need to."

Not knowing exactly why he was calling and not being all the way awake yet, Summer said, "Okay."

Tex chuckled on the other end of the phone. "First, you have to know what it is I do. If it has to do with something electronic, I can get information out of it. Phones, cameras, computers, credit card machines…anything."

"Are you a hacker?"

"Yes."

Whispering now, Summer said, "Is that legal?"

"I don't go around hacking into the FBI database for fun, Summer, if that's what you're asking. But if I need to find someone, or if one of my teams needs something, they'll find they have it."

"I don't understand how that's not illegal." Summer sat up in the bed, a little more awake now, and leaned against the headboard. She really wanted to understand this man. She heard the respect in Mozart's voice when he told her about Tex. She knew Mozart was an honest-to-God-hero, and he wouldn't champion someone who wasn't on the up-and-up.

"Let me give you an example. I hope you don't mind, but Mozart told me a bit about your situation. If you called me, as you're supposed to, if you run out of money for food and are hungry, all it takes is a few clicks and I can have the local grocery store deliver a week's worth of whatever it is that you want to eat, in about five minutes."

"But, that's stealing!" Summer, honestly shocked, informed him unnecessarily.

"I didn't say it wouldn't be paid for," Tex scolded.

Blushing, Summer muttered, "Oh."

"Yeah, Oh. I can arrange for food to be delivered to you remotely. I'd charge it to my credit card, or Mozart's, but it would be paid for. The point I'm trying to make here, sweetheart, is that you aren't alone out there. I can get whatever you need to do you remotely. I don't have to cheat or break the law in order to do it."

Summer let out a relieved breath.

Tex heard it and continued, "But, that isn't to say that I *wouldn't* do something illegal to help you if I needed to."

"You don't even know me though," Summer argued.

"I don't have to. You belong to Mozart. That's good enough for me."

Summer didn't have anything to say about that. On one hand she was appalled that Tex had actually said it out loud. It sounded so barbaric. But the other part of her, the part that had really listened to what Caroline, Alabama, and Fiona had told her about the men, rejoiced in being a part of their close-knit family. The thought of "belonging" to Mozart also made her feel warm and fuzzy inside. It was official, she was insane.

"Well, I'm good. I don't need anything, legal or illegal."

"You'll call me if you do?" When she didn't say anything, Tex warned, "Summer?"

"Oh all right. Jeez. You're just like Mozart."

"Thank you."

"It wasn't a compliment," Summer said petulantly, even though she was smiling.

"I know. And Summer, the next time you go out drinking with the ladies, try the Madori Sours, they're just as good as the Amaretto Sours."

"Wha-, how do you know what I was drinking?"

"There are security cameras everywhere, Summer."

Summer was just cluing into how serious Tex was about what he did. "Okay. I'll try them then. Next time." She could hear Tex laughing at her.

"Good. Now go back to sleep. You have another couple of hours before you need to be up and cleaning. *Call me,* Summer. For anything you need. I'm here when Mozart can't be."

"Okay, Tex. Thank you."

"You're welcome. Have a good day."

"You too. Bye."

"Bye."

Hanging up the phone, Summer could only shake her head. Mozart's world was one she never expected to find herself in, but she couldn't deny that she liked it. She liked how protective he and his friends were. They were bossy and liked ordering people around, but she could tell that deep down they were very caring men. And she figured women like Caroline, Alabama, and Fiona wouldn't be with them, if they were assholes. That had to mean something.

She snuggled back down into the covers and closed her eyes. She'd do what Tex ordered just because *she* wanted to, not because he told her to.

* * *

"HEY, Summer, can you come here for a second?"

Summer turned and saw Henry standing at the door to the office gesturing for her to come over to him. She wiped her hands on the towel she'd been holding and draped it over the cart. She moved the cart as much to the side as she could, out of the way of any guests that might walk by, and set the brake on it. The last thing she wanted was it rolling away and dumping all the stuff on the ground. Summer hurried across the parking lot to the office.

She entered to see Joseph leaning against the front desk with Henry standing behind it. Summer immediately tensed. Ever since the weird encounter she had with Joseph a few days ago, she'd been edgy and nervous around him. They hadn't spoken since then, but she'd caught him looking at her a few times.

"What's up, Henry?" Summer said as normally as she could.

"I've been talking with Joseph and he's got an idea and we could use your help."

"Okay, I'll do what I can."

Joseph took over the conversation. "I told Henry we could probably get more women to stay here if we spruced up the rooms a bit more. Women, after all, are the ones who most often make room reservations for family vacations. I think if we changed out the paintings on the walls and upgraded the bedding, it would go a long way toward helping raise business."

Summer looked at Joseph closely. The words coming out of his mouth seemed so incongruent to his looks. He was probably around sixty-five years old and had long, stringy, gray hair. He wasn't skinny and he wasn't fat. He was actually in pretty good shape for an older guy. But there was something about him, now that Summer was paying attention, that just wasn't right. Joseph talking about bedding and pictures just didn't go with what she thought a handy man would even care about.

She cautiously answered. "Okay, yeah, that sounds good. Was that what you wanted? For my approval and opinion?"

"Actually we need you for more," Henry told her. "I need for you to go with Joseph to town and pick out some things. We have no idea what women like, since you're female, you do. You guys can go this afternoon and get some stuff for a few of the rooms and we'll set them up and take pictures for the website tomorrow."

Summer stood stock still. Henry had never asked her to do anything like this before. She had no idea why he was suddenly interested in her opinion as a woman. Trying to get out of it she said, "Uh, I haven't finished cleaning the rooms yet."

"No problem. We don't have anyone renting them tonight, so they'll keep until tomorrow."

Shit. There went that excuse. Joseph hadn't said anything further, he was just standing next to the counter with his legs crossed at the ankle and smiling at her. Actually it looked more like a smirk. Summer had no idea what to say to get out of this, she'd never been any good at thinking on her feet. She usually came up with a good comeback about two days after the fact.

"Uh, okay."

"Great, here are the keys to my car. Joseph, go pull it around. Summer, meet Joseph out front."

"I have to make a phone call first," Summer blurted out. She couldn't get Tex's words out of her head. He'd keep an eye on her. If he could see what she'd been drinking when she'd been out with the other SEAL's women, maybe he could keep his eye on her while she was shopping with Joseph. Summer had no idea if that was even possible or not, but Tex *had* ordered her to call him if she needed anything.

"Okay, but make it quick. Time's a wastin'." Henry was feeling good about his decision to redecorate, and obviously wanted it done right away.

Summer pushed open the office door and made a beeline for her room. She pulled the keycard out of her back pocket and after entering, locked the door behind her. She went right to the phone and pulled the piece of paper with the phone numbers Mozart had left for her to the end of the table so she could read it. She'd kept it under the phone for easy reference.

She dialed Tex's phone number and listened to it ring. When it went to voicemail, Summer swore under her breath. Shit. He had to be there. She hung up and dialed the number again. When it again went to voice mail again, Summer sighed. She didn't have a choice but to leave a message.

Hey, Tex, it's Summer. I don't really know why I'm calling, except I needed some advice...or something. I've been asked to go into town with the guy Henry hired as a handy man for the motel. His name is Joseph. Normally I wouldn't think twice about it, but he's been...weird lately. Nothing bad, and I'm sure it's nothing, but since I don't have a car or anything I have to go with him. I thought that you could, maybe...shit. I don't know. Watch? You said there were cameras and you knew what I was drinking that one night....oh Jesus. I sound crazy. Anyway, okay, well, I have to go, he's waiting for me. I'll call you when I get back later and you can laugh at how paranoid I am. Bye.

Summer hung up the phone, took a deep breath, and walked to the door. She closed it carefully behind her, making sure it latched shut and saw Joseph waiting for her in Henry's old car. She smiled at Joseph nervously as she opened the door and closed it behind her. She looked behind her as they pulled out of the parking lot. *Big Bear Lake Cabins Motel* might be run-down and sad, but it held a special place in her heart because it was where she met Mozart. She'd do what she could to make it a success.

CHAPTER 14

Tex came back into his apartment after taking a short walk. He was so close to finding Ben Hurst he could taste it. He'd just needed a small break before hitting the computer again. He wanted to find the asshole for Mozart, and to get him off the streets. The man was a menace and had been extremely lucky over his lifetime. He'd apparently made a habit out of assaulting women and children. Avery Reed wasn't his first victim, and certainly wasn't his last. There was something obviously wrong inside the man's head. He had no remorse for what he'd done and what he continued to do. Hurst's short stints in jail had no effect on his behavior.

Tex had traced the man to the Big Bear Lake area a few months ago and that's why Mozart had ended up there. Tex smiled. He loved being able to have one up on a fellow SEAL. He could now claim for the rest of their lives that he was the one who basically introduced Mozart to Summer.

Tex settled into his chair and wiggled his mouse. His computer screen lit up and he was happy to see his chat box blinking at him. He eagerly clicked on it and saw the note from Mel. Smiling at her comment, he quickly responded. He loved talking to her. She was smart and funny. It was weird because he had no idea what she looked like or even where she was, but she entertained him and gave him a good break from everything else he had going on in his life.

Thirty minutes later, he signed off with Mel reluctantly. He had work to do. He wanted to nail Hurst and needed to find where the bastard was hiding. Tex clicked on the icon to open a new browser and out of the corner of his eye saw the red light blinking on his cell phone. When did he miss a call? He remembered suddenly that he hadn't taken the phone when he'd left earlier for his walk.

He listened to the message from Summer and heard what she didn't say. It was obvious she was feeling uneasy about the situation, but she had no idea how to get out of it. If she hadn't been uneasy, she never would have called him. Shit. If Tex had been able to talk to her, he would've told her in no uncertain terms not to get in the car with Joseph. He'd learned to listen to his gut, more times than not, it was right.

Tex looked at the time of the message. It'd been over half an hour since Summer had called him. Fuck. With purpose, Tex turned to his laptop and quickly brought up the security cameras he'd used to track Summer and the other women when they'd gone out. He rewound the footage about twenty-five minutes and combed through them all anxiously. He didn't see Summer in any of them.

Dammit. He quickly checked the other cameras that he was able to hack into, with no luck. Summer and the mysterious Joseph hadn't made it into town.

He checked the local law enforcement scanners. There had been no traffic accidents in the last half hour. He had no idea where Summer disappeared to, but he had a feeling the mysterious Joseph would turn out to be the man he'd spent the last few years tracking. Tex didn't know how he knew it, but with every minute that passed without sight of Summer, he knew he was right. Ben Hurst was at it again, and Tex had no idea how Mozart was going to react to the fact that the man who killed his little sister all those years ago, had now taken his woman.

* * *

SUMMER BLINKED SLOWLY. Fuck. She knew immediately she was in deep trouble. Just as they'd pulled around the corner from the motel, Joseph had hit her in the face hard enough to stun her. Her head had bounced off the side window and she saw stars. When Summer could finally think straight again, to try to open the door to get out, Joseph had already immobilized her. He'd pulled over on a side road and put a pair of handcuffs around her wrists behind her back, stuffed a piece of cloth in her mouth, and tied a gag around her head. Summer couldn't move and she couldn't talk. When she'd turned sideways and kicked Joseph as hard as she could in his ribs, he'd hit her again, this time hard enough to knock her out.

Now, here she was. Summer had no idea *where* she was, but she knew she wasn't safe. She choked back a sob. With the gag still in her mouth, she couldn't cry now. She was having a hard enough time breathing as it was. Why didn't she follow her instincts? She'd called Tex because she *knew* Joseph wasn't safe, but she didn't have the guts to say no. She moaned. Would she ever see Mozart again? Would she ever see *anyone* again?

* * *

TEX FRANTICALLY HIT the keys on his computer. Shit. Shit. Shit. He had to get Mozart and the rest of his team home. Tex shook his head. He spent too much of his damn life trying to get those SEALs back to the States when they were on a mission. It was uncanny how unlucky their women were. But there was no doubt in Tex's mind now that Hurst was Joseph. He'd called Henry at the motel and asked as many questions as he could about the handyman he'd hired.

Henry didn't know much about the man. He didn't know where he lived or even what his last name was. Henry had needed someone to do some grunt work around the motel, and Joseph had been his only applicant. Henry paid him in cash and had been happy with the work he'd been doing.

Tex hung up in disgust. Shit. Now what? He needed boots on the ground. This seemed to be one time when working from Virginia on the computer just wasn't going to cut it. He had to get Mozart home. Now.

* * *

"I've been waiting for you, Summer."

Summer glared at Joseph from across the room. She was in some sort of cabin, and it could have been anywhere in the mountains around the lake. She tried not to think about it, but instead, turned her mind to trying to figure out how the hell she was going to get out of the situation.

"I don't even know you, Joseph. Why would you be waiting for me?" Summer tried to keep her voice even, but she could hear the tremble in her voice. Joseph had taken the gag out of her mouth and even fed her a bit of food and given her some water. Summer had been reluctant to eat it at first, but after Joseph had eaten some of it to show it wasn't drugged, she'd given in. She knew she'd need her strength if she was going to get out of there.

"You have no idea who I am do you?"

"You're Joseph."

He laughed evilly. "I see your boyfriend hasn't really told you anything has he? You haven't spent time talking, I wonder what you've spent your time together doing?" Joseph sneered at Summer.

Summer didn't say anything, waiting for Joseph to get on with whatever it was he obviously wanted her to know.

"My name is Benjamin Hurst." When Summer didn't react in any way, he elaborated. "I kidnapped, raped, and killed Avery Reed years and years ago. In case *that* name doesn't ring any bells, I'll clue you in. I'm the man your boyfriend has been hunting since he was a teenager. I find it ironic he came up here to find me, and instead led me straight to your door. If he hadn't come back, I would've earned a bit of money working for Henry and slunk out of town as soon as the snow melted. Instead, I saw him with you. I couldn't resist."

"You killed his sister?"

"Oh yeah. But not before I raped and tortured her. There's nothing like the screams of a child, but alas, there aren't too many kids up here, so you'll have to do. And for the record, you *will* scream, Summer. I plan on raping and torturing you too, before I kill you. I've come a long way since little Avery. I know just how far to go before pulling back. I wouldn't want you to die before I'm ready."

Summer tried really hard to keep a straight face. Jesus. She couldn't think, she didn't know what to say. She kept her mouth shut and just watched as Joseph/Ben came toward her with the dreaded gag in his hand. She tried not to flinch, but couldn't help it. She was scared shitless.

"But first I need to go out. I can't risk you screaming so loudly that someone hears you, can I? Not that anyone would. We're so far out in the woods, it'd take a miracle for anyone to find you."

Before he could put the gag back in place, Summer spit out, "Mozart will find you and kill you. You might torture and end up killing me, but Mozart *will* find you. You'll wish you were dead when he does. You'll regret kidnapping me when the last thing you see is Mozart's face before he kills you."

Ben grabbed her jaw and squeezed so tightly, Summer couldn't help the whimper that escaped her lips. Her jaw opened involuntarily and Ben shoved the filthy piece of cloth back in her mouth. He quickly wrapped the piece of sheet around her head to keep the gag in place. When it was secured behind her, he leaned in and whispered, "I can't wait to see him, to show him what's left of your battered and beaten body. To watch him break down. I know he's a killer just like me. I want to see him lose it and kill out of anger. He's just like me, he just needs to be shown the way. Shown how cathartic it can be to take another's life."

Summer shivered. This man was crazy. She dropped her head. There would be no reasoning with him. She was as good as dead.

CHAPTER 15

Mozart clutched the arms of the seat in the military plane with all his strength. They'd been getting ready to head home when Wolf had gotten a message on their emergency satellite phone. The phone was only used in extreme emergencies back home. Mozart and the others had waited anxiously to hear what the issue was. Abe and Cookie were hoping like hell it wasn't anything to do with their women. Mozart wasn't too worried for himself, Summer was up in Big Bear working at the motel. But he was concerned for his friends.

When Wolf had come back to them and said bluntly that Summer had disappeared, Mozart at first didn't understand what he'd said.

"Did you hear me, Mozart?" Wolf had asked gently.

"What do you mean, disappeared? What was the message?" All Mozart could think was that maybe she'd decided she didn't want to be with him anymore and had just left.

"Tex got a hold of the Commander. Summer called Tex. The handyman at the hotel where she was working is Hurst. He's got her, Mozart." Wolf didn't beat around the bush.

Before he could jump Wolf and beat the crap out of him for lying,

Dude and Cookie grabbed his arms. "No! Not Summer! It can't be true! Tell me it's not true!"

"I'm sorry, Mozart. We're heading home now. He won't fucking get away with this."

Mozart clenched his teeth. Joseph was Hurst? Had he known Summer was his? Had he seen him around the motel? Had Hurst targeted Summer because of him? Deep down Mozart knew the truth. He had. He'd been the reason Summer was taken. He'd get her back. No matter what it took. Somehow he knew Hurst was waiting for him to get there. He wanted to confront him. He wanted to throw Avery in his face. Mozart was ready. Summer was all that mattered.

* * *

Summer sat stock still and watched as Ben carried someone into the little cabin over his shoulder. He dropped the slight woman as if she was nothing more than a sack of potatoes. The sound her body made as it thunked to the floor, made her wince.

Ben turned toward Summer. "Look what I found!" He sounded gleeful. "Another toy! I think I'll play with this one first before I start with you. I want you to see and know what's in store for you. I want you to think about it. To see it happening to someone else first." Ben squatted down in front of Summer. "Everything I do to her, I'll do to you. Every scream she makes, know you'll make as well. The anticipation is the best part."

Summer shuddered. She didn't recognize the woman lying unconscious on the floor, but she could see blood oozing out around a wound on the side of her temple. Summer shut her eyes, not wanting to see.

A blow to the side of her head brought her eyes open in a flash. "Keep your eyes open, bitch," Ben hissed. "If you close them, I'll make it hurt worse for her. Remember that." Summer nodded, knowing he'd do exactly what he said.

"I'll wait until she comes to, then we'll begin."

Summer allowed one tear to fall before ruthlessly pushing them back. This man wouldn't get any more of her tears. He'd enjoy them too much. She just had to hold on. She'd called Tex. Mozart would come. He had to.

* * *

As soon as they landed, Mozart turned his phone on. He needed to see if Summer had called him. Maybe it was all a misunderstanding. He had eight messages. He listened to them one right after another. Tears came to his eyes. The last time he'd cried was at Avery's funeral, but listening to Summer blithely talking about how her day went and saying she missed him at the end of every message made him die a bit inside.

What if your message space gets used up and someone important needs to leave you a message?

Jesus. Didn't Summer know that *she* was someone important? That there was no one he'd rather hear from, than her?

Joseph has been working on upgrading the rooms a bit... He's been a great help around here.

It tore Mozart's heart in two to hear Summer talking so nicely about Hurst, and having no idea who he was, *what* he was.

I like them. I like your friends. I'm so glad you have friends that will look out for you. And just so you know, I like you. I can handle what you do. I can handle your job. If you really want to be with me. I'm here.

HEARING her talk about liking Fiona, Alabama, and Caroline made Mozart feel good. He knew Summer would like them. Hearing her say she liked *him* and that she could handle what he did would have made him feel on top of the world, if she wasn't currently in the hands of a madman.

FIONA THOUGHT Joseph was creepy but I tried to tell her he wasn't, he's just a loner, like I was. But I'm not anymore. I have you.

ALABAMA COULD TELL he wasn't trustworthy. She knew. Why the hell didn't Summer see it?

SOMETHING WEIRD HAPPENED today with Joseph. He asked me if I was dating anyone.

MOZART CLOSED HIS EYES. Hurst knew. He *knew* Summer was his. Mozart had known it in his gut, but hearing Summer validate it, tore his heart in two. He clenched his fists. He had to get there in time. He had to. Mozart saved all of Summer's messages to listen to again later. He wanted to listen to them again when Summer was safe in his arms. He wanted to treasure them. A little voice inside his head tried to say that the reason he was keeping them was because if Summer died, he wanted to keep a piece of her, but he refused to listen. They'd get there in time. Hurst wanted him there. Mozart was convinced. Hurst wouldn't kill Summer until he'd arrived in Big Bear.

* * *

SUMMER KEPT her eyes open while Ben tortured the poor woman on the floor in front of her. She was gagged, like Summer. He'd tied her hands together and attached them to a stake in the floor of the cabin.

Her ankles were tied together with a piece of rope and then connected to a hook in the wall across the room. She was rendered helpless, stretched out on the hard cold floor, vulnerable and open for anything Ben wanted to do to her. To add insult to injury, Ben had also cut all of her clothes off so the poor woman lay naked on the floor whimpering. Ben had started his torture out by holding his hand over her mouth and nose while at the same time choking her with the other.

Ben laughed as she started turning blue, but let up on her neck and face at the last minute, letting her inhale precious oxygen to keep her conscious. In between choking her, he'd slap and hit her. Summer could see bruises all over the woman's body from the beatings she'd been given. The entire time Ben tortured the poor woman, he was looking at Summer.

"Watch, sweet Summer. See what I'm doing. See how she gasps for breath? This'll be you. I'll make you bleed just like she is. Your skin will bruise up even better than hers does. You'll have my marks all over you. At first you'll beg me to let you live, just like she's done. Eventually, you'll be begging me to kill you. You'll die all right. Just like she will. Slowly and painfully. Just how I like it."

Ben looked down at the woman beneath him for the first time. He leaned toward her and whispered in her ear. Summer couldn't hear what he said, but she saw the woman shake her head and mouth the word "no." Hurst just laughed and got up off her limp body on the floor. Whatever he'd said seemed to leave the woman broken and no longer willing to fight.

Ben didn't even look at the woman bleeding and gasping for breath. He came to Summer and leaned into her. His hands were covered in the woman's blood and he had a crazed look in his eye. He came way too close her for Summer's comfort. Ben took her face in his hands, smearing the woman's blood on her cheeks. He leaned in, and Summer could smell him. His body odor was atrocious. He'd been sweating and obviously hadn't showered in days, at least. He licked up the side of Summer's neck, laughing when she shook and strained against her bonds.

He brought his lips to Summer's ear, whispering intimately, as if they were lovers, "I told her you enjoyed watching. That you got off on it. I told her *you* were the one who wanted me to hurt her."

Summer glared at Ben. She was appalled at his words; the mental torture he was putting the other woman through was just as brutal as the physical abuse. She tried not to react in any other way to what he said though. Summer knew that was what Ben wanted, and she'd resist him with everything she could.

Ben was obviously pissed at Summer's lack of reaction. He undid his pants and pulled out his wrinkled and soft penis and proceeded to stroke himself until he was semi-hard. Summer looked away, repulsed. As Ben ran his hand up and down his manhood, he whispered about what he was going to do with Summer when it was her turn. When he'd gotten himself close to completion, his head went back and he groaned. Ben aimed his release at Summer and it splattered onto her. His cum landed in her lap and oozed down her restrained legs.

Ben's head came up and he laughed at the look of disgust on Summer's face. He brought his hand down to her lap and for a second Summer was confused, thinking he meant to clean it off of her, but then Ben palmed her cheek roughly in the hand he'd just run over his release in her lap. Ben smeared his semen on Summer's face and even ran his hand over her hair. The smell and feel of the wetness made her gag. Ben brought his hand back down to her face and squeezed Summer's cheeks until she couldn't help but grimace in pain. "Oh, Summer. When will you learn that I always fucking win?"

Ben turned and walked away, ignoring the pitiful whimpers from the bound and gagged woman on the cold floor. Summer waited until he left the room before closing her eyes and letting despair wash over her.

* * *

MOZART STOOD in the room at the base with his back to his friends listening as Tex's voice came from the speaker phone and told them everything he'd learned over the last day and a half. He clenched his teeth in frustration and fury. He wanted to be up at Big Bear Lake looking for Summer. He *needed* to be up there. But they had to wait to hear what Tex had found out. They needed his information.

"Apparently Hurst has been staying in the woods in various places in the summers. In the winter he finds small towns to stay in. He works as a handy man here and there earning the odd dollar. Every place I've tracked him I've found dead bodies in his wake. Children, teenagers, old women, it doesn't matter. Other than being female, he doesn't seem to have a type. But every single one of the bodies had been tortured and raped."

"*People*." Mozart growled suddenly from his spot against the wall. "Every single one of the *people* had been tortured and raped." He hadn't turned around and hadn't even spoken that loudly. Everyone in the room heard him though.

"Sorry, Mozart. Yes. All of the people that were found had been tortured before they were killed. It seems as if he chose Big Bear Lake for this winter to hole up. We were right, he was there, and it looks like he did know about you. He showed no interest in Summer until you left that second time. He targeted her."

Ignoring the pain coursing through his body at Tex's words, Mozart said, "Where did he take her?"

"I don't know."

Losing his cool for the first time since he'd heard the news that his Summer had been taken, Mozart turned around and yelled, "Where the hell is she, dammit? He's fucking torturing her. I know it. She needs me and I'm not there! I'm. Not. *There*!"

"We'll find her, Mozart," Wolf said in a low voice.

"When? After he's raped her over and over and gouged out her eyes? After she's nothing but a shell of the woman I left? When, Wolf? *When* will we find her? I thought Tex could find anybody!"

"I can, Mozart, when they're using modern technology," Tex responded calmly, his voice sounding eerie coming from the little speaker on the phone. "Hurst isn't using *any* technology. He's completely off the grid. No phones, no electric bills, no credit cards. He's living somewhere in the woods. Wherever he has your woman, it's in the middle of nowhere. It's too cold to have her tied to some tree, but it has to be a cabin or something."

"We need to get up there, Wolf," Mozart said hoarsely to his friend, not caring how he sounded. "Summer needs me. Now. Not in an hour, not tomorrow. Now."

"The helicopter's getting prepped as we speak, Mozart. We're going as soon as it's ready."

Mozart nodded.

The room was quiet for a moment, then Tex started talking excitedly. "Holy shit. Hang on. I'm getting a report from the cops up there about another missing woman. Elizabeth Parkins, twenty-two years old. Someone saw her being snatched right outside the local Walmart. Hold on....yeah, okay, I've got the surveillance video that was given to the police. Oh yeah, that's fucking Hurst all right. Let me just check something... "

Every man in the room held their breath. They could hear the clacking of the computer keys as Tex frantically typed on his keyboard.

"Yes! Okay, Elizabeth had her cell phone with her and it was on until about three hours ago. Cell phone towers pinged it as it traveled along State Road 38 and then up Polique Canyon Road toward Bertha Peak. Signal was lost about eight miles up the road. He has to be taking Elizabeth to his hideout. And if he has Elizabeth, there's a good chance that's where you'll find Summer."

Tex's excitement didn't carry to the rest of the SEALs standing in the room. They all knew if Hurst had taken another woman so soon after kidnapping Summer, he'd either already killed Summer, or he had something else horrible planned.

"Helicopter's here," Benny said quietly into the sudden silence in the room.

"Tex, stay in touch, let me know whatever information you get as soon as you get it," Wolf ordered as the team began to head out of the room to the waiting helicopter. Mozart was leading the way, they all knew if it would've sped up the timetable for leaving, he would've been running.

"Save her, Wolf," Tex said softly, obviously having waited until he could hear the others leave the room.

"We plan on it, Tex," Wolf returned, just as softly. He clicked off the phone and followed his team out the door. They had one of their own to find and rescue.

CHAPTER 16

Summer couldn't hold back her tears anymore. She'd been brave for as long as she could, now she was scared shitless. She grunted and twisted against the handcuffs. They were already tight, but as she struggled, they dug in even more. Blood oozed down her hands to drip on the floor below her, but Summer didn't even feel the pain anymore. Watching Ben hurt the woman in front of her, had finally broken her.

"Mumph, Peas stmp. *Peas*." The gag in her mouth prevented Summer from articulating what it was she wanted to say, but it was obvious Ben understood her mumbled words.

He laughed and held the lit cigarette once more to the poor woman's chest. She'd passed out about ten minutes ago, but Ben hadn't stopped. He continued to burn her flesh, pausing only to relight and puff on the cigarette each time it was snuffed out on the hapless woman's skin. Ben looked Summer in the eyes while he continued to hurt the woman lying motionless on the ground.

"Yeah, that's what I like to see. *Beg* me to stop, bitch."

Summer looked on in horror. He'd grown hard while torturing the poor woman. He was getting off on what he was doing. Even knowing she was playing right into his hands and doing exactly what he'd manipulated her into doing, Summer couldn't stop her whimpering behind the gag wrapped tightly around her face.

"Remember, this is gonna be you. Everything I'm doing to her, I'll do to you too. You want me to stop? You want me to wait until she's conscious again? I will if you want me to."

Summer shook her head frantically. Jesus no. Where was Mozart? She needed him more than she'd ever needed anyone in her entire life before.

* * *

"ARE you sure you're under control?" Wolf asked, eying Mozart intently.

Mozart simply nodded once.

"Because if you're not, you'll put her in even more danger."

Mozart nodded sharply again, but still didn't say a word.

Wolf just looked at Mozart for a second, then turned to the rest of the group. They'd spent the last thirty minutes scoping out the lay of the land. Hurst's cabin was sitting in a small clearing about two miles from the nearest gravel road. There was a four-wheeler parked in front of the door, obviously Hurst's transportation to and from the road. They hadn't found a car yet, but they hadn't looked for it. They were all focused on getting to Summer and Elizabeth.

The cabin was a piece of shit. It was small, only about two hundred or so square feet and it had two small windows, one in the back and one on the side. There was a sad looking front porch listing to one side.

Mozart clenched his hands at his sides. Standing there, listening to Wolf outline the plan one last time to the team was literally killing him. His heart was beating too fast and he could feel his breaths coming way too shallowly.

He was trained for this type of thing. They all were, but it was a completely different thing when it was someone you loved who was in danger. Mozart paused for a moment, letting his thoughts sink in. Yes. He loved Summer. It was quick, yeah, but it felt right. The feeling settled into Mozart's gut and didn't make him panic or feel trapped. He now knew how Wolf had felt when Ice had been kidnapped. This was the worst feeling in the world. He knew he should be taking deep breaths to calm his heart rate and ready himself for what was to come, but it was physically impossible.

Wolf, seemingly able to read his mind, turned to him. "Mozart, talk to me. Where are you at here?"

Liking the fact that Wolf wasn't ordering him around, but trusting him to know where he might be the most useful, Mozart answered tersely. "You take lead. I'll go in behind you." Wolf had been there. He'd let his team members take the front line to rescue Ice, and they'd delivered her back into his arms safe and sound. If Wolf had been able to do it, so could he.

Wolf put one hand on Mozart's shoulder briefly, before nodding and turning to the others.

"Okay, Dude, you take the side window and deploy the flashbang. After it's gone off, Cookie will make entry through the back window and Benny will go in through the side. Mozart and I will take the front door. Dude, you and Abe stand outside just in case Hurst decides to make a run for it. Our first objective here is to protect the women. Whatever it takes. Got it?"

All the men nodded solemnly. They knew what Wolf wasn't saying. They were ready.

"You all know it'll be crazy in there for a moment. That cabin isn't big enough to hold all of us comfortably, so be sure about your movements." Wolf paused for a beat then said, "Whatever you see in there, don't lose your heads."

"Fuck," Mozart said under his breath, knowing exactly what Wolf meant. He couldn't even think of Summer not being all right. He knew he should feel bad about the other woman as well, but his mind was filled with thoughts of Summer. He saw how she'd tried to be polite when she was literally starving and trying not to show it. He remembered how they'd laughed together while they'd cleaned the damn hotel rooms. Mozart even remembered how she'd felt in his arms. He had no idea what condition they'd find her in, and that sliced through him more than anything.

"Mozart, you have to keep your cool with Hurst. If he's alive when the dust settles, you can't go all vigilante on us. You hear me?"

Mozart jolted and his eyes careened with his buddy's. "Jesus, Wolf," he whispered dumbfounded, "I hadn't even thought about Hurst. All I can think about is Summer."

"Good," Wolf returned immediately. "I wasn't sure. You trust us right?"

"Yes, with my fucking life and with Summer's," Mozart said without hesitation.

"We'll take care of Hurst. He won't hurt anyone else after today. You have my word on that."

Mozart looked around. Every man was looking at him with determination and intent in their eyes. He relaxed. For the first time in his life something, no someone, was more important than his vendetta against Ben Hurst. He threw a silent prayer up to Avery, asking for her forgiveness in putting Summer first.

As if able to read his mind, Abe said, "Avery would want you to move on. No matter what, she'd want you to move on."

Mozart nodded. His heart finally slowed and he got a handle on the adrenaline coursing through his body. Abe was right. Avery would've been pissed at him for putting his life on hold. She'd tell him that Hurst wasn't worth all the effort he'd put into him over the years. She would've loved Summer.

"Let's do this."

The men nodded and everyone but Wolf and Mozart faded away silently into the woods to get into position.

Needing to say one last thing before everything went down, Mozart turned to Wolf.

"Make him pay."

"I got this, Sam," Wolf said, using Mozart's real name for the first time in a long time. "You take care of your woman, we'll take care of Hurst."

Mozart looked his friend in the eye for a beat, then nodded. No more words were needed.

Both men turned toward the cabin and waited. The shit was about to hit the fan.

* * *

SUMMER'S EYES WERE OPEN, but she wasn't seeing anything. She'd turned her brain off to protect herself. Ben Hurst was evil. He'd been torturing the woman, whose name she finally learned was Elizabeth, for hours. Every time Summer had closed her eyes, Ben had hit her in order to force her to open her eyes again. When she wouldn't stop closing her eyes, Ben had taken two pieces of duct tape and taped Summer's eyelids open. She physically couldn't close her eyes anymore. Summer wouldn't give up though. Ben might have physically made it so her eyes had to remain open, but he couldn't force her to *see* what he was doing.

Ben had no idea that even though Summer's eyes were open, she was seeing Mozart. Instead of seeing the long knife wound Ben had carved into Elizabeth's side, she saw the looks on the faces of the bitches maligning Mozart the first time she'd met him. Summer remembered how she'd run her hands up and down his chest, reveling in the feel of Mozart's cut body and seeing the look of jealousy in the other women's faces at her words.

Instead of seeing Ben's hands cruelly squeezing Elizabeth's breasts until finger sized bruises formed, Summer saw the look on Mozart's face as he palmed her own breasts and erotically pinched her nipple. The look of pure rapture and lust on Mozart's face would be engrained in her brain forever. Summer never thought she could make a man feel or look like that. The fact she'd done it without even being undressed, was even more of a miracle.

Instead of hearing Ben's threats of her upcoming torture, she heard Mozart calling her "Sunshine." She laughed inside at his exasperated mutterings of, "you're a pain in my ass," and thought about how she couldn't wait to find other ways to make him laugh and smile at her.

Instead of hearing Ben rant about how her mutilated dead body would never be found after he buried her deep in the woods, Summer remembered how safe she'd felt in Mozart's arms and how he'd purposely taken the side of the bed next to the door, just so he could protect her.

And instead of feeling the slaps and hits from Ben as he tried to terrify her with his threats, Summer remembered the feel of Mozart's arms around her as he walked next to her, stood next to her, and slept next to her.

Suddenly the room erupted into chaos. Because her eyes were taped open, she couldn't protect herself from the blinding flash of light that suddenly filled the room. The quiet of the day, the slaps, moans, and crying she'd gotten too used to hearing, were drowned out by the loudest noise she'd ever heard. Summer wished she could bring her hands up to her ears to cover them, to protect them, but they were still securely cuffed behind her back.

She was completely blinded by the flash of light that accompanied the loud bang and she felt physically nauseous from the loud noise. Summer shook her head, trying to get some of her senses back. She had no idea what was going on, but she wanted to stay in the place in her head where she'd felt safe in Mozart's arms.

Summer felt hands on her face, but still couldn't see who it was or what was going on. She tried to jerk out of way, but was held fast to the chair by the cuffs. She whimpered.

Finally a few words made their way through the ringing in her ears.

"...hold on...safe...fuck...help..."

Summer desperately tried to regain her faculties. She had to know what the hell was going on. Slowly she began to see shapes instead of the inky gray she'd been seeing since whatever had blown up had... well...blown up.

Her eyes hurt, were dry beyond belief, and Summer knew she'd been hoping Mozart would find her, but seeing his face in front of hers was a miracle she wasn't sure she could believe yet. She hoped she wasn't hallucinating. Summer jerked again, forgetting for a moment that her hands were still bound. She wanted to throw herself into his arms, but she couldn't.

"Thank fuck," Summer heard Mozart say. She watched as his face slowly came into more and more focus.

"Stay with me, Sunshine. I know you're in pain. I know the flash-bang fucked with your senses, just give it a minute and it'll be safe for me to help you."

Summer didn't really understand anything Mozart was saying, she was too glad he was there. He'd keep her safe. He wouldn't let Ben hurt her. Suddenly she remembered Elizabeth. "Mpsbth."

Mozart answered as if she'd spoken perfectly understandable English, "Cookie has her. She's okay."

Summer didn't look away from Mozart's eyes. She could vaguely hear a commotion going on behind him, but at the moment she didn't care. All she cared about was that Mozart was there with her. He was actually there. He wouldn't let Ben touch her again. Summer breathed heavily through her nose.

"All clear!"

At the words, Mozart moved quickly. He bought a knife up from somewhere and Summer felt the gag that had been tied around her face loosen. She whimpered and tried to spit out the bunched up cloth from her mouth. Her mouth was way too dry to be able to rid herself of the nasty piece of fabric.

Mozart put the knife on the ground, and gently took Summer's chin in his. "Hold still, Sunshine. Let me help."

He reached between her dry cracked lips and grasped the edge of the material that was in her mouth. Mozart didn't even bother to look at it as he flung it away once it cleared her lips. Mozart tried not to let the way she gasped for breath get to him. He couldn't. There were too many other things he had to do to help her first.

"I have to get the tape off your eyes, Sunshine," he whispered. "It's going to hurt. I'm sorry. I'm so sorry. It'll hurt for just a moment, then it will feel so good to be able to close your eyes. Okay? Do you understand?"

At her small nod, Mozart reached for the tape above her right eye. He had no idea if Hurst had known what he was doing, but he'd managed to get the tape on so that it was sticking to her eyelashes, eyebrows, and even some of her hair. Mozart hadn't lied. It was going to hurt coming off, but it couldn't wait for the hospital. Her eyes were bloodshot and dilated. She was in shock, and it had to be done.

Mozart wasn't sure if it would be better to rip it off, like a Band-Aid, but he decided to go slow and steady. When Summer didn't even moan as the tape ripped out the hair of her eyebrows and lashes, he knew her shock was worse than he'd thought. Seeing the little hairs on the tape as it came off, physically hurt him. Summer hadn't so much as whimpered throughout the ordeal though. As soon as the last piece of tape was off, Mozart watched as her eyes closed and she sighed.

Mozart stood up while saying, "Okay, Sunshine, you're doing great. I'm going to get these cuffs off then we're out of here."

"Don't touch me."

Mozart took a step back as if Summer had physically hit him. He'd wanted to hear her speak to him, to reassure him that she was okay, but hadn't expected her first words to be for him to get away from her. "What?" The word came out before Mozart could pull it back.

"Don't touch me," Summer repeated.

Ignoring what was happening behind him, Mozart couldn't give a shit about Hurst at the moment. His focus was centered on Summer, and only Summer. Who the hell knew what Hurst had done to her while they were trying to find her. He'd only gotten a glimpse of the young woman who'd been strapped to the floor, but if Summer had been through anything like what it looked like the young woman had been though, it was no wonder she didn't want to be touched.

"Sunshine, I have to touch you to get the cuffs off."

Mozart watched as her eyes opened to slits. Her words tore through him.

"I'm not clean. He jacked off on me. He wiped her blood on me. He spit on me. He smeared his fucking cum on my face and hair. I don't want him anywhere on you."

Mozart's stomach turned. Fuck. He brought his hand to her face and put it over her eyes lightly. "Sunshine, keep your eyes closed, I know they hurt. I don't give a fuck what he did to you. I'm here now, I'll take care of you. *Let* me take care of you."

"I...Okay." Summer's voice was so soft, Mozart could barely hear it, but he *had* heard it. He brushed the knuckles of one hand down her cheek briefly before standing up again. He pulled a set of handcuff keys out of his pocket. Handcuffs keys were generally pretty standard and they were a part of the team's general supplies they carried with them at all times. They'd come in very handy in the past when they'd gotten into some sticky situations as well as when they'd gone in for a hostage rescue.

Mozart made quick work of unlocking the cuffs and winced at the condition of Summer's wrists. They were covered in blood and he could see deep gouges in her wrists from fighting against the cuffs' hold. Mozart dropped the metal handcuffs on the ground and took hold of Summer's hands with his. He walked around her careful not to jar her and kneeled in front of her again.

"I'm going to pick you up, Sunshine, and take you outside and away from here. I want you to hold on to me, don't let go, and keep your eyes closed. It's bright outside and I know the light will hurt your eyes."

He watched as Summer nodded, then she squeezed his hands.

"Is Elizabeth going to be all right?"

Mozart thought about lying to her, but decided she needed to hear the truth. "I don't know. I've only been concerned about you."

He leaned over and picked Summer up and settled her into his arms. She immediately rested her head on his shoulder and wound her arms around his neck.

"His name isn't Joseph."

"I know."

"It's Ben Hurst. He said he's been torturing and killing women and kids for years."

"Shhhh, I know, Summer."

"He said..."

"Sunshine," Mozart said a bit more forcefully as he maneuvered them to the door of the small cabin. "I *know*."

Mozart looked back into the room for the first time. Cookie had cut Elizabeth free and was trying to tend to her injuries. Benny and Dude were holding a subdued Hurst. His pants were around his ankles and his face was bloody. Wolf was standing over Hurst holding his pistol in his hand. Wolf met Mozart's eyes as he stopped at the door.

Mozart knew what Wolf wanted to know, but he didn't feel capable of making the decision. Once upon a time, he knew he would've wanted to be the one standing over Hurst, making him beg for his life, but he just didn't care anymore.

Even with holding an injured and traumatized Summer in his arms, he felt lighter. He felt as if he'd finally let go of all the angst and bitterness he'd held since he was fifteen over what Hurst had taken from him. In a weird way, Hurst had brought him and Summer together. If it hadn't been for Hurst hiding out in Big Bear, he never would've met Summer.

Mozart just wanted to get Summer out of the cabin and into some fresh air. He needed to get her to a hospital and he needed to make sure she was all right. Nothing else mattered. Not even Hurst.

Mozart turned away from Wolf and left the cabin. He heard Hurst yelling at him as he left the cabin, but Mozart didn't care. Whatever the man had to say, it didn't matter anymore.

Mozart saw that Abe was standing outside. He met his eyes and walked toward him.

"We need to get her to a hospital."

"I've got the four wheeler ready. It looks like its got lots of gas in it. You can't drive and hold Summer at the same time and three people won't fit on it. We also need to get help for Elizabeth. I'll head down to the car and get a hold of Tex. He'll get a chopper up here."

Mozart wasn't letting go of Summer. Not until he had to. "I'm not leaving her."

"Of course you aren't. Don't worry, Mozart. She's made it this far, she'll be fine. I'll make sure Tex knows there'll be three people the chopper's picking up."

"Appreciate it." He turned to walk further away from the cabin and to get into the shade of some trees.

Abe turned to leave just as a single shot rang out from the cabin behind them. Abe stopped and turned around and looked at Mozart. Mozart hadn't veered from his path to the shade and in fact hadn't even turned around. Abe shook his head grimly, knowing what the shot meant. Hurst wouldn't be hurting anyone else ever again.

Finally, he shrugged, he had to get back to the cars and get a hold of Tex. Both women needed to get to a hospital immediately. They'd deal with Hurst and the aftermath of what had gone down later.

CHAPTER 17

Mozart sat next to Summer's hospital bed with his feet propped up on the end of the mattress and watched her breathe. He watched as Summer's chest slowly moved up and down and he counted her breaths. She was breathing about sixteen times a minute, which was still in the normal range, but was toward the top of it.

She'd scared him to death, and Mozart wasn't afraid to admit it. Tex had worked fast and they'd been taken to the Community Hospital of San Bernardino, the closest trauma center to Big Bear. Within a couple of hours, Ice, Alabama, and Fiona had arrived, along with the rest of the team.

Mozart had stayed by Summer's side and had refused to leave. He'd told the doctor that Summer was his fiancée, and every member of his team had backed him up. Summer hadn't even contradicted him. He'd been allowed to stay while they'd examined her physically. Her clothes had been put into paper bags for the police as evidence, and a crime scene investigator had arrived to document her injuries with photographs.

Mozart stayed in the room, even when the nurses had tried to chase him out before they gave her a sponge bath to clean her up. He turned his back, so as not to embarrass Summer, but he wouldn't leave.

Summer hadn't said much during the exams, but Mozart noticed that she constantly checked to see where he was. Hardly a minute went by where she wasn't searching for him. Mozart made sure to stay within her eyesight. If the doctor moved so he blocked Summer's view of him, Mozart would step to the side, so she could still see him. Someone else might not have even noticed she was doing it, but he'd noticed and made sure she felt as comfortable as possible during the uncomfortable exam.

While the doctors checked her eyes, Mozart had held Summer's hand and didn't complain a bit when her fingernails dug into his skin. It wasn't until he saw the damage that had been done to her wrists that he'd broken down. Mozart hadn't been able to stop the tears that fell silently from his eyes. He'd seen worse injuries in his lifetime, but it was what the deep gouges meant, that made him lose it.

He knew Summer had fought. She'd fought against what Hurst had done to Elizabeth. She'd tried to escape. Mozart knew she'd continued to try to escape her bindings, even when it was obvious she couldn't. Even as the blood coursed down her hands and dripped on the floor below, she continued to fight.

Summer had seen his tears and leaned into him. She couldn't touch him since the nurses were cleaning and stitching her wrists, but she still found a way to comfort him. She turned her head and nuzzled into his neck as he cried. She sighed as Mozart's arms went around her tightly. Summer had simply whispered, "I'm okay, Mozart," and continued to let him take her weight until the nurses were done. They'd given her a shot for pain and the last thing she'd said to him was, "please don't leave."

So here he sat. She'd asked him not to leave and nothing was going to tear him away from her side. Not his commander, not the United States Navy, not the damn President of the United States. Mozart would sit there until hell froze over if he had to.

Each one of the girls had tiptoed into the room to see how Summer was doing. They hadn't known her very long, but she'd obviously made an impression on them. Summer had slept through all of their visits. The girls had promised to come back the next day when hopefully Summer would be awake.

Caroline had to get back to Riverton, she was in the middle of a huge project at work and really couldn't spare even one day away, but she'd insisted on coming up to visit anyway. It meant even more to Mozart because he knew first-hand how much Ice hated hospitals. Mozart had pulled her aside and asked for a favor. Of course, Caroline had agreed with no questions asked. Mozart smiled, remembering. Caroline probably would have been pissed if he *hadn't* asked for her help.

Ice had given him a big hug and told him, "She'll be okay, Mozart. She'll want you here. I'll see you guys back home."

Mozart thought back to when Ice had been in the hospital. She'd also been kidnapped and tortured. He hoped Summer would be able to get past everything that had been done to her as well as Ice had. He knew Ice still had some nightmares. He and Wolf had even talked about it. But slowly she was getting over them, thank God.

Summer finally stirred. Mozart brought his feet down and stood up. He sat down on the bed next to her hip and leaned over her, being careful not to jostle her. He didn't want to freak her out, but he wanted to be close enough so she'd know he was there the second she opened her eyes. With his hands on either side of her hips, Mozart surrounded her with his heat and leaned in, watching as Summer struggled to fully awaken.

Summer squirmed on the bed, not wanting to wake up. She knew if she opened her eyes, she'd have to deal with all the crap that had gone down over the last day or so. She remembered almost every second she'd been held in the cabin. As much as she wished she didn't, Summer knew she'd never forget. Every single part of her body hurt, but she was alive. She tried to keep telling herself that.

Summer opened her eyes to slits trying to keep her panic down. She knew it would be a long time before she'd feel comfortable being by herself again. Summer jolted at seeing a pair of intense dark eyes right above her head. She immediately relaxed. She'd recognize Mozart's eyes anywhere.

"Hi," she said quietly, relieved at seeing him there.

"Hey. How are you feeling?"

"You want the truth, or the watered down version?"

"Always the truth, Sunshine. Always."

"My wrists hurt. My eyes are burning, I feel dirty and I'm worried about Elizabeth. But I'm so relieved you're here I'm not sure I can put it into words. It makes all the other things fade away." Summer watched as Mozart's face at first tensed at her words, but then relaxed.

"There's no place I'd rather be."

"I called Tex like you told me to."

"Are we going to talk about this now? Or do you need time?"

"I'd rather talk about it now. I don't think I can ignore it for too long. It'll eat away at me."

"Do you want me to get a psychiatrist in here for you? I know Ice still talks to one and she's helped her a lot."

"No, I just want you."

"You've got me, Sunshine. Scoot over."

Mozart waited as Summer moved a bit to the right, then he lay down right next to her and gathered her into his arms carefully. He heard her sigh in contentment.

"Is this even legal?"

"Don't care."

Summer smiled at Mozart's words. She knew he really didn't care about the hospital rules. She sobered. "This is what I thought about when he made me watch. I wasn't seeing what he was doing or saying, I was remembering how safe I felt when you held me just like this."

"You did good calling Tex, but dammit, Summer, I have to say it. You shouldn't have gotten in the damn car with Hurst in the first place."

"I know."

Mozart paused. He was all ready to deliver a gentle, but firm reprimand, and Summer took all the wind out of his sails.

She continued, "I had a bad feeling in my gut, which was why I called Tex. I was stupid. I shouldn't have let Henry goad me into it. I'm just sorry that the other woman got sucked into the situation. And I'm so sorry for you too. If I'd been smarter you wouldn't have had to go through it and be reminded of your sister."

Mozart chuckled. "You're the only person I've met who after being kidnapped and tortured, would apologize for it." Then he sobered. "Sunshine, I don't give a fuck about Hurst."

"But…"

"No, let me finish." When Summer nodded, Mozart pulled her more deeply into his arms and rested his head on top of her head.

"For most of my life I've been hunting that man. He's the reason I joined the SEAL teams. I wanted revenge for Avery. I wanted to kill him more than I wanted to serve my country, more than I really cared about rescuing people, more than anything else. It had consumed my life entirely. The only reason I was in Big Bear in the first place was because Tex told me Hurst had been there. But you know what? When we got to that cabin and revenge was in sight for me, I didn't give a damn. The *only* thing I cared about was you. I didn't see Elizabeth. I didn't see Hurst. I didn't see my teammates. I only saw *you*. I got to you as soon as I could and realized I couldn't care less what happened to that fucker. I knew my teammates would make sure he didn't get away, and that was good enough for me."

"What happened to him?"

"He won't be hurting anyone else ever again."

"Will you guys get in trouble? I'll say whatever's necessary to the police and the Navy so you don't in trouble."

Mozart could tell Summer was getting worked up and he tried to reassure her.

"No, we aren't going to get in trouble, Sunshine. Our CO knew where we were and what we were doing. The police are up at the cabin now taking photos and getting evidence. Tex has sent them everything, at least everything legal, he collected on Hurst over the years. They know he was a psycho. We won't get in trouble."

He relaxed a fraction as Summer's muscles loosened. After a beat she whispered in a voice so low, Mozart almost didn't hear her, "I was so scared."

"Aw, Sunshine."

"I know I called Tex, since you were out of the country on some mission. I tried to stay strong. I told myself that Tex would figure it out and help me, but I didn't know how."

"Tell me what you can about what happened. You have to get it out. I'm not a counselor, and that's probably what you need, but I also want you to talk to me."

"I'm scared."

"Of what? Me?"

"No. Well, kinda."

Mozart's arms loosened. Shit. She was scared of him? He prepared to get off the bed and give Summer some space.

"No! Please. I didn't mean it that way." Summer's arms tightened around Mozart, preventing him from moving away from her. "I'm not scared of *you*. I'm scared if I tell you what happened, you'll think differently about me. That you'll think I'm weak. I don't think I'm like the other women that your friends are with. Caroline is so put together. It happened to her too, but she's so strong."

"Summer, Ice is strong because of Wolf. She was a hot mess right after it happened. Hell, give yourself a break. It hasn't even been twenty-four hours, Sunshine. And you're right, I'll probably think differently about you after you tell me." When Summer jerked in his arms and tried to pull away, Mozart was the one who held on tight and pulled his head back so he could look in her eyes. "I'll be more proud of you than I am right now. I'll think you're so much stronger than I thought you were. I'll love you even more than I do right now."

Summer could only stare at Mozart in bewilderment. "Wha..."

"Yes, I love you. I've never said that to another woman before in my life. I never believed in insta-love before you. Even I know it's nuts. Hell, I haven't even been inside you yet, but I love you. If anything had happened to you, I don't know what I would've done. Now, tell me what happened. Give it to me. Let me help you though it." He pulled her head back down so it was resting on his chest again.

"Close your eyes, I know they're hurting. Relax, you're safe in my arms, now tell me."

"Bossy," Summer teased, bringing her hand up to his face and cupping it as she lay there. She ran her thumb over his cheek, realizing that he'd been through his own hell enough times that he most likely could help her work through what had happened.

She quietly described in a monotone what had happened up until the point where Hurst had taped her eyes open. Her voice broke. "He wanted me to watch. I just couldn't anymore. He got pissed and told me he'd make it so I didn't have a choice. I didn't want to see it. He might have forced my eyes open, but I refused to *see*. I thought about you. Your touch, your words, how it sounded when you called me 'Sunshine.' My eyes burned, they were so dry. The tape was pulling on my hair."

Mozart couldn't help it. "Shhhhh, Sunshine. I've got you. You're okay."

"When the bright light went off, I thought I'd been blinded. I was so scared."

"I'm so sorry…"

"No, you don't understand. When I was finally able to see again, the first thing I saw was *you*. You were blocking everything else out. I thought I was still dreaming at first. Then you were wanting to touch me, and I didn't want his filth on you. You're everything that's good and clean. I didn't want that touching you."

"Sunshine, I love that you feel that about me. But I'm not clean."

"You *are*. You've made me feel things I haven't felt in all my life. When you're around, I forget everything else. I called Tex knowing he'd find you. Somehow, no matter how crazy it was, I knew you'd come for me. You said you'd always come for me."

"Fuck, Sunshine. You're right. I'll always come for you. But please, Jesus, please, don't get in a car with a psychotic serial killer who wants to taunt me with you again."

Mozart closed his eyes when he heard Summer giggle. How the hell she could laugh after everything she'd been through, was beyond him.

"Are there any more psychotic serial killers out there who will want to kidnap me just to taunt you?"

"Fuck no."

"Then okay, I won't get in a car with any again." Summer brought her head up and looked at Mozart seriously. "I love you, Sam Reed."

"Thank God." Mozart crushed Summer to his chest again, just as a nurse entered the room.

"What do you think you're doing? You aren't allowed on the patient's bed."

Mozart didn't even twitch. He wasn't moving.

"Sir? Did you hear me?"

"Yeah, I heard you, I'm just ignoring you."

"You can't ignore me. I'll call security!"

Mozart felt Summer try to get up, and knew he had to say something to appease the shrew of a nurse before it further upset Summer.

He picked his head up off the pillow while still holding Summer tightly to him. Mozart looked at the nurse and calmly stated, "My woman has been kidnapped and tortured by a serial killer hell bent on destroying me. She just spent the last thirty minutes telling me about how that sick fuck tortured her by taping her damn eyes open and jacking off on her. I don't give a flying fuck if it's against the rules of this hospital, but I wasn't going to let her go through that without feeling safe in my arms. I'm sorry if you have a problem with that, but I'm not moving until I'm sure she's okay and is comfortable with me getting up off this bed."

Mozart put his head back down on the pillow and waited for the explosion he figured was coming. He hadn't exactly been diplomatic.

"Uh, okay, I'll just come back in a bit then."

Summer and Mozart listened as the door opened and then shut again. Summer broke the silence by giggling again. "Uh, was that really necessary?"

"Yes." Mozart wasn't ready to let it go.

"I love you, Mozart. I don't think our life will be easy and calm."

"Yes it will. I can't handle anything like this again. Oh and you should know, Ice is arranging to have all your things moved from Big

Bear down to my apartment. She's also been given carte blanche to get you anything else she thinks you need that she doesn't see in your stuff. And I have to warn you, Sunshine, most likely you'll have a shit-ton of new clothes and shoes when we get home."

Not knowing what to expect from his announcement, Mozart tensed. He knew Summer was independent and didn't like it when he bought her things. Telling her she was being moved into his apartment in a different city went way beyond "buying her things."

"Okay."

Mozart was floored. "Okay?" He lifted Summer's chin so he could look into her eyes.

"Okay," Summer repeated.

"You're not freaking out. Should I expect a freak out later when you're more yourself?"

"Mozart, I just went through the worst thing I've ever been through in my life. I was scared out of my mind that I'd never see you again. I was scared that Ben would rape, torture, and kill me before I'd get to tell you how much you meant to me. I didn't really even like my job all that much and was already planning on leaving after the winter was over. I'm more than happy to move down to Riverton with you. I'll stay with you as long as you'll have me."

"You're such a pain in my ass."

Summer just smiled up at him.

"Kiss me?"

"With pleasure."

Mozart turned on his side until he was over Summer. He leaned down and gently took her lips with his own. He took his time, tasting and nibbling. When he felt her tongue reach out for his, he deepened the kiss, bringing his hand up to her cheek and holding her still, as the kiss turned carnal.

Before the kiss could go any further, they heard the door open again. Mozart reluctantly lifted his head. He didn't look away from Summer's eyes but brushed his hand over her head and tucked her hair behind her ear. He kissed each eye, each eyebrow, and finally her forehead before finally turning his head to see who had entered the room.

Seeing the doctor was leaning against the door jamb, smiling, Mozart shook his head and smiled in return. He shifted until he could get his legs over the side of the bed and he stood up. He pulled the chair closer to the side of the bed and sat down, grasping Summer's hand in his own before settling down.

"Doc, it's good to see you," he drawled semi-sarcastically.

The doctor laughed and pushed himself away from the door and came toward the bed. "Yeah, I bet. But I bring good news." He looked at Summer. "You're being discharged today. Your eyes will be okay. I'm prescribing some eye drops to help with the dryness. You'll find in a few days they'll be back to normal. Your other injuries will just take some time to heal. I'm sending you home with some pain killers. You need to use them if the pain gets to be too much. Don't try to be a hero. Relax, rest, and you'll be as good as new in no time." He paused, obviously wanting to say something, but not knowing how to say it.

Finally, he just blurted it out. "I think it's also a good idea if you talked to someone about what happened. I can get some referrals if you need them."

"I've got it under control, doc." Mozart said darkly.

When it looked like the doctor was going to protest, Summer broke in. "I will. I promise. Mozart is a SEAL, there are a lot of doctors on the base I can talk to. He's going to set it up for me."

"Okay then. Good. I wish you the best of luck. I would recommend that you follow up with your personal physician when you get home to make sure everything is healing up as it should. A visit to your optometrist would also be a good move, again, just to make sure everything is okay."

"Will do," Mozart answered. "I'll get that set up for next week as well."

The doctor held out his hand to Mozart. "It was good to meet you Mr. Reed. Thank you for your service to our country. We're all better off for the job that you do." Visibly flustered, Mozart shook his hand. Summer giggled again at his discomfort. Some badass SEAL he was.

The doctor turned back to Summer and held out his hand to her. Shaking her hand, he said solemnly, "And good luck to you, Summer. You're an amazing woman and I'm glad you beat that son-of-a-bitch!"

Flushing, Summer didn't say anything.

"Go ahead and get dressed and get your things together. We'll discharge you as soon as we can. It can get crazy around here, but we know that leaving is generally people's favorite thing to do." He laughed at his own joke and turned to leave.

"Doctor?" Summer's voice sounded loud in the room.

"Yes, Summer?"

"Can you tell me how Elizabeth is doing?" A knot formed in Summer's stomach at the look on the doctor's face.

"I wish I could, doctor-patient privilege and all of that."

"Oh. Okay. I just…"

Mozart put his hand to Summer's cheek and turned her head toward him. "I'll find out for you, Sunshine."

"I just wanted her to know…"

When she didn't say anything else, Mozart prompted her to continue. "Know what?"

"That I wasn't getting off on what he was doing."

"What the fuck?" Mozart couldn't have bitten off the words if he'd tried.

Summer hurried to explain, "*He* told her that. He told her that he was torturing her because I'd asked him to. That I wanted him to."

"Sunshine, I'm sure she didn't believe him."

"But what if she did, Mozart?"

"She doesn't," the doctor spoke from beside Summer's bed. He'd walked back over and was speaking in a low voice. "She isn't doing as well as you are, Summer. She needed someone to talk to. I was there when she spoke briefly with the crisis counselor. She knows he was torturing you too. She told the counselor that she felt bad for *you*."

Summer's eyes burned with fresh tears. "Thank you for telling me."

"You're welcome. Now, get dressed and get out of my hospital." He smiled as he said it so Summer would know he was kidding with her.

Mozart waited until the door shut behind him. "Don't."

"Don't what?"

"Don't feel guilty. What he did to you was just as bad as what he did to her. You were both innocent in all of this."

"I know. I just feel…I don't know what I feel."

"Feel glad that you're not there anymore. Feel relief that he can't hurt anyone ever again. Feel happy that you're going home with me."

"I do, Mozart. I do."

"Okay then. Let's go home."

CHAPTER 18

Summer sat cross legged on the bed as Caroline, Alabama, and Fiona climbed on as well.

"How are you really doing, Summer?" Caroline asked somberly.

"I'm okay. Really. Thank you for giving me the name of your counselor. I thought I was doing okay talking with Mozart, but I realized I was still holding back with him because I didn't want to hurt him. And I knew every time I had a nightmare he was hurting."

"I know. I still feel that way sometimes. Having an unbiased person that you know you won't hurt if you tell them the fears and thoughts in your head is really important." Caroline patted Summer's knee.

"I'm not sure how we got so lucky, but I'll tell you this. I thank my lucky stars every day that I was kidnapped by those sex slavers," Fiona said unexpectedly.

"What the hell?" Alabama exclaimed, smacking Fiona lightly on the shoulder. "How can you say that?"

"Because if I hadn't been held hostage down there in Mexico, I never would have met Hunter. I would still be living my boring life in El Paso."

"Yeah but..."

"No, no buts. I've spent a lot of time thinking about this. Things happen in our lives for a reason. Caroline, you were on that plane so you could smell that drugged ice. Matthew was sitting next to you so he could save everyone's lives on board. Alabama, you saved Christopher's life at that party. If you hadn't been there to lead him to safety, he might not be around today. Yes, everything you went through with him sucked, but the bottom line is that he's still around today because of you. I met Hunter as a direct result of what happened to me in Mexico. And Summer, there are so many ways to look at what happened to you, but the bottom line is that if poor little Avery hadn't been killed when she was little, you never would have met Sam, and Ben Hurst might still be out there killing people today." Fiona let her words sink in before she continued.

"We can piss and moan about our lives and the hell we each went through, but the bottom line is that we wouldn't be with our men today if our lives hadn't played out as they had. I'm dealing with my issues, and you guys are dealing with yours, but at the end of the day we get to fall asleep in the arms of our men…and I wouldn't change one minute of my life if it meant losing that."

"Wow." Summer couldn't really disagree with Fiona. She was right. It helped put everything in perspective for her in a way she knew she never would have come up with on her own. She sent up a silent prayer for Avery. She'd never get the chance to meet her, but she'd be grateful to her for the rest of her life.

When everyone was quiet for a bit, Fiona finally broke the silence. "Okay, enough of that. Caroline, get out the drinks. We need to party!"

Everyone laughed. Caroline had browbeat Matthew until he'd agreed to let her host their little get together in the basement of their house. Alabama had spent a lot of time there after she'd been arrested and Christopher had his head up his ass, and it had become the hangout place when the women wanted to get together and let loose. Their men weren't comfortable with them going out all the time, so to appease them, they let loose in the basement while the SEALs were upstairs waiting them out.

Alabama and Christopher usually crashed in the bed there in the basement, and Hunter always took Fiona home. Since this was the first time Summer had been invited, she wasn't sure what Mozart would do, but she figured he'd sweep her home as soon as she popped her head upstairs again. He'd been crazy protective, but Summer secretly loved every second of his Alpha protectiveness. She still sometimes looked over her shoulder thinking she saw Ben, but knew he was dead.

On their way home from the hospital, Mozart had explained what had happened at the cabin. Wolf had decided to bring Hurst in to face the justice system for what he'd done to not only Elizabeth and Summer, but for every woman and child he'd murdered over the years. Wolf knew every one of his teammates wanted to slit Hurst's throat for not only what he'd done to Mozart's woman and sister, but for all the women and children he'd tortured over the years. But when they'd gone to bring Hurst out of the cabin, he'd turned on Benny and tried to gut him with a knife he'd had in his pants pocket. Wolf had shot him right between the eyes and Hurst had fallen down dead.

They were all a bit pissed the man hadn't suffered more, but it had been deemed a case of self-defense. There was no way anyone was going to put a SEAL team on the stand for murder, not with Hurst's history and with the testimony of Summer and Elizabeth about what had gone on in the cabin.

Sitting in the basement of Caroline's house, drinking Sex on the Beaches, Midori Sours, and Screwdrivers, Summer never felt safer. She knew her SEAL and three others were upstairs impatiently waiting for their female bonding to be over. They might gripe and complain about it, but they all knew they'd give their women whatever they wanted.

After another two hours, the women finally took pity on the men, at least that was what they said to each other. Summer chuckled, knowing the other women enough to know they were all horny as hell and wanted nothing more than to jump their men.

Mozart hadn't wanted to rush her and they'd yet to make love, but Summer was hoping tonight was the night. She was more than ready. They'd had some pretty heavy make out sessions over the last two weeks, but she wanted more than that. She wasn't sure what Mozart was waiting for, but she was determined to break through his resolve tonight.

The women all tripped up the stairs laughing and hanging off one another. They burst through the basement door into the kitchen and laughed anew at the looks on the men's faces. Each woman stumbled over to her man.

Summer loved the smile that was on Mozart's face. He'd turned in his seat as soon as he'd seen her, and he now pulled her to stand between his legs.

"Did you have a good time, Sunshine?"

"Yeah, you have the best friends."

"They're your friends too, Summer."

"Oh yeah, *we* have the best friends." Summer beamed at Mozart.

"Oh yeah, you're ready to go." Mozart looked around at his teammates. Yeah, they were going. Wolf and Ice were oblivious to anyone around them. They were locked in each other's arms and in another five minutes would probably be going at it on the table. Abe had hauled Alabama up in his arms and was heading toward the basement door. Mozart bet they would also be more than occupied within five minutes.

He met Cookie's eyes across the table and they smiled at each other. They were the poor saps that had to drive home. It'd take them at least another half an hour before they'd be able to crawl into bed with their women.

"You have a key right? Wolf is always too occupied to bother with locking the door behind us," Mozart asked almost rhetorically.

"Yeah, I've got it. Go on, get Summer home. I've got this."

Mozart laughed. Fiona was sitting in Cookie's lap alternating between kissing his neck and sucking on his earlobe.

"God, I love girls-night-in," Cookie said, as he tilted his head to give Fiona more access.

Mozart just shook his head and looked back at Summer.

"Ready to go?"

"Yeah. I'm ready."

At the weird tone of her voice, Mozart took a hard look at

Summer. She was grinning at him a little crookedly. He could tell she was tipsy, but she wasn't falling-down drunk. "What?"

"Nothing, let's go." Summer took a step back and tugged on his hand. Mozart stood up and followed her to the front door and out to his SUV.

He watched as her eyes darted from side to side as he walked around the vehicle to get into the driver's side. He hated that she still felt the need to get a sense of her surroundings. If she hadn't been through what she had with Hurst, Mozart would probably be proud of her for being safe. But seeing her do it now just pissed him off. He knew he couldn't erase all her memories of that night, but he hated seeing her scared or even uncomfortable.

Mozart climbed in and pulled on his seat belt before starting the car. He felt Summer's hand on his as it rested on the gear shift.

"I'm okay, Mozart. Promise."

He lifted her hand and kissed the back of it. "You're more than okay, Sunshine. Let's go home."

The car was silent all the way back to their apartment. Both Summer and Mozart were lost in their own thoughts. After parking the car, Mozart kissed Summer's hand again.

"Stay put, Sunshine."

Summer nodded, she knew the drill.

Mozart came around the car and opened her door. She slid out and put her hand in his. They walked up to the second floor to the apartment. Mozart didn't let go of Summer's hand as he unlocked the door and they walked in. He paused, as he usually did and tilted his head to listen to the quiet apartment. Not hearing anything unusual, and not feeling any bad vibes, he dropped the keys on the table beside the door and shut the front door.

Summer turned in his arms and looked up at him. Mozart was always saying to her that she could tell him anything, that he wanted her to be honest with him. Well, tonight she was going to be honest. The alcohol helped a bit, but the words were all hers.

"It's time. I want you."

"Summer, you've been drinking."

"I don't care. I'm not drunk. Not even close. I feel good. I feel safe. I need you, Mozart. I need you in my arms. I need you inside me. I'm starting to feel like you don't want me that way..." Even she was surprised at the words that came out. She *had* started to feel like he might not see her in the same way as he had before she'd been kidnapped. Maybe being in Hurst's clutches was too much for him.

Almost before the last word left her mouth, Mozart's lips were covering hers. He yanked her into his arms. One arm went behind her back and up her spine, to hold her upper body to his, and the other hand slid into her hair, holding her head still for his assault on her senses.

Lifting his head after making her sway in his arms he growled, "Not want you? Jesus, Sunshine, I've spent every morning since we've left the hospital jacking off in the shower. The feel of you beside me in bed, your smell on my skin in the mornings and on my sheets, watching you laugh and gain your footing back after going through what you've been through...it's almost been too much."

When Summer jerked in his arms, Mozart refused to loosen his hold. "I want you to be sure. I want you to be ready for me. I can't get inside you and then let you go. If we do this, I won't let you go."

"I don't want you to let me go."

"Are you sure you're ready for this?"

"Yes, I've never been more ready in my entire life," Summer paused a moment. "Have you really been...you know...in the shower?"

"Yes. But it doesn't help. The second I walk into the room and see you in my bed I get hard all over again."

"I do too."

"What?" Mozart didn't understand what Summer was saying.

"I do that too...in the shower...after you go to work..."

Mozart leaned down and swept Summer off her feet. Without a word he carried her into their room and set her on her feet next to the bed.

"Clothes. Off."

Smirking at his lapse into caveman speak, Summer slowly pulled her shirt over her head. She watched as Mozart's eyes widened and he stood stock still, his hands motionless on the button of his jeans. Enjoying the fact that her striptease was rendering him immobile, Summer reached down and pulled off her tennis shoes one at a time, bending low so he could see her cleavage. She toed off her socks next and then loosened her jeans.

Wanting to spur Mozart into action, Summer asked cheekily, "Am I the only one that's gonna be naked tonight?"

"Fuck no." Mozart finally jerked into action. He whipped his shirt over his head and let it fall behind him without a thought. He then ripped open the button on his jeans and jerked them down his legs.

Summer grinned and eased her own jeans down her legs. Finally, they stood staring at each other in nothing but their underwear. Summer could feel her own wetness; she shuffled her feet. She could see Mozart was excited too. He certainly was big, she could see the outline of his manhood clearly through his cotton briefs. She reached behind her and unhooked her bra. She let it fall off her arms to drop at her feet. That apparently was enough to push Mozart into motion.

As Mozart took a step toward her, she stepped back. Finally, he was almost touching her and Summer could feel the bed at the back of her knees. With one more step, she sat hard on the edge of the mattress. Mozart went to his knees in front of her. He grabbed the side of her panties and growled, "Lift up."

Summer lifted her hips so Mozart could peel her undies down her legs. He wasted no time and as soon as the scrap of cotton cleared her ankles, he was up and pushing her back on the bed with a hand to her chest.

"Scoot back." As Summer scrambled to move backward on the bed, Mozart ripped his briefs off and then came up onto the bed and over Summer. He crawled on his hands and knees over her as she wiggled her way up the bed.

Satisfied with her location, Mozart dropped his hips onto hers and pressed down. Summer could feel his length against her heat and stomach.

"I want to go slow, but I'm not sure I can." Mozart put his forehead on hers and took a deep breath. "You can't touch me. If this is going to work, you can't touch me."

"Screw that!" Summer returned immediately. She brought her hand up to his scarred cheek. "Mozart, we have all the time in the world. I don't care if our first time lasts five minutes or five hours, because I know after the first time, there'll be a second. After the second, there'll be a third. After the third, there'll be a fourth. Eventually we'll make it to the shower and we can do to each other what we've been doing to ourselves. There aren't a ton of rooms in this apartment, but you do have quite a bit of furniture that I'm sure we can get creative on. Don't you get it, Mozart? I'm happy to just be here with you. I want to touch you and have you touch me back. Don't overthink it."

Mozart laughed. Summer was right. "You're right." He reared back a fraction then slowly brought his hips back down to hers and entered her at the same time. They both groaned. "Is this okay? Shit, tell me this is all right!"

"It's wonderful. Fantastic. If you stop I'll have to hurt you!" Summer put her hands on Mozart's butt and pulled him the last few inches until he rested against her as close as he could get. They both groaned.

"When we met, you bragged that I'd made you come three times before dinner...well, I can't promise that, because it's after dinner, but I can promise you those three orgasms."

Summer laughed and then they both groaned again.

"I can feel you clench on me when you laugh. I've never felt anything like it." Suddenly Mozart stilled. "Oh shit. Sunshine. I can't. You have to stop."

Summer continued to clench against his length. She squeezed him with her inner muscles as hard as she could. "Don't stop, Mozart. Please don't stop."

"I'm not covered baby. I'm not protected."

"I don't care."

Mozart stopped moving and reared back enough so that only the tip of his hardness was inside her. "Sunshine, are you on the pill?"

"No, but I was on the shot. I know it's not good forever, but I think it's still okay."

"I'm not willing to take a chance on a 'think.'"

Tears filled Summer's eyes, and Mozart leaned down and kissed them away.

"Don't cry, Jesus, don't cry."

"You don't want a baby with me?"

"I want *you,* Summer. If we decide down the line that a baby is what we want, we'll plan for it and make a baby with intent. For now? No, I don't want a baby. I just want you. I want to spend time getting to know *you*. I want to be able to go out to dinner and not worry about our child. I want to take trips with you. I don't want to leave you and a child while I go out on missions."

Summer took a deep breath. He was right. She wasn't ready for a baby either. "I want our first time to be just us. No latex."

Mozart took a deep breath. "I'm clean, I swear. I know I've been with way too many women in the past, but that was in the past. I haven't been with anyone since I met you. I get tested by the Navy."

"Okay, Mozart. I'm clean too."

Mozart laughed, Summer thinking she wasn't clean was almost a joke. Of course she was. "Of course you are, Sunshine. Okay, birth control. When was your last period?" Mozart laughed when Summer blushed. "Sunshine, you talk to me about other things, this shouldn't be embarrassing."

"But it is."

Mozart pushed inside Summer slowly and relentlessly until he couldn't get inside her anymore, then pulled out so that she only had his tip again. "Tell me."

"Bossy," but Summer said it with a smile. "I'm due to start in a few days."

"It should be safe. I'll pull out, if it won't bring back too many bad memories for you." Mozart couldn't help but think about what Hurst had done to her in the cabin.

"It's fine. It's not the same at all. I want to see you, feel you in me, but Mozart, there's still a risk." Summer smiled so Mozart would know she wasn't upset at him.

At her smile, Mozart grinned back. "I know it's not foolproof, but it's better than nothing. And you're right, I want our first time to be just us, with nothing between us. Now, lie back and let me concentrate, woman."

Summer giggled again and smiled as Mozart groaned. Her giggles quickly turned to moans as he pushed inside her again. All thought of laughing quickly left her mind as Mozart set about driving her crazy. It wasn't until Summer had climaxed a second time that Mozart began to thrust into her harder.

"Yes, baby, that's it. Take me. I'm yours."

Her words pushed Mozart over the edge. He pulled out quickly and started to release on Summer's stomach. He was floored when he felt her soft, little hand stroking him and coaxing more of his cum from his manhood. He watched as Summer used one hand to caress his softening length and the other to rub his release into her skin.

"Jesus. You're killing me, Sunshine."

"I love the feel of you on me."

Mozart lowered himself onto Summer. She brought her arms up in between them and Mozart could feel his wetness on her fingertips as she caressed his chest.

"I love you."

"I love you too."

They lay on the bed for a few minutes before Summer broke the silence. "I'll go to the doctor soon and start on the shot again."

"Okay, Sunshine."

"I want to feel you fill me up."

"*Yes*. I want that too."

Mozart peeled himself off Summer's chest and he smiled as she giggled once again.

"Uh, I think we need a shower."

"I recall you saying that when we first met too. Didn't you promise me 'one more round in the shower'?"

"I'm never going to live that down am I?"

"It was the best day of my life, Sunshine. I hope neither of us ever forget it."

"Me either."

"Let's go rock each other's world."

Summer smiled and took the hand Mozart held out to her as he stood by the side of the bed. She thought back to what Fiona had said earlier that night. Things happen in our lives for a reason. While being kidnapped and tortured by Ben Hurst hadn't been fun, it was a part of her being able to be where she was right now. Summer loved Mozart so much she couldn't imagine her life without him.

She took Mozart's hand and smiled all the way to the bathroom, ready to rock his world and to have hers rocked in return.

EPILOGUE

The team sat around the table at *Aces Bar and Grill* enjoying each other's company and ribbing each other good naturedly.

Jess, their usual waitress, put down a round of beers.

"Here you go, guys."

"Thanks, Jess. Hey, you got your hair cut," Benny said.

Jess looked up in surprise at the good looking group of men, locking eyes with Benny.

"Uh yeah, it was…uh...always in my face." Jess nervously smoothed a stray lock of hair behind her ear.

"Hmm, I guess I've never see it down, you've always had it pulled back when we've seen you here."

"Yeah, well, I needed a change."

Hearing the bartender calling her name, Jess looked over and saw the bartender gesturing at her. She turned back to the table. "I'll be back in a bit to see if you guys need anything else." She then turned and limped over to the bar to pick up another order to deliver.

Dude brought up the subject they were talking about before their drinks arrived. "As I was saying, you guys are pathetic!" He rolled his eyes at the men sitting around the table. "Seriously, you never want to go out anymore, you stay home all the time. You're all a bunch of fuddy duddies now that you have women."

"Hey, you're just jealous," Mozart shot back, laughing at his friend.

Dude wouldn't admit it, but he knew Mozart wasn't exactly wrong. He'd never really thought about settling down until he'd watched his friends find women to love one by one. And the women they'd found were awesome. He didn't like that they'd had to rescue Ice, Fiona, and Summer from awful situations, but he was pleased as all get out that they were now safe and with his friends.

Because most of their team was married now, the CO had backed off sending them on some of the more extreme missions they'd been on in the beginning of their careers. And both Dude and Benny were okay with that. They weren't as young as they used to be and the last thing any of them wanted to do was come home and have to tell one of their women that they'd lost their SEAL.

But Dude wasn't sure where he was supposed to find a woman of the caliber of his teammates'. He knew he wasn't the best candidate for a woman. He was too stubborn and needed too much control in his life. He tried not to let it bother him, but every time he saw Ice run her fingers down Wolf's face and laugh when she felt his stubble on her skin, or when he'd watch Fiona run her hand over Cookie's head, Dude knew in his gut he most likely wouldn't ever have that.

His left hand was too badly scarred, too mangled, too ugly to have a woman really take him seriously. He'd seen it time and time again. He'd meet a good looking woman while out at the bars and they'd be hitting it off, but when they saw his left hand they'd always back off.

He looked down at his hand. He was missing parts of three fingers that were blown off by the toe-popper on one of their missions. He was actually lucky it had been his left hand, and even more lucky to have only lost part of his fingers. He could still be a SEAL and he could still work with explosives, but it'd really put a crimp on his love life.

His wants in the bedroom was another reason Dude figured he'd never find a woman to settle down with permanently. It was one thing for a woman to want to play in the bedroom with him for a while, but another to accept the way he was full time. It was a novelty for a few nights to be told what to do and how to do it while in his bed, Dude had learned that more than that, women just plain didn't want long term.

Dude mentally shrugged. The hell with it.

The men were startled when Wolf's cell phone rang. They watched as he answered it and they all sat up straighter when they saw his muscles get tight.

"Right, yeah, I'll get him on it. Thanks." Wolf hung up the phone and turned to Dude.

"Bomb threat at the big grocery store on Main Street. They're asking for an ordinance expert."

"I'm on it." Dude stood up quickly, already thinking about what he might find. The local police department would sometimes call on the military when they needed extra help. This apparently was one of the times when they felt like the extra help would be needed.

"Be safe. Let us know if you need anything."

Dude raised his hand in acknowledgement of Wolf's words, then he was gone.

* * *

Download the next book in the SEAL of Protection Series:

Protecting Cheyenne

PROTECTING CHEYENNE

SEAL OF PROTECTION, BOOK 5

Living in Southern California, Cheyenne was used to seeing hot military men as she went about her daily business. An anonymous encounter at the grocery store cemented her crush on one such man. He was big, built, and incredibly easy on the eyes, but it wasn't as if he would ever really notice *her*.

Always in control of any situation, Faulkner "Dude" Cooper knows explosives. As a bomb expert, he's lived through many high pressure situations. Disfigured by a bomb while on a mission, he's used to being looked at with pity. When he's called to a local supermarket to assist the local PD, the last thing he expects to find is a generous act of kindness performed by a beautiful, amazing woman. Enchanted by her selflessness in the face of danger and intrigued by her actions to save civilians she didn't know, Dude's hooked.

Dude was able to save Cheyenne from the group of thugs trying to take her life, but when the past comes back to haunt them both, sometimes having the knowledge and the desire isn't enough to beat the countdown of the clock.

**Protecting Cheyenne is the 5th book in the SEAL of Protection Series. It can be read as a stand-alone, but it's recommended you read the books in order to get maximum enjoyment out of the series.

To receive special offers, bonus content, and news about my latest books, sign up for my newsletter:

www.StokerAces.com/contact.html

ACKNOWLEDGMENTS

Thank you to my awesome Facebook friends who spent a night brainstorming various 'jobs' that Cheyenne could hold. I thought about making her a drywaller, but then decided that wasn't quite right. Ha! Thanks for keeping it real and helping me out with suggestions and helping to make my characters "real."

To Phyllis, my inspiration and model for 911 operators everywhere. Thank you for all your do. Thank you for suffering through your own kind of PTSD. While I've never been there, anyone who has ever had to call 911 to get help, thanks you and is thankful you were there to help them.

For Cathy, Celeste, Beth, Phyllis, Karen, Wendy, Alicia, Mickey, Chris, Mandy and all my other LGBT friends and readers…keep on keepin' on.

CHAPTER 1

"911, what is your emergency?"

"Is this the police?"

"Yes, this is 911, what is your emergency?"

"My cable went out and I can't get my shows."

"Ma'am, this line is for emergencies only."

"Yeah, I know. This *is* an emergency. My DVR isn't working and I have to see what happens to Toni tonight."

Cheyenne sighed. Jesus, she hated these calls. "Have you tried calling your cable company?"

"Yeah, but they weren't answering."

"What do you want me to do?" Cheyenne was shorter than she probably should've been, but this was an emergency line and she was exhausted. She didn't have the time or patience for this crap.

"Can you see if you can get through to them for me? I need them to fix this now."

"Okay, hold on. Let me see what I can do." Cheyenne put the woman on hold and plunked her head on the desk in front of her. She took three deep breaths then sat up straight again and clicked the caller back on. "Okay, I got a hold of them and they said you should call them back. They'll see what they can do for you."

"Oh my God, thank you so much! I appreciate it."

"Have a good night, ma'am, and I hope Toni is all right."

"Yeah me too! Thanks again. I'll call them right now."

Cheyenne clicked off the phone again and sighed deeply. Working as a 911 operator sounded much more glamourous than it was in reality. Most nights she had at least one or two people calling in with the most ridiculous "emergencies." Technically, she was supposed to report them and give the info to her supervisor, but it was usually just as easy to get the person off the phone, quickly and politely, than try to report them and get them in trouble.

It never made sense to Cheyenne to take up a police officer's time to go out and give a warning to these types of people when the officer could instead be concentrating on finding bad guys or helping people that honestly needed assistance.

Cheyenne turned back to her laptop sitting next to the other computer and electronic equipment on her desk and clicked back on the movie she'd been watching.

Typically, Cheyenne was the only phone operator on duty for her small section. She worked the second shift, which she loved, but she could go hours with no calls at all. She learned quickly to bring something to do, otherwise she'd die of boredom. She wasn't typically a "night" person, but working from three in the afternoon to eleven at night suited her. She could sleep in, do errands in the mornings, and still have time to get to work in the afternoons.

The job was much harder than Cheyenne had thought it'd be when she'd first applied. She didn't mind talking to people. Giving out basic first aid advice was kind of exhilarating; she enjoyed being able to help keep someone alive or even simply calm them down until the paramedics or police officers could get there. Lately, however, Cheyenne had been feeling antsy and discontented. It wasn't until she read an article online about post-traumatic stress, that she understood her feelings.

Every time she answered the phone was potentially a life and death situation. Cheyenne would spend anywhere from three to twenty minutes on the phone with someone, helping them, working through whatever issue they had…only to hang up once the police or paramedics arrived, not knowing what the final outcome was.

Oh, sometimes she'd see a story on the news and recognize the situation as one she assisted with on the phone, but most of the time she had no idea how things turned out. Was anyone arrested? Did anyone die? Were they okay? By the end of each night Cheyenne was so full of adrenaline, that it'd take quite a while to get to sleep when she got home.

Perhaps even worse than the not knowing, was that Cheyenne was lonely. She spent her time at work talking with others, but she never really got to know them. She spoke with people on what many times was the worst day of their life. Only once in the five years she'd had her job, had someone tracked her down to thank her. Once.

Working second shift made it hard to make and keep friends, never mind finding time for romance. She worked five days on and four days off. She wasn't really a party girl and usually didn't go to the bars. She knew people from her station at work, but they typically had opposite schedules than she did, so they couldn't exactly socialize together outside of work.

Cheyenne recalled a conversation she'd once had with her mom. She'd called to try to get some sympathy after a hard day at work where she'd had to try to console a woman who'd found her husband dead in their home. It had been emotional and Cheyenne had cried at the woman's grief after she'd hung up. She should've known better than to try to get any sympathy from her mother.

"I don't know why you get so worked up over people you don't even know, Cheyenne," her mom had scolded.

"Mom, they call me when they need help. Most of the time they're freaked out and just need someone to tell them it'll be okay. That's me."

"But, honey, you're always getting emotional over your job. Why can't you find a normal job, like your sister?"

Cheyenne had just sighed. She knew most people didn't understand what she did or why she did it, but she'd always hoped her family would come to understand and support, rather than mock, her.

She wished she was closer to her sister, but ever since they'd been little, Karen had been ultra-competitive with her. Cheyenne never understood it because she couldn't care less about competing with her sister, but since Cheyenne had been a "surprise" when Karen had been five, she supposed the adjustment of being an only child to being the big sister of a baby, hadn't been a smooth one.

Karen was a paralegal to a criminal lawyer in town and Cheyenne knew her mom loved to brag to her friends about her "successful" daughter. Cheyenne had learned to keep her hurt about how her mom treated her to herself. There was no use trying to change her now, she'd never understand.

The phone rang, startling Cheyenne out of her reverie, and her heart rate immediately skyrocketed. There was no way to tell what kind of situation she'd be trying to help the caller with. She pushed "pause" on her movie, and picked up the phone.

CHAPTER 2

Faulkner "Dude" Cooper stared stonily at the woman behind the counter at the gas station. He was wearing jeans and a T-shirt and was paying for the gas he'd just put in his car, as well as a coffee and six pack of doughnuts. Hell, breakfast of champions it wasn't, but he'd just run ten miles and lifted weights for half an hour. Six measly doughnuts wasn't going to hurt him. He'd pulled his wallet out of his pocket and reached in to pull out a twenty dollar bill. Dude hadn't thought about his hand, he'd gotten used to working around the missing parts of his fingers.

He looked up just in time to see the woman looking at his hand in horror. Dude sighed and held out the bill impatiently, waiting for her to take it.

He should be used to the reactions his hand got, and for the most part he was, but every now and then it still caught him by surprise. Dude's teammates on his Navy SEAL team didn't give a shit about his hand, and their women were just as easy going about it. Thinking about it, Dude realized that not once had any of them acted like his hand was repulsive. That thought was enough to let him ignore the looks, like the one the cashier was giving him.

Just to be perverse, Dude held out his left hand for his change, forcing the woman to once again look at his mangled hand. He smirked at her with a grin that didn't reach his eyes and pocketed the change. Shaking his head, Dude grabbed up his snack and coffee cup, and headed back out to his car.

He stuck the doughnuts under his chin, and opened his door with his now-free hand. Dude snagged the sugary snack from its resting place in his throat and sat down in the driver's seat. He took a sip of the coffee, grimaced at the taste of burnt convenience store sludge that tried to pass itself off as coffee, and started the engine. He drove forward and out of the parking lot.

"I bet she would've acted differently if she knew I was a SEAL," Dude thought bitterly to himself. He shook his head. He was getting more and more maudlin as the days went on. He had to shake himself out of it.

He pulled up outside of Wolf and Ice's house. Ice never failed to cheer him up. The two had met when the plane they'd been in had been hijacked. Ice had smelled the drug in the ice in the drinks they'd been served, and Wolf, Mozart, and Abe had managed to take out the terrorists. Of course the FBI double agent had figured out Ice had something to do with the plot being foiled, and arranged to have her kidnapped and tortured.

After she'd spent too much time in the hands of the terrorists, the team had been able to rescue her, but it had been touch and go for a while. Ice had been Dude's introduction into what real love was. His own family hadn't been the touchy-feely type and he'd always felt as if he'd let them down. His parents wanted him to go to college, but he'd decided to enter the military instead. They'd wanted him to choose the Marines, and he'd gone into the Navy. They'd wanted him to be a doctor, he'd chosen the SEALs. Dude didn't go home much anymore. He only felt awkward and uncomfortable, knowing he'd disappointed them.

Dude left the crappy cup of coffee in the holder in the car and headed toward the front door. He smiled when it was thrown open before he could even knock.

"Faulkner!"

Dude went back on a foot as a blonde dynamo threw herself into his arms. He smiled, and mock-chastised her. "Jesus, Summer, take it easy on an old man would ya? And how many times do I have to tell you to call me Dude?"

"Whatever! I'm not going to use that ridiculous name. I don't care if you were a champion surfer in high school. You are not a 'Dude' and I won't call you that! And you're not old! If you're old, I'm absolutely ancient." It was an old joke between the two of them. "It's good to see you. It's been a while."

"How are you?" Dude asked seriously.

"I'm good."

"No, *how are you?*" Dude used his "I'm in control voice" knowing Summer wouldn't be able to resist telling him what he needed to know. Summer had been through hell at the hands of a serial killer. Dude had been just a second too late, or he would've been the one to have killed him. Wolf had pulled the trigger before Dude or Benny could get their k-bars out and slit Hurst's throat.

"I'm okay, Faulkner. I swear," Summer told him before hugging him again.

"All right, come on, let's get off the front porch and get inside."

Summer grabbed Dude's mangled left hand and towed him into the house. If he hadn't already been rejected that day, he probably wouldn't even have noticed. He marveled at the fact Summer didn't even flinch. She'd never, not once, been disgusted at the sight or feel of his hand. That thought made Dude feel slightly better, and gave him hope that there were other women out there that would feel the same.

They walked into the kitchen where Wolf, Ice, and Mozart were sitting around the table. Summer let go of his hand and immediately went to Mozart. He pulled her into his side and curled his hand around her waist. Mozart kissed the side of her head, and Dude smiled as Summer put one hand around her man's shoulder, and the other curled around his at her waist.

"Hey, Dude. Glad you could make it." Mozart greeted his teammate with honest enthusiasm.

"You know I feel like a fifth wheel around you guys."

"Whatever," Caroline said, rolling her eyes. "We love when you and Kason hang out with us. Just because you're single doesn't mean we don't want you around."

"I know, I was teasing." Dude tried to put sincerity into his words, but was afraid they fell flat when he saw the worried looks in his friends' eyes.

Dude pulled out a chair and settled into it at the table.

"What's for dinner, Wolf?" Dude asked, knowing the man was probably grilling up some sort of meat on his new fancy grill in the backyard.

"New York Strip Steaks for us and grilled chicken for the ladies."

"Awesome, don't want to waste the meat on the women."

"Hey!" Summer grumbled, scowling at Dude.

"Kidding!"

Everyone laughed and relaxed. Dude really enjoyed hanging out with his friends. Somehow they made all his other worries and concerns disappear.

The group spent the rest of the evening laughing and talking about nothing in particular. By the time Dude left, he'd forgotten the feelings of rejection he'd momentarily felt earlier that evening.

CHAPTER 3

"J*ust another boring day in my life*," thought Cheyenne as she pushed her cart around the grocery store. She was in day two of her four days off in a row. She'd slept in that morning and decided to get the grocery shopping out of the way. She hated to cook and usually ate herself out of house and home before forcing herself to go to the store. She lived on packaged food and easy to make processed food. She had no inclination to learn to cook. Cheyenne figured she was somehow missing the "cooking gene" or whatever it was that made other women want to learn how to make delicious meals.

Besides that, Karen was an excellent cook, it was just one more thing her mom used to measure her against her sister, and Cheyenne always came out the loser. Cheyenne mentally shrugged. It wasn't as if she had anyone to cook for anyway.

She wished she had a best friend, or even a good friend to hang out with, but after Cheyenne graduated from high school, she lost touch with the few friends she did have. Oh she went out with people from work when they could all get off work at the same time, and she'd honestly call them her friends, but she didn't have that one special woman to hang out with that a lot of other people had. She'd always wanted a best friend, but she was happy with the casual friends she did have.

Once again Cheyenne thought about her job and how it should be more fulfilling than it was. She thought saving people's lives would be exciting and rewarding, but all it turned out to be was stressful and boring at times. *I'm 32 years old, I should be doing something interesting with my life. I should be traveling, or even married by now.*

Cheyenne's life depressed her. She lived in Riverton, California, near the Navy base. She saw men and women in uniform every day. She'd once thought about joining up to "see the world" as all the recruiting posters claimed, but she really was too much of a coward to go through with it. Besides, there was no way she'd be able to pass the physical tests. She wasn't fat, but Cheyenne didn't think she'd be able to do even one pull up, and running was completely out of the question.

Cheyenne found military men fascinating. She assumed it was because she didn't really know any, but like many woman, she found a man in uniform irresistible. She wasn't living in a fantasy world though, she knew they could be mean and ugly, just like any other person. She saw the stories in the newspaper all the time about killings and beatings and such that happened on and around the base, not to mention manning the phone lines and hearing and getting help for domestic incidents that sometimes involved members in the military, but it didn't keep her from fantasizing about men in uniform in general.

There was one man that she saw on a semi-regular basis at the grocery store who immediately came to mind when she thought of the Naval Base. He wasn't usually in his uniform at the store, but she always knew it was him. He was fairly tall, had dark hair and he was built. Cheyenne was ashamed to admit that she'd stalked him around the store one day, watching as he filled his cart with healthy food, nothing like the pastries and processed crap she always bought.

He was always polite to the people around him. He even helped her get a can of something off the top shelf once and smiled at her as he'd done it. Cheyenne had beamed the rest of the day like a schoolgirl. She didn't know his first name, but she knew his last name was Cooper. It was sewn onto the front of his uniform. She'd only seen him wearing it on one occasion, but she knew she'd never forget it. He filled it out in all the right places. She had no idea what kind of job he did in the Navy, as she didn't know what all the patches on his uniform meant, but it honestly didn't really matter to her. Ever since Cheyenne had seen him in the store, she refused to shop anywhere else, just in case she'd run into him again.

Cheyenne found it interesting to people watch as she went about her day. Since she had to sum up a person after only a brief conversation at work, she'd gotten really good at it. One of her favorite things to do was imagine what people's lives were like just from looking at them. Cheyenne looked around her in the grocery store…it wasn't very crowded, which was good because she preferred to do her shopping when there weren't hordes of people around.

There was a lady walking in front of Cheyenne in the produce section. She was wearing three inch heels and a skin tight dress that barely covered her backside. *I don't know how people wear those things. I bet she's an undercover police officer, she's just gotten off duty where she tried to arrest men soliciting prostitutes and is getting some food before she heads home.* Cheyenne looked at a college aged man standing at the meat counter. *I bet he's having a barbeque today and is trying to decide what to buy to grill for his buddies.* Cheyenne continued her daydreaming as she wandered around the store. She wasn't in a hurry, because the only plans she had that day were to go home and finish the book she'd started the day before.

Cheyenne started up the frozen food aisle and noticed five men standing around near the pharmacy. As the store was pretty empty, they really stood out. They didn't have carts with them and they were dressed all in black. About the time her brain processed the fact that something wasn't right, she heard yelling, and the men all pulled out pistols from somewhere hidden in their clothing. Cheyenne stood frozen. When she'd wished for more excitement in her life she really hadn't meant something like this! She started inching backwards to get out of the aisle and out of sight of the men, but one noticed her and started down the aisle toward her pointing the gun directly at her.

* * *

DUDE LAUGHED AT HIS FRIENDS. They loved eating at *Aces Bar and Grill.* It was their go-to place for both drinks and food. They'd tried to get everyone together at least once a week. The bar might not be big, and it certainly wasn't a chain, but the food was delicious and, perhaps most importantly, wasn't overrun with tourists.

If Dude was honest with himself, he knew it didn't matter where they ate every week. He loved his friends and their women. He loved to rib his teammates as much as he could.

"You guys are pathetic!" Dude teased, rolling his eyes at the other men on his SEAL team. "Seriously, you never want to go out anymore, you stay home all the time. You're all a bunch of fuddy duddies now that you have women. I'm impressed you even left your houses at all today."

"Hey, you're just jealous," Mozart shot back, laughing at his friend.

Dude laughed with his friends, knowing Mozart was right on so many levels. He looked around and was thrilled to see the happiness on his friends' faces. Their women were perfect for them.

The men were startled when the sound of Wolf's cell phone pealed. They watched as he answered it and they all sat up straighter when they saw his muscles get tight. A phone call could mean nothing more than a telemarketer had somehow gotten a hold of Wolf's unlisted number, or it could mean they were about to be shipped out to an undisclosed location.

Dude watched as the four women around them also tensed, waiting to hear what the news was.

"Right, yeah, I'll get him on it. Thanks." Wolf hung up the phone and turned to Dude. Not beating around the bush he stated urgently, "Possible bomb threat inside the grocery store on Main Street here in Riverton. They're asking for an ordinance expert."

"I'm on it." Dude stood up quickly, already thinking about what he might find. The local police department would sometimes call on the military when they needed extra help. Their commander had no qualms in reaching out to the team when he knew they'd be able to help.

"Let us know if you need anything."

Dude raised his hand in acknowledgement of Wolf's words, then he was gone.

* * *

CHEYENNE HAD NEVER BEEN SO SCARED in her life. She'd seen movies and read books where the heroines were brave and smart-mouthed the bad guys. Somehow it had always worked out for them though. Cheyenne didn't think smart-mouthing back to these scary men would help her, or anyone else around her, in any way shape or form. They were mean, and somehow Cheyenne knew they wouldn't hesitate to pull the trigger and kill any one of them.

Apparently they wanted to rob the pharmacy in the back of the grocery store of their drugs, but unfortunately, their plan had failed. Three SPs, Naval Shore Patrols, happened to have been in the store at the time they tried to rob it. Guns were drawn and a stand-off ensued. Cheyenne had been trapped in the store, along with two other women, and the five gunmen. They'd hauled them all to the back corner of the store.

The SPs had managed to get all of the other customers out of harm's way and out of the building in the chaos that had ensued once the gunmen had pulled out their weapons. It seemed like forever had passed since they'd taken over the store, when in actuality it had only been about an hour and a half. The gunmen were mad and desperate. Cheyenne could tell they were getting more and more anxious as time went on. Occasionally she'd hear mumblings of a loudspeaker outside the building.

The two women trapped with her were hysterical. They were both pretty young, maybe in their early twenties. Each time one of the gunmen would look their way, they would plead with them to let them go, that they had families, that they had children, that they were married...whatever they thought would sway the gunmen into showing mercy and letting them go. When that didn't work, they just sat huddled together and cried.

While Cheyenne was also scared to death, she didn't figure that crying would do much good. These guys were obviously high on some kind of drug and they only cared about getting away. Since there were five of them, Cheyenne knew there was no way she and the other women would be able to "make a break for it," anyway. They were stuck until this standoff was over, however "over" occured.

She thought about her coworkers. Had anyone called 911? Had one of her coworkers answered the call and sent out for more help? Cheyenne wished with all her heart she'd never stepped foot in the grocery store that day. That's what wanting to eat got her. What she'd give to be sitting in the control room at work and organizing the rescue from the outside. She'd never thought much about being a victim herself. She was always the one helping others, she never considered that *she'd* be the one needing help.

Cheyenne was brought back to her present situation when one of the gunmen, the biggest and meanest looking, stalked over to their corner and snarled, "Today's a good day to die."

This, of course, got the cashiers even more hysterical than they already were. He laughed with a cruel low grunt. Cheyenne knew he was enjoying making them scared. She just sat there dry eyed and tried to tamp down her terror.

"Here's the deal, ladies," the scary man sneered. "We can't get out of here until those cops get out of the way, and they aren't going to do that unless we make them, that's where you come in."

Cheyenne sucked in a deep breath, knowing whatever he had in store for them wasn't going to be good.

"Since I'm in a good mood today..." Cheyenne couldn't help but snort under her breath. She apparently hadn't been quiet enough with her scorn because the man glared at her nastily before continuing. "I'll let you all decide who gets to deliver my message to the cops outside."

Cheyenne could practically feel the nervous energy coming off of the cashiers. She knew they were dying to be the ones to take the message out of the building. But Cheyenne wanted to know what the catch was. There was no way this evil man was just going to let one of them walk outside and go free. They were their ticket out of there and Cheyenne knew it.

The gunman walked away, but called back to them, "Stay put bitches, I'll be right back with the message."

As soon as the man was out of earshot, the cashiers started arguing with each other.

"I need to get out of here," the blonde said.

"No way, *I* should be the one to deliver the message, you aren't married, no matter what you told him," the other woman argued back.

Their voices got louder and bitchier as they argued with each other.

"Yeah, but I have to be here to take care of my mom, you know she's not doing well," the blonde shot right back.

Cheyenne sighed. She didn't bother joining in their argument. She was glad the two women hadn't turned on her yet, they weren't even *considering* her to be the one to get out of there with the message. She was basically invisible to the women. But that was okay, Cheyenne was single, had no husband or kids...essentially she was expendable.

The women stopped their arguing as the man came back toward them holding a box. Cheyenne shuddered, knowing that whatever was in that box wasn't good. They'd all assumed he'd come back with a piece of paper with the gunmen's demands written on it. No one had expected a box.

The man carefully put the package on the floor and turned toward them, with his hands on his hips as if daring them to defy him. "Here's the message...it's a bomb."

Cheyenne gasped and shrunk back from the innocuous looking box on the floor, just as the two cashiers did the same thing.

"The message is, that if they don't let us out of here, we'll blow up this bomb and everyone in the store. Shrapnel will blow for fucking miles...anyone in the vicinity of the building will die...holes punched throughout their body," his voice trailed off as he laughed. Then he glared at them all again and said, "You have three minutes to choose who will take the message outside. I'm sure it won't be hard to decide. After all, whoever gets to take it, will be free." He again laughed, but Cheyenne couldn't hear any humor in the laugh. He stalked off to converse with his fellow gunmen, leaving them there to figure out who would be the one to carry the deadly bomb outside to the cops.

Cheyenne turned to the two women; they all just looked at each other. Predictably, the cashiers started to cry. Cheyenne wasn't very far from crying herself, although she willed the tears away. If she was going to die, she wasn't going to do it sniveling.

Whispering, Cheyenne turned to the two women. "It sucks, but he's right, whoever takes this outside will be free."

"But, it's a bomb," the blonde woman croaked, not able to tear her horrified eyes away from the box sitting in front of them.

"What if it's not?" the other woman said. "I mean, what if they just want us to *think* it's a bomb to scare us, but it's really only a piece of paper in there?" Cheyenne thought about it. The girl was right, he could be trying to scare them and it wasn't anything.

"Are you crazy enough to take a chance on that?" the blonde whispered.

The other cashier's shoulders slumped. "Hell no."

"Well, I know I don't want to risk it. These guys are crazy. I'm not sure I'd trust them to know how to build a bomb, nonetheless build it sturdy enough to withstand being carried through the store."

Unfortunately, Cheyenne agreed with her.

As if realizing she was there for the first time, the cashiers turned toward her. "What about you?"

"Uh..." Cheyenne couldn't think of anything to say, but the blonde didn't give her a chance anyway.

"I don't see you wearing a ring, so you aren't married. Do you have kids?"

Cheyenne shook her head honestly, knowing where this was going.

"Then you have to do it. We have families, people who depend on us."

When Cheyenne just stared at them, the dark haired woman joined in with the pleading, but at least she was nice about it. "Please," she begged.

Finally after another moment, knowing it was probably the best decision, Cheyenne decided to just go with it. If all it took to be free from this nightmare was a moment of danger to walk that damn box out the door, it'd be worth it. "I'll do it," Cheyenne croaked to the other women. "I know you both have families. Hopefully it won't come to anything; we'll just have to believe that." The women nodded and didn't say anything.

The gunman stalked back over to the frightened women and demanded, "So? Who's taking my message outside?"

Cheyenne stuck her chin up and said simply, "Me." She really didn't like the wicked smirk that came over the man's face as he turned to her.

"Then get up, bitch, I gotta prepare my gift for the cops."

Cheyenne slowly stood up, regretting with every fiber of her being what she was about to do. She knew this wasn't going to end up well for her. She just knew it.

* * *

DUDE PACED outside the grocery store. He hated waiting. So far no one knew much about what was going on inside the building. The SPs that were in the store when the robbery had started had done a great job in getting almost everyone out, but they said there were still some civilians inside. He wasn't sure how many, and the gunmen weren't really talking except to say if they weren't allowed to leave, then they would set off a bomb and blow everyone up. That was where he came in. Everyone knew he was the best, all he needed was a chance to diffuse the bomb, but no one knew if they would have that chance.

Dude heard one of the police officers say, "Look!"

He turned and watched through the plate glass window as two women walked across the front of the store toward the front door. They were holding each other and walking quickly. There was no sign of any of the gunmen. Had they sneaked out? Was that even possible? He watched as the women exited the store and crept toward the line of police cars.

"Stop right there," one of the police said through his bullhorn. "Turn around, put your hands on your head and get down on your knees." The women did as he asked. Four police officers cautiously peeled away from the line of cars they'd been standing behind as cover, and approached the women with their guns drawn. They grasped them by their hands, which were behind their heads, had them stand, and practically dragged them back behind the police cars.

Dude listened in as the cops quickly interrogated the women on the spot, trying to get more intel as to what the hell was going on.

"How many gunmen are there?"

"Five."

"What kind of firepower do they have?"

At the blank look from the women, Dude rolled his eyes as the officer explained that he wanted to know what kind of guns the bad guys had.

"Oh, they each had a little gun, but the leader guy had like, two of them, and a long gun too," the blonde explained, wringing her hands dramatically.

"Did they let you go? How'd you get out of here?"

This time it was the dark haired woman that answered. "They wanted one of us to take a message out here to you guys, but then the big guy said the message was a bomb. The other lady said she'd do it and the guy took her in the back. They left us alone, and we decided to get the hell out of there, we didn't want to get blown up. We ran toward the front of the store and by the time they noticed us, we were too close to the door, so they had let us go. But they're pissed, that's for sure."

"So there's only one other hostage inside?"

At the nods from both women, the officer asked again, "You're sure?"

"Yeah, positive," the blonde said frantically nodding. "Yeah, you heard her say the message they wanted us to take out here to you was a bomb? Neither of us wanted to take it, and we have family, there was no way we could've done it. The other lady volunteered."

Dude clenched his teeth. Volunteered his ass. More likely the two young women flatly refused to do it and the other woman was left, literally, holding the bag.

Dude was getting itchy. He wanted nothing more than to get his hands on that bomb…if there was one. At this point he truly didn't know if anything the gunmen, or the hysterical women, said could be believed. There were no doubts that everyone in the area was in danger, however. The gunmen were unstable, armed, and getting more and more desperate. They wanted out of the store and Dude knew they'd do anything to get what they wanted. He wondered what their next move would be.

They didn't have long to wait.

* * *

CHEYENNE SWALLOWED HARD. She was boring Cheyenne Cotton…the woman that nothing exciting ever happened to, how had she ended up with a fucking bomb duct taped to her body? She thought they were going to make her *carry* the bomb outside…to show the cops they were serious, but the gunman had different plans. He'd made her hold the bomb against her stomach then started taping it to her. Going round and round and round her with the tape, until she couldn't move. *Then* he flicked a switch near the bottom of the device and taped her up some more. He'd activated the bomb and taped the whole thing so much Cheyenne couldn't see any of it through it all. But she could feel it ticking against her chest. She was going to die. Damn it all to hell.

* * *

DUDE WATCHED as five men inside the store walked toward the front door. He wished like hell his team was there. He hadn't had time to call Wolf once everything started happening, and now all the police with their guns drawn were making him really nervous. Dude had no idea where the supposed bomb was in this cluster fuck, just that his hands were itching.

All of the police had their weapons pointed at the men as they walked to the front of the store and could be seen on the other side of the big plate glass windows. There was no way they were getting out of this. The men were walking in a triangle/rectangle formation with a woman at the point, shielding them. They were pushing her ahead of them as they walked. When they got to the front door it was opened a crack.

One of the men yelled out, "You let us walk out of here and we'll let her go, you don't, she'll die, along with all of you, courtesy of the bomb she's currently fucking wearing!"

Dude turned his attention to the woman. He hadn't really been focused on her as the men came into sight, he'd been concentrating on escape routes and trying to ascertain what type of fire power the men had. Looking now, Dude couldn't see anything on the woman other than miles of silver tape. It looked like they had used multiple rolls to mummify her in the heavy tape. Dude honestly couldn't tell if there was a bomb under all that tape or not, the gunmen could be bluffing. But Dude knew they couldn't treat the situation as anything *but* a bomb threat, for their own safety and that of the woman who was as white as a ghost and being held tightly by what would have been her upper arm if it hadn't been encased in tape. If the look on her face was anything to go by, there most likely was a bomb under all the silver tape holding her still. She looked freaked and terrified out of her mind. She obviously knew, as did the officers all around him, that the odds of her getting out of whatever fucked up situation this was without getting hurt…or killed…were extremely low.

As soon as the man who'd yelled the threat shut the front door, all hell broke loose. Apparently the snipers had gotten the approval to take the gunmen out. There were five men inside the store, but there were also more than enough snipers to go around. Not only were they near a Navy base where SEAL snipers were plentiful, the local SWAT team had their own cadre of the deadly officers as well.

The standoff had been going on for well over four hours Dude knew everyone wanted it to end. Glass went flying in all directions. He *knew* the snipers were good at their jobs, but he hoped like hell they hadn't missed and hurt the woman. The situation was chaotic and shooting through glass always held a modicum of danger. The woman was an innocent bystander, a terrified bystander. Dude had only gotten one quick look at her, but he'd been impressed at how she'd been holding herself together.

She was scared, yes, but she hadn't screamed, hadn't tried to wrestle herself out of the arms of the gunmen, and amazingly hadn't been crying. If nothing else, Dude hoped the sniper's bullets hadn't hit her to reward her for her stoic behavior in the face of extreme danger.

* * *

CHEYENNE FLINCHED as the glass in front of her shattered. She immediately ducked as low as she could go, which wasn't too far since she was bundled up in the tape. As she crouched on the floor, she was more than aware of the ticking of the bomb against her stomach. More glass shattered around her and Cheyenne felt a spray of wetness against her face and back. One of the gunmen sagged against her and she lost her balance, falling toward the front door of the store. Cheyenne couldn't throw out a hand to stop her forward momentum and ended up wedged against the glass that hadn't been shattered by the gunfire by the weight of at least one of the men who'd been terrorizing her for the last few hours.

Cheyenne quickly glanced around, taking in the broken glass, the blood on the floor, and the bodies of the five men around her. Damn, she was amazed she was still alive. Every one of the five men who'd held her hostage was lying dead on the ground. She'd always been impressed with the skills of snipers, but she was even more so now seeing their prowess up close and personal.

She took a deep breath; and knew she was losing her mind when she was thankful she could still feel the ticking of the bomb against her body. Falling hadn't set it off, thank God, but it was still active and ticking away. She had no idea how much time she had before it exploded, but Cheyenne figured she was going to die. She didn't see any way to get the damn thing off of herself without it blowing up, but she didn't want any innocent people to die with her.

Cheyenne managed to use the shaky glass in front of her to brace with her shoulder and push herself upright. She scooted away from the body of the man leaning against her back, the man she'd thought of as the leader of the gang. His eyes were open and staring sightlessly toward the ceiling. He looked almost as scary dead, as he was alive... just without the maniacal smile he'd shown her as he'd taped her up. She stepped to the left, around the bodies of the other men littering the tile at the front of the store...stepping around the broken glass and rapidly spreading blood pools, and walked backwards toward the aisles in the store. Cheyenne kept an eye on the front parking lot, willing all the cops and rescue personnel to stay away as she made her way away from all the commotion in the parking lot, away from the people so she didn't kill them as the bomb blew up.

* * *

As soon as the dust settled, Dude was running toward the store along with about ten of the other officers who'd been waiting and watching the front of the grocery store. He didn't have a gun, but he wasn't concerned, he was there for the bomb, the other officers would take care of peripheral safety. Time was of the essence. It always was when bombs were involved.

Dude heard the officers shouting to someone, "Stop, don't move," as they moved forward. He saw the bodies of the gunmen on the ground by the door, but didn't see the woman who'd been trussed up like a mummy. When Dude got further into the store and looked down one of the long aisles, he saw her, still bound up in all that tape, backing away from the officers as they moved toward her.

They were all yelling at her to stop, to surrender. She was shaking her head and saying "No, no, don't come near me, you don't understand."

The woman was as pale as the tiles under their feet, and her dark hair, which had been in some sort of ponytail or braid at one point, had mostly come loose and was hanging limply around her face. She had blood sprayed on her face and right side and she was stumbling a bit as she backed away. Dude couldn't stay quiet anymore.

"All of you halt," he ordered in his best Alpha voice. The officers stopped at once, guns still drawn and mostly pointed at the ground instead of at the bound woman, but she kept backing away from them all, ignoring the command in his voice.

"Let me through," Dude urged as he elbowed himself to the front of the line of officers. He turned his back on the woman and spoke to the twitchy men in front of him, "If that *is* a bomb she has strapped to her under all that tape, I need to get to it. I can't do that if she keeps backing away. Give me a moment."

The officer in charge nodded, knowing exactly who Dude was and why he was there. "You have two minutes, she might be in on it with them. We won't put our guns down. We've got your back."

Dude nodded, not agreeing with the officer about the terrified woman being in cahoots with the gunmen, but knowing he had to work quickly to get to the bottom of whatever was going on. He knew the local cops were used to working with the military, but they were on edge and their adrenaline levels were sky-high. He'd learned to control his adrenaline high through his training. "Just let me talk to her," Dude told the officer curtly and turned back toward the woman.

She'd steadily backed herself halfway down the snack aisle and hadn't stopped while he'd momentarily stopped to talk to the officers. Dude stepped toward her, leaving the line of officers behind him without a second thought. He knew they'd split up and were coming in behind him and probably around the next aisle to cut off her retreat. It's what he and his team would do if they were in this situation. Dude knew he had to figure out what was going on before that bomb went off and they were all killed.

"Why don't you stop and talk to me, it's okay, it's over, the men are dead, you're okay." Dude kept his voice low and soothing, but put just a hint of the man he was behind his words with the hopes she'd respond to the subtle command.

Cheyenne just shook her head, didn't they understand? She *was* the bomb for crying out loud. What was he doing? Why was this man coming toward her? She didn't listen to his words, she just wanted to get away from him and hide somewhere in the back of the store. She figured she could find a place to hole up so when the bomb exploded it didn't kill anyone...well, anyone but her. But holy cow, from what she could see through the tears in her eyes, the man in front of her was gorgeous. She didn't want to be responsible for killing him. Hell, he probably had a family, a wife, kids...she couldn't kill him.

She kept backing up. Cheyenne could barely see through her unshed tears. She would not cry, she would not cry, she had to get these people out of here. Through her panic, Cheyenne heard something behind her, she turned and was horrified to see two police officers at the end of the aisle. They'd cut her off. Shit, they were all going to die after all she'd tried to do. She turned sideways, so her back was to the shelves and shut her eyes tightly. A couple of boxes of something fell off the shelf behind her, but she didn't bother opening her eyes to see what it was. At this point, making a mess was the least of her worries.

"Ma'am," Dude said again, seeing her stop after spying the officers at the end of the aisle. "Can you hear me? Look at me and talk to me, tell me what's going on."

Cheyenne opened her eyes and looked more closely at the man who'd followed her down the aisle for the first time. He didn't have a weapon, but was standing about ten feet from her. His hands were at his sides, palms out, showing her he was no threat. But Cheyenne knew he was close, too close. If she could just get him to back off, maybe he'd somehow survive when the bomb went off.

"Please," she croaked, then cleared her throat and tried again. "Please, you have to get out of here....just go..."

Dude saw her trying to hold her composure together, and his impression of her rose. "You know we can't do that, these police officers have to make sure you're all right and that you aren't an accomplice." Dude saw her eyes widen in surprise. He'd purposely tried to shock her, so she'd stop and listen to him. "Yeah, I know, seems unlikely to me, but they're just doing their job, no matter what you or I say to them. Why don't you help us and we'll all get out of here and have some lunch." Dude tried to get her to smile just a bit.

It was obvious his attempt at humor fell flat, when she flung her words at him. "No, you have to go, all of you. I'm not 'in' on anything." Cheyenne gestured to her chest with her chin. "This bomb is going to blow up and kill everyone." Her voice dropped and she changed tactics, begging now, "Please, just go, I don't want anyone to die."

Dude suddenly understood and his stomach clenched with respect. She wasn't trying to get away; she was trying to *protect* them. He hadn't been sure there even *was* a bomb, but now that he was closer to her, Dude could see a lump in front of her body that could be anything, but with the way she was acting, it probably was exactly what the bad guys had said it was. If that bomb *did* go off, there was a good chance many of them *would* die, or at least be badly hurt.

Dude abruptly turned away from the woman who was obviously scared to death, and to the officer in charge who'd followed at a close distance behind him down the aisle.

"Get your men out of here, *now*!" Dude bellowed. "That bomb strapped to her chest could go off and we need to clear the area. I've got this."

The officer took one look at Dude's serious face, and ordered his men back.

Dude turned back to the woman as the officers backed away from the aisle on each end, and made their way toward the front of the store. "Okay, they're leaving, now will you let me help you?"

The woman resumed her relentless retreat away from the front of the store now that the officers weren't blocking her way.

"No, you have to leave too, don't *do* this to me." Cheyenne looked at the man in horror, suddenly recognizing him as "Cooper," the military guy she'd semi-stalked in this exact grocery store. Oh my God. It was even more important he just let her go. *He* couldn't die. Not him.

Dude ignored her words and strolled steadily toward her and said again in the low commanding voice that, in the past, women had a hard time disobeying. “Look, you’re wasting my time. I’m a bomb ordnance technician, if anyone is going to prevent that bomb from going off and killing you, me, and anyone else nearby, it’s going to be me, so for God’s sake stop backing away from me and let me help.”

Cheyenne stopped, surprised by his words and the tone of his voice, and let the man get closer to her. As he came up toward her, she whispered, “I don’t want you to die.”

“I’m not going to die if you let me take a look at that bomb. If you don’t, then we’ll both *definitely* die because I’m *not* leaving you.” Dude was slightly surprised at the words that left his mouth. It wasn’t like him to be reckless, or to let himself be swayed by a woman, but there was something about the bravery and self-sacrifice of *this* woman that touched him deep inside. She had been one hundred percent honest with him, he could tell. She’d honestly rather just lock herself away in a back room and let herself be blown up, then allow anyone the chance to help her, just in case she couldn’t be helped. It wasn’t acceptable in Dude’s eyes.

Dude reached out and took her arm, or what he thought was her arm…it was hard to tell since it was under miles of duct tape, and steered her toward the back of the store. “You’re right though, we have to get away from the windows up front, come on.”

Cheyenne let herself be led away from the front of the store and the officers and onlookers that had congregated there.

Dude led the woman into the small room behind the meat counter. He helped her lean against one of the butcher tables where the meat was packaged and stared at the tape around her body, trying to work it all out in his head before he tackled it physically.

“Talk to me,” Dude said to the trembling woman now standing in front of him. “Tell me what they said as they put this on you and how it’s attached.”

Cheyenne didn’t like the fact this man was here with her and in such horrible danger, but she didn’t know what else to do. She really didn’t have a choice. He seemed to know what he was doing. She couldn’t get the tape off herself, and she certainly couldn’t disarm the bomb. She took a deep breath and did as he ordered. Maybe, just maybe, she could give him something that would help get the damn bomb off of her.

"He didn't say much. He asked me to hold it in my hands, which I'm still doing, and they started with the tape. Once I was mostly taped up, he flicked a switch near the bottom, and then taped me up some more. I can feel it ticking against my body."

The man hadn't looked her in the eyes since they were in the aisle; he was wholly focused on the contraption and her mummified body, as if he had x-ray vision and could see under the tape.

"I'm afraid I might hurt you trying to get some of this tape off," Dude started to tell her, looking up in surprise when the woman let out a sharp laugh.

"I think the tape will hurt less than the damn bomb going off...go ahead, do your worst."

Dude looked up at her for the first time. She was splattered with blood, a tear had escaped from her right eye, and she had what looked like the beginning of a black eye, but she was still standing there in front of him, with a bomb strapped to her chest, and making a smart ass comment. Amazing.

"By the way, my name is Dude."

Cheyenne sighed, did it matter? Yes, she thought it *did* matter. "Dude?"

Knowing she'd probably ask, Dude had purposely given her his nickname. "Yeah, it's a nickname. When my buddies in boot camp heard I'd spent most of my time in high school surfing, instead of studying, the name stuck."

"What's your real name?"

"Faulkner. Faulkner Cooper. What's your name, hon?"

"Cheyenne Cotton," she told him softly.

"Well, Cheyenne, let's get this thing off of you." Dude pulled a chair over toward her and sat down to work.

After ten minutes of Dude trying to get the tape removed, without either hurting her, or prematurely triggering the bomb, Cheyenne said urgently, "Promise me something."

Dude didn't look up but replied immediately and honestly, "Anything."

"If you can't get this thing off, you'll get the hell out of here."

Dude *did* look up at that. "Sorry, Shy, I can't promise that, anything but that. Ask me to take you out for dinner, ask me to come to your house and rake up your leaves in the fall, hell, ask me to kiss you, I'll agree with no complaints. But leave you? Not gonna happen."

Cheyenne started a bit at the nickname he'd used. No one had ever shortened her name before. It felt intimate. She liked it, but now wasn't the time or the place to acknowledge it. She ignored his other words, figuring they were said to make a point in the heat of the moment. "You don't know me," Cheyenne continued desperately. "You don't owe me anything, I'm a nobody. Look at you, you're gorgeous, and you're an honest-to-God hero, I know you are, you should *not* give up your life for mine. I'm just not worth it."

Cheyenne took a deep breath and babbled on, not giving Faulkner a chance to say anything. "I don't have any close family, I'm not married, no one will miss me. I just *know* that you have loved ones who'd be mad as hell if you got killed. Look at you, you survived one bomb already, don't let this one kill you, I couldn't stand it." Cheyenne's voice trailed off.

Dude didn't stop fiddling with the tape or with the bomb after her passionate speech, he just kept his head down and continued with what he'd been doing. Cheyenne shifted nervously, if he was pissed she'd mentioned his hand, too bad, maybe it would make him leave.

"How do you figure I've survived one bomb already?" Dude asked, not addressing her other points. They weren't worth him giving them the light of day. But he was honestly curious as to her train of thought and how she'd figured out he'd survived an explosion in the past. Dude also figured it'd distract her and let him keep working. She was pretty persistent, something he usually admired, but right now he wanted her concentrated on something else.

"Well, um, your hand…I figured since you're here now trying to get this damn bomb off of me and you said you were a bomb…order…

whatever...and well...I just thought..." Cheyenne trailed off, not sure what she even really wanted to say.

"Well, you're right. I *do* do this for a living. I'm a bomb ordnance technician in the Navy, among other things. I can't say I'm a hero, but I have a whole team of men that depend on me being good at my job. And, hon, I *am* good at my job. Damn good. The bomb that took three of my fingers notwithstanding, I know what I'm doing. I'll be damned if those yahoos get the best of me."

Cheyenne was silent for a moment, but couldn't stay that way. This was too important. "Please, Faulkner..."

Dude cut her off, not letting her finish her thought. "Hush, you're ruining my concentration," he told her not harshly, and not truthfully. He was one hundred percent focused on the bomb in front of him. Dude was sweating now and he was just getting past all the tape to the actual bomb underneath. He could see Cheyenne's hands now, and he had access to the bottom switch, just where she'd told him it was. Dude was in luck, it looked like a fairly simple switch, but he couldn't be certain. He wouldn't put Cheyenne's life, or his own, at risk on a hunch. He needed to uncover a bit more of the bomb itself to be sure.

Dude was impressed with Cheyenne. He knew she was scared to death, but she was holding herself together. He didn't know too many people, soldiers included, that would've done what she did...try to get everyone else out of harm's way. He told her so as he continued to work.

Cheyenne shook her head. "That's not true," she told him.

"Tell me how the other two women were able to sneak past five armed men and get out while you were being strapped to this bomb?" Dude asked her, already figuring he knew the answer, but wanting to see if Cheyenne would come clean.

Cheyenne was silent.

"That's what I thought," Dude said after a moment. "You volunteered, didn't you? Then you created some sort of distraction..." He took the time to slowly reach up and brush her darkening eye gently before turning back to the contraption taped to her belly, and finished his sentence, "...that allowed them to escape out the front door."

Cheyenne sighed. Faulkner was pretty smart, but Cheyenne hadn't been able to simply to be led like a lamb to the slaughter to have the bomb taped on. She'd struggled just enough to make sure the men's attention was all on her, and before the biggest guy had hit her, she'd caught the other women's eyes and gestured nonverbally toward the door, hoping they'd understand. They did. They'd snuck out as the men were subduing her. A black eye was worth it to Cheyenne.

"Just like I told you, I don't have anyone, they do, it was better this way." Cheyenne looked at the top of Faulkner's head as he continued to try to get to the bomb. She watched as sweat trickled down the side of his face. He wiped it off with his shoulder and kept working. Cheyenne wished her hands were free so she could wipe the sweat out of his eyes for him, but that was crazy. No, it was creepy, she'd just met the man for goodness sake.

Cheyenne couldn't believe this was "Cooper"...the man she'd daydreamed about for weeks and had followed around this very store once. He was just so gorgeous...she certainly hadn't dreamed *this* was how he'd be touching her though. The touch of his hand on her face had been short, but it'd sent shivers shooting down her spine nevertheless.

Cheyenne looked at Faulkner's mangled hand to distract herself. She meant what she'd told him. She knew he was a hero, and while his hand wasn't pleasant to look at, Cheyenne also knew what someone looked like made no difference as to the person they were inside. That hand was pure magic as far as she was concerned. If it was going to get this bomb off of her, she didn't care what it looked like. He was missing half of his middle three fingers on his left hand, but she noticed it didn't slow him down at all. He was still able to use what was left of his fingers to maneuver around the bomb. She wondered what it would be like to feel his hands on her...

Dude worked in silence for a bit longer before Cheyenne told him out of the blue, "I know you, you know."

That surprised Dude and he took his attention from the bomb for a second and looked up briefly and met Cheyenne's eyes before dropping his gaze and concentrating on the device again.

"Really?" he said. "Have we met?" Dude didn't know if he would remember her or not. She wasn't exactly looking her best at that moment, but what he saw, he liked.

Cheyenne nodded and told him, "I guess we haven't really *met,* met, I've *seen* you around."

Dude nodded, gritting his teeth, he was getting to a tricky part. "Ah, it is a small town," he told her absently.

"It was actually here, we were both shopping, we passed each other in an aisle, and you helped me get a can down from the top shelf. I told you I could probably use the bottom shelf to step up and get it myself, but you insisted, for my own safety, that it was your duty to keep me out of danger...." Cheyenne's voice trailed off and she mentally smacked her forehead in consternation. She hated her tendency to sometimes ramble. "I know you don't remember, that's okay, I'm sure it's just your nature to help people." They were both silent as Dude worked and merely nodded to acknowledge her words.

Dude took a deep breath. It was now or never. He thought he'd discovered the line that was connected to the C4 that was strapped to her chest. He could see the bomb also had at least two pounds of nails inside it. If it went off it *would* send shrapnel flying. They would certainly be dead, just as the gunman had said. He didn't want to think about what Cheyenne's body, or his own, would look like if those nails went flying.

Dude looked up at Cheyenne. "I've reached enough of this damn bomb so I can disarm it. Are you ready?"

Cheyenne looked into his eyes. He didn't look nervous, he was calm and matter of fact. She tried to calm her heartbeat. If he was confident enough not to quake in his boots, she would be too. "I'm ready," she told him with far more bravado than she felt. Before he moved, she quickly asked, "Do you mind if I close my eyes?"

Dude chuckled, feeling amusement for the first time since he'd arrived on scene and had seen this woman. "I'd close mine too if I could," he softly told her with a smile.

Cheyenne squeezed her eyes shut. She was still all mummified in the duct tape, still couldn't move much, but she felt lighter just by having him there.

Dude cut the last wire and waited.

Cheyenne's eyes flew open to see Dude looking up at her expectantly. "What?" he asked her urgently. He didn't *think* there was a secondary trigger, but it could be possible.

"I don't feel it ticking anymore," Cheyenne told him. "Was that it?"

Dude smiled and stood up, scooting the chair back as he did. He swiped his forehead with his bicep, removing the sweat that had built up there. "That was it. Let's get out of here," Dude told Cheyenne, reaching for her arm to guide her out of the store.

Cheyenne shook her head and pleaded with him. "Please…please take the rest of this tape off me now, before we go out there."

Dude studied Cheyenne critically. She'd held up extraordinarily well. He'd worked in some situations where he had had to knock civilians out because they were hysterical and wouldn't let him concentrate on working. This woman had not only stood there without moving, but she'd kept her calm at the same time. Dude really didn't want to hurt her though, and he knew removing the tape *was* going to hurt.

"Cheyenne," Dude started to deny her, but she interrupted him, frantically struggling against the bonds of what was left of the tape around her body. Now that the bomb was removed it was as if she couldn't stand the feeling of being bound.

"Please, Faulkner, I can't move…I can't breathe…need to get out of this…I…" she stopped and panted a bit and looked at the floor. Cheyenne took a deep breath and stopped moving, obviously trying to get herself under control. "Never mind, I'm okay. Let's go."

Dude couldn't help the feeling of rightness that went through him at the sound of his real name coming from between this woman's lips. Oh, Ice and the other women used his name all the time, but somehow it sounded different coming from Cheyenne. Dude stopped her from stepping away from him with a hand on her tape covered arm. She hadn't asked for much of anything during the whole ordeal, Dude figured he could give her this. "Calm down, Shy. Let me see what I can do. Lean back against the table."

Cheyenne braced herself back on the table while Dude reached over and grabbed a large pair of scissors that had been sitting on the table behind them. He regretted not having his k-bar knife with him. Since he'd been at *Aces* with the guys, he hadn't bothered to put it in his pocket before heading out for the night. Dude made a mental note to start carrying the damn thing with him wherever he went from now on.

He started at the bottom of the tape roll at her side and slowly snipped his way upward. The tape didn't move as he snipped, as it was stuck to her arms as well as to her clothing and the remnants of the bomb. Dude then went to her other side and did the same thing. She wasn't exactly free, but it was a start. He continued snipping around her on the tape until he'd gotten most of it cut.

Finally Dude looked at Cheyenne and said, "I don't want to hurt you, but taking this tape off your arms *is* going to hurt."

"I don't care," Cheyenne urged. "Just do it."

She flinched when he ripped off the tape on her left arm. Cheyenne knew that most of her arm hair had probably gone with the tape, but she was afraid to look. She scrunched her eyes closed as she heard Dude take a deep breath.

"How bad is it?" Cheyenne asked him softly.

Dude took a deep breath and tried to calm himself. He didn't know what kind of adhesive was on the tape, but it'd been strong. There were places on her arms where some of her skin looked like it had been taken right off with the tape. It was red and blotchy, and extremely painful looking. You wouldn't know it to look at Cheyenne though; she stood there stoically, waiting for his answer.

"Well," Dude started. "It's not too bad. I tried to be careful, but it's gonna be painful for a while. Please don't make me do that again," he said, referring to her other arm.

Cheyenne sighed. How could she refuse him when he'd done so much for her already? What was left of the skin on her arm where the tape was removed hurt bad, but she figured pragmatically that it would've hurt a lot more if she'd been blown up into tiny pieces. "Okay, thank you for at least loosening it up."

They looked at each other for a moment, each lost in their thoughts. They'd just been through a pretty intense experience.

Cheyenne looked at Faulkner and liked what she saw. She thought he was older than her, but not by much. He had dark hair, and dark eyes, which were looking at her as if she was the only other person on the planet. Cheyenne had always loved a man in uniform, and this man wore his well. She didn't know what he was thinking, but she kind of liked the intense look in his eyes as he peered down at her.

Dude looked down at the woman standing in front of him with respect. He didn't like to admit it, but he was used to women being weak, his teammates' women notwithstanding. The women he dated certainly were. Part of that was their submissive sexual desires, but it was more than that. Dude was used to taking charge and controlling those around him, but he hadn't had to do much to take charge with Cheyenne. She was strong, and did what needed to be done, regardless of her feelings or what she wanted to do.

Dude couldn't have stopped his hand from moving up to her hair to smooth it away from her flushed face if his life depended on it. "You're an amazing woman, Cheyenne Cotton." Dude lingered a beat as he ran his mangled hand over her hair to her shoulder, then he said, with a touch of regret, "Let's get out of here."

Dude carefully steered Cheyenne toward the front of the store. He put his hand on her lower back and they started walking to the front door. Cheyenne stopped when she saw the crowd that was outside the store. Of course there were police officers and military men around, but she also saw a lot of TV vans and cameras. She should've realized the media would be there, but she'd been worrying about other things...namely living through the last hour or so.

Cheyenne took a deep breath and said quietly to the man standing patiently next to her, "I know it's asking a lot...but....." she paused, nibbling her lip, trying to work up the courage to ask a huge favor of the strong military man standing next to her..

"Yes?" Dude prodded her gently.

"Will you hold my hand as we go out there?" Cheyenne looked up at him. "I know it doesn't mean anything, but I don't think I can face all of that," she gestured toward the front of the store with her head, "right now." Cheyenne could feel her face flame. She was so embarrassed, but she'd never felt as alone as she did looking at the mob she'd have to go through when she walked out the door.

Dude felt something shift deep inside of him. She was covered in grime and blood, she still had tape wrapped around most of her, her arm looked like it was horribly painful and all she wanted was someone to hold her hand. It was such a little request, but in his eyes it was huge. Women didn't usually ask him for favors, they waited for him to dole them out. Dude's respect for Cheyenne, in the face of everything she was feeling and going through, rose dramatically, and it was already pretty high.

He must have hesitated a bit too long before answering, because Cheyenne suddenly shook her head, looked down and mumbled, "Never mind, it was stupid anyway. Let's go," and started toward the door.

Dude caught her right hand in his left before she could take two steps and before he even thought about the fact she'd have to hold his injured hand. He'd made it a point never to hold a woman's hand with his injured one. Ever. "Cheyenne," he said softly, "it's not stupid. There's nothing I'd like better than to hold your hand as we face the lions together. Come on." The words were nothing but one hundred percent truth. Dude wasn't above lying to get cooperation from someone, but he wasn't lying now. The feel of Cheyenne's fingers in his was something Dude knew he'd never forget. She wasn't disgusted, she wasn't repulsed, she simply tightened her fingers around his and held on for dear life, as if she couldn't feel the scars and missing fingers on his hand. On the outside, she looked calm and composed, but the tight grip on his hand proved it to be a façade.

Cheyenne gripped Faulkner's hand tightly in hers, swallowed hard, put her chin up, and took a deep breath. She started for the front door, hand in hand with the larger than life man next to her and knew, even with everything that had happened to her in the last few hours, she'd never forget this moment. Holding this man's hand, letting him support her in that small way, meant more to her than any other gesture he could've made. She'd needed him and he hadn't hesitated to step up to the plate. Not only step up, but not make her feel bad for asking in the process.

Cheyenne blocked out the questions from the reporters, the police officers' demands, the lights, the noise…all of it, and concentrated on holding on to Faulkner's hand and following him wherever he wanted to lead her.

CHAPTER 4

Cheyenne sat in the lobby of the emergency room waiting for her taxi. The walk from the front of the store to the ambulance was a nightmare she didn't want to think about. The only good part was Faulkner's strength as he helped clear the way for her. At one point she'd been jostled hard enough that she would've fallen to the ground if it hadn't been for Faulkner. He'd taken his hand out of her own and wrapped his arm around her waist and curled her into his body. Cheyenne hadn't even been ashamed to lean into him and let him help her.

With everything she'd been through in the last few hours, it had felt so good to be held tight and safe against Faulkner's side and let him deal with making sure they made it through all the people safely. He'd helped her over to the ambulance and made sure she'd settled into the gurney without any issues. Once she was sitting and stable, Faulkner had kissed the top of her head briefly and squeezed her hand one last time. The last Cheyenne had seen of him was as he'd backed out of the ambulance. He'd given her a smile and a half wave before the doors shut in his face.

She'd spent the last three hours in the hospital. She'd given her statement to the police about what had happened, at least what had happened from *her* viewpoint. The nurses had removed the rest of the tape, which had been more painful than Cheyenne had thought it would be, and had both arms gooped up with lotion and antibiotics and who knew what else.

The first time Cheyenne had looked in the mirror, she'd been shocked. She was a mess. She was splattered with blood and her hair was hanging limply against her head. Fortunately a nurse gave her a pair of scrubs she could change into and let her brush her hair. Cheyenne supposed she was lucky, but the only thing she could think about was getting home and into a nice hot shower.

The problem with that was she wasn't supposed to get her arms wet for the next twenty four hours because of the bandages and the antibiotic mixture they'd smeared on her arms. The nurses had helped as much as they could in trying to get the blood out of her hair, but Cheyenne knew until she had a shower, she wouldn't feel clean.

She sighed. Cheyenne hadn't seen Faulkner since he'd helped her into the ambulance and squeezed her hand. She didn't expect to see him again really. After all, he was just doing his job. He'd go home and probably shoot the shit with his friends about what a crazy day he'd had, and then continue on with his life, just like she would...except first she had to *get* home.

Since her car was still in the grocery store parking lot, Cheyenne had to call a taxi. It really was pathetic that she didn't have one person she felt comfortable in calling and asking to come get her. There was no way in hell she was calling her mom or sister. They'd never let her live down her bad luck. A shitty day would just get worse if she involved either of them. Eventually she'd call and explain everything that had happened, but it'd have to be on a day she felt better able to deal with them. And that day certainly wasn't today.

Cheyenne knew she was a loner. She didn't really mind, except for times like this. She could've called one of her friends from work, but she hated to rely on other people, and besides, they weren't really the kind of friends that she felt comfortable calling out of the blue to pick her up from the hospital of all places. So, she'd simply called a taxi and now was waiting to go home. Home to her lonely apartment.

Cheyenne still had two days before she had to go back to work and she planned on crashing in bed and sleeping for one of those days, then she'd take the longest shower known to man, and *then* get herself together and back into the routine of her life.

Cheyenne laughed out loud, making the little old lady sitting in the hospital waiting room look at her disapprovingly. She still had to get some food. She'd been at the grocery store that afternoon for a reason. She had some cans of cream of mushroom soup and salad dressing, and that was about it. *Screw it. I'll order in until I can I get back to the store.* Cheyenne knew she'd never shop at the grocery store she'd been held hostage in again, even if it was where she'd first seen Faulkner. And even if it was a popular store for other men in uniform. It wasn't that she thought she'd be taken hostage again, it was just…she didn't know. She wasn't comfortable with the thought of entering the store again.

The taxi finally arrived outside the automatic doors. Cheyenne made her way outside, verified the car was there for her, and climbed into the backseat that smelled slightly of body odor and cigarette smoke. After giving directions to the taxi driver, Cheyenne put her head back on the seat, deliberately not thinking about how many germs and nasties might be lurking on the headrest, and closed her eyes. She felt weird. The painkillers the doctors had given her were obviously doing their job because she wasn't in any pain, but they also made her a bit woozy. She probably shouldn't be driving once she got to her car, but it wasn't too far to her apartment from the parking lot of the grocery store. She'd be extra cautious. She'd be fine. She always was.

* * *

DUDE COULDN'T STOP THINKING about Cheyenne. She had to be the bravest person he'd met in a long time. Her actions reminded him a lot of Ice's. Hell, all of his teammates' women for that matter. Cheyenne had faced what happened to her with courage and she hadn't panicked. From the first time Dude had seen her backing away from the officers trying to keep them from harm, to the last look he had of her smiling bravely at him as he left her in the ambulance, she'd been grace personified.

He didn't want to leave her, but Dude knew he had to give his statement to the local cops and get back with his CO. He'd spent a good hour going over what had happened inside the store with Cheyenne and what he'd done and seen. Since Dude wasn't related to Cheyenne, there was no reason, or really any excuse, for him to go with her to the hospital.

The press had been relentless. Dude knew it was their job, just as it was his job to give a report of what had happened, but this time was different somehow. Each time they asked the police department's representative probing questions about Cheyenne and where she lived and what she said and what she thought and what she did, Dude just wanted to rail at them and tell them it was none of their damn business and to leave her alone. Cheyenne was a grown woman, she could handle herself...she didn't need him. But there was something about her that made him want to wrap her in his arms and protect her from the world anyway.

* * *

THE TAXI PULLED up in front of the grocery store. *"Was it just this morning I was here?"* Cheyenne thought ruefully. Seriously, it felt like it'd been days since she'd walked into the store intent on buying enough to fill up her pantry so she'd be good to go for a good long while.

Cheyenne painfully eased out of the back seat after paying the driver. As the taxi pulled away, she started walking toward her car. She'd parked near the back of the lot that morning, as was her habit, to try to get a little extra exercise. As she approached her car she heard the sound of a vehicle pulling up behind her.

Feeling extraordinarily cautious after everything that had happened, Cheyenne quickly turned and watched as a huge pickup came to a stop and Faulkner hopped out. Cheyenne looked at him in confusion. What was he doing here? She looked around to see if anyone else was there that he was meeting. There was no one else. The parking lot was deserted, it was only the two of them.

Dude eyed Cheyenne as he neared. She looked perplexed to see him. She also looked tired…and adorably cute. She was wearing blue scrubs from the hospital, no doubt because her clothes were ruined. They were big on her, and it looked like if she moved the wrong way, the pants would fall right off of her. There were dark smudges under her eyes, which made her black eye even more prominent, and both arms were bandaged from wrist to elbow, and probably beyond, but Dude couldn't see because of the scrubs she was wearing.

"Hi again," Dude said softly as he came to a halt in front of Cheyenne.

"Um…Hi." Cheyenne said haltingly. "What are you doing here?"

Dude laughed and looked her in the eye. "I started thinking about how you probably drove to the store today, and since you were taken to the hospital in the ambulance that somehow you'd have to get back here to get your car. I wanted to meet you at the hospital and see how you were doing and give you a ride, but when I called, they told me you'd already been discharged. I'm sorry I missed you."

Cheyenne looked at the man in front of her in confusion. "You called? Why would you do that?" she asked, not thinking about how rude it sounded until it was too late. "I…I...mean," she stammered, eager to make sure Faulkner didn't take offense.

Dude chuckled. "I know what you mean, Shy, and to be honest I'm not sure why…I just wanted to be sure you were okay and to see if I could help you in some way. What did the doctor say?" He gestured at her arms with his chin.

"Uh, okay, well, I'm okay. They just bandaged my arms to make sure they wouldn't get infected or anything. They're covered in some slimy horrible goo that makes me want to scratch. I'm not supposed to get them wet, which is ridiculous because the goo is gross and I feel disgusting after everything that happened today. I don't have any food in my apartment, which isn't surprising considering I was in the damn store in the first place this morning. My food is probably still sitting in my cart in the middle of one of the aisles, and I'm hungry, and I don't know if I can eat anything because the pills they gave me are making me feel really weird."

Cheyenne's words faded in the air around them and she immediately closed her eyes. Holy shit, had all that crap really just spewed out of her mouth? She was mortified.

"Aw, come here, Shy." Dude felt his heart melt a bit more at her words. She was adorable. Whatever drugs they'd given her were obviously making her much more talkative than she probably normally was. He'd known a few sailors and marines who reacted the same way to painkillers. They'd talk and talk and talk seemingly without any filter. It was a hell of a lot cuter on Cheyenne.

Without waiting for her to move, Dude took a step toward her and pulled her into his arms. He relaxed as Cheyenne melted into him. He'd been half afraid she'd rebuff his attempt to soothe her. Dude heard her sniff once, then felt her bury her nose into his neck. Her breath was warm against his skin and Dude tilted his head just a bit until he was touching her with his cheek.

"You smell good."

Dude smiled. That wasn't what he thought she'd say. She was constantly surprising him.

"Thanks." Dude stood in the dark parking lot holding an amazing woman and realized he didn't want to let her go. "Can I take you home?"

"I need my car."

"I don't think you should be driving. I don't know you all that well, but I imagine if you were in your right mind you never would have told me all of that other stuff. Am I right?" He felt her nod reluctantly against him and smiled. "Okay then. I'll take you home. I'll arrange for your car to get to your apartment." Dude knew he could call any of his teammates to come and get it and drive it home for her.

Cheyenne was too tired to argue or even protest. It felt so good to be taken care of, she couldn't remember a time when someone had offered, or who she allowed, to take care of her. At that moment Cheyenne would've probably agreed to anything Faulkner said.

She startled when he spoke again, "I gotta hear you say it's okay, Shy."

Cheyenne forced herself to look up at the man holding her. She looked into his eyes and saw nothing but sincerity. "Okay, but if you're really a serial killer can you please kill me quickly? I've had a really bad day." Her words came out softly, but with one hundred percent honesty.

Dude laughed out loud and brought his hand to Cheyenne's cheek. "Painkillers really loosen your tongue, don't they?" He asked rhetorically. "Don't worry, Shy, I promise I'll get you home in one piece. You're safe with me."

"I *feel* safe with you. I don't know why or how, but I do. Thank you, Faulkner. Seriously. I know you probably have better things to do than lug my ass around. But I appreciate it. I do. Really."

Dude pulled back and kept a hand around Cheyenne's waist, and steered her toward his truck. "I know you do, hon. Come on, let's get you home. We don't want you turning into a pumpkin. Do you have your keys?"

"Yeah, my purse was delivered to me at the hospital by one of the cops when he came to get my statement. I have no idea how they found it in the chaos of the store, I sure as hell couldn't have just slung it over my shoulder and pranced out of the store with you."

Dude nodded, glad he wouldn't have to pick the lock to her apartment to get her inside. He would've done it, but it wasn't exactly the first impression he wanted to leave Cheyenne with. He opened his passenger door and helped her sit, then reached over and buckled her in. Dude closed the door and made his way around to the driver's side. He settled into the seat and looked over at Cheyenne. Her head was resting against the headrest and she was turned toward him.

"What is it, hon?"

"You're hot. I'm assuming you know this." Cheyenne sounded like she was imparting some deep dark secret to him.

"Shy..." He didn't disagree, but he didn't agree either. She was extremely charming all drugged up. Dude shuddered to think about her actually driving in this condition.

"Seriously, you *are*. I don't know why you're here though. Did you lose a bet or something? Are your buddies around somewhere ready to bust out and laugh?"

"What?" Dude was getting pissed. Cheyenne couldn't mean what it sounded like she meant.

"Yeah, no one who looks like you has ever taken a second look at me before. I'm just me. You're…well…you're sex on a stick."

Dude didn't even smile at her words. She had to be kidding him. "Hon…"

"No, really. I know I'm not a troll. I'm passable, I actually think I've got great calves, and I like my arms…at least I did before I had the hair completely ripped off of them. Let me tell you, I don't think duct tape is gonna become the new fashion fad anytime soon. But I'm not the kind of woman you probably are with all the time. I bet chicks throw themselves at you. When you go out to the bar I bet you always leave with someone right? Oh shit! I bet you hang out with a gang of hotties don't you? Jesus, You leave a wake of devastation behind you wherever you go, don't you?"

Dude raised his right hand and covered Cheyenne's mouth lightly. He didn't know whether to be pissed at her assumptions, or to be flattered. When she stayed silent, and simply looked at him with wide eyes, he told her, "Cheyenne, first, there's no fucking bet and I'm kinda pissed you'd even accuse me of something like that. I think you're exquisite. Funny. Cute. Interesting. And there's nowhere I'd rather be than right here, right now, with you. Second, yes, I have a group of friends and we hang out, but almost all of them are either married or in a serious relationship. We don't leave a wake of anything behind us, because we only have eyes for our women." Dude didn't even stop to think about what he was saying, that he was suddenly including Cheyenne in his thoughts and words.

"I hope like hell when you wake up in the morning and the pain pills have worn off you'll remember this conversation and want to hang out with me and my friends. You're like them more than you know."

Dude smiled at the look on Cheyenne's face. She hadn't picked her head up off the head rest, but watched him with serious eyes.

"But you're perfect..." She mumbled the words around his hand and would've said more, but Dude interrupted her.

"I'm not even close to fucking perfect. I'm kinda a slob, I have a tendency to throw my shit on the floor until it annoys me too badly and I have to put it in the hamper. I have a temper, but I'd never raise my hand to you or any other woman. I'm controlling and like to be in charge. And..." Dude held up his left hand, reminding Cheyenne of his disfigurement. "Enough women have told me this is disgusting, or just plain gross, for me to think I'm anything but perfect."

Cheyenne didn't even think. She brought her hand up to his and grasped it tightly and brought it to her mouth. She kissed each mangled stub of a finger as she spoke. "Those dumb bitches don't know what they're talking about. You're perfect, Faulkner. These little scars don't mean dick. Wait, yes they do. They mean a lot. They mean you're a hero. That you've suffered helping our country, helping people out of shitty situations. I don't know what kind of situations, 'cos if you told me, you'd probably have to kill me, but I don't really want to know anyway 'cos I'm kinda a wuss. But if those women rejected you because of your hand, they're complete morons. Seriously." Cheyenne closed her eyes, still feeling dizzy, and at the same time wanting to concentrate on the feel of Faulkner's skin against her own, and brought his hand to her cheek, missing the look of endearment on Dude's face.

"Your skin is so soft, except here." Cheyenne rubbed her face against his scars. "It's rough and where your fingers were, the skin is raised and bumpy. It feels so good against my skin. It's like a massager. I can only imagine what it'd feel like..."

Cheyenne stopped abruptly and Dude could see her blushing. Was she really going to say what he thought she was? "Go on, Shy, this I want to hear."

Cheyenne let go of his hand, but Dude continued to brush his fingers against her cheek.

"Uh, anyway, those women were idiots."

"God, you're fucking sweet."

Cheyenne opened her eyes and saw the intensity in Faulkner's. She wanted to close her eyes, the cab of the truck was filled with a weird vibe, but she couldn't.

They stared at each other for a moment before Dude's hand left her cheek and went behind her neck. He pulled her toward him and kissed her forehead and stayed close with his lips resting against her for a moment, before pulling away.

"Let's get you home, Cinderella, before the clock strikes midnight."

"I love that story," Cheyenne sighed dreamily.

"Why doesn't that surprise me?" Dude said absently as he started up his truck and headed out of the parking lot.

Cheyenne giggled at his words and fell silent.

"Where am I going, Shy?"

"To my apartment."

"Yeah, I got that, but where is that?"

"Oh. Shit. These are some crazy drugs."

"Yeah." Dude waited a beat, then reminded her of his question.

"Sorry. I live at Oak Tree Apartments on Copper and Fifth."

"I know where that is. Thanks, I'll get you there. What apartment?"

Cheyenne turned to him again and teased, "Are you *sure* you're not a serial killer?"

Dude laughed at her again. "I'm sure."

"Okay, I'm 513 in building four."

"Close your eyes, Shy, I'll get us there in a bit. You rest and I'll wake you up once we've arrived."

Cheyenne did as Faulkner said. She closed her eyes again and relaxed into the seat. "Thank you for the ride, Faulkner. I didn't have anyone else to call." She couldn't stop the words.

"You're more than welcome. Now shush."

Cheyenne smiled, but didn't open her eyes. Her head was swirling too much to fall asleep, but it was heavenly to be able to relax and not worry about anything for a while.

CHAPTER 5

Cheyenne opened her eyes and groaned. She knew exactly where she was and everything she'd said and done the night before. She would've been happy if she could've forgotten it all, but she wasn't so lucky.

Last night, Faulkner had pulled up to her apartment building and helped her out of the car. He'd half carried, half walked, her up to her apartment and taken her keys out of her hand when she couldn't seem to get the key into the lock.

Cheyenne was embarrassed Faulkner had seen her apartment. She was a slob, as he'd claimed to be. She knew it, but it was her little secret. Not anymore. She wasn't going to agree with him when he'd talked about how he didn't like to pick up his clothes from the floor. It was somewhat manly and macho when a man did it, but when a woman had a messy house, somehow it was pathetic. Faulkner had opened her door and laughed outright at seeing her mess. Cheyenne had tried to explain when she was home from work she just never felt like cleaning or picking up around her apartment, but he just laughed off her explanations.

"The two of us together would be a mess. But at least I know you aren't perfect now, Shy."

Cheyenne had looked at Faulkner as if he had three heads. "Of *course* I'm not perfect, Faulkner. *You're* the perfect one."

"I think we've had this conversation once already. Come on, let's get you to bed."

He'd led her into her bedroom and pulled back the covers. He'd tucked her in, scrubs and all, kissed her on the forehead again and whispered, "Sleep well, Shy. I'll see you tomorrow."

Cheyenne hadn't thought much about it then, she'd been too tired and frazzled from the drugs coursing through her system, but now, in the light of day, it was freaking her out. Faulkner would see her today? Had they made plans and she didn't remember? Cheyenne didn't know if she was ready to spend time with Faulkner...normal time together that was. Without bombs, bad guys, drugs and her being a damsel in distress. She figured he'd get as far away from her as possible, especially after her diarrhea of the mouth last night. Cheyenne buried her head into her pillow and groaned, remembering how she'd actually told him he probably hung out with a gang of hotties. Who said things like that? Darn drugs.

Cheyenne sat up, ready to get out of bed and tackle the shower, when her bedroom door opened and Faulkner strolled in.

What the freaking hell?

Cheyenne pulled the covers back up her body until she clutched them under her chin.

"Good morning, Shy. I hope you feel better this morning?"

Cheyenne could only stare at Faulkner in stupefaction, and nod.

"Words."

Cheyenne had forgotten that about him. Faulkner liked to hear verbal confirmation of his questions. "I feel better."

"Good. I made you some breakfast, we can eat after you shower."

"Breakfast?" Cheyenne could only stare at Faulkner in bewilderment. "I don't have anything to eat in my apartment. I'm pretty sure that was one of the four hundred and fifty four things I blabbed to you last night, that I now wish I hadn't."

"You've got food now. I called Fiona, the wife of one of my teammates. She went shopping this morning and brought over a shit ton of food. It should be enough to last you for a while."

"Fiona?" Cheyenne tried to shake herself out of the weird dimension she felt like she'd fallen into.

"Yeah, Fiona. Now, come on. Get up. Let's see about removing those bandages. We'll see how they look and if I think your arms look good enough, you can shower. You can do that after the bandages are gone."

Cheyenne tilted her head at Faulkner, but did as he asked. She swung her legs over the side of the bed and sat on the side.

Dude put a hand under her elbow and helped her stand. When Cheyenne had her legs firmly under her, he backed away and waited for her to make her way to the bathroom, which was connected to the little bedroom.

Cheyenne walked in front of Faulkner into the bathroom.

"I'll give you a minute to take care of business, then I'll be back to help you with those bandages."

Cheyenne thought she couldn't have been any more embarrassed than when she'd remembered what she'd babbled last night to the gorgeous man waiting for her in her bedroom, but she'd been wrong. She hurried through using the toilet and brushing her teeth and was standing in front of the sink with her head down, leaning on her hands when Faulkner returned.

He stood behind her and rested his hands next to hers on the counter. Cheyenne could feel his heat along her back. His body was one big muscle and she loved how he felt against her. She felt safe and cared for. It was crazy, but it was also a feeling she knew she couldn't get accustomed to. She should be more freaked that this man, this stranger, had apparently spent the night in her apartment, and was still there, but she couldn't muster up the outrage. He'd done nothing but take care of her. Cheyenne knew she could trust him, but she wasn't sure why he'd spent the night.

"Why are you here?" Cheyenne asked seriously, lifting her head to look at Faulkner in the mirror.

"Because you need me."

"But we don't know each other."

"We know each other better than some people do after a couple of dates."

"Yeah, but we haven't even *been* on a date."

"Which is something I mean to remedy soon."

"Do you have a comeback to everything I say?" Cheyenne was frustrated with Faulkner's calm and rational answers to everything she brought up.

"Yes. Now, are you ready for the bandages to come off?"

Cheyenne nodded, then rolled her eyes when Faulkner didn't move, but just raised his eyebrow at her instead. "Yes, I'm ready for the bandages to come off."

Dude merely smiled at her. He stepped back a foot and let her turn in his arms. He reached behind him to pull out a wicked looking knife from somewhere behind him.

"Jesus, Faulkner. Is *that* necessary to carry around?"

He looked down at the k-bar knife in his hand. "Yeah, Shy, it's necessary. I'm just sorry I didn't have it with me yesterday when I was trying to remove all that damn tape from your arms. It was in my truck, but it was a huge fuck up on my part not to have it on me."

Dude wasn't going to say anything else, but the knife had saved his life more than once. He brought it up to her arm and said, "Stay still." He wasn't going to cut her, he'd rather face ten terrorists with no weapon than hurt this woman, but her standing still would certainly help make *sure* he didn't hurt her.

Dude felt Cheyenne go stiff and smothered the smile he could feel forming on his face. He felt lucky as hell she'd been as trusting of him as she had been so far. If she'd told him how she'd woken up and found a man she barely knew in her apartment after a hell of a day, and didn't immediately kick him out, he would've paddled her ass. But since it was him, and since he knew he'd never hurt even one hair on her head, he didn't say a word at her easy capitulation.

He ran the knife up the bandage on her right arm, easily slicing it. Dude put the knife on the counter and took both hands to peel back the white gauze slowly and easily. He winced at the rough looking patches of skin that had been irritated by the removal of the tape.

"They look good," Cheyenne said with satisfaction looking down at her arm that had been uncovered.

"Good?"

"Yeah, you should've seen them yesterday. That stuff they put on my arm is obviously miracle goo!"

They both laughed and Dude grabbed the knife again and made short work of the bandages on Cheyenne's other arm. When those too had been removed, Dude stepped back. "Okay, Shy, I think you're okay to shower. Hop in and get clean. I'll be in the kitchen waiting for you. Take your time."

Cheyenne nodded and watched as Faulkner backed out of the small bathroom and closed the door behind him. She shook her head in bemusement. She'd planned on spending the day loafing around and being lazy. She had no idea what the day held in store for her now. She didn't know why she trusted Faulkner. Maybe it was because she'd seen him in the store before. Maybe it was because he was in the military. Maybe it was because of the extreme situation she'd been in the day before and he'd been gentle, and had saved her life. Whatever it was, Cheyenne knew it was probably stupid, but she couldn't muster up any alarm that he was in her apartment, and had apparently been there all night. Shrugging, she turned toward the shower and turned on the water, letting it get hot as she removed the scrubs she'd slept in.

Cheyenne spent way too long in the shower, but it felt heavenly. She scrubbed her skin as hard as she dared, and could stand. The hot water felt like it washed her worries away along with the dirt and grime from her ordeal the day before.

She finally turned off the water and stepped from the shower stall. Sitting on the counter was a change of clothes that definitely hadn't been there when she started her shower. Cheyenne blushed furiously, knowing Faulkner had been in the room while she'd been completely naked just a few steps away. Had he seen anything? Did he like what he might have seen?

Cheyenne had been honest with him in that she didn't think she was horrible looking. She did like parts of her body, but others she could take or leave. Cheyenne wasn't huge, she wasn't skinny. She didn't have long hair, she didn't have short hair. She didn't have lavender or ice blue eyes, she had normal brown eyes. She wasn't short, but she wasn't tall either. She was right smack in the middle of everything. Pretty darn normal. Her mom and sister had told her often enough that she was nothing special, and while Cheyenne knew she shouldn't listen to what they said, in this case they were more right than wrong.

Cheyenne quickly dressed in the clothes he'd left on the counter, blushing at Faulkner's choice of underwear. It was obvious he had to dig deep in her undie drawer to find the black lace nylon thong. She normally didn't wear such a thing, and she knew it'd been buried under the more practical cotton and nylon bikini underwear. She wasn't going to put them on, but she couldn't resist. She felt tingly and beautiful knowing Faulkner had picked it out and she was now wearing it.

He'd also pulled out a pair of gray sweat bottoms and a V-neck shirt which plunged way too deep for Cheyenne's peace of mind. The bra he'd also dug out of her drawer was the one push up bra she owned. She'd bought it on a whim, thinking it might make her feel sexy, but it hadn't, it'd made her feel uncomfortable and like she was falsely advertising something she didn't have. But now, wearing it because Faulkner had picked it out? She got it. She felt sexy.

Cheyenne looked at herself in the mirror when she'd finished dressing. The bra made her have more cleavage than ever before, and it definitely lived up to its name. It pushed her boobs up and accented them inside the low cut shirt. Cheyenne knew she should probably put on a regular T-shirt, and probably one of her regular bras, but she made herself walk out of the door of the bathroom and into her room.

She might never have a chance like this again. She had no idea where this, whatever this was, was going to go, maybe nowhere, but she'd ride the wave for as long as she could. She'd be a fool not to. She had no idea what Faulkner was still doing there. Cheyenne had been honest, too honest, thanks to the pain killers, last night when she'd questioned what Faulkner was doing with her, but it was no more clear now in the morning when her mind wasn't clouded by drugs as it was last night.

Cheyenne walked into the main area of her apartment, and stopped abruptly and stared. Faulkner was standing in her kitchen at the stove holding a spatula over a steaming pan that held what looked like an omelet. He looked up when she entered the room as if he could sense her there.

"Hey, you look a lot better."

His words were innocuous, but the look in his eye was anything but. Cheyenne watched as his eyes went from her feet, up her legs, stopping at her chest for a moment, then coming back up to meet her eyes.

"Thanks."

They looked at each other a beat longer than was truly comfortable, or polite, before Dude looked back down at the omelet he was making. He took a deep breath and tried not to imagine how the underwear he'd picked out would look on her without the sweats and shirt in the way.

He'd opened her drawers looking for something for Cheyenne to wear after her shower and came face to face with her underwear. It was stuffed into a drawer haphazardly, with no organization and nothing was folded. Dude had been stunned for a moment, then, as if he was watching from far away, saw himself shifting through the cotton until he'd seen the miniscule little black thong on the bottom of the pile of material. He'd plucked it out without thinking and rubbed his thumb over it.

The same thing had happened when Dude had found her bras. They'd all been sensible and comfortable, except for the black lace number with the strategic padding. Dude wasn't an expert, but he knew what the extra material in the corner of the cups was for.

Sneaking another look up at Cheyenne, Dude knew she'd at least put on the bra he'd picked out. He could see more than a hint of her cleavage as she pulled herself up on the stool at the bar that ran along the edge of the kitchen. He smirked as a slight blush came over her face. She'd caught him looking.

Dude turned and grabbed one of the plates he'd placed next to the stove and expertly scooped up the omelet and transferred it to the plate. He took a fork, placed it on the plate and brought it over to Cheyenne.

"You didn't have to cook," Cheyenne tried to protest.

"I know. Eat."

"I didn't have anything in my fridge but salad dressing...You said someone named Fiona brought all of this?"

"Eat, Shy."

Dude smiled as Cheyenne dutifully picked up the fork and cut into the omelet. He didn't move from her side until she'd taken a bite and closed her eyes in enjoyment. He went back to the stove and broke more eggs into the still hot pan. Dude divided his attention between Cheyenne eating and his own omelet.

By the time he finished making his own breakfast, Cheyenne was eating her last bites. She suddenly looked at him in embarrassment. "I'm sorry, I should've waited for you. Jesus, I'm horrible."

"It's fine, Shy. If you'd waited, yours would've been cold."

"But..."

"I said it's fine." Dude knew he was being a bit harsher than the situation called for, but he couldn't help it. It was a part of who he was. He was used to being obeyed. It came from being a SEAL and being in situations where obeying was second nature and necessary for survival. He wasn't into total control and the bullshit that went along with the BDSM lifestyle, but he certainly needed to be in control when he went to bed with a woman.

Dude hadn't really thought about what that might mean in a real relationship, because he'd had never *had* a real relationship. As most of his buddies had done before they'd settled down, he enjoyed picking up women. He'd take them home and have an excellent time for the night. But after that one night, they were gone. Every woman had known the score and none had any complaints, at least none they'd verbalized to him. They'd all willingly turned over control to him and left the next morning, but Dude had never really thought about how it would work for more than a night.

He shook his head. Dude wanted Cheyenne, and not like he'd had other women. He *liked* her. As he'd told her the night before, she was interesting and fun. Those weren't adjectives he'd used to describe women in the past that he'd liked. Hell, he hadn't even bothered to get to know any of the women he'd taken to bed before. That probably made him a dick, but he couldn't change his past now.

Liking a woman and wanting to get to know her before sleeping with her, was new for Dude. He'd also never invited his friends into any relationship, whatever kind of relationship he had with Cheyenne, before. He'd *never* gone out of his way to have a one-night-stand interact with his friends. But here he was, one day after meeting Cheyenne, and he'd voluntarily reached out to his friends for her help. Fiona had been overjoyed to help him out and go shopping for food. Dude hadn't wanted to leave Cheyenne while she was hurt and loopy from whatever drugs the staff at the hospital had given her, so he'd called Cookie, but gotten Fiona instead. She'd bought enough food for at least a month.

Dude had spent the night on Cheyenne's couch, waking up at least once an hour so he could pop his head into her room and check on her. She'd been dead to the world. She hadn't even stirred when he'd stood by her bedside. And the one time Dude had actually touched Cheyenne, she'd groaned and rolled *toward* him, not away from him. It had been harder than Dude had thought to leave her room after that.

Now here he was, bossing Cheyenne around and generally pushing himself on her. Dude knew he should leave and give her some room, but he honestly didn't want to.

"What were your plans for the day, Shy?"

Cheyenne looked over at Faulkner as he ate. She pushed her plate away and leaned on her elbows. "I hadn't really thought much about it. I usually just hang out on my days off."

"Hell, I didn't even ask what you do for a living. I'm sorry."

Cheyenne shrugged. "It's okay. It's not like we've really had a chance to chat about our lives. Besides, it's not that interesting really. I answer the phone when people call 911."

Dude lowered the forkful of omelet he'd been about to put in his mouth and looked at Cheyenne incredulously. "What?"

Feeling nervous and not knowing why Faulkner was being weird, Cheyenne repeated, "I'm a 911 operator."

"So you help save people's lives when they're in desperate need of someone to help them."

It wasn't a question, but Cheyenne treated it as if it was. "Well, I guess, yeah, but it's actually boring a lot of the time and we get a lot of calls that aren't emergencies we have to deal with."

"Don't downplay it, Shy," Dude scolded. "You help people through some of the worst times in their lives. You're there for them when they reach out. That's amazing."

Feeling uncomfortable with his praise, Cheyenne just shrugged.

Dude tilted his head and looked closer at her. He'd been amazed at her occupation. It wasn't as if he couldn't imagine her doing it. She'd stayed calm the day before in the face of her own mortality, and now he knew why. She had a lot of practice dealing with her emotions in extreme situations. "How do you deal with the stress of the job?"

"What?" Cheyenne was startled by Faulkner's question.

"I said, how do you deal with the stress of your job?"

"Uh, I read? I hang out here at home?"

Faulkner looked at her closely. Cheyenne hadn't answered his question, she'd pretty much answered in the form of a question. "You don't deal with it, do you?"

"It's not a big deal."

"It *is* a big deal, Shy. Hell, even me and my buddies know we have to let off steam after a mission. You have to let it go somehow."

"I know you work with explosives, but what do *you* do, Faulkner?" Cheyenne asked defensively. She wanted to get the attention off of her and since he brought it up, she'd go with it.

"I'm a SEAL."

Cheyenne looked at him in horror. Oh fucking hell.

"No, just no, this isn't right."

Dude put his plate away from himself and leaned into Cheyenne. He didn't like her tone of voice. "What do you mean it isn't right? What I feel about you is as right as I've felt in a long time, Shy."

"I mean, you really *are* a hero. What the *hell* are you doing here?"

Dude stood up and crowded Cheyenne until she leaned back against the bar counter. He put his hands on the counter behind her so he was hovering over her and she couldn't possibly ignore him and what he wanted to say.

"As far as I'm concerned, *you're* the hero, Shy." Dude ignored Cheyenne as she shook her head in denial and continued. "You help people every day. Every damn day. You're their lifeline when they need it. They reach out and you're there."

"But I don't save them. Most of the time they're already dead or dying, or at least someone they know is."

"Shy, Jesus." Dude watched as Cheyenne began to shake.

"No really, most of the time I have no idea what happened, what the outcome is, but I watch the news. Sometimes I see. All I do is call the cops and the paramedics, Faulkner. I call people like *you* to come and do the real saving."

Dude felt sick inside. He didn't like to hear Cheyenne feeling this way about herself, about her job. "Shy, I have a story to tell you. Will you listen with an open mind and really hear what I'm about to tell you?"

At Cheyenne's nod, he simply raised his eyebrows at her.

"Sorry, yes, I'll listen."

"I'm a disappointment to my parents." Dude could tell Cheyenne was about to protest, and he cut her off. "I'm not telling you this to make you feel sorry for me or anything. Just listen."

Cheyenne nodded and watched as a muscle ticked in Faulkner's jaw. Whatever he wanted to tell her was serious.

"I skipped school one day when I was about thirteen. I came home from surfing, expecting to get shit from my parents for skipping, and saw blood all over our kitchen. My parents weren't there. There was no note or anything. I had no idea where they were or what had happened. All I knew was that the house was empty and there was a shitload of blood on the counter, sink, and even on the floor of our kitchen. I completely freaked out. I dialed 911 and was hysterical. The lady who answered the phone was an angel. She got me calmed down and asked me to answer some simple questions. She used a technique I've since heard will engage the right side of the brain and make people think less with their emotional side, and more with the rational side of their brain. She asked what my name was, she asked how old I was, and she asked what my address was. I'm sure you use these techniques too, but by the time she got to the next question I was able to think a bit more clearly.

"I looked around and saw a butcher knife resting next to the cutting board along with a slew of vegetables. While I described what I was seeing, the 911 lady had been doing some investigating of her own. She told me that my mother had been signed into the emergency room by my father. She'd cut herself badly while making dinner and had bled all over the place while she'd waited on my father to help her wrap it up and put pressure on it."

Dude smiled as Cheyenne put one hand on his bicep and stroked him. She was still looking up at him, brow furrowed, and chewing one lip. Unconsciously, she was trying to soothe him. Dude liked that.

He quickly went to finish his story and make his point. "I was embarrassed as all hell that I'd jumped to conclusions and thought my parents had been stabbed and kidnapped. I never forgot the feeling of relief I had when that lady answered the phone. She was my lifeline, and I don't know what I would've done if she hadn't been there for me. *You* do that for people Shy. You're a lifeline for every person having a crisis that calls and you pick up the phone. I don't know that lady's name, I never met her and never had a chance to thank her properly. I regret that to this day. I wish you could meet every single person you help, Shy. I wish you could see first-hand how much you help them."

Dude paused and brought his scarred hand to the back of Cheyenne's neck. He tilted it up to his and forced her to look into his eyes. "What you do is important, Shy. You touch more lives than you'll ever know. The people you talk to will never forget you and what you do for them, even if their loved one doesn't survive. Own it, hon. Be proud of yourself."

Cheyenne closed her eyes briefly, loving the feel of Faulkner's thumb at her chin and his pinky on the back of her neck. It felt awesome. "I'll try," she whispered.

"You do that." Dude got closer into Cheyenne's space and brought his other hand up from the counter to her side. He stroked his thumb against her waist. "I'm going to kiss the hell out of you, Shy. Then I'll probably touch you way too intimately for having just met you yesterday. I can't stop thinking about you wearing the thong I picked out for you and having it snug against your core as we sit here. Once I force myself to pull away from you, hopefully before I go too far, I'm going to get out of your hair for a few hours. I have some things I have to do, but I'll be back later. I'm going to take you to meet the most important people in my life…my SEAL team and their women. Then I'll take you back to my place and you'll spend the night in my bed while I sleep on the couch. When I finally take you, I want to make sure we're both ready for it. Do you have a problem with any of that?"

Cheyenne tried not to hyperventilate. There were so many things wrong with what Faulkner said, but she wanted every single thing with a desire that boarded on desperation. "I have to work tomorrow," she managed breathlessly.

She watched as Faulkner smiled widely and a bit wickedly. "Okay, I'll bring you back here before your shift so you can change and do whatever it is you have to do to get ready. Will that work? Any other objections?"

Cheyenne went to shake her head, caught herself and said instead, "No, Faulkner, no objections."

The look in his eyes was electric. "You expressed a thought last night, and you should know that I can't wait to show you how my hand feels against your…skin, Shy." Dude lowered his head, not giving her a chance to respond to his words, and proceeded to kiss the hell out of her as he promised.

He didn't ask, he didn't ease into the kiss, he dove in and took over. Dude didn't give her a chance to take control. He thrust his tongue into Cheyenne's mouth and aggressively took her. He used his teeth, tongue, and even his lips. He teased, nibbled, bit, and stroked her. Within moments, Cheyenne was twisting and turning in his grip, lost in the passion they were sharing.

Dude grabbed hold of her wrists with his right hand and brought them behind her. He held them at the small of her back, encouraging her to arch into him. Dude took his left hand and brushed his knuckles against her breasts, now even more prominently displayed in her low cut shirt and the push up bra.

Dude eased away from Cheyenne's mouth, ignoring her whimper of protest and looked down at his hand caressing her chest. He could see her nipples poking through both the lacy bra and the cotton of the T-shirt.

"Normal? Jesus, Shy, look at you. You are *anything* but fucking *normal*."

Without giving her a chance to say or do anything else, Dude dropped his head and licked a line between her breasts. He held her still with one hand still clutching her wrists behind her back and the other rested just under her breasts. He could feel her heart hammering against her chest as if she'd run a marathon.

"Beautiful. So beautiful," Dude murmured, pulling back once more. He looked up into Cheyenne's eyes again. "You have no idea how badly I want to take you to the ground, strip off all your clothes and spend the rest of the day tasting you and discovering just how good you feel under me. No fucking clue. This is *not* a one night stand, Shy. Say it."

"Not a one night stand."

"Good. Yeah, no way one night would be enough." Dude struggled with himself. Cheyenne was so beautiful, helpless in his arms, waiting for whatever he was going to do with her next. He knew he was treading on thin ice. He was testing his control to the limit, but he had to taste her.

"Hang on, Shy. I have to feel your nipple on my tongue just once before I let you go." Dude leaned back and took his mangled left hand and stretched the V-neck of her shirt to one side. He was probably ruining it, but he didn't fucking care. He moved it over enough until he could see the edge of the lace on the cup of her bra. Holding her shirt, he used one of the stubs of his fingers to move it out of the way. It only took an inch and her nipple popped out of the cup of her bra and Dude could see it harden further as the cold air of the room hit it.

Cheyenne had large areolas and her nipple was a shade darker than the skin around it. Dude took the nail of his thumb and flicked it over her nipple. He watched as Cheyenne groaned and arched into his touch, pushing herself closer to him. "Fuck. Beautiful." Dude leaned down and sucked Cheyenne into his mouth hard. Just as he'd done with the kiss, he didn't start out slow. He sucked hard and used his teeth to pull on her nipple and elongate it further. Dude felt her arms jerk against his hold as she squirmed against him.

He let go of her nipple with a pop and looked down. If they hadn't been wearing clothes, Dude knew he would've been inside her. They were pressed together intimately and he could swear he could feel Cheyenne's heat through both their clothes.

As his thumbnail continued to flick over her nipple, Dude leaned in and whispered in her ear, "Oh yeah, that thong is soaked, isn't it, Shy? I'd love to brush it up against my cheek now that you've been wearing it. I imagined what it'd feel like, what it'd smell like as I pulled it out of your drawer, but I'll kill to have my hands on it now." Dude heard Cheyenne whimper, and she tilted her neck to the side, inviting him to play.

He sucked her earlobe into his mouth and bit down. Then Dude moved to her neck. Not caring, he began marking her where everyone would be able to see it. Purposely choosing a place where his mark couldn't be hidden, he sucked Cheyenne's skin into his mouth.

"Are y-y-you giving me a hickey?" Cheyenne stuttered, not fighting him, but tilting her head giving Dude more room to work. "What are we, fifteen?"

Waiting until he'd sufficiently bruised her neck with his mouth, Dude finally lifted his head to check his handiwork. "Hell yeah I'm marking you. I want you to think about my mouth on you, my fingers on your nipple, and your legs squeezing me tight every time you look in the mirror, Shy."

Watching as his fingers plucked at her erect nipple Dude repeated, enunciating each word clearly, "This is not a one night stand. I don't think I'll get ever get enough of you."

Finally, with regret, Dude knew he had to stop or else he *wouldn't* stop. He leaned down and gave her nipple one last long lick, loving how hard she was for him. He licked his way over to her cleavage and tasted her between her breasts one more time. He reluctantly tweaked her nipple one last time with his thumbnail and eased the cup of her bra back over so it covered her breast once more. He leaned in and took her mouth with his again. His left hand shifted so it was up at the back of her neck.

Dude eased back so the only places they were touching were his hand holding her wrists at the small of her back and his other hand on her neck. He waited patiently, with a wide smile on his face, for Cheyenne to open her eyes.

When she finally pried her eyelids up, he was right there, watching as she blushed a fiery red. "You're delicious, Shy. I'm sorry you were caught up in that situation yesterday, but I'm not sorry we met. If that was the only way you could come into my life, then I'm glad you were there. I'm a selfish asshole, but that's how I feel."

Dude waited, when Cheyenne didn't say anything, but continued to look up at him calmly, he continued. "I like you, Cheyenne. I think you're amazing. I'm a demanding son of a bitch in the bedroom, but if this interlude was any indication, we're going to get along just fine."

Cheyenne struggled for the first time, realizing just how much Faulkner had bossed her around. When he didn't let go of her she belatedly glared at him. Her glare obviously had no effect, because he just laughed and held on to her wrists tighter.

"I loved feeling you next to me. I loved feeling you flex against me. If at any time you honestly don't like what we're doing, just tell me. I swear I'll hear you, Shy. Okay?"

"Okay," Cheyenne agreed immediately. Faulkner hadn't done anything she didn't like so far. It might not be very women's lib of her, but she loved not having to think about anything but enjoying the feelings Faulkner was invoking in her body. She liked that he took charge of their lovemaking.

Dude finally let go of her hands and took a step back from her. He looked down at her in appreciation as she shifted, trying to regain her equilibrium. He ran his index finger down the stretched out V of her shirt, and dipped low between her breasts. Finally he shut his eyes and sighed.

"Okay, now that you think I'm a sex fiend, I'm leaving. I have some stuff to do related to yesterday. I have to debrief my commander and check in again with the police. I'll be back around three to pick you up. We'll be heading to Wolf and Ice's house. They're having an impromptu picnic today.

"Impromptu?"

Dude smiled. "Yeah, as soon as Fiona dropped off the food last night, she called her girl posse and they arranged this get together today so they could meet you." At the startled look in Cheyenne's eyes, Dude leaned in and rested his forehead against hers. "They'll love you, Shy. Trust me. Remember when you said this wasn't a one night stand? This is what I mean. I would never bring a one night stand over to my friend's house to meet my team and their women."

"You made me say that."

"I didn't make you say anything. You said it of your own volition."

"But..."

"No, no buts," Dude cut her off. "This. Is. Not. A. One. Night. Stand." He enunciated quietly and firmly.

Cheyenne smiled. "Okay, Faulkner, whatever you say."

Dude just shook his head at her. She was so damn sweet. His smile dimmed and he looked at Cheyenne seriously. "You all right with this. With us?"

"We just met. It's fast."

"It is. But it feels right. Yes?"

"Yeah."

"Okay then, I'll pick you up at three."

"Okay, Faulkner. I'll be ready."

Dude stepped completely away from Cheyenne. As he backed away from her, he didn't take his eyes off hers until he got to the front door. "Rest today, Shy. Take it easy, don't overdo it. I'll see you later." Then he turned and opened her door. Right before leaving, Dude turned back to Cheyenne. "Lock this behind me." He waited for her to nod, then he disappeared out the door.

Cheyenne padded over to her front door. She dutifully turned the dead bolt and put on the emergency chain, then sagged against the door.

Holy hell, was all she could think to herself as she closed her eyes and smiled.

CHAPTER 6

Cheyenne fidgeted nervously as she sat in the truck seat next to Faulkner. He'd come back to her apartment later that afternoon just as he said he would. Cheyenne had spent the day freaking out about what she was supposed to wear to this "get-together" with his friends, what he was really doing with her, why she was even letting him come back and get her…and any other little thing that came to her mind.

This wasn't her. First of all she wasn't the type of woman to move so quickly with a man. Hell, the last man she'd dated, they'd dated for a month before he'd gotten to second base. Secondly, she wasn't the kind of woman men fell for, but God, it felt nice. She'd daydreamed about Faulkner. Ever since she'd seen him in the grocery store, innocently shopping for food, she'd dreamed he'd take one look at her and declare his undying love. It was stupid, but as her family was constantly telling her, she had her head in the clouds.

Cheyenne had spent the day, between freak outs, cleaning her apartment from top to bottom. She could admit she was lazy, but knowing Faulkner had been in her craptastic apartment all night, looking at her sloppiness, was too much.

So she cleaned. Cheyenne washed all the dirty dishes that were sitting in the sink, vacuumed, picked up all the junk mail she usually just threw on the coffee table and sorted through it. She wrote out a couple of checks for bills that were due soon and she did a few loads of laundry.

Looking around, Cheyenne figured she probably should dust, but that was going just a bit too far. She never understood dusting. What was the point? It wasn't as if dusting a piece of furniture would make the dust in the air disappear. As soon as she finished wiping down the bookshelf, or table or whatever, the dust in the air would settle right back down...so it was really just a waste of time. Cheyenne also didn't figure Faulkner would even see or care about some dust.

Finally in the early afternoon, Cheyenne knew it was time to see about figuring out what she was going to wear. Cheyenne left on the thong undies with a secret smile. Over the course of the day she'd gotten used to them, and if she was honest with herself, she wanted to please Faulkner by keeping them on.

After trying on, and dismissing, what seemed to be half her wardrobe, Cheyenne settled on a pair of low rider jeans, which weren't too low, she wasn't eighteen years old anymore, a black knit sweater that had a scoop neck in front that showed a hint of cleavage, but not enough to be slutty. Cheyenne did consider for about four point two seconds wearing the push-up bra she'd had on before, but decided against it. Yes, Faulkner had picked it out for her to wear earlier, but it seemed too weird to wear it when she was going to meet his friends.

There was nothing she could do about the bruise Faulkner had left on the side of her neck, but if she was being honest with herself, it made her smile every time she looked at it. She'd only had a hickey once before in her life, back in junior high school. The boy who'd given it to her had sucked way too hard on her and the bruise that had resulted was horrific. She'd worn a turtle neck for at least a week until it had healed enough not to be gruesome looking. But Faulkner's mark, was subtle. He'd applied just the right of pressure to mark her, but not to make her look like she was thirteen and experimenting with sex.

Her shirt had long sleeves to cover her still-healing arms, which was one of the most important check boxes for Cheyenne for the night. She didn't want to stand out too much when she met Faulkner's friends, and if she wore a short sleeve shirt, she certainly would. She put on a pair of black flip flops with sparkly rhinestones along the material on the top, and finished off the outfit with a pair of dangly fake diamond earrings.

Cheyenne couldn't really do anything about her black eye though. She'd never really learned how to put on make-up and figured if she tried now she'd look like a teenage girl playing with her mom's make-up kit for the first time. She swiped some mascara over her lashes and put on some peppermint flavored lip balm. She stuck the tube in her pocket for reapplication later. She never wore lipstick, but was addicted to flavored lip balm.

Cheyenne figured she looked passable. She'd never win any beauty pageants, but she thought she looked pretty good. The shirt was one of her favorites and the jeans looked good on her. The thirty minutes before Faulkner arrived at her apartment Cheyenne spent pacing the small living room and biting her thumbnail. It was a nasty habit that she'd mostly broken, in part because her sister had teased her unmercifully about it, but she couldn't seem to make herself stop doing it when she was stressed out.

She'd also packed a small overnight bag. Faulkner had informed, not asked, her that she'd be spending the night at his place that night. She wasn't sure if he really meant it, but if he did, she wanted to be ready. Cheyenne knew it was a little weird, and way fast, but what the hell. She decided to live in the moment. Faulkner said, and had made her agree, that whatever was going on with them wasn't a one night stand, but she wasn't sure she truly believed him. She'd go with it though. If all this turned out to be *was* a one night stand, she wasn't going to complain about it. Cheyenne had obsessed about the military guy in the grocery store long enough that there was no way she could, or would, turn him down now. Hell, people had one night stands all the time. She decided to live a little and worry about it all later.

Cheyenne packed a T-shirt and pair of stretchy boy-shorts to sleep in, as well as a casual outfit to change into the next day, another pair of jeans and a V-neck T-shirt this time. Faulkner said he'd bring her home before her shift tomorrow, so she could change into her work clothes then. Cheyenne threw in the things she needed for the morning–shampoo, toothpaste, things like that, and she was done.

Finally when Cheyenne thought she was going to have a heart attack, Faulkner was there. She opened the door and watched as his eyes did a full body sweep. When his eyes finally met hers, it was obvious he liked what he saw.

"Maybe we can stay in instead."

Huh?

"What?"

Dude shook his head as if to clear it. "Fuck. No, we have to go, everyone is waiting for us."

"You don't want to go anymore?" Cheyenne's thumb came up to her mouth unconsciously. If Faulkner had taken one look at her and decided he didn't want to take her to meet his friends anymore, she was going to die.

Dude saw the look of uncertainty in Cheyenne's eyes and mentally kicked himself. He took a step forward until he was in her space. Satisfaction ran through him when she didn't step out of his way.

He put his right hand on her arm and brought his scarred left hand up to her face. In the past he never would've even thought about touching a woman with his mangled hand, but Cheyenne didn't seem to mind it in the least. In fact, if her words and actions in the car the night before were any indication, she enjoyed it.

"Shy, I want you to meet my friends more than anything. They're going to love you, you're going to love them. But the second I saw you, the only thing I could think about was how you'd look lying on your bed, looking up at me the same way you did when I opened the door. I'm trying to go slowly here, to prove to you, and me, that this isn't a one-time thing. I've never had to hold myself back before, so I'm learning as I go. The words popped out of my mouth before I could stop them."

Cheyenne was looking up at him with wide eyes. Faulkner could see her nipples peak through the knit shirt she was wearing. He shut his eyes for a moment then opened them again and willed her to understand.

"I say what I mean, Shy. If I didn't want you to meet my friends, you wouldn't. If I wanted to be your friend, and only your friend, you'd know. I'm a simple man. If I'm tired, I sleep, if I'm hungry, I eat. But know this…I want you. I want nothing more than to take you into your bedroom and watch as you take your clothes off for me. I want you to watch me, just as you are right now, as I strip for you. I want to take you hard and fast, then I want it slow and sweet. I want you in your shower and on every piece of furniture in my house. I want to take you from behind as your hands are tied together behind your back, and I want to watch as you take me down your throat until I explode. All these thoughts ran through my mind in the split second after you opened the door and I saw you. That's why I said what I did, not because I don't want you to meet my friends. Got it? Don't doubt me, Shy."

Cheyenne could only look up at Faulkner. Her brain was officially fried. She could feel how slick she'd gotten with his words and she knew if she looked down she'd be embarrassed at how tight her nipples had gotten with his words.

"I got it. You certainly put any fears I had to rest about whether or not you wanted me to meet your friends."

"Good. One more thing."

"Yeah?"

"You're not wearing the bra I pulled out earlier. Why?"

Cheyenne blushed, she wasn't sure Faulkner would've noticed. "You can tell?"

Dude loved the rosy hue that bloomed over Cheyenne's face and neck. He'd wanted to pull her into his arms and cart her off to her bedroom more than he wanted to breathe, but he controlled himself… barely. "Yeah, I can tell. You've got beautiful tits, Shy. They don't sag and sit high on your chest. But when you were wearing that bra earlier, they were pushed up even higher, and the cleavage it created made me want to bury my face between your flesh and spend hours worshiping you there. So yeah, I can tell."

Dude brought his right hand up to her chest and caressed the top of her breasts that were showing above the scoop neck of her shirt.

"I...uh...Do I look okay in this sweater without it?"

Dude didn't like the uncertainty in Cheyenne's words. Damn. He mentally kicked himself again. He was saying all the wrong things tonight. He knew Cheyenne wasn't confident in herself and how she looked. He'd have to work on that.

"I think I already covered how 'okay' you look in that shirt, Shy. And on second thought, my teammates might be married, but I don't want them ogling you all night, and ogle they would do if you were wearing that bra. I think I'll have to make sure you only wear your sexy lingerie when we're alone." Dude watched as Cheyenne gave him a small shy smile.

Dude pulled Cheyenne forward, put his right hand under her chin and lifted her head so he could get at her with the perfect angle, and kissed her long and deep. The kiss was over way too quickly, but Dude knew he had to get them out of there. Every word he'd spoken was the God's honest truth, and if he didn't get them gone, they wouldn't go.

Dude pulled back. "Peppermint. Every time I kiss you, you taste different."

"It's my lip balm," Cheyenne told him softly.

"I love it." Dude left his right hand under her chin, forcing her to look at him, and took his left hand and curled his remaining fingers down and ran the stubs of his fingers over the mark on the side of her neck, her collarbone, then down over the swells of her breasts. Without looking away from her eyes, Dude moved his hand lower and ran his hand over the nipple on her right breast. Feeling it peak even more than it was before, he finally looked down.

"Damn, Shy, You're so fucking responsive."

"I haven't been before," Cheyenne said the words without thought, then cringed. Shit.

Not freaking out over her mention of being with other men, Dude commented, "Oh man, we're going to have fun aren't we?" Taking a deep breath, Dude moved his hand so it gently grasped her arm. "Did you pack a bag? You're coming to my place tonight."

Cheyenne nodded shyly at him, and pointed to her bag sitting next to the door.

Dude took a deep breath, the sight of her pre-packed bag, knowing she'd done what he'd asked of her without balking, did something to him. Yes, he'd told her to, but ultimately she made the decision to do it. It was what he loved best about being with submissive women. They held all the power. He could order Cheyenne around all he wanted, but in the end, she was the one who allowed it or not. Dude leaned down and grabbed the small bag, suddenly wishing it had a lot more in it, and said, "Come on, we have to go. Now."

Cheyenne smiled at him. Faulkner liked to boss her around, it was obvious he liked to be in control in the bedroom, but she could still get to him. She liked that.

Now they were sitting in his truck on the way to Ice and Wolf's house.

"Tell me about your friends again?" Cheyenne asked as they headed down the road.

"Wolf is the team leader. Ice is his woman and she's a chemist. She saved his life when they were on a plane that was hijacked."

"I remember that! Holy shit! That was *your* SEAL team?" Fascinated by the blush that stole over Faulkner's face, Cheyenne waited for him to continue.

"Yeah, that was us. They went through a whole bunch of shit, but eventually Caroline moved out here to be with him. They recently got married. Then there's Abe and Alabama. Things were great with them until Abe said some shit after Alabama got arrested and he fought like hell to get her back. I don't think I've ever seen a couple more in love and connected at the hip than those two. As SEALs, we're born and bred to protect others, but Abe certainly fucked up by not protecting Alabama's emotions. Thank God she forgave him.

"Cookie and Fiona were the next to get together. Fiona was kidnapped by a sex slave ring and taken over the border. Cookie was the one to go in and find her and bring her out. Mozart and Summer are the most recent of us to get together. Mozart had been hunting the man who killed his little sister when he was a teenager and somehow the man found out about Summer and wanted to torture Mozart by taking his woman. Benny and I are the last ones of our team without women."

Silence filled the cab of the truck when Dude had finished speaking. He turned to look at Cheyenne. She was staring at him incredulously.

Dude chuckled. "Yeah, it sounds crazy, but I swear they're all normal people and they're gonna love you."

"Maybe we should go back." Cheyenne was freaking out. A chemist? Sex slave ring? Arrested? Kidnapping? She was in way over her head.

"Nope. You don't see it do you?"

"See what?"

"Think about how *we* met, Shy."

"Oh hell."

"Exactly. Now when people talk about us they'll talk about how I saved your life when you had a bomb strapped to your chest. That's just as dramatic as the way my friends met their women. Relax, Cheyenne." Dude turned to her as they stopped at a red light and put his hand on her knee. "I would never put you in a position where you'd feel unwelcome. You might be a little uncomfortable at first, it's hard to meet new people, but I know by the end of the night you'll have four new girlfriends and you'll have the respect of the guys on my team. Just relax."

Chewing on her nail, Cheyenne said, "Okay, I'll try."

Dude pulled her thumb out of her mouth and pulled it to his own lips and sucked on it for a moment before letting go. He laughed at the wide eyed look Cheyenne was giving him.

"Don't chew on your nail. Anytime I see you doing it, I'm going to do that same thing. I don't care where we are. Keep that in mind."

"Uh..."

Dude just laughed and patted her on her knee as he turned his attention back to the traffic.

Deciding to be amused, rather than pissed, Cheyenne finally laughed at him. "I'm not sure that's really a deterrent, Faulkner."

He just grinned at her. "Oh, I think you'll find it is if you don't want to find your nipples hard as rocks and squirming in your seat in front of others. I bet I could have you doing both just by sucking on that thumb." Dude laughed as he watched Cheyenne shift in her seat.

He didn't filter the words that came to his mind, just shot them out there. "Jesus, Shy, if my words can do that to you, you're going to love what my mouth can do."

"Stop, Faulkner. Seriously. I don't…I can't…"

Dude sobered quickly at seeing her unease. "I'm sorry, Shy. I'll tone it down. I keep forgetting how new this is to you and that you aren't used to it."

"I just…Fuck. Why can't I talk around you?"

"You could talk last night," Dude reminded her.

"Yeah, that's because the evil doctors drugged me up. I didn't know taking hard core prescription drugs loosened my tongue like that."

The car stopped in front of a small house in a cute neighborhood. There was a small porch and there were various cars and trucks parked in the driveway and along the street. Cheyenne didn't think she was ready for this after all.

"Hey, look at me for a second, Cheyenne."

She turned her head and wiped her hands down her thighs. Cheyenne was feeling more nervous about meeting Faulkner's friends than when she'd been waiting to answer her first emergency call at work.

"If you want to go, we'll go. We don't have to do this now."

That wasn't what Cheyenne thought Faulkner would say. "But you wanted me to meet your friends."

"And I still do, but I don't want you to make yourself sick over it. I rushed this, I know it, I'm sorry. But I like you. And I wanted you to meet the most important people in my life. We'll have plenty of time to do this later. It was a stupid idea."

Cheyenne watched as Faulkner reached for the keys still hanging in the ignition. She put her hand out and placed it on his forearm, stopping him from starting the truck again.

"I'm nervous, I won't deny that, but I want to meet them. I *do*. I don't get out much, Faulkner. It wouldn't matter if I met them today or three months from now, I'd still be nervous, partly because I'm meeting new people, but also because they're so important to *you*. I like you." Cheyenne dropped her eyes and fiddled with a string hanging off of the seat in front of her. "What if they don't like me? What if we have nothing in common? I…I want to get to know you better and knowing how important they are to you, I know we could never last if they didn't like me."

Dude knew this was an important moment and he struggled to find the right words so Cheyenne would understand. "Trust me when I tell you they'll like you, Shy. Alabama was a janitor when she met Abe. She spent her evenings cleaning offices in buildings. Caroline is a chemist, but she'd just lost her parents when she met Wolf. She was on her way across the country to a new job because she had no ties to California. No one reported Fiona missing when she was taken. She didn't have any close friends or family that worried about her. Summer was divorced and was flat broke when she met Mozart and was working as a maid for a dump of a motel. These are not women who'll judge you. I promise. And in case it wasn't already obvious, I like you too. And in the extremely low chance you don't get along with the other women, I'll still want to get to know you better." Dude paused for a moment then said, "It's your choice, Shy. I'd never force you to do anything you didn't want to do. *Anything*."

Cheyenne knew there was more to what he'd said than simply meeting his friends, but she put it aside for the moment.

"Okay, let's go. Shit. I had a damn bomb strapped to my chest, how hard can this be?"

Dude laughed and reached out for Cheyenne. He pulled her to him for a quick hard kiss then let her go. "Wait there, I'll come around."

Cheyenne rolled her eyes, but waited for Faulkner to come around the truck and open her door for her.

He tucked her arm in his and they ambled up the front walk to the house. Cheyenne took a deep breath and steeled herself for whatever was going to happen. She decided right there to do whatever it took to enjoy herself. These people were important to Faulkner, and she wanted them to like her more than was probably healthy. She warned herself not to be a dork, a spaz, or a flake. She'd just be herself. Hopefully that'd be enough.

CHAPTER 7

"Faulkner!"

Cheyenne took a step back as the front door burst open and a brunette dynamo slammed into Faulkner. He took a step back and laughed as his arms came around the woman and lifted her off her feet.

"Hey, Alabama. How are you?"

"It's been too long since we've seen you!" Alabama pulled back and kissed Faulkner on the cheek. Suddenly turning and pinning her eyes on Cheyenne, Alabama said, "Oh shit, I'm sorry, it's just been too long since I've seen him. That was so rude of me. Jeez."

Cheyenne relaxed a bit. She immediately liked this woman. "It's okay, really."

Dude leaned down, kissed Alabama on the cheek, then turned to Cheyenne. "Come on, Shy, let's go inside and I'll introduce you to everyone."

Cheyenne nodded and smiled at Alabama as they made their way inside. They went into the living room and Cheyenne froze. Shit. She knew there would be a lot of people there, but seeing them all in the same place at the same time was daunting. Looking around at the muscular men, Cheyenne sighed. She knew it. She leaned into Faulkner and stood on tiptoe. He leaned down toward her so she could reach his ear and she told him earnestly, "I knew it, you *do* hang out with a gang of hotties!"

Dude threw his head back and laughed. God, his Shy was fucking hilarious.

Cheyenne looked at Faulkner with a small smile on her face. She loved when he laughed. She remembered how serious he'd been at the store when he was working on the bomb. Being able to put some levity into his life seemed like the best gift anyone could have given her.

"Girl, you're officially one of us now. I've never seen Faulkner laugh like that before. Ever."

Remembering where they were and who they were standing in front of, Cheyenne blushed and looked at the woman who'd spoken.

"I'm Caroline. It's so good to meet you. When Fiona called and said that Faulkner needed her to get some food over to your apartment, it was all we could do not to all bust over there. We're so glad you came over today. I'm sure you're freaked, we all were when we had to meet each other. Just know you aren't alone."

Cheyenne smiled, liking the other woman immediately. It seemed there was a lot of "saying it like it was" around these people.

"It's good to meet you too, Caroline. Thanks for having me over today."

A big man came over to stand next to Caroline. He looked older than the other men, but he was absolutely gorgeous. He had large muscles that Cheyenne could see rippling under his shirt.

"Let me make the introductions before you have to use mind-melding skills to figure out who everyone is."

Before he could continue, Caroline poked him in the ribs and looked up. "And tell her everyone's real names. You can't just use nicknames."

Wolf smiled indulgently down at Caroline. "Yes, dear."

Caroline rolled her eyes.

Cheyenne smiled again and relaxed a fraction. They all seemed so…normal. Faulkner put his arm around her waist and she turned to him for a moment. He smiled down at her then leaned down. "Told you they'd like you," he whispered.

Cheyenne just shook her head. She'd only been there for like two point three minutes, the jury was still out in her mind, but it did look good…so far.

"I'm Wolf, or Matthew if you prefer, and this is Caroline, my wife. Sometimes you'll hear us call her Ice, that's her nickname."

Cheyenne watched as Matthew looked down at Caroline with so much love, and lust, it made her blush. She tried to ignore the big man standing next to her, and concentrated on the introductions.

"Over there is Mozart, or Sam, and his woman Summer. Next to them is Cookie, or Hunter, and Fiona. Then there's Abe, whose real name is Christopher, and Alabama. And that lonely looking guy over there is Benny, or Kason. He's the last one of us to find a woman."

"Hey!" Benny protested, "I've got women!"

Everyone laughed.

Cheyenne laughed with everyone else, but inside was quaking. How in the hell would she ever remember who everyone was? She was horrible at names. The first thing she did every time the phone rang at work and she asked the person on the line what their name was, was write it down on a sticky pad next to her keyboard. Shit, she already forgot most of the people's names already, and she was *just* told them all.

"Everyone, this is Cheyenne Cotton. Please don't freak her out tonight. Keep all the scary and weird stories to yourself. I don't want her to run screaming from the house."

Cheyenne waved self-consciously at the group. God, this was awkward.

"Okay then," Caroline said, taking charge of the group. "Matthew, you and Christopher go and grill up the steaks. Anyone want to help me with the rest of the grub?"

Cheyenne immediately spoke up. The last thing she wanted to do was stand around while everyone else got the food ready. "I will."

Caroline smiled at her. "Great. Thanks. I could use the help."

Cheyenne went to follow Caroline into the kitchen, but Faulkner wouldn't let go of her waist. She looked up at him questionably.

He just looked at her intently for a moment.

"What?" Cheyenne whispered, suddenly wondering if she should've offered to help after all.

"Thank you."

"For what?"

"For being here. For helping. For trying, for me."

"They seem very nice, Faulkner. I'm glad you brought me."

Cheyenne could tell there was more Faulkner wanted to say, but instead he leaned down and kissed her on her forehead. He let his lips linger for a beat longer than was probably proper in front of his friends, with a woman he'd met only the day before, but he soon brought his head back up.

"Go make me food, woman."

Cheyenne laughed and smacked him on the arm. "Whatever, *Dude*."

Dude squeezed Cheyenne's waist affectionately and let her go. She headed off to the kitchen smiling.

* * *

CHEYENNE LOOKED around the crowded room contentedly. The evening had been wonderful. She'd relaxed much sooner than she'd thought possible. The women were funny and cheerful and didn't care if they said something stupid or silly in front of her or the men.

And the men. Holy smokes. Cheyenne actually pinched herself at one point to make sure it was really real. That she was really sitting in a house with six incredibly hot men chit-chatting. It was surreal.

She hadn't remembered everyone's name, and she certainly didn't know which nickname went with which man, but ultimately it didn't matter. She just went with the flow, and no one seemed to notice.

"I'm stuffed. Jesus, Caroline, did you have to make so much damn food?" Fiona complained. She was sitting in an easy chair on Hunter's lap. Cheyenne could see Hunter's hand absently stroking her hip.

"I might have overdone it a bit, but it was all so good wasn't it?"

"I think if I ate one more bite I would explode like the guy in that Monty Python movie did," Alabama grumbled laughing.

"I loved that movie," Cheyenne spoke up. Parroting the line from the movie, she said in a fake British accent, "I couldn't eat another bite."

Everyone laughed, and Cheyenne smiled at them all.

"How's school going?" Dude asked Alabama, knowing she was working toward her degree.

"It's good. It's the helicopter parents that are really crazy. There was one mother that actually came to class to take notes for her kid. It was ridiculous. It's hard sometimes to be in classes with teenagers who have no idea what the world is really like though. If they had any idea how precious an education is they'd work harder at it and not take it for granted."

"That is so true," Summer said. "I worked my butt off for my degree and loved every minute of working in Human Resources."

"I remember when I worked at a University in Texas I'd have to deal with those kind of parents every day. I even had a parent call once for her *thirty one* year old son. He couldn't figure out how to order a transcript. It's crazy!" Fiona added, shaking her head.

Cheyenne would've loved to have asked questions, but kept her mouth shut and just let the conversation flow around her. Hopefully in the future she'd get to know these women better and would have a better understanding of what made them tick and she could contribute to the conversation and not feel weird about it.

"Ice, did you ever figure out that new compound you were working on?"

Caroline laughed at Benny's question. "Do you want the technical answer, or the short answer?"

Knowing she could go on all night about chemicals and what she did, Benny smiled and told her, "The short answer."

"Yes."

Everyone laughed when Caroline didn't elaborate.

"Good job then. Congratulations."

"Thanks, Benny. Hopefully in the future it'll mean a lot of people won't have to go through such horrible treatment for some of the worst diseases out there if it does what we think it should."

There was quiet for a moment in the room, then Summer asked, "So what do you do, Cheyenne?"

Cheyenne shifted uncomfortably on the couch. Faulkner was sitting next to her and of course he noticed. "Summer," he warned his friend, knowing Cheyenne was still working through her feelings about her job and hating that Summer had unintentionally put Cheyenne on the spot.

Cheyenne quickly broke in, and put her hand on Faulkner's thigh to ease him. "No, it's okay. It's not a big deal. I answer phones for a living."

"Oh, so you're in customer service or something?"

"Not exactly. I'm an emergency services operator."

No one said anything for a moment, then Fiona asked apologetically, "What does that mean exactly? I'm sorry if I should know, I just don't."

"Oh no, don't feel bad, I should've explained better. I answer the phone when people call in with an emergency. If there's a fire or someone's having a heart attack or something like that."

"You answer 911 calls?" Caroline asked in a weird voice.

Cheyenne looked at Caroline who was sitting across the room in another big fluffy arm chair. She too was sitting in her man's lap, and Cheyenne watched as Matthew's eyes immediately went to his wife. He didn't look happy at the tone of her voice. He looked worried.

Cheyenne tensed. Oh shit. Was Caroline offended? Did she have a bad experience with 911 in the past?

"It's okay, Shy," Dude murmured next to her, sensing her discomfort. He put his arm around her shoulder and pulled her into his side.

"Yeah, I answer 911 calls," Cheyenne told Caroline carefully.

Cheyenne watched as Caroline unfolded herself from Matthew's lap and stood up. Cheyenne risked a glance at the other people in the room. The women's faces were soft, the men's weren't exactly hard, but they weren't relaxed either. Something was happening and Cheyenne had no idea what it was.

Caroline came across the small room to stand in front of Cheyenne. She went to her knees in front of her and put her hands on Cheyenne's knees.

Cheyenne didn't know what to do. She risked a quick glance at Faulkner, but his eyes were locked on Caroline. Cheyenne turned back to the woman kneeling at her feet nervously, not knowing what to expect.

"Thank you. It's obvious you have no idea how important what you do is."

Cheyenne didn't know what to say, so she said nothing.

"I've always wished I could've met the 911 operator that helped me."

Oh shit, Cheyenne didn't know if she was ready to hear this story. She tensed and Faulkner tightened his hold on her and grabbed her left hand with his scarred one. Cheyenne gripped his hand as if it was the only thing standing between her and the firing squad.

Cheyenne heard Faulkner tell Caroline, "I already told her this, Ice, but I'm not sure she really understood. Tell her your story. Maybe between all of us we can convince her how she changes people lives."

"Faulkner..."

"Shhhh, Shy. Listen."

Cheyenne turned back to Caroline, then flicked her eyes up to Matthew. He was looking at Caroline with affection from his seat across the room. He'd sat up and was resting his forearms on his knees. He looked relaxed, but Cheyenne knew he could be across the room in a heartbeat if he needed to be.

"When I lived in Virginia, I was followed home from work one day. Matthew and the rest of the team were away on a mission. I'd just started my job and didn't really know anyone yet. A man broke into my apartment and I had to hide in my shower. I was really scared and called 911 almost without thought. Every kid is taught from a young age to call when they need help, and that's just what I did. I didn't have a long conversation with the lady on the other end of the line, but she was awesome. She didn't panic and had the police on their way within seconds of hearing what my problem was.

"I have no idea who she was or what her name was, but she was my lifeline. I'll never forget her. So on behalf of that lady, and for anyone who has ever called 911, thank you. Thank you for being there. Thank you for caring enough to try to help us. Just thank you."

Cheyenne watched as Caroline's eyes filled with tears and she lay her head down on Cheyenne's knee. Cheyenne lifted a hand and put it on the back of Caroline's head. "I...you're welcome." Cheyenne didn't know what else to say, she was uncomfortable and touched at the same time.

Caroline finally lifted her head and gave Cheyenne a watery smile. "You, my friend, will have good karma for the rest of your life because of what you do."

Cheyenne was embarrassed and hoped the conversation would soon switch so it wasn't focused on her anymore. She still wasn't ready to jump up and down with glee about her job, but Caroline and Faulkner had started her on the path to thinking that maybe she really did make a difference in the world. At least for some people.

"So...how about them LA Kings huh?" Benny said, trying to lighten the mood of the room, and succeeding.

Everyone laughed. Caroline stood up and wiped the tears from her eyes. She walked back to Matthew and he pulled her into his lap and kissed her deeply.

Cheyenne watched as Matthew put his hand on the back of her head and shifted her until she was lying sideways over his lap. Her legs were dangling over one of the arms of the chair and her upper body was supported by Matthew's arm. Wow.

Cheyenne shifted in her chair and shivered when Faulkner whispered in her ear. "Told you *you* were amazing."

She just smiled.

After a bit more time had passed, Hunter turned on the television.

The group was feeling mellow after the large meal, emotional revelations, and spending time with good friends.

After watching a mindless sitcom, the evening news came on. Cheyenne stiffened in surprise when she heard the newscaster say her name. They all watched in fascination as the anchor spoke while a clip from the day before was shown.

"In other news, Cheyenne Cotton was released from the hospital last night after suffering only superficial wounds in the bomb threat at Kroger yesterday afternoon. Five men were killed after they strapped a bomb to Ms. Cotton and tried to negotiate their way out of the store. A bomb ordinance technician from the Navy was called in to defuse the explosive. Here they are leaving the store after the bomb was neutralized."

Cheyenne watched in shock as a video of her and Faulkner coming out of the store was shown. She looked pale and she was holding his hand as he led the way across the broken glass from the front of the store toward the ambulance. She watched as they were surrounded by reporters and Faulkner put his arm around her waist to steady her. The clip ended and the camera panned back to the anchorman sitting behind a desk as he finished his story.

"The five men who were killed, seemed to be working independently. As of now, the police can't confirm or deny if they were part of a gang. The authorities are withholding their names because of the ongoing investigation. Ms. Cotton has declined any interviews and the Navy isn't releasing the name of the bomb technician that defused the bomb and saved many lives yesterday. We will continue to investigate the story and will report back with any new information. Next up is Tina with the weather for the week..."

No one said anything for a moment until Mozart breathed, "Jesus, Cheyenne, we had no idea that was *you*. Are you all right? Should you even be out and about?"

Cheyenne couldn't help but giggle. Jesus, these guys were all the same. Protective to the bone. "I'm okay. Faulkner got there in time."

Dude spoke up. "The bastards wrapped her up in so much duct tape it took me ten minutes to get to the damn bomb. The tape ripped off parts of the skin on her arms and you can see the black eye she has from the assholes as well."

Cheyenne glared up at Faulkner. "I can talk, you know."

"I know, but what would come out of your mouth would probably be something like, 'I'm fine, thanks for asking,'" Dude said in a high pitched voice, mocking her.

Cheyenne could hear the other women giggling. She tried to keep her mouth from twitching, but couldn't. It was funny, dammit.

"Well, I *am* all right, Faulkner, and it was nice of them to ask."

That made everyone around the room laugh out right.

"You guys are hilarious," Fiona told them. "We're so glad Faulkner was there yesterday. Seriously, he's the best at the bomb thing."

"The bomb thing?" Dude mock growled.

"Yeah, the whole bomb thing."

Cheyenne watched as the group bantered back and forth. She'd never had friends like this. Hell, her own family didn't tease each other at all. When Karen picked on her, it had been vicious, and not teasing at all. This was nice. She really liked Faulkner's friends.

Cheyenne didn't realize she was fading until she heard Faulkner say, "It's time for us to go. Shy can't keep her eyes open."

At that Cheyenne forced her eyes to open all the way and watched as Faulkner stood up and shook his friends' hands.

"Yeah, it's time for all of us to get going too. PT is gonna suck in the morning," Mozart groaned.

"You want to use the restroom before you go, Cheyenne?" Caroline asked politely.

"Please."

Cheyenne followed Caroline down a hallway to the small guest bathroom tucked away. Caroline turned to her before she entered.

"I was serious about what I said in there, Cheyenne."

Cheyenne merely nodded. She didn't really want to get into it again. She liked Caroline, but there was only so many "thank you's" she could handle in one night.

"I'm so glad you and Faulkner are together. He deserves someone like you in his life. I'd probably be dead if it wasn't for him and the rest of guys in there."

"I'm not sure we're actually together, Caroline," Cheyenne told her honestly. "I mean, we just met yesterday, under pretty extreme circumstances."

"I know you think that, but you don't really understand these guys. The only time we met any woman of Faulkner's was when we met at *Aces Bar and Grill* or a restaurant. He was never serious about any of them. Ever. He had a wall up. He's a black and white kind of guy. He's either one hundred percent in, or he's not. And believe me, girlfriend, he's one hundred percent into you. As much as I like you, I have to say this. Faulkner is my friend. Don't hurt him. If you aren't into him, leave now. I'll call you a taxi. He'll be pissed, but he'll get over it. If you don't want a long term relationship with him, don't lead him on."

"But..."

"Let me finish. Please."

At Cheyenne's nod, Caroline continued. "These guys fall fast. They're really big teddy bears under all their gruffness. Faulkner wants you. I can see it. We can all see it, but I'm not sure *you* see it. If you just want to sleep with a SEAL, please find someone other than Faulkner."

"Are you kidding?" Cheyenne didn't want to piss Caroline off, but she really couldn't believe the words that were coming out of her mouth.

"No."

"I mean seriously, you think I *wanted* to come over here tonight? Really? When the gorgeous man I've been semi-stalking in the grocery store saves my life and seems to be, by some freaking miracle, interested in me, wants me to come and meet his teammates and friends, do you think I *wanted* to go with him? I knew you guys would judge me. I *knew* it. I don't make friends easily. I didn't know how you guys would take to me. I wanted you to like me and I wanted to like you back, but I thought it was too soon. But I did it. Because I want to be with Faulkner. I'm into him. I'm so into him that if he wanted to tie me to his bed and have his wicked way with me tonight, and every fucking night, I'd do it, without a second thought. I trust him that much."

Not noticing the attention her raised voice was garnering from the group who was now standing at the end of the hall behind her, gaping at them, Cheyenne continued.

"I appreciate you looking out for your friend, I really do, but I don't appreciate you insinuating that I just want to bag a SEAL. Jesus, Caroline, I've lived in Riverton most of my life. You think any SEAL has ever *wanted* me before? It's not like I can pick one off the street like I'm ordering take out. I have no idea what Faulkner sees in me, and I'm still hoping he's serious and not just playing with me, but I can guaran-fucking-tee you that as long as he's interested in me, I'm his."

Cheyenne was breathing hard when she finished. She noticed Caroline was smiling at her. What the hell was she smiling about? She figured it out when an arm went around her waist, and one went around her chest and she was pulled back into a hard body. Faulkner.

"I'm interested in you, Shy."

Not looking behind her and not moving, Cheyenne looked at Caroline, who was no longer trying to hide her amusement and whispered, "Please tell me he didn't hear all of that."

"Sorry, Cheyenne, I think they *all* heard it."

Cheyenne closed her eyes as she heard the rustling of clothing and the quiet footsteps of more people joining them in the narrow hallway.

"Jesus Christ." She couldn't say anything else. All Faulkner's friends had heard her lose her shit on Caroline, the apparent matriarch of the group? Fuck.

"Okay, we're leaving now. Thanks for the meal, Ice. Wolf. I'll see the rest of you in the morning." Dude was all business. He shifted until Cheyenne was against his side and he put an arm around her waist, making sure she stayed there, and led her through the group of people now smiling at them.

"Bye, Cheyenne, it was nice meeting you."

"We'll call you soon!"

Cheyenne heard Caroline's voice say through her embarrassment. "We're having a girl's day out shopping soon, I'll call ya!"

The rest of the men added their goodbyes as well and Faulkner herded her out the front door to his truck. He opened the passenger door and got her seated and comfortable. Then Cheyenne watched as he rounded the front of the vehicle and got in next to her. Without a word, he started the car, did a U-turn in the middle of the road and drove down the street, presumably to his place.

CHAPTER 8

Cheyenne didn't say anything on the trip to Faulkner's house. She was embarrassed beyond belief that Faulkner, and all his friends, had overheard her. She wasn't upset about *what* she'd said to Caroline though, every bit of that was dead-on true. She appreciated the fact Caroline was trying to protect her friend, but jeez, Caroline should've known by just looking at Cheyenne, she wasn't like that.

But knowing all of his friends, and Faulkner himself, had heard what she'd said was embarrassing as hell. Even now he hadn't said much to her. He'd been quiet all the way to his house. Cheyenne had half expected Faulkner to take her back to her own apartment and drop her off without a word, but he hadn't.

They pulled up to a small, well-kept brick house with only a small overhang over the front door. There was a long driveway which led to a one-car garage along the side and back of the house. The yard was well maintained, with no overgrown bushes lining the sides of the house, and the grass seemed to be freshly mowed.

Faulkner turned into the driveway and pulled to the end and shut off the truck. He didn't open the garage, simply got out and came around to Cheyenne's side of the vehicle. He helped her out, then opened the back door and grabbed her overnight bag from the back seat. Still without speaking, he put his hand on her waist and steered her to the back door. He put the key in the lock and led her inside.

They entered into a laundry room that had a basic washer and dryer in it. Without giving her a chance to look around, Faulkner all but pushed her through the small, but functional kitchen, and into the living room. Faulkner had a huge television mounted on the wall, not surprising, and a couch and love seat set in an L arrangement around a small coffee table.

The walls were a slight gray color that offset the dark browns of the couches. It was definitely a masculine looking room that fit Faulkner to a tee.

Still not stopping, Dude encouraged Cheyenne to keep walking. He steered her into a bedroom in the back of the house. Once he entered, Dude dropped her bag and turned Cheyenne in his arms until he was holding her upper arms and she was looking up at him.

"I'm sorry…"

Dude cut Cheyenne off before she could get anything else out. "Don't you fucking be sorry. You have no idea how much your words meant to me. I don't even know where to start. First, I'm pissed that Caroline had the nerve to try to warn you off."

"She loves you, she was looking out for you."

"I don't give a shit. It was rude. But, having said that, if she hadn't confronted you, you wouldn't have said what you did and I wouldn't have been there to hear it. I think your words are gonna stay with me forever. I knew you weren't thrilled to go over there tonight, but after we talked, I thought you were okay with it. But you weren't were you? You did it because you thought I wanted you to. You did it for me."

Looking at her, as if waiting for her agreement, Cheyenne gave a small nod.

"Yeah, you did it because you wanted to please me."

Again, when Faulkner didn't say anything else, Cheyenne nodded again, giving him the reassurance he needed. For once he didn't demand she say the words.

"You're into me. You said it. I heard it. All my friends heard it. I'm not letting you take it back."

"I don't want to take it back. I'm not an idiot, Faulkner. As much as you push me and boss me around, if I didn't want to be with you, I wouldn't be. If I didn't want to be standing in your bedroom right now, I wouldn't be here. I'm not a complete moron."

Cheyenne was fascinated at the affects her words were having on Faulkner. She could see his pupils dilate. His fingers squeezed her biceps a bit harder and she saw him clench his teeth before he continued.

"You have no idea what I see in you."

Cheyenne just shook her head at him, agreeing. She had *no* idea what he saw in her.

"Jesus, Shy, it's everything. You're level headed, you're loyal, you're independent, you're humble and shy, but then you're all piss and vinegar when you have to be. You're a walking contradiction and it turns me on so much I can't stand it. But hearing you say you trust me? That you'd let me tie you to my bed? You have no idea what you've shared with me. I don't think you even understand your own needs, or mine, but I'm going to be there to help you figure it out. You said you were mine as long as I'm interested. Well, Shy, I'm interested and you're fucking mine."

Embarrassed, Cheyenne whispered, "Are you talking about BDSM?"

"Go sit on the bed, Shy," Dude ordered, not answering her question and dropping his hands from her arms and taking a step back.

"What?"

"Go sit on the bed. Do it."

Not understanding, Cheyenne took a step backward. Faulkner matched her steps. Every time she took a step back, he took a step forward. She took another, then another. Cheyenne kept her eyes on Faulkner's as she slowly backed into the room until the back of her legs hit the mattress. She sat, still looking up at Faulkner. Without thinking she brought her thumbnail up to her mouth and chewed on it. She was nervous as all hell. What was going on here?

"Not BDSM, Shy. Never that. I'm not down with labels. Who we are together is who we are. Nothing more, nothing less. But think about what just happened here. I asked you to do something and you did it. Why?"

Cheyenne thought about what he said. "I don't know."

"You know."

"Because you asked me to and I wanted to please you."

"Exactly. That's what this is about. I want to please you and you want to please me. We do that by me taking charge. It's what I need, and you submit to it so beautifully." Dude dropped to his haunches in front of her. He took the thumb Cheyenne had been chewing on and brought it to his mouth. "What'd I tell you I'd do if I caught you doing that again?" He waited for her to answer.

"That you'd do the same thing."

"Damn straight." Without looking away from Cheyenne's eyes, he took her thumb into his mouth. He nibbled on the pad, then wrapped his tongue around it. He sucked, he caressed, he bit.

When he finally let go, Cheyenne felt boneless. "Seriously, is that supposed to be a deterrent, Faulkner? 'Cos I have to tell you, it's really not."

Dude chuckled at her words and wrapped his bad hand around hers. "Mine, Shy. You said it. I heard it. My friends heard it. Thank God I wasn't on a mission and was available to be there yesterday. Oh, someone else probably would've been able to disarm that bomb, but it wasn't someone else. It was me. We have this combustible connection that I've never felt before. We'll figure this out as we go. But I'm warning you, I don't think I'm going to lose interest in you anytime soon."

"Okay." It was all Cheyenne could think to say. It wasn't like she was going to argue with him.

"Okay. Here's how tonight will work. You get changed into whatever you've brought to sleep in. I know I told you I'd sleep on the couch tonight, but I don't think I can. I'll sleep in here with you. In my bed. Nothing will happen. I promised you that. You can trust me. I want you relaxed, and I want you to get used to me, to get more comfortable with me before we explore that part of our relationship. We'll get up in the morning, I'll make you breakfast then drive you home so you can get ready for your shift. We'll figure out the rest as we go."

Cheyenne noticed immediately that he wasn't asking. He was telling. She thought about it for a moment. Realizing she was okay with everything he'd said, she simply nodded as if Faulkner had actually asked for her approval.

He smiled and leaned over, bringing his mouth inches from hers. "You please me, Shy. Fuck, you please me. Now, go get changed."

Dude stood up and helped Cheyenne to her feet. He watched as she padded over to her bag, picked it up, and headed toward the little bathroom connected to the bedroom. The door closed behind her and Dude sagged onto the bed. Jesus, he was screwed. He'd barely known Cheyenne for a day and he was so far gone it wasn't funny. He'd always thought insta-love was a fallacy, something romance authors made up to sell books.

But he was knee deep in it. It was scary as hell, especially for someone used to being in control of every aspect of his life, but Dude welcomed it all the same. Sleeping next to Cheyenne, and not being inside her, would be one of the most difficult things he'd ever done, but he couldn't deny the thought of holding her in his arms all night sounded like heaven. He'd never, not once, spent the entire night with a woman. Oh, he'd catnapped and dozed after having sex, but he'd always woken up and left before the night had ended. Looking back, he knew it made him somewhat of an asshole, but it was the way he was and the way it had to be. But now, just the thought of holding Cheyenne in his arms all night felt right. Instead of the panicked feeling he usually got at the thought of having to deal with a woman "the morning after," Dude couldn't wait to see what Shy looked like first thing in the morning.

He left the bedroom, not wanting Cheyenne to feel awkward when she came out of the bathroom. Dude killed some time in the kitchen making sure he had what he needed for breakfast in the morning. Figuring he'd given Cheyenne enough time, he made his way back to his bedroom.

Seeing Cheyenne in his bed made him feel funny. He swallowed once, hard. Without a word he went into the bathroom. Knowing Cheyenne didn't have a direct line of sight into the room, he didn't bother closing the door. The room smelled like her. It smelled of toothpaste and some sort of sweet lotion. Dude took a closer look at the bottle on his counter, Gingerbread. Fuck. He'd never be able to think of Christmas again without thinking about her and her damn gingerbread lotion. Dude supposed it should have irritated him, her stuff strewn all over his counter, but instead it thrilled him.

He brushed his own teeth then stripped off his clothes down to his boxers. He usually slept nude, but knew that wasn't happening tonight. He probably should've pulled on a shirt, but Dude couldn't resist the thought of having Cheyenne close to his skin. He was pushing his control, but he couldn't stop himself.

He walked back into his bedroom to see Cheyenne lying on his bed and the covers up to her chin. She was obviously nervous and unsure.

Not wanting to prolong her anxiety, Dude strode across the room, turned off the light then turned back to the bed and pulled back the covers next to her. He climbed in and immediately turned over and pulled Cheyenne into him.

He arranged her so that she was up against his side, with her head resting on his shoulder. Dude put one hand around her and placed his other hand on her waist.

Dude relaxed when he felt Cheyenne's hand flatten against his chest. He relaxed further when he felt her muscles loosen and finally melt into him.

"Comfortable?"

"Surprisingly, yeah."

"Why surprisingly?"

"I've never spent the night with a guy before."

At Faulkner's sharp inhalation of breath, Cheyenne hurriedly explained. "No, Jesus, Faulkner, I'm not a virgin. Jeez. Relax. I just meant I've never slept in the same bed all night with a guy."

"I don't want to hear you talk about another man when you're in my arms and in my bed again, Shy, but just saying, they were idiots.

I'm getting more satisfaction out of having you here in my arms and knowing you'll be here in the morning, just like this, than I ever have fucking a woman before."

Cheyenne propped herself up quickly and tried to glare at Faulkner in the darkness. "If I can't talk about other men, you can't talk about fucking any other women either," she snapped, irritated.

Chuckling, Dude raised his hand and soothed it over her back, feeling the soft cotton of her sleep shirt. "You're right, I'm sorry, Shy. I won't do it again."

"I mean, I know you've slept with a shit-ton of women, but I don't want to hear about them."

"It hasn't been a shit-ton."

"Whatever."

Dude chuckled. "All I meant, was that I've never felt as satisfied as I do right now, simply holding you."

"Good save." Cheyenne smiled. How could she stay mad at Faulkner when he said something like that?

"Go to sleep, Shy. I've got you."

"I know." After a moment Cheyenne whispered, "You didn't kiss me goodnight."

"I can't. If my mouth touches you, I'm lost. I'll taste whatever flavored lip shit you used, and it'll go straight to my head. It's bad enough I'm lying here smelling the gingerbread lotion you used tonight. I'm imaging how your skin will feel under me and how good you'll smell when I finally go down on you. If I even get a hint of gingerbread mixed with your slick arousal, I'll lose it. So it might be a simple good night kiss to you, but it's a slippery slope that I'm holding on at the top of with my fingernails. So just shush and close your eyes. You'll get your kisses. I promise, Shy. Just not tonight, and not right now."

Giggling softly, Cheyenne simply said, "Okay."

"Sleep, Shy. For the love of God, close your eyes and sleep."

Dude lay in the dark waiting for Cheyenne to fall asleep. It didn't take long. The excitement of the last couple of days and the nervousness she'd felt tonight had obviously taken a toll on her.

Dude hadn't lied to her. Holding her in his arms was one of the most satisfying things he'd ever felt. Knowing she was just the kind of woman he needed and that Cheyenne wanted to please him was heady stuff. It wasn't just that he had a woman in his bed who Dude knew would be open to just about anything he wanted to do to her. It was that he had *Cheyenne* in his bed who would be open to anything he wanted to do to her. *That* was what made his control hard to hold on to. He never expected when he'd been called to a bomb threat that he'd meet his match, but Dude knew he'd spend the rest of his life thanking Christ he had.

When Cheyenne mumbled in her sleep, Dude clutched her closer to him and smiled as she quieted. He knew they'd moved really fast and he'd have to back off a bit so as not to scare her, but he wasn't going to let a day go by without making sure she knew he was thinking about her.

CHAPTER 9

Cheyenne smiled at the text message from Faulkner.

Thinking about you.

He never used shorthand when he texted her. He always spelled out every word and never used cute little emoticons in his messages. Not a day went by without him texting her at least once.

She thought back to their first morning together. She'd woken up and opened her eyes to see Faulkner staring down at her. She'd been on her back and he was propped up over her on an elbow. He'd taken her hair and smoothed it behind her ear.

"Morning, Shy."

"Good morning."

They'd just stared at each other, but when he'd lowered his head as if he was going to kiss her, Cheyenne sprang into action. There was no way she was letting him get near her with morning breath. She could feel how dry her mouth was. Yuck. When she'd explained, he'd merely laughed and let her up to head into the bathroom.

He'd cooked her breakfast as he'd promised. They'd spent a lazy morning together, getting to know each other better. Cheyenne found out Faulkner loved to read and had no issues reading romance books. He'd winked and told her it was "research."

When he'd dropped her off at her apartment, he'd kissed her long and hard. Cheyenne had decided on green apple lip balm that morning and she could tell how much he liked it by his reluctance to let her go. She smiled at the memory.

Then in typical Faulkner style, he'd simply held out his hand and demanded her cell phone. She'd unlocked it, given it to him, and watched as he programed in his numbers. He dialed his own phone and let it ring once, so he'd have her number as well.

He'd given it back, brought her lips to his once again with a hand at the back of her neck, given her one more deep kiss then let her go.

"I'll talk to you later," and he was gone.

Faulkner had been true to his word. She'd gotten several texts from him during her shift. He demanded she let him know when she got home. He didn't like the thought of her going home at eleven at night.

Cheyenne just rolled her eyes at his demanding text. She'd been working second shift for so long, the late night hours didn't faze her anymore. She told Faulkner as much, but he merely told her that while she might not care that criminals tended to be more active and would troll for victims when the sun went down, but *he* did.

While she might pretend it annoyed her, deep down Cheyenne knew she was lying to herself. She loved that Faulkner was worried about her. It felt good.

Over the last two weeks their schedules were out of sync, so they hadn't been able to spend the night together again. It had worried Cheyenne until Faulkner reassured her.

"I don't care if it's a year before we're able to get together, Shy, you're mine. We have all the time in the world. Stop worrying about it."

Thinking about his words could still make her tingle and feel better, no matter what was going on in her life.

Cheyenne needed his text today more than usual. She'd talked to her mom that morning and heard all about how Karen had been involved in a big case that had won in court. Her mom had bragged about Karen for twenty minutes straight before even bothering to ask Cheyenne about how her day went.

When Cheyenne had told her how she'd helped a man deliver a baby after he'd called the emergency line, her mom had actually said, "Cheyenne, when are you going to get a real job?"

Cheyenne had merely sighed and listened absently until her mom had finally said she had to go. She was meeting Karen for lunch. It always hurt knowing her mom and Karen got together regularly, and never bothered to invite Cheyenne.

So looking at the three words on her cell phone from Faulkner made her feel good.

Miss u 2. :)

Cheyenne put her phone aside when the phone on the console in front of her rang.

"911, what is your emergency?"

The voice on the other end of the phone sounded completely calm, which was highly unusual. "Yes, I'm looking for a Cheyenne who works as a 911 operator."

Cheyenne frowned. What the hell? She couldn't tell if the person on the other end of the line was a man or a woman, it was muffled and soft.

"Do you have an emergency? This line is for emergencies only."

Cheyenne heard a dial tone in her ear. She shivered. That was really weird. She didn't really keep her job a secret, but she'd never had someone ask for her specifically when they'd called. She tried to see if she could see what number the call had come from, but the person hadn't stayed on the line long enough and they were using a cell phone. The data simply wasn't available.

Her cell phone dinged with a text message.

I'm picking you up after work tonight.

Forgetting the weird call, Cheyenne snatched up her phone excitedly.

Don't u have pt in the am?

I don't care.

But u'll be tired

I said I don't care. This has gone on too long. I need to see you.

Cheyenne smiled happily. She needed to see Faulkner too. They'd gotten to know each other pretty well over the last two weeks. He'd call when she was working and they'd chat until she had to answer the emergency line. Faulkner never cared that she'd have to hang up with him immediately when that happened. He'd merely told her to text when she was done and could talk again.

It'd worked out really well. Cheyenne had found out all sorts of things about Faulkner and about his friends. She loved how loyal he was and how loyal it seemed his friends were back with him. She learned that he liked to cook, but hated to do laundry. He admitted he'd read his first romance novel as a dare by Caroline, and that he'd actually enjoyed it.

Cheyenne had shared about her mom and sister and how she'd always felt second fiddle to them, then had to listen to a lecture from Faulkner about how wrong they were and how he and all his friends thought she was an amazing human being.

Talking with Faulkner always made her smile.

Cheyenne would always remember the conversation they'd had one night after she'd gotten home from her shift. She'd uncharacteristically texted him to see if he was awake. She typically didn't like to wake him up late at night because she knew he had to get up so early, but she'd had a horrible phone call and desperately wanted to talk to him.

He'd texted back immediately and told her to call him.

"What's wrong, Shy?"

"I just...I had a hard night."

"What happened?"

"Just a call."

"It's never *just* a call, not if it upsets you. Tell me."

"I probably should let you go, you have to get up in like, three hours."

"Cheyenne..."

Not able to resist him when he used *that* tone of voice, and knowing she honestly really did want to talk to Faulkner about it, she told him.

"A woman called, hysterical. She went into her twelve year old son's room to check on him and found him hanging in his closet. He'd wrapped a belt around his neck and killed himself."

"Oh, Shy..."

Faulkner's sympathy almost broke her, but she continued quickly. "She told me he'd been quiet lately. She knew he was struggling at school. Seventh grade is tough on all kids I think. I know I hated it, and myself, most of the time. She said she was a single mom and hadn't had the time to check in with him lately, not the way she should've. He was gay and had told his mom that some of the other kids had been picking on him. She blamed herself, Faulkner. She said that it was all her fault. I talked to her until the paramedics got there and tried to revive her son. By what she'd told me I knew he was probably already gone, but I kept her busy until help arrived. She didn't want to hang up with me. She wanted to tell me all about how great her son had been. She said he was an artist and wanted to grow up to work in animation. It wasn't until the police told her she had to hang up and talk with them, that she finally let me go." Cheyenne had sniffed once. "It was tough."

"She'll never forget you were there for her though."

"I'll never understand people as long as I live, Faulkner," Cheyenne complained sadly. "Here was this kid, full of potential, a good kid, and other people made him feel like he was less of a person just because of his sexual orientation. Less worthy. It's just not right. It's not fair."

"Listen to yourself, Shy. *Hear* what you just said."

Cheyenne stilled.

Dude continued, hoping she was really hearing him. "Your sister has done that to you her entire life. And now even your mom does it, knowingly or not. They put you down and make you feel like what you do for a living isn't as important as what Karen does."

"Holy shit, Faulkner, you're right."

"Of course I am."

Cheyenne chuckled, in spite of the heavy conversation they'd been having. "Thank you, I needed that."

"I know, baby. I'm sorry you had to go through that, but don't ever think I'd rather sleep than listen to you and help you work through a tough call. I'll be pissed if you do it after tonight. Got me?"

"Got you." She'd hung up and slept soundly that night. Usually after a tough call she tossed and turned most of the night reliving it over and over.

Cheyenne startled when her cell phone buzzed in her hand. She'd been so lost in her thoughts of the past, she hadn't texted Faulkner back.

We'll figure out your car later. I'll be there at 11:10. Is that enough time?

Cheyenne quickly typed out a response.

Y, can't wait

Cheyenne couldn't wait until the end of her shift. While she'd enjoyed getting to know Faulkner over the last couple of weeks via texts and phone calls, she was more than ready to see him in person again. She didn't know if he was just giving her time to get used to him or if he really had been busy, but at this point she didn't really care.

She really hoped the chemistry they'd had before hadn't waned. She didn't think it had, but what did she know about men like Faulkner?

Cheyenne sat back and drummed her fingers on the tabletop. Only two hours to go until her shift was over.

CHAPTER 10

Cheyenne waved to David, her relief operator, and headed out the door. Faulkner had texted her ten minutes ago to say he was outside and ready whenever she was.

She'd closed up her station and explained what had gone on that night to David. Luckily, so far it had been pretty quiet, all things considered. She put her purse over her shoulder and pushed out into the dark parking lot.

Faulkner was parked under one of the lights in the lot and was standing outside leaning against the passenger door of his truck. Cheyenne walked toward him with a wide happy smile on her face.

Suddenly feeling shy, and not really knowing why, they'd talked on the phone almost every day, but it was different being face to face with Faulkner again. It was much easier to bare your soul to someone when you weren't looking them in the eyes.

"Hey."

"Hey. The night go okay?"

Cheyenne loved that Faulkner always asked about how her shift went. "It was good, kinda boring actually."

"Boring is good."

Cheyenne nodded in agreement.

"Come here."

Cheyenne shivered at the tone of Faulkner's voice, and went to him.

Dude wrapped his arms around Cheyenne and breathed her in. Tonight she smelled like vanilla. He smiled at her penchant to wear sweet food-smelling lotion.

"I wonder what flavor your lips are tonight." Without giving her a chance to answer, Dude leaned down and stole the kiss he'd been desperate for since the last time he'd kissed Cheyenne. He ran his tongue over her lips, tasting cherry, before plunging into her mouth. She opened willingly to him and Dude loved feeling her hands grab onto the back of his shirt as he continued his sensual assault.

Before he could go too far, he pulled back. "Cherry. Yum." Dude watched as Cheyenne's lips quirked up into a smile and she turned her head to the side adorably. "Let's go, it wouldn't do to get caught necking in the parking lot of a public service building."

Cheyenne looked up at Faulkner again and simply nodded. He reached over and opened the door for her and once again waited until she'd settled in the seat before shutting the door and walked around to the driver's side.

"Where are we going?"

"Your place."

Cheyenne wasn't expecting that. "Mine?"

"Yeah. Yours. You don't have any of your stuff, so we'll go there, you can pack, then we'll go back to my house."

"Why don't we just stay at my apartment tonight? If we're already there…" Her words tapered off at the look Faulkner was giving her, then she asked, "What?"

"Because the first time I make love to you will be in my bed, in my house. I've been dreaming about seeing you splayed out on my sheets waiting for me. I've jacked off to the thought of you in my space the entire time we've been apart. I'm done waiting. You're mine, and you'll be mine tonight in every way possible."

Cheyenne just stared at him. Wow. That was intense. She loved it. She smiled. "Okay, Faulkner, whatever you say."

He smiled back. "Get used to saying those words, Shy. I fucking love hearing them come from your lips."

Cheyenne wasn't surprised when Faulkner leaned over to her and captured her lips again for one more intense kiss before he pulled back and started the truck. He pulled out of the lot and headed toward her apartment, leaving three cars sitting in the parking lot, one of which wasn't empty.

* * *

FAULKNER HAD WALKED her up to her apartment and stood in the living room while she packed. It didn't take her long, but Cheyenne made sure to pack a couple of outfits. She was off for the next few days and didn't know what Faulkner had planned. She figured it'd be better to be safe than sorry.

She walked out of her bedroom and said, "Sorry it took so long, I'm ready."

Faulkner didn't come toward her, just stood next to her window looking out. He turned when she spoke and simply looked at her. Finally he said, "Be sure about this, Shy. Be sure it's what you want and not something you're doing because I want it."

"I've never been more sure of anything in my entire life, Faulkner."

"Then come on, let's go."

The ride to Faulkner's house was quiet, but electric.

Finally when they were a block from his house, Dude broke the comfortable, but intense, silence. "When we get home, go into the house. I'll give you five minutes before I follow you. Make sure you do what you need to in the bathroom. When I get there, I want to see you in my bed, naked, covers pulled back, not covering you. Lie on your back with your arms over your head. Keep your head turned toward the door so you'll see me the second I walk in. Don't speak. Do you have any questions or concerns before we get there?"

Cheyenne felt her nipples peak at his words. My God, Faulkner was completely one hundred percent serious. This was really going to happen, and it was going to happen his way. Cheyenne tried not to hyperventilate. "Will I get a safe word?"

"Fuck no," his response was immediate. "You don't need a safe word. You don't like something, just tell me. I told you I'm not into games. But I promise you, Shy, you'll like everything we do. I'm not into pain, yours or mine. If you need to stop me, I'm not doing it right." He paused a beat. "Anything else?"

Cheyenne shook her head.

"Words."

"No, Faulkner. I'm good. I'm so good, I'm about ready to go off without you even touching me."

Cheyenne saw Faulkner smile quickly, a small satisfied smile, before he banked it and ordered. "Don't. You don't come until I say you can."

"Jesus," Cheyenne muttered under her breath.

The cab of the truck was silent until Faulkner stopped the truck in his driveway.

"Go on, Shy. Five minutes. Remember what I said."

Dude watched as Cheyenne headed into his house, her bag over her shoulder. He'd given her his key and she didn't hesitate for one single second to take it and make her way quickly through the door. Dude put his head on the steering wheel.

The past two weeks had been hell. He'd made up reasons why they couldn't get together in person. He'd done everything he could to try to slow things down, to really get to know Cheyenne and to have her get to know him. Two weeks really wasn't a long time in most normal relationships, but this one didn't seem "normal" to him. He felt deep in his gut that Cheyenne was meant to be his. They were both in the right place at the right time to meet. Dude hadn't believed much in fate before, even after seeing his friends and teammates find the women of their dreams in the most unusual of ways. The two weeks apart had given Dude a good understanding of what made Cheyenne the person she was today, and made him fall for her all the more.

When he'd heard about how her mom and sister treated her, he'd wanted to march over to their houses and give them a piece of his mind. The only thing that stopped him, was that he knew Cheyenne would've been embarrassed if he'd followed through.

Dude had opened up to Cheyenne about his likes and dislikes, and he honestly felt as if they'd becoming closer as a result. His libido hadn't liked it, but Dude *did* like the feeling of this relationship being different from the others he'd had. In the past he hadn't wanted to get to know a woman before taking her to bed. All he'd cared about was getting her off, then getting himself off. With Cheyenne, he didn't want to take her to his bed until he knew more about her and what made her tick.

She was sensitive and shy. Passionate and repressed. Emotional and closed off. She was a mass of contradictions and she absolutely fascinated him.

Dude looked at his watch. Two minutes to go. He opened his door, shut it behind him and pressed "lock" on his key fob. He leaned against the door with his feet crossed at the ankles. Tonight would be telling. He hoped like hell Cheyenne would enjoy it.

If she didn't, then they had no future. It was that simple. Dude was the way he was. He'd been honest with her. He wasn't into games, or pain, or the other crap that came with what people thought the BDSM lifestyle was about. He'd read some of Caroline's erotic romances. Some were all right, but it wasn't for him. He didn't need the kneeling, serving, and floggers, but he *did* need the control. Knowing a woman trusted him to let him lead their lovemaking was heady and was what excited him.

From what Dude had seen, Cheyenne needed him to be in control too. She took too much on herself. Between her job, her family, and her independent lifestyle, the few times he'd taken control, she'd melted in his arms.

He looked at his watch again. One minute. He pushed off the truck and headed toward his house. He'd never been so excited, or hard, in his life. He was ready to take what was his.

CHAPTER 11

Cheyenne lay on Faulkner's bed and waited. She could feel her heart beating quickly. She knew her breathing had increased. She gripped the slats of Faulkner's bed frame so hard, she figured her knuckles were probably white. He hadn't told her to grab hold of them, but when Cheyenne had seen the bed again, she couldn't stop thinking about being tied to it.

She worried about her body, would Faulkner like it? Most of the time in the past when she'd had sex, the room had been dark and the men hadn't bothered to try to check her out all that much before they'd gone for the gusto.

Cheyenne had turned on the light in the bedroom and decided to leave it on. She'd used the restroom and slicked herself up with her gingerbread lotion, remembering his words from two weeks ago. She swiped her lips with her favorite flavor, cake batter, and tore her clothes off. Not bothering to look at herself in the mirror, she'd rushed into Faulkner's bedroom to make sure she was in place when her five minutes was up.

Faulkner was right. Cheyenne wanted to please him. He'd asked her to do something and she wanted nothing more than to follow his directions to the letter. She knew that in pleasing Faulkner, she too would be satisfied.

Not knowing how much time had passed, Cheyenne kept her eyes on the bedroom door. The last thing she wanted was to be caught not looking when Faulkner walked in. Besides, she wanted to see his first unguarded reaction when he saw her.

She clenched the slats of the bed above her head. How much time had gone by anyway? The anticipation was killing her.

Then Faulkner was there. His eyes bore into hers as he entered the room. Cheyenne kept her mouth shut, he'd ordered her not to talk. She knew she was breathing too fast, but she was nervous as hell. Cheyenne bit her lip, trying to keep any words back. Faulkner was intense and beautiful, and all hers.

She watched as he stalked, yes stalked, across the room until he stood over her.

"Nice touch with the slats, Shy. Don't let go until I tell you to."

Cheyenne smiled up at him and nodded, thankful he'd noticed her efforts.

"Wonder what flavor you're wearing tonight?"

The question was rhetorical since Cheyenne knew he didn't want her to speak. She waited for him to take her lips, and pouted when he didn't.

Instead he leaned down and put his nose in her belly button. He didn't touch her anywhere else, but Cheyenne sucked in a breath all the same.

He breathed in and stood up again. "Fuck me. Gingerbread. You wear that for me?"

Cheyenne nodded, not taking her eyes off Faulkner.

"God. Fucking perfect."

Cheyenne watched as Faulkner unbuttoned his shirt slowly. One button at a time. Cheyenne couldn't help but squirm on the bed.

"Still, Shy."

Cheyenne immediately stilled. Crap. It was harder than it seemed. She'd always scoffed at the women in her books that would whimper and moan when their men told them to stay still. She was just realizing how much harder it was than it seemed to be still. Those authors obviously knew what they were talking about.

Cheyenne sucked in a breath when Faulkner sat next to her on the bed, still wearing his pants, but devoid of his shirt. Her eyes eagerly roamed over him. He was built. She knew he worked out every morning with his team, but Jesus, she'd never seen an eight pack before.

"You like the feel of my hand don't you, Shy?"

She nodded immediately, lying. She didn't like it, she loved it.

"Let's test that shall we?"

Cheyenne sucked in a breath as Faulkner went right for the kill. He didn't mess around by touching her stomach or shoulders or face. He went right for her breasts, and her nipples that were drawn up into hard peaks. He rubbed his scarred fingers over her breasts until Cheyenne thought her heart was going to beat out of her chest.

She opened her mouth to plead with Faulkner to do something, and at the last second remembered. She shut her mouth.

"Perfect. Thank you for trying so hard. I love watching your restraint."

Dude brought his index finger to her lips and rubbed against them, smearing her lip balm over his finger. He smirked at her and brought his finger down and rubbed the balm he'd pilfered from her lips over her nipple, then leaned down. Cheyenne tensed, she'd wanted his lips on her again since the first night. She'd dreamed about it.

Faulkner nipped and sucked and completely drove her crazy. He brought his hand up and continued to torture the first nipple as he moved his mouth to the other. Finally he covered both her breasts with his hands. Cheyenne could feel her nipples stabbing into his palms. He rubbed and caressed her as he spoke.

"Is that cake?"

Cheyenne just smirked at him.

"Oh, I'm going to like this game. I wonder how many different flavors you have? We could really have fun with them. But I think I need a different taste in my mouth now."

Dude tried to still his racing heart. When he'd walked into the room and saw Cheyenne had followed his directions to the letter, and then some, he'd almost lost it right there. She was fucking beautiful. She was a feast to his senses.

Taking his time, he slid to the end of the bed, never losing eye contact with Cheyenne. He positioned himself between her legs and slowly slid them further apart. "Bend." He tapped her knees and smiled as she immediately bent her legs until he could lie down comfortably between them.

"I hope you're comfortable, Shy. I plan on spending a lot of time down here." Dude leaned down and inhaled. "Oh yeah. Gingerbread and you. There's nothing better."

He got to work driving his woman crazy. Bringing her to the edge and pulling back over and over again, Dude knew Cheyenne was going to orgasm like she never had before. He looked up at her, not slowing his fingers as they continued to caress and tease her.

"Look at me."

Waiting until Cheyenne's eyes drifted down and met his, Dude continued. "You've been so good, Shy. So fucking responsive. You've done everything I've asked. You followed my directions to the letter. I've never been more pleased before. *Never*. Let go. As many times as you can. For me. No words, but don't hold back your reactions either. I want to hear you."

As soon as the words left his mouth, he leaned down and sucked on her bud, hard. Cheyenne exploded. It was as if she was waiting for his explicit permission. She cried out in delight and arched her back, riding his fingers. Dude rode out Cheyenne's first orgasm and built her up to another. She bucked and moaned, but didn't speak. She was amazing.

Dude regretfully pulled his finger out of her snug sheath and leaned down for one more long lick. He felt Cheyenne shudder under him. He couldn't wait anymore. He had to have her. She was still twitching and Dude hoped she'd have at least one more orgasm left in her.

"Legs down."

As soon as Cheyenne dropped her legs bonelessly to the bed, Dude shifted until he straddled her hips. He unbuckled his jeans and eased the zipper down carefully. He watched as Cheyenne licked her lips. He looked down and the head of his dick was peeking out the top waistband of his boxers. He wasn't surprised. He'd been harder than he ever had been before in his life for the last half hour.

Meeting Cheyenne's eyes again he said, "Eyes on mine, Shy." He chuckled as she reluctantly brought her eyes up to his. "You'll get to see it all you want in a moment. But for now, keep your eyes on mine."

Dude eased off the bed and quickly shucked his pants and boxers off. He opened the drawer to the nightstand next to the bed, and grabbed a condom, all without breaking eye contact with her. He opened the wrapper without looking, and covered himself with the latex. He resumed his position on the bed over Cheyenne, but this time got on his hands and knees. He lowered himself just enough so that the only part of him that was touching her was his manhood.

"Feel that?" he whispered, "It's all I can do not to plunge into you with one stroke. To fill you up so completely you don't know where you end and I begin."

Dude watched as Cheyenne's eyes dilated until he could barely see the brown color of her irises anymore. "You want that?"

He watched as Cheyenne nodded frantically. He teased her a bit more. "You sure?" When she nodded again and licked her lips, Dude asked, "Maybe you're tired?"

As she shook her head desperately he said seriously, "What you do to me, Shy. I can't wait anymore. I thought I could tease you some more, but I can't. I need to be in you." With that, Dude lowered himself and fit himself to her core and pushed. He drove inside her until it was just as he'd told her *she'd* feel. He didn't know where he ended and she began.

She was hot and wet and felt better than anything Dude had ever experienced before.

"Please," Cheyenne croaked out. "I want to touch you."

Not caring or reprimanding her for speaking, Dude groaned, "Yes, God yes."

At his words, Cheyenne loosened her grip on his bed slats and drove one hand into Faulkner's hair, and the other gripped the muscles on his back.

"Oh God, Faulkner. I can't keep quiet anymore. Please don't make me."

"Whatever you need, Shy. Whatever you need."

"I need you. I need you to move. I need your hands on me. You feel so good. God, you have no idea. I've never...I mean no one has ever... Fuck. I can't think. You're so hard, everywhere. I have no idea why you want me, but I'm here, I'm yours. Jesus, Faulkner. Yes." It as if being allowed to speak again broke a dam inside her. Her words spewed out without thought, but with extreme emotion.

Dude's thrusts got harder the longer she spoke. It was obvious she wasn't thinking, just speaking what she felt. Dude never felt more like a man.

"Yes, Shy, tell me what you need."

"You. I need you. Harder. Please. It feels so good. Yessssss."

Dude kept his eyes open and watched Cheyenne's face. Her eyes were scrunched up tight and her head was thrown back. She was moaning and squirming in his arms as she bucked up against him even as he thrust into her. Cheyenne held on to him tightly and never let go, even when he thrust especially hard, she was right there with him.

Her eyes finally popped open and looked him in the eyes. "Faulkner, Fuck. Yes. I'm going to..."

Dude reached down and rubbed his thumb over her clit, hard. All it took was two hard strokes and she exploded again. Dude gritted his teeth against the feeling of her inner muscles clenching rhythmically against him and her body twitching and bucking up against him. He held his orgasm back by the skin of his teeth and when Cheyenne stopped quivering against him, he put both hands on either side of her head and growled, "Look at me, Shy. Watch yourself take me over the edge. Watch what you do to me. You. Only you."

Cheyenne felt boneless. She opened her eyes at Faulkner's demand and watched his face as he thrust into her. She saw the second his release came over him. He thrust against her once, twice, then after the third hard thrust, stayed buried to the hilt. His eyes never fully closed, but did shut into slits. Cheyenne watched as the vein in Faulkner's neck throbbed and he gritted his teeth and grunted. It was sexy as hell and she'd done this to him. Cheyenne brought a hand up to Faulkner's neck and gripped him tightly.

Finally the muscles in his body lost their rigid tone and he blew out a breath. "Jesus, fuck."

"I think that's my line," Cheyenne teased dreamily.

Dude collapsed onto Cheyenne's chest with a grunt. He heard her squeak in surprise and then felt her arms go around his back and pull him into her. He was never letting her go. Never.

CHAPTER 12

What r u up 2 2day?

We have a meeting with our commander then we have more PT.

U always have pt.

Yeah, and you love the results.

Ok that's true. :)

Cheyenne smiled as she texted Faulkner. He was so funny. She loved talking to him this way. Somehow it seemed more intimate and made her feel closer to him. The last month had been a dream. They didn't get to spend the night with each other every night because of their schedules, but when they did, they made the most of it.

What are you doing today?

Lunch w/ mom and sis.

I wish you would wait until I could go with you.

I'll b ok.

Wait until I can go with you.

Sorry, that only wrks in bed.

Damn. Thought I'd give it a try.

Laughing out loud and ignoring the funny looks she was getting from the people around her in the coffee shop, Cheyenne continued to text.

It's only lnch. I'll text when done.

Call me instead. I want to hear your voice to know you are okay.

I'll b fine.

Call. Me.

Oh ok mr. bossy.

Later

Ltr

Cheyenne turned her phone off and put it in her bag. She sat back waiting for her family to arrive. She'd purposely picked the little coffee shop, knowing her sister would hate it. She wasn't proud of herself, but she rationalized at least this way their lunch would be kept short.

She stood up as Karen and her mom walked into the shop. Karen looked impeccable as always. She was wearing a brown skirt that was a proper knee length. She'd paired it with a white button up shirt and a brown suit jacket. She was wearing brown heels and had her hair up in a complicated looking twist.

Cheyenne's mom was just as put together. Dressed in a pair of gray slacks with a pale pink angora short sleeve sweater, a pair of low heels, and her hair up in a bun, the gray in her hair matched the pants she was wearing perfectly.

Cheyenne felt frumpy next to her family, but shook off the feeling. It was her day off. She wasn't going to worry about dressing up. The jeans, fitted T-shirt, and flip-flops she was wearing were fine. She'd put her hair up in a ponytail to keep it out of her face.

"Hey Mom, Karen."

"Cheyenne, how many times do I have to tell you to take more care with your appearance?"

Cheyenne sighed. No "hello," no "how are you doing," her mom just jumped right in with the criticisms. Nothing ever changed. "Mom, it's my day off..."

Her mom cut her off. "That's no excuse. You never know who you'll run into while you are out and about and it pays to look your best. Look at your sister. She always looks impeccable. How do you expect to attract a man if you don't put any effort in?"

"Actually..."

Cheyenne was cut off again, this time by her sister.

"I can't believe the news isn't sick of your little incident yet. I mean really. I think a month and a half is enough already."

Cheyenne looked at Karen in bewilderment, forgetting she was about to tell her mom that she *had* attracted a man, a hell of a man. "What are you talking about?"

"You didn't know? There was another special on you last night. Well, at least on what happened. I don't know why you won't just talk to the press already. It would probably get them off your back."

"*Another* special?" Cheyenne didn't know what her sister was talking about.

"Yeah. *Another* special. The news station has done a couple of shows highlighting the various people that were involved in what happened. They highlighted all of the guys the police killed, and touched on you. They weren't allowed to talk about the military guy that was involved though. I felt kinda bad for the men that were killed. They all had families and such sad backgrounds."

Cheyenne couldn't believe what she was hearing. "Are you shitting me?"

Her mom immediately rebuked, "Cheyenne, watch your language."

Cheyenne turned to her. "Are *you* shitting me?"

"Cheyenne Nicole Cotton, language," her mom scolded her again.

Cheyenne turned back to Karen. "I can't believe you said that. You're supposed to be my *sister*. My flesh and blood. Do you know what they *did* to me?"

"You look okay to me. Jeez, Cheyenne, you've always been such a drama queen."

Cheyenne shook her head and leaned toward her sister. "I invited you guys today because I wanted to try to get to know you better. I've always felt bad we didn't get along. But I can't believe you'd say something like that to a stranger, nonetheless your own flesh and blood. Those men you are busy feeling sorry for, *hit* me. They threatened me with guns. They scared the crap out of me. They strapped a fucking *bomb* to my chest and wouldn't have thought twice about blowing me to bits. And you have the gall to sit there and tell me about how you feel bad for *their* families? That they had such hard lives that what they did was okay? The next thing you're going to say is that you think the cops were in the wrong for shooting them."

"I do," Karen immediately returned, a hateful look in her eye.

Cheyenne nodded once. She calmly put her napkin on the table in front of her.

"Look, maybe we..." her mother began.

Cheyenne interrupted her mother. "I'm done. You're cold, Karen. I have no idea how you got that way, but you are. I don't know what I did to you to make you hate me so much, except for being born, and I don't think I can take any blame for *that*. All I've ever wanted is a big sister I could hang out with and look up to, but you never gave me a chance. I don't want to see or talk to you again. If you have more sympathy for a bunch of thugs than your own sister, you're no family of mine."

It wasn't Karen that spoke up, but her mom. "Cheyenne, you can't do that. You don't mean it."

"What do *you* think, Mom? Do you feel sorry for those guys too?"

"Well, it wasn't as if the police gave them a chance to give up did they?"

"I'm done with you too," Cheyenne whispered immediately, tears gathering in her eyes. "All my life I've tried to be good enough. I've done everything I could think of to make you feel a fraction of pride toward me as you do for Karen. But it's obvious you don't and can't. So that's fine. Don't call me again. Just leave me alone."

Turning on her heel, Cheyenne left the coffee shop. She beeped her car doors open and climbed in on autopilot. She wasn't surprised when she didn't see either her mom or Karen storm out of the coffee shop in pursuit of her. They were probably inside gossiping about her and reassuring each other that they'd said nothing wrong.

Cheyenne drove to the beach. She'd always loved the sound of the waves against the sand. It usually relaxed her, but not today.

She'd had no idea the media was airing "specials" about what had happened to her. She felt sick inside about the spin they were putting on the men who'd taken her and the two other women hostage. They'd terrorized her. Cheyenne honestly thought she was going to die and it had scared the shit out of her.

To think there were people who felt *sorry* for those men was sickening. That her own flesh and blood felt sorry for the men, was disheartening and made her feel more alone than she'd ever felt before.

Cheyenne sat facing the ocean on the stone wall that lined the parking lot. She'd been so happy. She'd just spent the last four nights in Faulkner's bed and every single night, that week and when they'd been together in the past month, he'd made her body hum. He'd shown her how good "submitting" to him could be. She trusted him with her life.

Just when things were starting to look up for her, her own damn family had to ruin it. She should've known Karen would be jealous of the media attention she was getting, even though Cheyenne had always refused to speak to the press.

Cheyenne should've waited for Faulkner to have lunch with her family. She'd honestly thought she could work on repairing their relationship though. It was her *mom*. Moms were supposed to love all their kids equally, but *her* mom never had.

Pulling her feet up onto the wall in front of her, Cheyenne linked her arms around her shins and put her cheek to her knees. How long she sat like that she had no idea, but eventually her butt went numb and she had to move. Stiffly she released her legs and let them fall to the ground. She wasn't ready to leave yet, but knew she'd better get in touch with Faulkner. He'd wanted her to call him when she was done with lunch, but Cheyenne hadn't wanted to talk to him, or anyone else.

She walked to her car and grabbed her phone out of her purse. She walked back toward the beach and set off down the sidewalk until she got to a part of the beach that wasn't as crowded. She kicked off her flip-flops and wandered into the sand. Finding a place that seemed as good as any, she sank down.

She turned on the screen to her phone and winced. Three texts and a phone message. All from Falkner. The fact that even with what she'd said, neither her sister nor her mom had tried to get a hold of her, cut deep.

She looked at the texts first.

Just checking in. How was lunch?

I haven't heard from you. Call me.

CALL ME.

Somehow, even though it was written, she could sense Faulkner's irritation with her. Cheyenne really didn't want to listen to the voice mail from him. He was probably pissed at her. She couldn't deal with someone else being pissed at her.

Scrolling through her contacts, Cheyenne hesitated over Caroline's number, then clicked "send message."

One night after dinner, Faulkner had taken her cell and programmed in all his teammates numbers. He'd even added in all of the women as well. She'd protested, telling Faulkner that she didn't even know them, but he'd ignored her and done it anyway.

Then, bizarrely, he'd pointed to one name he'd put in her phone and told her seriously, "If you are *ever* in trouble and can't get a hold of me, call Tex."

"Tex? Who is that? Is that another nickname for one of your teammates?"

"Tex is a former SEAL who lives in Virginia. He can find anyone. It's a long story, but suffice it to say, he's had a hand in helping us protect all of my friends' women at one time or another. I'd trust him with my life. He's got connections we can't hope to have. Just promise. Okay?"

She had.

But this wasn't a situation where she wanted to talk to a stranger, and she wasn't in trouble. She just needed a friend. She quickly typed out a text.

Hey Caroline, it's Cheyenne. U around?

The response came almost immediately.

Hey C. what's up?

Suddenly Cheyenne didn't know what to say. She didn't know why she'd texted Caroline in the first place.

Cheyenne? U ok?

Yeah. Got a sec to talk? Can I call?

Of course.

Cheyenne took a deep breath. She had to start somewhere. She liked Caroline and the other women and she needed a friend. She hit Caroline's number and waited for her to pick up.

"Hey, Cheyenne."

"Hey."

"Seriously, are you okay?"

"Yeah. I need some advice."

"Let me guess, about a certain SEAL we both know?"

"Yeah." Cheyenne let out her breath. "I think he's mad at me," she whispered, not knowing why she was whispering.

"What'd you do?"

"I was supposed to call him, and didn't. He sent three texts and the last one was all capital letters."

Caroline laughed. When Cheyenne didn't join in, she sobered. "Hey, you're serious aren't you? Look, I piss Matthew off all the time, but he gets over it."

"I don't want Faulkner to yell at me," Cheyenne's breath hitched. "I've had a bad day. But the longer I wait to call him, I know the madder he'll get."

"Where are you? You aren't home are you?"

"No. I'm sitting on a beach watching the sun go down because I'm a wuss. I can't go home because he'll find me and yell at me. He's…he's bossy. And I…fuck. This is embarrassing."

"I get it, Cheyenne. We all know Faulkner is a lot more intense about his bossiness than the other guys are. But, Shy, he won't yell at you if he knows you've had a bad day."

"Everything has been so good between us. I like the way he is…the way we are…I don't want to ruin it."

"Listen to me. These SEALS are intense. They're big, bad, and brash, but as I told you when you were at my house, inside they're big teddy bears. All you have to do is be honest with him. Tell Faulkner that you're sorry you didn't call but you needed some time. Then apologize for it and let him make your day better."

When Cheyenne didn't say anything Caroline continued. "Oh, Shy. What happened?"

"I…don't…I can't…"

"Okay, you don't have to tell me. But please, let Faulkner know where you are. He's probably worried sick about you. It's how they are. Do you want me to call him?"

"No, I'll do it. I just needed…a pep talk I guess."

"I'm so glad you called me. Seriously. Call me anytime you need to. I can't promise to be able to explain half the things these guys do, but we can at least put our heads together and try to figure it out. And just so you know, when the guys get sent out on a mission, we all get together and get completely drunk the first night. It's our own brand of a support group."

Cheyenne giggled, as she supposed Caroline meant for her to.

"And we're still going shopping one of these days. I promise to get the girls together sooner rather than later. Okay? You'll come with us?"

"Yeah, I think I'd like that. Thanks."

"Okay. Cheyenne? Call Faulkner and let him know where you are. Trust him to take care of you. It sounds like you already trust him to do so at home…"

Cheyenne knew what Caroline was getting at, and blushed.

"Trust him in the light of day too. He needs that from you."

"Okay. Thanks, Caroline."

"Anytime. I'll talk to you soon."

"Okay, Bye."

"Bye."

Cheyenne clicked the end button and stared down at her phone. The message waiting icon mocked her. She couldn't do it. She couldn't listen to Faulkner's message right now.

Arguing with herself for a good five minutes, Cheyenne finally bit her lip and opened the text app. She needed to at least text him.

Hey. Sry I didn't call

The response was almost immediate.

Where are you?

I'm ok.

Shy, where are u? I'm worried about u.

Cheyenne looked at the latest message from Faulkner. He'd used shorthand. He *never* used text language before. Was he really that stressed out?

I'm at S Mission beach. I'm ok. There r a gazillon people around. Was about to head back.

Stay put. I'm on my way.

Plse don't be mad.

I'm not mad.

I shld hve waited 4 u 2 go 2 lunch with me.

It's okay. I'm not mad.

Promise? I can't deal with mad right now.

Shy, I'm not mad. I'm worried as hell. I just want to get to you.

Ok. Drive safe. I'm ok.

I'll be there as soon as I can.

Cheyenne took a deep breath. Just connecting with Faulkner via text was enough to make her feel a bit better. She looked down at her phone and contemplated listening to the message he'd left. Nope, she couldn't do it yet. She'd wait until she felt better. Stronger. She curled her arms around her drawn up legs again, her favorite position lately, and waited for Faulkner to come to her.

CHAPTER 13

Dude's hands shook as he drove toward South Mission Beach. Cheyenne was right, it wasn't secluded, there probably *were* a gazillion people around, but he still worried about her. He'd been upset when she hadn't called after her lunch should've been over, but that only lasted about five minutes. It wasn't like Cheyenne to let him worry or to not contact him. Concern had taken over the anger quickly.

Obviously the lunch with her family hadn't gone well. Dammit. Dude had a lot more experience in dealing with disappointed parents than Cheyenne did. He'd wanted to be there to be a buffer, to make sure they didn't say anything cutting. His instincts had obviously been right on. Something had happened.

Now Dude only wanted to get to Cheyenne and comfort her. Whatever it took. He'd been so relieved when Caroline had called him and told him she'd just talked to Shy and that she was okay. She'd told him briefly about how Shy had wanted to call him, but had waited, then the longer she waited the more she thought he'd get angrier and angrier. The thought saddened Dude. It was obvious they needed to have a talk.

Cheyenne's need to please ran deep, but Dude didn't want her afraid to talk to him for any reason. And he certainly didn't want her to be scared of him, of how he'd react to anything she'd tell him.

After the longest thirty minutes of his life, Dude pulled into the parking lot at South Mission Beach. It wasn't as crowded as he'd seen it in the past, which he was thankful for. It meant he could easily find a place to park. He pulled out his phone and sent a quick text to Cheyenne.

I'm in the parking lot. Where are you?

Her answer came immediately.

left dwn the beach.

Dude pocketed his phone and started walking. He found Cheyenne not too far down from the parking lot. She was sitting forlornly in the sand, watching the ocean, not looking for his arrival.

Not bothering to take off his combat boots, Dude trekked out to where his woman sat sadly in the sand. He stopped behind her and eased himself to the sand. He bracketed her body with his, knees on either side of her, and wrapped his arms around her. He rested his head on her shoulder and waited.

Cheyenne felt cocooned in Faulkner's arms. He sat still and quiet behind her as he took her into his arms. She felt warm for the first time since she'd left the coffee shop that afternoon. She sighed. She needed this, she needed Faulkner.

"Hey," she said softly.

"Hey."

"I should've called. I'm sorry."

"It's okay, Shy."

"No, it's really not. I'm sorry if I worried you. I just...I thought you'd be mad. You asked me to call you and I didn't. Then it all just snowballed in my head. The longer I went without calling you, the madder I thought you'd get."

Her voice fell enough that Dude had to lean forward and turn his head to hear her.

"I don't like it when you're mad at me. Even though you haven't really even *been* mad at me yet, I can't stand the *thought* of you being mad at me. I think that's what it was. I want to make you happy."

"Shy..."

Cheyenne interrupted him. "And now, I've disappointed you. I don't know which is worse really. Fuck, I'm not like this. I'm not a wuss. The only thing I can say in my defense is that I've had a bad day."

Dude had enough of this. He scooted himself around until he was sitting at Cheyenne's side. "Stop, Shy. I'm not mad and you didn't disappoint me. You worried me. There's a huge difference."

"I didn't mean to."

"I know. But we need to talk about this. We should've talked before now and that's on me. You aren't used to this. I love how we are. I love how you do what I tell you in our bed. I can't tell you what it means to me. I crave that. I need that. But outside the bedroom? No. I love the contradiction that is you. You're not afraid to call out my friends when they say dumb shit. You're brave enough to take on an entire police department when you have a bomb strapped to your chest. You're compassionate enough to allow assholes to strap said bomb to your chest, just so two other people don't have to go through that."

He kissed the top of her head and continued. "I'm going to get mad, Shy. I'm probably going to yell at some point. It doesn't mean I don't love you. Don't be afraid of me. Don't be scared to tell me to fuck off. If I overwhelm you, tell me. Remember when I told you we don't need safe words? It still holds, Shy. If you need me to back off, just say the word and I will."

"You love me?"

"Yes. I know it's soon, and crazy and I'm not even sure how it happened. I've waited for you my whole life. Not someone *like* you, but *you*. I know you don't have the experience to realize this, but what we have in the bedroom is unique. Unique and special. It's something I've never had with anyone else, ever. And it's not just about the sex. It's about who you are as a person. We've gotten to know each other over the last month and I *like* you Cheyenne." Dude's voice dropped. "I'm sorry your family disappointed you."

Cheyenne's eyes immediately filled with tears. "I should've known better, Faulkner. They've been like that my entire life. But when

Karen told me she felt bad for those guys' families, I lost it. I couldn't believe she had more empathy for them than me. *Me*! Her flesh and blood. And Mom didn't say a word in my defense." After a beat Cheyenne said sadly, "I think I disowned them today."

"Good."

At Faulkner's heartfelt comment, Cheyenne peered up at him.

Dude repeated himself. "Good. You don't need that shit in your life. I'm your family now. Me and the guys. And of course their women."

He paused. As much as Dude wanted to demand she return the words to him, he moved on. She'd say them when she was ready.

"We have to talk about today a bit more, Shy."

"I won't do it again, I swear. I know I have this need to please you, but hearing you remind me it's okay to say no to you makes me feel better."

"Did you listen to the message I left you?"

Cheyenne was quiet for a moment. Then she shook her head.

Dude tsked at her. "Listen to it."

"I will."

"Now."

"I said I'd listen to it later, Faulkner."

"Give me your phone." Dude knew he was pushing it. Hell, he'd just told her that if he pushed her too hard or if she didn't want to do something all she had to do was let him know and he'd back off. But he couldn't back off of this.

Sighing, Cheyenne handed it over. She watched as Faulkner pushed some icons on the screen then turned the microphone toward them. He'd pushed play on the message and put it on speaker.

Cheyenne tensed. Oh shit, she didn't want to listen to what he had to say when Faulkner was right there…

Hey Shy. I'm worried about you. I'm sure something happened at lunch with your family. Will you please call or text me? If you need space, no problem, but I just need to know you're safe. Hope to hear from you soon.

The message ended and Cheyenne swallowed. "You weren't mad."

Cheyenne looked up at the man sitting beside her. She'd been so afraid he'd yell at her, she'd totally underestimated him.

"No Shy, I wasn't mad. I told you, I was worried."

"I'm sorry."

"No more apologies. We're still learning about each other. We're still getting to know each other and figuring out the dynamics of our relationship. As I said, I'm sure there'll be times I'll be mad, just as there'll be times you'll be pissed at me. It's called a relationship, Shy. It's normal and healthy. If you need space, just let me know, I'll give it to you, but only if I know you're safe while you have it. Deal?"

"Deal. Thank you, Faulkner."

"You're welcome, Shy. Now, can we please go home?"

"Yeah. We can go home."

Dude stood up and held out his hand to Cheyenne. She grabbed it and he helped her stand up. His eyes glittered as he looked at her.

"What flavor today?" Dude leaned in and took her lips in a quick hard kiss. He ran his tongue over her lips as he pulled back. "Grape. Yum."

Cheyenne just shook her head at Faulkner and licked her lips, trying to get her equilibrium back.

Dude took her hand and towed her back to the parking lot. "As much as I'd like to refuse to let you drive, I think you'd probably get irritated with me if I demanded that, wouldn't you?"

Cheyenne simply nodded. "I'm okay to drive, Faulkner."

"Okay. I'll see you at home?"

"Yeah, home."

They smiled at each other and Dude gave her one last kiss before making sure she was buckled up in the seat. He shut the door behind her and turned around to head to his truck. He couldn't wait to show her how much she meant to him tonight. Cheyenne might not have said the words, but she showed him with her actions every day that he meant something to her. Dude would be patient. At least he'd *try* to be patient.

CHAPTER 14

Cheyenne giggled at Summer and Alabama. Caroline had called Cheyenne that morning and told her they were all going out. It was about a month after the horrendous lunch with her family and Cheyenne had blossomed under Faulkner's affection.

Their love life continued to be scorching hot and Cheyenne loved every second of it. There was something so freeing about being able to let go and have Faulkner make all the decisions. And it was something he excelled at. He knew exactly what to say and do to maximize her pleasure. Cheyenne knew she'd never get enough of him.

She hadn't yet told him she loved him. She had no idea why, just that she was waiting for the perfect time. Cheyenne wanted it to be romantic and meaningful. Saying it in the middle of sex didn't seem right, but right afterwards wasn't either. Faulkner wasn't the "go out to a fancy restaurant" type of guy, so that was out. So Cheyenne was struggling. She knew it was dumb, she should just say it, but so far she hadn't. The longer she waited the more the pressure to come up with the perfect time overwhelmed her.

Caroline had made it a point to include Cheyenne in their "girl's night out" festivities ever since Cheyenne had called her from the beach. The other women were hysterical. Cheyenne's respect for them had risen. She'd heard all of their stories over the last month at one time or another. Cheyenne couldn't believe what they'd all lived through, but when she'd tried to tell them that, they'd just laughed and said what *she'd* been through was just as impressive.

So now that Cheyenne had gotten over her nervousness, she loved hanging out with them. Sometimes she'd have lunch or dinner with just one of the girls, and other times it was all of them.

Cheyenne had slowly gotten to know the other guys on Faulkner's team as well. Caroline was right, on the outside they were all growly and gruff, but deep down, they *were* teddy bears.

It took an interaction between Hunter and Fiona for Cheyenne to finally "get" what Faulkner had tried to tell her that day on the beach.

Fiona and Cheyenne had gone out for lunch and made an impromptu decision to watch an afternoon movie. Not even thinking, they'd muted their phones and enjoyed the flick. After it was over Fiona looked at her phone and said, "Uh oh."

"What?"

"I was supposed to call Hunter after we were done with lunch so he could pick me up. He hasn't been able to get in touch with me, or you." She giggled. Actually giggled.

"Isn't he going to be pissed?"

Fiona had looked Cheyenne in the eye and said, "No. He'll be upset with me. He might yell, but I know deep down it's all stemmed in worry *for* me. There's a big difference between anger that is straight up anger, and anger that comes as a result of love."

It had clicked for Cheyenne. When Hunter had arrived at the theater to pick up Fiona, she watched as Hunter ranted and raved at Fiona. He'd lambasted her for being inconsiderate and selfish. Fiona had taken it in stride and apologized over and over. Hunter's anger blew itself out quickly and he took Fiona in his arms and held her tight.

It all made sense after seeing Hunter's reaction. Cheyenne hadn't brought it up with Faulkner yet, but she would. She knew he'd been extra careful lately not to upset her, and Cheyenne knew it had to stop. He was a SEAL, and more of a man than anyone she'd ever met.

He had to let his feelings out. Cheyenne knew she had to convince Faulkner she wouldn't freak out if he did let them out on her now.

So tonight Caroline had called and informed her that they were all going out. Since Cheyenne wasn't working, she'd readily agreed.

Now they were sitting in *Aces,* their favorite bar, drinking amaretto and midori sours and doing the occasional shot. Summer and Alabama had challenged each other to see who could do a shot with no hands, drinking from the far side of the glass. It was obvious they'd fail, but it was hysterical to see them trying to strategize.

Cheyenne looked over at Mozart. He was sitting on the other side of the room pretending not to watch them. The guys had said the girls could go out all they wanted, as long as one of them was there to watch over them.

The guys pretended to be disgruntled about it, but Caroline had told her they all secretly loved it. She'd further informed Cheyenne that the girls only went out because of the incredible sex that followed when they arrived back home. She'd explained how their men loved doing them while they were drunk, so they encouraged the behavior by going out at least once a month.

Cheyenne giggled remembering how Caroline had told her about one episode with Matthew one month. She couldn't resist leaning in and whispering to Caroline that Faulkner had tied her up like that just last night. The look on Caroline's face was priceless. Cheyenne couldn't wait to see how Faulkner "did her drunk." If it was better than how he was giving it to her now, she was in serious trouble.

A pretty waitress, with short black hair and a tired look on her face, had been serving them. The other women seemed to know her as they called her by name, Jess, and joked with her as if she was one of the group.

Cheyenne told her friends that she felt bad that Jess kept walking back and forth from their table to the bar because she had a limp, and offered to go to the bar to get the drinks herself. The women had told her that it would embarrass Jess and not to worry about it. So Cheyenne had dropped it and after another shot or two stopped thinking of their waitress as handicapped, and instead as more of a savior from above who delivered drinks just as they needed them.

Cheyenne watched as Fiona counted to three and Summer and Alabama leaned over and grabbed the shot glass with their mouths and teeth. As they tried to grab the glass with their teeth and lean backward to try to down the shot, more liquid spilled down their chests than went into their mouths, soaking the front of each of their shirts in the process.

Laughing uncontrollably, Caroline, Fiona, and Cheyenne could only watch as the two women tried desperately to sop up the liquid before it ran all the way down their chests to their pants.

"So who won?" Summer asked with a crooked grin.

Cheyenne just shook her head. "You guys are such dorks. I think you both lost. Okay, let's go get you cleaned up." Cheyenne stepped between them and the three ladies made their way wobbling to the restroom at the bar. Stopping by Mozart, Summer kissed him long and hard. Sick of waiting, Alabama grabbed her arm and pulled.

"Come on, girl. You can do that later. It's girl's night out, not date night. You have to wait just like the rest of us have to."

Summer pulled herself out of her man's arms. Before continuing to the restroom, Summer leaned in and whispered something in his ear. Cheyenne watched as he smiled lazily and nodded, obviously pleased at whatever naughty thing Summer had told him.

The trio continued to the bathroom and they all piled inside. For a small bar, the restroom was surprisingly spacious. It was also very clean, which was one of the reasons the group always chose to come to *Aces*. There was nothing worse than having to pee while drunk in a filthy bathroom…at least that was what Caroline said.

Since Cheyenne hadn't ever tried to pee while drunk in a dirty bathroom, she couldn't argue one way or another, but she did appreciate not having to hover over a dirty toilet seat. It was much nicer to be able to sit on the seat, knowing it was clean.

"Boys are so lucky!" Cheyenne called out while relieving herself.

"What the hell are you babbling about, Cheyenne?" Alabama called out from the next stall over.

"Boys. They can stand up and pee. They don't have to worry about dirty bathrooms or filthy toilet seats."

"Lucky shits!" Summer screeched from the other side of Cheyenne.

The girls giggled and finished their business and were washing their hands, laughing about the trials and tribulations of women having to pee in public restrooms, when the door opened and a woman walked in. She had long brown hair and was wearing a pair of black jeans and a black long sleeved T-shirt.

"Hey!" she said cheerfully. Looking at Cheyenne she said, "I know you, you're that woman who was on the news a while back right? You were at that store when those men were shot weren't you?"

Cheyenne froze. She hadn't ever been recognized before, and there was something about the way the woman had asked about her, that sounded wrong.

Before she could affirm or deny the woman's words, Summer spoke up for her. "Hell yeah, she kicked *ass*! Those assholes didn't have a shot in hell at getting out of there. Our Cheyenne was too smart for them." She turned to Alabama and gave her a high five.

Cheyenne didn't take her eyes off the stranger. Her buzz was quickly fading. The woman didn't look happy. In fact she looked pissed.

"One of those assholes was my brother," she said in a low voice as she pulled out a pistol.

"Oh, Fuck," Alabama said quietly.

"Okay, look, I'm sorry, I didn't mean it." Summer tried to back pedal and apologize.

"Too late, bitch. You can't say something like that then in the next breath say you didn't mean it. You meant it. Just for that, you're coming with me too."

"Coming with you?"

"Yeah, we're all going for a ride."

Cheyenne tried to think fast. "Look, it's me you're pissed at...not them. They weren't there. I can tell you anything you want to know. I can tell you the last thing your brother said. Let them stay, just take me."

"Fuck that. The second we leave, they'll be on the phone calling in your military friends. No way in hell. You all have to come with me."

"How are you going to get us all to go with you?" Alabama asked steadily, as if she wasn't falling down drunk a minute ago.

The woman moved quickly and grabbed Summer's arm. She pulled her off balance and into her. The woman snagged her around the neck and tightened her hold, while also holding her pistol to the side of Summer's head. "If you don't come with me, I'll kill her. Right here in front of you. I'll blow her fucking brains out. What's it going to be?"

The woman was obviously stronger than she appeared, either that, or she was under the influence of some sort of drug. Summer struggled briefly, but wasn't able to break the woman's hold.

Cheyenne and Alabama watched helplessly as Summer struggled to breathe. It was an easy decision.

"Okay, we're coming. Don't hurt her. Please."

The woman eased up on Summer's throat a bit. "Don't try anything. I know one of your military friends is out there. We're going out the back door. Act normal or I'll fucking shoot her. I don't have anything to lose. After Hank was killed, my world went to shit anyway."

Cheyenne believed this woman would kill Summer if either of them made any wrong moves. Cheyenne's eyes filled with tears. Dammit. She didn't want to put her friends in danger. Summer had already been kidnapped once, she didn't need this. Cheyenne knew she had to get her new friends out of this somehow.

It wouldn't be long until Sam realized they'd been gone too long, especially with Summer being his. He'd come and look for them and when he couldn't find them, surely he'd know something was wrong.

Cheyenne and Alabama preceded the crazy woman out of the restroom and toward the back door.

It was almost scary how easy it was for her to kidnap them right out of *Aces*. There was an SUV idling in the alley. A large man was sitting behind the wheel of the car and he glared at all of them as they exited the bar.

"What the hell, Alicia? I thought you were just going to get the store bitch? Who the hell are these other bitches?"

"I couldn't leave them all in there, Javier! Jesus! The second I left with her, the others would've been on the phone getting the military guys after us! Shit. Let's get the hell out of here."

Cheyenne tried one more time. "Please, don't take them, leave them here, they won't call anyone. I swear."

"Hell no, get in the car, bitch. Remember what I said. I'll kill your friends if you even *look* like you're planning something. I don't give a fuck about them, so you know I'm not lying."

"I'll do whatever you want. I promise. Just don't hurt them."

Cheyenne watched as an evil smile slid across Javier's face. "I see what you mean, Alicia. Good going. She'll be good as gold to keep her friends safe…won't you, sweetheart?"

Cheyenne swallowed the bile that crept up her throat. Shit. They were in serious trouble.

* * *

MOZART SHIFTED ON HIS SEAT. He couldn't wait to take Summer home and show her how much he loved "girls night out." She'd whispered in his ear that tonight was the night she was going to allow him to restrain her. They'd been working up to it. She still had nightmares about Ben Hurst and when she was restrained and helpless in his clutches. They both knew he wasn't Hurst, but sometimes the heart and the head differed in opinion.

He loved seeing the women drunk. They were cute and actually hilarious. Mozart only wished he could've filmed Summer and Alabama trying to down that shot without using their hands. Abe would've gotten a kick out of it.

The guys might bitch and moan to the women about having to babysit them, but the truth was, they all fought for the chance to watch over them each month. The women would laugh themselves silly if they saw the elaborate ritual they went through every month, each trying to outdo the other, for the chance to sit in a damn bar for a few hours watching the women tie one on. There were enough women now that it'd probably be a good idea to have two of them there when the ladies were getting drunk, just to be safe.

Mozart checked his watch. It'd been fifteen minutes since Summer and the others had passed him to go to the bathroom. He knew women tended to spend more time than men in the restroom, but fifteen minutes was pushing it. Gesturing at Caroline, who was also checking her watch, he gave a chin lift and motioned toward the bathroom.

Caroline leaned over to Fiona and told her she'd be right back. She passed Mozart and headed to the restroom. Mozart frowned when she returned before even a minute had passed.

"They aren't in there."

"Are you sure?"

"Sam, the bathroom only has three stalls, it's not like it's the size of a football stadium. There's no one in there."

They just looked at each other. Caroline reached for her phone. "They didn't text me."

Mozart pulled out his own phone. "Me either. Fuck."

They turned and almost ran into Jess, the waitress.

"Hey, Jess, have you seen Alabama, Summer, or Cheyenne? They went to the restroom about fifteen minutes ago and never came back."

Jess looked worried. "I'm sorry, I didn't see them at all. I was busy over there," Jess gestured toward the other side of the bar. "I was taking that large party's orders and then helping get the drinks ready."

Caroline and Mozart nodded and hurried back to the table. "Fiona, did any of the others text you by any chance?"

Sensing their urgency, Fiona checked her phone and shook her head after seeing she had no new texts.

Mozart didn't waste any more time. He dialed Wolf first.

"Hey, Mozart, ready to call it a night yet?"

"Summer, Alabama, and Cheyenne are MIA. They went to the

restroom twenty minutes ago and disappeared. I haven't searched the premises yet, but wanted you to know."

"Caroline and Fiona?" Wolf's voice was clipped and businesslike.

"Right here with me."

"Put Ice on."

Mozart handed the phone to Caroline.

"Hey, Matthew."

"Ice, I need you and Fiona to stay close to Mozart. I'm calling the team, but until we know what the hell is going on I need you safe. Got me?"

"Of course, Matthew. I'll stay right here and won't let him out of my sight."

"Thank you, baby, please stay safe," Wolf said softly and with feeling before switching back to his no nonsense voice. "Put Mozart back on."

Caroline handed the phone back to Sam without a word.

"Yeah."

"Do a recon, then call Tex if you don't find them. He'll be able to track their phones. I'll call Dude and Abe and let them know. Call Benny and Cookie and tell them to meet you at *Aces*."

"Got it. Call if you find anything."

After hanging up with Mozart, Wolf clenched his fists momentarily before sighing and scrolling through his contacts. Neither Abe nor Dude were going to be happy to hear their women were missing.

* * *

CHEYENNE SAT in the front seat of the SUV, huddled in misery. Alicia had crawled in the back seat with Summer and Alabama. She held the gun jammed into Alabama's side. Javier kept sneering at Cheyenne and winking at her viciously. It was seriously creeping Cheyenne out.

She tried to think through what was happening. So far, all she knew was that one of the men at the grocery store that day was Alicia's brother. She hadn't been able to figure out how Javier fit into everything yet.

The duo wasn't talking about where they were going or what was going to happen once they got there. The kidnapping was obviously pre-planned.

They drove for what seemed like hours, but was probably more like forty minutes or so, and pulled onto a dusty road. They bumped over the rough ground for at least a mile before coming to a stop outside a tiny house.

Alicia forced Alabama and Summer out, while Javier kept Cheyenne from exiting by latching tightly onto her arm and not letting go.

"Where is she taking them?" Cheyenne shrieked. "Let me go. "No, don't take them. Shit. No." She struggled against Javier's hold until he finally took his fist and rammed it into the side of her face.

"Shut the fuck up. Damn. Seriously."

Cheyenne shook her head. Her ears were ringing and she groaned. Shit that hurt. She tried a different tactic. "Look, if it's money you want, I can get it for you. I've got twenty thousand dollars in the bank, it's yours if you just let my friends go. They didn't do anything, they have nothing to do with this. Please don't hurt them, just take me and we'll go and get the money."

Javier didn't answer, but instead rolled down the passenger window and yelled, "Hurry the fuck up, Alicia, we ain't got time for this shit!"

"Keep your pants on, Javier. Fuck! I'm gettin' there!"

Before Javier could roll the window up again, Cheyenne yelled out the open window to her friends. "Hang in there you guys! I'm sure the guys are coming!"

"Your fucking Navy SEALS aren't coming, bitch." Javier growled at her.

Cheyenne was sick of this. "They *are*. They'll find you guys and shoot you down just like the snipers did to Alicia's brother!"

"If they come, they'll die."

Cheyenne stared at Javier, trying to decide if he was talking smack or if he was serious.

"We wired the entire place."

At the look of horror on Cheyenne's face, Javier laughed. "Poor, poor, Cheyenne. Not only will you lose your friends, but you'll also lose your precious SEAL. We've got cameras hooked up so we can watch too."

"But I thought you didn't know my friends would be here with me."

"Of course we did. We put on a show that you fucking bought hook, line, and sinker. Do you think we don't know that bitches can't pee by themselves? We figured you'd be with at least one of your friends. Having two? That'll just keep your SEALs occupied that much longer."

"No, Jesus, no."

"Yes, Jesus, yes." Javier mocked.

"Who are you? Why are you doing this?" Cheyenne asked desperately trying to figure out a way out of the horrible situation she found herself and her new friends in.

"Because one of those assholes was *my* brother too. Alicia and I met while filming a segment for one of the news shows. We watched you, hung out in the parking lot where you work. Memorized your schedule. We decided to band together to get revenge. Revenge is always sweeter when shared, don't you think?"

Cheyenne sobbed once, then choked it back. She flinched when she heard a gunshot ring out into the countryside. "Summer? Alabama?" she cried out frantically.

"We're okay!"

Cheyenne sighed in relief, then heard another gun shot. "Stop fucking shooting at my friends!" she screeched, hoping Alicia could hear her. Javier just laughed next to her, obviously not concerned about Alicia in the slightest. He rolled the window up, so Cheyenne couldn't hear what was happening in the little cabin anymore.

Cheyenne watched as Alicia exited the cabin. She didn't come straight to the car though. Cheyenne observed as she took wire and circled the cabin twice, making sure to twist the wires together as she went.

"She's setting the wires for the bomb," Javier told her, sounding as if he was telling her the weather forecast for the day. "The cabin is rigged to blow. There are trip wires all over the place. All it will take is one wrong step by your precious SEALs and your friends will be blown to bits right in front of their eyes."

"No," Cheyenne breathed. "Please, leave them alone."

"Sorry, sweets. Too fucking late for that."

Cheyenne thought she was hyperventilating. Had Alicia shot Summer or Alabama? Were they inside the cabin dying right now?

Alicia came running back toward the SUV. She tore open the back door and was laughing as she plopped her butt on the seat and slammed the door behind her. "All set. The first shot scared them, but the second one shut the blonde up."

"No! What did you do?" Cheyenne tried to turn in her seat to she could leap over and hurt Alicia, but Javier just laughed and twisted the arm he still had in his grasp cruelly.

Cheyenne contorted her body to try to take the pressure off her arm as Javier twisted it in his grasp. He kept on twisting until Cheyenne heard a *pop*. The most incredible pain she could ever imagine swept over her, almost making her pass out. "Aahhhhhhh."

Cheyenne heard Javier and Alicia laughing through her pain.

"Did you break it?"

"Nah, just pulled it out of socket. That should keep her docile."

Cheyenne concentrated on not throwing up all over herself, the car, and Javier. She had no idea how she'd get out of this. How her friends would get out of it. She didn't even know if Summer was still alive. If Alicia had shot her, how long did she have before she had to see a doctor or she'd die? Cheyenne moaned. They were all in big trouble.

CHAPTER 15

Wolf, Abe, Mozart, Dude, and Benny surrounded an alley in the heart of the city. Cookie was back at *Aces* with Ice and Fiona, guarding them, waiting for intel from the team.

Wolf and Abe approached from the south while the other three SEALS approached from the north. Tex had traced the women's cell phones to this location. There was a large dumpster up against the wall and the men could hear sounds coming from inside it.

Cautiously and soundlessly the men approached. They had no idea what they would find inside, but all five men were fully concentrated on the dumpster. Wolf covered the south while Benny covered the north entrance. Mozart cautiously approached the dumpster, brought his flashlight up and without making a sound, lifted the lid.

After he peered inside, he lowered the lid and closed the dumpster carefully, then quickly backed away.

"Bomb," he said tonelessly.

The five men wasted no time retreating until they were standing at the end of the alley.

Mozart told his friends what he'd seen.

"All three cell phones are in there, strapped to a small bomb. I don't think it can do much damage, but we need to call it in."

"Do I need to go and check it out?" Dude asked, knowing he'd be able to tell with a glance how dangerous the bomb was.

"No, it's obvious they ditched the phones and they're just fucking with us," Abe commented with disgust.

"Fuck. I'll call Tex back and tell him to keep looking," Benny said, pulling out his phone and punching buttons while he said it.

"What the fuck is going on?" Dude growled out to no one in particular.

"This has to be connected to whatever happened in that grocery store. The bomb is just too much of a coincidence," Wolf theorized as the team stalked down the street back to Wolf's SUV. "Call Cookie, have him talk to Ice and Fiona again, see if he can't get *any* more information. Anything would help us at this point."

"They are never fucking going out again without us there, not even to pee." Dude was at the end of his rope. This was worse than the day Cheyenne had lunch with her family. At least then he knew she'd just had a bad day and was laying low. This? Some fucker had her who was smart enough to ditch their cells *and* create a hell of a diversion with them.

Benny piped up as they got to the SUV. "Tex is calling the cops to let them know about the explosive in the dumpster. He's as pissed as we are. He's seeing what he can find on surveillance tapes, although *Aces* doesn't really have good coverage. Since they had three women, they had to have had a bigger type car."

"Why do you think they all went? I mean if they were kidnapped by one person, it would've been hard to overpower them all," Benny further mused.

"Threats. He had to have threatened one of them. You know our women," Abe said in a low pissed off voice. "All he had to do was threaten to kill or hurt one of them and the others would've done whatever he said without a fight."

Out of the blue, Mozart turned away from the vehicle and stalked over to the nearest building and punched the wall. Blood immediately flowed from the broken flesh on his knuckles. Wolf and Benny went to him and put their hands on his arms, ready to restrain him if he went to punch the wall again.

Instead, Mozart put both hands against the wall and leaned heavily on it, head down. "Summer can't go through this again," he said in a low tortured voice. "She'll break. If she's fucking broken when I find her, someone's gonna die."

"We'll find her, Mozart," Wolf told his friend earnestly.

"Yeah? When? After she's been violated? After she's been tortured again? Seriously, you *know* what happened with Hurst last time. She can't go through this again."

"I know, Mozart. I know. Tex will find them. You know he can find anyone."

"He fucking better."

No one said a word for a moment. Thoughts about what the three women were going through flitted through each man's head. Finally Mozart pushed off the wall and walked up to Dude and Abe.

"I'm so fucking sorry you guys have to experience this. I'd hoped I'd be the only one to have to know what it feels like to have my woman stolen from me. I don't know who or what we're up against, but we have to get them back. Yesterday."

"We will, Mozart. We fucking will," Abe told him.

Dude didn't say a word. Hatred was burning in the back of his eyes. It was bad enough his friends' women were taken. But no one took *his* woman away from him. Cheyenne was his. He felt like a dog with a bone. Shy had said it straight out. She was his.

Dude *loved* Shy. It was all suddenly clear to him now. He didn't get it before. Oh he knew he had feelings for Cheyenne and he'd thought he'd loved her, had even told her so, but he hadn't understood how his teammates could put everything they'd ever known aside for a woman. But now? He fucking got it. When Fiona had run because of flashbacks and Cookie was out of the country? When Abe realized how badly he'd hurt Alabama and how much his words had shredded her? When Summer had been taken and Mozart had been frantic to find her? Even when they were in the middle of the ocean and Wolf had stepped aside and let someone else run the mission to rescue Ice...Dude finally understood.

Love. His friends loved their women with all they had, just as Dude loved Cheyenne. She was his. It didn't matter that this was the twenty first century and women didn't "belong" to anyone anymore. It didn't matter that Cheyenne was independent and could function perfectly fine on her own without him.

Deep down, some basic instinct they had, insisted that the women were theirs. Theirs to protect, to feed, to clothe, to love. Theirs. Cheyenne was *his,* dammit. He needed her in his life, in his house, in his bed. Hell, he just needed her around. To see her smile, to see her chew on her damn thumbnail. To love. That's what love was. It wasn't simple affection, it wasn't enjoying her company. It was all consuming and in the very marrow of his bones.

"Let's go," was all Dude could get out between his clenched teeth. He was on edge. He knew Mozart and Abe were feeling the same way. Their women were in danger. This was probably the most important mission they'd ever been on. The team was already close, but now, they were functioning as one. Wolf knew it could've easily been Caroline. It was pure chance that it hadn't been.

The men climbed back into the SUV without a word. This shit had to end. Whatever this shit was, it totally had to end.

* * *

Two hours later, the entire team convened around a small cabin about twenty miles outside the city. Caroline and Fiona had gone back to Caroline's house and were accompanied by three SEALs from another team on the base. Wolf wasn't putting their safety to chance. The women had accepted the protection without a word, which pissed all the men off because it meant the women were feeling vulnerable and freaked by everything that had happened. Usually Ice would've flipped out on Wolf and argued against having any strangers in their house, but she'd just kissed him, hugged him hard, and told him to bring her friends home.

Tex had come through again. Just when the men thought there was no way Tex would be able to help them this time, he figured it out. The man could find a damn needle in a haystack, from a thousand miles away.

He'd used some sort of math/physics/engineering algorithm to study the traffic patterns, along with cell phone usage and surveillance cameras to pinpoint the exact damn vehicle the women had been taken in. Once he'd found the car, it was a simple matter, Tex's words, to hack into the government's satellites and track it.

Everyone on the team knew what Tex was doing was illegal, but no one said a word. If it helped get their women back, no one gave a fuck.

Tex had been able to track the car to this shitty little cabin. It was eerily quiet. Too quiet. Something was definitely not right. Dude wanted to yell out Cheyenne's name, to see if she was okay, to see if she was even in the damn building, but he wouldn't. This mission was on communication lockdown. If the kidnapper was in there, they wanted to surprise him.

Dude led the way to the cabin, every few steps he scanned the area, looking for…something. He wasn't sure what. The hair on the back of his neck was sticking straight up. This wasn't right. He signaled for everyone to hold up.

Everyone stopped immediately and waited for Dude. Taking his eyes off the ground, Dude looked around. He willed his brain to see what his eyes weren't. Finally he stopped and turned his head back to where he was just looking. There.

"Fucking camera in the tree," he tonelessly said to his teammates through his mic.

After a moment Wolf said, "There's one over here too."

"Here too," Abe chimed in.

"Wolf, the bastards are watching us," Dude commented unnecessarily.

"But are they watching from inside the cabin or from elsewhere?" Benny chimed in, asking what everyone else had been thinking.

Without waiting for Wolf to approve of his actions, Dude yelled out. His voice carried across the clearing to the house. "Shy? Summer? Alabama?"

The men waited. Hoping.

"Here! We're here!"

"Thank fuck!" Abe breathed, recognizing Alabama's voice.

"Don't come in!" Alabama continued to yell from inside the cabin. "The bastards have rigged the entire place with some sort of explosive!"

Every man froze in place. Dude looked around, now that he knew what he was looking for, it was easy to see. The wires around the cabin weren't hidden all that well. He'd been so concerned about looking for hidden trip wires, he'd missed the obvious ones right in front of him. The kidnapper had obviously thought he was being sneaky by placing some wires around the cabin in the path, hoping the SEALs would step on them and set off the bomb. Idiots.

"Is Summer in there with you? Cheyenne?" Mozart called out.

"Summer is. They took Cheyenne though."

"They? Jesus, how many people are involved in this?" Cookie muttered through the mic.

"Okay, sit tight, sweetheart. Anyone else around?" Everyone could tell Abe wanted nothing more than to rush into the cabin and see for himself that Alabama was all right, but he was too well-trained to do anything to fuck up the mission, especially when explosives were involved.

"No, it's just us in here. But, Summer's hurt."

With Alabama's words, the anxiety level of the men suddenly shot up. Dude blocked out the fact that Cheyenne wasn't in the cabin and got to work trying to piece together how the explosives were set up and how to disarm them. The faster he figured it out, the faster they could get to Summer and Alabama, and the faster he could find Shy.

"Benny, you and Cookie work on dismantling the cameras. Be careful, the bastards might have rigged those too. Leave one up and running. I'll call Tex and give him a head's up on the cameras, he might be able to backtrack the signal and find the fucking nest. They have to be watching us for a reason. Let's use their voyeurism against them. Fucking assholes."

* * *

CHEYENNE COULDN'T BELIEVE this was happening to her again. Once again she was covered in miles of duct tape. Her shoulder was screaming at her. Javier really *had* pulled it out of its socket when he'd wrenched it in the car. She supposed the tape holding her still was probably helping her keep it immobile, but it still hurt like nothing Cheyenne had experienced before.

The duo had driven her back into the city and to an apartment building. They'd broken in through a door in a back alley and dragged her down the stairs to the basement where they'd begun the process of taping her up.

Javier and Alicia had cackled the entire time they'd wrapped her in tape. Unlike in the grocery store though, they'd wrapped three bombs up this time. Then Alicia thought it'd be funny to wrap the tape around her neck and head too. Luckily Javier had stopped her before she could cover her mouth and nose with the stuff too.

So now Cheyenne was literally mummified. She couldn't move. She was lying on the floor, ankles, legs, body, arms, head, all taped up. Cheyenne almost laughed thinking about how much all the tape must have cost.

She couldn't help herself. She couldn't run, she couldn't get out of the way, she could only lay on the ground and watch Javier and Alicia. Cheyenne closed her eyes, she'd had enough of watching them. Apparently being horrible human beings in the middle of a kidnapping made them horny. They'd had sex on the floor right next to her. Since she'd been mummified she couldn't move, she couldn't do anything but close her eyes and wish like hell Faulkner was there.

After getting off, Javier pulled out a hand-held device and hunkered over it with Alicia, the two of them cackling with glee and laughing manically. It was the video feed of the cabin. They were watching as the SEALs made their way to the cabin.

"I wish this had sound!" Alicia complained. "But it's fucking great. Look at them, all in stealth mode. I can understand what you see in them, they're hunky and hot...too bad they're all going to get blown up...along with your stupid friends."

Cheyenne struggled on the floor. No! Dammit no! She stopped struggling when all it did was make her shoulder hurt more. She wasn't going anywhere. She had to believe the guys knew what they were doing. They weren't going to just barge in to the cabin without being cautious. Dude would see the explosives. He had to.

"What the fuck are they doing? Why aren't they going in? You said they would rush right up to the door and bust in!" Javier complained to Alicia.

"Well, I figured they would. We had two of their women. They're hotheaded military guys! That's what they're supposed to do!"

"Well, they're not! Look! That one guy sees the camera! Fuck!"

The two were quiet a moment as they watched the action play out on the little black and white handheld device. After another few minutes, Javier sighed in exasperation.

"We gotta get out of here. Obviously they're gonna get the girls out. Fuck this."

"What about her?" Alicia whined.

"That part of the plan doesn't change. In about eight hours she's gonna blow up, so who the fuck cares."

"But she knows who we are..."

Javier growled and got in Alicia's face. "Yeah, and so do those bitches that are about to be rescued. You think they aren't gonna tell those SEALs who we are? Huh?"

"But we can't just leave *her* here...she's going to tell them we're headed to Mexico."

"In about eight hours she's gonna be dead so who. the. fuck. cares."

"All right, all right, jeez. Keep your pants on. Shit. Should we change the timing so that thing goes off sooner?"

"Too late, dumbass. We already covered it all up with the tape," Javier said impatiently. "Leave the TV here with her. We don't want to have it with us in case they can somehow trace it back. Besides, she can watch her friends either get rescued, or blown to bits. Seems fair to me."

Cheyenne watched as Alicia threw her head back and cackled at Javier's suggestion. She then came over to where Cheyenne lay helpless on the floor, and propped the little device up next to her head with a box.

"There you go, bitch. I hope they all get blown to pieces. You can watch and then wait for your own bombs to go off and blow *you* to pieces."

"You're a piece of shit," Cheyenne croaked out.

"No, you got my brother killed and you got Javier's brother killed. *You're* the piece of shit."

Cheyenne could only watch as the two kidnappers gathered up their stuff and left without a backward glance. She looked around, knowing that if the bombs did go off she'd die, but probably more importantly, so would a lot of other people.

She was underneath an apartment complex. People *lived* there. If the bombs went off it would surely do some damage to the building itself. It might even collapse. If it did, no one would even find her body...if there was anything left to find. Cheyenne suppressed a sob. She couldn't cry. There was nothing worse than snot running down your face when you couldn't wipe it away. There was still time though. Eight hours. Maybe Faulkner could find her in time.

She turned her attention to the little television screen propped next to her. Cheyenne could barely make out the cabin, but she saw the SEALs walking around it and leaning over. Hopefully they were able to make it safe enough to get Summer and Alabama out. Hopefully Summer wasn't dead. She could only watch as the best people she'd ever met, worked frantically to rescue her friends.

Cheyenne drank in the sight of Faulkner. She'd know him anywhere. She'd spent weeks memorizing every inch of his body, at his command. She knew the placement of every scar, every mole, every nook and cranny. Cheyenne had no idea if she'd ever see him in person again, or be able to feel his body against hers, so watching

Faulkner move around the small cabin, she memorized everything about him all over again.

* * *

DUDE STOOD off to the side and observed Abe holding Alabama and Mozart comforting Summer as Cookie made sure she was stable enough to be transported down to the city. Summer had been shot, but luckily the bullet had only grazed her upper arm. Alabama had immediately done some basic first aid and stopped the bleeding. She'd be okay.

Dude was relieved both women were all right, but the burning in his gut wouldn't stop. Where the hell was Cheyenne? What was *she* going through? He stood back from the others, fists clenched, wanting to do something, but not sure what it was they could do yet.

Remembering the cameras in the trees, he looked up at the one they hadn't taken down yet. Tex was working on tracing the feed. Were the bastards watching them now? He kept his eyes on the camera, it was easier than watching his friends holding their women.

* * *

CHEYENNE DIDN'T KNOW how much time had passed since Alicia and Javier had left. She'd kept her eyes on the blurry little black and white screen in front of her. The angle wasn't great, but she could still make out when the group went into the cabin and when both Summer and Alabama came out.

Her heart about stopped when she saw Summer being carried by Sam, but relaxed a bit when she saw she was moving and holding on to her man of her own accord.

Even though it was torturous to see her friends so close, but so far away, she kept watching. After a moment she noticed Faulkner. He was standing off to the side, not interacting with his friends in any way. He was looking up at her…well up at the camera. Cheyenne could imagine she saw the tick in his jaw. They knew the cameras were there. They *knew*.

A single tear fell from Cheyenne's eye before she brutally swallowed them down. If they knew about the cameras then they had some plan. She had to believe that. Cheyenne had no idea how they were going to get her out of *this*, but if anyone could, her SEALs could.

Cheyenne continued to watch until the group finally moved out of camera range. They were obviously leaving. The feed continued to play but all Cheyenne could see were the trees gently blowing in the wind and the cabin sitting forlornly in the clearing.

She hoped with all her being that she hadn't just seen the last of her friends...and of Faulkner.

* * *

"COME ON, let's go. We have to get Summer to the hospital," Wolf ordered, heading back for the SUV.

Dude finally took his gaze off the camera and looked at his teammates. Wolf was looking at him with concern. Benny and Cookie just looked pissed and Mozart and Abe looked relieved to have their women back, but they also looked determined.

"No one fucks with this team. And no one fucks with our women and gets away with it," Abe said with feeling. "We're not stopping until we find her, Dude."

"The woman's name was Alicia and she called the guy Javier," Alabama said suddenly. "They said some of the guys in the grocery store that day were their brothers."

With those two sentences, it finally all made sense.

"Revenge," Cookie said, stating the obvious.

"Obviously making bombs and being an asshole runs in the family," Summer quipped from Mozart's arms.

No one laughed, but everyone appreciated her attempt at levity.

"We can't leave yet. What if Cheyenne is up here somewhere? We'll lose too much time if we all head back to the city and then have to come back up here once Tex traces that feed."

Benny was being practical, and it sucked. He was right. Dude didn't know whether to continue to search the woods nearby, or to head back down to the city. He closed his eyes and bowed his head, thinking.

Okay, so these were siblings to the guys killed. They wanted revenge. Would they want to stash Cheyenne up in the woods where they could torture her, or would they bring her back into civilization for some reason?

Dude raised his head, knowing deep in his gut his conclusion was right. "They're in the city."

Without asking how Dude was so sure, the men strode toward the car.

Alabama wasn't so sure. "But Dude, they brought us up here, why wouldn't they have stashed Cheyenne somewhere up here too?"

Not slowing down, Dude tried to explain. "They want revenge. You guys were a diversion. They wanted us to waste time up here. They took her back down to where there are people. They want to hurt Cheyenne, yes, but they also want to hurt us. They know what we do, killing as many people as possible is their goal. They want to show that SEALs aren't perfect, that we can't always rescue people as I did that day in the grocery store."

"But that's crazy," Alabama whispered.

"Yeah," Dude agreed, but said no more.

It was a tight fit in the SUV, but no one complained. Their mission wasn't done. Cheyenne was still out there…somewhere.

CHAPTER 16

Seven men stood around a table on the Naval base. The team's CO, Commander Hurt, had joined them and was listening to the information Tex was giving them.

"The camera feed definitely leads back into the city. Because of all the buildings and interference, it's hard to pinpoint exactly where."

"Try." Dude's voice was strained. It was obvious he was hanging on by the merest thread.

"I am, Dude. I swear to Christ, I am. Have the police had any luck in breaking Alicia and Javier yet?"

Wolf had contacted the commander and he in turn had contacted the police as soon as they'd left the cabin. He'd explained who the people were that kidnapped Summer and Alabama. Both women had said they were more than willing to press charges.

Javier and Alicia were dumb enough to still be in their apartments packing to flee out of the country. They'd been taken into custody without trouble, but were refusing to say anything about Cheyenne. They denied having anything to do with the kidnappings and denied even knowing who Cheyenne was.

Wolf answered Tex, "No, they aren't saying anything. Alicia let something slip though, and it might be nothing, but she said she might be willing to talk in the morning. We don't know why the morning will make a difference though."

"It's another bomb," Dude said into the silence that followed Wolf's statement. "It's the only thing that makes sense. They've stashed her somewhere and immobilized her with a bomb, just as their brothers did in the store. She'll talk in the morning because it'll be too late then. The bomb will have gone off."

Surprisingly, it was the commander who lost it. "God *damn* it! Get me the fucking Police Chief on the phone *now*!"

No one was really sure who Commander Hurt was talking to, but Tex apparently decided he was talking to him. "Connecting now, Sir... Ringing...you're on."

"Yeah?" A voice barked out from the speaker sitting on the table in the room.

"Chief? Listen, this is Commander Hurt. There's been a development in the case..."

The Commander proceeded to explain their suspicions to the Police Chief and why time was of the essence. The Chief agreed to put more pressure on Alicia and see if they couldn't get her to tell them where they'd stashed Cheyenne.

"Tex..."

"I know, I know, I'm working on it."

"We're running out of time," Dude's voice finally cracked. He could sense it was almost too late. He knew he'd need every second he could get to try to get Cheyenne out of whatever fucked up situation the two yahoos had put her in. *This* was what his entire SEAL career had prepared him for. *This* was why he was a natural with explosives. To save this woman's life. To save his woman's life.

"Dude, I swear to God I'm going to find her. Those schmucks aren't very fucking smart, they sure as hell aren't smarter than me. Mother fuckers." Tex's rant stopped abruptly. "Wait...oh fucking hell. Are you shitting me?"

"What? Jesus Tex. What?"

Every man in the room turned their complete attention on the innocuous looking phone sitting on the table.

"Okay, I'm not one hundred percent sure, but I don't want to wait to *be* completely sure. I've narrowed the feed down to a city block. There are three buildings. An office building, an apartment building and what looks from the satellite photos to be an abandoned old factory. I think there are plans to turn it into some fancy-ass duplexes or something."

Wolf turned to Dude. "Which one?" He had complete confidence that Dude would know.

Dude closed his eyes to think. He couldn't be wrong about this. Yes, all the buildings were close together, but for all the people involved, for Cheyenne, he couldn't be wrong. He worked through the situation out loud.

"Okay, the abandoned building is out. That wouldn't cause enough damage. They wanted people hurt or killed. They want to make a statement. Both of the other buildings have people in them. Tex," Dude's eyes opened and he began to pace, "tell me about the layouts of each."

They could hear Tex clicking on his computer keys. "The office building is a four story building which houses seventeen different organizations. They're split over the four different floors. Elevators in the NW corner as well as in the middle. Stairways in the SW and NE corners. The apartment building is also four stories high. There are twenty apartments on each floor for a total of eighty apartments. Seventy five of the apartments are currently occupied. There are two vacant apartments on the second floor, one on the third and two on the fourth. There are three elevators in the lobby and two stairwells. Both are emergency stairwells with exits to the street."

"Entrances?" Dude barked, still pacing.

"The offices have two emergency exits leading out to the street from the stairwells. There are two main entrances into the building and there seems to be a security desk in the lobby checking employee IDs and accepting packages. The apartment building also has two entrances, both are swipe card access, but no security desk in the lobby. There's a mail room on the first floor, accessible to the general public, but there's a swipe card door that leads from the mailroom into the lobby."

"Basements? Access to them?"

"Both buildings have basements, negative on the access for the office, but both stairwells in the apartment access both the basement and the roof."

Dude was heading for the door to the conference room before Tex had finished speaking. "She's in the basement of the apartment building," he said as he reached the door.

No one asked how Dude knew, no one questioned him. It was uncanny how Dude could figure things out sometimes. If he said Cheyenne was in the basement of the apartment building, she was in the basement of the apartment building.

The commander was barking into the phone at Tex. "I'll notify the Police and Fire Chiefs...set off the alarms remotely Tex, clear both those buildings and get people out of the area. I don't know how much time we have, but we have to get everyone out."

Dude was focused on Cheyenne. The commander was right, he didn't know how much time he had, but in his gut he was afraid it wasn't going to be enough.

* * *

CHEYENNE HEARD the alarms in the building above her pealing. She had no idea what time it was or how much of the eight hours had passed since Alicia and Javier had left. Her shoulder didn't hurt anymore, she figured it was because it was numb. She knew when a shoulder was pulled out of its socket it was a matter of time before blood flow was stopped.

Her eyes went back to the black and white screen. She couldn't take her eyes from it. It was the last place she'd seen Faulkner and she needed to hold that memory in her head.

Cheyenne hoped like hell the sounds of the fire alarm above her head meant the building was being cleared. She couldn't think that it was because of her. She wouldn't get that hope built up inside her, only to have it dashed.

The trees swaying at the cabin on the screen mesmerized her. The door to the cabin was open and every now and then would slowly creep shut, then be blown open again a couple of minutes later. She kept her attention on the little screen. It was better than thinking about her own situation, or about how many people might die because of her.

* * *

DUDE WAS COMPLETELY FOCUSED on the building in front of him. His Shy was there, he could instinctively feel it. The set up was perfect. The stairwell door in the alley had been propped open with a small rock in the doorjamb. The door wasn't able to latch because of the small obstruction. It was where Alicia and Javier had to have entered.

Dude turned to Benny and Cookie. "I'm going down there alone."

"No you aren't," Benny immediately returned.

"Look, we all know what we're going to find down there and I'm the only one who can get her out of it."

"No, you aren't, Dude," Cookie argued. "We're a team, and you're wasting fucking time. Wolf has it under control up here. We're going down there with you and we'll figure out how to save her. Now shut the hell up and move your ass."

Cookie was right. They didn't have any time to spare. Dude turned on his heel and headed down the stairs. The three men turned the corner and stopped dead. Dude had been right. Cheyenne was there, but she was in deep trouble. They all were.

Cheyenne thought she heard something, but didn't bother to turn her head away from the screen. She wanted to stay in the moment, to remember watching as her friends were saved. Suddenly she felt a hand on her cheek. No, she felt *Faulkner's* hand on her cheek. She'd recognize that scarred and rough touch anywhere. Was she dreaming?

"Shy, I'm here."

Cheyenne forced her eyes away from the screen and looked up. It *was* Faulkner. And Hunter. And Kason. Oh shit.

"No. Just go, seriously. Please. Just go."

"We've been here before, Shy. Just let me help you. I'll get you out of this."

"No, Faulkner, you can't. This isn't like last time."

"The hell it isn't. I'm not letting you go, Shy. You're mine. You said it. I take care of what's mine. Remember?"

Cheyenne couldn't hold back the sob. She looked over at Kason and Hunter and whispered, "Please, he can't this time, take him and go."

"Fuck no, Cheyenne, he's not leaving and neither are we," Cookie said harshly, his eyes roving over her body, trying to come up with a plan of action.

"Cheyenne, the others are evacuating the building. They're getting everyone out and away. We'll just get this shit off you and Dude will take care of whatever's underneath and we'll get you out too."

Bizarrely, Cheyenne didn't react to this statement, she simply turned back to Faulkner and asked in a weirdly monotone voice, "How long has it been since you rescued Summer and Alabama?"

Dude looked down at his watch, then back into Cheyenne's eyes. "About six hours."

"They said eight hours. It's probably been about seven by now. There's no way you can figure all this out in an hour."

"Bullshit, Shy. An hour's a piece of cake. Hell, I thought I'd only have minutes. Trust me."

"I do, Faulkner, I do, but..."

"No. No buts. You do or you don't. Period, Shy."

Cheyenne looked deep into Faulkner's eyes. She tried not to think about being blown to bits, to think about *him* being blown to bits right next to her. He hadn't asked for much from her, only her submission and along with that, her trust. She trusted him to take care of her sexually, she trusted that he'd never willingly hurt her, she had to trust him here too. This was what he did.

"I trust you and I love you."

Cheyenne watched as Faulkner closed his eyes briefly. When he opened them again, there was determination shining in them. He pressed his lips together then told her, "When I get you home, you're going to pay for waiting until *now* to give me the words, Shy."

When she opened her mouth, he waved her off, completely focused on what he had to do again. "Tell me what's under this tape. Tell me everything you can."

"There are three bombs as far as I know. One between my knees, one at my belly, and one on my chest. They were ticking before they strapped them to me. I can't feel my arm. Javier dislocated my shoulder before they taped me up."

Blocking out her comment about her shoulder for a moment, Dude asked, "Which one did they wrap up first? And can you breathe all right? Anything else wrong I need to know about before I start?"

"They started with my feet. I couldn't kick them if they were taped together. They immobilized me and started from my feet and worked their way up. And yes, I can breathe okay." Cheyenne paused a moment then said softly, "I'm scared, Faulkner."

"Me too, Shy, me too," Dude said unexpectedly, "But I swear, I'm getting you out of this."

"I know you are. Don't worry about hurting me. I can take it. Do whatever you need to in order to get the tape off and these damn bombs disarmed."

"There's no need for you to hurt, Cheyenne," Cookie said, pulling something out of his pack. "Dude, I have some morphine here."

"Do it," Dude didn't even hesitate. He knew he was going to have to hurt Shy, and he wanted to make sure he kept it to a minimum.

"Oh fuck, Faulkner, you know what those kinds of drugs do to me."

Dude smiled for the first time in hours. He quickly leaned down and kissed Shy's duct taped forehead and looked her in the eyes. "I don't give a fuck what comes out of your mouth, baby, as long as you're alive and breathing."

"Cheyenne, I'm going to have to inject this into your thigh. I can't see exactly where it's going in, so I apologize in advance for causing you any pain."

"Hunter, it's gonna hurt a lot more to be blown to pieces, so I don't give a damn about where you stick me, just shut up and do it already."

Benny chuckled at the crankiness of her voice as Cookie quickly inserted the needle through the duct tape around her thigh.

Still looking into Faulkner's eyes, Cheyenne told him, "Don't wait, get it done."

As much as he wanted to wait until the morphine took effect, Cheyenne was right, he didn't have the luxury of waiting.

"Benny, come up here to her head, don't touch the tape around her head that can come off later. Start on her chest. Be extremely careful. Don't touch the device at all. Loosen up what you can. Cookie, do the same starting at her hips. I'm going to start down here. Remove only what's necessary to get to the devices, nothing else."

The three men got to work.

Dude pulled out his K-bar knife, as the others did the same, and sliced at the tape around Cheyenne's ankles. He had to actually saw through the material because there was so much of it. Alicia and Javier had spent some time wrapping her. They hadn't wanted her to be able to get out of there easily. Hell, they hadn't wanted her to get out at all.

At last Dude freed her ankles. Once they were separated it was easier for him to cut through the tape holding her legs together.

He finally got to the explosive device between her knees. He took precious time to free as much tape from above and below the device as he could.

"Faulkner, the last time you were between my legs like this, you ordered me not to come, I don't think that'll be an issue right now."

Dude couldn't help but smile. Jesus, he couldn't believe how the filter of Cheyenne's words turned itself off when she had some drugs in her system. "Shy…" he started to warn her, but she interrupted him.

"No, I know. I know you like to boss me around and you know I love it. I'm just saying, you don't have to tell me to hold back. I'm not going to. I swear."

At Cookie's choked laughter, Dude explained to his friends. "It's the drugs, she says whatever she's thinking, with no filters."

"Obviously," Cookie observed, still smiling.

"Faulkner?" Cheyenne asked, sounding completely out of it.

"Yes, Shy?" Dude didn't look up from what between her legs.

"I do love you, you know. I was trying to figure out when to tell you, but the longer I waited, the harder it was to find the best time. I was going to make you dinner one night, but forgot I had to work, and besides I'm a shitty cook. Then I was going to tell you when you had me on my knees for you, but that didn't seem right either, and besides it wasn't as if I could really talk with my mouth full anyway. Then I was going to wait until you untied me that one night…God that was hot…but anyway, I fell asleep too soon. It didn't seem right to just blurt it out…but I do. I love you so much. You're everything I ever wanted in a guy. In *my* guy. I never knew I wanted to submit, but you make it so easy. I-I-I don't know what I'll do if you decide you don't want me anymore."

Dude paused for a fraction, he had to respond to the pain he heard in her voice. "Shy…"

"No! I know, I'm probably fucking this up somehow. I feel like I'm floating, but I just, I'd do anything for you. You have to know. I'll even leave you alone if you want me to. It might kill me, but I'll do it."

"I'm not letting you go, Shy."

"Oh. Okay. Good. 'Cos I like you holding me."

Dude shook his head and concentrated on the device again. "Fuck," he said quietly. "Cookie, Benny, stop. They've connected the three bombs to each other. I can't disarm this one without disarming the others at the same time."

Never one to let an opportunity to rub something in go by, Cookie said, "Looks like you needed both of us here after all, didn't you?"

"Fucker," Dude said lightly, knowing Cookie was right. There was no way he could disarm all three bombs at the same time. He needed both his teammates there.

"Hunter?"

"Yeah, Cheyenne?"

"How's Fiona? I bet she was really worried. And she didn't see Javier did she? I don't want her freaked out. I know she's still dealing with those assholes from Mexico kidnapping her. Not that Javier got her, but still. I'm worried about her. I miss her. We didn't get to finish our shots..."

"She's okay, Cheyenne, don't worry about her."

"Yeah, all right, she has you. I'll try not to. But I've never had best friends before. That's what friends do, they worry about each other."

There was silence as the three men continued to try to remove enough tape to safely get to the bombs underneath. Every time they had to peel some of the tape away from her skin they cringed. The red blotches underneath the tape looked bad.

"Okay, the first two are uncovered, how're you doing up there Benny?" Dude asked urgently. Time was ticking away. Too much time. He wasn't going to get a second chance.

"Almost done, Dude."

"Kason...I like that name. Why do you go by Benny?"

Benny opened his mouth, but Cookie answered before he could.

"He earned his nickname fair and square, Cheyenne. No matter if he says differently."

"Ooooooh, I sense a good story there," Cheyenne slurred. "Can you see my arm guys? Is it still attached? I can't feel it at all. That can't be good can it? Faulkner?"

"Yeah, baby?"

"I love you."

"I know."

"Aren't you going to say it back?"

"Yeah, when you're out of this fucking building and I have you safe in my arms in my bed and you've just come for me three times and I'm sure you'll never be in this kind of fucked up situation again."

"Uh, Faulkner?"

"What?" Dude's voice was all business. As much as he loved Cheyenne, he was trying to concentrate.

"That was a lot of swear words, but I can't wait."

Dude blew out a breath, but didn't answer her.

"Okay guys, here's what I need you to do. See that little red wire running under the device? On the count of three you need to pull it out. Pull it as hard as you can. It has to pop out. We have to do it at the same time. If we don't, they'll all go off."

"Oh God, don't. Please don't." Cheyenne said suddenly, she started squirming under them, and Benny put both hands on her shoulders to try to keep her still. Dude hadn't been sure she was understanding what they were doing, but with her words he knew she did. She knew exactly. "Just leave it, fuck. Don't. Kason, Hunter, just go, take Faulkner with you. Don't." She started trembling hard.

Dude checked his watch. He had time, barely, but he had time. He moved up to Cheyenne's line of vision. He sandwiched her head between his hands and leaned down to her.

"Cheyenne, stop it."

She stopped moving, but he saw tears falling from her eyes for the first time since they'd arrived. She'd been so strong, but when it got too real, she finally broke.

"I can't. I want to touch you, Faulkner, and I can't. I've never been so scared in my life, not for me, but for *you*. I can't be the reason Fiona loses her man. I can't be the reason Benny never meets the woman who's out there waiting for him to protect her. I can't be the reason you die. If I die, it'll be okay, you'll find someone else, but I can't kill you. Please, Faulkner, please."

Dude could feel his heart breaking. He leaned down and kissed the tears falling from her right eye, then did the same on the left side.

"Shy, I'll never find anyone else. Ever. You're it. Period. Done. End of story. I've waited for you my entire life. If I have to go a day without tasting what flavor lip shit you've put on, I won't survive. If I can't see you night after night stretched out on my bed, waiting for me to come to you and do whatever I want, if I can't feel you surrounding me, squeezing me, my life isn't worth living." Dude's voice dropped to a whisper. "I love you, Shy. We're in this together. Okay?"

"You don't *ask* me stuff, Faulkner."

"Sorry." Dude held back the chuckle. She was so fucking cute even covered in tape. "I love you, Shy. We're in this together."

Cheyenne sniffed. "Can you please wipe my nose? I can't get to it and I can't stand feeling snot run down my face."

Dude smiled and used his sleeve to wipe the errant tears off her face then to clear the fluid away from her face that had leaked out of her nose.

"Can I please disarm this fucking bomb and get us out of here now?"

Cheyenne nodded.

Dude leaned down one more time and kissed her lips. "Hang in there, this is almost done."

He moved back down her body to the device between her knees.

"Is Summer okay? I mean Alicia and Javier left the camera thingy for me to watch. I think they were wanting me to have to watch you guys get blown up or something, but you're way too smart for that aren't you? Anyway, I heard Alicia…"

"On the count of three. One…"

"…shoot. Twice! And she told me she shot Summer, and I wasn't sure if she was dead or not, but I saw you guys carry her out and she was holding on to Sam, so I thought she looked okay and you guys weren't freaking out or anything. But it was awful. Is she…"

"Two…"

"…okay? I mean it couldn't have been fun to have been kidnapped, *again*. Fuckers. And Caroline? Is she okay? I mean it had to have sucked to have been sitting in *Aces* and to find out we were missing. Where are Fiona and Caroline? Is someone watching…"

"Three!"

"…them because Alicia and Javier know who they are and are still out there. They're planning on flying out of the country. Did you guys know that? They told me…stupid jerks, so you should be sure…"

"Cheyenne."

"…to track them down before they get out of the country. Can we steal them back if they go to Mexico? I can never remember all the rules about that sort of thing. I want to go out again with the girls. Next week. No tomorrow. We didn't get..."

"Cheyenne."

"...to finish our girl's night out and that was the first girls night out I've ever had. I was having fun dammit. It's not fair. It wasn't our fault stupid people had to go and ruin it..."

Cheyenne's words were suddenly cut off. She looked up to see Faulkner kneeling by her side and saw Kason and Hunter standing above her.

"It's over, Shy."

"You turned the bombs off?"

Dude smiled at her wording. "Yeah, we turned them off."

"Can we go home now, Faulkner? I want to sleep for a million hours in your bed. With you. Naked. Preferably with you inside me."

"Soon. First I need to get you to the hospital."

"But Faulkner, I don't wanna go to the hospital. I just want to be with you."

"You'll be with me, Shy. I'm not leaving your side and I want to see anyone *try* to peel me away."

"Okay then, but soon? You'll take me to bed?"

"Yes, Shy. Soon."

Looking up at Hunter and Kason, and seeing the broad grins on their faces, Cheyenne demanded, "What's so funny? I don't think there's anything funny about any of this." Her eyes went back to Faulkner. "Tell them to stop laughing."

"You're so fucking cute, Shy."

"No, I'm not," she retorted immediately. "I haven't been able to put on my lip balm in hours, my lips don't taste like anything, and I want to make sure they always taste like something different so you want to keep kissing me. I'm covered in fucking tape, *again,* but this time I know it's gonna hurt like hell when they take it off. I have no idea how they're going to get it out of my hair without cutting it all fucking off. I can't feel my arm and I'm afraid they're going to have to cut that off too. I'm just so tired of being scared and now I'm going to cry again and I still can't wipe my own snot off my face."

Dude leaned down and lifted Cheyenne into his arms. "Wipe your snot on me, Shy, I can handle it. I swear to Christ you aren't going to feel anything when they take the tape off, they aren't going to cut your hair off and you'll still have your arm when you wake up."

Dude felt Cheyenne nod against his shoulder where she'd buried her head and then wiped her face on his shirt, obviously taking him at his word and wiping her face on him to stop her snot from running down her face. He smiled.

"And another thing, I want to kiss you no matter if you're wearing flavored lip crap or not."

"Okay. I want to hold you."

"You will. Just shush now. Let me take care of you."

"You always take care of me."

"Damn straight."

CHAPTER 17

Cheyenne groaned and opened her eyes. The room was dark, but she knew immediately she was at the hospital. There was no mistaking the smell of antiseptic, old person, and sickness. Feeling panicky, she looked to her right and sighed.

Faulkner was there. She remembered bits and pieces of the last few hours, and he'd kept his word and not left her side. He'd carried her out of the basement into the bright sunlight of the day. There had been cameras and people yelling for information, but Faulkner had ignored all of them and his teammates had escorted him, shielding them from the cameras, to the waiting ambulance. He hadn't left her there this time though, he'd sat at her head and kept his scarred hand on her forehead the entire trip.

The emergency room had been expecting them and Cheyenne had been whisked to the back behind a flimsy curtain. A doctor had come in, almost immediately, and taken stock. Cheyenne didn't remember much after that, only that she'd been given another shot and in panic had looked to Faulkner.

He'd dipped his head to hers and whispered, "Trust me."

She'd nodded and was out.

Cheyenne watched as Faulkner breathed in and out. The rhythm of his breaths were steady and even. She'd watched him sleep enough to know he was sleeping deeply instead of the light cat-naps he was wont to do here and there.

She swore under her breath when the door opened and Faulkner jerked awake. He probably needed the sleep and it'd just been rudely interrupted. Cheyenne kept her eyes on Faulkner and was rewarded with his bright smile when he saw she was awake.

He stood up and came over to her side. "Hey, Shy. How do you feel?"

"Terrible." Her voice croaked a bit but she was honest, as usual.

Faulkner actually chuckled at her answer. She frowned at him.

"Give it a bit of time, Cheyenne, you'll feel better soon."

Cheyenne turned to see a man standing by her bed. She didn't recognize him, but he was obviously her doctor.

"We were able to remove most of the tape without pulling off your skin this time. It'll take a bit of time for the hair on your arms and legs to grow back though."

Cheyenne remembered for the first time how the tape had covered her head. She moved her good arm up as if to feel for herself if she was indeed bald, but Faulkner intercepted it and kissed her palm before engulfing it in his own scarred hand.

"My hair?"

"That was a bit more problematic. Your man here," the doctor gestured at Faulkner, "refused to let us shave it, but we did have to cut some of it to get the tape out."

Tears gathered in the corners of Cheyenne eyes, but she refused to let them fall. It was stupid to cry over something like that. She was alive, Faulkner was alive, her friends were alive. Her hair would grow back.

"It looks fine, Shy," Falkner whispered in her ear. "It's just shorter than it was. Trust me."

Damn him for continuing to say that. She *did* trust him, but it was still scary not to see for herself. She bit her lip, then nodded at Faulkner. The smile that came over his face was all the reward

Cheyenne needed. She'd walk through fire in order to see him smile at her like that. To know she pleased him.

The doctor continued speaking, "Your shoulder is going to take a bit longer to heal. You were lucky in that it was only a subluxation." At the blank look in Cheyenne's face, the doctor explained, "Sorry, that means it was only a partial dislocation. We didn't have to do surgery to put it back in place, we just manipulated it here in the ER. That doesn't mean it's not going to hurt. We want to watch you carefully since it was dislocated for a long period of time. You'll need to baby it for a while. There are some studies that show keeping it in a sling doesn't really help it much, so just do what you can and be careful. If the sling helps, use it. If you get tired and need to take a break from it, do so. I've written out a prescription for some pain killers. I recommend that you use them for the first day or so, then you can wean yourself off of them."

"No drugs," Cheyenne insisted. "I hate the way they make me feel."

Dude chuckled from beside her. "I have to agree with her in this. They really make her not herself, but I know if I ever need any information out of her, how to get it."

"That's not funny, Faulkner," Cheyenne chided him.

"But it's true."

Ignoring Faulkner for the moment, Cheyenne turned back to the doctor. "When can I go home?"

"Today."

Cheyenne sighed in relief.

"We have to get the paperwork in order and put you on the list for discharge, but you should be on your way in a couple of hours."

Faulkner stuck his hand out for the doctor to shake. "Thanks for everything, Doc. I mean it."

"You're welcome." He shook Faulkner's hand then turned back to Cheyenne.

"You're a very lucky lady, Cheyenne. You have quite the champion here. He wouldn't leave your side and insisted on overseeing the removal of all that tape. I wouldn't let him slip out of your grasp."

Cheyenne looked up at Faulkner and smiled. "No way, he's mine and I'm not letting him go."

* * *

CHEYENNE WAS DOZING on the bed, waiting for the doctor to come back and give them the all clear. She was ready to get out of there.

She heard Faulkner say, "What the hell?" and she opened her eyes to see her mom and sister walk into her room.

"No, hell no. You aren't staying."

"Uh, we're here to see my daughter," Cheyenne's mom said hesitantly.

"No you're not, you're here to upset her," Faulkner retorted.

"Cheyenne, really. Who is this?" Karen sneered. "He obviously doesn't have any manners. Should I call security to have him removed, Mother?"

Before Faulkner could say anything, Cheyenne spoke up. "Please, Karen, by all means, call security, but it'll be to remove the two of you and not Faulkner."

"Really Cheyenne, seriously. We've talked about this, you have to stop being a drama queen."

"Why are you here?" Cheyenne asked, trying to scoot up in the bed.

Faulkner leaned over and helped her into a sitting position, Cheyenne spared him a quick smile in thanks before turning her attention back to her family.

"We're here because you're family," her mom said, somehow sounding bored.

"Are you?" Cheyenne heard Faulkner growl from beside her. She put her hand on his and squeezed. She was thankful he was there, but she had to handle this herself.

"Of course we are! She's my daughter and Karen's sister."

The silence in the room grew awkward. Cheyenne refused to break it. If they were here for a reason, they'd get to it soon enough.

"We saw on the news that you were kidnapped again."

Cheyenne waited for her sister to get to the point.

"Seriously, it seems like your job is obviously putting you in danger, if you'd just find something a lot less dangerous, this wouldn't keep happening to you."

Cheyenne squeezed Faulkner's hand as hard as she could. She could feel every muscle in his body tense at her sister's words.

"How exactly is it my fault I got attacked when I was grocery shopping, Karen? And how exactly is it my fault that the 'poor family,' as you called them, if I recall correctly, felt the need to avenge their brothers and come after me? My job had nothing to do with this. I sit in a room and answer a telephone. That's it."

"But, Cheyenne, look at your sister," her mom spoke up, obviously once again supporting Karen and not bothering to think about how much her words could hurt her other daughter. "She works for the justice system, she helps put bad guys behind bars, you just answer a phone."

"Mom, she doesn't put bad guys behind bars, the lawyers do. She answers phones and does all the dirty work for the lawyers who do the real work. How is her job any different from mine?"

"I'm fucking done with this," Dude couldn't keep quiet anymore. "Your daughter doesn't 'just answer phones,' she is the lifeline for people who call needing help. Sometimes she's the only thing between someone living and dying. She walks people through first aid, she gives comfort, she helps bring the police and paramedics to people who need it. She's on the front lines every day working her ass off with no thanks and no rewards for it. There's no 'just' about anything Cheyenne does. I'm fucking proud of her for what she does, but that's not the fucking point here. As her *family*, you should've been at her side last night when she was brought in. You should be proud of her because she's your flesh and blood, not because of what she does for a living. You should be ashamed of yourselves."

Dude heard both women gasp, but he continued.

"Cheyenne also told me she disowned you both because of the way you acted the last time you saw her. That means she's done with you. *Done*. If she decides she wants to give you another chance, that's up to her. Not you. She probably will, because she's a big softy, but I'll tell you this right now, if you ever disparage her again, you'll never have another chance to talk to her. I'll bar you from her life. I won't allow her to be talked down to and I won't allow you to hurt her any more than you already have. So leave. Both of you. Think about what you're losing. If you don't care, that's on you, not Cheyenne."

Cheyenne watched as Karen's lips tightened. "Come on, Mother, if Cheyenne wants to hang out with this low-life, let her."

Her mom took another look at Cheyenne and turned to follow her daughter out of the room without a word.

Dude put his thumb against Cheyenne's chin and turned her face toward him. He looked into her eyes for a moment then sighed. "I'm sorry, Shy. Not sorry I told them off, but sorry you had to deal with that today of all days. Don't listen to a word they say. You're amazing. What you do is amazing. I'm crazy about every inch of you."

"Thank you, Faulkner. I'm glad you were here."

"You didn't need me here, you held your own just fine, but I'm glad I was here too."

Putting her so-called family behind her once and for all, Cheyenne knew they wouldn't change. She'd lived her entire life trying to please them and hadn't gotten anywhere. She'd probably cry about it later, in Faulkner's arms, but for now she was over it.

"Can you check with the doctor and see how much longer it'll be until we can leave?"

"Of course. I'll be right back."

"I'm okay. Really."

"I know you are, Shy. I love you."

Cheyenne smiled as Faulkner opened the door and checked the hallway for any sign of her family. Obviously not seeing them, he smiled back at her then closed the door behind him.

Cheyenne snuggled down into the bed, sliding her butt back down until she was lying flat again, and closed her eyes. Maybe she'd just take a short nap while she wanted for Faulkner to get back and get her out of here.

* * *

CHEYENNE SETTLED into the seat of Faulkner's truck with a sigh. She was so glad to get out of the hospital it wasn't funny. They'd exited through the back exit because, unfortunately, the media had camped out at the front doors. The entire story of her re-kidnapping and the subsequent bomb threat to her, as well as to an entire city block, was huge news. Not to mention the fact that the abductors were related to the men who'd done the same thing a few months back.

Cheyenne knew Faulkner wouldn't let them get anywhere near her, and it allowed her to relax. He'd take care of her.

"Are you up to a short stop on the way home, Shy?"

Cheyenne looked over at Faulkner. He looked rumpled and tired, but she'd stop wherever he needed to with no questions. It didn't matter that she was wearing another pair of borrowed scrubs and desperately wanted a shower. If Faulkner wanted to stop somewhere, she was okay with it.

"Of course. Stop wherever you need to. I'm fine."

Dude leaned over and tagged Shy behind the neck and drew her to him gently, careful not to jostle her shoulder. "You *are* fine. And thank you."

He let her go and started the truck. "I need to tell you something before we get home. You'll find out soon enough, but I wanted to give you some warning."

"What?" Cheyenne asked suspiciously.

"You're moving in with me."

"What? Faulkner! You can't ask that already, it's too soon!"

"I'm not asking, Shy. Remember? You told me that when we were in the basement of that damn building. I don't ask. I tell."

"Well, yeah, I kinda remember that, but Faulkner, this is soon."

"It is, but you love me. I love you. I'll never love anyone else. I'll never let you love anyone else. So you're moving in. We might as well start the rest of our life now. We've missed enough time together. I'm not letting you spend another damn night in anyone's bed but mine."

Cheyenne felt her insides melt. She pressed her lips together and tried not to cry. "I never thought I'd be here."

"Where?"

"Here. With you. In a relationship where I'd feel comfortable enough to let someone make these kinds of decision for me. Where I didn't have to worry about having a bad day at work, knowing I'd have someone who'd listen to me and comfort me. Where I didn't have to compete for affection. Where I didn't have to justify my actions to someone. I never thought I'd be this happy, Faulkner."

"I can't promise it'll all be sunshine and roses, Shy."

"I never asked for that. I'm not an idiot. I work weird hours. You're in the military. You're a SEAL. I know you'll be sent off to do something I can't ask about and will never know about. But you know what? You'll come back to me. I couldn't have lived through...hell, *we* couldn't have lived through what we did to have it taken from us now. When you have to go, I'll cry, I'll pout, I'll be sad. But I'll hang out with the girls. We'll drink too much in the safety of someone's house, I'll go to work, I'll continue on until you come home. Then you'll boss me around, deny me orgasms, then give them to me over and over again until you're satisfied. Then you'll fuck me until we're both noodles, then we'll do it all again. And I'll love every second of it."

Dude smiled over at Cheyenne. "I love you."

"I'm not done."

"Sorry, Shy, by all means, continue."

Cheyenne smiled at her man. Fuck she loved him. "I figured something out. And once I did, I got it."

"What'd you figure out?"

"I figured out that when and if you get mad at me it's not because you're necessarily *mad* at me. It's because you're worried about me." She paused a fraction then continued. "And I know you told me this, but I didn't *really* get it. That day on the beach, when I was scared to call you because I was afraid you'd be mad...it's because my sister would get mad at me. She'd get furious and scream at me. She scared me and that's what I understood anger to be. But then I saw it with Fiona and Hunter. We went to a movie and she forgot to text him.

When she did finally get in touch with him, he yelled and ranted and raved, but through it all, Fiona was stoic. She wasn't afraid of him. When he was done he hugged her so hard I thought her ribs would break.

"He was worried about her. He was mad because he thought she'd had a flashback. He didn't know where she was and he thought she could be in trouble. I got it. So I don't want you to ever be afraid to yell at me. I know you won't hurt me, and I know you're mad because you care about me, because you're worried. I get it now."

Dude had to pull the truck over. Jesus. He pulled into a parking lot of a business that was right off the road. He put the truck in gear and opened his door. He strode around until he got to the passenger side. He opened the door and immediately leaned in, resting both hands on the seat next to Cheyenne.

"Shy, I swear to God, you have to stop doing this to me when I'm driving." Dude smiled at her then moved so his hands on her thighs. "I love you. I love you so much it scares the living hell out of me. I worry about you all the time. All the fucking time. You could be in the other room and I worry if you're okay. Are you hungry? Cold? Happy? Sad? Content? I have a feeling you're going to see me 'mad' a lot. I'm thrilled to pieces you told me, but know that I'm going to do everything I can to not yell at you or get mad. I don't want you to lose your independence. Hell, I love that about you, but you have to promise to keep me updated about where you are and when you might be getting home.

"Text me, call me, leave me a note, whatever it takes, just tell me. You want to go out for lunch? No problem. Text me. You want to go shopping with the girls? Great. Spend all the fucking money you want, but tell me that's where you'll be. If you're stopping to get gas before coming home? Let me know. Because I swear if you're two minutes late I'm going to worry. I'm not being controlling, I'm not being an asshole. I'm *worrying* about you. I can't handle you being taken out from under my nose again. I swear I can't. If I don't know where you are for five minutes I'm likely to call the team and track your ass down."

Cheyenne put her good hand on Faulkner's cheek. "I promise."

"Oh and you should probably know, you and all the other girls will have fucking tracking devices on just about everything you own."

"What?"

"Yeah, we worked with Tex and he's ordering them and will set up the software."

"Uh, that's a bit over the top, Faulkner."

"No, it isn't. Caroline was taken by an FBI traitor and hauled out into the middle of the ocean so they could dispose of her body. Alabama was living on the fucking streets and no one could find her. Fiona was taken into a foreign fucking country and about to be sold as a sex slave and Summer was kidnapped by a murderous, bastard, pedophile rapist. And you, you had three fucking goddamn bombs strapped to you and were hidden in the basement of an apartment building. It's not over the fucking top at all."

"You're swearing a lot, Faulkner."

Dude just shook his head and dropped it to his chest and closed his eyes for a moment, trying to get himself back under control. Figures that instead of bitching about the fact he'd just ordered tracking devices so he'd be able to find her no matter what she was wearing, carrying, or where she was going, Cheyenne concentrated on his language.

Dude lifted his head up again and leaned in to kiss her. He took Cheyenne's lips in a hard, deep kiss then drew back and smiled. "I can't place it."

"Pomegranate."

Dude shook his head again and ran his tongue over his lips. "Delicious."

He kissed Cheyenne on the forehead then backed up and closed her door. He jogged back around to his side and jumped in. "Okay, we're going to be late, I'll just blame you and your penchant for wearing flavored lip crap."

"Okay," Cheyenne agreed with a smile, not knowing what they were going to be late for, but not caring either.

Dude drove until they pulled into a familiar parking lot. Cheyenne beamed at him.

"Are you serious?"

"I figured since you bitched so much about not getting to finish your girl's night out, that there was no time like the present. Although, you'll have to deal with it being a friend's night out instead. Everyone's inside waiting on us."

"Thank you, Faulkner. I love you."

"I love you too, Shy. But don't think I've forgotten about you not saying the words until we were in a life and death situation. I owe you for that."

"I'm sure you'll make me pay...tonight."

"Damn straight I will. When we get home I'll help you remove your clothes and get you situated on our bed. I can't tie your arms, but I'll tie your legs until you're spread eagled and can't close them. You'll not touch me and not move an inch while I take my fill of you. You won't be allowed to come until I say, and Shy, I'm pissed you made me wait to hear you say it."

Cheyenne smiled, his words said he was pissed, but the carnal look in his eyes said otherwise.

"Then I'll take you hard, while you're still tied, and see how many times I can make you explode before I fill you up."

Cheyenne's ears rang and she could feel her own harsh breathing.

"Do we have to go inside?"

"Yes. And you'll not drink anything alcoholic. You still probably have some morphine in your system and I won't chance it. You can have orange juice, but no soda, your body needs nutrients, not crap right now."

"Okay, Faulkner."

"When I say it's time to go, we're going. Don't argue with me. I know you're probably more tired than you're letting on. And your shoulder probably hurts too. That over-the-counter painkiller probably isn't cutting it. But I wanted to give you this, Shy. I'll give you anything and everything you want if it's in my power."

"Okay, Faulkner."

"I love you, Shy."

"I love you too."

"Okay, let's do this so we can go and welcome you to your new home."

"Our new home."

"Yeah, *our* new home."

EPILOGUE

The large group of friends sat at the table at *Aces*. Cheyenne, Summer, and Alabama had insisted on coming back to the bar at the first opportunity. Their men, of course, wanted to boycott the place altogether and never set foot in it again, but the women put their foot down.

"I won't allow those jerks to run us out of the best bar in town. We love this place." Summer had argued with Mozart until she was blue in the face, and he, as well as Dude and Abe had still refused.

They'd only given in when the women made plans to go back on their own. Of course that made all the men change their minds in a heartbeat. They wouldn't let them go back without them.

The moment Cheyenne stepped inside *Aces*, she'd frozen, but Faulkner was right there at her back. He put his arms around her and pulled back into his hard body. They'd stood in the middle of the entrance, not moving. Faulkner leaned down and whispered in her ear. Cheyenne could feel the breath from his words tickling her ear.

"You can do this, Shy. You're not alone. You just stand here as long as you need to. I'm here."

His words gave Cheyenne the strength to take a deep breath. She intertwined her fingers with Faulkner's, rubbing her thumb over the stubs of his fingers for a second, then she turned in his arms and laid her head on his chest, wrapping her arms as far around his back as she could without hurting her shoulder.

"Thank you, Faulkner. I love you."

"I love you too, Shy. Come on, let's get a drink."

After that, entering *Aces* became easier. It had gotten to a point where Cheyenne and the other women would meet up at the little bar at least once a week. Sometimes they'd be by themselves and other times they'd go with their men.

The men also still went there to unwind as well, with their women's blessing. Typically they'd have a women's night in and a men's night out at the same time. The men could go out and have a beer or two, and the women would hole up in Caroline's house and do whatever it was that women did when they got together.

Three months had gone by since the women had been kidnapped and for once, everything had been quiet. The team had left twice on missions, but they were short and they hadn't been out of the country for more than four days for each one.

The team sat around the table nursing their beers and Cookie laughed when he caught Dude looking at his watch for the third time in the last twenty minutes.

"Suck it up, Dude, seriously, you can go one night without ordering Cheyenne to service you." Cookie said the words softly, for Dude's ears only, wanting to tease him, but not wanting to share his secret.

"Shut it, Cookie, I warned you not to spread that shit around. I know you heard what Cheyenne said in that basement, but that stays between the three of us."

"Don't worry, Dude, I might tease you about it, but I'd never break your, or her, confidence that way."

Dude just snorted. Cheyenne had left for her shift that afternoon and he'd taken her hard that morning. She was always willing to do whatever he wanted to try, and that morning he'd gotten creative. Dude had blindfolded her, tied her hands behind her back, and played with her back passage for the first time before taking her hard. Dude loved that Cheyenne trusted him enough to try things she wasn't sure about. Their lovemaking that morning took the ultimate trust, and Cheyenne had not only tolerated him making love to her in a new way, but if her moans were any indication, she'd enjoyed it and wanted more.

The waitress, Jess, limped up to the table and put another round of beers on the table. She turned to leave without her usual friendly conversation.

Benny grabbed a hold of her upper arm as she turned to go. "Hey, Jess, how've you been? Haven't see you around lately."

Benny, and the other men frowned at the grimace that came over the waitress's face. Benny quickly let go of her arm and she stepped back a foot and glanced at the men around the table then back down to the tray she was holding in her hands.

"Uh, yeah, I've had some stuff going on at home."

"Everything okay?" Benny asked, not liking how she'd flinched from him. He wasn't the biggest man around the table, but he wasn't exactly small. He knew he could be scary, but Jess *knew* him. She knew all of them. She'd been serving them all for a while now.

"Yeah." Her tone was flat, and while not unfriendly, it wasn't inviting further conversation, which was unusual for her.

Benny watched as she glanced around the room furtively and then simply turned away from the table and limped with her funny little gait, back to the bar.

"That wasn't normal," Dude commented unnecessarily.

"No shit." Benny returned, his eyes not leaving the waitress as she gathered another set of drinks from the bar.

Dude watched as Benny took a deep breath and turned back to the group. They could tell he didn't want to let the odd encounter with the waitress go, but he did anyway. The conversation turned back to their normal friendly chatter until finally Benny was the first to call it a night.

"I know you guys all have women to get back to, and I should be the last one to leave, but I'm just not in the mood anymore. Say hey to all your women for me. I'll see you at PT."

Dude and the rest of the team watched their friend leave. They were worried about him. Benny was now the odd-man out. The only man on the team that didn't have a woman to worry about, to love. They couldn't lose him. They might pick on him, but Benny was an important part of their team. No one wanted to see him put in transfer paperwork to another SEAL team.

After Benny left, the rest of the guys decided they might as well call it a night too. They all had women waiting for them. Dude's thoughts turned back to Cheyenne. He looked at his watch. Perfect. Eleven. She'd switched to first shift and didn't have to work through the evening anymore. After work that afternoon she'd gone over to Caroline's house for dinner and to visit for a few hours.

Even though she'd been visiting with her friends, Dude had told her to leave around a quarter to eleven and head back to their house. He planned it so she'd arrive home just before he would, and he'd told her just how to be waiting for him. She always followed his instructions to the letter. He had a bag in the truck waiting with new toys he'd picked out just for her. Dude couldn't wait. He was the luckiest bastard alive.

Find out what happens in Benny's story

Protecting Jessyka

PROTECTING JESSYKA

SEAL OF PROTECTION, BOOK 6

Kason "Benny" Sawyer was the last single man on his Navy SEAL team. He loved his teammates like brothers and respected each and every one of their women. They'd all been through hell and they deserved their current happiness. But seeing the love between his friends and their women made it tough to be the odd man out all the time.

Jessyka Allen had a good life, until it wasn't anymore. Finding herself in an impossible situation, with no noticeable way out, her job was an escape. Working at the small Bar and Grill put her in contact with some wonderful people, who Jess figured couldn't ever understand what she was going through.

Being a SEAL, Benny thought he knew the true meaning of teamwork and friendship. But Jess would show him that everything he *thought* he knew about sacrifice, trust, and love, paled in comparison to what she brought into his world.

**Protecting Jessyka is the 6th book in the SEAL of Protection Series. It can be read as a stand-alone, but it's recommended you read the books in order to get maximum enjoyment out of the series.

To receive special offers, bonus content, and news about my latest books, sign up for my newsletter:

www.StokerAces.com/contact.html

NOTE FROM THE AUTHOR

After the first few SEAL of Protection books came out, I started to get questions from readers if "Jess," from *Aces Bar and Grill*, was going to get a story. I always smiled, proud that the little teasers of Jessyka I'd put in the other books had done their job . . . made readers interested in her story.

I wanted to have a heroine who was disabled, but it didn't faze her. She didn't talk about it, it didn't slow her down . . . it was just a part of who she was and a normal part of her life.

I've seen comments from readers who complained that each story in the series was the "same". I've tried really hard to make them different, but I *am* a fan of the damsel in distress . . . and while most of my heroines are tough women in their own right, they all need a hand in the end.

With that in mind, I tried to make Jess's story a *bit* different. I hope you'll see what I mean when you read it.

Thank you all for your support of the SEALs. From the messages I've received online, to the support from readers at book signings, to the day in and day out encouragement from my PA, Amy—thank you.

As long as you, the reader, keeps on enjoying my stories, I'll keep writing them.

Enjoy Jessyka and Benny's story.

CHAPTER 1

Benny pushed away the plate of microwaved food sitting in front of him at his little table in his kitchen. He loved to cook, was quite good at it even, but he had no desire to whip up a grand meal for one.

Ever since his SEAL teammates, and friends, had found the loves of their lives, they'd spent less and less time together. It wasn't as if Benny begrudged his friends finding a woman to love and protect. He loved Ice, Alabama, Fiona, Summer, and Cheyenne as if they were his own sisters. He'd fight and die for them, simply because they loved his friends. But now he could see what was missing in his own life.

Benny had seriously considered asking for a transfer to another SEAL team. He knew it would rip his guts out to do it, but he didn't know how much longer he could go seeing what his friends had, and knowing it was out of his own reach.

He took a long drink from the glass of water he'd poured to go with his crappy dinner and thought back to the last time they'd all gotten together at *Aces Bar and Grill*. It was a small bar, but was always clean and was relatively peaceful. It was, admittedly, a pick up bar, that's how they found it in the first place. But since they'd been eating and drinking there for a while, it now felt more like home.

Benny knew he and his friends turned heads wherever they went. They used to go to the bar to hook up with women, but as each team member found the woman meant just for them, their reason for meeting up there changed. Now they enjoyed the atmosphere and the camaraderie they shared. But they were SEAL members. They were muscular men, who women seemed to find attractive.

Benny was the youngest on the team. He was six feet tall with short brown hair. Women in the past had told him he had unique eyes, the color of molten chocolate. Benny didn't know about that, he'd always thought they were just plain brown.

Over the time Benny and his teammates had been going to *Aces*, they'd gotten to know the names of the servers and bartenders, and everyone in return, knew who their team was as well. Unfortunately, it was also the place where Cheyenne, Summer, and Alabama had been snatched right out from under Mozart's nose while the girls were there for a night out. Luckily it ended all right and no one was seriously hurt or killed.

Last week the entire team had gotten together for dinner, drinks, and conversation to try to push out the bad memories of what had happened there. Benny knew if it had been up to his friends, they never would've stepped foot in the place again, but the ladies, being the strong stubborn women they were, had insisted. They'd laughed, and the women had even shed a tear or two, but in the end, it had been the right decision to go back.

But something was bothering Benny about their visit. He couldn't get the look on Jess's face out of his head. Their usual waitress had limped up to their table, with the little lopsided gait she had, and when he had gently taken hold of her arm to keep her from leaving right away, she'd grimaced.

Every man around the table had taken notice, and hadn't liked it. It didn't take a genius to see it had hurt when Benny had taken hold of her arm, and he hadn't grabbed her, hadn't squeezed, had just stopped her from leaving. Now that Benny thought about it, Jess hadn't been acting the same. When they'd first met her she'd been bubbly and easy-going, always laughing and joking with all of them.

But last week, she'd been quiet and kept her eyes downcast. The long-sleeved shirts were new too. In fact, the more Benny thought about her, the more worried he got. Whoever was abusing her was smart. He was keeping his hands off her face, where the abuse would be the most obvious. If Jess had come in with a black eye or a split lip, none of the guys would have hesitated to say something.

But if he was leaving bruises or hitting her on her body where her clothes hid the marks, no one could be certain. Benny didn't like the thought of Jess being hurt though. He knew that for sure.

He hadn't really thought about Jess in *that* way . . . until now. She'd just always been there. She was a part of the bar experience. She was a good waitress, always refilling their drinks, always laughing with them, but giving them room when they needed it.

When the girls had been kidnapped from the bar, Benny knew Jess had immediately huddled with Fiona and Caroline to keep them calm. She'd taken them into a back office and stayed with them until the team thought it was safe for them to leave.

Thinking back, Benny suddenly felt bad. They'd taken advantage of her hospitality and nurturing nature. They'd taken their women away, but left Jess there without a thought to *her* safety.

Benny just couldn't reconcile how good Jess had been with the team's women and how caring she was, with someone who'd stay with a man who abused her. There had to be a reason, but Benny couldn't think of what it might be.

He pushed up from his kitchen table, suddenly on a mission. He couldn't go another moment without checking on Jess. He had a bad feeling in his gut, and a SEAL never dismissed those feelings.

Jess was probably fine. She was most likely at the bar and she'd call out a greeting, just as she always did, when he walked in.

Mind set, Benny grabbed his keys from the basket by the door and was headed to his car before he'd really made a conscious decision to move.

As his forgotten microwave dinner sat congealing on the counter, Benny pulled out of the parking lot of his apartment complex.

I'll just go and grab a burger, it's not like I'm really checking on her. I'm hungry. If she's there, great, I'll assuage my curiosity and then come back home. I'm sure she's fine. I'm just overreacting.

CHAPTER 2

Jessyka Allen sighed. Her week had sucked. Actually the last month had sucked. She sighed again. Shit. Her *life* sucked. She had no idea how she'd gotten to where she was . . . stuck, with not many options open to her. She never thought she'd be the type of person who'd stay with someone who hurt her, but here she was.

It was always so easy to say, "The first time someone hit me, I'd be gone," but in real life it turned out it was much easier to say than to do.

Jess had grown up in a suburb of Los Angeles. Her parents weren't rich, but they weren't poor either. She was able to get the clothes she wanted and she had good friends in high school. She wasn't the most popular girl in school, but she also wasn't an outcast either.

Jessyka had been born prematurely, and as a result, one leg was shorter than the other. She didn't have any big dramatic story to tell about it, but it meant she limped, she'd always limped. She was teased growing up about it, but Jess had learned to mostly ignore people when they were rude.

There were times when her legs hurt, mostly because she had to overuse the muscles on her right leg to compensate for the shorter length of her left. Her parents had wanted her to try shoes with a lift on them, but Jess had hated them. They were mostly ugly and it was obvious the left shoe had a much larger sole on it than the right. So she limped.

She met Brian her junior year and they'd been friends throughout high school. It wasn't until they had graduated and taken classes at the local community college together that they'd started dating. Brian was fun and Jess had enjoyed spending time with him. After dating for a few years, it was obvious they weren't going to ever get married or have a future together. Brian had a temper, and Jess was completely laid back. She refused to fight back with him when he did turn on her, and that usually made him even angrier.

After they'd stopped being boyfriend and girlfriend, their relationship improved. Brian seemed to settle down and didn't seem as angry.

When Jess's parents moved across the country and she needed a place to live, Brian offered to let her move into the extra bedroom in his townhouse. Jess agreed on the spot. It had seemed to be the perfect arrangement.

It seemed even better when Jess met Tabitha. Tabitha was Brian's niece. His sister lived in a townhouse in the same complex as they did. Tabitha was ten when they'd met and Jess loved her on sight. She was a chubby kid, but had the biggest heart. Brian's sister, Tammy, was a mess though. She was a single mother and worked all the time. When she wasn't working, she still wasn't around much, so Jess became like Tabitha's second mother.

Tabitha was an unusually sensitive child though. She took everything to heart. Jess had seen Tabitha cry her eyes out when she'd seen a dead feral cat on the road next to the apartment complex one day. Jess had tried to console her, but Tabitha stayed in a funk for at least a week after that.

Brian didn't have any patience for his niece. He told Jess she was a baby and a whiner and would never get anywhere in the world.

Over the last four years, Brian had turned his harsh words onto Tabitha too. He didn't care who he put her down in front of, and he started haranguing Jessyka as well. It had gotten to a point where Jess knew Tabitha was depressed. She'd tried to talk to Tammy about it, but Tammy had blown her off and told her to mind her own business.

In the last couple of months, Brian had started to lash out at Jess again. It had started with words, but had quickly escalated to shoving, pushing, and, finally, hitting. Jess never knew what would set him off. He was completely unstable. One minute he'd be laughing and the next he'd be in her face screaming at her, telling her what a crippled loser she was.

Jess knew she had to get out, but she'd gotten complacent. Being a waitress didn't bring in that much money, and she knew she didn't have enough to move out on her own just yet. She could probably fly to Florida and live with her parents for a while, but she didn't want to leave Tabitha. The girl was fourteen and something wasn't right.

Jessyka worried about her all the time. Tabitha was withdrawn and sad. Jess spent as much time as she could with her and tried to cheer her up. It was hard though, because after the last time Jess had tried to talk with Tammy about her daughter, Tammy had told Tabitha Jess wasn't welcome in their apartment anymore.

So now Tabitha had to either come over to her apartment, and risk having Brian be there and messing with her head, or they'd have to go out. If they went out, Jess had to spend money on lunch, ice cream, or whatever. Money she should be saving to get her own place. It was a vicious circle, but Jess knew she couldn't abandon Tabitha. She loved her and Tabitha needed her. So she stayed.

Jess figured she could take it. It wasn't as if Brian was *really* hurting her. She could take the bruises. It was no big deal.

But deep down, she knew it *was* a big deal. Jess worked in a bar. She'd seen it time and time again with the patrons. She'd seen how the violence escalated. Jess felt stuck. She wanted to go, but knew leaving would mean bad things for Tabitha. She just didn't know what to do anymore. It felt like she had the world on her shoulders.

Jess rolled her head to try to release some tension and winced. Damn. She'd forgotten about her shoulder. Brian had wrenched it that afternoon before she'd left to go to work. Jess had been visiting

Tabitha and had come back into the apartment with just enough time to change before having to leave for work.

"Where have you been?" Brian had inquired nastily.

"Visiting with Tabitha." Jess kept her voice flat, knowing if she threw any attitude, Brian would make her pay for it.

"I don't know why you bother. She's fat. She'll always be fat. She's stupid too. Tammy tells me all the time what a moron she is and how embarrassed she is by her."

"She's not stupid, Brian. I've read some of the stories she's written. She's actually very talented and I know she's going to be a famous author someday."

"What the hell do you know, crip? You're just as stupid as she is. Working as a damn waitress in a fucking bar. What a loser. You know everyone just makes fun of you behind your back don't you? I've seen them. You limp around the bar and everyone just laughs and bets on if you'll drop a tray or not."

Jess stared at Brian, not believing the words that were coming out of his mouth. How had they gotten to this point? What had she done for him to have such horrible feelings about her? They used to be friends.

Misunderstanding her look, Brian continued. "Surprised, crip? Yeah, they all laugh at you, especially the military guys. I bet you have fantasies about them doing you? Well, give it up. They only like the beautiful, perfect ladies."

Brian's words struck her hard, just as he'd meant them to.

"What's happened to us, Brian?" Jess couldn't help the words, she'd been thinking them and with his harsh words, they just popped out. "We used to be friends."

"Friends don't sponge off one another," he immediately returned. "I've been working my ass off for that construction company, and you bring home pennies and pretend you're putting in your fair share. Jesus, Jess, I can't believe you haven't already figured this out."

"But, Brian . . ." Jessyka started, not surprised when he interrupted her.

"No, Jess, you're pathetic." He came toward her and Jess took a step back.

"You limp around all day, you dress in drab shit clothes, and you expect everyone to love you." Brian grabbed her upper arm and squeezed, trying to make his point.

"I work my ass off and you coddle my niece. My sister hates you, you just don't see it. Fuck, I don't know why I put up with you."

Without warning, Brian lifted the hand that wasn't holding her and put it around her neck. He backed them up until she hit the wall behind them.

Jess drew in a quick breath and brought both hands up to grasp Brian's wrist.

"Brian, please . . ."

He squeezed her throat. "No, I'm done with this shit. You have until the end of the month and I want you out. Seriously. You have nine fucking days."

Jess just looked up at Brian. It didn't even look like the Brian she knew. His face was contorted with an irrational anger she'd never seen before. She opened her mouth to speak, to tell him whatever he needed to hear to placate him, but he tightened his grip on her neck.

Shit. He wasn't letting go. Jess's hands clawed at Brian's hand around her throat and wiggled, trying to make him lose his grip.

Finally, with a smirk, he let go. Before Jess could catch her breath and get away from him, he'd wrenched the arm he still had in his grasp, spun her around, and held it up against her back.

"I'm serious, crip. Nine days. Got it?"

Jess could only nod frantically and try to block out the pain of Brian wrenching her arm at an unnatural angle. She swallowed painfully, and prayed he'd let go of her.

When he did, Jess didn't even look back, just fled up the stairs to her room. She'd slammed the door and locked it behind her. Not that the flimsy lock would keep Brian out if he really wanted in, but it made her feel marginally better.

Now Jess was at work. She had to figure out what she was going to do. She didn't want to go back to the townhouse, even for the nine days Brian had given her, but she had nowhere else to go. None. She also didn't want to leave Tabitha. Somehow she knew the girl was only hanging in there because of her. Jess knew if she said it out loud to anyone, it'd sound conceited, but she knew, deep down inside, if Tabitha thought Jess had abandoned her, she'd break.

Jess picked up the heavy tray and tried not to wince. She had no idea what she was going to do, but she had to get through her shift first. Then she'd think about it.

* * *

BENNY PULLED into the parking lot of *Aces* and turned off his engine. He had no idea what he was really doing, but something in the back of his mind wouldn't let him let this go. Something was wrong, and he liked Jess. He didn't really know her, but he liked her nonetheless.

He pocketed his keys as he walked to the front door of the bar. Entering, it took a moment for Benny's eyes to adjust to the darkness. It was later than he'd been there in a long time. Usually the team and their women came around dinner time and ended up leaving around ten or so. At eleven, the bar was busy and the lights had been dimmed.

Benny looked around and didn't see Jess. He made his way to the bar and sat on a stool on the end so he could see the entire room. He ordered a draft beer and took his time nursing it. Ignoring the looks the two women across the room were giving him, he wasn't there to pick up a woman, he kept his eyes peeled for Jess.

Finally he saw her. Jess was his age, probably late twenties or early thirties. She had pale skin, which somehow made her look more fragile than she was. She was shorter than his six feet by a few inches. She was curvy, and as Benny noticed for the first time tonight, she filled out her clothes in a way which was sexy as hell.

She was struggling to hold on to a tray filled with empty bottles and glasses and make her way across the crowded bar. Benny stood up and went toward her.

It looked to Benny that Jess was limping more than usual. He had no idea why she limped, he only knew that she always had. They'd all noticed it the first time they'd met her at the bar, and when Wolf had commented on it, she'd given him a death stare. No one had asked about it again. She was entitled to her secrets, and besides, it was kinda rude for Wolf to have asked in the first place.

He reached Jess just as she got bumped by someone behind her. She would've gone flying, but Benny grabbed the tray with one hand and her waist with the other. He spun them in a move that would've gotten them high points if it was being scored, and saved her, and the tray, from sprawling on the floor.

"Thanks," Jess breathed, thankful she wasn't sitting in the middle of the grimy floor surrounded by broken glass.

"You're welcome."

The voice was low and strangely familiar.

Jess looked up. Wow, it was one of the SEALs. She wasn't sure of his name. She'd heard all of their names more than once, but it was confusing as hell because sometimes she heard their nicknames and other times their real names. She couldn't keep them all straight.

The man continued to hold her to him, finally she shifted, trying to break his hold. He held on for another beat then finally let her go, brushing his hand along her hip in the process.

Jess held back a shiver. "I'll take that." She gestured toward the tray he was holding up. Some of the bottles had fallen over, but nothing was broken.

"Lead the way, Jess, I've got it."

Jessyka stared at him for a beat. "You know my name?"

"Yeah, I've only been eating here with my friends for an eon now and you're always our server. I know your name."

Jess blushed. Shit. Of course he knew who she was. She shook her head and tried to play it off. "Just checking. Come on." She turned her back on him and led him back to the busy bar. When they got there he finally allowed her to take the tray out of his hands and she placed it on the bar.

Turning back she said, "Thanks again, that would've sucked to have spilled all those bottles." Looking around she asked, "Where are your friends?"

Jess knew this guy was always here with the other SEALs. She'd watched them with a bit of jealously over the last few months. Most of the men were now either married or in a serious relationship. Jessyka had watched how they treated their woman. It was a mixture of tolerance and protectiveness with a bit of caveman thrown in. But it wasn't over-the-top. It looked delicious. If Jessyka had a man who looked at her like those men looked at their women, she didn't think she'd ever give him up.

"Don't know."

"What?"

The man smiled at her as if he knew she had slipped into a daydream for a moment. "I said, I don't know where my friends are. They're probably all at home with their women."

"Then why are you here?" Jess paused, then blushed. "Oh, never mind. Sorry. Yeah, why does any single man come to the bar? I'll just . . ." Her embarrassed words were cut short.

"I'm not here to pick up a woman, Jess. I'm here to check on you."

"Me?" Jess just looked at him incredulously.

"Yeah, you. I'm worried about you."

"Uh, I don't mean to be rude, but you don't even know me."

"Jess, remember what I said earlier in this conversation. I've been coming here for a while now. I know your personality has changed over the last few months. I know while you always limp, it's gotten worse. I know that the last time I saw you, I touched your arm and you flinched. I know you used to wear cute little tank tops and short sleeves, now you're wearing a damn turtleneck. This is Southern California and I can't remember the last time I've even seen someone wearing a fucking turtleneck. I'm a Navy SEAL, gorgeous, I've been trained to be observant. Maybe someone else wouldn't notice, but I have. I don't like it when women grimace when I touch them. I don't like knowing *why* they might do that. So I'm here because I'm worried about you."

Jess just stared at the handsome man standing next to her, baffled. As usual, her mouth opened before her brain could stop it. "I don't even know your name."

He smiled and shook his head. "Will you ever stop surprising me?" It was obviously a rhetorical question, because he continued without letting her answer. "I'm Kason. Kason Sawyer."

"Is that your real name or nickname?"

"Real name."

After a beat, Jess asked, "Are you going to tell me your nickname? I know you all have them."

"No. I don't like it, but I earned it fair and square. The guys call me by my nickname, but you won't."

"But . . ."

"Are you all right?"

"Kason . . ."

"Don't lie to me, Jess."

"Jessyka!"

She turned to see the bartender gesturing at her then to the drinks he'd lined up at the waitress station.

"I gotta go."

"When do you get off tonight?"

Jess stared at Kason for a moment. It wasn't that she didn't trust him. Hell, if she couldn't trust a Navy SEAL, she couldn't trust anyone. She was just still confused about why he was there. Jess didn't actually believe it was because he was worried about her. Yeah, he probably did notice all those things about her, but he didn't know her. So he couldn't *really* be worried about her.

"Two."

"I'll wait."

"Kason . . ."

"I said, I'll wait."

Jess looked at him for a beat, then turned abruptly and headed for the drinks she had to deliver. She didn't have time to worry about Kason. He'd get tired of whatever game he was playing and bolt. She had more important things to worry about. Namely, where the hell she was going to live and how she was going to come up with enough money to find a place of her own in nine days.

CHAPTER 3

Benny watched as Jess worked the rest of her shift. Focusing one hundred percent of his attention on her, he could see she was definitely not the same person as he'd met when they first started coming to the bar. Oh, she was still efficient and good at what she did, but she was different.

She used to touch people all the time. She'd lay a hand on their arm, or she'd touch their hand briefly when they handed her money. She used to laugh more and flirt more. She didn't smile as much and she didn't flirt at all.

She was completely focused on the job at hand . . . getting drinks to patrons and collecting money. The more Benny thought about it, the more he was bothered by her clothes as well. All waitresses knew in order to increase tips, it was good to wear clothes that showed a little skin. Benny couldn't see any skin on Jess except for her face and hands.

Benny knew Jess was uncomfortable with him being there, but he didn't let it stop him. He joked with the bartender and rebuffed every woman who approached him. He was here for Jess, nothing else. He wasn't even tempted by any of the ladies that came on to him. In the past, he probably would've jumped at the chance to spend a sexually charged night with any of the women that were there, but not tonight. He was completely focused on Jess.

Benny watched as two o'clock came and Jess cashed out. She shoved her tips into the front pocket of her jeans and disappeared down the hall where the office was. She came back a moment later with her purse over her shoulder and headed for the door, without looking around for him.

Benny quickly followed her and gave a chin lift to the bouncer. "I've got it. I'll make sure she's safe."

The bouncer nodded, he knew Benny, had seen him around and knew he was a SEAL.

Benny came up next to Jess as she walked into the parking lot. "Can I take you home?"

Jess stopped in the middle of the lot and turned to Kason. "Why are you following me?"

"We've already been over this, but I can rehash it if you need me to."

Jess shook her head impatiently, at the end of her rope. "Look, Kason, I've had a bad week. Hell, a bad month, and I don't need you fucking with me. I've seen your friends. I'm too young for all of you. I don't do one-night stands. I'm not looking for a military guy. I'm broke, crippled, and too tired to deal with whatever it is you want out of me tonight. So just back off and let me go. Okay?"

As if he didn't hear a word she said, Kason simply said, "Let me take you home."

Jess sighed and looked down at the ground. She looked back at the bar then turned to Kason. "I usually take the bus."

"Please."

"Fuck. All right, Kason. You can take me home."

Benny took Jess's elbow in his and steered her the other way to his car. He clicked the locks as they were walking up and opened the door for her. He waited until she was seated before closing the door and walking around to the other side. Still without a word, he started the engine and pulled out of the lot.

"Where to?"

Jess startled. Duh, of course he didn't know where she lived. "I live in the Pinehurst townhouses over on Sunshine Way. Do you know them?" Jess watched as he nodded.

"Put your head back and close your eyes, gorgeous. Relax. I got this."

Jess blew out a half laugh and did as Kason said. It wasn't because he ordered it, it was because she was exhausted. She hurt. She was tired. She was stressed. The small break to let down her guard was unexpected, but appreciated.

Jess felt the car slow after a while, then stop. She opened her eyes and started in surprise. They weren't at her place.

"Where the hell are we?" She demanded.

Benny turned in his seat so he was facing Jess. He'd driven to a local park that he knew wasn't too seedy, and parked the car. He was going to talk to her whether she wanted to or not.

"I know we don't really know each other, but you need a friend, Jess, and I'm it. I'm not fucking with you. You aren't too young for me. Hell, we're probably only like five years apart in age. I'm not looking for a one-night stand with you, I don't give a damn how much money you have and you aren't fucking crippled. If I hear you say that about yourself one more time, I'm gonna take you over my knee. And you'll never be too tired to let me be a sympathetic ear for you. That's what I want. Now talk."

Jess just looked at Kason for a beat, thinking back to what she'd said to him in the parking lot of the bar. "Did you really just address every single thing I said earlier? How did you remember all of it?"

"Jess, focus."

"I *am* focused, Kason!" Jess exclaimed. "Seriously! That was impressive."

"Did you hear what I said?"

Jess nodded and rubbed her temples. "Yeah. I'm sorry. I was being honest when I said I'd had a bad day. I'm sorry for being a bitch."

"You aren't a bitch."

"I can be."

"I have no doubt." Jess watched as Kason chuckled. "All of my friend's women can be. It's not a big deal. But I meant what I said earlier tonight. I'm worried about you. Talk to me. Please?"

"I don't know what you want me to say. I feel awkward." Jess picked at a thread hanging off the bottom of her shirt. "I'm not in the habit of spilling all my problems to people I don't know."

"I'm Kason. I'm a Navy SEAL. I've been in the Navy for about ten years. I love my friends. I'd give my life for any one of them and the same goes for their women. I love to cook and I'm good at it. I can pick a lock faster than anyone else on my team. I hate my nickname, but the guys won't change it. It's an inside joke between us now. Hell, if they *did* let me change it, I probably wouldn't. My favorite color is brown. I'd love to own a piece of land someday where I could go days without seeing anyone. Most of the time I don't like people, they're rude and conceited and self-absorbed. I've seen more shit in my lifetime than any person has a right to. I love dogs and hope to have at least four when I get my piece of land somewhere. I'll always be a bit rough around the edges, but if I ever find a woman who can put up with me, I'll put her first in all things in my life. I've seen how my teammates are with their women and I want what they have. I'm the odd man out on my SEAL team right now and I hate it. I've been thinking about transferring, but haven't told any of them yet."

He stopped talking and Jess just stared at him. Finally she whispered, "Why did you tell me all that?"

"I want to get to know you, Jess. I'm spilling my guts to you in the hopes it'll make you feel less awkward and so you'll talk to me about what the hell is going on with you."

Jess licked her lips and picked at her thumbnail. She thought about what Kason had said. He really had shared some pretty personal stuff with her.

"Jess," Benny said taking hold of one of her hands so she had to stop picking at her fingernail. "Look at me."

When she did, Benny continued. "I consider us friends. We've known each other for a while now. We might not be the type of friends to go and get a manicure together and spend all day shopping, but I've seen you around enough to know when something is different. Let me help. Or at least let it out. It'll help. I promise."

Jess sighed. She loved the feel of her hand in his, but knew she couldn't get used to it. She decided to copy him, but start with the easy stuff first.

"My name is Jessyka . . . spelled y-k-a, not i-c-a. I think my parents were drunk when they filled out the birth certificate." She smiled so he'd know she was kidding. "I grew up around LA and my parents are now living the high life in Florida. I like the color pink and I love dogs, especially hounds. I want a basset hound, a bloodhound, and a coonhound when I can get a place of my own. I'm currently a waitress and I make crap money at it, but interestingly enough, I like it. I meet lots of neat people." She smiled at Kason, but stopped talking. Now for the hard stuff.

"It's my roommate."

Benny sighed in relief. Thank God, she was talking to him about what was really bothering her. He loved hearing more about Jess and her life, but he wanted to know more about what was going on with her. Hopefully he'd have time to get more into the easy stuff later. "What about her?"

"Not her, him."

Benny tensed. A guy? She was living with a guy? He knew there was a guy involved somehow, but she was living with him? Fuck. "Go on. What about him?"

"Long story short, we met in high school, started dating while we were taking classes. After we graduated, we stopped dating, but were friends. I moved in with him because I needed a place to stay and he didn't seem to care. We're . . . having issues now."

"Why the hell would he want to stop dating you?"

"Huh?" Jess couldn't figure out how Kason's mind worked. He never said what she was expecting him to.

"Why weren't you dating? What the hell is wrong with him?"

"Nothing, I guess. We just didn't have a spark anymore."

"Moron."

Jess wasn't sure she heard Kason's mumbled word right, but she continued on without asking him to repeat it. "So anyway, we're having issues and I need to move out. But I'm worried about his niece. She's . . . vulnerable, and I'm afraid if I move out she'll do something rash."

"Does she live there too?"

"No, but she lives in the same complex and I see her all the time. She spends all her time, when she isn't at school and I'm not at work, with me."

Kason squeezed her hand. "I know you're leaving some important chunks out here, gorgeous, because I'm not seeing the problem so far." He brought his other hand over and ran his index fingers over the material of her shirt at her throat. "But I'm guessing part of it is whatever you're hiding under this."

Jess jerked back away from his touch, afraid he'd pull down her turtleneck.

"Easy, Jess," Benny murmured, drawing back and giving her some space.

"It's . . ."

"Don't tell me it's nothing," Kason growled out, not sounding like the easy going man she'd been talking to for the last fifteen minutes. Jess thought it was almost scary how he could change so quickly.

"And don't flinch away from me. Fuck." He put both hands on the steering wheel and leaned his forehead against his hands for a moment before turning his head, leaving his head resting on his hands, and looked at her.

"We were on a mission once. I can't tell you where and I can't tell you why, but suffice to say it was in a country that didn't have the kind of women's rights we have here in the United States. I've never been so disgusted in all my life watching the women over there get beaten, kicked, and berated openly. No one cared. No one stood up for them. Kids were married off at age twelve to men four times their age. You never, *ever* have to worry about me physically hurting you. I know you probably don't believe me, but dammit, Jess. Try."

Jessyka took a deep breath. "I know it Kason. I do. It's just . . ."

"I know what it's just," Kason reassured her. "What can I do to help you?"

"What do you mean?"

"I mean, I'm your friend. What can I do to help you? Do you need help moving? Do you want me to get the girls to meet with your friend so she has some other good role models to look up to? Do you need money? Want me to beat up your roommate? Tell me what you need."

"You want to help me?"

"Jesus, Jess," Benny teased. "Pay attention! Yes, I want to help you."

"I-I don't know."

"Okay, well, why don't we start with exchanging phone numbers? That way when you figure it out, you can let me know." Benny didn't push, even though he wanted to.

"Uh, okay. Yeah. I'd like that." The more Jess thought about it, the more she *did* like it. She needed time to think about Kason and his offer of friendship and help.

They exchanged numbers and there was silence in the cab as they punched in each other's contact information. Jess startled when her phone vibrated with a new text. She smiled seeing it was from Kason, and looked up at him.

"Figured I'd make sure you didn't give me a pizza delivery boy's number."

Jess just shook her head and looked down at the text he'd sent.

I'm always just a text away.

She looked up at Kason, not knowing what to say.

"I know we didn't really solve anything, but I hope you know I'm one hundred percent serious when I say I want to be your friend, Jess. You aren't alone and if you need anything, just call me. I'll be pissed if you don't. I sure as hell don't want you going back to your place with that fucker there, but you don't know me well enough yet to let me put you up somewhere. Use my number if you need it. Please."

"I have no idea why you want to be my friend, but thank you. It's been a long time since I've felt like I've had one."

Having the urge, and not resisting, Benny reached out a hand and slowly caressed Jessyka's face. Then he slid his hand around until it was resting on the back of her neck and he drew her gently and awkwardly in the small space of the car toward him. He leaned over and kissed her forehead and then rested his head against hers.

"Trust me, Jess."

Benny felt her nod slightly. He leaned back, squeezed her neck reassuredly, then let go.

"How about we get you home? It's late, you're tired, and I've got to get up in about an hour and a half for PT."

"Okay."

When Benny pulled up to the townhouse Jess said she lived in, he put the car in park and said, "Stay."

He then walked around the car and opened the door for her. Jess just shook her head and climbed out. Kason walked her all the way to the front door, even though she'd insisted she was fine. He leaned in and once again kissed her on the forehead. "I'll see you later. Be safe."

Jess nodded and when Kason pulled back said, "Thank you."

"You're welcome. Don't be a stranger. I expect you to text."

"Okay."

"Okay."

"Bye, gorgeous."

"Bye, Kason."

Jessyka opened the door and cautiously entered the townhouse. The last thing she wanted was for Brian to be there waiting up for her. He wasn't. The place was quiet. Jess quickly headed up the stairs to her room and sighed in relief when she was in her room with the door locked.

She hated being scared of Brian, but she could still feel his fingers wrapped around her neck. He'd been pissed, and she hadn't even done anything. She knew nine days was too long. She had to do something sooner than that.

The phone Jess had been clutching in her hand vibrated. She looked down and smiled.

Sleep well. Talk to you later.

She didn't know how the hell she'd gotten lucky enough to have

Kason decide he wanted to be her friend, but she certainly wasn't going to complain. It seemed like the only good thing that had happened to her in the last year.

Nite. ltr.

She expected that to be the end of it, but her phone vibrated again soon after she'd hit send.

You're one of those people who write in text speak aren't you?

Jess couldn't help the small laugh that escaped her mouth. She couldn't remember the last time she'd laughed out loud.

Appntly so. Don't txt & drve

I'm at a stop light. Good night, gorgeous.

Gd nite

Jess turned off her phone with a smile. Maybe tomorrow, well today, would be a better day. It certainly started out all right.

CHAPTER 4

Benny couldn't stop thinking about Jessyka. It'd been days since he'd seen or talked to her, with the exception of the few texts they'd exchanged. They had all been initiated by him, but she'd always responded, which made Benny feel a little bit better.

He hadn't had a chance to get back to the bar, but he also didn't want to seem like a stalker. Benny trusted Jess would get a hold of him if she needed to. He couldn't force her.

The bottom line was that Benny liked her. He couldn't say he really knew her all that well, but he hadn't lied when he'd told her that he liked what he'd seen so far.

Benny had a conversation with Dude about Jess the night before. He'd gone to his house to have dinner with him and Cheyenne. It seemed like the guys were "passing him around" like a lost puppy. Each week someone new would ask if he wanted to come over for dinner. Benny never refused, first because he liked his friends and their women, and second because it kinda sucked sitting at home alone.

Benny supposed he could go out and find a woman to bring home for the night, but he didn't really have the urge, especially since his little chat with Jessyka.

After dinner and a movie, Cheyenne had gone up to bed, and Dude had asked Benny how he was doing. Benny took the chance to bring up Jess.

"Remember the waitress at the bar the night we all went out last?"

"Yeah, Jess, right?"

"Yeah. We all saw the shape she was in that night. I couldn't get her out of my mind. I mean, I feel like I know her, with how much time we spend in that damn place. I think we've only been served by someone different a few times."

Dude had nodded. "Yeah, she looked a bit rough. Didn't like the way she flinched when you touched her."

"Yeah, me either. I went to the bar the other night and she looked even worse."

"In what way?"

"She was wearing a fucking turtleneck."

"Are you shitting me?"

"No."

"What'd she say about it?"

"Well, nothing about that specifically, but she's got some stuff going on and she's stressed out about it. She lives with some guy she used to date. Apparently he's kicking her out."

"Sounds like that's probably for the best."

"Yeah, but I still don't like it. I gave her my number, but shit, Dude, I'm still worried about her."

"Want to call Tex to do some recon?"

"Yeah, but I won't."

"Why the hell not? I would. You know I've got Cheyenne monitored 24/7. I won't allow some asshole to take her again."

"I still can't believe you guys got all the women to agree to that shit."

"You don't understand."

Benny nodded. "You're right. I don't, not really. But just because I don't have a woman of my own doesn't mean I don't understand wanting to keep them safe."

"I didn't mean . . ."

"Yeah, it's okay. I know what you meant. I like Jessyka, Dude. I don't really know her that well, but I'm concerned about her. I don't like that she's living with a guy. I really don't like that she's living with a guy who has given her a deadline to get out of the townhouse they share. I don't like that she feels like she has to stay for his niece who has some self-esteem issues. I don't like that he probably grabbed her and hurt her. And I really don't like that she doesn't have the money to move out."

"What are you doing about it?"

"I don't know."

"Can I give you some advice?"

"Please do. I wouldn't have brought all this shit up if I didn't want your advice, Dude."

"Don't give her space. It sounds like she needs help. If she's as independent as Cheyenne and the other women, she won't reach out. She'll keep on trying to do it all herself. Don't give her a choice."

"What if she gets pissed?"

"Who the fuck cares. She gets pissed, she gets pissed. Then she'll get over it. If it's the right thing to do, and she needs the help, give it to her. Eventually she'll thank you for it."

Benny thought about that for a moment. "You're right."

"Of course I am, Benny-boy."

Benny just rolled his eyes at his friend. "Thanks, man."

"You're welcome. Now go home. My woman is upstairs, and if she's being good, she's doing what I told her to and she's waiting for me just as I asked."

"Jesus, Dude, I don't need to hear this."

Dude just smiled.

"I'm out of here. When you let Cheyenne up for air, thank her for dinner for me."

"Will do."

Now, Benny thought back to the conversation with his friend and knew he had to get on it. He didn't want to wait anymore. He wanted to know how Jess was doing and if she wasn't going to call him, he'd have to go to her.

He stirred the spaghetti sauce on the stove and tested the noodles. They were almost done. Pasta was an easy meal to make for one, and Benny usually had leftovers. He always made the sauce from scratch, there was nothing worse than the bottled crap in the store.

Hearing his phone vibrate, Benny looked over. It was a text from Jess. He smiled and picked up the phone.

I need you.

Benny's muscled clenched immediately. The three words looked so stark on his phone screen. He didn't even hesitate.

Where are you?

Sittig at entrnce to apartmnts

On my way

Benny took the time to turn off the burners, but that was about it. He quickly stuffed his phone in his pocket and headed for the door. He was in his car and headed for Jess's place about thirty seconds after he'd hit the *y* on his last text.

Knowing it was dangerous, but not caring at the moment, he texted Jess back while he drove to her.

Are you ok?

He waited impatiently for her response.

No

Fuck.

Do you need a doctor?

Maybe

Benny pressed his foot down on the gas. Double fuck.

Are you safe where you are?

I think so

Get somewhere where you know you're safe

I don't know where that is anymore

Call me

Fuck the texting thing. Benny needed to hear her voice. His phone rang and Benny put it on speaker as he answered.

"Jess?"

"Yeah, it's me."

Her voice sounded low and scratchy.

"I'm on my way. It'll probably take me another ten minutes. Will you be okay? Should I call an ambulance?"

"No."

"You're scaring the shit out of me, gorgeous. Talk to me."

"Tabitha's gone."

"What do you mean? Who's Tabitha?" Benny didn't like the monotone sound of Jessyka's voice. It sounded like she was in shock.

"She killed herself."

Benny pushed the car a little faster. He was going way over the speed limit, but Jess needed him and he wasn't there.

"Jess . . ."

"I told her yesterday I was leaving and she killed herself."

It came to Benny suddenly who Tabitha was. Shit. "Why aren't you inside?"

Benny had to figure out what was going on.

"Brian was mad."

Fuck. He knew what was going on now. "Okay, gorgeous. Stay put. I'm coming for you all right? Just hunker down there and I'll be there in a second."

"He . . ."

"Shhhh," Benny interrupted. He didn't want Jess to relive anything else until he was there with her. "I'll be there in a moment. You can tell me everything when I'm there with you. Just hang on."

"I'm so tired, Kason. You said you were my friend right? I need a friend."

"I'm your friend, Jess. You can rest as soon as I get there. I'll take care of you."

"Okay."

"Go ahead and hang up, Jess, I'm a block away, I'll be there before you know it."

"Okay," she repeated in the same eerie monotone voice she'd been using.

The connection was cut.

Benny clenched his fists around the steering wheel until his fingers turned white. Jesus fuck this was messed up. He felt like he only had snippets of the story, but what he had was bad enough.

He got close to the turn off into Jess's complex when he saw her. She was sitting on the curb, her hands wrapped around her knees and she was leaning over staring at the ground. She didn't move, even when the headlights from his car shone on her. Benny slammed the gearshift into park and got out. He approached Jessyka carefully so as not to startle her.

"Jess?"

Her head whipped up at the sound of his voice and she looked ready to bolt. When she saw it was him she sagged and sighed, "Kason."

Benny didn't hesitate, but went over to her and sat next to her. What he really wanted to do was pick her up and hold her, but until he knew what was wrong and where, and if she was hurt, he couldn't.

Jess's face was tearstained and blotchy from crying. The shirt she was wearing was torn at the neck and was hanging off one shoulder. Benny could see her bra strap highlighted against her shoulder. He couldn't see much more of her than that, but the ripped shirt was enough to make him want to kill someone.

Benny put his hand on the back of Jess's head and held it gingerly. "Where do you hurt, gorgeous?"

"Everywhere."

"I need you to be more specific, Jess. What happened and where did he hurt you?"

Ignoring the first part of his question, she answered the second. "It hurts to breathe. Brian punched me in the stomach. My back hurts because he pushed me and I fell into the corner of the coffee table. My leg hurts because it always hurts when I've pushed it too far. My face hurts because he slapped me a few times and my neck still hurts from the other night." She paused a moment and then said softly, "And my toe hurts because I stubbed it walking over here to sit and text you."

Benny couldn't help but smile at that last part. There was absolutely nothing to smile about, but Jess was so earnest about her poor toe.

"Do you think you can walk to my car?"

Jess looked over at the still-running car sitting about four feet from where they were sitting and said, with a hint of her old spunk, "I think I can manage it."

Benny didn't even smile. "Okay, then up you go. I need to get you out of here." He helped Jess stand up and steadied her when she wobbled. Benny put an arm around her waist and took most of her weight as she hobbled unsteadily to his car. Even though it was only a few feet to the car door, Benny wasn't convinced Jess *could've* made it by herself.

He shut the door and jogged around to the driver's side. Benny had a million questions for her, but he wanted to get her out of there first.

Before he left, Benny leaned over Jessyka and grabbed hold of the seat belt and buckled her in. She hadn't moved since he'd helped her sit, and it was really worrying him.

"Hang in there, Jess."

He watched as she nodded.

Benny tried not to peel out of the parking lot, but he heard the tires squeal as he did a U-turn and turned right toward the emergency room. He wasn't going to take any chances. Jess looked like crap and he didn't like the distant look in her eyes. She said she hurt everywhere, well the doctors could make sure that nothing was broken and that she wasn't bleeding internally. She hadn't said she was assaulted, but maybe she was embarrassed and ashamed about that. Maybe she didn't feel like she knew him well enough to admit it. Just the *thought* of her being hurt that way made his adrenaline spike.

Benny pulled up to the emergency doors and reached over and gently put his hand on Jess's cheek. "We're here."

Her eyes had been closed the entire time they'd been driving, and now she turned her head to look to see where "here" was. Benny watched as her face blanched. "No, please. I don't want to."

"I'll be right here. You have to, Jess. You know it."

She was silent for a moment and when she didn't protest further, Benny knew she was hurting more than just a little bit. He wanted to kill Brian. He didn't know what he looked like, or even where he was at the moment, but he didn't want to kill anyone as badly in his life, as he did Brian right now.

"Come on, gorgeous, let's get you inside."

Benny helped Jess out of the car and when she faltered with her first step, he simply picked her up. He felt something inside him melt when she wrapped her arms around his neck and rested her head on his shoulder.

Benny strode up to the reception desk. "We need a doctor."

"What's the problem, Sir?" The woman managed to sound business-like and bored at the same time. Benny ground his teeth together.

"The problem is that my friend has had the shit beaten out of her. She's in pain and she needs to be checked out to make sure nothing's fucking broken inside and she isn't going to die of internal bleeding or anything."

Taken aback for a moment, the lady stared at Benny.

Benny felt Jess's hand curl around the back of his neck to try to calm him, and the goose bumps that followed her movement shot all the way down to his toes. That had never happened to him before . . . and to happen now, in this situation, was almost unbelievable. He tightened his hold on her and held her a little closer.

"Okay, Sir, if you would just follow me down the hall we'll get her settled and a nurse will be in to examine her as soon as possible."

Benny ground his teeth together at her obviously fake polite tone and held Jess tightly as he followed the receptionist down the hall.

He placed Jess on the bed carefully then went to sit in the chair next to it.

The receptionist made a tsking noise and said, "Sorry, Sir, only relatives are allowed to be back here with the patient. You'll have to wait out in the waiting room."

"Oh hell no," Benny said impatiently. "I'm staying." He sat in the chair and reached over to grasp Jess's hand. He kissed the back of it and ignored the sputterings of the woman still trying to get him to leave.

When she finally left, Jess turned to Benny and said with the first hint of a smile he'd seen since he'd found her earlier that night. "You're going to get in trouble."

"I don't care. I'm not leaving."

Five minutes later, a nurse pulled back the curtain and a security guard was standing next to her.

"Sir, you'll have to step out into the waiting area while we take a look at your friend," the nurse explained.

"No."

"Sir . . ."

Benny broke into her explanation and looked at both her and the security guard as he spoke. "I got a text from my friend, Jess, tonight," he gestured at Jessyka on the bed with his chin and continued. "She said she needed me. She has no immediate family in the area. The girl she loves like a sister killed herself today. Her roommate and ex-boyfriend beat the crap out of her, as you can see. She's in pain and frightened, and she called *me*. I'm a Navy SEAL and I can protect her. I'm not leaving her side. I'll plug my ears and sing a song if there's medical shit you don't want me to hear. I'll do whatever it is you want me to do . . . except leave."

His voice lowered as he pleaded with the strangers to let him stay. "Please. She needs me."

And she did. They could all see it. Jess's hand was gripping his tightly and she looked between Benny and the security guard apprehensively.

"Ma'am? Do you want him to stay?"

Benny knew they had to ask, but it still pissed him off. He knew they probably thought he was the one who beat her up, but he didn't care. He wasn't leaving, no matter what they thought.

Jessyka obviously knew what they were thinking too. "Yes. God, please, let him stay. I feel safer with him here. If he's here I know Brian can't get to me. Please . . ."

The nurse glared at Benny. "Okay, but if you cause any problems I'll kick you out so fast you won't know what hit you. Navy SEAL or not."

Benny could only nod jerkily. They were letting him stay. He immediately dismissed the nurse and looked back at Jess. "You're damn right he won't touch you while I'm here. Just relax. They'll make it so you don't hurt anymore and then I'll get you out of here. Hang in there for me."

Benny sat with Jess, while the nurse, then the doctor, examined her. He moved when they told him to, but he never lost touch with Jess. Benny kept a hand on her head, then her arm, then her foot, then back to her head. Wherever the doctor wasn't examining, Benny was there, touching her, reassuring her that she wasn't alone.

Now that they were in the light, Benny got a good look at Jess's neck for the first time. It took all he had not to stalk out of the room and hunt Brian down. She had bruises on her neck in the shape of fingers. The bastard had choked her. It was obvious they were a few days old, so it hadn't been done tonight. No wonder she'd been wearing a turtleneck when he saw her last.

Benny took some deep breaths and tried to stay in the moment. He couldn't go off half-cocked when Jess needed him.

When the doctor was done with the exam, Benny sat in the chair he'd originally been sitting in and took hold of Jess's hand again.

"It looks like nothing is seriously wrong. You were lucky, Jess," the doctor said gently. "Your face will probably bruise and you'll most likely have a black eye. I don't feel any broken ribs or anything. That spot on your back will be painful for a while, but I'll get you some pain killers and if you take it easy for the next couple of days, you'll be able to be up and around with no issues."

"She needs to speak with the police before she goes," Benny told the doctor.

Benny thought Jess might protest his words, but she merely nodded as if she'd already resigned herself to the inevitable.

"Okay, I'll be back with the Sergeant and those pain killers I promised. Just relax."

There was silence in the room for a moment after the doctor left. Benny raised the hand that wasn't clutching hers and brushed it lightly over her forehead. Then her cheek. Then her shoulder. Finally, he brushed each bruise on her neck with the back of his hand.

"I wouldn't have let you go back there if I'd known."

Jess obviously was on the same wavelength as he was because she responded, "I know."

"I hate he did this to you."

"I know."

"You're not going back there."

"I know."

Benny smiled for the first time that night. "Is that the only thing you're going to say?"

"Maybe."

He got serious again. "I meant what I said tonight. Brian won't touch you again."

Benny didn't hear her response because a police sergeant entered the little room. For the next thirty minutes Jess rehashed what had happened that night.

Finally when she was done, the cop asked her, "Can I talk to you for a moment alone?"

Benny knew what that meant. Like any good cop, he wanted to make sure Benny didn't have anything to do with what had happened and that it wasn't actually *him* that had beaten Jess up.

Benny saw Jess was about to protest. Needing a moment to get himself together after all he'd heard, Benny stood up and leaned over Jess. He kissed her on the forehead and said softly, but not so softly that the police officer couldn't hear him. "I'll be right outside, gorgeous. No one's getting past me. Okay? Finish up here and we'll leave." He leaned up and met her eyes confidently. Whatever Jess saw in his eyes obviously was enough, because she nodded and said softly, "Okay."

Benny nodded at the officer as he left the room. Doing just as he told Jess he would, he leaned against the wall outside her room and waited. He closed his eyes, hearing her words echo in his mind. He knew he'd never forget them.

"He told me it was my fault."

"He punched me in the stomach and told me I was ugly."

"He wouldn't let go of my throat even though I was gouging my fingernails into his wrist."

"He kicked my hip saying that it wouldn't matter since I was already a cripple."

Benny clenched his teeth and pulled out his phone and clicked on Wolf's number.

"Hey, Benny."

"Wolf, I have a situation, I need a couple days leave."

Wolf's voice changed from laidback to serious in an instant. "Of course. I'll clear it with the Commander. Anything we can do?"

"Maybe. I'll keep you up to date. Remember Jess, the black haired waitress from the bar?"

"Of course."

"She called me tonight. I'm at the hospital with her and will be taking her back to my place. I know Ice and the others will want to . . . just give me a couple days before you set them loose on us . . . okay?"

"Of course. Anything we can do on our side?"

"Yeah, get with Tex on a Brian Thompson." Benny gave Wolf his address. "He beat the shit out of Jess tonight, and apparently has been doing it for a while. He has a sister. Her kid killed herself today."

"Fuck, Benny. Are you sure you don't need us over there?"

"Thanks, man, but I got it. Cops were here tonight, but I don't need that asswipe getting any ideas and deciding to try to get revenge or to try and find Jess."

"We'll take care of it for you. Just call if you need anything else."

"I will. And, Wolf? Thanks."

"Anytime. It's what a team is for."

Benny hung up feeling a bit better, but still way too jacked up. Jess's words still echoing in his brain. *"He kicked me"* . . . *"He punched me"* . . . *"He wouldn't let go of my throat"* . . .

Jess was a hell of a woman, and he knew a lot of strong women. Benny knew Jess wouldn't think that way about herself, but he had to make her see it.

The police officer stuck his head out the door, and seeing Benny standing there, told him he was finished talking with Jessyka. Benny nodded and went back to Jess's side.

After another ten minutes, they were on their way home. The doctor had come in and given Jessyka some pain killers along with a prescription for more if she needed them and a few more warnings to take it easy.

Jess had insisted on walking out on her own, but Benny was right by her side the entire way. They slowly made their way to the waiting area, where Benny, seeing she was fading, plunked her in a chair and ordered in a gentle voice, "Wait here."

Benny knew Jess was still in pain when she didn't argue with him, but only sat where he'd indicated.

He rushed out and got the car he'd had to move earlier, and went back inside to collect Jess. She was sitting on the chair clutching the sides so hard her knuckles were bone white.

"Come on, gorgeous. Let's get out of here."

Benny bent down and gathered Jess into his arms, and he sighed, pleased when she didn't protest.

He strode out of the hospital with Jess in his arms. He settled her into the passenger seat and headed for his apartment.

"What hotel are you taking me to?" Benny heard Jess ask groggily from beside him.

He whipped his head around to look at her incredulously. "You're not going to a fucking hotel. You're coming home with me."

"But, Kason, that's not fair."

"Did you not hear me in the hospital when I said I wasn't leaving your side?"

"Kason, you can't stay with me all the time. I knew you just meant while we were there. And I appreciate it, I do, but this is crazy. You don't know me."

"I wish you'd fucking stop saying that. I know you Jessyka, with a y-k-a, Allen. I know I can't keep you by my side 24/7. It's not practical for either of us. But for the next couple of days I can. We'll talk through what happened with you. We'll talk about Tabitha. You'll cry and let me hold you while you do it and my team will make sure Brian knows he's never to contact you again. Once that's done, we'll figure out what to do about your living situation. But for now you're coming back to my apartment and I don't want to hear anything else about it."

Benny took a deep breath and looked quickly at Jess to see what affect his words had on her. Incredibly she was smiling.

"What are you smiling at?"

"Thank you, Kason. I had no idea where I was going to go tonight. So thank you for taking that burden from me for the moment."

"You're welcome. Now shut your eyes and relax."

"I've heard that before."

"Yeah, well this time when you open them we'll be at my house instead of a park."

Jessyka did as Kason asked, and was asleep within moments.

CHAPTER 5

Jess came awake slowly. She turned her head and opened her eyes only to see Kason watching her from the driver's seat of the car.

"Oh, are we here?"

"Yeah."

When he didn't say anything else, Jess asked, "Are we going in?"

"Yeah. You just looked so peaceful and relaxed, I didn't want to wake you up." Kason lifted a hand and brushed Jess's hair behind her ear. "Stay put. I'll come around."

Jess could only nod. Kason had a weird look in his eyes. She couldn't really place it, but it looked an awful lot like tenderness. Jess couldn't remember the last time someone had looked at her like that. She liked it a lot.

Kason opened the door for Jess and held her elbow as she got out of the car. He leaned in and grabbed her purse and helped her to his apartment. It was on the lower floor and he had the door opened and her shuttled inside before she could really get a good look around the complex.

"I thought living on the first floor was more dangerous than living on an upper floor?" Jess asked, blurting out her thoughts without really thinking about them. She watched as Kason smiled at her.

"For a single woman? Yeah, it is. For me? Not so much. Besides, I'm not really comfortable living in a building with other people. I don't know what they're doing and if they burn the place down, I want to be able to get out without having to jump off a balcony or something."

"I hadn't thought of that."

Kason laughed and encouraged Jess to keep walking into his apartment with a hand on her lower back, careful to keep away from the large bruise on her back from where she'd been pushed against the coffee table earlier that night.

Jess looked around. Kason's apartment was nothing special. She hated to even think it, but it was true. The walls were white and he had, of course, a giant TV attached to the wall. There was a huge sectional couch with a beat up coffee table sitting in front of it. The kitchen was behind the couch. It was pretty typical for an apartment. Fridge, four burner stove, microwave, dishwasher and a small bar-type counter with two stools. Jess could see two pans sitting on the stove. One had water and noodles in it and the other was filled with some sort of red sauce.

She turned to Kason. "I interrupted your dinner? I'm so sorry!"

"Not a big deal, Jess."

"No, really. I'm sorry."

Kason had gotten Jess to the sectional and he helped her ease down into it. He'd placed her in the middle of one of the sides and after she'd sat down, he picked her feet up and swung them on the cushions.

Without a word he unlaced both shoes and put them on the floor, under the coffee table, out of the way. Benny grabbed a throw pillow from the side of the couch and helped arrange it under Jess's head. Once he was done, Benny leaned in and put his hands on either side of her. His voice was low and controlled.

"I don't give a fuck about dinner. I can re-make dinner. I can't re-make you, Jess. So yeah, if you text me and say you need me, I don't care what I'm doing, I'll always drop it and come to you." He paused, as if he was letting his words sink in. "Got it?"

Jess could only nod. She wasn't sure she *did* get it, but it was obvious Kason had strong feelings on the subject, so she let it go.

"Are you hungry?"

Jess shook her head.

"Are you in pain? Can I get you anything?"

Jess shook her head again.

"Okay, get comfortable. I'll be right back."

Jess watched as Kason stood up and headed down a hallway off of the living room. She closed her eyes, trying desperately to stay in the moment and not let her mind go back to what had happened that night.

Kason was back a couple of minutes later. He was now dressed in a pair of badly cut off sweat pants and a T-shirt that looked like it had been in its prime about twenty years ago. His feet were bare and his hair was mussed, as if he'd run his fingers through it a few times. He was carrying two pillows and a fuzzy blanket. He put them on top of the coffee table and went into the kitchen, still without a word.

Jess heard the faucet running and the refrigerator opening. Kason came back around the couch and she could see he was carrying two glasses of water. He put them on the coffee table as well. Then he turned and looked down at her as if trying to decide where to sit. Finally he went to her head and gently lifted the pillow so he could sit down. Then he propped the pillow on his leg and gently eased Jess's head back down. Benny's hand came to rest on her forehead and stayed there. Every now and then his thumb would move in a small caress over her hairline, but otherwise he was still.

When he didn't say anything, Jess looked up at him. Kason had his head tipped back so it was resting on the back of the couch with his eyes closed.

"Kason?"

"Yeah, Jess?"

"Are you okay?"

His head came up and he looked down at her. "Yeah. I'm okay. I'm just so relieved you're here and that bastard didn't hurt you any worse than he did. I'm trying to come up with a way to have you talk to me about what happened where you don't have to re-live it all, but I'm not having any luck."

Jess closed her eyes at Benny's words and said in a small voice, "Do I have to talk about it?"

"Yeah, I think you do. Jess, look at me."

Jess took a deep breath and opened her eyes. Kason was leaning over her now, one hand had moved to her cheek and just laid there, the other he put on her stomach.

"I've been there, gorgeous. Not exactly where you are, but I've been captured while on a mission. We were . . . asked . . . to give up information . . . but we wouldn't. I had a cousin who killed himself too. Cookie's woman lived through Hell after being kidnapped by sex traffickers down in Mexico . . . and she had a breakdown because she didn't talk about it with anyone.

"I've been there, Jess. I know how important it is to talk it out. I'm probably not the best person you can talk to, but I'm here now and I'm your friend. Talk to me. Tell me what happened. Get it out. Then tomorrow in the light of day, we can start to figure out where to go from here. But for now, here tonight, let me have it. I'm your friend, Jess. Give it to me."

Jess scrunched her eyes closed. "I-I . . ."

Before she could finish her sentence, even though she didn't really know what she was going to say, Kason was moving. He stood up and encouraged Jess to sit up as well. He sat on the other side of her, then lay down so his back was to the back of the couch. He pulled Jess down until she was lying in front of him. Her back to his stomach. He curled one arm around her waist and pulled her back until she was completely surrounded by him.

"Am I hurting you?"

"No," Jess whispered back, even though every time she moved she *did* hurt. She closed her eyes again. She curled her arms up until they were in front of her and her hands were resting under her cheek. She could feel every inch of Kason behind her. His legs were bent, as were hers, and they were touching from her feet to her head. The warmth of his body seeped into hers as if he was her own personal electric blanket. She hadn't realized until that moment how cold she'd been. She shivered.

Kason leaned over her and snagged the blanket from the coffee table. He awkwardly spread it over their bodies, carefully tucking it in around Jess so that every inch of her body was covered. He lay back down and Jess felt his lips on the top of her head.

Jess could feel Kason waiting. "I don't know where to start," she told him honestly. So much was running through her head she didn't know how to tell him anything.

"Take your time. I'm not going anywhere. Start wherever seems right."

After a few moments, Jess started.

"I met Tabitha when she was ten. She was overweight and sad. I could see the sadness right away. But she was so smart. She could write stories that made me cry. At ten, Kason. She was that good. Her mom worked two jobs, so she was never home. Brian . . . well, he wasn't much of an uncle. I tried to make up for it. I'd take her places, we'd go exploring. We'd laugh, we'd have a good time. Every time when I dropped her off back at her place, she'd be happy. Then the next time I'd see her, I'd have to cheer her up all over again. This happened over and over. All the time. As she got older she retreated into herself even more. I tried to help. I tried to talk to Tammy about it, but she just got mad at me. I tried to talk to Brian, but he told me he didn't care. That Tabitha was fat and ugly and I might as well not bother."

Jess took a breath and felt Kason's hand rubbing up and down the side of her body. It was rhythmic and soothing. He hadn't interrupted her to ask questions, he was just listening. It felt good.

"It was earlier this year that Brian started getting physical with me. I always knew he had a temper, but after we broke up and were just friends, he seemed to have a handle on it. That's why I moved in. He was more like the fun-loving guy I knew in high school. I don't know what happened. Something *had* to have happened. It was like a switch went off in him. One day he was laughing with me over me spilling something in the kitchen and the next day he was grabbing my arm and flinging me across the kitchen telling me I was a worthless cripple."

"Drugs."

"What?"

"Drugs. It's the only thing I can think of that would make his personality change so drastically like that," Benny said in a low confident voice.

Jess thought about it. Kason was probably right. She didn't know who Brian was hanging out with at the construction site, but something had to have triggered his change in personality. Drugs made as much sense as anything else.

"I hadn't thought it could be drugs affecting him," Jess said. "Whatever it was, it scared me. But when Brian started belittling Tabitha when she was visiting, I knew I couldn't bring her there anymore. I was scared for her. I was scared for me. I didn't know what to do. I wanted to get out. I'm not an idiot, Kason, I swear I'm not. I *knew* I shouldn't stay with someone who was hitting me, but if I left, Tabitha wouldn't have anyone on her side. I struggled with it for a while."

"I know. I could see your struggle when we came into *Aces*."

Jess nodded against Kason, but fell silent.

"What happened tonight?"

"I knew I had to get out. If Brian had no problem choking me, how far would he go? I knew I couldn't stay until the end of the month, even if that meant I wouldn't get to see Tabitha. I contacted a women's shelter and they said they'd take me for a while until I could get the money to get my own place."

Jess felt Kason's muscles clench behind her. The arm around her waist tightened a fraction. She could feel him consciously loosen his grip on her.

When she didn't continue, Kason urged, "Go on."

"So I got some of my stuff together and put it by the door. I went over to talk to Tabitha. Tammy was out, so we stayed in and I talked to her for an hour. I explained what happened with Brian and why I was leaving. I told her I wasn't leaving *her*, but I couldn't live with Brian anymore. I warned her about him. Told her not to listen to anything he said to her, that she was a beautiful person inside and out." Jess's breath hitched and she forced back a sob. She had to get through this.

"She hugged me and told me not to worry about her, that she'd be okay. We both cried a little bit. She gave me a copy of the newest story she'd written. I felt pretty good about it when I left. I'd been so scared to tell her, but Tabitha was strong. She was encouraging and said she understood. But Kason . . . she didn't. She was lying."

"It's okay, Jess, I've got you. Finish it."

Jess could feel Kason's arms tighten around her. She burrowed further into the blanket and his arms.

"A little while later, I'd arrived home when Brian came in. I was getting the last of my stuff together and he slammed the door open. He came right up to me and punched me in the stomach without saying anything. I fell back against the coffee table and he ranted at me. He screamed that Tabitha was dead. That she'd taken a bunch of pills and was dead. There wasn't a note or anything, but I know why she did it."

"No, Jess. You will not take this on yourself. I won't let you," Benny said firmly.

"But Kason . . ."

"No. You did nothing wrong. You didn't kill her. She was a fourteen year-old teenager, whose mother didn't take care of her emotionally. She was overweight and probably picked on at school. She was a loner who didn't have any friends. She was the creative type. I could go on and on, but your words to her today did *not* make her do this. She obviously had it already planned. Think about it for a second."

Jess didn't want to think about it. Kason continued anyway, even when Jess shook her head.

"Maybe she was hanging on for *you*. Maybe she was just existing in her life as you were in yours, because she was worried about you. Once she knew you'd be okay, and were getting out, she felt free to do what she felt she had to do. I'm not condoning it. I don't think anyone should end their life in order to escape emotional issues, but Jess, you can't blame yourself. You're a victim here too."

Jess couldn't speak. It just hurt too badly.

"Turn over, gorgeous, let me hold you."

Jess awkwardly turned around in Kason's arms until she was facing him. She buried her head into his chest and sniffled.

"Finish it, Jess. What else did Brian do?" Benny knew. He'd heard the story as she told it to the officer in the hospital, but he wanted her to get it all out here and now, safe in his arms.

"Nothing he hadn't already done before. He called me a cripple. Made fun of me. Kicked me, smacked me around, then threw me against the wall. He said if I was leaving to get the hell out. I didn't hesitate. I just grabbed my purse and left. I don't have any of my stuff. I don't have anything."

"You'll get your stuff, Jess. Don't worry about that. I'll take care of it. And you have something. You have me. I'm your friend. I have your back. You don't have to go to the women's shelter. I have two bedrooms. It's a crappy apartment, but you aren't homeless. You can stay here as long as it takes to save up enough money for a place of your own."

At Kason's words, Jess burst into tears. She couldn't hold them back anymore. Kason didn't tell her to hush, he didn't tell her it would all be okay, he just held her. He rocked her and ran his hands up and down her back.

Jess had no idea how long she'd been crying when she finally found herself out of tears. She was exhausted, completely drained. She opened her eyes and saw she'd soaked Kason's shirt.

"I got you all wet."

Kason chuckled above her. "I've slogged through the pits of hell on missions. I survived Hell Week. I've trudged through jungles without a shower for a week. A few tears and some snot doesn't bother me in the least."

His words made Jess blush. She hadn't even thought about snot! "Jesus. Well, I'm sorry anyway, this isn't the jungle or Hell Week."

She could feel the chuckle rumble through Kason's chest. It felt nice.

"Do you want some water or anything?"

Jess shook her head. She was comfortable right where she was. "I don't want to move."

"Okay." Jess felt Kason's hand on the back of her head. He pressed until her cheek was once more resting on his chest. "Go to sleep. We'll figure things out in the morning."

"But . . ."

"Jess, I'm tired. You're tired. It's been a hell of a day. Just relax. Trust me. I've got you. You're safe, just sleep."

"Okay." Jess paused then quickly said, "Thank you. For everything."

"You're welcome, Jess. Thank *you* for contacting me. It means a lot. Sleep now."

Jessyka didn't think she'd be able to sleep, but surprisingly, she was out of it within moments. She never knew that Kason stayed awake for another hour, simply enjoying the feel of her in his arms. She never heard him mutter softly, "You'll always be safe if I have anything to say about it."

CHAPTER 6

Benny tried to be quiet in the kitchen as he fixed Jessyka a good hearty breakfast. He was still going through all she'd told him last night. He had a lot of work to do in order to help her, but first he wanted to get some food into her.

All his life, Benny had felt a need to protect people, but his thoughts about Jess were way beyond anything he'd ever felt before. He'd been a horndog in the past, sleeping with women for a night and then not thinking twice about how they were feeling when he never called them again. But Benny had never found anyone who he actually liked. Who he wanted to get to know outside the bedroom. But with Jess, he found that he wanted to know everything about her. He wanted to know who her friends were, her favorite foods, her everyday routine, just everything.

Benny had never been friends with a woman before. He supposed it was cliché, but there it was. He used women and they used him. Now that he thought about it, he was friends with his teammates' women, but that was different somehow. They were already taken. There was no chance of them wanting to be in his bed, and he certainly didn't want to be in theirs. But Jess? Yeah, Benny could admit he wanted her in his bed, but along with that was the fact that he just plain liked her. She was strong, hardworking, witty, and she was compassionate. She didn't look at him and see a conquest. At least he didn't think she did.

He knew Jess was different when the thought of her in his kitchen didn't freak him out. He didn't like when people tried to "help" him when he was cooking. He was meticulous about it, and had been made fun of on more than one occasion by his teammates and their women, but it was just the way he was.

The first thing he'd thought of this morning was a vision of Jess standing next to him as they fixed breakfast together. Benny supposed it was partly because he'd held her all night. The feel of her body next to his was unlike anything he'd felt before. In the past he'd cuddle with a woman because it was expected of him after sex, not because he felt any real connection with her. That probably made him an asshole, but he couldn't force feelings when there weren't any there.

But with Jess, Benny had been completely satisfied holding her all night. He didn't feel the urge to have sex with her, he just wanted to hold her and make sure she felt safe.

Benny was brought out of his musings when he saw Jessyka's head pop up from over the couch.

"Sleep well?" he called out, stirring the eggs in the bowl he was holding.

Jess turned her head and saw him in the kitchen. "Surprisingly, yeah."

"I've got an extra toothbrush and toothpaste in the bathroom. I don't have any girly soap or shampoo, but you can use mine if you want to shower." Benny watched as Jess's eyes got big. Yeah, she wanted to shower.

"Clothes will be an issue until Dude gets here this morning with your stuff, but in the meantime, I put one of my shirts in the bathroom along with a pair of boxers. They'll be big on you, but they'll do until later."

Jess blushed, hoping Kason couldn't see it. Just the *thought* of wearing his underwear made goosebumps break out all over her body. She tried to tamp down her reaction. Kason was her friend, no matter how sexy he was, she didn't want to ruin the best thing to happen to her in the last year.

"I'd love a shower, thanks." She stood up and swayed a bit, catching herself on the couch.

Before she could take a step, Kason was there with a hand on her elbow, steadying her.

"Are you okay? I should've asked that first."

"I'm good. I just stood up too fast."

"How's the hip?"

"Kason, I'm okay. I promise." Jess watched as he backed off, still looking worried.

"If you don't mind, take a few steps so I know you won't face plant on my floor the second I turn my back," Benny demanded, wanting to see for himself that Jess could walk.

He watched as Jess did as he asked. She looked okay, she had her normal limp, but it didn't look any more exaggerated than he'd seen it before. He headed back to the kitchen and the words popped out before he could stop them.

"Brian's a fucking idiot. You're not crippled. I love your gait." Benny watched as Jess turned to him with an incredulous look on her face. He decided to play it off as nonchalantly as he could. Sometime between his making breakfast for her and coming to her side to make sure she didn't hurt herself, he'd decided she was his. Benny couldn't have all these protective feelings about her and not want to keep her. He'd give her as much time as she needed, but he hoped in the end, whenever that might be, she'd want to keep him right back.

"I don't know why you have that limp, but I'm assuming somehow your left leg is shorter than the other. I've watched you for several months now. Jess, it's sexy as hell. You don't get that, but I do, and so do my teammates. When you walk, you sway. Because of the difference in the length of your legs, your hips have an exaggerated back and forth movement to them. From behind, your ass just begs to be caressed. From the front, your sway makes your breasts move with your body. Again, it's sexy as all hell. For Brian to call you crippled just means he doesn't appreciate the female form. And

Jess, your form is abso-fucking-lutely perfect. Own it, because I swear to God, every man in that bar appreciates it. Swear to fucking God."

Jess stood in the entrance to the hallway that apparently led to the bedrooms and bathroom. She simply stared at Benny, not knowing what, if anything, she was supposed to say to him.

Benny smiled and continued to beat the eggs, getting them just the right consistency before he poured them into the pan to make an omelet. He'd gotten to her, as he'd meant to, but every word out of his mouth had been the truth. It was time she stopped believing the words that asshole spewed to her for too damn long.

"You taking that shower, gorgeous, or are you just going to stand there staring at me?"

Jess turned and fled down the hallway, ignoring Benny's laugh as she hurried away.

Thirty minutes later Benny heard the bathroom door open. He turned to the hallway and waited for Jess to appear.

She walked into the living area of the apartment and he could only stare at her. Her black hair looked shiny and clean and he could smell the scent of his soap wafting out into the room. But what really caught his attention was her body. Jess was wearing his clothes and that made his heart beat faster.

She walked slowly over to the stools at the bar counter and pulled herself up. Benny could see more of her body than he'd seen in a long time. The boxers left her legs bare and the shirt covered most of her upper arms, but her forearms were exposed. The shirt was also big enough that it kept falling off one shoulder. He watched as she hitched it up with her hand as she sat.

Benny clenched his fists and tried to calm himself down. The bruises on her forearms were highly visible against her pale skin. The marks at her throat were fading, but it was obvious what they were as well. He hadn't gotten a good look at her legs before she'd sat, but Benny knew he'd see bruises there too.

He turned to the stove and poured the egg mixture into the steaming pan. "I hope an omelet is okay for breakfast." Benny thought he sounded pretty normal, especially for the murderous thoughts that were coursing through his brain.

"It's more than okay. I haven't had an omelet in forever. Thank you, Kason."

"You don't have to thank me for every single thing I do, Jess."

"I feel like I do."

"Well, you don't. You are *not* a guest in this house. You live here too. I'm sure you'll do your part as well. Think how annoying it'll be if we go around thanking each other all the time." Benny tried to lessen the blow of his words by smiling.

Jess grinned back. "Okay. I'll try. I'm just not used to anyone doing anything for me like this. Brian never did."

"Well, one, I'm definitely not Brian. And two, you better get used to it."

It was obvious Jess was going to ignore his words from earlier, and that was okay with Benny. He didn't want to rush her, but he'd do whatever he could, say whatever he needed to say, to erase the hurtful words she'd most likely heard too many times from the jerk she'd lived with.

He put a glass of orange juice in front of her and turned back to the stove to flip the eggs.

"What time do you go into work?" Jess asked.

Benny turned back to her resting his palms on the edge of the counter behind him. "I'm not going to work for a couple of days. I'm taking some leave."

"You can't do that."

"Why not?"

"Well . . . because."

Benny laughed at her. "That's not an answer. Look. You can't possibly think I'm going to just leave you here by yourself the day after I took you to the emergency room do you?"

"Uh . . ."

"Not happening, Jess. We've got shit we have to do. First up, Dude'll be bringing some of your stuff over. At some point we have to go over there and get the rest of your things packed. I'm not letting you go back there without me or one of the guys with you. We need to find out the details of the funeral for Tabitha. I won't allow you to be harangued by Tammy or Brian, so if I need to arrange a time for you to say your good-bye to Tabitha in person, that's what I'll do. You need to call the women's shelter and tell them you won't need the room you arranged with them. You also need to talk to your boss and tell him what's going on and figure out your work schedule. On top of all that, the girls will want to come over and see for themselves that you're okay. I've bought you some time with that, but I expect that will only last for a day or two, so you have to brace for the onslaught."

"I don't understand," Jess whispered, completely overwhelmed.

"What don't you understand?" Benny came over to the bar and leaned on it, giving Jess his complete attention.

"I can do all those things, you don't have to stay home from work."

"Jess, it's what friends do for each other. You aren't alone anymore. I've got your back. My friends have your back."

"I don't think it's what friends do. I mean, I've never had friends that have done anything like this before."

Benny reached over the bar and put his palm on Jess's cheek. "You have friends that do that kind of thing now, gorgeous."

Jess couldn't help it, she leaned her head to the side and brought her hand up and put it over his on her face. "Thank you," she whispered.

Smiling, Benny teased, "What did I tell you about saying 'thank you' all the time?" He put his other hand on the back of her neck and pulled her gently across the bar, kissed her on the top of the head then let go. "Do you need to take a pain pill?"

Jess had only a moment to feel disappointed Kason had removed his hands before he'd changed the subject. She thought about it for a moment. "No, I think I'm all right." At Kason's frown, she quickly added, "But if I hurt later, I'll take one. Promise."

"Okay, I was just going to suggest that it might be good if you took it with food. Here you go, omelet with tomatoes, green peppers, onions, red peppers, chorizo sausage, a little bit of bacon, and of course topped with a ton of shredded cheese. I have sour cream and salsa if you want to add a southwest flair to it."

"Are you shitting me?"

"Nope, dig in."

"I've never met a man who can cook."

"Well, you've met one now. Eat."

Jess picked up the fork and looked up at Kason. "What are you eating?"

"Mine's cooking now."

"I'll wait." Jess put down her fork.

"No you won't. Eat, Jess. It'll get cold. Mine won't take long."

"But that's rude," she pouted.

Benny laughed. God, she was cute. "No, it's not. Not if I tell you to eat. Do it. Seriously, it's much better when it's still hot."

"Oh all right. But next time *you* eat first."

Benny wasn't going to agree with Jess, but he smiled at her anyway. He was glad to see her in a relatively good mood. Benny had no idea what her frame of mind was going to be when she got up that morning. She had a hard day yesterday and she was going to have another few tough days. Jess would never completely be able to put the loss of Tabitha behind her, but maybe, just maybe with a little luck and a lot of support, she could deal with it and move on.

Benny agreed with her last statement about eating first, knowing he lied as he said it. "Okay, Jess, next time I'll eat first." He watched with satisfaction as she closed her eyes and groaned as she chewed the first bite of the omelet. Amazingly, Benny felt himself grow hard. Fuck. He had to control himself. He didn't want to scare her away. He turned back to the stove.

"Jesus, Kason. This is awesome."

Benny shrugged. "It's just an omelet."

"Uh, no. It's not. It's . . . hell, I don't have the words, but I'm sure if you were on one of those cooking reality shows you'd win hands down."

"Thanks, I think. Now quit talking and eat."

Jess just shook her head at him and did as he requested.

Not long after they'd finished breakfast and Jess had done the dishes, at her insistence, there was a knock at the door.

"Stay put, I'll get it," Benny said.

Jess knew it was an order, even though he'd used a gentle tone. She stood next to the bar by the kitchen and waited to see who it was. Benny opened the door and one of his military friends came in.

"Hey, Dude, Thanks for coming over. Did you have any issues?"

"Nope, didn't see anyone. Just got in and grabbed the bag. It was right where you said it would probably be."

The man turned his piercing eyes onto Jess. She felt completely naked standing in the room in nothing but Kason's shirt and boxers, but forced herself to come forward and thank the big man for bringing her bag over. "Thank you so much!"

"Are you fucking shitting me?"

Jess was taken aback at the harsh words coming out of Benny's friend's mouth and involuntarily took a step away from him.

"Dude . . ." Benny warned in a quiet voice.

"You didn't tell me he tried to fucking choke her, Benny."

Jess brought her hand up to her throat and tried to cover the lingering marks. She'd honestly forgotten about them. Benny had made her feel so comfortable and relaxed around him, she hadn't even remembered her bruises.

"I told you there was a reason she was wearing a turtleneck."

"The only reason a woman should feel obligated to wear a fucking turtleneck when it's seventy fucking degrees outside is if she needs to cover up the angry marks a man made on her neck the night before because she doesn't want anyone to see and because some asshat guy doesn't want anyone to ask any questions and get his ass thrown in jail."

Holy crap. His words made Jess shift where she was standing. This guy was intense, but he hadn't made a move toward her and his words came off as concerned somehow at the same time being very scary. It was obvious he was pissed at Brian, not her. She'd sensed he was somehow more intense than the other men that she'd met at *Aces*, but up close, he was kinda scaring the shit out of her.

Dude continued his mini-tirade. "You having those marks on your neck means that asshole you lived with needs a lesson in manners and the proper way to treat a woman." Dude walked further into the apartment and came to Jess.

Jessyka's eyes moved to Kason. He said he wouldn't let anyone hurt her. She couldn't run, for one, her hip wouldn't allow it, but two, she had nowhere to go in the small space. She took a breath. Kason looked calm. Whatever his friend wanted with her, it wasn't to hurt her. His non-concern about his friend hurting her allowed her to have the courage to stay where she was as the big SEAL came toward her.

Dude gently took her chin in his hand and raised her head. Jess felt his other hand brush against her neck. Then he dropped her chin and picked up one of her hands, he pushed the sleeve of her shirt up to examine the bruises on her upper arm, then did the same on the other side. "He cause that limp?"

Jess shook her head, she couldn't get a word out of her tight throat if her life depended on it.

Dude cocked his head as if determining if she was telling the truth or not. Whatever he saw apparently was enough, because he turned on his heel and headed back to the door. "I'm calling Wolf. We'll get the rest of her shit today. You take care of her." Then he was out the door and gone.

Jess let out a breath and looked at Kason again. He was standing at the now closed door.

"Come here."

Jess didn't think. She went to him. She limped across the room and straight into Kason's arms. As they closed around her, she breathed easy for the first time since the knock on the door happened.

"He's a little intense," Jess commented, even if it felt like the understatement of the year.

Benny laughed. "You don't know the half of it. You okay? Dude would never hurt you, but you didn't know that."

"I *did* know it. Okay, well, not at first, but you said you wouldn't let anyone hurt me and you didn't move when he came toward me, so I figured I was okay."

"Jesus, Jess. Thank you for trusting me."

"I thought we weren't supposed to thank each other," Jess said with a grin, looking up at Kason as he held her in the circle of his arms.

He laughed. "You got me there. Okay, let's tackle one thing at a time today. Go get dressed. I'm assuming you have some clothes in the bag Dude brought." Benny gestured to the bag sitting on the floor that Dude had dropped by the door when he'd stalked inside.

"Once you're dressed, we'll handle the other shit. Obviously we can cross 'getting your stuff' off the list, Dude and the guys have that covered."

"How will they know what's mine and what's Brian's?"

"They'll figure it out, and if they don't, who fucking cares. If they miss anything, I'll get it for you."

"I can't ask you to . . ."

"You didn't ask. I offered." Benny interrupted Jess before she could finish her thought and leaned down, grabbed her bag and handed it to her. "Now get changed. As much as I like seeing you in my shirt, we have shit we have to do, and I'm not letting you leave the apartment looking like sex on a stick. Get moving." Benny let go of Jess and turned her gently to face the room. He gave her a little push to the small of her back.

"You guys must take lessons in 'bossy,'" Jess said, laughing as she limped toward the hallway. She looked back to see Kason's eyes on her ass as she walked. She faltered a bit remembering what he'd told her earlier.

She watched as Benny's eyes came up off her ass and up to meet her eyes. He merely winked and dropped his eyes again. Jess could only laugh and shake her head as she limped out of sight down the hallway.

CHAPTER 7

Jessyka sat on the couch at Kason's apartment and tried not to cry. She'd cried enough for one day.

While the morning had started off all right, the rest of the day had sucked. She'd called her boss at the bar and he'd been horrified at everything that had happened. Luckily, since she was a good employee, he'd given her an entire week off.

Next, Jess had contacted the women's shelter and let them know she was safe and with a friend. Jess loved how Kason had put his hand over hers when she'd said that.

Then Kason took over and called Wolf. Dude had already talked to him and the rest of the SEAL team had arranged to go over to her old place and collect her belongings. Caroline, who was apparently married to Wolf, insisted on accompanying them. Jess had wanted to go too, but Kason waved her off and continued making arrangements without her involvement.

Jess had been pissed, but after Kason had explained that she had to go and see about Tabitha, she relented. He was right. If his friends could go over and get her things without her, why shouldn't she let them? Deep down inside she was relieved she wouldn't have to face Brian or the townhouse where she had such horrible memories again.

The last thing on the list was Tabitha and the reason the rest of the day had sucked. Kason had pulled some strings and talked to the caretaker of the funeral home. The guy had explained that Tammy had requested to have Tabitha's body cremated. She hadn't even arranged a service for her daughter.

Kason arranged for Jessyka to be able to go and say her goodbyes. Jess had no idea how he'd done it . . . surely it wasn't as easy as calling up and saying they wanted to see a body . . . she technically wasn't even related to Tabitha . . . but somehow Kason had done it. They'd arrived at the funeral home that afternoon. The caretaker had led them to a back room and left them alone with Tabitha's body.

Jess had stood paralyzed by the door, staring at the gurney. She knew Tabitha lay under the sheet and she didn't know if she could handle seeing her.

"I can't," she said quietly, her voice hitching.

"Take your time, Jess." Kason wrapped his arms around her from behind and pulled her into his body. She melted into him, desperate for some support.

"I can't," she repeated despondently.

"Okay."

Jess didn't move and neither did Kason.

After what seemed like forever, but was probably only a minute or two, Jess took a hesitant step toward the body on the platform, then stopped. The sheet was almost obscenely white. She wished like hell Tabitha would sit up suddenly and say "surprise!" and giggle the way Jess remembered she used to do when she was younger.

"What if she doesn't look like Tabitha? I can't have my last glimpse of her that way."

"Stay here." Kason put his hands on her shoulders and pressed down. He leaned down and spoke quietly into Jess's ear. "I'll take a look and let you know. Do you trust me?"

"Yes." Jessyka's answer was immediate and relieved. "I shouldn't ask you to . . ."

"Jess, look at me." Benny came around her and stood in front of her, blocking her view of the body under the sheet. He put his finger under her chin. "I can handle this. I'm a SEAL. This won't be the first dead person I've seen. Okay? Trust me to know if you can handle this."

Jess could only nod. She briefly leaned forward and put her forehead on Kason's chest, needing that contact. Her hands came to his sides and gripped his T-shirt in her fists. She felt Kason's hands come around her and enfold her into his body. They stood like that for a minute or so, then she felt Kason's arms loosen. He kissed the top of her head and then gently spun her around so she was looking at the door.

"Give me a second."

Jess simply nodded again. She heard the rustle of the sheet and then nothing. Then Kason was back.

"It's okay, come on."

Jess took a deep breath and turned around. Kason put his arm around her and they walked to Tabitha's side together.

Kason had pulled the sheet down enough so Tabitha's face was the only thing visible. Jess choked back a sob. It looked like she was sleeping. Tabitha was pale, but otherwise she looked just like she had the last time Jess had seen her.

Jess lost it. She didn't think she'd ever cried that hard. Kason had been so patient and kind with her too. He'd held her and murmured words of encouragement. He hadn't rushed her, as a lot of men might have. Jess thought they were in the room for at least an hour. Every time Jess had decided she was ready to go, she couldn't make herself leave.

Finally she was ready. Jess thought she'd gone through all five stages of grief in that hour with Tabitha. First she had tried to deny she was really dead. Tabitha had looked so normal, that she hadn't believed she could be dead at first. Then she'd gotten mad. Tabitha had no right to kill herself. It was selfish and inconsiderate of their friendship. Then Jess had moved to the bargaining stage. Kason had to reel her back in from that one. She'd gone back to the "if only" statements she'd made the night before. Kason gently reminded her that it wasn't her fault and there wasn't anything Jess could have done to make the outcome any different.

Finally she cried. Hard. It was depressing as hell to see such a wonderful person, lifeless. The world would never get to read her wonderful stories, they'd never get to see what an awesome person Tabitha was. Finally, Jess had moved to acceptance. Tabitha was dead. She wasn't in pain anymore. Jess didn't have to worry about her friend being overly sensitive to everyday life events.

Jess knew she'd revisit all of the same feelings she'd just gone through sooner rather than later though. An hour wasn't enough to completely heal, but she knew she felt as okay as she did, because Kason was there with her.

Jess had kissed Tabitha on the forehead, crying a bit again, feeling the coldness of her skin, and finally let Kason tug the sheet back up and over Tabitha's face.

"Come on, gorgeous, let's get out of here."

Jess had nodded and they'd left. Kason thanked the caretaker and he'd taken them to the same park he'd pulled into not too long ago when he was taking her home from work that first night. He hadn't said anything, but just helped her out of the car and they'd made the short walk to a bench. They'd sat on the bench and talked about Tabitha, and about nothing important for over two hours. Finally, after Jess's stomach had growled, Kason had helped her up and taken her back to his car and back to his apartment.

Now she was sitting on his couch, comfortable and warm, and trying not to cry. Jess felt like she'd been crying all day. She hated being such a wimp, she'd never been one to feel sorry for herself. She needed a distraction. She got up and made her way to the kitchen.

"Can I help?"

Benny looked up at Jessyka. She'd been strong all day and he was so proud of her. He wanted to make a good home-style meal for her. He'd never invited a woman to assist him in the kitchen before. It was his space, the place he went when he needed to decompress. But the thought of having Jess standing next to him helping him, felt right. It felt like the next natural step in their relationship . . . whatever that was.

"I'd like nothing more than for you to help me, Jess."

Jessyka tilted her head, somehow knowing there was more to his words than she was understanding, but she wasn't feeling up to figuring it out right now.

"Where do you want me?"

Benny chuckled, if Jess knew where he really wanted her, she'd probably run screaming from the apartment.

"Come'ere. You chop the veggies while I put together the lasagna."

"You're making lasagna? Isn't that . . . complicated?"

Benny leaned toward Jess and got in her space. "What? You don't think I can do complicated?"

Jess swallowed hard. There were times when she thought Kason wanted more from her than just friendship, like now, but then other times he acted just like a buddy, like a friend would. "I-I-I'm sure you can." She hated how her voice stuttered.

"I can do complicated, gorgeous. Promise. I like to cook. I'm good at it. This is gonna be the best lasagna you've ever eaten."

"If the omelet this morning was any indication, I'm sure it will be."

They worked around each other in the small space. Jess would reach for a knife around Kason as he worked on layering the sauce and noodles in the pan. He would stretch over her and snatch a slice of green pepper off of the cutting board as she chopped. They laughed and joked with each other. It was just what Jess needed. She felt normal.

"Here, taste this."

Jess turned to see Kason holding a wooden spoon out to her with a dollop of sauce on it. He had one hand under the spoon to catch any sauce that might drip. "Guarantee it's the best sauce you've ever tasted."

Without thinking, Jess took hold of Kason's wrist on the hand that was holding the spoon and leaned toward him. She opened her mouth and looked up at him just as she closed her lips around the spoon. She almost choked at the heat pouring out of his eyes. She pulled back and licked her lips, letting go of his wrist.

"Good, isn't it?" Benny asked, not taking his eyes off of Jess's lips. He took his thumb and wiped the corner of her mouth where some errant sauce lingered. He suppressed his groan as her tongue came out and licked right where he'd just been touching.

"Jesus, Kason, that *is* the best thing I've ever tasted."

Her innocent words made Benny's libido sit up and take notice . . . again. She hadn't meant anything by what she'd said, but his mind immediately went into the gutter. Her words accompanied by the visual of how she'd opened her mouth, held on to his wrist and how her eyes looked up at him with open honesty and anticipation, made him immediately harden in his jeans. He knew she'd look exactly like that kneeling at his feet as she prepared to take him into her mouth.

"Just wait until you taste the finished product, gorgeous," Benny managed, keeping his lower body turned away from her, swallowing hard, trying to remember the tough day she'd had. She didn't need to deal with his obvious desire on top of everything else.

After Benny put the lasagna into the oven to cook, he suggested they eat the salad while they were waiting for the main dish. He could hear Jess's stomach growling and didn't want her to have to wait another hour to eat. They sat at the bar and munched on the salad. They talked about nothing important, until Benny saw some of the sadness lift from Jess's eyes.

The only thing that happened while they were eating that Benny didn't like, was when he reached across the bar for the salt shaker. Jess had startled and almost fallen off her stool trying to get away from his reaching arm.

Benny had stopped immediately and looked at her in concern. "Just getting the salt, Jess," he soothed.

"Yeah, I know . . . sorry." She blushed in embarrassment and wouldn't meet his eyes.

Kason put his hand on her forearm lightly and stroked her with his thumb as he spoke. "Don't be sorry, but I hope you *do* know you have nothing to be afraid of with me or with any of my teammates. We might be big and mean, but you are *never* in danger of being hurt or hit when we're around."

"I know Kason. I *know*. I just . . . it's just instinctive. You can't erase years of me being cautious in one night. Just be patient with me."

Slowly Benny brought his hand up to Jess's cheek. "As long as you know you're safe, I'll try to be patient."

"I know I'm safe."

"Okay then, will you please pass the salt? I should've asked in the first place instead of being rude and reaching for it. My mom would've smacked the back of my head if she'd been here." He smiled at her, lightening the mood once again.

Jessyka laughed and shook her head. Kason never did what she thought he would. She leaned over, grabbed the salt and handed it to him.

Later, after they'd eaten dinner, and Jess had admitted it *was* the best lasagna she'd ever eaten, they were sitting on the couch watching a football game on the television. Jess wasn't really paying attention, but she didn't want to be rude and tell Kason she hated the game. She was going over in her head all that had happened and what she should do next with her life.

There was a knock at the door and Benny stood up. "Stay."

"What am I, a dog?" Jess mock grumbled, but didn't move as Benny got up to answer the door.

He opened it to see his teammates standing there. "Hey."

"Hey, Benny. Got the stuff," Mozart told him gruffly.

Benny looked at his friends, none of them looked happy. "What the fuck happened?" he asked softly, not wanting Jess to hear them if something went awry.

"Let us in, Benny," Wolf said seriously.

Benny opened the door and the five men entered and stood around the small space. They all looked at Jessyka, who was now standing by the coffee table. They all noticed she kept the couch between them.

"Hey guys . . ." she began, but stopped when no one returned her greeting.

Benny came over to her and put his hand around her upper arm gently and led her over to the men. "Before you guys say what you need to, let me formally introduce you. I know you know Jess, hell, we've seen her almost every time we've eaten at *Aces*, but everyone, this is Jessyka, with a y-k-a, Allen. Jess, this is Wolf, Abe, Mozart, Cookie, and you already met Dude."

Jess looked at the men. They were certainly good looking, and big, and right now having all their attention on her was a bit unnerving. She was used to them being with their women and not really paying any attention to her. "Hi," was all she could squeak out. She looked back to Kason.

"Did that asshole do all that to you?" Cookie growled.

"Here we go again," Jess said under her breath. She'd made it through Dude's inspection earlier, she wasn't feeling up to another, or four, others.

"Yes, Brian hit me. He hurt me. I'm okay. I have bruises, but they're healing. I'm here, I'm not there anymore. I don't limp because of him. I was born with one leg shorter than the other. I just had the best fucking lasagna I've ever eaten and am feeling fairly mellow after a long, shitty day. Can we please move on?"

Surprisingly, she watched the men's mouths quirk as if they wanted to laugh, but they didn't.

"Yeah, sweets, we can move on," Mozart said for the group.

"Thank God," Jess commented, barely resisting the urge to roll her eyes.

"So we went by today to get your stuff," Wolf said grimly. "There was a lot of shit sitting out by the dumpster, we had a bad feeling about it and when we checked it out, figured it was yours."

Jess gasped. Brian had thrown her stuff away?

Wolf continued. "We loaded it all up to bring to you, and Dude and Abe went to 'speak' with Brian."

"I take it the talk didn't go well," Jessyka said, figuring Brian probably tried to act all macho with the men standing in front of her. He never did know when to keep his mouth shut and when it was appropriate to voice his displeasure.

"Yeah, it didn't go well," Abe responded dryly.

"What'd he do?"

"For starters he copped an attitude with us, which wasn't smart. Then he insulted you, his sister, and someone named Tabitha."

Jess drew in a breath, just hearing Tabitha's name brought back the intense pain she'd felt earlier that day. She'd been able to bank it during dinner and while sitting with Kason, but simply hearing her name brought it all back in an instant.

Kason put his hand on her lower back and slowly massaged her there. His touch pushed the feelings back just enough so she could focus again.

Abe continued, not commenting on her indrawn breath, "We were going to just take a look around and get out of his hair until he started with the threats."

The air in the room turned electric. Jess didn't know how else to describe it. The men were pissed. They were pissed then and they were obviously still pissed now. "Threats?"

"Yeah, telling us he'd fuck you up worse the next time he saw you wasn't his best choice of words. Dude convinced him of the error of his way of thinking," Abe said.

"What did you do?" Jess whispered, horrified, looking at Dude.

"Don't worry about it, Jess," Wolf told her confidently. "Brian won't touch you again."

Jess was horrified. "But you guys could get in trouble. I don't understand why you'd risk your career for me. I know around here all it'll take is one person complaining about something you did and taking it back to the base. Your military career could be hurt because of me."

Dude walked up to Jess, as he had that morning, and put his finger under her chin again. Jess knew she should probably be more freaked out than she was, but as she'd told Kason earlier that night, she knew these guys wouldn't hurt her. But it was obvious they liked to make sure whoever they were talking to, *saw* them while they were talking. Kason's hand on her back went a long way to making her feel safe and comfortable though.

"He won't touch you again," Dude repeated what Wolf had just said. "But, if you see him, turn and walk the other way. Don't engage him. You let one of us know and we'll deal with it."

He wasn't asking. He was telling.

Jess pulled her face out of Dude's grip and looked at the men. "I don't understand any of this, but fine. I don't want anything to do with him ever again, so it's no problem for me to walk away from him."

"We looked around your old place and gathered what we thought was yours," Cookie told her. "Unfortunately, it looked like he'd already removed most of it. What we did find by the dumpster was either broken or destroyed. We found a few bags of your clothes though. But don't worry, Fiona and the other women are already on a mission to replace every piece of clothing that might have been destroyed . . . plus enough clothes for you to wear one outfit a day for the next year and not have to repeat anything."

The other men chuckled, obviously knowing their women and their shopping habits.

"But I can't pay them back," Jess fretted, turning to Kason.

"You don't need to pay them back, Jess," Benny reassured her.

"But . . ."

Wolf interrupted Jessyka before she could protest further. "Jess, this is what friends do. We know you, we like you. You were in a hell of a situation. Any one of us should've done something sooner, but we didn't."

"I don't understand."

"We saw you all the time, Jess. I'm sure Benny has explained this to you. We saw how you were changing in front of our eyes, week after week. We didn't know for sure what Brian was doing to you, but we had our suspicions, but none of us *did* anything. That's on us. This is our way of making it right. And I'd just like to see you *try* to tell Ice or the other women you won't take the things they get for you. If you think we're bad, you haven't seen anything yet."

The men all laughed. Jess didn't know what to say.

Dude hadn't moved, but now leaned down and kissed Jess on the cheek. "I advise you to just go with it, Jess. You won't win." He chucked her under the chin and backed away. "I'll go and get what we brought."

Wolf came up to Jessyka next and kissed the other cheek. "Hang in there, sweetie. Things will get better quickly. Promise."

The other three men came up in sequence and kissed her as well. They all added their support and left to make sure all her things were brought inside.

Jess looked up at Benny. "Your friends are all so nice."

"They're *your* friends now too, Jess."

She blinked. She supposed they were. Jess didn't know how she'd gotten so lucky, but she silently threw a prayer toward the sky. Maybe Tabitha was watching out for her and making sure she was all right. Jess closed her eyes and smiled a small smile.

CHAPTER 8

"Come on, Jess! You have to try that on!" Summer's voice rang through the store.

Jess shook her head. "Summer, I've tried practically everything in the store on already. I'm tired, I'm broke, and I'm ready to go home!"

"Just one more store, you have to see the new stuff they got in!"

Jess sighed and followed Summer out of the store. Kason's teammates' women were awesome. They were funny and down to earth and Jess liked them from the moment they met up that day. She figured she would, since she'd seen them in the bar every week. They never snapped their fingers at her, they were always polite, and they were all great tippers.

She pulled out her phone to text Kason. She'd gotten used to texting him whenever a funny thought struck her. He always responded, sometimes not right away, but at least within a few hours.

Summer is drvig me crazy! Save me!

His response was almost immediate this time. *Too much shopping?*

Y!

Kason didn't text back, but Jess wasn't worried. He'd never failed to come through for her. The last month had been unreal for Jessyka. She'd been nervous about living with Kason, but shouldn't have been.

He'd set up his extra room for her, provided her with a little TV of her own, so when she needed her own space, she'd have a place to go. He'd given her five hundred dollars so she could buy what she needed. Jess had insisted it be a loan, and Kason had agreed, but she had a feeling she'd have a fight on her hands if she actually tried to pay him back.

So Jess made sure she earned her keep around the apartment. When she did her laundry, she threw his in too. She vacuumed and cleaned the dishes when he cooked.

She quickly learned he was anal about his kitchen and about cooking. Caroline had looked at her like she was an alien from another planet when Jess had told her that she and Kason frequently made dinner together. Caroline explained that Kason never let *anyone* help him. Ever. Even his teammates. The kitchen was his domain and was off limits to anyone when he was cooking.

Jess had been shocked, Kason had never said anything to her about it. She'd confronted him about it one night and all he'd said was, "I don't mind when *you* help me."

Jess had let it go because honestly, it was one of her favorite times, when they stood side-by-side in the small kitchen preparing dinner.

When Kason had to work late, Jess always made sure she had something waiting for him when he got home. Jess knew she wasn't as good of a cook as he was, but Kason never made her feel as if what she'd made was any less delicious than what he'd make for himself.

He admitted that most of the time when he lived by himself he just threw a pre-packaged meal in the microwave and ate that for dinner. Jess had been appalled, but Kason just laughed.

Jessyka admitted to herself that she was at a point where she wished for more with Kason, but she honestly had no idea what he thought about her. He touched her all the time. He'd kiss her on the head, he'd put his hand on her waist or the small of her back to steer her around furniture or to where he wanted her to go. When they watched TV, he'd put his arm around her and she'd snuggle into his side, but Jess hadn't seen any signs from him that he wanted anything more than friendship.

Kason hadn't held her in his arms since that first night. Every now and then when Jess would have a nightmare she craved the feel of Kason's arms around her, to make her feel safe, but she'd lay in her bed, wide-awake, by herself, waiting for her terror to fade.

Living with Kason made her appreciate what he and his teammates went through to stay as in shape as they were. They worked out, or did PT, almost every morning. They would run ten miles along the beach, swim, bike, lift weights . . . not to mention the mock situations they participated in on the base to keep up to date in extraction techniques or whatever. They were always having meetings and other things they couldn't talk about.

They were very busy men, but every time Jess had called or texted Kason, he'd responded. Jess had no idea how he did it, but it made her feel very special. She'd never felt that way before. Brian had certainly never come running when she lowered herself to ask for his help. She remembered one night when they'd actually been dating, she'd called to let him know she had a flat tire and was nervous since it was late and dark and he'd reprimanded her for calling him because he had to get up early and work. Jess had ended up calling the auto club and it had taken over an hour to get the tire changed before she finally was able to get home. She'd quickly learned not to bother asking for any help from Brian again.

Jessyka had no idea how to find out if Kason actually liked her as more than a friend. She was scared to rock the boat. What if he didn't? She would feel so awkward around him and it would probably ruin their friendship. She felt like she was in junior high and was obsessing over a crush. Jess knew the first step to trying to move their relationship to the next level was to move out of his apartment. She needed to get a place of her own, then maybe she could dip her toe in the waters and see if maybe, if she was lucky, Kason might want to take their relationship past friendship.

Jess startled when Summer's phone rang. They were power-walking down the mall toward the big department store at the other end.

"Hey, Mozart. *Pause*. I'm shopping with Jessyka. *Pause*. Really? *Pause*. But . . . *Pause*. Okay, see you soon. *Pause*. Love you too. Bye."

Jess held back the smile that threatened to erupt.

"Oh, Jess, I'm sorry, but that was Mozart. I have to go."

"Is everything all right?"

Jess couldn't help the grin that came over her face when Summer blushed. "Yeah, he got the rest of the afternoon off . . . he wants me to come home."

"No problem, Summer. We can shop later."

"Yeah."

Jess pulled out her phone as Summer led the way back through the mall toward the exit that would take them to her car. She shot off a quick text.

Thnk u. U're a lifesvr.

Anything for you gorgeous.

"Summer, can you drop me off at *Aces*? Since I have some extra time I need to stop by and pick up my schedule for the next two weeks. I also want to talk to my boss and see if I can't get some extra hours scheduled."

"Everything okay? Do you need money?"

"You guys are always offering me money," Jess mock grumbled. "No, I'm fine. I've just been thinking about getting out of Kason's hair and moving into my own place. I've just about got enough saved, but if I can get a few more hours I think I can have what I need to be comfortable in another couple of weeks."

Summer got a weird look on her face and looked at Jess as they walked. "Have you spoken to Kason about this yet?"

"Well, no, but I'm planning on it."

"I think you should do that before you make any plans or sign any leases."

"Of course I will, Summer. I'd never disrespect him like that. He's been too much of a good friend to me."

Summer continued to look at her weirdly.

"What? Why are you looking at me like that?"

"What do you think of Kason?"

"Why are you asking me that? You know I like him."

"Yeah, but do you *like* him, or only like him?"

"Are we in junior high school now?" Jess voiced the thought she'd had earlier.

"Just answer the question, Jess." When Jessyka was silent, Summer stopped walking and turned toward her friend. "Look, Caroline is the one who usually does this, but it looks like I have to since you brought it up. Jess, Kason likes you."

"Yeah, I'm his friend, I like him too."

"No, quit acting coy. He *likes* you. Jesus, Jess, do you think he'd let any ol' woman live in his apartment with him? The man is private. He is closed off. Don't take this the wrong way, but he used to have one-night stands all the time. He's never let anyone cook with him before. No. One. But here you are. Living with him. Sharing cooking duties. Texting him to save you from evil girlfriends who want to shop with you." Summer smiled at her last words to take the sting out of them.

Jess blushed, embarrassed Summer knew she'd texted Kason to get her out of the shopping trip.

"What I'm trying to say, is that he wants to be more than friends with you. We don't know what he's waiting for, but I expect it's for you to show him some sign you want that too. If you don't, by all means, move out. Find your own place. Move on. But if you *like* him, let him know. I guarantee he won't leave you hanging."

"What if it ruins our friendship?"

"Oh, Jess. It won't. I swear. Out of all of us women, you and Kason have known each other the longest before you got together . . . that is *if* you get together. For most of us it was an instant attraction. While we fought it for a while, it was still quick. But you guys have known each other for *forever* compared to the rest of us. Yes, you're just now really getting to know each other, but you have a base that none of us had because you've lived together as friends. And that's a good thing. All I ask is that you treat him with care. We love Kason. Think about it, will you?"

Jess could only nod. Did Kason really like her more than a friend? She tried to think back through the last month. She tried to analyze their encounters, his touches . . . Summer interrupted her thoughts.

"Stop thinking so much about it, Jess. Just go with it. Tell him you want to talk to him tonight and let him know how you feel, that you want to know if he has any desire to take your friendship to the next level. If he doesn't, he'll tell you. You can proceed with your plans to get your own place and that will be that. But if he does want to move things along, you'll never find another man more willing and eager to please you and keep you safe, than a Navy SEAL. I can promise you that."

"It scares the crap out of me, but you're right, Summer. Thank you."

"You're welcome." Summer took Jess's arm in hers and pulled her to the exit. "Now text him and let him know I'm dropping you off at the bar and to come and get you in about an hour."

"You're as bossy as your man . . . did you know that?"

"Yeah, I learned from the best. Now, come on, let's get out of here. I expect you to call or text me the minute you come up for air."

"You're that sure of what Kason's answer will be?"

"Oh yeah. You have no idea what's coming." Summer smiled a secret smile as she pulled Jess to her car. She couldn't wait to get a hold of the other girls and tell them their plan had been set in motion. Hopefully the next time they saw Jess, she'd be one of them for real.

CHAPTER 9

I'm rdy whenvr u r 4 u 2 pk me up at bar

I'll be there in twenty minutes. Stay inside until I get there.

Jessyka rolled her eyes at Kason's text. She always acted annoyed at his commands, but deep down, didn't mind. It meant he cared about her. Brian had always been annoyed when she'd asked him to pick her up anywhere, so it was a nice change. She hated to constantly compare Kason to Brian, but the differences were so acute, she couldn't help it.

Jess put the phone down and put her elbows back on the bar. It was mid-afternoon, past the lunch crowd, but before the dinner and bar rush. She'd spoken to her boss and he'd been more than willing to add on some hours for her.

Jess supposed most people would hate working as a waitress, but she honestly enjoyed it. Every day was different and she was good at it. She didn't need to write down orders, she could make change in her head, and she'd excelled over the years at being the type of waitress each group or person wanted. Sometimes she was their friend, other times she kept her interactions to a minimum and more business-like. She even knew how far to take the flirting so it wouldn't be interpreted as a come on.

Jess was lost in her own thoughts about what she was going to say to Kason that night when Brian and a bunch of other men walked in. She hadn't seen him since the night he beat the crap out of her and Tabitha had died. Brian's eyes locked on hers right away. The look he gave her made Jess's heart stop for a moment. Brian had a cast on his arm that went from his fingertips all the way up to his shoulder.

Feeling sick and frightened, even though they were in a public place and there were people all around, Jess grabbed her phone and went into the back of the bar and to the office. She knocked on the door and her boss answered.

"Can I wait in here for Kason to pick me up?"

"Of course, babe. Anything wrong?" Mr. Davis was a big man. He'd been in the Navy for a few years, Jess had no idea how long, but after he'd gotten out he'd bought the bar and had been running it ever since. He'd told her several times how he was thinking about retiring, but Jess would believe it when she saw it. He loved *Aces*. It was his baby.

"My ex just came in. That's all."

Her boss stood up, ready to rush out into the bar area. Kason had sat down with him and had a talk with the bar owner. He wanted to make sure he knew that Brian was dangerous and to keep him away from Jessyka if at all possible. He'd agreed immediately. Mr. Davis might be a retired Navy sailor, and not a SEAL, but he still looked able to defend Jess from anyone who might want to hurt her.

Jess put out her hand toward Mr. Davis, trying to reassure him and make sure he didn't rush out into the bar and kick Brian out. "No, it's okay. He didn't do anything, he just makes me nervous. If I can just wait in here, I'm sure it'll be fine."

"No problem. I know you have those SEAL friends now, but know if you need anything, I'm here for you."

"Thanks, Mr. Davis. I appreciate it. Seriously."

Jess waited in the office, playing solitaire on her phone, until it vibrated.

Here

Jessyka stood up and put her purse over her shoulder. "Thanks, Mr. Davis. Kason's here. I'll see you tomorrow. Thanks again for the extra hours."

"I'll walk you out. And of course you can have the extra hours, Jess. Why you'd doubt I've give them to you is beyond me. You're the best server I've ever had."

Jess shook her head at the man and smiled. She wasn't sure that was true, but it was nice of him to say.

She headed back into the bar next to her boss, nervously looking around for Brian. He was sitting at the other end of the large room, on the other side of what constituted the dance floor at night, glaring at her. His eyes turned into slits and he mouthed something at her. Jess didn't stick around to try to figure out what it was. She walked as fast as she could, without looking desperate, to the door of the bar.

They got to the door and Mr. Davis opened it for her. Jess was relieved to see Kason standing at the passenger side of his car, not too far from the exit. Jess waved at her boss and limped over to Kason as fast as her legs would carry her and hugged him tightly when she reached his side. Her only thought was to feel his arms around her . . . to feel safe.

"Hey. What's wrong?"

"Nothing, can we just go?"

Benny pulled back from Jess and held her by her upper arms and looked into her eyes. He looked back at her boss, standing in the doorway of the bar then back to Jess. Something was definitely wrong, but a parking lot out in the open wasn't the place to discuss it. She looked okay otherwise, no visible injuries and that made Benny feel better.

"Okay, Jess, we're going. Hop in."

Jess didn't waste any time and climbed into the safety of his car. Kason closed her door and she watched as he stalked around the hood and got into the driver's seat. He put the car in drive and headed out without a word.

Jessyka couldn't resist, and turned her head around to look back at the bar as they pulled away. The door was now shut and no one came out, no one followed after her. She breathed a sigh of relief and turned back to the front windshield.

It wasn't until Kason spoke that Jess realized she probably should've been a bit more circumspect in her actions.

"I don't know what the hell you're looking for, but you better be ready to talk to me when we get home."

Jess looked over and saw a muscle ticking in Kason's jaw. His hands were flexing on the steering wheel and his body was tight. Uh oh.

"I'm okay, Kason. Nothing happened."

"But something freaked you out."

Shit. He was too smart for his own good. "Yeah." Jess put her hand on Kason's thigh and felt it jump under her touch before relaxing a fraction.

No more words were spoken as Kason drove them back to the apartment. He parked and came around the car and helped Jess out. He put his hand on the small of her back and followed her to the door. He unlocked the locks and guided her in. Once inside, Kason threw his keys into the basket by the door and crossed his arms over his chest.

"We're home. Spill."

Jess didn't hesitate. She put her purse on the table next to the bowl of keys and turned to Kason. "Brian came into the bar while I was waiting for you."

"Fuck."

"It's okay, he didn't talk to me at all."

"Then why are you all jacked up, Jess?"

"It sounds stupid."

Benny took a step forward and pulled Jess into his arms. He put one hand behind her head and pressed it into his chest. The other he wrapped around her waist until they were touching from their hips up to her head. "It's not stupid." His voice eased a bit.

"He looked at me funny."

Instead of laughing at her, Benny simply asked, "In what way?"

Jess took a deep breath, inhaling the scent of Kason. She'd never grow tired of it. He smelled like the soap he used that morning and . . . man. She had no idea how to describe it. It was probably a mixture of his sweat and his natural scent, but it was an immediate aphrodisiac to her. Jess could feel her nipples tighten. It was completely inappropriate, but she couldn't help it. Remembering he'd asked her a question, she finally answered him.

"He was pissed. He came in with a group of men and he looked right at me and glared. I went into the back to Mr. Davis's office to wait for you. When you got there and I went to leave, he squinted his eyes at me and mouthed something. I don't know what it was because I hightailed it out of there."

"Good girl," Benny soothed. "You did good."

Without looking up, Jess told him, whispering, "He had a cast on his arm."

"Yeah, I know."

At that, Jess did look up. "You know?"

"Yeah, the guys did that to him when they went to get your stuff."

Jess could only stare at Kason in surprise and dismay. She could only parrot his words back to him. "The guys did that?"

"Yeah. I told you he was being an ass. They had to convince him they were serious. He now knows if he fucks with you again, they'll fuck with *him* again. Simple."

Jess put her head back on Kason's chest and tried to work out in her mind what she thought about what his friends had done.

"You need to talk this through?"

"Maybe."

"Okay, let me make us something to eat. You go take a hot bath, try to relax. It'll be ready in about an hour. That enough time?"

Jess nodded, but didn't move out of Kason's arms.

Benny loved the feel of Jessyka in his arms. He wanted nothing more than to carry her into his room and strip off all her clothes and make her relax the best way he knew how, but he had to know she wanted it first. He pulled back and put his hand on her cheek.

"An hour?"

"Yeah, okay, Kason."

Benny couldn't resist and he leaned to her and kissed her forehead. Then her nose, then for the first time since she'd moved in with him, he touched his lips to hers. He kept the contact light and unthreatening. "Go run your bath, gorgeous."

Benny watched as Jess licked her lips, as if tasting him all over again. "Okay," she whispered before stepping away from him.

Jess turned and limped away and Benny repressed the groan that threatened to come out of his throat. He wasn't kidding when he'd told her a month or so ago that her gait was sexy as hell. Her hips swayed seductively back and forth as she walked. It was more of a turn on to watch her walk than any practiced runway model he'd ever seen. Part of the allure was that she had absolutely no idea how sexy she was. None. No idea at all. Totally clueless.

Benny turned to the kitchen. He had an hour to whip up some comfort food for his woman. He knew Jess had some heavy thoughts running around in her head, but Benny hoped after they talked she'd be okay with what was happening.

Fifty minutes later, Jess wandered out of the back hall. She was wearing the same T-shirt she'd borrowed the first day she'd been there. Benny smiled. She'd refused to give it back, claiming he'd given it to her and she wasn't giving it back. Benny had no problem with that at all. She could steal any shirt of his she wanted. He loved seeing her in his clothes, and could imagine what she wasn't wearing underneath it.

Her hair was wet. It wasn't quite long enough to go back in a scrunchie, but it was getting there. Jess had explained how she'd cut her hair because Brian had liked to yank on it to get her attention. Kason had held back the harsh words he wanted to say and had simply told her he liked her hair short or long, as long as she was happy with it.

Jess was flushed from the heat of the bath and Benny could see a sheen of sweat on her brow. She was gorgeous and Benny knew he'd never wanted a woman as badly as he wanted this one.

"Go sit on the couch, we'll eat there."

"Can I help?"

"Thank you, no, I got it. Let me spoil you."

"You're always spoiling me."

"Yeah, so let me keep doing it. Sit." Benny smiled as he said it so Jess would know he was teasing. He relaxed as she smiled back and went to do as he'd asked.

Benny got together the plate with dinner on it as well as napkins. He stuck two water bottles under his arm and headed over to Jess.

"Jesus, Kason, you should've let me help. I could've carried something."

"I said I got it." Benny leaned down and let Jess take the bottles out from under his arm. He turned and put the plate on the coffee table and settled in next to her. He yanked the blanket off the back of the couch and pulled Jess into his side. He put the blanket over her lap, making sure she wouldn't be chilled after her bath.

Then he reached out and grabbed the plate of food and leaned back again, resettling Jess against him.

"What'd you make?"

"Pizza roll ups."

"From scratch?"

"Yeah."

Jess smiled, his words said yes, but his tone said "duh."

Jessyka reached for one of the crescent rolls and Kason held them out of her reach.

"Uh uh. I got this." Benny picked up one of the homemade pizza rolls and blew on it, making sure it wouldn't burn her when she bit into it. He took a bite, and finding the temperature acceptable, held it to Jess.

She looked at him, incredulously.

"Open."

When Jess started to raise her hand to take the roll from his hand, Benny held it up out of her reach. "Open," he repeated.

Jess opened her mouth and didn't take her eyes off of Kason's as he brought the roll down to her mouth. He placed part of it between her teeth and she bit down. Some of the sauce dripped out, but before it could fall, Kason caught it with his finger. He brought his finger up to his mouth and sucked on it, licking away the red sauce he'd just wiped from her mouth.

Neither looked away from each other. Jess finished chewing the first bite and Kason held the rest of the pizza up to her lips. She opened dutifully, and felt Kason's thumb brush against her lip as she closed her lips around the delicious crescent roll.

Kason continued to feed her. He took turns between eating himself, and feeding her. Each time, he took a bite of the roll first, making sure it wasn't too hot, before letting her take a bite.

Jessyka felt weird. She knew she was supposed to be freaking out about Brian and what the SEALs had done to him, but she just didn't have it in her at the moment. Between the bath, being held in Kason's arms, and him feeding her, she was one big marshmallow.

When the pizza rolls were gone, Kason leaned over and placed the now empty plate back on the coffee table. He leaned back to the couch and turned, taking Jess with him.

Benny held on to the woman in his arms as he turned them around on the couch. He moved so he was on his back and Jess's back was to the back of the couch. She was half lying on him and half lying on the couch. Her head rested on his shoulder and one of her arms was lying over his stomach. He had one arm wrapped around her shoulders and the other rested lightly on her hand on his stomach. He sighed in contentment.

Benny hadn't allowed himself the luxury of cuddling with Jess since that first night she'd been in his apartment. Oh, she'd leaned into him on the couch while they watched TV, but it wasn't like this. He wanted to give her space. He didn't want to push her into anything she might not be ready for. But he wanted her. He wanted her more now than he did a month ago. Benny knew all the important things he needed to know about Jess, except for one. How she felt about him.

Benny had spent the last month fantasizing about her. It wasn't enough he woke up hard and had to take care of it before he could go to PT, but every night he went to bed hard, imagining how Jess looked spread out on her bed just one door down from him. He'd had to wash his sheets a lot more often now that Jessyka was living with him.

"Are you comfortable? Your leg doesn't hurt?"

"I'm perfect, Kason. This is perfect."

Benny pulled Jess toward him and kissed her forehead once before settling back again. "Good. Now, talk to me."

Jess didn't hesitate, but laid out what she was thinking. "It's not that I care about Brian, because at this point I don't. But I'm worried about the guys. What if Brian goes to the cops? What if they get in trouble? What if Brian goes after Caroline or any of the others? What if . . ."

"Shhhh, hang on, gorgeous, let me address your fears one by one, okay?" Benny waited until Jess nodded against him before continuing. "First, Brian won't go to the cops. It's already on file what he did to you. Remember, they took pictures in the hospital. Brian knows it'd be his word against a SEAL's. Who do you think would win in that battle?" Not waiting for her response he went on.

"Wolf talked to our Commander about what happened, essentially giving him a head's up. Of course he didn't give him all the details, but enough that if he heard about it through official channels he could defend the team. And lastly, there's no way in hell Brian would go after the women. He knows he's outmanned and outgunned. Besides, they're all monitored 24/7."

"What do you mean?"

Benny sighed. He had no idea how Jess would take this. He knew he had to give her some background. "How much of the history of the girls do you know?"

Jess looked up at Kason. He sounded so serious. "I know some, but obviously not enough if the look on your face is anything to go by."

Benny put his hand on Jess's head and encouraged her to lay back down. "Wolf met Caroline on a plane that was taken over by hijackers. They survived it, but the bad guys came after her and kidnapped her.

Alabama fled from Abe because he did a dumbass thing and hurt her. It was weeks before we could find her. She'd been living on the damn streets. Cookie met Fiona when he was sent into Mexico to rescue another woman that had been taken by white-slavers. She'd been in captivity for about three months when we got her out and no one had even known or cared she was gone. Summer was taken by a man who'd kidnapped, tortured, and murdered Mozart's little sister when he was in high school. Cheyenne had a bomb strapped to her chest... twice. And finally, you know what happened to Cheyenne, Summer, and Fiona when they were taken from the bar not too long ago."

Benny took a deep breath. Now the hard part. "All the guys got together and agreed this shit had to end. We have a friend who lives in Virginia . . . Tex. He used to be a SEAL, but got hurt and now does some computer shit from out east. He can find anyone. We've literally used him to save the lives of every single one of the guys' women. He does illegal crap we pretend we don't know about, and he knows people in every branch of the military and probably in every state. We overlook anything illegal he might do because it's effective and has saved us more times than not. He monitors the girls. They're tracked all the time. Every day, every move they make."

"But, Kason . . ."

"I wasn't done. Let me finish then I'll answer whatever questions you have." Benny waited for Jess's agreement, then continued. "They know about it. They agreed to it. They all have issues related to what happened to them. It makes them feel better knowing their men will be able to get to them if, God-forbid, something happens again. The work we do is dangerous. The last thing we want is for some asshole we captured, injured, defeated, whatever, to come back and try to get revenge by taking our women. Their shoes are tracked, their bags, some of their clothes. They even have several pieces of jewelry that have tracking devices in them. Jess, if you remember nothing else, remember this. The women know about it and agreed to it. This is not us being manipulative, controlling assholes, which I admit, we all can be. But this is not that.

"So while Brian doesn't know about any of that, the guys made it clear if he even *thinks* about coming after their women, he'll pay. And how he'll pay would be completely unconnected to us. Tex knows people. I know for a fact he's as close to a team of Delta Force operatives as he is with us. Payment could be arranged without any of us being involved in any way."

"This sounds like the mob or something, Kason. I don't like it."

"I know, and I'm sorry, Jess. But it's how we are. We're a family, yes, sort of like the mob, but we don't go around hurting and intimidating people for the hell of it. In fact, I think this is the only time the guys have taken Tex up on his repeated offers to allow him to be involved."

Benny let his words sink in. The silence stretched out for at least five minutes, but it didn't feel uncomfortable.

At last Jess spoke, "You really think I'm safe? He won't come after me?"

"I really think you're safe. If I didn't think so, I'd tell you. I'd tell you so you could be more vigilant, more aware. I'd never hide that from you."

"Are you tracking me?"

Finally. It was the question Benny had expected from the second he'd mentioned tracking the other women. "No."

"Why not?"

That was *not* what he expected her to say. "I told you the girls know about the devices. I would never do that to you without your consent."

Without looking up, Jess said in a voice that cracked, "I think it'd make me feel safer."

"Then I'll set it up." Benny didn't hesitate in agreeing.

"But Kason, it's different for me. I'm just . . ." Jess paused thinking about how she wanted to word her thoughts and about what Summer had told her that day. "I'm not *with* you. I'm just your friend. It's not the same."

Benny slid out from under Jessyka and moved her until she was flat on her back on the couch and he was leaning over her. He had one elbow next to her head and his hand curled around the side of her neck.

"How honest can I be with you right now, Jess? I've been pretty forthcoming tonight. Can you take more?"

"From you? Yes."

Benny didn't hesitate or prevaricate. "I want you. Yes, you're my friend, but I want more. I want to be your lover. I want you to sleep in my bed. I want to see you lying on my sheets naked and waiting for me. I want to see you in the shower in the mornings while I'm shaving. You're already doing my laundry and cooking for me when I'm not home to do it for myself. We're already acting like a couple, just without the intimacy. I wanted to give you space. I wanted you to be sure. I've been sure for a while now. I've wanted you in my bed since about a week after you moved in."

"Is that all you want, Kason? Because I don't think I can handle just a sexual relationship with you. I'm too emotionally involved."

"Hell, no, that isn't all I want. If all I wanted was to get off, I could do that any day of the week. I want *you,* Jess. You have no idea how badly I want you, all of you. I want to be free to hold your hand whenever and wherever I want. I want to pull you down in my lap and wrap my arms around you when you come up to me at *Aces.* I want to claim you, to make it so no other guy looks at you while you're walking with your sexy gait. I want everyone to know you're mine. Can you handle that?"

"Yeah, I think I can," Jess smiled at Kason, happier than she'd been in a long time.

They both looked at each other, breathing heavily.

"Did we just agree to 'go together'?"

Benny laughed. "I haven't heard that term since I was in the seventh grade. And no, we didn't agree to 'go together.' You agreed that you're mine. You agreed that I'd take care of you and keep you safe. You agreed to sleep in my bed, shower in my bathroom when I'm in there too, and let me put my hands and lips on you whenever and wherever I want."

"Uh . . ."

"I'm going to kiss you now, Jess, and I'm not stopping until we're both so exhausted, we're comatose in my bed."

Benny waited for her agreement. He'd never do anything she didn't want him to do.

"God, please, Kason. I've waited forever to really feel your lips on mine."

Benny lowered his head to take what was finally his.

CHAPTER 10

Benny didn't ease into the kiss, he slammed his lips onto Jessyka's and felt goose bumps form on his arms as she immediately opened for him. Jess wasn't coy, she didn't hesitate, she took all he gave her.

He plunged his tongue inside her mouth and reveled in her taste. Benny had never gotten so turned on by a mere kiss before. If he hadn't waited so long to be inside her, to be right where he was, he could've spent all night simply kissing her. But he was too impatient. He needed to see her, all of her. Benny needed Jess in his territory, on his bed.

He broke the kiss and pushed himself up. Benny could feel his hardness push deeper into the vee of Jess's legs. He smiled and groaned as he felt her hips push up against him.

"You are so fucking sexy, and all mine. Come on, I need to get you in my bed." It didn't seem too fast, they'd gotten to know each other very well over the last month, and it felt right, now that they'd cleared the air, to take the next step.

Benny levered himself up and off the couch and held out a hand to Jess. She didn't hesitate, but immediately put her hand in his and allowed him to pull her up and off the couch, the blanket falling unnoticed by either of them to the floor.

"Walk in front of me, Jess. I want to see your hips sway and know that soon I'll have them all to myself. You have no idea how badly I've wanted to see those hips and that ass on my sheets."

Jess blushed, but did as Kason asked. Feeling bold, she exaggerated her limp as she made her way down the short hallway, smiling as she heard Kason groan. He was fun to tease, especially when she knew her teasing would end with her satisfaction, at least she hoped it would.

She entered his room and inhaled deeply. It smelled like him. She turned around once she entered and faced Kason.

He was ripping his shirt over his head. "Take off your shirt, gorgeous. Let me see you."

Without thinking twice, Jess began to unfasten the buttons on her shirt.

Benny stalked over to her and brushed her hands away from her shirt. "Too slow, lift your arms."

Jess just smiled at the impatience in his voice. Soon Kason's mouth was at her neck. "I saw how you reacted to Dude's words all those weeks ago about marks on a woman's neck. I need to see *my* mark on you. I need everyone else to see it as well."

Jess had never had so much fun during foreplay or sex before. "Well, since we're 'going together,' I suppose it's mandatory to have a hickey too."

She felt Kason's lips curl up into a smile before she groaned and let her head fall back. He sucked hard on her neck and she felt his teeth nip and his tongue soothe over her skin as he did it. His other hand was busy on her breast. Kason hadn't removed her bra yet, but his fingers played over and under the cup, teasing her nipple into hardness.

"Oh God, Kason. Yeah. That feels so good."

Without removing his hand from her breast, his other hand brushed down Jessyka's side. Benny raised his head long enough to murmur in a satisfied voice, "Goosebumps," then he returned to her neck.

He kept his lips on her, but backed them up until her legs hit his mattress. Benny kept pushing until Jess had no choice but to sit. Finally his head came up and he looked into her eyes as both hands went to her breasts. He played and teased there, running his fingers under her bra and over her nipples, before backing away and merely running his hands over the cups themselves.

Jess ran her own hands up and down his body as he caressed hers. Kason's chest was amazing. Hard and cut. He didn't have an ounce of fat anywhere on him, at least not that Jess could see. She couldn't help herself, and brought her fingers up to his nipples and pinched them.

Benny groaned and grabbed Jess's wrists. "Oh no, much more of that and this'll be finished before we even start."

Jess mock-pouted at Kason. "But I want to play too."

"Oh, you'll get to play, don't worry, but it's my turn first. You're lucky enough to be able to get off several times, while we poor men have to settle for one at a time."

"Several times?" Jess asked in bewilderment.

"Oh shit. Really? You don't already know this? Fuck, this is gonna be fun. Take off your bra and lean back."

Jess could only watch as Kason took a step back from her. She immediately felt the loss. Jess quickly put her arms behind her and undid the hook on her bra. She let it fall off her arms and onto the floor and she scooted back on the bed and lay back, as Kason had asked.

"Close your eyes and just feel."

She immediately shut her eyes. Jess knew at this point she'd do just about anything Kason asked of her, and they both knew it.

Jess felt Kason's hands at her waistband. He undid the button of her jeans and she heard the zipper lowering. But instead of pulling them off, he simply ran his fingers around her stomach and the waistband.

"I've spent weeks wondering what you look like here. Do you shave? Are you completely bare? Or do you trim down here so that you only have a small patch? Maybe you don't do anything and you're as wild as your personality. Do I dare guess which one it is, gorgeous?"

When Jess opened her mouth to answer his rhetorical question she felt one of his fingers press over her lips. "No, don't tell me. I want to find out on my own."

Finally Kason tugged off her jeans. She was mostly naked, covered only by her black cotton panties. Jess's breaths came out in pants. She was so ready for this.

"Open your eyes, look at me."

Jess's eyes popped open and met Kason's. "Beautiful. You look beautiful against my sheets, in my bed." His words made her nipples tighten further. His eyes roamed over her body then came up to her eyes.

"Once we do this, I'm not letting you go, Jess. Be sure."

"I'm sure." Her words were strong and immediate. "If we do this, you're mine too. It goes both ways."

"Shit yeah, it does. I'm yours, you're mine. Fuck, I love that."

Jess smiled. Kason's language got dirtier and dirtier the more turned on he got.

Prolonging the anticipation of knowing what she looked like under her panties, Benny leaned down and tasted her nipple for the first time. Jess wasn't overly endowed, but what she had was perfect. Benny didn't know sizes, but she fit in the palm of his hands perfectly. He squeezed her breasts and then brought his index fingers and thumbs to her nipples. "You like to tease, Jess?"

Jessyka arched her back. God, his fingers felt so good. She moved restlessly under him. "Jesus, Kason, please!"

"Please what, gorgeous?"

"I don't know!" Jess looked up to see the broad smile on Kason's face.

"Oh yeah, this is gonna be fun."

He lifted his hands off of her and leaned back on his knees above her. Benny's hands went to the waistband of his own jeans and he torturously eased his zipper down. As soon as the zipper got below a certain point, the head of his cock poked through the hole in his boxers.

Jess couldn't help but giggle.

Benny smiled. He'd never laughed during sex before. Everything felt new with Jess.

"He looks excited to come out and play."

"Oh, he's excited all right, but he'll just have to wait. I have stuff I gotta do first."

"Stuff?"

"Stuff," he confirmed with a smile.

Jess watched as Kason leaned to the side and shucked his jeans one leg at a time. He then scooted down on the bed until his face was right over her now damp panties. He drew his index finger down over the seam, then back up.

"Soaked."

Jess moaned. "Yeah . . . please."

"For me."

"Yeah, Kason. For you."

"I like."

Jess didn't answer him that time, knowing he was playing with her. Instead she bent her knees and spread her legs.

"Oh yeah, I can smell how much you want me. You do want this, right, Jess?"

"Duh, Kason. Yeah. Can you please get on with it? 'Cos I'm dying here."

Apparently her words pushed Kason over the edge because he reached to the bedside table and grabbed a knife. He flicked it open and looked up at Jess.

She didn't even flinch, just raised her hips and murmured, "Oh, fuck yeah."

Benny smiled. "You aren't worried what I'm gonna do with this?"

"You'd better be cutting my panties off and going down on me if you know what's good for you."

Benny laughed. Jess was fucking perfect. This was a side of her he'd sensed was lurking below her beaten-down persona. Brian had bent her, but hadn't broken her. "Don't move." He placed one hand on her stomach and pressed down, making sure she wouldn't inadvertently twitch or move. Benny didn't want to cut her, just the elastic on the underwear she was sporting. He put the blade under one side of the cloth at her hip and tugged upward. It didn't take much pressure, Benny, as did every good SEAL, kept his blade razor sharp. He then moved to her other hip and did the same thing. He flicked the blade shut and threw it toward the nightstand. It clattered to a stop, resting against the wall.

Knowing nothing would stop him now, Benny slowly peeled down the front of Jess's panties and sighed in appreciation. She wasn't bare, but was well trimmed. She'd shaved the lips of her sex, but left a nice sized patch of hair above. He ran his fingers over it. "Fuck woman," he breathed, then lowered his head.

Jessyka had been nervous about what he'd think of her grooming choice, but soon forgot everything, including her own name. Kason had been right, females certainly *could* go more than once, as long as they had a man who knew what he was doing.

And Kason *definitely* knew what he was doing. It wasn't until she'd begged him to stop, that he'd sat up and wiped his hand over his mouth. "God, you taste good. I swear, Jess, I could do that all night."

Jessyka smiled weakly up at him. She'd only had one lover before Kason, and Brian certainly didn't compare at all. "Your turn, Kason."

"No, now it's *our* turn."

Kason slid off the bed and stood up so he could remove his boxers. His cock was hard and straining upward. It certainly didn't look comfortable to Jessyka. He opened the drawer next to the bed and pulled out a brand new box of condoms. He quickly opened the box and grabbed one and put it on. He crawled back on the bed and over to Jess.

"Are you ready for me?"

"I think I've been ready for you all my life."

At her words, Jess watched as Kason's face got soft and he leaned down to kiss her. She felt him ease inside her at the same time. He went slowly, somehow understanding how long it'd been for her. When he was all the way in, he sighed and pulled back just enough to see her face.

Jess could see the strain on his face. He was holding back. She hated it. "Let go, Kason. I can take it. I won't break."

"It's been a while for you, gorgeous, I don't want to hurt you."

"You won't hurt me. God, Kason, you prepared me so well, after two orgasms, I'm soaked. I can take whatever you have. Let go. Make me yours."

"You fucking *are* mine." It was as if his words loosened something inside him. He pulled back and slammed into her. Jess could feel his balls hit up against her body as he bottomed out. She put her arms around him and dug her fingers into his butt.

"Yes, Kason. Again. Do that again."

He did it again, then again. Kason arched his back and his hips pounded into her. Jess leaned up and latched onto his pectoral muscle, right next to his nipple. She sucked in as hard as she could, using her teeth to nibble while she was sucking. If Kason could mark her as his, Jess could do the same right back.

When she was satisfied she'd left a good sized mark, she pulled back and looked up. Kason was smiling down at her, obviously having watched her mark him. "Satisfied?"

"Oh yeah, mine."

"Yours. Fuck, Jess. Yours."

Benny had never felt so connected to another person in his life. He thought the bond he had with his SEAL team was tight, but it was nothing compared to this. Watching her mark his skin was sexy as hell. He wanted to crawl inside Jessyka and never leave. He wanted to imprint her on his skin and imprint himself on hers in return. With that thought, Benny's heart sped up and he couldn't get the image of his release all over her skin out of his mind.

"I want to do something."

"Yes, anything."

Benny smiled. Jess didn't even know what it was that he wanted, but she'd agreed nonetheless.

"I want to paint you with my come. Mark you."

"Yes, Kason, God yes. That's hot as hell."

"Give me one more gorgeous, one more time, then it'll be my turn."

Benny leaned up and reached down between their bodies to rub Jess's clit. He continued to pound into her, but rubbed against her bundle of nerves at the same time. Benny felt Jess's inner muscles squeeze and flutter around his dick as she came closer and closer to orgasm.

"That's it, Jess, that's it. Let go. Give it to me."

Jess put her head back and dug her nails into Kason's biceps. "Oh yes. God that feels good. I'm coming . . ."

Benny could feel the second Jessyka lost it as her inner muscles contracted and gripped him tightly as he continued to push his way in and out of her tight sheath throughout her climax. The second Jess stopped shaking, Benny pulled out and yanked off the condom. There was no way he could hold off his own release any longer. "Look at me, Jess. Watch what you do to me."

Jessyka opened her eyes and looked down. She'd never seen anything more erotic in all her life. Kason was still straddling her, but he was stroking his cock quickly up and down, aiming at her stomach. She reached for him, wanting to feel his hardness in her hand, but was too late. He threw his head back and erupted. Jess watched, fascinated as Kason continued to spurt in pulses throughout his climax. She brought her hand down to her stomach and smeared his release into her skin, even as he continued emptying himself onto her.

Benny finally opened his eyes after what seemed to be the most intense climax he'd ever had, only to see Jess running both her hands through his release on her stomach. When she saw him watching, she reached down further and caressed his softening cock, squeezing one last stream of fluid from him.

"God, that was sexy as hell," she told him, no artifice in her face or tone. "I loved watching that, and I love feeling you on me."

Benny brought one of his hands up to her face. "Taste me." He couldn't stop the order if he tried. But Jess, being Jess, didn't hesitate. She brought one of her hands up to his wrist and guided his thumb into her mouth. Benny could feel his own wetness from her hand as she held his wrist. She licked and sucked all of his release off his finger, then nipped the pad of his thumb as she let go.

Benny let himself drop down gently on top of her. He could feel the wetness between her legs as she drew one leg up and over his hip. He could feel his own release between them on her stomach just as he could feel her wet hand run over his back and down to his ass.

He chuckled. "We need a shower."

"I like us like this. It's real. Raw. I've never had it this way. It was always polite and neat."

"I don't want to hear anything about how it used to be again," Benny warned, not lifting his head.

"I only meant that this means something to me. I like it. I like us. Some people might think this is gross, but I think it's natural and real. Can we just stay here for a bit?"

"Of course. But don't blame me when you're sticky and uncomfortable."

Jess laughed. "Okay. I won't. Promise."

Later that night, much later, after a shower which included both of them climaxing again, Benny thought about how he'd gotten to this point in his life. He was happy for the first time ever. Genuinely happy. He might not know how he'd gotten there, but he knew he never wanted it to change.

CHAPTER 11

Jessyka looked over at Fiona as they pulled up to Caroline and Wolf's house. She wasn't sure about this. While she liked all of the women, a slumber party was a bit beyond what she was used to.

"Maybe you should take me back home, Fiona."

"No way. This is tradition. Every time the guys get sent off on a mission we all get together and get drunk and cry and worry about them, then we get on with life until they get home. You're one of us now, so you belong here with us."

The whole "being one of them now" was still so unreal to Jessyka. It hadn't taken long for the guys, and their women, to figure out her and Kason's relationship had changed. Hell, the guys had taken one look at the hickey on Kason's chest the first time they'd had PT and known. The same with the girls when they'd seen the not-so-subtle mark Kason had left on her neck.

Jess blushed, but Summer had just given her a huge hug and said, "Told you so."

A week after Jess and Kason had solidified their new relationship, the team had been called on a mission. They couldn't say where they were going or when they'd be back. That was the hardest part about being with a SEAL. They'd get called off on the spur of the moment and couldn't say anything about where they were going or when they might return.

Jess had cried a bit, but Kason just held her tight and told her to trust him. That he knew what he was doing and so did the team. They'd be back as soon as they could.

So here she was, packed for a slumber party of all things. Mr. Davis had given her the night off from *Aces* and she was apparently stuck until she could escape in the morning.

"Hey you guys! It's about time you got here!" Caroline was standing at the front door waving frantically at them.

"Looks like they started without us," Fiona said laughing as she got their bags out of the trunk of the car.

And they *had* gotten started without them. Once they'd gotten inside it was obvious Caroline and Alabama were already three sheets to the wind and Summer and Cheyenne weren't too far behind them.

"We're so glad you're here, Jess! Seriously! We just *knew* Kason would find someone soon, we just had no idea it would be *you*! You're awesome!"

Jess could just smile at her.

"Here! You have to catch up! Try this! We just invented it tonight!" Alabama thrust a glass filled with what looked like milk in it. "I know it looks gross, but try it anyway!"

Jessyka took a small sip, dreading what it would taste like, and looked up in surprise.

"Ha! Told you it was good! Tastes like the milk left over after you've eaten a bowl of cinnamon cereal doesn't it?"

"Oh my God! That's *exactly* what it tastes like! What is it?" Jess couldn't believe how good the drink tasted. She wasn't one for the taste of hard alcohol, but she couldn't really taste anything in this.

"It's Rum Chata and vanilla cake vodka."

"Rum what?"

"Don't ask, just drink!"

And they did. Eventually they moved their party to the basement and lay sprawled on the bed, floor, and a fluffy chair in the corner of the room.

The room was slowly spinning around Jessyka, but she felt like she was floating, so it was okay.

"I don't like it when the guys are gone," Cheyenne said in a lull in the conversation.

"We don't either, but we have each other, and it gets easier," Caroline said confidently.

"How can it get easier? They're out there getting shot at or something worse," Cheyenne grumbled.

"Because they're good at what they do. Because they'll come home. Because we're tough as nails Navy SEAL women and we have to deal with it," was Alabama's answer.

Asking what she never would've asked if she hadn't been drinking for the last three hours, Jess piped up. "Aren't you nervous without them around? I mean scared for yourself?"

Not beating around the bush, Fiona asked for clarification. "You mean like someone's gonna kidnap us again?"

"Well, yeah. Or hurt you, or rob you, or something."

"No. We have Tex," Fiona said matter-of-factly.

"Tex. Kason said something about Tex," Jess said absently.

"You mean he hasn't programmed your phone with his number yet?" Summer asked in bewilderment.

"No, I don't think so," Jess said honestly.

Fiona didn't say anything else, just pulled her cell phone out of her pocket and hit some buttons. Soon they all heard through the speaker, the ringing of a phone.

"Hey, Fiona, what's up?"

"Tex!"

"Yeah girl, you called me. What do you need?"

"Kason hasn't programmed your number into Jess's phone yet," Fiona said, as if this was a federal offense.

"Yeah, well, he hasn't set up tracers yet either," Tex replied calmly.

"Are you kidding?"

All eyes in the room turned to Jess. She looked at all the women looking at her and threw both her hands up as if to say, "don't look at me."

"This is not acceptable at all!" Fiona exclaimed to no one. Remembering Tex was on the line she leaned down and said too loudly into the speaker, "Tex!"

"How much have y'all had to drink tonight?"

"Whatever, listen, Tex. You have to get some thingies on Jess!"

"I will, once Benny tells me he's talked to her about it."

Jess thought it was about time she broke in and prevented world war three. "I know about the tracking thingies. Kason told me about them."

Five sets of eyes swiveled to her and Jess swallowed hard.

"And?" Cheyenne demanded.

"And what?" Jess prevaricated, not knowing exactly what it was she was supposed to say.

"Are you gonna be all high and mighty and disapprove or what?" Alabama's tone was a bit belligerent and Jess immediately got defensive.

Forgetting Tex was still listening, Jess let the women know exactly what she was thinking. "I don't disapprove. Shit, knowing what you guys all went through, I'm amazed you're still upright and functioning normally in society. If I'd been through what you had, I'd probably be in a fetal position on the floor crying and moaning and not wanting to see anybody ever again. I figure part of the reason why you're so awesome is because of your men. So you know what, if I was you, I'd want to have a GPS surgically implanted under my skin, like a microchip that dogs get. To know that you have a man who'd do anything to protect you, to go so far as to want to know where you are every minute of every day just so he knows you're safe? Hell yeah, I want that. But I'm not you. I haven't been stolen out of my bed at night. I haven't been kidnapped by scary people wanting to do scary things. I'm just me. And besides, Kason hasn't asked me. He told me about you guys, but he hasn't told me he wants to put a tracking thingie on me. So there."

It was a lame finish to her impassioned speech, but Jess wound down quickly after blurting out the truth. The truth that she hadn't been able to get off her mind since Kason had told her about how all the other women were tracked. He hadn't brought it up again and she didn't know if it was because he didn't want her like that, or because he thought she'd disapprove or what.

"Jessyka, go upstairs and get your purse."

Jess turned to look at the phone in confusion. "Huh?"

"Go upstairs and get your purse. Bring it back down to the basement. We'll wait for you," Tex repeated, as if talking to a child.

"I'll get it!" Cheyenne yelled, leaping up and stumbling up the stairs as if she was an eight year old and not thirty two.

They heard Cheyenne clomping back down the stairs not fifteen seconds later. "Got it!" she yelled, almost tripping and landing on her face as she got to the last step.

"Jessyka, open it up and look in the side pocket," Tex's voice was calm, but at the same time it was obvious he wasn't asking, he was telling.

Jess did as Tex asked and pulled out a small black square. It was about the size of her thumbnail. "What the hell is this?"

"It's a tracking thingie!" Fiona cried happily.

"But, Tex, you said that you hadn't . . ."

"I said *I* hadn't. I didn't say Benny hadn't already taken care of it."

The room was quiet for a moment, everyone taking in what had just happened.

"Kason put this in my purse?" Jess whispered looking down at the innocent looking small black device in her hand incredulously. "But I thought he didn't . . ."

"No, he wanted to," Tex interrupted Jessyka before she could continue. "He called me about a week ago and said he wanted me to track you the same way I tracked everyone else. I refused."

"Tex!" Summer admonished. "That's mean!"

"Let me finish, darlin'. I refused because he hadn't gotten your permission yet. I won't ever track any of you women without you approving it. Benny was planning on talking to you about it, but then they got called away. He was in a panic because he hadn't been able to talk to you yet and he didn't want to rush it, but he also didn't want to go on a mission and leave you vulnerable. I agreed to one tracking device in your purse. I've got all the others waiting to be set up for when he gets back home."

"Why did he panic?" Jess asked, her words slurring a bit. She was obviously more drunk than she thought.

"Because every damn time they go on a mission it seems like one of you girls gets in trouble. So in order to prevent that from happening this time to you, Jess, he wanted you tracked before he left. Are you guys going to get in trouble this time? I swear to God, every time they leave I'm stuck to my chair making sure nothing goes wrong with you ladies."

"Nothing's going to go wrong!" Caroline told him with authority. Of course her statement would've been a bit more believable if she hadn't hiccupped in the middle of it.

"Right. Okay, if ya'll would just stay in that basement for the next whoever knows how long until they get home, I might believe it."

"Tex! It's not our fault. It's the other assholes' faults!" Fiona exclaimed.

Tex sighed. "Okay, Fee, you're right. Jess?"

"Yeah?"

"Put the black thingie back in the side pocket of your purse and zip it up again. Make sure you take your purse with you whenever you go out...okay?"

Jess did as Tex asked, feeling a warm glow inside. Kason had wanted to make sure she was safe. It should've felt creepy, but instead it just felt good to know he cared that much.

"Now, pull out your phone, it's why you guys called me in the first place." He waited until Jessyka told him it was done. "Go to your contacts and look for my name.'"

Jess scrolled through, cursing when she accidently pushed too hard and pulled up a different contact. "Damn phone." Finally she made it to the T's and turned the phone around as if the girls would be able to read it from where they were sitting and as she drunkenly wiggled it around in the air. "Hey! Look guys! Tex is already in my phone!"

Tex just sighed over the connection. "Yeah, Benny programmed it in. Now you know. If you need anything, you call me. Okay?"

"Yeah." Jess said it distractedly, thinking about when Kason might have taken her phone and programmed Tex into it without her knowing.

"Summer!" Tex barked out unexpectedly.

"Yeah?" Summer responded immediately.

"What's my number?" Tex demanded.

Summer immediately recited ten numbers back to him.

"Fiona, your turn."

Fiona dutifully also told him what he wanted to know, without looking up the number in her contact list.

Tex did this again with Caroline, Cheyenne and then Alabama. All three women didn't hesitate and repeated his number back.

"Memorize my number, Jess," Tex said seriously. "It's important. People today don't bother to learn anyone's number anymore. What would you do if you didn't have your phone but you needed to call someone? You'd be in trouble, that's what. I'm going to call you back tomorrow night and you had better know it. I'm serious, Jess."

"He *is* serious," Cheyenne whispered in a stage whisper that was more of a shout than a whisper. "He did the same with me and when I couldn't immediately give it to him he sicced Dude on me. And while I love what my man does to me, I don't particularly like punishment spankings. I prefer the erotic ones."

Jess looked at Cheyenne in disbelief.

Cheyenne giggled. "Too much information?"

"Jesus. Okay, I'm hanging up. Ya'll had better not be planning on going anywhere tonight, you're way too blitzed."

"Don't worry, Tex, we're stayin' in," Caroline reassured him. "Thanks for talking to us. We love you!"

The other women all joined in the Tex lovefest until he finally hung up laughing.

"Is he really going to call me tomorrow?" Jess asked in disbelief.

"Yes!" all five women said at the same time.

"We'd better start practicing now so you have it down!" Cheyenne was completely earnest with her words.

They spent the next two hours laughing and giggling. Jess learned Tex's number both forward and backward. Everyone agreed that her plan to recite it to him both ways the next night was genius.

Finally they wound down. Jess thought the night had been a blast.

"Thanks, you guys, for inviting me."

"Thank you for coming over. We know we can be a bit over the top sometimes, but we love our men so much and we're so lucky they all found cool as shit women. Can you imagine if one of us was stuck up and a pain in the ass?"

Everyone laughed at Caroline's words, thinking about how awful it would be if one of them was mean.

Just as everyone was falling asleep, Fiona said into the darkness of the room, "It's not fun being taken and not knowing if anyone knows where you are. You hit the nail on the head tonight, Jess. To know we have a man who'd do anything to protect us, to go so far as to want to make sure someone knows where we are every minute of every day just so they know we're safe? It's a dream come true and probably one of the only reasons we're not curled into a fetal position on the floor, as you so elegantly put it. I'm sure other people would think it's creepy and wouldn't understand at all, but we all agree that it makes us feel safe instead of stalked."

Jessyka was amazed at the amount of recall Fiona had of her words earlier that night. Her impression of the woman went up a notch, and it was already pretty high.

No one said a word and one by one they all fell asleep. Secure in the knowledge that while their men might not be in the same time zone, or even the same country, they were still being watched over by their very own guardian angel named Tex.

CHAPTER 12

All six of the SEALs let out a breath of relief as their plane touched down. They'd actually completed a mission without hearing from Tex that one of their women had been kidnapped, lost, tortured, or somehow otherwise hurt.

It seemed as if things were calming down for the group, and the men were thankful. Their women had all been through enough in their lives. It was about time they could just settle down and live a "normal" life.

"Jess found out about what you all did to Brian," Benny commented to Wolf as they were getting ready to de-plane.

"Yeah?"

"Yeah."

"And?"

"She was more concerned about you guys than him."

"You keeping her?"

The question wasn't completely unexpected, and Benny answered from the heart. "Hell yeah."

"Good. Ice likes her."

"What trouble do you think they got into while we were gone?"

"No idea, but it couldn't have been anything horrible since we didn't get yanked back by Tex."

Benny and Wolf laughed together. As much as Wolf bitched about the trouble the women got into from time to time, they both knew he wouldn't have it any other way.

"We meeting up at *Aces* tomorrow night?" Wolf asked loudly enough so all the guys could hear him.

Before anyone else could respond, Benny asked, "Can I check on Jess's work schedule? I'd like for her to be able to be there as one of us, and not as our waitress."

"Yeah, of course. Sorry, should've thought of that," Wolf apologized.

"No big deal. I'll let you all know in the morning. We'll shoot for the first night she's off, if that's okay," Benny told his friends.

The tarmac was deserted when they got off the plane, no one knew when they'd be returning, so none of the men expected a welcoming party.

The men walked briskly into the small building, ready to get the debrief over with so they could get home to the women who would be surprised, and happy, they were home and safe.

* * *

JESS THOUGHT she heard something and sat up in bed, her eyes straining to see through the darkness of the room. Before she could move or make a plan of action, she saw a shadow in the doorway. Jess threw herself off the side of the bed furthest from the door and landed hard on her hands and knees. The bed sheet tangled around her body and she fought to free herself before whoever it was in her room could get to her.

"Jesus, Jess, it's me."

Jessyka froze for a second, then every muscle in her body relaxed. She recognized that voice. "Kason?"

Then he was there. He picked her up off the floor, tangled sheet and all and sat on the side of the bed holding her in his arms. "Fuck, I'm sorry, gorgeous. Yeah, it's me. We're back."

Jess hugged Kason as hard as she could and buried her face into his neck. Her heart was still beating a million miles an hour. Suddenly she leaned back and smacked him on the arm. "You scared the crap out of me!"

Benny let out a short laugh then got serious. "I'm sorry, Jess. Seriously. I'm not used to having someone waiting for me in my bed."

"You should've texted me and let me know you were back."

"You're right, I should've and it won't happen again," Benny immediately agreed contritely. He buried his face into the side of her neck and breathed in her unique scent. "Fuck it's good to be back. It's even better to come home and see you in my bed."

Benny relaxed his muscles and laid back on the bed, pulling Jess with him. She sat up, straddling his waist and looked down at him.

"I can't see you. Are you okay? No new holes? Everyone else all right too?"

"No holes, gorgeous. We're all fine. It was an easy in-and-out thing this time."

"Thank God. I worried about you."

"And I worried about you." Benny paused, not knowing if he should really say what he was thinking, then decided he might as well. "It feels good to have someone to worry about and to be worried about in return."

"Yeah."

They lay on the bed for a moment before Benny sat up, taking Jess with him. "Okay, let me up and out of these clothes, then you can give me a proper welcome home . . . more proper than crawling around on the ground hiding from me."

"Jerk," Jessyka said laughing. "I wouldn't have been crawling around on the floor if you'd let me know you were coming home."

"Uh huh, give me a second and I'll show you how sorry I am."

Jess moved off his lap and felt Kason stand up. "Hurry up then, I'm feeling a need for you to apologize." She heard him laugh and she scooted up on the bed so she'd be ready for him. Jess peeled off his T-shirt she'd been wearing to bed and waited. The mattress on the bed dipped and suddenly Kason was there.

Jess sighed in relief. She hadn't lied. She *had* been worried about him, and it was the best feeling in the world to have him back in her arms. To be back in his arms. She had no idea how she'd thought for a moment what she had with Brian was love. The feelings she had for Kason were so much bigger. She felt like the luckiest woman ever.

* * *

"Hey!"

"Hi, Jess!"

"Yo!"

Jessyka smiled at the greetings she got from the girls. Most of the SEALs just did the manly chin-lift thing, but that was okay with her. "Hey, everyone! Great to see you!" Jessyka walked around and sat in the empty seat at the table. All the guys were there, along with their women as well. It was a lively group, and Jess was happy to be a part of it. She turned and smiled at Kason, who had sat next to her after pulling out her chair.

"Thanks for postponing this until tonight. I couldn't get off before now."

"Hey, thanks for agreeing to come. We know you work here just about every night, I'm sure it's a pain to come on your night off," Alabama told Jess with a smile.

"No biggie. I love this place."

"Hey, Jess, can I take your order?" Jessyka looked up to see Ella, one of the waitresses at the bar standing by the table.

"Yeah, can I get an amaretto sour?"

"Sure thing."

"Draft for you?" Ella asked, looking at Kason.

"Sounds good."

Jess put her hand on Kason's leg. She loved him. She hadn't told him, but she supposed it was probably obvious. They hadn't moved from their bedroom for at least a day after he'd gotten home. They'd ventured out to grab something to eat, but Kason had dragged her back to his bed as soon as they'd finished.

Between bouts of lovemaking, Kason had talked to her about his job, his friends, and about his upbringing. He'd reiterated how he wanted to buy a plot of land when he retired and enjoy his life away from people and their drama.

Jess had even brought up the subject of Tex and the tracking devices.

"The girls called Tex while I was at their house and brought up the tracking thingies," Jess said cautiously. She didn't want to assume anything.

Kason didn't flinch. He continued to run his hand up and down her back as they lay together, both recovering from intense orgasms. "Yeah?"

Since Kason didn't seem perturbed, Jessyka continued. "He told me about the one you put in my purse."

"Yeah, I didn't have time for more than that before I left. I meant to talk to talk to you as soon as I got back . . . but we got sidetracked." Kason had grinned at her.

Jess bit her lip. She didn't want to ask. If he wanted her to be safe, like the other women were, then he'd ask her about it.

"Hey." Kason had seen her unease. He turned her on her back and loomed over her. "Are you upset about it?"

Jess shook her head and looked up at him.

"Okay, now's as good a time as any to talk about this." Kason had taken both her hands in his and pinned them above her head. He put his weight on her hips so she was immobile. "You mean more to me than anyone ever has in my entire life. If something happened to you, I don't know what I'd do. I've seen enough evil in my life to be scared shitless at the thought of you disappearing and me not being able to find you. I want Tex to be able to find you with the push of a button if he needs to. Please tell me you're okay with that."

Jess thought about making him squirm, but the bottom line was she wanted that too. "I'm okay with that."

"Thank Christ."

The sex that followed had been amazing. Probably even more amazing than any other time before . . . and that was saying a lot. Needless to say, Jess thought it was pretty obvious they had deep feelings for each other. For now she was fine without the words, but she knew she wouldn't be able to hold them back for long.

The conversation around the table at the bar was lively. The guys loved to tease each other about anything and everything. It was a side Jess had never seen, she'd only seen their friendliness and politeness to her as a waitress, and their concern for the women sitting next to them.

The subject of Benny's nickname came up and Jess leaned in, eager to hear the story of how he got it. The other women had shared their men's nicknames with her, but they'd all admitted to having no idea of how Benny got his name.

"So we've been thinking Benny, now that you have a woman of your own, it might be time to change up your nickname," Wolf told him casually, absently running his fingers over Caroline's shoulders as he spoke.

"Yeah, we have a couple in mind, what about Chef? Or Lock, since you're the fastest lock picker on the team?" Cookie asked Benny, taking a long pull of his beer.

"Sure, either of those would be great," Benny answered enthusiastically.

"What about Stud, or Turtle, since you were the last to find yourself a woman?" Abe teased.

"No, I have it! Sloth!" Mozart joined in, laughing.

Benny was starting to figure out that the guys were just fucking with him . . . again.

"What the hell ever, assholes," he murmured.

The guys all laughed.

"Face it, you're never gonna live 'Benny' down," Dude said, not unkindly.

"How did he get that nickname anyway?" Cheyenne dared to ask.

"We are *not* sharing that story!" Benny ordered his friends.

Wolf just smiled. "Well, it was one night when we were visiting this crappy bar in a small country in Africa . . ." His voice trailed off and he got a hard, angry look on his face as he looked toward the door of the bar.

As if in a Monty Python movie, everyone's heads swiveled to see what Wolf was scowling at. Brian had just walked into the bar, along with a group of men.

Jess didn't recognize any of the men that were with Brian, but she shivered anyway. She hated that Brian continued to come to the bar.

"What the fuck is he doing here?" Dude said angrily, voicing what everyone was thinking.

"He comes in all the time," Jess told her friends softly.

Everyone's heads swiveled around to now stare at Jessyka.

"He does?" Fiona asked. "But isn't that . . . weird?"

"Yes, it's fucking weird!" Benny exclaimed. "Why didn't you tell me?" he demanded from Jess.

"He hasn't done anything. He just comes in with his friends and has a few drinks. I've always avoided serving them and he hasn't caused any issues. He hasn't even talked to me."

"I don't like it," Benny said, frustration in his voice. "I don't trust him."

"Me either," Wolf stated. "Maybe it's time we had another word with him."

"Oh no!" Jess said leaning forward and dislodging Benny's hand from her back. She spoke quickly, trying to head off a confrontation. "It's fine. Seriously, I'd tell you if he did something, but he hasn't. He's stayed away from me. Promise!"

Jess met each one of the men's eyes around the table. She could tell none of them were happy.

"If he says one word to you, Jess, we're going to have another 'talk' with him. We expect you to tell Benny if he does anything."

"I will, I swear." Jess looked over to Kason. His teeth were clenched and a muscle in his jaw was ticking. She turned to him and put her hand on his cheek. "I swear, Kason. He hasn't really even looked at me since that one time I already told you about."

Benny took her hand off his cheek and kissed the palm before putting it on his thigh and holding it there. He brought his other hand up to the side of her neck and brought her in for a long, slow, and extremely inappropriate for being in public, kiss. When he leaned back, his thumb rubbed against her cheek. "If he so much as fucking looks cross-eyed at you, I want to know."

He watched as Jess nodded at him. "I will."

Benny looked over at the table where Brian was sitting, and caught his eyes briefly, glaring at him, before Brian turned away back to his friends.

Talk around the table was a bit stilted after Brian arrived. Jess sighed. "This sucks. I'm sorry guys."

"Not your fault, Jess," Dude answered before anyone else could.

"I still feel bad. "Maybe I should just go, then you guys can . . ."

"Shut it, Jess," Abe said. "You will not take this on yourself and we are not leaving."

"But . . ."

"No."

Abe's voice was hard and Jess knew she should shut up.

Caroline broke the uneasy silence of the group. "So, Jess, did Tex call you after our sleepover?"

Jess smiled at her friend, grateful for the change of topic. "Yeah, he called and yelled at me when I recited the number he thought was wrong back to him. When he figured out I'd just repeated it backwards to him, he was speechless."

"*Tex* was speechless? I don't believe it!" Alabama said in amusement.

"Yeah, he then lectured me for ten minutes straight on why I should be taking everything more seriously. It wasn't until I apologized for the twentieth time that he finally let me off the hook."

The girls all laughed.

Deciding to bring up the topic of the tracers before any of the other women could, and before they could embarrass her about what she'd said at their get-together, Jess commented, "Oh and Kason talked to Tex and he sent the tracers."

"About time, Benny," Dude told him in a low voice.

"Yeah, well, between finding the right time to inform Jess she belonged in my bed and the mission, I didn't have the time." The guys all laughed at Benny as Jess blushed scarlet.

"It's good you got on that. Jess, what're you wearing tonight?" Dude asked, wondering what tracking devices she had on.

Jessyka couldn't believe they were actually talking about this as if it wasn't a big deal. She decided to go with it since she'd brought it up in the first place. She fingered the small gold stud in her left ear. "Well, this is one of them. I've also got one in my purse and Kason drilled a damn hole in my shoe last night and put one there too."

"Don't feel bad, Jess," Cheyenne told her. "Faulkner put one in my bra!"

They all laughed.

"Good idea, Dude!" Mozart exclaimed, then looking at Summer said, "I'll get with Tex in the morning for a new shipment."

"Yeah, me too. Great idea," Benny enthused.

"You guys are all crazy," Jess said without thinking.

"Crazy about our women," Wolf told her seriously. Then putting both elbows on the table he leaned in and Jess couldn't look away from his piercing gaze. She felt Kason's hand on the back of her neck, holding her affectionately, but her attention was all on the man across from her.

"I'm sure you've had a conversation with the ladies and with Benny about this, but let me reiterate something. We don't take this lightly," He gestured around the table to the other men. "There's a lot of evil in the world and we'll do whatever it takes to try to keep it from touching all of you. But if it does, those unassuming little devices will give us a leg up in finding you and keeping that evil from affecting you. Got it?"

"I got it, Wolf," Jess whispered and nodded at him. She'd found it was easier for her to call the guys by their nicknames, except for Kason of course, because that was how Kason talked about his friends and how she'd learned their names.

She continued in a low voice, so no one else in the bar would hear what they were talking about. Jess knew no one else would understand. "And for the record, I'm all for it. I wouldn't have agreed to it if I wasn't. And if I'm ever in a situation where evil comes for me, I'll feel comforted knowing you guys are on your way to get to me."

"Damn straight," Cookie said with feeling, pulling Fiona into his side and kissing the top of her head.

"Whew, okay, enough of the serious talk," Summer said with a smile. "When are we all getting together again to go shopping?"

"You and your shopping!" Caroline laughed.

The rest of the night was spent laughing and joking. The only awkward moment was when Brian and his friends got up to leave. But he didn't once look at their table or act like he knew they were even there.

Jess sighed in relief, glad to have gotten through another encounter with her ex with no drama. She'd had enough drama to last her a lifetime.

Finally Wolf stood up and pulled Caroline with him. "Well, guys, Ice and I are calling it a night. We have the morning off from PT, so I'll see you all in the office."

"When we are having our next ladies' night?" Alabama asked before Caroline was dragged away. Everyone at the table knew why the couple was leaving already, and they all knew they'd all be following suit not too much later.

"How about this coming weekend?" Jess threw out, knowing she had the weekend off.

"Sounds good. See you all here around eight?" Fiona asked.

Eight was a bit early for a night of drinking fun, but they all wanted to be sure to get home at a reasonable hour, because their men liked to keep them up much later, enjoying the effects the girls' night out had on them.

"Perfect! Whose night is it to watch us?" Cheyenne wanted to know.

The guys had decided after Cheyenne, Summer, and Alabama had gotten snatched right under their noses while enjoying a girls' night out, that anytime the women went out, one of them would be there to watch over them and make sure they were safe.

"We'll have to figure it out, but there will be at least two of us here," Cookie said resolutely.

"Okie dokie!" Caroline chirped easily. "See you this weekend!"

After Caroline and Wolf left, the other couples quickly followed suit. They finished up their drinks and the guys paid the tabs.

Jess walked out, held securely against Benny's side. She looked up at him. "I still don't know why they call you Benny."

"And you never will if I have any say about it," Benny said, kissing the top of Jess's head as they walked toward his car.

"Do you want me to call you Chef, or Stud, or Turtle?" Jessyka knew she was pushing Kason's buttons, but it was so fun.

"Not if you know what's good for you," Kason growled at her.

Jess laughed.

On the way home, Jess asked Kason a question that had been nagging at her for a while, ever since she'd found out about the tracking devices. "Does it bother you that Tex knows where we are at all times and you guys don't?"

"No." Kason's voice was resolute.

"Why not?"

Kason looked over at Jess as they stopped at a red light. "It doesn't bother me in the least because I know he has your best interests at heart. I don't give a fuck if he knows you're in the bathroom, at work, at Caroline's, or shopping at the mall. The peace of mind it gives me, gives all the guys, to know if somehow the worst happens and you disappear, we can find you by making a quick phone call to Tex. That's worth him knowing your whereabouts 24/7. There's no one we trust more with your lives than Tex."

"Okay."

"Any other questions, gorgeous?"

"No."

"Good. Because in about ten minutes, if I play my cards right, you won't be able to remember your own name, nonetheless anything about any damn tracking device."

Jess smiled at Kason and ran her hand up her chest until she got to the top button of her shirt. She played with it, swirling her finger around it. Seeing Kason's eyes locked to her finger she playfully said, "Light's green, Chef."

Kason put his eyes back on the road and put his foot on the gas. "Nine minutes, gorgeous."

Jess smiled again and said, "Can't wait."

CHAPTER 13

Benny leaned over and kissed Jessyka as if it was the last time he'd ever see her. He pulled back, not letting go, and laughed at the dreamy look on her face.

"You gonna get out or sit here all night?"

Jess opened her eyes and looked at Kason. God, she loved it when he kissed her as if he couldn't get enough of her. "Maybe I'll stay here and you can kiss me again."

Benny smiled at her. "As tempting as that is, you need to get in there and chat it up with your girls. I can't wait to get you home tonight and show you what Dude loaned me."

Knowing how Dude was, because Cheyenne couldn't keep her mouth shut about how well her man gave it to her and how dominating he was sexually, Jess could feel herself grow wet. "Are you freaking kidding me? Kason, that's just mean."

Benny pulled Jess to him again, but this time put his mouth at her ear. "I know you've been talking to Cheyenne so you have an idea of what I mean. I've got a pair of restraints attached to the headboard that have your name all over them. I can't wait to get you home, strap you down, and drive you crazy over and over again until you're begging me to fill you up."

Jessyka shivered in Kason's hold. "Jesus, Kason," she breathed, "Are you *trying* to kill me?"

"No, Jess, I'm trying to make sure you don't forget about me while you're getting crazy with your girls. I'm trying to drive you as crazy as you make me."

"I could never forget you and I think you've succeeded in driving me crazy!"

"Did I tell you tonight how beautiful you look?"

Jess only nodded. Yeah, he'd shown her as well. He'd taken one look at her in her tight jeans and spaghetti strap top and he'd declared they were going to be late. He'd pushed her into their room and proceeded to show her exactly how nice he thought she looked. She was now twenty minutes late and found herself wanting to go right back to the apartment and test out the restraints Kason had borrowed from Dude.

"Well, you are. Every time I think I've seen you at your best, you go and prove me wrong." Benny kissed her one more time, quick and hard, then set her back into her seat. "Go on, gorgeous. Call me when you're ready for me to come and get you. I'll see you later."

"Okay." Jess got out of the car and turned back at the last minute. She watched as Kason rolled down the window.

"Everything okay?" Kason asked.

Jess nodded and took a deep breath. She'd been holding back for too long. If he wanted to get her hot and bothered and leave her hanging, she'd drop a bomb on him too. "I just wanted to let you know that I love you, Kason Sawyer. I can't ever forget you. I think about you every minute of every day and thank God you came to check on me that day in the bar. You're more than just my friend. You're my everything. I'll see you tonight."

Jess backed away from the car, watching as Kason's jaw got tight and he curled his fingers around the steering wheel.

"You'll pay for that tonight," he taunted with a grin as he watched Jess head to the front door of the bar.

"I'm counting on it, Chef!" Jess called back, smiling at him. She felt great. She'd finally told Kason what was in her heart and he hadn't thrown it back at her.

She heard his car leave the parking lot as she opened the door to *Aces*. Jess took a quick look around and sighed in relief at not seeing Brian. He'd been coming to the bar more and more, and it was completely unnerving her.

He hadn't ever said anything to her, but she knew he was up to no good. The SEALs were right to be unhappy that he was hanging around, but she hadn't wanted to rock the boat by having them do something else to Brian. Jess was very thankful to see both Cookie and Dude at the bar. They'd obviously been the ones to draw the lucky straws. Jess felt safer with them there.

Caroline and the others had let Jess in on a secret. The guys grumbled about who would be the ones to watch over them when they went out, but Caroline knew they each coveted the spot. Earlier Caroline had called her laughing because Kason was upset he hadn't won the right tonight and he'd even tried to bribe Cookie and Dude into switching with him and letting him be at the bar tonight.

Caroline had overheard Kason saying that since it was the first girl's night out since Jess and him were together and that *he* should get one of the babysitting spots. The other guys had just laughed at him.

Jess made her way over to the other girls at the round table in the corner. It was the same table they always sat at when they went out.

"Hey guys!"

"Look who finally decided to join us!" Summer laughed as she hugged Jess.

"Yeah well . . . you know how it goes . . ."

Everyone laughed, because they did know.

The night was filled with a lot of laughter. Summer and Alabama agreed not to challenge each other to any weird shot competitions, as the last time they did, three of them ended up being kidnapped from the bar.

For the most part, the women didn't overindulge. Maybe they were getting old, but they'd all agreed it was nice to just have a drink or two and girl talk, instead of getting completely hammered.

At one point in the night, talk turned to babies.

"Last week I realized I'd missed my period. I hadn't noticed at the time, but when I did, I was freaking out. I refused to take a pregnancy test until Matthew finally forced me to," Caroline told them ripping up a napkin sitting on the table.

"Are you telling us you're pregnant?" Fiona gasped.

"No. Jesus, no. I wouldn't be here drinking if I was!" Caroline told them. "But it scared the hell out of me. Matthew was the calm one."

"How did he react to you not being pregnant?" Summer asked.

"He was fine, perfect actually. He told me that he wanted whatever I wanted."

"Do you want kids?" Alabama asked.

"I don't know. And that makes me feel horrible," Caroline admitted in a low voice. "I mean, in all the romance books I've read and in most television shows, when a couple falls in love, the culmination of that love is *always* a baby. It's like their love isn't validated until she gets pregnant. Then they live happily ever after. But I'm enjoying my time with Matthew. My parents were older when they had me, and I'm just not convinced it's what I want." She paused a moment, then looked up at her friends. "Does that make me a horrible person? I feel so selfish."

Summer got up and walked around the table until she was standing next to Caroline's stool. "No, you aren't a horrible person. And you know what, who cares if it's selfish? I mean seriously, who says women have to have kids when they get married? Where is it written that a couple's love isn't 'solid' unless they have a rug-rat or two running around? You guys need to do what feels right to the both of you."

Caroline leaned her head against Summer's shoulder. "Thanks, Summer, you always make me feel better. What about you guys?"

No one said anything for a moment. Then Cheyenne shared her thoughts. "I know I'm relatively new to your group, but I agree with you Caroline. I love Faulkner so much. I want him all to myself. All the time. I can't imagine having to give up one second of my time with him right now. I love how we are together and I can't imagine giving that up. But, I think I do want kids—someday. I know how protective and loving he is with me, and I'd love to see him with his child."

"I agree, the press and social media today make it seem like we are complete selfish bitches and not a normal member of society if we don't want kids. What right does anyone have to tell us that we should be popping out babies as soon as we get with a guy? Aren't there enough unwanted kids out in the world already? I should know, I was one of them." Alabama finished huffily.

"To no kids!" Fiona raised her glass. "At least until *we're* ready, and not when everyone else says we should be ready!"

"To no kids!" Everyone shouted and took a big swallow of their drinks. Summer walked back around to her seat at the table.

"Hey, who wants to try an experiment?" Jess asked everyone after a moment.

"Hell yeah, what kind of experiment?" Cheyenne asked eagerly.

"Everyone has their phones right?" When everyone nodded, Jess continued. "Let's send a text to our guys and see how long it takes them to get back to us. Whoever's guy is the last to respond has to buy the next round."

Everyone laughed. "Perfect!" Caroline exclaimed. "But we all have to say the same thing, otherwise it wouldn't be fair."

"Good idea, let's see . . . how about something short and sweet . . . and we can't ask a question so they *have* to respond," Jessyka declared.

"How about something like, 'It's so hot in here, I just took my panties off?'"

Everyone erupted into laughter. "Oh my God! That's perfect, Cheyenne. I'm not even going to ask how you thought of that one!" Summer exclaimed. "And we have to show each other what our guys say in response too!"

"Okay, but since Hunter and Faulkner are at the bar, Fiona, you and Cheyenne will need to go to the restroom, so they'll really think you did it."

"Good idea, Jess. Come on Cheyenne, let's go!"

The other girls watched as Cheyenne and Fiona tripped across the room toward the bathroom. Neither was surprised when Faulkner casually got up and stood in the hallway that led to the bathroom. The last time Cheyenne went to the restroom in a bar, she disappeared. Faulkner wasn't going to take a chance on that ever happening again.

The girls left the restroom and laughed hysterically after seeing Faulkner standing there watching them.

They came back to the table and continued to giggle uncontrollably.

"Okay, everyone get your phones out, but try to hide them from the guys at the bar," Caroline ordered. "Type in the message and don't hit send until we're all ready."

When everyone was done typing, Caroline counted down. "Three, two, one, *send*. Okay, now everyone put your phone in the middle of the table. We'll see whose vibrates first."

Everyone giggled as they waited. Then Cheyenne's phone suddenly wiggled on the table.

"Why am I not surprised?" Caroline said laughing and rolling her eyes.

Cheyenne picked up her phone and everyone watched as she blushed furiously.

"What did he say?" Alabama asked, leaning toward her.

Cheyenne turned so her body was blocking her actions from her man sitting at the bar and showed Faulkner's return text. *Did I give you permission to remove them? Hope you're comfortable sitting on that stool because I'm taking you over my knee when we get home.*

"Jeez, Cheyenne, you lucky bitch!" Caroline said, completely serious.

Cheyenne giggled and put her phone back into her pocket. "I know you guys know how Faulkner is with me, but I swear I've never been happier."

Caroline put her hand on Cheyenne's and said seriously, "Just because he's a bit more dominant in bed with you than our guys are with us doesn't make it wrong. If you guys are happy with what you are, who the hell cares what everyone else thinks."

Everyone around the table nodded their agreement. Suddenly two more phones started vibrating.

Jess leaned over and picked her phone up, read Kason's words, and smiled. "He said, 'Are you ready for me to pick you up yet?'" Jess typed out a short negative return text and put her phone away. "What did Cookie say Fiona?"

Fiona laughed and showed everyone the phone. *What game are you girls playing?*

They all laughed and turned and waved at the two men at the bar. Hunter had seen them laughing and he and Faulkner had obviously shared that they received the same text.

"Three more to go!" Jess said with glee. She couldn't remember when she'd had a better time. It'd been a long time since she'd hung out with girlfriends.

The next phone vibrated and Caroline snatched it up. She threw her head back and laughed and showed them all Matthew's response. *Fuck I love girl's night out!*

They all leaned forward and stared at the two phones left on the table. Alabama and Summer both looked ready to jump out of their skin. Finally Alabama's phone vibrated, then Summer's did too, five seconds too late for her to have won.

"Damn! Mozart's gonna pay when we get home!" Summer said laughing.

Abe's return text had said, *Bet we don't make it home before I can make you explode* and Mozart's said, *You're going to pay for that . . . in the best way possible.*

Everyone agreed that while Summer might have lost the bet, they were all going to be winners that night.

CHAPTER 14

Benny waited impatiently for Jessyka to text or call him to come and pick her up. The words she'd said right before she'd entered *Aces* for the night, echoed around in his brain. Jess loved him. He'd known it already, there was no way she could respond to him the way she had if she didn't love him.

He wanted to show her how much he loved her in return, before giving her the words back. It figured she'd say them when he couldn't do anything about it.

But Benny had the night all planned. He'd been serious when he'd told her what he had in store for them tonight. Benny had spoken at length with Dude about his lifestyle. And while Benny knew he'd never be a hardcore dominant as Dude was, he found there were aspects of it that he found interesting and wouldn't mind trying out.

Jess had never complained when he'd held her down or ordered her around in their bed. He knew she liked it. Benny figured he'd take it just a step further and see if she also enjoyed being physically restrained. If so, Benny knew they had a lot of fun nights experimenting ahead of them. He didn't need to be in control in the bedroom, like Dude did, and he knew Jess liked to take the reins sometimes, which he had no problem with. But, it was fun to mix it up now and then and try new things.

When Jess had texted him the naughty note about her panties, it had taken all he had not to get in the car right then and pick her ass up and drag her home. He wanted to give her the night out she'd been looking forward to, but it was killing him.

Finally around eleven, Benny's phone rang. He didn't recognize the number, but answered anyway, figuring it had to be Jess.

"Hello?"

"Is this Kason Sawyer?"

"Yeah, who the hell is this?" Benny's voice was curt and impatient. He didn't like getting calls from people he didn't know, but who obviously knew him.

"I work at the bar where Jess and the girls are at. Your SEAL buddy told me to call and tell you trouble's brewing and that you need to get down here. Go to the alley in the back and enter that way. He'll make sure the door is open."

"What kind of trouble?" Benny asked, but the person on the other end of the line had hung up. "Fuck," Benny couldn't hold back the expletive.

This is the last time they go to that fucking place by themselves.

Benny thought about calling either Cookie or Dude to verify what whoever was on the phone said, but didn't want to take the time. He knew he was being a dumbass, but all he could think of was Jess. Everything he'd ever been taught in his SEAL training said to wait, not make rash decisions, to get all the intel possible before entering into an unknown situation, and perhaps most importantly, relying on his teammates to help him . . . but he couldn't wait. Not when it was his Jess that could be in trouble.

He grabbed his keys and shoved his phone in his pocket and raced out the door. He jogged to his car and started it up. Not bothering with his seat belt, Benny threw the car into drive and pealed out of the parking lot toward the bar.

As he pulled into the parking lot, the bar looked quiet, maybe too quiet. Benny had no idea what was going on, but he wasn't taking any chances. He parked his car at the far end of the lot, out of direct line of sight of the door and silently made his way to the alley behind the bar. He pulled his K-bar knife out of its sheath and held it loosely in his hand. He had no idea what trouble he was walking into, but he wanted to be prepared for anything.

Benny saw the back door to the bar and made his way forward. He reached for the handle of the door and pulled, surprised to find it locked. The hair on the back of his neck was standing straight up and he suddenly knew he'd fucked up . . . huge. Hell, it was as if he hadn't spent ten years of his life learning the basics about dangerous ops. Benny wanted to kick his own ass. He had to get a hold of Wolf and the others immediately. He turned around to head back around to the front to find out what the fuck was going on and to call his teammate, but didn't make it two steps before everything went black.

* * *

"Holy shit, Jess, please stop! My stomach hurts so bad!" Fiona begged as they all doubled over with laughter again.

"I can't help it if I see some crazy shit here at the bar," Jessyka defended herself. She'd been telling the girls stories about some of the weird things people did when they were drunk. "There was even this one time when a group of women came in and tried to do a shot from the opposite side of the glass!" That made the girls all double over with laughter again.

"Hey, we were amazing at that!" Summer bragged, knowing exactly what Jessyka was talking about.

"Yeah, you were. You'll have to teach us all how to do it!" Jess agreed and smiled. She couldn't remember the last time she'd laughed so hard. Feeling her phone vibrating in her pocket, Jess eagerly pulled it out, excited to see what Kason would have to say to her. She'd been ready to go for at least an hour, but didn't want to be the first one to bail.

I've got your boyfriend. Don't say anything to the others or I'll kill him. Come outside through the back door.

Jess frowned as she re-read the text. It said it was from Kason's phone. Was he playing a joke on her?

Kp yr pnts on Kason, Ill be hme sn

She clicked the screen off and lifted her head ready to share Kason's impatience with her friends. Over the last few hours Jess had learned they didn't keep anything from each other, and she loved the openness and non-judgmental attitudes of her new friends.

Her phone vibrated again and Jess smiled and looked down to see Kason's response. She gasped instead. There was no note, only a picture of Kason on the backseat of a car. He was obviously unconscious and there was blood smeared on the side of his face. Trying to figure out if what she was seeing was for real, another text came though.

I'll fucking kill him and won't think twice. Get your ass outside and if you say anything to anyone, or warn them, I'll know and he'll die.

Jess thought fast. There was no way she could sneak out the back. Dude and Cookie were way too paranoid about that back hallway and door. She also didn't think the girls would let her go to the bathroom alone, and one of the guys would watch them if they did go.

I cnt go out the bk. Hve to go out frnt. Dnt hrt him. I'm cming

Jess tried not to panic. She didn't want to be one of those girls who was too stupid to live. And walking out the door would certainly make her just that. She didn't want to be kidnapped, but how the hell could she do anything differently? Jess knew the guys would figure it out quickly. They had to. She knew Tex was tracking her. She didn't think he just sat in front of his computer and watched their movements all day, but hopefully it would look weird when he did finally take a look to see that she went from the bar to . . . wherever she'd be taken when she stepped outside. Hopefully it would be to Kason.

What sucked was that no one had ever thought about the *guys* needing to be tracked. It had always been the women. Everyone had always been so concerned about one of *them* being taken again. They didn't even think that one of *them* could be kidnapped or put in danger. All it would've taken is one measly device attached to a piece of clothing, or a watch or a shoe or something, and Kason wouldn't be in this predicament. Hell, *she* wouldn't be in this predicament.

If Kason had a tracking device she would've immediately told Dude or Cookie and they would've taken care of it while she stayed safe, but now she was put into a position where if she didn't do exactly as whoever was on the other end of Kason's phone demanded, she could lose the best thing that ever happened to her.

Jess didn't want to risk ignoring whoever it was that had texted her, because she had no idea where Kason was. She didn't know who was behind the kidnapping. Was it someone from a mission he'd been on? She couldn't imagine the guys being so careless as to let one of their enemies know where they were, but she had no other idea who might be responsible. Jess was scared to death, but knew Kason's best chance was to get whoever it was to take her to him and hope Tex was watching.

You have three minutes. I'll kill him if you aren't out here.

Jess closed the phone without bothering to answer and took a deep breath. Showtime.

"That was Kason," she said to the girls, hoping she sounded normal. "He's waiting outside. Guess he got too impatient and wanted me to call it a night already. That text got him thinking I suppose." Jess laughed, knowing it wasn't her usual easy-going laugh, but she wasn't *that* good of an actress.

"Don't do anything we wouldn't!" Caroline laughed as she hopped off her stool and came over to give Jess a hug. "We'll do this again soon!"

It looked like she'd fooled her friends. Jess nodded in agreement and hugged each of the women. If she held on a bit too long and squeezed a bit too hard, no one said anything.

"I'm going to go and say bye to the guys."

Everyone nodded and turned back to their conversation. Jess took another deep breath. It was one thing to trick her friends, but fooling the SEALs would be another thing altogether. How much time had passed? She had no idea, but knew she had to step this up.

She limped quickly over to Cookie and Dude. "Hey guys, Kason just texted, he's outside waiting for me. I teased him a bit too much before we got here I think." She looked up at Dude. "Guess that little talk you had with him went over well. He said he has plans for me tonight." Jess smiled up at Dude.

"You all right?" Dude asked, taking her chin in his hand.

Damn, guess she wasn't as good at this acting thing as she thought. Jess closed her eyes briefly and prayed he'd let her go. "I'm good, Dude. Swear. Hell, what can go wrong? Tex has me bugged up ten ways to Sunday. I can't take a step without Tex and you guys knowing where I am, right?" Jess knew she was overdoing it, but she had to try to give them some clue. Maybe Dude and Cookie wouldn't get it right away, but hopefully they'd figure it out sooner rather than later.

"Right. Remember you can always say no and Benny'll stop."

Jessyka flushed. Jesus. Dude was talking about her sex life as if he knew exactly what Kason had in store for her tonight.

Dude chuckled, obviously enjoying her embarrassment. "All right, sweetie. Go on home. We'll see you later."

Jess gave Cookie a hug and wished with all her heart she could say something to these men. She knew they'd take action in a heartbeat, but she couldn't stop seeing the words, *I'll kill him,* flash in front of her eyes or get the picture of Kason lying motionless and bleeding out of her head. She wouldn't risk his life. The guys would find her, and hopefully Kason, soon.

Jess headed for the front door of *Aces,* wondering if she'd ever see it again. She turned and waved at the girls. They wavered in her sight a bit because of the tears in her eyes. Jess beat the tears back. Fuck that. She wouldn't cry. She had to be strong. She had two tracking devices on her at the moment, they'd show Tex, and therefore the others, where she was. They had to.

She opened the door and stepped outside and looked around. Jess had no idea where it was she was supposed to go. Suddenly an arm wrapped around her from behind and a cloth was shoved over her mouth and nose. She struggled, but quickly became overwhelmed from the fumes on the cloth. The last thing Jess thought about before she went unconscious was that she hoped Tex was as good at tracking people as the guys said he was.

CHAPTER 15

Jess wrinkled her nose and turned her head to get away from the horrible stench currently filling her nostrils. When the smell didn't abate, she brought her hand up to smack whatever it was away, but her hand was caught in a harsh grip and forced to her side.

Finally she opened her eyes and looked into the brown eyes of her ex. He was holding a little white capsule under her nose that was emitting a noxious smell.

"Brian," she breathed.

"Yeah, it's me, babe. Glad to see me?"

Jess struggled in his grip. "Let go."

"You're going to do exactly as I say if you want your precious SEAL to live. Got it?"

"Where is he? What did you do to him?" Jess refused to give in to Brian ever again. Maybe it wasn't the smartest thing to do, but fuck it. She was done cowering from him. She'd heard all about what Caroline and the other women had been through, and if they could be brave, so could she.

"I've only done to him what his friends did to me. I've been waiting for this moment for a long time. Come on, crip, let's go."

Brian hauled Jess to her feet and kept a strong grip on her arm. She swayed, still trying to fight the effects of the chloroform.

"Now, you're going to walk, bitch. I've hidden him out in the woods so he wouldn't cause any trouble. I didn't want his asshole friends to find him before I was done with him . . . and you."

Brian pushed Jess toward the trees next to where he'd parked. It was the same park Kason had brought her to in the past when he wanted to talk. Jess bit back a bitter laugh. How ironic.

She stumbled over the uneven ground and tried to keep her pace up. Brian had a light on his hat to help him see as he walked, but Jess had to rely on the meager light coming from it to show her the way. Every time she faltered, Brian would shove her. She fell each time he put his hands on her. The uneven length of her legs had never made hiking easy, and walking through the woods in the middle of the night, and not on an established path, wasn't making it easier.

She fell for the tenth time and Brian brought his foot back and kicked her in the hip, hard. "Get the fuck up, bitch. Swear to God, I have no idea why I wasted so much of my time with you."

Trying to ignore the pain in her hip, and to give it time to stop throbbing before she had to use it again, Jess asked, "Why *did* you Brian? If you hated me so much why the hell did you ask me to move in?"

"Tammy needed a fucking babysitter. You were there. So we decided you'd do."

Jess stared at Brian in disbelief. "You decided I'd *do*? That's all I was? A means to an end for you?"

"Yeah, that's all you were. A means to a fucking end. Then the stupid bitch killed herself. We were making good money off of her too."

"What?" Jess breathed, not believing what she'd heard.

Brian squatted down next to Jess, smiling evilly. "Yeah, she was a good fuck for my buddies. They paid us in drugs and they got . . . teenage pussy. Too bad she was so fat though, we could've gotten double if she wasn't such a fat ass."

Jess saw red. She had no idea Tabitha was being abused. None.

She'd trusted Brian. She hadn't really liked him much at the end, but she had *no* idea he was so twisted. Jess reached out and shoved Brian as hard as she could. "She was your niece! How could you *do* that? That's *sick*!"

Brian stood up and hauled Jessyka up by her hair. As she scrambled to get her feet under her and to take the pressure off her scalp, Brian put his face to hers and sneered, "All she was good for was fucking. I got my drugs and she got some dick. Besides, who do you think came up with the idea anyway? Yeah, her fucking mother. Don't put this on me, Jess, I was just doing what mommy dearest wanted."

Jessyka felt sick. She'd lived with Brian for years. She had no idea Tabitha had been going through what she had. No wonder she'd ended her life. It hadn't been because Jess was moving out, but she'd ended up being more of a catalyst for Tabitha getting the courage to end her own torment. Hell, for all Jess knew, Brian was telling Tabitha he'd hurt *her* if she didn't comply.

"Now, *walk*. Or I'll drag you the rest of the way by your fucking hair."

Jess knew Brian would do exactly as he threatened. She'd never been so scared of him as she was right now. Before, she'd only been worried he'd smack her around. But now? Knowing how depraved he was? Knowing what he'd done to Tabitha? Jess was terrified. Where was Kason? What had Brian done to him? For the first time Jess realized that Brian might have already killed him. He was obviously crazy enough.

Jess stumbled along in front of Brian as best she could. Her hip hurt worse than it had in a long time. Brian kicking it certainly hadn't helped. The pain reminded her of the one time she'd decided she could do a 5K charity walk. She'd done it, but her hip had hurt for at least a week afterwards. The difference in the length of her legs didn't allow her to walk for long periods of time, nonetheless a forced march over uneven ground like this.

While Jessyka fell a few more times, Brian didn't kick her, he just hauled her up time and time again and forced her to keep walking.

Finally Brian came to a halt and grabbed Jess's arm. He pointed to the right as if he knew exactly where he was going. "In there."

"What? Where?"

Brian pushed her hard until Jess fell on her hands and knees. "*There*."

Jess lifted her head and saw Brian pointing toward a break in the trees. How the hell did Brian know where they were going? There was no difference that Jess could see from where they'd just came from and what the trees looked like ahead of her, especially in the dark. She had no idea how far they'd come either. Her faltering gait was misleading. It could have been one mile or four.

Jess stood up slowly, repressing the groan of pain she could feel on the tip of her tongue, and crawled to where Brian was pointing. She moved the branches out of her way and suddenly came face to face with Kason. And he was absolutely livid.

CHAPTER 16

"Lookie what I found, SEAL man!" Brian cackled as he propped a flashlight in the crook of a tree nearby. Ignoring the daggers shooting out of Kason's eyes, Brian put his boot on Jess's butt and shoved until she fell with a cry right in front of Kason.

Jess heard Kason grunt and saw him struggle against the ropes that were holding him to a large oak tree. She stared at him in dismay.

Kason had dried blood on the side of his face, obviously from the cut at his temple. Brian had wrapped cloth around his head and shoved it into his mouth so he was effectively gagged. He'd been tied by what seemed like miles of rope. Kason's hands were behind his back, putting his body at an awkward angle as his back couldn't lie flush against the tree he was tied to. His legs had been tied together at the ankles, then wrapped up with the same rope as was holding him the tree at his knees and thighs as well. He also wasn't wearing any shoes or socks.

Somehow it was seeing his bare feet, so vulnerable in the middle of the forest, that got to Jess the most. "I'm so sorry," she whispered before Brian grabbed her by the hair and hauled her upright once more.

"Fuck!" Jess couldn't stop the word from escaping.

"He's not so high and mighty now is he?" Brian murmured into Jess's ear as if he was a lover whispering sweet nothings. "Now he knows how it feels to be helpless, just like I did when his buddies came to visit me. Seems to be a fair exchange if you ask me." Brian threw Jess away from him and she once again landed on all fours in front of Kason. She was sick of being on the ground.

Jess thought fast. She had to do something. Brian was bat-shit crazy. She didn't want to think about what he was going to do to them. She had to buy some time. Jess knew there was no way she could save them both, but all she had to do was give the others time to find them. She wasn't a SEAL, she wasn't a soldier. Hell, Brian outweighed her by a lot and she couldn't overpower him. But maybe she could trick him somehow.

Kason was the vulnerable one here. She knew he was a SEAL and a super soldier, but seriously, he was trussed up so tightly there was no way he was getting loose. Hell, if he could've gotten loose, he would've while Brian was back at the bar grabbing her. It was up to her to save him. The tables were turned for once. It was up to her to protect Kason until his friends could get to them. And she had no doubt they would. It was what they did. She only had to give both her and Kason time for that to happen.

The terror Jess had been feeling since she realized it was Brian that had taken both her and Kason melted away and a feeling of calm came over her. She had no idea if this was what happened to Kason and the others when they were on a mission, but she was going to go with it.

Jess looked up at Kason again and mouthed, "I love you," then turned back to Brian. Ignoring the sounds coming from Kason, she said, "Brian, seriously, why didn't you just talk to me before all this? Do you really think I wanted to hang around Tabitha? Seriously? She *was* fat. It was actually a bit embarrassing to go out with her. Do you know how much she'd eat? Jesus, I was actually a bit impressed. I only hung out with her because I was trying to do what I thought *you* wanted me to. "

Brian didn't look convinced. Jess kept talking, staying on the ground and trying not to look aggressive at all.

"You know the day she took all those pills? I brought them to her." Jess's stomach rolled at the lies she was telling Brian, but she *had* to get him to believe her. "We'd talked about it. Oh, she never told me she was having sex with your friends, but she said she was thinking about seeing if taking the pills could make it better for her. I might have egged her on a teensy bit."

Jess could feel Kason's eyes boring into the back of her head, but she continued on. "I told her that maybe if one pill made the sex better, taking more would make it feel even better. She asked me how many she should take and I told her to take the whole fucking bottle."

At Brian's look of disbelief she rushed on. "I know, it's absolutely ridiculous, but she trusted me and believed me. I told her to take them as soon as I left so they'd be able to go into effect by the time your friends got there. She wasn't that smart."

"You always said she *was* smart," Brian said deadpan.

"Well, yeah, because I didn't want to offend you. She *was* your niece! If you had just *told* me she was your ticket to the drugs, I might not have encouraged her so much. But you were the one who was always complaining about her. I thought I was doing you a favor!"

Jess tried not to throw up. She silently sent a prayer up to Tabitha asking for her forgiveness for the absolute filth that was coming out of her mouth. Jess couldn't think about what Kason thought about her right now, she just kept talking.

"And really, Brian, now that I've had it rough with him," Jess pointed over her shoulder with her thumb at Kason, "I get it. I get what you like now. I like it. I want it like that with you. We were always so sweet and vanilla. I bet that's not how you *really* like it is it?"

Jess's heart was beating hard in her chest. She was getting to the meat of her plan and it could go wrong in a big way if she wasn't careful.

Seeing Brian's eyes light up in interest and lust, Jess forged on. "Yeah, I bet you like to tie your women up don't you? He tied me up once, and I liked it. I know you like to hold me by my hair, but I haven't done that in the bedroom before. Bet I'd get off on it."

Jess reached behind her and under her shirt. She unsnapped her bra and kept talking as Brian's eyes followed her movements. "I haven't ever tried drugs either. I bet that makes it even hotter, doesn't it? Does it make you feel like you're floating?" Jess pulled her bra strap down one arm and took her arm out of the strap, keeping herself covered by her shirt as she moved. "Have you and your friends shared a woman before? That's another thing I haven't done yet either. Kason's been too possessive. But I bet your friend's hands would feel good on my tits as you shove your dick in me."

Jess pulled her other hand out of her bra strap and pulled the bra off completely. She dropped it behind her on the ground, once again ignoring the furious sounds coming from Kason. She was breathing hard. Jess had no idea if she would get out of this in one piece, but she had to try. She arched her back and put her hands on her hips, making sure to pull her shirt taut at the same time, showing off her nipples, which were clearly visible in the cool night air against the stretched tight cotton. Jess slowly stood up, still talking.

"Have you done that, Brian? What about an unconscious girl? What is it called? A roofie? I bet that'd be fun. Imagine being able to do whatever you want with someone and they can't complain about it. I can't say I want to be the one drugged though, I'd rather watch." Jess laughed, hoping it didn't sound to Brian as fake as it did to her own ears.

"What are your fantasies, Brian?" Jess held her breath. This could go wrong so quickly, but dammit she had to do something.

"I fantasize about fucking you right here in front of this asshole. I want to shove my dick down your throat until you're choking on it, testing your gag reflex. Would you like that, Jess?"

Jess gulped. Fuck. "Oh yeah, you know I've always loved your dick. What else? You'd like it if I fought, wouldn't you?"

"Oh yeah, because when you settled down and accepted the inevitable, it'd be perfect."

"What about if you had to chase me first?"

The sounds coming out of Kason were nonstop now. He was grunting and obviously trying to talk, but Jess ignored him. It looked like he figured out her plan and wasn't happy.

"You think you can outrun me, Jess?" Brian asked with a sneer. "You're a cripple. You wouldn't get five steps before I'd be on you."

Jess lifted her arms and gathered her hair on top of her head, making sure to arch her back at the same time. She knew her breasts were jiggling under her shirt and fear was making her nipples peak. She threw her hip to the side, ignoring the twinge of pain the action caused.

"Of course I can't outrun you. You know how badly I walk and run with my hip. But you could give me a head start . . . make it more exciting for you."

Jess held her pose, but rejoiced inside as Brian actually considered her words. She tried to sweeten the pot a bit. She lowered her arms and put her hands on her hips again. "Tell you what, you give me a two minute head start. You can watch which way I go. If you catch me in two minutes, I'll let you and your buddies fuck me at the same time, as long as you share your drugs with me."

"And if it takes longer than two minutes?"

Jess wanted to jump up and down like a little kid, even though she knew she was still in deep shit. She had him. Brian was going to go for it.

"Then your buddies are out, but I'll let you stick your huge cock down my throat right here in the woods."

Jess couldn't come up with anything else at the moment. Hopefully Brian was cocky enough to believe he'd be able to get her within the original two minute time frame. And more hopefully, Tex and Kason's friends would hurry up and get to them.

"Oh, you'll take my cock, Jess, whether it takes two minutes or two seconds."

Jess smiled what she hoped was a seductive smile at Brian.

"Looks like your boyfriend isn't too pleased with you."

Jess didn't want to turn around and look at Kason. She was disgusted with her own words, she could only imagine what Kason thought. But knowing Brian had pointed it out because he wanted her to look, she turned.

The fury on Kason's face, Jess expected to see. His eyes were blazing with it. His toes were curled and every muscle in his body was taut. But under the fury, Jess saw the concern, compassion, and even love in his eyes. She quickly turned back around. Shit. She couldn't do what she needed to if she kept looking at Kason. She needed to stay removed from it all.

"So, want to play catch-me-if-you-can?"

Brian cocked his head at her and said, "You know, I regret not talking to you now. If I'd only known what a kinky little whore you were, we would've gotten along much better."

Jess smiled and winked at Brian, but didn't say anything.

"Yeah, sure, I'll bite. I have nothing to lose. You aren't getting away from me on that gimp leg. It's gonna feel so good to hear you scream as I take you, Jess. You always were a limp fish lying under me, so still. I can't wait to feel you squirm as I take what I want, how I want, and whenever I want. Your two minutes start . . . *now*!"

CHAPTER 17

Wolf smiled over at Caroline who was sitting in the seat in his car next to him. She was tired from the alcohol she'd drank that night with her friends and she turned her head to look at him.

"I love you, Matthew."

"I love you too, Ice. Have a good time?"

"You know I did."

Wolf put his hand on Caroline's thigh and moved it slowly upward. "Tired?"

Caroline put her hand over his as it moved up her body. "Never too tired for you."

They smiled at each other until the light turned green and Wolf had to turn his attention back to the road.

His phone vibrated in his pocket and Wolf leaned to the side. "Ice, can you grab my phone and check to see what that text is about?"

Caroline groped Matthew's butt as she pulled his phone out of his back pocket. She smiled as he groaned and said under his breath, "Watch it, or you'll pay for that later."

She smiled and looked down at the phone. She swiped the face of the phone, put in Wolf's password and clicked on the text message. It was from Tex. Caroline frowned, it was late in California, but it was *really* late in Virginia.

"Who's it from?"

"Tex."

Wolf sat up in his seat, losing the easy going vibe he had going on. "What does he want?"

Caroline read the message and her eyebrows scrunched together in confusion. "I have no idea."

"What does it say?"

What the hell is Jessyka doing in the middle of Brant park?

The phone in Caroline's hand started ringing. She startled and almost dropped it, but then immediately handed it over to Matthew, knowing something was wrong.

Wolf took his phone and seeing it was Abe, swiped it to answer the call.

"What?"

"Did you get a text from Tex?"

"Fuck. Yeah, you too?"

"Yeah."

"Call Cookie, I'm calling Dude. We'll see if they know what Tex is talking about."

Wolf ended the call and took the time to ask Caroline a quick question before he called Dude. "Jess was there tonight, right?"

"Yeah, she left around eleven." Caroline looked at her watch, "About forty minutes ago. She said Kason texted her and was anxious to get her home. She said goodbye to us and the guys, then left out the front door."

Wolf didn't respond, but quickly clicked on Dude's number.

"I got it too," Dude said by way of greeting.

"Did you sense anything weird when Jess left tonight? Ice said she got a text from Benny and decided to leave."

"Not really, or I wouldn't have let her leave. But given what's going on now, she did comment on how she was all bugged up and that Tex could find her if he needed to."

"She knew," Wolf deducted quickly.

"Yeah, that's what I'm thinking," Dude agreed.

"Why wouldn't she just tell you guys something was wrong?" Wolf didn't understand what Jess had been thinking.

"What if the text she received wasn't really from Benny?"

"Fuck."

Wolf turned the wheel and guided his car into a large parking lot. He did a wide U-turn and headed back to the street. "Head back to the bar, we'll meet there. I'll try Benny, then Tex."

Wolf clicked off the phone without bothering to say goodbye. Caroline was silent next to him. He took the time to silently run his hand over the top and back of her head to reassure her, then pulled up Benny's number.

The phone rang, and went to voice mail after four rings. "Fuck." Wolf didn't bother trying again. If Benny didn't answer, something was horribly fucked up. He pushed the number for Tex.

"I haven't been able to get a hold of Benny," Tex said as he answered the phone.

"Me either. I've got the guys, we're meeting back at *Aces*."

"Okay, everyone's about the same distance away. I take it Jess shouldn't be in the middle of Brant Park?"

"Fuck no."

Wolf could hear Tex tapping on computer keys in the background. "Okay, she's moving deeper into the woods. Looks like she's headed smack dab to the middle of the park."

"Keep me updated, call me if something changes."

"Will do."

The connection was cut.

Caroline whispered from next to Wolf. "What's going on, Matthew? Did someone take Jess?"

Wolf sighed. "Yeah, Ice. I think someone took Jess."

"I don't understand. Did she walk outside knowing someone was out there?"

"What would you do if someone threatened me, and told you if you didn't go with them, they'd hurt me?" Wolf knew what Caroline's answer would be, and wasn't really expecting her to answer.

Caroline looked at Matthew in horror. "Oh my God. We didn't even think about that."

"Yeah," Wolf agreed grimly and pushed the gas a little harder. The team had to figure this shit out, and quickly. Not only was one of their women in danger, it looked like their teammate was as well.

* * *

JESS RAN AS FAST as she could. She knew she wasn't moving quickly enough, but the further she could get away from Kason, the better chance Tex and his team had of getting to him before Brian could get back and hurt him after dealing with her.

The branches scratched Jess's face as she blindly ran in the dark. She'd started out running in the opposite direction from where Brian had left the car, then as soon as the leaves had obscured her from Brian, she turned ninety degrees and changed direction. She did this once more until she hoped she was headed back the way they'd originally come. Jess had no idea where she was, or even how far it was. All she cared about was keeping as far ahead of Brian as she could.

When Brian got a hold of her he was going to hurt her. Jess knew it, she wasn't an idiot. But she also knew if Brian took the time to do all the things she'd taunted him with, that meant that Kason would have a better chance of getting free or being rescued by his team.

There was no way she could keep ahead of Brian, but if she zigzagged enough, and tried to hide more than run, maybe, just maybe she'd buy herself, and Kason, enough time.

Jess couldn't believe Brian and Tammy were as cold-hearted and psychopathic as they were. She refused to cry about Tabitha now. How scared and confused the girl must've been. Shaking her head, Jess tried to put it out of her mind. She had to figure out how to get both her and Kason out of the current mess they were in. She'd grieve later . . . if she had a later.

Jess had purposely left her bra behind because she knew it had a tracking device in it. The strip tease had done its job in distracting Brian, but it had also been the only way she could think of to be able to leave a tracking device behind for Kason. Jess also had a thingie in her shoe, but there was no way she could leave her shoe behind, especially since she had to run through the damn woods. It had to have been her bra.

Jess fell for the fourth time, but immediately forced herself to get up. She had to keep moving. She couldn't stop. Every painful step meant she was one step, hopefully, closer to rescue, but most importantly, one step further away from Kason and the danger he was in from a pissed-off Brian.

* * *

WOLF PULLED into the parking lot of *Aces* and slammed on the brakes. He put the car in park and hurried over to his friends.

"Anything?"

"No, nothing looks out of place here," Mozart said in a crisp business-like voice.

The men huddled together, trying to hash out what had happened when Alabama called from across the parking lot.

"I think that's Kason's car!"

The men all turned and headed to where Alabama had pointed. Shit, they were fucking losing it. They should've seen his car first thing, they'd all been too eager to talk with each other than to scout out the scene first. They had to get their act together if they were going to get Benny out of whatever bullshit he was in. Without touching anything on the car they walked around it.

"Doesn't look tampered with," Abe observed. "But why'd Benny park it here and not directly in front?"

"What if he was lured here too?" Cookie mused.

Wolf took his phone out and called Tex and put him on speaker. "Benny's car is here."

"Hold on."

The team waited impatiently as Tex searched for something on his computer. They all knew time was of the essence. It always was. Every second counted. They all remembered how Cheyenne had been saved. If they'd waited too long, the bombs that had been strapped to her body would have gone off and killed her and hundreds of other people as well.

"Benny received a call from the bar around ten. Call lasted about twenty seconds," Tex said in a brusque voice.

"Okay, so someone lured him here and told him something was going down and he had to keep it on the down-low." Wolf turned in circles, checking out the area as he reasoned out what had happened earlier that night. "He didn't call us, so the person probably threatened Jess in some way." Wolf walked toward the side of the bar. "He didn't want to go in the front door, so he snuck around the side thinking he'd be able to get in through the alley."

Wolf, Abe, and Dude entered the alley while Mozart and Cookie stayed in the parking lot, keeping their eyes on the women who were huddled together around Wolf's car.

The team searched the alley for something, anything, to give them more information about what had happened to their teammate.

"There!" Abe pointed. They all saw the blood spots on the ground and Benny's K-bar lying open and clean on the ground.

"Okay, so whoever it was, took Benny by surprise. They incapacitated him, then sent Jess a text saying if she didn't go with them, they'd hurt or kill him."

"I have a feeling that's right on, Wolf," Tex said from the phone Wolf was still holding. "I hacked into her phone. I'm sending the picture to Abe that was sent to Jess from Benny's phone."

The men waited, and when Abe's phone vibrated, they huddled around it.

"Dammit!" Dude exclaimed upon seeing the picture of Benny unconscious and bleeding on the screen. "No wonder she did exactly what they wanted her to when she saw this."

Wolf was moving back to the parking lot. "Status on Jess, Tex?"

"She's been stationary for about seven minutes now. Still in the middle of the park."

"Okay, we're headed there now," Wolf told him. "I'm keeping you live on my phone, let me know if anything changes."

Wolf stalked toward the five women standing near his car. He pulled Caroline into him as he reached her side. "We're going to get them back. I need you guys to go into the bar and stay there. Don't fucking move until we get back. I don't care if you get a text or a call. Don't. Move. Got it?"

Ice hugged her man tightly, then pulled back. "Got it, Matthew. Tex has us. You go."

Wolf loved Caroline. She was tough when she needed to be and practical as all get out. She knew just what to say to calm him down. "Thank you, Ice." He kissed her once, hard, then backed away. He watched as his teammates said a quick passionate goodbye to their women as well, then they turned back to him.

"We'll take my car and Dude's. Let's get this done."

The men nodded in agreement and without a word, split up into the two cars and they all headed toward Brant Park to find their teammate and his woman.

* * *

JESS GRUNTED as Brian tackled her and she landed hard on her knees, then her stomach. The light from the lantern on his hat shone crazily around them. She knew it was only a matter of time before he caught up with her . . . but she'd made it further than she thought she would. Brian roughly turned Jess over until she was on her back. He grabbed both her wrists in his and braced them above her head. He sneered down at her and Jess flinched away from the light shining in her eyes from his hat.

"Tag." Brian sing-songed and then laughed at his own joke.

"You caught me!" Jess said, still trying to buy time.

"Fucking right I did." Brian pulled Jess to her feet and shoved her in front of him until he got to a sort of clearing. He shoved her and Jess fell on her hands and knees. Jesus, her hands and knees were going to be permanently bruised before this was all said and done. Before she could move, Brian was behind her. He grabbed her hips and pulled her back until his cock rested against her ass. He thrust against her as he described exactly what he was going to do to her.

Jess blocked out Brian's voice, refusing to listen to the disgusting words coming out of his mouth and desperately looked around for something she could use as a weapon. There was a lot of trash in the small clearing . . . it'd obviously been used as a camping spot for some unfortunate homeless person at one time or another.

She looked to her right and saw the last thing she expected to see in the middle of nowhere. It was part of a cinderblock. Jess had no idea how it had gotten there, perhaps a homeless person had lugged it in thinking it could be used for something, but whatever the case . . . right now it was a godsend.

If she could only get to it.

Brian pulled her back to her feet by her hair, his favorite way of handling her apparently, and shoved her up against a tree. "I'm going to fuck you right here. You're going to take everything I've got. I'll fill all your holes with my cock, then we're going back to your boyfriend and I'm going to watch as *you* put a bullet in his brain. Then you'll come back to my place with me and I'll tie you to my bed and you'll serve as my little honey pot for my friends. Anytime I want drugs, you'll take my friends any way they want and you'll be fucking quiet about it or I'll arrange for your other friends to die as well. You want that? You want to kill your little girlfriends or their men? I'll fuck them before I kill them too. Defy me, Jess. I fucking dare you."

Jess couldn't breathe. She couldn't think. All she could see was Kason tied against the tree, bleeding from a bullet hole in his forehead that Brian had made her put there. Other images flew through her brain, one after another. Alabama lying dead on the floor, Fiona tied up and begging Brian's friends to leave her alone. Cheyenne, Summer, Caroline. She couldn't even think about the guys. They were her friends. No fucking way was Brian doing this. He was a monster. He sold his own niece for drugs and scarred her so badly she felt she had no way out but to take her own life.

Jess lunged away from Brian, taking him by surprise. She got about three limping steps away when Brian managed to stick out his leg and trip her. Jess fell hard once again and Brian threw back his head and laughed at her.

"Fuck, that was funny. You're still trying to get away from me. When are you going to learn that you're nothing but a fucking cripple, Jess? No one wants you. You're nothing and nobody. Do you think I believed your sob story back there? Hell no, I know you loved that fat bitch. You're mine now and I'm not fucking letting you go again just so you can go to the cops. I'll fuck you, and my friends will fuck you, and you won't ever get away from me again. I'll chain you to the bed and you'll never see the light of . . ."

Brian's words ended abruptly. He never saw the cinderblock that came toward his face. The last thing Brian knew was his feeling of triumph over the stupid crippled woman who was lying at his feet.

* * *

"Wolf, we got problems." Tex's words were sharp and biting. Wolf and Dude had just pulled into the parking lot at Brant Park. There was one other car in the lot.

"Talk to me," Wolf told Tex brusquely.

"I've got two marks now. One is stationary in the same place it's been for the last fifteen minutes. The other is moving. It started off heading north, then it turned back and is now coming toward you and the parking lot."

"What the hell?" Cookie said under his breath, hearing Tex's words.

"We'll stick together as long as we can, but if the tracks split up too far, we'll need to follow them separately," Wolf said, already setting out into the trees in the park.

The team agreed, and quickly followed Wolf, flashlights in hand lighting up the area as they started toward the beacons.

"What's going on, Tex? I know you can't see us, but are the marks still doing the same thing?"

"Affirmative. The one still isn't moving, and the other has now stopped too. Head north-northwest from the parking lot and you should run right into whoever has the tracker."

The men picked up their pace. They could run all night if they had to, but it looked like they only had to go a short distance before they'd come across the first tracking beacon that had once been on Jessyka.

The men pushed themselves hard. There was so much at stake. They'd been in brutal life-and-death situations before. Situations that included rescuing their own women, and this situation was just as important as any they'd been on before, perhaps more so. One of their own was in trouble. Not only one of their own team, but his woman as well. The stakes were twice as high.

"Tex?"

"Situation static," Tex told Wolf, indicating nothing had changed from the last time he'd reported in.

Wolf didn't bother to respond, he and his team just kept moving. "Spread out, we don't want to miss anything in the cover," Wolf urged the others.

The men fanned out until they were about ten feet apart, and still moving northwest through the thick foliage, their flashlights moving crazily in the darkness.

It was Dude who found Jess first.

"Here!"

The other men changed course immediately and closed in on Dude.

All five men stopped at the edge of the clearing and stared at the scene in front of them.

Jessyka was there, and so was her ex-boyfriend, or what they thought was Brian.

Dude edged slowly toward Benny's woman.

"Jess? You're safe now."

Jessyka didn't respond. She was crouched by Brian's body, breathing hard. She was holding on to a broken piece of cinderblock with both hands. They could all see the blood that had splattered over her upper body.

It was obvious Brian wasn't going to leave the park alive.

"Jess." Dude's voice lowered and he used his Dominant voice. "Put down the cinderblock."

"No."

The men all looked at each other. Jess's voice sounded off.

"He won't touch the others. I won't let him."

"He's not going anywhere. We'll make sure of it." Dude tried to reason with Jess.

"No! *I'll* make sure of it. I'm not a cripple. I'll fucking show him crippled."

Dude couldn't help the inappropriate smile that crept across his face, but looking down at the woman in front of him and the smashed in skull of Brian, made the smile disappear quickly.

Wolf had eased around behind Jess and Dude met his eye. They didn't want to do it this way, but they had to get Jess out of there. Dude nodded at his teammate.

Wolf came up behind Jessyka and circled his arms around her lifting her upper body up and off the ground.

Jess shrieked and kicked backward, dropping the heavy cinderblock in the process. "No! Let me go!"

"Shhhh, you're safe now, Jess. It's Wolf. I've got you."

"Wolf! He's gonna hurt Caroline. Make him stop!"

Her urgent words made Wolf's heart ache. "He won't hurt her, sweetie. You made sure of that. Come on." Wolf turned Jessyka around so she couldn't see Brian's body on the ground. "Talk to us. We're all here. Tex tracked you. Where's Benny?"

It was as his words snapped her out of wherever her mind had taken her. "Oh my God, Kason!" Jess wiggled in Wolf's arms until he loosened them enough so she could turn and face him. She grabbed hold of his shirt, leaving dark smears of blood on his navy blue shirt, and looked up at him. "Kason! You have to find him! He's hurt!"

"Okay, Tex'll lead us there."

"I'm coming too."

"No, you're not," Wolf had no sooner had the words out of his mouth when Jessyka stepped backward and had turned and started hobbling painfully back into the woods.

Cookie swooped in and picked her up with one hand under her back and the other under her knees. "Come on, Jess, it's obvious you're in pain. Let Wolf, Dude, and Mozart go and get Benny for you. Is there anyone else out here?"

Jess struggled in Cookie's arms. "Let me go, Cookie. Please. Damn, I need to be there. He's so pissed . . ."

"Jess. Is there anyone else out here?" Dude bit the words out. He'd stepped over to Cookie and took hold of Jess's chin with his hand, forcing her to look at him.

Jess whimpered and panted hard. Finally she whispered, "I don't think so. I only saw Brian. But I don't know how he got Kason out here. He might've had help."

Dude kissed Jess on the forehead and said quietly, "We'll bring him to you, Jess. Hang in there."

Jess could only nod, then she watched as the three men left the clearing heading into the woods back the way she'd come as she was running from Brian.

Cookie and Abe headed back to the parking lot without another word. Jess laid her head on Cookie's chest and prayed they'd find Kason in one piece. She had no idea if he'd forgive the words she'd said while trying to placate Brian, but ultimately it didn't matter. As long as he was alive, she knew she wouldn't have done anything differently.

CHAPTER 18

Wolf, Dude, and Mozart followed the path that Jess had taken through the foliage. They could see where she fell and how hard she'd tried to keep ahead of Brian. It was obvious she'd been running for her life, and Benny's.

It wasn't too far from where they'd found Jess, and with Tex's directions, that they stumbled on their teammate. Benny was tied to a tree and had almost freed himself. There was rope still bound tightly around his legs, but the bindings that had been wrapped around his torso and the tree were hanging loosely.

Wolf stepped up to him with his K-bar knife and quickly sliced through the gag and the ropes around his torso. Dude cut through the bindings around his legs at the same time.

"Mother *fucker*," Benny spat out as soon as the gag was removed. "He's got Jess. We have to find her."

"We've got her, man. She's safe. Tex called us. We found her right before we got here to you."

Benny eased his legs to the side and leaned over and put his forehead on the ground. "Mother fucker," he said more quietly into the dirt. "Mother fucking fucker."

Dude put his hand on Benny's shoulder and squeezed.

Pulling himself together, Benny lifted his head and asked, "Brian?"

"Dead."

"Thank you."

"It wasn't us. He was dead when we got there. Jess killed him."

"Mother fucker." This time Benny's words were a whisper.

"She had a cinderblock in her hand when we found them. Brian was dead. Looks like Jess must've hit him at least a dozen times," Mozart told Benny quietly.

"Is she okay?" Benny asked, immediately climbing to his feet awkwardly. It was obvious his legs had fallen asleep after being tied to the tree for so long.

"She seems so."

Benny took a step, then swore. He'd forgotten his feet were bare.

Wolf sat down and started unlacing his boots. Without a word he took off his socks and handed them to Benny. Benny took them gratefully. It wasn't ideal, but having the wool socks between his bare feet and the rough ground would have to do. They'd done this before in an emergency. Hell, "The only easy day was yesterday" was the SEALs mantra. It was second nature to all of them to do what needed to be done.

While Wolf and Benny got prepared for the trek back to the parking area, Mozart picked up Jessyka's bra from the ground. "Pretty fucking smart," he murmured under his breath.

They all understood what she'd done. She knew there was a tracking device in the lining of her bra and she'd somehow removed it so that Tex could track Benny. If she hadn't left it behind, there's no telling when they would've found him. It looked like Benny probably would've freed himself before the night was over, but the tracking device simply sped up the process.

Benny stood up and without a word, took the garment from Mozart and stuffed it into the pocket of his cargo pants.

They left the area much slower than when they'd entered it, leaving the ropes on the ground for the police investigation that was sure to follow the clusterfuck of a night.

The four men didn't speak on their way back to the car, each lost in their own thoughts. Wolf on how close they'd come, once again, to losing one of their women. Mozart on how thankful he was that they'd decided to tell their women about the tracking devices, Dude about how much he admired Benny's woman, and Benny on how much he regretted dropping his knife when he'd been knocked unconscious, he could've gotten out of the damn ropes holding him to the damn tree way before Jess had been involved. But more importantly, how he couldn't wait to wrap his arms around Jessyka and not let go for days. She'd scared the shit out of him and he couldn't wait to see her for himself, to make sure she was all right.

* * *

JESS HUDDLED into the blanket Abe had wrapped around her shoulders when she'd settled into the passenger side of Dude's car. Abe and Cookie had stood on either side of her, efficiently guarding her and making her feel safe in the process. Abe called the cops and Cookie called Tex. Tex had heard what had happened in the clearing as he'd been on the line, but he also relayed back to Cookie that Wolf and the others had found Benny and were on their way back to the car.

Jess heard Cookie tell her Benny was all right as if she was in a tunnel and he was standing at the end of it. She couldn't believe it until she saw Kason with her own eyes. She couldn't get the image of him tied to a tree, helpless, out of her mind. Hell, intellectually she knew that didn't even come close to the kind of situations he'd probably been in as a SEAL, but *she* hadn't ever seen him in any of those situations.

She *had* seen him tied to the tree tonight, helpless, and she didn't know how else to get that image out of her mind other than to see him upright and alive and well. She could only see him with a hole in his forehead as Brian had threatened . . . and until she saw with her own eyes that he was okay, she knew she'd continue to see him that way.

Jess heard sirens in the distance, but didn't bother to look toward the road. Her eyes were fixed on the woods in front of her. She strained to catch a glimpse of Benny and the others. Finally she thought she saw lights winking in the distance. Jess heard Tex tell Cookie that they were almost to them and she stood up.

Neither Abe nor Cookie tried to stop her, but they did wince in sympathy as she painfully made her way to the edge of the forest. Her hip hurt, badly, but nothing would keep her from Benny. She hoped like hell he still wanted to see her after everything she'd said and done.

Finally the lights got closer and Jess could make out the forms of the men coming toward her. She dropped the blanket and made her way as fast as she could toward the bobbing lights.

Benny looked up and cursed. His crazy woman was obviously in pain, but she was coming at them as fast as her limp would allow.

He jogged ahead of his teammates and gathered Jess into his arms. He pulled her off her feet and buried his head in her neck. "Fuck," was all he could say. Benny knew when his teammates passed him and continued on to the cars, but he didn't care. All he could do was feel Jess's heart beating against his own.

Finally pulling his head back a fraction, Benny put her on her feet and put his hands on each side of Jess's head and forced her head up to meet his eyes. "Are you all right, gorgeous?"

Jess could only nod. She couldn't think of anything to say. She was in Kason's arms. She didn't know if she'd live to be here again, if he'd live to be there again. Finally, she said the only words she could, "I love you. I love you so much."

Benny crushed his lips to hers with a short but intense kiss, then tucked her back into his arms. With one hand on the back of her head and the other around her waist, he picked her up again and started toward the cars and his teammates. Jess's legs bumped against his as he walked, but he didn't give a damn.

Jess knew she should probably put her legs around Kason's waist to help him walk, but she couldn't. Her hip was screaming in pain and the thought of moving it was just too much. So she dangled in his arms and let him carry her however he wanted.

By the time Benny got to the cars, the police had arrived, along with an ambulance and a fire truck as well.

He carried Jess over to the ambulance and motioned with his chin for the paramedic to open the back doors. Benny climbed inside, never letting go of the most important thing in his life. It wasn't until he shuffled over to the gurney in the vehicle, that he loosened his hold.

"Let go, gorgeous, let's let the paramedics look you over."

Jess didn't loosen her hold. "I'm fine, Kason. Promise," she murmured against his chest.

"I believe you, but humor me."

At that point, Jess would've done anything Kason asked of her, so she finally pulled back and lay back on the crisp white sheet.

"Don't leave me?" Jess whispered as Kason stood up.

"I'm not going anywhere. Just moving out of the way." Benny moved up to the very front of the small space until he was kneeling next to Jess's head.

Benny watched as the paramedic asked Jess questions about how she felt and if she hurt anywhere. She claimed she didn't, except for her hip. She explained how one leg was shorter than the other and when she overdid it, her hip would ache.

Sometime in the middle of the examination, a crime scene investigator stuck her head inside the ambulance and asked if she could take pictures of Jessyka. She'd agreed and closed her eyes as the flashes from her camera went off. The crime scene tech took at least a thousand pictures, at least it seemed that way to Jess.

After she finally left, Benny asked the paramedic if he could have an alcohol wipe. He used it to gently wipe the splattered blood off of Jess's face, neck and hands. Finally, once she'd been thoroughly cleaned and the EMT was satisfied that she wasn't in imminent danger of passing away, Benny allowed the man to take a look at his own head.

The wound on Benny's head was shallow and not life threatening, even if it had bled a lot.

After refusing to be transported to the hospital and they'd both signed a piece of paper called an "Against Medical Advice" form that absolved the ambulance employees and medics of responsibility over them if they fell ill, Benny helped Jess shuffle out of the vehicle. As soon as she stood on her own feet by the bumper, he picked her up again and headed back to his friends and the police.

He wanted to talk to Jess alone. He needed to lay her on his bed and just hold her. He'd come way too fucking close to losing her tonight and he needed to feel her skin on skin.

"Benny, Lt. Walker needs your statement. Jess's too," Wolf told him in a soft voice.

Benny nodded, he'd expected it.

"He needs to talk to you separately."

Benny felt Jess's hand convulse against him, then loosen, as if she forced herself to let go. He hated this. Ignoring the officer and his teammates standing next to him, he put Jessyka's feet on the ground and leaned back and waited. Finally her eyes came up to his.

"I'll be right here. You'll be able to see me the entire time. Tell him everything, Jess. It'll be okay." He watched as she nodded and took a deep breath.

Jess let go of Kason and took a step backward. She could do this. She lived through the night, this was nothing in comparison. She might have to go to jail, but she felt comforted in the fact that if she was arrested, Kason and the guys would do what they could to get her a lawyer and hopefully get her out on bail. It scared the shit out of her, but Kason was alive . . . she could do anything now.

Lt. Walker gently took Jess's elbow in his and helped her over to his car. He sat her down in the front passenger seat of his cruiser and he crouched down in front of her.

"She okay?" Abe asked Benny softly, watching from a distance as the officer spoke with Jess.

"Yeah, she'll be sore for a while. She overworked her hip tonight, but otherwise she's remarkably good."

"She'll probably need to see a therapist after what she did to Brian."

Benny thought about it. Jess hadn't seemed to be traumatized to him, but he didn't really know for sure. "I'll talk to her."

"If she needs someone, she can talk to Dr. Hancock. She's done wonders for Fee," Cookie spoke up.

"Thanks, man." The voices fell away and all Benny could see was Jess. She was huddled in on herself in the cop car and he needed this to be done so he could see to her. He hoped like hell the man wasn't planning on cuffing her and hauling her off to the station, but he didn't know what Cookie had told the cops when they'd been called. But knowing Cookie, he probably explained the situation in a way that Jess would be safe from immediate arrest. Finally the police officer stood up and put his hand on Jessyka's shoulder. He walked back over to the SEALs.

"To put your minds at ease, I don't see any reason to bring her down to the station and arrest her tonight. But, she'll have to come in and give a complete statement. I'll need to get all of your statements as well, but I'm thinking it can wait until the morning. We've taken pictures of her and the crime scene techs are out in the park taking pictures there. Anyone have any objection to coming into the station tomorrow and officially talking with the investigators?"

The men were relieved. It was late. Their women were still at the bar waiting to go home. Wolf had called Caroline and let her know that Jess and Benny were safe. They all wanted to go home and hold their women.

"No problem, Lieutenant. Thank you. We'll be there as soon as we can," Wolf answered for all of them. He also knew Tex would be gathering any and all evidence to deliver to Lt. Walker as well. What he'd dig up would go a long way toward exonerating Jess and Benny.

"Appreciate that. The crime scene techs should be done with the scene in there . . ." the officer gestured into the woods, ". . . soon. We'll see you tomorrow . . . well, later today."

All Benny could think was, "Thank God." He turned on his heel and headed to Jess. She held up her arms as he came toward her and waited for him to get her.

Benny leaned down and picked her up with one arm under her knees and the other behind her back. Jess wrapped her arms around him, as she had before, and tucked her face into his neck. He carried her back over to Dude's car and got into the backseat. The other men quietly climbed in as well, Abe in with Dude, Jess, and Benny. Mozart and Cookie joined Wolf in his car.

Dude turned on the engine and pulled out of the parking lot and headed back to the bar. Not a word was spoken as they traveled the short distance. Finally pulling into *Aces* parking lot, Dude shut off his car and said, "I'm fucking proud of you, Jess. I don't know all that went on out there, but you obviously used your head and you survived. From what I can tell, you protected Benny. We found the tracking device you left behind, it led us right to him. Good job."

Jess buried her head deeper into Kason's neck and simply nodded, too overwhelmed to even answer the big man in the front seat. His voice had been gentle, but it was still too much for Jess right then. All she could see was the pictures Brian had put in her head that night. Of Cheyenne and the other women, hurting, or dead.

Dude climbed out and opened the back seat of his car for Benny. "You need any help?" he asked Benny.

"I got it. Thanks man. I owe you."

"You don't owe us dick, and you know it."

Benny just smiled at his friend. He settled Jess into the front passenger seat of his car and buckled her in. He kissed her forehead and closed the door. He jogged around to his side, still in Wolf's borrowed socks, and climbed in. He eased out of the lot and headed back to his apartment. He couldn't wait to hold Jess close and forget how they'd both come way too close to being killed or seriously hurt.

CHAPTER 19

Benny held Jess against his side as he fumbled with the key to his apartment and opened the door. He didn't take his arm from around her waist as he took most of Jess's weight and propelled them inside. He dropped the keys in the bowl by the door and shut and locked the door behind them.

Without letting go of her, Benny walked them to the counter and snagged the small envelope off the counter that held two pain pills left over from Jess's hospital visit the night Tabitha had died. She hadn't needed to use any more after that first night, and Benny had put them in a large bowl filled with odds and ends on the counter.

Benny then turned and made his way down the hallway to the master bedroom. Jess hadn't said a word, she simply clung to Benny's side and went wherever he led her.

He took them inside his bedroom and into the master bathroom. Benny walked her over to the toilet seat.

"Sit, gorgeous, give me a second."

Jess did as he asked. She eased down, with Benny holding onto her waist. Once she was sitting, Benny took his hands away from her and grabbed a cup from the counter and filled it with water. He shook out the pills and held them out to Jess along with the cup of water. She took both without protest and quickly swallowed the pills. She drank half the glass of water before handing it back to him.

Jess watched as Kason turned from the sink and pulled the shower curtain back. She fidgeted on her seat. She couldn't quite read Kason's mood and she was getting worried. She didn't think he was mad at her, but since he wasn't talking to her, she didn't know for sure.

Kason tested the temperature of the water and Jess kept her eyes on him as he then grabbed his shirt and tore it off over his head and dropped it on the floor. He eased the socks off his feet then turned to look her in the eyes as he unbuttoned and unzipped his cargo pants and dropped those to the floor as well. Jess's eyes widened as Kason then dropped his boxer briefs to the ground. He stood in front of her completely naked, the most handsome man she'd ever seen. He was hard in all the right places. He had muscles on top of muscles. Jess was confused, as it was obvious Kason wasn't aroused, and wasn't getting ready to have shower sex. His manhood hung flaccid between his legs. Jess hadn't often seen him when he wasn't turned on, and she wasn't sure what to make of whatever was happening.

Benny knew he was probably freaking Jessyka out, but he couldn't think of anything other than getting her clean and then holding her safe in his arms. The words she'd hurled at Brian tonight kept pinging around in his brain. He knew exactly what she'd been doing and he'd never felt more helpless in his life. He was very rarely helpless, and found he hated the feeling.

When the water was a comfortable temperature, he stepped over to Jess. She hadn't moved, that alone told him she was probably in more pain than she'd ever admit to.

"Arms up," Benny told her in a low voice. Jess immediately complied, and he helped ease her shirt over her head. Once the shirt was removed, Benny held out his hands palm up. "Let me help you stand." Jess wasn't wearing a bra, it was still in the pocket of his cargos, so there was no need for him to help her to remove it.

Jess put her hands in his and he took most of her weight as she stood up. Benny kneeled down, feeling Jess's hands rest on his shoulders for balance, and untied both her shoes and eased them off her feet. Then, still kneeling, he unbuttoned and unzipped her jeans and carefully pulled them down her legs. He tapped her right foot and she shifted until it was off the ground. Benny steadied her as she stood on one foot. He pulled the leg of her jeans off that leg, then repeated the same actions on her other side.

Benny meant to keep everything clinical and medicinal, but he couldn't help himself. Having her so close to him, and in one piece, he couldn't stop himself from reaching forward and drawing Jess to him. Benny lay his cheek on her belly and wrapped his arms around her and rested the palms of his hands on her back. He felt Jess's hands go to his head and gently caress him as he took comfort from having her safe in his arms.

Finally Benny looked up from his crouched position in front of her. "You're okay, aren't you, Jess?" he whispered, feeling raw inside.

"I'm okay," Jess whispered back.

Benny nodded and rested his forehead against the small pooch of her belly for a moment. Finally, he took a deep breath and pulled back an inch. He took hold of her panties on each side of her hips and drew them down her legs. He held Jess steady as she stepped out of them.

Benny stood up fully and wrapped his arm around her waist again and helped her to the side of the bathtub. Not allowing her to step over the deep side of the tub because he knew it would only cause her pain, Benny lifted her bodily into the shower. He closed the curtain after he stepped in with her and eased them both back until the water was hitting Jess's lower back.

He put both hands up to the side of her head and gently tipped it back until the water was running over her head. "Close your eyes, Jess, let me wash away the night."

Benny felt Jess melt into his hold. He gently squirted some of her shampoo into his hand and lathered up her hair. He washed and rinsed her hair twice before working in a handful of conditioner.

While the conditioner was doing its thing, Benny turned Jessyka until her front was facing the warm spray of water. When she went to protest, Benny shushed her with his words. "Let me, gorgeous. Let me clean you."

Jess nodded and Benny squirted some of his body wash into his hands. He needed her to smell like him. He wanted to rub a small piece of himself into her skin. He ran his hands over her chest and belly, then moved to her arms and hands. He carefully ran his soapy hands over her neck and face, making sure to leave not one inch of the skin that had been sprayed with Brian's blood unclean. Squirting more soap into his hands, he then moved to her legs. He briskly cleaned her sex, then rubbed her back. Once Benny was convinced Jess was clean and there wasn't one speck of Brian's blood left on her, he turned her back around and gently rinsed the conditioner out of her hair.

Then while Jess stood in the spray of the water, Benny quickly ran soap over his own body, not bothering to watch what he was doing, he kept his eyes locked on Jess. He took a step toward her and she stepped back until the water was hitting Benny, and not her. After a quick rinse, Benny reached around Jess and turned off the water. He then pulled her into his side again and opened the shower curtain.

He grabbed a towel and dried every inch of Jessyka's body before wrapping the towel around her. He lifted her out of the tub.

Benny watched as she turned to the sink and picked up her toothbrush. He wiped himself down quickly and then wrapped the towel around his own waist. Benny picked up his own toothbrush and followed Jess's lead. When they were ready, he took both their towels and threw them on the floor of the bathroom, not caring if they sat in a wet heap on the floor all night, he picked Jess up as he had in the park. He put both arms around her and lifted her up until her feet were off the ground and clasped her to him. Her front to his front, then carried her into the bedroom. He gently put her down, pulled back the covers and encouraged Jess to climb in. He followed behind her after turning off the overhead light.

It was now nearing dawn. Between the kidnapping, her running through the park, being rescued, and then being questioned by the police, the morning sky was slowly lightening as the sun made its way across the globe.

Benny wrapped both arms around Jess and pulled her to him. She buried her face into his chest and went to wrap one leg around his.

"No, Jess, I don't want any strain on that hip."

Benny put his own leg around hers instead, and pulled her into his body.

They were both quiet for a moment, enjoying the feel of each other's body, skin to skin. Jess broke the silence. "I wasn't sure I'd ever feel this again."

"I can't decide if I want to beat your ass for everything you did tonight or make love to you until the only thing you can feel and think about, is me."

"Do I get a choice? I choose door number two."

Benny smiled for a moment at her words, then got serious again. "Seriously, Jess, I think you took ten years off my life when I saw him push you into that clearing. He threatened to kill you if I didn't do exactly what he said. I bided my time, thinking I'd be able to get away after he got me where he wanted me. I didn't know exactly who was behind tying my ass to that tree, he had me blindfolded as he led me out there, until I saw him shove you to the ground in front of me. What the hell were you thinking?"

Jess didn't even raise her head, but instead snuggled closer to Kason and his arms got even tighter around her. "He sent me a picture of you bleeding and unconscious."

Without letting her continue, Benny barked, "So?"

Jess finally lifted her head at that. "So?"

"Yeah, so? Jess, I'm a SEAL. There's nothing you could've done, as a civilian, to help me."

"That's not exactly true." Jess was getting mad now. "You're not invincible, Kason. No one knew you were gone. No one knew where you were. Only some asshole who took your picture while you were *unconscious* and *bleeding* and sent it to *me*. Tex couldn't find you in the middle of a fucking forest for God's sake with nothing to go on. I knew I was tracked. I knew he could find *me*. I figured if I could get to you, you'd figure something out and Tex could rescue both of us. I didn't know you'd be all tied up without any damn shoes on."

She hiccupped and continued, obviously on a roll. Benny just let her get it out. Jess was so damn cute when she was riled up. He didn't think he'd ever get sick of watching her.

"I knew Brian was an asshole, but I didn't know he was *that* much of an asshole. I did the only thing I could think of. He wasn't going to let me just waltz on out of there. It's not like I could've said, 'Hey, I'm just going to take my bra off because it has a tracking device in it.' Dammit, Kason, what the hell are you smiling at?"

"I love you, Jess."

Jess stopped mid-rant and stared at Kason. Her face crumpled and she bit out, "Oh fuck."

Benny smiled tenderly at her and pulled her into his chest again.

"I love you so much, Kason. I was so worried about you."

Benny heard her words mumbled in his chest and he put one hand on the back of her head and caressed her.

"I know, gorgeous, I love you too."

"I d-d-didn't know what to do."

"You were amazing."

"You weren't wearing any s-s-shoes," Jess wailed, obviously having reached her breaking point. "They were r-r-raping T-T-Tabitha."

"I know, I'm so sorry."

"I d-d-didn't know, Kason. I swear I didn't."

"Of course you didn't, Jess. I'd never think that about you.

"I made all that stuff up that I told him."

"Jess. Hush. I *know*."

"He was going to go back and kill you. He s-s-said he was going to make me put a b-b-bullet in your head. Then he said he was going to r-r-rape Caroline and fuck the other girls. I didn't want his filth to touch them. I didn't want you to d-d-die." Jess lifted her head and looked Kason in the eye. "I killed him. I hit him with that cement block. Then I did it again. I didn't stop even when he was on the ground and not moving. All I could see was Tabitha, and you, and Cheyenne and the others . . . I'm not sorry. I'd do it again if I had to."

Benny reached up and took Jess's head in his hands and held her still. He saw her red-rimmed eyes and her running nose. She'd never looked more beautiful. "Good for you. I'm so fucking proud of you, I can't stand it. You didn't back down, you thought on your feet and you did what you had to do. I'm not thrilled you were out there in the first place and that you put yourself out there though. I'm sorry as hell I couldn't rescue or protect you, but you did it for yourself. I fucking love you so damn much."

Benny kissed Jess once, hard, then drew back, not letting go of her head. "I'm sorry you had to kill him, I'd never want that on your conscience, but I'm not sorry he's gone."

Jess bit her lip, then pouted. "I didn't get my night you promised me."

With her words, Benny knew Jess was going to be all right. He didn't see any angst in her eyes at taking Brian's life. He knew it might hit her later and she might feel remorseful, but he was thankful she wasn't broken as a result. He'd still suggest she get counseling until they were both a hundred percent sure she was okay, but for now he was relieved as all get out that she seemed to be okay. Benny kissed her forehead and brought her back into his hold. "You'll get your night, gorgeous. I promise." After a beat he asked, "How much pain are you in?"

"On a scale of one to ten?" Jess asked groggily, snuggling deeper into his arms.

"Yeah, on a scale of one to ten."

"Around a twelve."

Benny made a distraught sound in his throat and made like he was going to get out of bed.

"If you move one inch I'm going to have to hurt you," Jess grumbled, tightening her arms around him. "Yes, I hurt. But all I want to do is lie here with you. Feel you against me. I didn't know if I'd ever have this again. I took the pills, they'll kick in soon enough. I'll be okay. Please, Kason. Give me this. I *need* this. I promise I'll feel better when we get up. I haven't run in years and my body is reminding me why I shouldn't go on long romantic walks or run through the woods away from a crazy psychotic asshole. Please? Just hold me?"

"If it's not better later, you're going to the doctor."

"Promise. Thank you. I love you."

"And I love you too, gorgeous." Benny kissed her on the top of the head. "Sleep. Tomorrow, well later today, we'll start the rest of our lives together."

"That sounds good."

Benny held Jessyka as she fell asleep. He knew they had a lot to figure out in the next few days. The team had to give their statements to the police. Jess would have to continue to deal with the legal ramifications of having killed Brian. Benny didn't think it'd be an issue based on how Brian had hurt her before. Benny also hoped there would be some evidence in his townhouse about his drug activities.

They'd also have to deal with Tammy. If what Brian had told Jessyka was true, she was just as guilty in the pimping out of her daughter as Brian was. Benny also knew Jess would have to psychologically deal with everything she'd learned that night. They'd spent the last few hours hyped up on adrenaline and he knew she hadn't had time to process everything that had happened.

But Benny figured she'd be all right. Everything he'd told her tonight was true. Jess was tough and smart and she'd done well in trusting Tex to bring his team to their rescue. She'd been put in a horrible situation that neither he, nor any of the other guys had even thought about. They hadn't thought someone would use *them* to lure the more vulnerable women into a dangerous situation. They'd have to do some soul searching about that. They'd all thought tracking the women would keep them safe, but it was obvious they'd missed the huge flaw in that thinking. Brian was an idiot, but he'd managed to find the one thing that would present Jessyka to him as if on a silver platter. Jess had done the best she could in a fucked up situation, and the bottom line was that she'd trusted Tex and the rest of the team to get to both of them in time. Thank god they had.

Benny held Jess long into the morning as the room slowly brightened. He watched her breathe in and out and he never felt happier. She was alive. He was alive. They loved each other. He felt like the luckiest man alive.

CHAPTER 20

"You know you were a bonehead, right?" Wolf asked Benny, completely relaxed with one arm thrown over Caroline's shoulders as they sat at a table in *Aces* a week after Benny's kidnapping.

"Shut it," Benny responded to his team leader and friend.

"Seriously," Dude joined in, not willing to let it go. "I wasn't allowed to go into that basement and get Shy out by myself, I don't know why you think *you're* superman or something and could rush in singlehandedly and save your woman." Dude's words were teasing, but they all knew there was more than a kernel of truth to them.

"Look, I could sit here and give you all a load of shit about how I thought I had it under control and how it wouldn't have been a big deal if I hadn't been taken by surprise, but we all know that's a load of crap. I fucked up. I admit it. I should've immediately called one of you, or hell, even Tex, to see what the situation was. I've been trained better than that. Hell, if anyone on one of my teams did that shit I'd have blown a gasket on them."

Benny looked down at Jess. She had one hand resting on his thigh and he could feel the heat from her hand burning into his leg. He almost lost her. She'd had to do the unthinkable and kill a man, because he ignored all his training and leaped before he looked. "All I can say is that when Brian said that Jess was in danger, I could think of nothing but getting to her as fast as I could."

His teammates all nodded, knowingly. They'd all been there. They understood better than anyone else. "But I've learned my lesson. No more lone wolf shit from here on out. Even if, God forbid, this happens again. We're a team. Always. We all need each other. I won't forget again."

"See that you don't," was Abe's response. His harsh words were tempered with a smile. Benny relaxed, glad the well-deserved ass kicking was out of the way.

"I have no idea how I got so lucky to be sitting here with all of you today," Jessyka told the men and women around her honestly and with emotion clear in her voice. "I mean, I always knew the military was a close-knit group, but I had no idea it'd be like this."

When Caroline went to say something, Jess held up her hand to stop her and continued speaking. "I saw you week after week in the bar. I watched as each of you guys," she motioned to the men, "found a woman who was perfect for you. Abe, you always put the women you dated first, but they obviously didn't care about you. Then you found Alabama. I watched as she made sure you had refills of your beer, she ordered you food when you came to the bar after working all day, she even made you go home before everyone else when she knew you were tired."

Jess watched as Alabama leaned her head against Abe's shoulder and he kissed the top of it and turned his attention back to her. "And you, Cookie. You had to go all the way to Mexico to find Fiona, but you were tenacious in your quest to make sure she always felt safe. In return, she always does her best to give you what you need, whether that be giving you the chair against the wall, or a shoulder rub when you're tense. Mozart, you were suffering. You held a grudge against everyone and it was obvious to see. Summer helped you let that go and cling to love instead. In the end, your love for her was more important than revenge for yourself."

Jessyka hurried to finish. The looks the guys were giving her were going to make her start bawling any second now.

"And Dude, I know you never realized it, but you never used your left hand for anything, you always kept it in your lap. You didn't realize that the fact you only have part of a hand didn't mean jack squat to anyone around you, and if it did, they weren't good enough for you anyway. Cheyenne was made for you. She never saw you as incomplete or wounded. She only sees your heart.

"Caroline, you and Wolf were the catalyst that started all of this." At their looks of amusement she continued. "I know, you think I'm crazy, but I wanted to be just like you guys. The other guys here did too. They saw what a good, healthy relationship was supposed to be like. Shortly after you moved here, the rest of the guys stopped being such horn dogs and started paying attention to what they really wanted in their lives.

"I knew you were all friends, but I thought that was as far as it went. I had no idea that not only are you all friends, you're family as well. I wanted to be a part of this, but never in a million years dreamed I would be, not like this." Jess turned to Kason. "I love you so damn much. I'd do anything for you. I'd walk right into the hands of a crazy psycho every day of my life if it meant keeping you safe."

Benny growled at her and leaned over and lifted Jess into his lap so she was sitting sideways and still facing their friends.

Jess continued talking from within Kason's arms. "I used to think that therapy was for wimps." When Hunter looked like he was going to say something, Jess continued quickly. "And I thought I'd be fine after what happened . . . but thanks to Fiona urging me, and some soul searching, I've realized that it's okay to need to talk to someone about what happened. My situation is way different than Fiona's, and Alabama's, and Summer's and even yours, Cheyenne, but just because I find talking to the doctor about what I did, and what Brian and his sister did, soothing, doesn't mean I'm crazy or that I'll need to see a shrink for the rest of my life. I have more respect for the eleven of you sitting around this table than I ever have for anyone in my entire life."

Jessyka took a deep breath, glad she'd said what she needed, and wanted, to say before anyone could interrupt her. The couple of visits to Fiona's therapist had helped a lot, even though she didn't think, at first, she needed to see her. She'd most likely continue to see her to talk through everything that happened, but for now, she was good with everything.

"I think, however, that we've all had enough drama in our lives. Can we please, maybe, just live like normal people without being lost, kidnapped, or used for someone's revenge for at least a few weeks? I mean, what else could we go through?" Jess finished exasperatedly.

Everyone moaned and shook their heads.

"Jesus, Jess, you can't say that shit," Cookie groaned. "Seriously, you've just jinxed us."

"No way, we're through. We're destined to live easy-going normal lives from here on out. After all, we've all found men of our own, we're good," Caroline said this as if she was laying down the law.

"That's true. Now that we've found our men and settled down, we shouldn't have any more drama," Cheyenne agreed with Caroline.

"We haven't all found our mate though," Jess pointed out.

"Uh, I hate to burst your bubble, gorgeous, but none of us are letting you girls go. You're stuck with us," Benny said while nuzzling the side of Jess's neck.

"Tex," Jessyka said matter-of-factly. "He's a defacto part of this team too. And from what I understand, he isn't with anyone."

The group was silent for a moment, then Dude spoke up. "Hon, we haven't really sat down with Tex and talked through any of this shit, but he's even more sensitive about his leg than I am with my hand."

It was true. Tex talked a good game when it came to the prosthetic he wore ever since he'd been medically retired from the Navy, but everyone was aware that he joked a little too much about how he was crippled and laughed when women turned him down once they found out about his injury.

"But Dude, Tex is a part of this team. He *has* to find his perfect match. Face it, if we all somehow found each other, he will too." Jess leaned back against Benny, resting her head on his shoulder and her cheek on his chest. She wrapped an arm around his shoulders and idly played with his hair at the nape of his neck. "I don't know how, and I don't know where, but you guys have all said it yourself. Tex can find anyone no matter what. I have a good feeling about this. He'll find his woman, one way or another."

* * *

THOUSANDS OF MILES AWAY, on the other side of the country, Tex tapped rapidly on his keyboard.

Mel? Are you there? Haven't heard from you in a while.

After a few minutes with no response, Tex tried again.

I'm worried about you. Please. Talk to me. I miss your sarcasm. ;)

When there was still no response, Tex tried one last time to connect with the woman he'd been chatting with online for the last few months.

If you don't answer me, I'm going to have to do something drastic to make sure you're all right. I know you never wanted to talk on the phone, or exchange photos, but I have to know you're okay. I've already given you my cell number, please call me.

Tex got up and adjusted his prosthetic before walking into his kitchen to grab something to eat for dinner. He brought his plate back into his computer room and glanced over the three monitors sitting on his desk, then he looked over at the GPS coordinates that were constantly displayed on a map. He smiled. All his friends, and their women, were currently at *Aces*, most likely eating and hanging out as friends did.

Tex loved each and every one of them, and he was pleased he played a part in keeping them together. Using his computer and his skills to track people down, made him feel good, when most days he didn't feel very worthy. He'd missed feeling as if he was part of a team when he retired. He lost the adrenaline rush that came from successfully completing a mission when he'd left.

He'd been cut off from everything he'd loved and hadn't had a chance to figure out what he was going to do with his life. The Navy had been his life. But he'd always been good with computers. And between his computer skills and some of the nefarious people he'd met in his life, he'd found his new niche.

If he felt jealous of his friends and the wonderful women they'd found to spend the rest of their lives with, Tex would never let on.

Tex thought back to the conversation he'd had with Jess, Benny's woman, the other night. She'd called to thank him for noticing so quickly something was weird the night Benny had been used as a lure to get her out of *Aces*. She'd ranted and raved at him that it was asinine to only track the women. She'd had a compelling argument, telling Tex that if he'd been tracking Benny the night he'd been kidnapped by her crazy ex, she never would've had to put herself in danger.

When Jess had put it that way, Tex couldn't disagree with her. Thus, the six big bad Navy SEALs he'd gotten to know very well over the last months, were now all owners of shiny new tracking devices.

The men had balked about wearing the trackers when they were out of the country on a mission, but Tex had pointed out that he was the only one who knew about the devices, and it couldn't hurt to have the extra protection when they were in foreign countries doing the dirty work that was too dangerous for most other military teams. They'd agreed to put the devices in their packs as a concession. Tex wanted to point out that packs could be lost or stolen, but the women had been so relieved, he'd dropped it.

Tex turned back to his computer screen, trying to put his friends out of his mind. Hopefully they'd seen the last of the drama they'd all been through over the last year or so.

He clicked some buttons on his keyboard and stared at the chat box he'd just been using to talk to Melody.

User unknown

Tex frantically clicked more buttons, then swore under his breath and leaned back in his chair and put his hands behind his head. She'd deleted her account. She wasn't just logged off, she'd severed the only connection they had with each other.

They'd been talking for months, and she'd never given any overt indication that anything was wrong, but Tex still sensed there was something. Obviously he was right. He knew her well enough to know she was too polite to just up and disappear without a word . . . at least he thought he did.

They hadn't gotten into anything sexual, but they'd definitely shared some intimate thoughts. Melody was the only person he'd told how useless he felt and how, even though he'd ultimately begged the doctor to remove his mangled leg, he hated the fact that he wasn't whole. He'd even opened up to her about the phantom pain he still felt all the time in his leg, a leg that wasn't even there.

Melody had understood. She'd said all the right things. But thinking about it now, Tex realized she'd never *really* told him anything about herself. Oh, he knew she liked to eat Mexican food and that pink was her favorite color, but she'd never opened up to him about the things that really mattered in her life.

He pushed up the sleeves on the shirt he was wearing and crouched over his keyboard. If Melody thought she could erase their connection as easily as deleting her user account, she had another think coming.

The SEALs always said he could find anyone, it was time to put his skills to use . . . for himself this time. Something was wrong. He'd find Melody and figure out what it was. Hopefully he wouldn't be too late.

* * *

Find out what happens in Tex's story

Protecting Melody

PROTECTING JULIE

SEAL OF PROTECTION, BOOK 6.5

Julie Lytle is working hard to turn her life around. Being kidnapped by sex traffickers changed her drastically, but having grown up the spoiled daughter of a senator, Julie wishes she could've changed just a little sooner. Shamed by her behavior toward the woman rescued alongside her, and further embarrassed and guilt-racked over the way she treated the SEALs who risked their lives on her behalf, Julie is desperate to make amends.

With help from a D.C. acquaintance who'd endured her own harrowing experience, Julie connects with Patrick Hurt, Commander of the SEALs who'd saved her life. If she can prove she's not the same person who mistreated his team, he'll grant her request to meet them —but not before the protective, sexy man makes a surprising request of his own.

**Protecting Julie is a part of the SEAL of Protection Series. It can be read as a stand-alone, but it's recommended you read the books in order to get maximum enjoyment out of the series.

CHAPTER 1

Julie sat up in bed and gasped in fright, throwing herself off the side of her double bed and landing on her hands and knees on the floor with a thud. She immediately scuttled to the nearby wall and collapsed against it, curling into a small ball. Her arms went around her legs and squeezed even as she buried her head into her knees and sobbed.

It'd been almost a month since she'd dreamt she was back in Mexico. Julie had hoped the nightmares had stopped for good, but it was obvious that moving across the country to California and starting her life over wasn't the magic cure-all to make them stop. She loved her daddy with all her heart and knew everything he'd done was out of concern and love for *her*, but she'd thought that maybe she was still dreaming about the hell she went through because she was living in the house she'd grown up in and in the town where she'd been kidnapped. She was twenty-eight years old, more than old enough to move out of her father's house and be on her own.

But at that moment, remembering what had happened to her, she wished she was back in her daddy's house, where she'd always felt safe, even with the continued nightmares. Julie knew it didn't make sense...she moved to California to try to get away from the nightmares, but even when she was at home she knew she could wake up her daddy and he'd talk to her and comfort her until she felt better.

She was a completely different person now than the naïve young woman who'd been kidnapped and almost sold into a prostitution ring south of the border about a year and a half ago. Julie didn't like to remember how she'd acted when the Navy SEAL had found and rescued her.

Truth of the matter was, she'd been terrified, frightened out of her skull, and she'd lashed out at the woman who'd been held in the same hellhole, and who'd handled everything that had happened to them a thousand percent better than Julie had.

Julie forced air into her lungs slowly, remembering what her therapist had told her. When she was overwhelmed and felt the panic attacks coming on, she needed to concentrate on breathing. In. Out. In. Out. Slowly but surely, Julie felt her heart rate slow and the adrenaline coursing through her body start to wane.

She stood up and braced herself on the mattress as she made her way around the end of her bed into the small bathroom attached to the equally small bedroom. Julie splashed some water on her face and steadied herself with her hands on the counter. The water dripped from her chin as she looked in the mirror.

What she saw made her wince. She had lines furrowed in her forehead. Her eyes were slightly bloodshot and her short brown hair hung around her face. Her cheeks were sunken in and even though she knew she'd gained the weight back from her time spent in the hands of the kidnappers, but because of the nightmares and the fact that she wasn't eating well, even all these months after she was rescued, she was still too skinny.

Her five-foot-two frame was naturally small, but now, at a little over a hundred pounds, she looked even more fragile.

"Get it together, Julie," she told herself in a firm voice, glaring at her reflection. She sighed and reached for the towel hanging on the rack next to the utilitarian bathtub/shower combo. She dried her face and headed back into the bedroom, straightened the covers and climbed back into bed.

Julie thought about her plans for the next day, sure they were why she'd had the nightmare. It was time. She'd put it off for way too long, but it was finally time.

After she'd gotten back home from Mexico, and after a few visits with a therapist her dad had scheduled visits for her with, Julie knew she had to find the SEAL team that had rescued her so she could thank them. But no matter how much she'd begged her dad, he'd claimed he had no way of getting ahold of the SEALs and had suggested she should move on with her life.

Ironically, it had been one of her acquaintances who had given her the information she'd needed so she *could* get on with living.

* * *

STACEY KELLOGG WAS the daughter of a senator who worked with Julie's dad. She knew Stacey from all the political parties they'd attended with their families. They'd belonged to the same country club in Virginia and had even played tennis together a couple of times in the past.

Julie had been horrified when she'd learned Stacey had been kidnapped by an ex-boyfriend. He apparently decided that if she wasn't with him, he didn't want her being with anyone. He went on the run with her for a week and a half. Julie didn't know all the details of what she went through, but what she had heard, it had been a harrowing ordeal for her.

The fact that they'd both been held against their will was what gave Julie the strength to approach Stacey. Even though their situations weren't exactly the same, she figured she and the other woman shared something unique. She'd sought Stacey out at the club a few months ago, before moving to California. Stacey had been eating, and Julie had approached and traded some superficial greetings, then asked if it'd be okay to talk to Stacey alone.

They'd moved off to a group of comfortable easy chairs in the corner of the large lounge and they'd spoken for over an hour. Julie knew Stacey was dating a Navy SEAL, who'd been involved in her ultimate rescue, and hoped he'd be able to somehow assist her in finding the SEALs who'd helped her. Stacey hadn't promised anything, but said she'd ask her boyfriend, Diesel Bonds. They'd exchanged phone numbers and when Julie didn't hear anything for a week, figured Stacey had blown her off.

But when Stacey had texted her and asked to meet, Julie was shocked, but pleased. They'd gotten together at a restaurant, and Julie had been surprised to see a gorgeous man with Stacey.

After they'd sat down at a small table, Stacey said happily, "Hey, Julie, it's good to see you again."

"Hi, Stacey. You too."

"This is Diesel. We talked about him last week."

Julie nodded and held out her hand. "It's good to meet you. Thank you for your service. I know those words are somewhat cliché, but I mean them from the bottom of my heart."

"You're welcome."

Diesel shook her hand, then returned his arm to the back of Stacey's chair. It was a protective posture, and Julie couldn't help but envy her for having a man who wanted to shield her from anything and anyone who might cause her harm.

Stacey didn't beat around the bush. "You said you wanted to know who rescued you."

Julie nodded and pressed her lips together nervously.

"Why?" It was Diesel who asked.

"Because I was a bitch." Julie laid it all out on the table. "There I was in the middle of the Mexican jungle. I'd been violated, I hurt, I was hungry and scared out of my skull. This guy came into the hut I'd been shoved in. He surprised me, and I acted like he was trying to pick me up at a bar." She shook her head in disgust, remembering her actions that day in the jungle.

"There was another woman there. She'd been there a lot longer than me, and seeing her, freaked me out. I knew that could be me. When I finally understood how long she'd been there, I realized how screwed I really was. So I lashed out. I was rude and bitchy. All I wanted was out of the jungle and out of the country. I wanted to be home. I'm embarrassed to admit that, even hurt and hooked on drugs, the other woman was acting so much better than me, it wasn't even a comparison. Even the SEAL thought so. And that made me think that maybe he'd decide I was too much trouble, and he'd leave me in the jungle. It was a stupid thing to think; of course he wasn't going to leave me there. But it made me act even bitchier."

Julie lowered her eyes, embarrassed. Her voice dropped to a whisper, "I'm ashamed that I didn't even thank them. His team showed up with a helicopter, the SEAL was hurt as we were hauled up into the chopper, and I didn't even bother to turn around and say 'are you all right' or 'thank you.' Not to any of them."

"What makes you think that they want to hear your thanks?" Diesel asked without rancor.

Julie looked up at the hard man in front of her. She avoided Stacey's gaze. She forced herself to keep eye contact with Diesel. "I'm sure they don't. I know they were all glad to see the last of me. I can only imagine their conversations once I was gone. I know it's selfish, but I need to do this. I..." Julie's voice trailed off, not sure what she could say that this super SEAL sitting in front of her would understand.

"I don't know what team got you out. It wasn't SEAL Team Six; that much I know. We don't talk about our missions; even within the brotherhood, they're top secret. But I know a guy. His name is Tex. He lives out here in Virginia. He used to be a SEAL, but was medically retired after losing part of his leg in a mission. I'll call him. See if he knows who was on the team that rescued you. He seems to know everything about everyone. But, Julie, I can't guarantee he'll tell me."

Julie sat up straighter in her chair. "I know, but I appreciate you even asking. Seriously. I know I'm still being selfish. No one in their right mind would want to see me again after the way I acted, but I swear I'm a different person now," she said earnestly.

"You don't have to convince me, Julie," Diesel said gently. "People can be unpredictable in hostage and rescue situations. You probably remember it worse than it really was."

"I don't think so," Julie said honestly. "I was pretty horrible."

"Hey, I heard you're moving?" Stacey asked, trying to move them on from the uncomfortable topic.

"Yeah. I can't stay here any longer. I love my dad, but it's time for me to move on. I can't stand politics, and my dad loves it, of course. I feel smothered living in his house. I need to get out, do something useful with my life. Being in charge of his house and being a hostess for his political parties just isn't fulfilling anymore. I need to...give back."

"Give back?"

Julie tried to explain, "Uh-huh. I feel like I've gotten a new lease on life. Those men found me and gave me a chance to be a better person. I blew it with them, but I'm ready to prove that I'm not the selfish bitch I was down there, and that I'm pretty sure I was before I was kidnapped."

"I'm sure you weren't that bitchy," Diesel protested.

"Thanks, but yeah, I was." Julie said ruefully. "While I wish I could move across the country and earn my own living without any help from anyone, I know I can't. So my dad is helping. But my idea is to move out to California and start my own nonprofit agency."

"Really? Isn't that harder than it sounds? Don't you have to have a business degree or something?"

Julie nodded. "Yeah, probably. But as I said, my dad is helping. He has some friends out there who will be helping me with the paperwork, marketing, and the day-to-day running of the business. He's gonna pay them until I can get my business on its feet and take over the payroll."

"What will you be doing?"

"I was watching one of the daytime talk shows and got the idea. I have a knack for fashion, so I want to see if I can start a thrift store of sorts, but full of designer clothes. I figure lots of women out in California are rich and probably have dresses and clothes they don't wear anymore. I want to get them to donate them to my secondhand store. I could sell as much as possible and also give outfits to people who need nice dressy clothes for interviews. The money I raise after paying expenses I could donate to various programs to help struggling women."

There was silence around the table for a beat before Julie hurried to say, "I know, it's kinda stupid, but I couldn't think of—"

"It's not stupid," Stacey said quickly. "I think it's awesome. It's a great idea."

"Well, it's not like I'm doing it by myself. I need my dad's money to start it up and the people he knows to help me, but I'm hoping that once I learn more about it, I'll be able to contribute more as time goes by and eventually be one hundred percent responsible for the day-to-day expenses."

"I think it's a wonderful idea," Stacey said resolutely.

"Thanks." Julie looked up in relief as the waitress approached the table. The conversation had gotten pretty awkward for her.

They ordered sandwiches and there was no more talk about SEALs, rescues or charities as they ate their lunch. As they were leaving, Diesel shook Julie's hand and held on when she would've pulled back.

"I wasn't there when you were being rescued, but I wanted to say, if you do get to meet the SEALs who helped you, let them see the woman who ate lunch with us today. They'll forgive you."

"Do you really think so?" Julie's voice was low and worried.

"Yeah."

"Thanks, Diesel."

"You're welcome. Don't forget to stay in touch with Stacey and let her know how things go for you out there in California."

Julie looked at Stacey. "I'd like that."

"Me too," Stacey agreed. "Good luck with everything."

"Thanks."

Julie watched as Stacey and Diesel walked across the parking lot to his sports car. She observed Diesel opening the passenger door and waiting for Stacey to get settled. Julie sighed. In her old life, Julie might've been jealous and catty and would've tried to flirt and steal Diesel from Stacey. But not now. They were a great couple, and while

Julie might've been jealous of their obviously close relationship, she was also happy for Stacey.

It was great that Stacey seemed to be moving on after her kidnapping, Julie smiled and waved as Diesel pulled out of the restaurant parking lot.

Julie had packed up her small SUV and left Virginia to drive across the country a week later. She still hadn't heard from Diesel or anyone named Tex, but she couldn't wait for them to get ahold of her. It was time to start her new life out in California.

It had been a month and a half since she'd arrived in Riverton before she'd finally heard from the man Diesel had called Tex. Her phone had rung, and even though the number said "unknown," Julie had answered it anyway.

"Hello?"

"Is this Julie Lytle?"

"Yes, who's this?"

"My name is Tex. I heard from Diesel Bonds that you had some questions about your rescue?"

The voice on the other end of the line was deep with a southern accent. He almost sounded bored. Julie's heart immediately started beating faster.

"Yes. I wanted to thank the men who came all the way to Mexico to rescue me."

"They would've done the same thing for anyone."

Julie winced. Wow, this Tex guy didn't pull any punches. "I know. But I...I was mean. And I feel bad. I didn't say thank you when the men dropped me off, and I wanted to make sure they knew I'm thankful for all they did."

"I can't tell you the names of the men," Tex said bluntly.

Julie's heart dropped. "Oh, okay."

"But I can give you the phone number of their Commander. You can talk to him and if he thinks it's appropriate, he'll get you in touch with the SEALs."

"Okay. Yeah, that sounds great," Julie enthused.

"I'm not sure I'd get too excited," Tex warned. "Commander Hurt's awfully protective of the men under his command. If I had to say, I'd give you a thirty/seventy shot of being able to thank the men in person. Hurt will probably tell you he'll pass the message on for you."

"It's better than no chance," Julie said resolutely.

Tex laughed under his breath. "Optimistic."

"Yeah, it's more than I had this time yesterday."

"True."

"I...thank you."

"Don't thank me," Tex chuckled. "You still have a hard road ahead of you."

Julie straightened her spine. "I can do it."

"Good luck. Now. Got a pen?"

Julie fumbled with her purse and got out a pen and a receipt from a fast food restaurant she'd eaten lunch at that day. "Ready."

Tex gave her a phone number and once again wished her luck.

* * *

NOW JULIE WAS LYING in bed, thinking back over the last month and a half and all that had changed in her life, and trying to recover from the nightmare and subsequent panic attack she'd had earlier. Tomorrow she'd call this Commander Hurt guy and get him to agree to let her talk to the SEALs who rescued her. No problem.

She closed her eyes and tried to relax. Tried to pretend that she wasn't as nervous as she'd ever been in her life. As the sun rose in the sky, Julie was no closer to being relaxed than when she first woke up from her nightmare.

CHAPTER 2

"Hello?"

"Uh, hi. My name is Julie and—"

"How'd you get this number?" Patrick Hurt wasn't often surprised, but to hear a soft feminine voice on the other end of his work phone was out of the norm. And he didn't like abnormal.

"Tex gave it to me. My name is Julie Lytle—"

"Tex? Why the hell would Tex give you my number?"

"If you'd let me talk, I'll tell you."

Patrick barely held back the snort of laughter that threatened to escape. It'd been a long time since he'd been spoken to with such… snark. As the Commander of an elite SEAL team, he'd gotten used to being treated with respect. "By all means then…tell me." He heard the woman take a deep breath before she continued.

"As I was saying, my name is Julie Lytle. I got your number from Tex. I wanted to thank the Navy SEALs who rescued me from a hellacious situation, and Tex told me you were their Commander. I know you probably can't give me their names, but I'd like to meet them and thank them in person for saving my life."

"No."

"I'd appreciate…uh… No?"

"That's right. No. The missions the SEALs undertake are top secret. It would be against protocol for them to be jaunting to meet-and-greets so they could be thanked. It's their job, ma'am. That's all."

"First of all, I get that what they do is top secret, but since I was *there*, it's not secret to *me*. And secondly, I don't care if it *is* their job, this was the first time I had to be saved, and it wasn't just a job to *me*. Thirdly, I'll flat out say it—I was a bitch and I need to make it right."

Patrick sat back in his chair in his office and ran a hand through his dark hair. He didn't need this shit today. "Look, Julie, was it? I'm glad they saved you, I am, really. But don't you think the fact you were a bitch would mean they don't want to see you or get your thanks?"

"Yes," she immediately returned, and Patrick's respect for the mysterious woman rose a notch. She continued. "I know they don't want it, but they deserve it. I swear I won't be obnoxious, I won't fawn all over them. I won't go to the press. We can meet in a back alley somewhere if that makes you more comfortable. I just..." Her voice trailed off.

Patrick didn't say anything, letting the silence stretch, and as he expected, she started talking again to fill the awkward break in conversation.

"I was about to be sold to a bunch of really scary guys. They'd already taught me what to expect when I was sold, and let me tell you, the thought of being a receptacle for who the hell knows how many men's lust wasn't a good one. Your team saved me from a fate worse than death and I just want to look them in the eye and say 'thank you for giving me my life back.'"

Patrick clenched his teeth and mentally swore. Julie Lytle. The name clicked with the mission she was talking about.

He'd heard a lot about the infamous Julie, and she was right, she *had* been a bitch. He knew Cookie and the others wouldn't really want to hear her thanks. They were glad to deliver her into her father's arms and see the last of her. Not to mention, Patrick didn't think Fiona needed the reminder of what had happened. The last thing he wanted was to put her in a position where she'd have another flashback.

But there was...sincerity...in Julie's voice that he hadn't heard from many other victims and people they'd rescued. Patrick was a pretty good judge of character, he had to be after being a SEAL himself and now commanding the team from behind the scenes.

"Julie. Yeah, I remember you, and I have to be honest. I don't think the guys would want to see you again."

"Oh. Okay." Julie's voice was soft and Patrick could tell she was on the verge of tears. "I appreciate you taking the time to talk to me anyway. If it's not too much to ask, could you at least tell them I called and thank them *for* me? It's not the same, but it's better than nothing."

Patrick made a split-second decision that he hoped he wouldn't regret. "Thursday afternoon. Four o'clock. I'll meet you and we can talk about it. If I think you're honestly sincere and you're doing this for the right reasons, I'll consider letting you meet the men."

"I'll be there. Where are we meeting?"

"Pacific Beach up by La Jolla."

"Okay. How will I—"

"I'll find you," Patrick told her, knowing what she was going to ask. He could find out what she looked like easily enough. It wasn't as if her kidnapping was a secret. It'd been all over the media after she'd returned home.

"Great. I'll see you there in a couple of days then. And Commander Hurt? Thank you. Seriously. You don't know what this means to me."

"Thursday. See you later."

"Bye."

"Bye."

Patrick hung up his phone and put his hands on the back of his head and leaned back in his chair. He wasn't a man who generally liked surprises, and he'd just had a whopper of one dropped in his lap. He didn't really have a plan, but he'd play it by ear. Once again the SEAL motto came to his mind. *The only easy day was yesterday.* How true.

* * *

JULIE SMILED as she hung up the phone. She knew it wasn't a done deal, but she felt on top of the world. Meeting with the SEAL Commander brought her one step closer to being able to move on and right the huge wrong she'd done. All she had to do was meet up with the SEALs, then she'd really be able to put the entire episode behind her and concentrate on her new life.

In the past month, she'd worked harder than she ever had before, and she was loving every second of it. She'd scoped out the country clubs and made pitches to several women's groups. The two women and one man her father had found to help her were wonderful.

They'd helped her find the cutest little storefront in Mission Valley. She'd had a logo designed and the store decorated. There were comfortable chairs scattered around the inside for customers or their spouses to sit in. She put in a free little coffee bar, so shoppers could get a snack and a drink. The clothes were all professionally cleaned and displayed after being donated. It honestly looked like a small boutique instead of the secondhand store that it was.

Business had been really good. Julie knew she'd been successful so far because of the help she'd gotten from her dad, but she'd also worked her butt off. She'd spent most of her day either meeting with people to drum up interest, or networking. She'd also gone around the area to other thrift stores scouring the racks for designer clothes she could purchase and fill her own racks with.

Julie hoped with the amount of connections she was making she could continue to grow and garner interest in her venture. She'd spoken with a few managers of some battered women's shelters in the area and had a meeting set up for the following week with a woman who ran one of the local Boys and Girls Clubs. There was also a teen center Julie wanted to check into as well. She'd expanded her idea of donating interview clothes to women in need, to also wanting to donate fancy dresses for teenagers who couldn't afford to buy one for their prom.

The bell over the shop door tinkled as three women entered. Julie put aside her excitement over being able to speak to Commander

Hurt in a few days and turned to the women to give them her welcome spiel.

"Hello, welcome to *My Sister's Closet,* feel free to look around. All the clothes have been donated and are the real thing. Versace, Hermès, Ralph Lauren, Prada, Kate Spade, Chanel, Gucci...you name it, we have it. I think you'll find the prices very reasonable. If you have any questions, feel free to ask. Dressing rooms are in the back, and help yourself to a cup of coffee if you'd like."

The women nodded politely at her and wandered over to the racks to start browsing. Julie couldn't help but hear their conversation as they laughed and joked with each other.

"Oh lord, Caroline, check this out, it'd be adorable on you!"

"Ha, no way in hell, Alabama. That thing is hideous."

"But it's Vera Wang!"

"Don't care, it's still butt ugly!"

The women laughed and moved on to look at more clothes. Julie held back her sigh. She missed hanging out with her girlfriends. Granted, her so-called friends back in Virginia didn't seem as close as this group of women did, but still. She'd been working so much she hadn't had time to try to meet anyone in California yet. She'd have to do something to remedy that.

Julie turned her attention to the spreadsheet on the computer in front of her, trying not to be rude and listen in on the conversation of the three women in the back of the store, but the light music couldn't drown out their happy chatter.

"Do you think Sam would like this?" One of the women asked the others.

"Uh, yeah. Are you kidding? He'll have you out of it as soon as he sees you."

They all giggled.

Finally, after an hour of browsing the store, the trio came up to the cash register to check out.

"Find everything you wanted?"

"No way, this store rocks! I wanted just about everything I saw in my size. We'll definitely be back."

Julie went into her recruitment speech as she rang up their purchases. "Well, we're constantly getting new stuff in because everything in here has been donated, so if you have any designer clothes at home that you either don't want or don't fit anymore, I'd be glad to take them off your hands. All donations are tax deductible and you'd of course get a receipt. We're also working with the local women's shelters to give free outfits to women who have interviews, but don't have the appropriate clothing to wear and can't afford to buy anything. And starting in the spring, I want to offer the same kind of service for prom dresses for the local teens who can't afford to purchase a new dress."

"Wow, really? That's awesome," one of the women exclaimed. "I don't have anything designer, that's just not me, but I bet some of the women on base might. And heck, between all of us and the guys, we could probably find people to donate."

"That would be great!" Julie gushed. "Here, take a business card. I'm willing to pick stuff up too, if that would be easier for someone. Just email or call and we'll figure it out."

"My name is Caroline. This is Alabama and Summer," the woman said, holding out her hand.

Julie shook it and said, "Good to meet you. I'm Julie."

"We haven't seen your store before, are you new?"

"Yeah, I moved here from the East Coast about a month and a half ago. I'm still getting set up, but so far I love it out here."

Summer laughed. "Yeah, what's not to love? Sun, sand, and hot sailors."

They all chuckled. Julie finished ringing up the purchases and handed the bags to the three women. "Seriously, thanks for coming in and checking the store out. I'd appreciate any word of mouth reference you can give me. I'm honestly not in this to make money, I want to help others."

Summer looked at her with a critical eye, but didn't say anything.

Julie hurried to elaborate. "I know, that made me sound like I'm bragging or doing this for publicity's sake, but it's not that, honest. I needed a change in my life. My dad is helping me finance the business, so I'm okay there, but I had a life-altering experience, and had someone help me out, so I just want to pass it on. Pay it forward. You know, karma and all that."

"Well, this seems to be a good way to do it. We wish you the best of luck. I'm sure you'll see us in here again, with our friends next time."

"Friends?"

"Yeah," Caroline chimed in. "There's six of us. We're like a girl posse or something. Our men don't get to see us dressed up all that much, but I think if we could find some kick-ass dresses we'd knock their SEAL socks off."

"SEAL?" Julie couldn't help but ask. Seems like everyone had SEALs on their minds.

"Uh-huh. We're all partnered with SEALs. It's a tough job, but someone has to do them…I mean *it*." Alabama piped up for the first time. All the women laughed and Julie waved and smiled as they left her shop.

At first Julie thought it was fate that the three women who happened to be with SEALs came into her shop just as she hung up from talking with Commander Hurt, but then she shrugged. She was smack-dab in the middle of SEAL country. It really wasn't that odd, all things considered.

The rest of the day went by fairly quickly. A few more customers wandered in and Julie tried to plan out in her head what in the heck she was going to say to the Commander when she met up with him in a few days. She had to make him understand she was a changed person. Different than she was all those months ago, when she'd met his SEALs.

She could hear in his voice that he knew all about what she'd done and the horrible things she'd said to his team and to the other woman who was rescued with her.

Julie beat down the remorse. No. She was different now. She'd make him see it, he'd hook her up with the men who saved her, and she could get on with her life. Easy-peasy.

CHAPTER 3

Julie sat on the small wall watching the waves crash on the shore. There was a surprisingly large amount of people milling around. Julie was a good swimmer, but hadn't made the time to check out any of the local beaches. This one was perfect. There was a lot of sand as opposed to rock, as a lot of the western coast seemed to have. It looked as though there was a slope from the beach into the water. It didn't just drop off. This allowed kids to stand at the water's edge and shriek as the waves crashed and moved up and down the coastline. There was also what looked like a large sandbar a hundred feet or so from the beach.

There were several surfers in the water. The waves weren't huge, it wasn't Hawaii after all, but some were big enough so the surfers could stand up and ride them for a little bit before they broke. Julie supposed most of the serious surfers probably got there early in the morning, at least that was what she'd always heard. She had no first-hand experience with surfers and their preferred hang-ten time.

Julie looked down at her watch. She was early. She never used to be, but now that she had to meet with people for whom time was a premium, she made it a point to always arrive about ten minutes early. It was the polite thing to do. She didn't want anyone to decide not to do business with her because she was late for a meeting.

She looked around, swinging her feet. Her toes barely brushed the sand below her. She'd kicked off her flip-flops when she'd sat down and was enjoying the afternoon sun on her legs and toes. It'd been tough to decide what she wanted to wear. Julie wanted to project a sense of sincerity and honesty, but really had no idea how to do that. She'd settled on a pair of respectable jean shorts that came down to just above her knees and a light-pink tank top. It wasn't revealing or low-cut, but seemed about perfect for the eighty-five-degree day. She would've looked stuck-up and snotty if she'd worn a business suit, and she also didn't want to look slutty.

After having a few days to contemplate about what she wanted to say, Julie wasn't any closer to figuring it out now than she was when Commander Hurt first suggested the meeting. Finally, after two more nightmares and many sleepless hours, she decided she'd wing it.

Patrick sat in his car and watched Julie. She was sitting on the containment wall around the beach area. She smiled at the antics of a couple of kids near her, and she occasionally glanced at her watch and over at the parking lot. She looked the same as the pictures he'd had Tex send over, but there was something different about her. Patrick couldn't put his finger on it. Finally, knowing he couldn't put it off anymore, he climbed out of his car and made his way to her.

He had no idea what decision he was going to make about allowing her to meet up with Cookie and the other guys, but he'd give her the benefit of the doubt for now. She'd sounded sincere on the phone, and if it was what she needed to move on from the experience, who was he to deny her?

"Hi. You must be Julie."

She looked up at him with a smile and hopped off the wall onto the sand. She smiled at him as she bent down awkwardly to grab her shoes. "Yeah," she replied and held out a hand. "Julie Lytle. Commander Hurt?"

"Patrick. Call me Patrick." He shook her hand, pleased when she gripped his tightly, then let go.

"Patrick then. It's good to meet you. Thank you for agreeing to meet with me. I appreciate it."

He shrugged. "It's the least I could do."

"Not really, but thank you just the same. So..." Her voice faded as she looked around. "Where should we—"

"How about we walk?" Patrick suggested.

"Okay."

Patrick had come prepared for walking along the sandy beach, and kicked off the worn pair of flip-flops he had on and easily stepped over the wall she'd been sitting on a moment ago.

"Wow, you're tall," she commented dryly, eyeing him up and down. He was wearing a navy-blue T-shirt that did nothing to hide his huge biceps. He might be a Commander and not go on any missions any longer, but he obviously still worked out. The cargo shorts he was wearing were knee-length and had holes on each leg, one above his left knee and another on the left thigh. They were well-worn and looked comfortable as hell. He was also wearing a pair of sunglasses. The entire package made her think of Tom Cruise in the movie *Top Gun*.

He grinned down at Julie. Now that they were both standing in the sand, Patrick could see just how tiny she was. He'd read her stats in the report from the mission in Mexico, but seeing her five-foot-two-inch frame in person was a different thing. "Six-one probably does seem tall to you, but I'm honestly not all that big compared to a lot of guys."

She shrugged. "Okay, if you say so."

They started off down the beach. Neither seemed to be in a hurry, so they took their time. Finally, Julie delved into the reason they were there. "I'm sure you read up on whatever secret files you guys keep on missions so you know what happened down in Mexico." She knew if she tried to downplay how she'd acted, it'd make her look as if she wasn't owning up to her actions. "But I'd like to explain what happened, how I got there, the real story, not the crap the media came up with...before you make your decision...if that's all right."

She watched as he simply nodded and hurried to continue before she lost her nerve.

"I was at a bar with a group of friends. Well, they weren't true friends, just people I knew. They were daughters and friends of some of the politicians my dad works with. We got together almost every weekend to let off some steam. I know, I'm honestly too old for that crap, and what 'steam' could we possibly have to 'let off,' but it was what we did. I went to the bathroom by myself, which I know is unusual for a girl."

She looked up at Patrick with a small smile, but he wasn't even looking at her. His gaze was directed at the long line of beach in front of them. She sighed and continued, deciding to cut out the extra commentary he obviously didn't care about and get to the point.

"When I came out of the bathroom, someone grabbed me from behind and stuck a needle in my arm before I could even think about screaming or struggling. He put a hand over my mouth and pulled me out the back door, which was conveniently located next to the restrooms. I was shoved into the backseat of a car and we were leaving before I'd gotten my wits about me. Then it was too late. Whatever he'd shoved into my veins was taking affect. The last thing I remember was the men speaking to each other in Spanish before I passed out.

"I have no idea how long I was out, but I woke up naked and tied hand and foot to a cot. I was thirsty and scared and I hurt. I heard more Spanish and then a man was there. On top of me. Leering down at me as he raped me. I was still confused and didn't fully understand what was happening. I lay there, disconcerted and terrified out of my brain. Finally, after three more men took their turns, they untied my wrists, threw my clothes at me, told me to get dressed and led me to a dark hut in the middle of a jungle. I had no idea what country I was in or what was going on."

Julie felt Patrick touch her lightly on the arm. "Come on, let's sit."

She looked to where Patrick was gesturing and saw a large tree, which had fallen over. They made their way over to it and Julie was thankful that Patrick gave her a hand and helped her climb up on it so she could sit. He leaned against the tree as she got settled and crossed his arms over his chest, his shoes dropped to the sand beneath them.

"If it's too painful, you don't have to continue."

"No, I want you to know why this is so important to me."

Patrick nodded and held her gaze.

Seeing no censure in his eyes, Julie took a deep breath and continued.

"So there I was, dumped in the middle of a dark hut, with no idea where I was or what was happening. The other woman, she tried to talk to me, tried to comfort me, but all I could do was cry. I wouldn't listen to anything she had to say to me. I was in denial and didn't want to hear her. I knew if she'd been there for as long as she said she had, that I was in trouble. I knew I wouldn't be able to deal with what had happened to me over and over again for another three months. So when your SEAL came in, all I wanted to do was get out of there. Anywhere was better than that damn hut, where I could be taken away and assaulted again. When he somehow sensed the other woman in the building, I was afraid taking any more time would make the bad guys find us and kill your man. Then they'd tie me down and hurt me again."

Julie wiped away the tears she hadn't realized she was shedding and continued, trying not to break down in sobs. "I begged him to go, to ignore whatever it was he heard or saw. I had tunnel vision or something and all I could think of was getting the hell out of there. I'm so ashamed of what I did. Out of everything that happened down there, that's the one thing I can't get out of my head. That if he'd listened to me, that poor woman would still be captive. She'd be..." Julie's words faded off. She couldn't even say what she knew would've become of the other woman if she'd been left.

"Thank God he didn't listen to me, though. He went to the other side of the hut, got the other girl, and we all tromped through the jungle. It's not an excuse, but I felt horrible. I hadn't eaten, I was scared, and I said unforgivably nasty things. I knew the other woman was stronger than I was. She was a good person, trying to be nice to me, letting me have more food than she should've. I knew she felt guilty because the SEAL was sent in for me and not her, and I think at the time, I felt that way too. But I swear to you, I didn't want him to get hurt."

Julie looked up at the sexy man standing next to her, not saying anything, not letting anything he was thinking show.

"When I saw him bleeding as he was hauled into the helicopter, I knew it could've been me. When they let me off, I didn't say goodbye, I didn't say thank you, I simply walked away from them and never looked back, so damn grateful to be back in my father's arms I couldn't think of anything else. It wasn't until hours later I'd started thinking about all that had happened and feeling ashamed of myself. Everyone told me how brave I'd been, and how horrible what had happened to me was, but I knew the truth."

"And what's that?" Patrick asked.

"That I was a coward. Everything I did in my life was for myself. I'd been selfish and conceited and self-centered. I didn't care about that other woman. I just wanted to get *myself* out of the situation. I didn't care about the SEAL, I just wanted out of the jungle. I didn't care about the other guys on the team, I couldn't even tell you what they looked like. I was only concerned about myself."

"I think anyone in your situation would've been the same way."

"Yeah, that's what everyone told me, but I know it's a lie."

"A lie?"

"Uh-huh," Julie said. "Because I was there. I saw that other woman. *She* wasn't like that. Her first concern was for your SEAL. She even worried about *me* and I certainly didn't deserve an ounce of her sympathy. Your SEAL wasn't like that. He was willing to give his life up for mine, even though I didn't deserve it."

"Julie, I don't think—"

"No. I'm right. But I'm trying to change. I'm really trying. I know a lot of people see me as stuck up and a rich daddy's girl. I even moved out here with my dad's money. I wouldn't have been able to start my business without him, so in a way, I'm still being selfish. But I'm hoping that everything I'm trying to do now to help others will somehow balance out my karma a little."

Julie swallowed and hurried to finish. "I just want to do what I should've done all those months ago. A simple thank you. Tell all of them face-to-face that I appreciate what they did for me and what they do for our country. I won't take much of their time, and I know they probably don't want to hear it from me. But, I'd be more appreciative than you'd ever know if you helped me do that."

"I'll help you."

Julie let out the breath she'd been holding and felt tears well up again. She beat them back by brute force.

"On one condition."

Oh shit. "Anything," she told Patrick honestly, looking up at him, not having the first clue what his condition might be.

"Go out on a date with me."

CHAPTER 4

Patrick hadn't thought ahead of time what he was going to do, but as he leaned against the tree listening to what she'd gone through at the hands of the human traffickers, and everything she was doing now to try to change her life around, he'd found himself admiring her.

It was crazy. This was *Julie*. The bitch. He'd heard from Cookie and the others what a pain in the ass she'd been. How she'd encouraged Cookie to leave the hut knowing Fiona was still there chained to the floor. How she'd complained and bitched the entire walk to the helicopter. And even how she'd walked away from all of them without a word.

The more he thought about it, the more Patrick knew the team needed to hear from her. They needed to know everything she'd just told him, but it was her story to tell, not his.

He'd give her the chance she needed to thank the guys and he'd warn them ahead of time to give her a shot. But watching her fight to tell him her story, watching her work her way through it, made him respect her.

Patrick was a hard man. Over twenty years in the Navy, most of those as a SEAL, had made him that way. But he'd never been so moved by a story as he'd been by Julie's. It would be up to Cookie if he wanted to let Fiona meet Julie as well, so he wasn't going to let either woman know of the other's existence until the guys had met with her.

"A date?"

"Yeah. You know...dinner...maybe another walk on a beach...a date."

She looked at him in confusion for a beat. "So you can find out more about what happened down there? Why I was a bitch?"

Patrick stepped in front of her and put his hands on the rough bark of the tree at her hips, realizing he was probably overstepping his bounds after she'd just poured her heart out to him and knowing he was still practically a stranger to her. He leaned forward, trying to make sure she really heard him and saw he was serious. "No. Because despite the difference in our ages, I'm attracted to you."

"To *me*?"

Patrick chuckled and looked her in the eyes. "You."

He watched as she struggled to come to terms with what he said. When she did respond, it wasn't what he thought she'd say. "You aren't that much older than me."

He pulled back. "How old do you think I am?"

"Um..." She wrinkled her nose as she contemplated him. "Thirty-five?"

He burst out laughing. When he had himself under control, he told her, "I appreciate that, but no, I'm not thirty-five."

When he didn't say anything else, she asked, "Then how old are you?"

"I don't think I'm going to tell you."

"What? Why? I thought only women were sensitive about their ages."

"I'm not sensitive about it, but I don't want to give you any reason to say no."

The laughter died on her face and she gazed at him for a beat. "If I say no, does that really mean that you won't help me make it right with your SEALs?"

"No. I might be a dick, but I'd never force you to go out with me. I know I said I'd set up a meeting on one condition, but I lied. I'll do it if you agree to see me again or not."

"Okay."

"Okay to the fact that I lied about the condition, or okay to going out on a date with me?"

"Both."

Patrick nodded and moved back a fraction, holding out his hand. "Come on, I'll walk you back to your car."

Julie put her hand in his and jumped off the tree. Patrick didn't let go of her and bent down to pick up their shoes. He handed hers to her and snatched up his own. He continued to hold her hand and turned them back around the way they'd come, back to the parking lot.

Julie was silent for a bit, but then said, "I don't know anything about you…other than your name is Patrick, you aren't thirty-five, and you're in charge of a Navy SEAL team."

Recognizing that she needed some reassurance, Patrick began talking. "My name is Patrick Hurt, my nickname is Hurt, for obvious reasons. I'm not thirty-five. I used to be a SEAL myself and I've been on some intense missions in my life. I like what I do now, working behind the scenes, coordinating things. I've lived here in California for what seems my entire life. My parents are both still alive, they live up north of Los Angeles. I don't have any blood brothers or sisters, but have plenty of men and women I call my family. I've never been married, I don't have any kids floating around out in the world." He paused, looking down at Julie. He waited until she looked up at him, then continued.

"I'm not impulsive. I think through everything I do before I do it. Missions, what I'm going to eat for dinner, the route I'll take home each day, how many calories I can eat based on how much I work out. Some people have called me anal."

"But…"

Patrick knew what she was going to say. It was what he wanted her to realize. "Yeah, asking you out was impulsive and out of character for me. It should tell you that this isn't a pity date. It isn't to pump you for more information. You've piqued my interest and I want to get to know you better. I like *this* Julie."

"I like her too."

"Good." They'd arrived at the parking area. "So...is next Saturday too soon?"

"Too soon?"

"For our date."

"Oh, no. Saturday's fine. What time?"

"What time are you free?"

Julie looked up, obviously trying to remember her schedule. "I have a meeting at nine in the morning with a woman who runs an after-school program for at-risk teens, then the store opens at ten. I work until four and have another meeting with a counselor from one of the high schools."

"You're a busy woman," Patrick observed as he put on his shoes.

She shrugged. "I guess. I like being busy. Keeps me from thinking too much...about stuff."

"Do you want me to pick you up, or do you want to meet me somewhere?" Patrick wanted to give her the option. It wasn't very smart to let a man pick her up at her home on a first date because if things didn't work out, the man would then know where she lived. He was completely trustworthy though, and if they didn't click on their date, he'd leave her alone, but it was ultimately her choice.

Julie bit her lip as she contemplated his question. He liked how she really thought it through before answering. "I think I should meet you somewhere. That way if we decide to end things early, it won't be awkward if you have to drive me home."

Patrick didn't quibble. "How about if we meet at six-thirty at the new steak place that opened up near here."

"Which one?"

"The one where you pay a flat fee and get as much meat as you can eat. They bring it around to your table until you're full and tell them to stop."

"Oh, *Fogo de Chao*? That Brazilian place? I've heard of it, and people have said it's wonderful."

"That's the one."

"Okay."

"We'll play it by ear after that."

"Sounds good."

Julie turned to him. "Thanks, Patrick. Seriously. I know you didn't have to meet me today, and you didn't have to listen to me, and you certainly don't have to let me meet your guys, but it's appreciated. More than you'll know."

Patrick lifted her hand and kissed the back of it. "You're welcome. I'll see you Saturday night. Be safe out there."

"I will. See you next week."

Patrick watched as Julie walked to her nondescript car and left the parking lot. He wondered for a beat what the hell he was doing, but when he thought about it, and it felt right, he decided to go for it. He was the type of leader who, once he made a decision, he went with it.

And he was going with it now.

CHAPTER 5

Julie stood at the counter at *My Sister's Closet* the following Friday afternoon, talking to her dad on the phone. He checked in frequently, and Julie knew she'd never take it for granted again.

"Hey, Daddy. How are you?"

"I'm good. How's my baby?"

Julie rolled her eyes. His baby. Whatever. "Things are great here. I had a meeting this morning with a woman who runs an after-school program for teenagers. It was an impromptu thing on my part. I have a meeting next week with another director of a different teen center, but I was passing the building on my way to work and decided to stop and see if anyone was in and would talk to me. We worked out a deal where some of the oldest girls would start volunteering at *My Sister's Closet*. In return, they'd get a clothing allowance."

"Sounds like things are going well."

"They are. I love it out here."

"I'm glad. I've been worried about you."

"I know, and I appreciate it. What's going on there? Anything new in the world of politics?"

"Actually, since you brought it up, there're rumors going around that Senator Kellogg might be making a bid for the Presidency. He wants to get the nomination and backing of the Republican Party."

"Wow, really? That's Stacey dad...right?" Julie asked incredulously. "Are you okay with that Dad?"

"Of course. What? Did you think *I* wanted to be President? No way."

Julie breathed out an exaggerated sigh of relief. "Okay, then. Good."

They both laughed.

The door chimed as a group of women entered the store. "Hey, Daddy, I gotta go. Customers."

"Okay, Princess. Stay safe out there and don't forget to call your old man once in a while."

It was a running joke between the two of them. "I will. Love you, Daddy."

"Love you too, baby. Talk to you soon."

"Bye."

"Bye."

Julie turned to the women, ready to give her welcome-to-the-store speech, and recognized three of them from the other day. "Oh, hi! It's good to see you guys again."

"Hi, Julie. Told you we'd be back! When Fiona and the others heard about this place, they had to see it for themselves!"

"Well, take your time, look around, do your worst!"

The women all laughed and dispersed around the store, checking out what had come in since the last time they were there and seeing what deals they could find.

Julie kept one eye on the group of women, making sure they didn't need any assistance with anything, as she thought about her date the next night with Patrick. She'd honestly been surprised he'd asked her out. She'd thought him extremely handsome from the second she'd laid eyes on him, but never in a million years thought he'd ask her on a date. She still thought it had something to do with the fact he felt sorry for her. But she was willing to give him the benefit of the doubt.

He'd sounded sincere enough when he'd told her he wanted to get to know her better.

"Excuse me, I have a question."

Julie's thoughts were interrupted by the words spoken nearby. She immediately turned her attention to the woman standing in front of her. "Of course, what can I—"

Julie's words cut off abruptly when she looked up and saw who was standing at the counter.

"Oh my God," the woman said in a low shocked voice. "It's you."

Julie wasn't sure what to say, but didn't get a chance to say *anything*. Caroline had come up behind her friend. "What's wrong, Fiona?"

Fiona. Julie hadn't remembered the other woman's name until Caroline said it and she looked into the eyes of the woman she'd spent some of the worst days of her life with. Fiona looked a hell of a lot better than the last time she'd seen her. Healthy. She looked healthy and happy now. Julie looked down, not able to meet Fiona's eyes, and saw a wedding band and huge diamond ring on her finger. She'd gotten married. Then she remembered what Caroline had told her when she was in the store the previous week. They were all with SEALs.

Could it…? Oh lord.

"Julie, right?" Fiona asked.

Julie couldn't read her tone, but nodded and spoke quickly, wanting to get this done before Fiona stormed out and took all her friends with her. "I'm sorry…" She trailed off uncomfortably. Could this situation be any worse?

"You know each other?" Caroline asked in confusion, looking between Fiona and Julie.

"Yes, I—" Fiona said.

"No, not really," Julie mumbled at the same time as Fiona.

Julie wanted to sink into a hole and never reappear again.

"So is it yes or no?"

The other women had converged on the counter and Julie felt decidedly ganged up on, even if that wasn't their intent.

"Julie was the woman in Mexico with me," Fiona explained softly.

The store got so quiet, the only sound was the music playing through the speakers and the occasional car passing outside.

"Oh."

Julie thought the one word out of the blonde woman, who she remembered as Summer, summed it up concisely. The disgust and scorn for the woman Julie had been back in that hot jungle came through loud and clear.

"What are you doing here?" A woman with black hair asked brusquely. "You own this store? I thought you lived out in DC?"

Julie nodded. "Yeah, I just opened last month. I moved out here. I needed a change."

"Hmm, well, I forgot I have a meeting. Sorry, we have to get going."

That time it was the brunette who'd been in with Summer and Caroline who'd spoken. The other women agreed and they all shuffled toward the door, putting the clothes they'd picked up down on a table near the cash register.

"I'm sorry!" Julie blurted again before they could leave the store, never to return. "I'm so sorry. I was a bitch. I was scared and took it out on you. There's no excuse for the things I said to you or the things I did. I was horrible and you didn't deserve any of it. I hope you're... okay...and if I live to be a hundred I'll never forgive myself for what I did out there."

Fiona didn't say anything, but her friend did. Alabama put her hands on her hips and faced Julie. "Fiona told us some of what happened while you guys were on the run in the jungle, but I'm guessing she didn't tell us everything, if your trite little apology is anything to go by." Her arms dropped and she took a step toward Julie. Caroline grabbed her arm before she could get any closer.

"Easy, Alabama."

Alabama leaned toward Julie and hissed, "You were going to *leave* her there. Who *does* that?"

When Julie didn't respond, Alabama turned on her heel and hooked Fiona's arm in hers. "Come on, Fee, let's get out of here."

Julie watched as the women filed out of the store. The perky bell tinkled as the door closed behind them, leaving an eerie silence only broken by the music playing. Julie bent her head and rested her hands on the counter in front of her, not caring that her tears splashed onto the paperwork she'd been working on before the women had entered not five minutes earlier.

"That was a disaster," Julie said to nobody. "This whole thing is a disaster. What am I doing?" She lifted her head, walked to the door, locked it, turned the sign to closed, and woodenly walked to the back of the store, away from the windows, away from the world.

She sat in one of the armchairs and curled into a ball, hugging her knees. And she sobbed.

CHAPTER 6

"I can't believe she had the nerve to move *here*," Alabama groused. "I mean seriously."

"I know, and to open a store, here, where Fiona lives. I mean she treated Fiona like crap down in Mexico, why would she want to start a business here when her dad lives out in DC?"

"And she used her daddy's money to open it too. She's so spoiled."

The nasty comments continued around the table as the six women regrouped after having their world rocked that afternoon. Caroline was silent as the others continued haranguing Julie and her existence in their little corner of California. She noticed that Fiona was also quiet.

"You all right?" Caroline asked Fiona during a lull in the conversation. "That couldn't have been fun."

"I'm okay," Fiona told her friend. "I just..."

"What?" Caroline urged. She was concerned and didn't want her to have any kind of flashback, just as she'd had before. She thought Fiona was past that, but seeing Julie again could easily make her regress in her healing.

"Did she sound sincere to you?" Fiona looked Caroline in the eyes as she asked.

"Sincere? I'm not sure—"

Caroline cut Alabama off. "Yes, she did." She looked at Alabama. "I know you're protecting Fiona and that you're just as upset about this as the rest of us are, but think about things for a second. Okay?"

Alabama bit her lip and waited for Caroline to keep talking.

"We liked Julie when we were there last week, right?" When Summer and Alabama nodded, she continued. "She was funny, gracious, and super open. If asked after we left the store if we thought she was a bitch, would any of you have agreed?"

"No. I liked her. That's why we all went back today. We wanted to support her. It seemed like she was doing such a good thing with the store," Summer said softly.

"Exactly," Caroline agreed. "If what she told us is true, she's trying to help out the community. Jess, she's giving some of the dresses in there to teenagers who can't afford a prom dress." Caroline knew her words would strike a chord with Jessyka because of her work with at-risk teens.

"And you all know, because we talked about it before we went over there today, that she's also donating clothes to women's shelters to provide them with appropriate clothes to wear to interviews. I just can't reconcile *that* woman with the one who was in the jungle with Fiona." Caroline took a deep breath. "What do *you* think, Fiona?"

"I have no idea. It doesn't make sense. I was there, I heard what she said and saw what she did. She looks the same, but...not. She never met my eyes when we were in the jungle. She always looked above my head or at the ground when she spoke. She kept a tight grip on Hunter's shirt the entire time we were fleeing."

"But she wanted to leave you there, Fiona," Cheyenne said softly, having heard the entire story from Caroline one night.

"Did she?" Fiona asked, almost rhetorically.

"What do you mean?" Summer asked.

"I'm trying to remember exactly what she said when she and Hunter were about to leave and something made him turn back around one last time." Fiona paused and bit her lip, obviously trying to remember what was said back when she was being held captive.

"She was scared, like I was. She'd just been brought in, and recently had been …uh…you know." Fiona closed her eyes as if that would help her recall Julie's exact words. "'We have to go. I want to go'."

"See? She wanted to leave you there and get out."

Fiona shook her head slowly and raised wide eyes to her friends. "No, I don't think so. Now that I think about it, I felt like she did in that hut at one point too. I would've done anything to get as far away from there as possible. But I'd become resigned. She wasn't yet. She was scared and wanted out. If I had to guess, I'd say she was only thinking about getting away from the men who'd hurt her."

"You don't think she meant to leave you, per se, but instead was focused on escaping?" Caroline tried to clarify.

"Yeah," Fiona whispered.

"But what about the rest of it?" Alabama demanded, not harshly. "You've told us how she hated the food, complained about you suffering from the effects of the drugs, and even how she didn't care if Hunter got hurt or not."

"I don't know. I wasn't in her head, so I just don't know what she was thinking. But why do I suddenly feel horrible about that entire scene back there?"

"She was crying," Caroline mentioned in a soft voice. "We were all walking out of her store and I looked back. She was standing at the register, looking off into space, and tears were running down her face."

After a moment of silence, when none of the women said anything, struggling with their own thoughts about how they now felt a little sorry for Julie, but still were pissed off for Fiona about all that had happened to her down in Mexico, Caroline stood up from her chair and went behind Fiona. She wrapped her arms around her friend's chest and put her chin on her shoulder as she hugged her. "You gonna be okay? Do we need to call Dr. Hancock so you can talk this through?"

Fiona hugged Caroline back as well as she could in their awkward embrace. "No, I'm okay. It just makes me appreciate Hunter more for his eerie sixth sense he seems to have at times, and thank my lucky stars I got out as relatively normal as I did. Yes, I still have some flashbacks, but I have all of you guys, and Hunter, and everyone else on the team. Who does Julie have?"

Everyone was silent as Fiona's words sunk in.

CHAPTER 7

Patrick looked down at his watch for what seemed like the hundredth time that night. Seven o'clock. It looked as though he'd been stood up. Stupidly, he hadn't given his cell phone number to Julie, so she couldn't call and let him know if she was running late. Hopefully she had an emergency or something had come up, rather than her truly standing him up. After telling the hostess it looked as if he wouldn't be eating dinner after all, he got in his car and drove to Mission Valley.

He knew Julie's store was there, it was amazing the information Tex could come up with on short notice. Her store, *My Sister's Closet*, was nestled between a small bookstore and a kids' boutique that sold baby and toddler toys and clothes. The lights in the store were off, except for the security lighting, which gave off just enough light to deter any wannabe burglars.

Patrick had Julie's home address, but knew if he showed up there, he'd be a total creeper. He drummed his fingers on the steering wheel, trying to decide if he should call her or not, he'd gotten her number from Tex, finally deciding to give her some space. If Julie was having second thoughts about going on a date with him, he wouldn't push.

He didn't want to bring up any bad memories or trigger any kind of flashback. Patrick knew Fiona suffered with them and the last thing he wanted to do was make Julie more uncomfortable. He blew out a breath and murmured, "Fuck, this sucks." He pulled out onto the road and headed home. Maybe he'd get lucky and she'd call him on Monday and let him know what was going on.

* * *

JULIE HUDDLED ON HER BED, concentrating on her breathing. She'd had a hell of a nightmare, one she hadn't had in a long time. She'd halfway expected it though, maybe that's why she dreamed it tonight.

She was walking away from the hut she'd been held captive in and she'd looked behind her as she followed the SEAL into the jungle. In her dream, he hadn't turned around. He hadn't noticed Fiona on the other side of the room. He'd left with Julie in tow and they'd abandoned Fiona back in the hut. As they fled she looked back and Julie saw Fiona sitting in the room, and there was a spotlight above her, shining down. The other woman was kneeling in a small circle of light. The chain was around her neck and she was completely naked.

Julie could see bruises all over the other woman's body and she was bleeding from several large cuts on her face, head and chest. Her hand was outstretched toward Julie and she kept saying, "Why, Why did you leave me here? You knew what would happen to me."

Julie had jerked awake, sweating and shaking. Even though she knew it wasn't what had happened, she knew it very well *could* have happened. If the SEAL hadn't been as good at his job as he was, it would have. And that ate at Julie's conscience. It was as if she had to have the dreams every now and then to remind herself who she really was. A woman who'd leave another to live a horrible existence and to most likely die a slow, painful death.

Tonight was supposed to have been her date with Patrick, but Julie knew there was no way she could show up. After seeing Fiona and her friends at the store, it was obvious she'd never be forgiven, because what she'd done was unforgiveable. The SEALs agreeing to listen to her was a pipedream. She'd been a job to them. Nothing more, nothing less. They'd moved on; she had to as well.

So she'd stood up Patrick. He'd understand.

But Julie still felt bad. How long had he waited for her? Had he sat at the table looking at his watch, wondering if she was all right? Then when he'd finally decided she wasn't coming, was he mad? Julie bet he didn't get stood up very often. He was so good-looking. No one in their right mind would stand him up.

And that was the thing—she was obviously not in her right mind. She'd been insane to think anything she'd done to change herself and her lifestyle would balance out the horrible person she'd been.

Julie dug the palms of her hands into her eyes and rubbed, trying to get the horrific image of Fiona in the hut, blaming Julie for leaving her there, out of her mind. Finally, she shook her head and reached for her cell. Even though it was the middle of the night, she'd call and leave a message for Patrick. It was the polite thing to do. She hadn't grown up the daughter of a politician for nothing. As a politician, her dad might be able to be a jerk and demanding, but as his daughter if she was rude, she opened herself up to ridicule and censure by the press, and she didn't want that to blow back on her dad. Julie had to let Patrick off the hook.

She dialed the number Tex had given her, knowing Patrick wouldn't be at work and she could leave a message and could take the cowardly way out and not speak with him personally. Julie waited impatiently for the message to finish so she could talk. Finally, after the beep, she spoke quickly.

"Hi Patrick, it's Julie. Sorry I didn't show up tonight…something came up. And I've thought about it more and I won't need your help with what we talked about. It was a dumb idea anyway and selfish on my part…as usual. Thank you for your service to our country. Bye."

As far as blow-off messages went, it was pretty lame, but at least it was done.

Julie threw the phone back on the nightstand and curled up on her side, hugging her pillow. Tomorrow was a new day. She'd be fine. It was a big city. She'd never see either Patrick or Fiona and her friends again. No problem.

* * *

PATRICK SAT with three of the SEALs under his command: Cookie, Wolf, and Dude. They'd been discussing the upcoming training they'd be taking part in during the next week.

"How're things at home with Caroline, Wolf?"

"Good, although you'll never guess what happened this past weekend."

Patrick raised an eyebrow, waiting for him to continue.

"The girls ran into Julie. You know, Julie from the rescue we did down in Mexico, where Cookie found his Fee?"

Patrick looked sharply at Cookie. He was sitting back in his chair with both arms crossed over his chest, looking pissed. "Julie Lytle?"

"Uh-huh."

"And?"

"The girls were pissed. Words were spoken. Caroline said Julie tried to apologize to Fiona, but they hustled her out of the store pretty quickly."

Patrick understood why Julie had stood him up now. His heart hurt for her, but first he had to see where Cookie's head was at.

"Cookie?"

"What?"

"How's Fiona? She pissed?"

He shook his head. "You know Fee, she sees the good in everyone."

"So she wasn't upset?"

"I didn't say that. She was upset. Had a nightmare that night. We talked it through and I think she's okay now, but I'm keeping an extra eye on her. Caroline and the others are helping. But we talked about it. She feels bad for Julie."

"Bad?"

"Yeah. Julie seems to be trying really hard to make a difference in the community. She's volunteered her time and has been doing what she can to help battered and abused women and teens."

"What do you think, Cookie?"

Cookie shrugged and sat up in the chair, leaning his elbows on his knees. "I only care about Fiona. If she wants to think Julie's changed, then I'm all for it. But if she doesn't ever want to see her again, I'll do everything I can to convince Julie to move back to Virginia. I realize that makes me sound like a dick, and it's possible even if she stays, Fiona won't run into her, but I won't chance it. Fiona means the world to me and I'll do whatever it takes to make sure she's in a safe and healthy place and that she'll never suffer another flashback again...if I can help it.

Patrick thought about Cookie's words. Julie certainly had a hard road to travel to get back in his good graces, but he didn't think that was what Julie really wanted. She knew she'd never be best friends with the SEALs who rescued her. She only wanted a chance to apologize and to thank them.

Suddenly Patrick really wanted her to have that shot.

"I talked to Julie before the girls ran into her," he admitted.

"What?" Wolf questioned sharply.

"What the hell, Hurt?" Cookie exclaimed at the same time.

"Are you fucking shitting me?"

The last was from Dude, arguably the most intense of the SEALs on the team. Patrick held up his hand. "Hear me out."

When the men nodded, he continued. "Tex gave her my number. She called wanting to see if she could find out who the SEALs were who rescued her so she could thank them, and apologize."

"A day late and a dollar short," Dude grumbled.

"She knows it," Patrick confirmed. "She knows she fucked up and she wanted to make it right. I'm surprised Tex gave her my office number, but she never would've found out anything about you or how to get hold of you without Tex. Luckily he let me be the middle-man between you and her. She made a good case on the phone for wanting to apologize to you, so I went and met with her. I think she's sincere."

"It wasn't cool of her to talk to the girls," Cookie complained, knowing he was being unreasonable. It wasn't as if Julie planned for Fiona and the other women to go into her store.

"I think that was purely by chance. At no time did she mention to me about wanting to see Fiona, Cookie. She was sorry about what she did, but she didn't talk about tracking her down at all. I don't think she even knows you guys are married. Think about it, Julie owns a secondhand shop that carries high-end designer clothing. Of course your women are gonna find out about it and make their way there. It was only a matter of time before they ran into each other. And neither Julie nor Fiona are dumb. I'm sure they recognized each other immediately."

No one said anything for a moment.

"And just so we can get it all out on the table here…full disclosure and all that…I asked her out."

"You *what*? Jesus, Hurt, you can't do that!" Cookie exclaimed and stood up sharply, leaning toward his Commander with his body braced on the table with his hands.

Patrick ignored Cookie's outburst. "I can and I did, but you'll probably be happy to know she stood me up."

At his Commander's words, Cookie sat back down and ran his hand over his head. "She did?" he asked in a calmer voice.

"Yeah. We were supposed to go to dinner Saturday night."

"The girls ran into her on Friday," Cookie said solemnly.

"I know that now, I didn't then. I'm thinking after meeting them, she went over in her head whatever was said between them and she figured she might as well give up on the idea of seeing you guys."

"I think, Cookie," Wolf said carefully, "it might do you some good to meet with her. To hear what she has to say."

"I don't know, guys. You weren't there. You didn't hear how horrible she was when Fee was counting backwards to take her mind off of the fact she was going through withdrawal from the shit they'd been feeding into her veins. You weren't there when she bitched that all I had to give her to eat was granola bars. You didn't see the guilt in Fiona's eyes when she didn't think there was enough food to eat." Cookie shook his head and repeated, "I just don't know."

"Well, I think you'll have some time to think about it," Patrick told him. "I'm fairly certain I have my work cut out for me if I want to get her to agree to go out with me again."

"You really liked her that much?" Dude questioned.

"Yeah. There's just something about her. It's like she's a ten-pound terrier standing up to an eighty-pound pit bull. She's scared out of her mind, but acts like it's no big deal and that she can't be hurt by anything."

"So you feel protective of her," Dude stated. "I can understand that."

Patrick knew he could. He was very protective of Cheyenne. "Yes and no. She's been through hell and clawed her way back to the other side. She fascinates me. Many people wouldn't be as well-adjusted as she is after going through what she did. Cookie, I *know* you understand that. I figure if she can own up to what she did wrong and have the guts to try to do something about it, then I can admit that I admire her for being brave enough to go after what she feels she needs and that I want to get to know her better."

"I can't say I'm thrilled about having her around if things between you and her go well, but I'm also not that big of an asshole to say I never want to see her. I trust your judgement, Hurt; if you say you see something redeemable in her, I have to believe you. If it comes to it, and she still wants it, I'll meet with her and let her have her say."

"Appreciate that, Cookie. If I can get her to see me again, I'll see if I can make it happen."

The men stood up and Wolf clapped the Commander on the back. "Good luck, man. Women never do what you think they're going to."

CHAPTER 8

How in the hell she could have the worst luck on the planet and keep running into the seven people she least wanted to see again in her life, was beyond Julie's imagination. She knew she had a lot to atone for, but seriously, she couldn't get a break.

A week after the disastrous encounter in her store, Julie almost ran into Summer in the grocery store. She'd apologized profusely and rushed off without giving the other woman a chance to say anything.

Then on another day, Julie was driving down the road and happened to look at the car next to her at a red light, only to see Caroline sitting behind the wheel of an SUV. It seemed like Fiona's friends were everywhere.

But that wasn't the end of her torture. Julie had been visiting yet another teen center and had come face-to-face with Jessyka.

She'd somehow stumbled through some small talk and when she'd met with the director of the center, the woman had explained Jess was a frequent volunteer and a staunch supporter and friend to most of the girls who participated in the after-school programs.

Just when Julie thought she was over the worst of the accidental run-ins with the people who knew how awful of a person she could be, Patrick strode into her store as if he shopped there every day of the week.

"Hello, Julie."

"Uh, hi." She stared at him for a moment, and when he didn't say anything else, she nervously filled the silence between them. "Sorry about the other week. Did you get my message?"

"Uh-huh."

"Oh, okay. Yeah, well, something came up. I'm sorry I didn't get ahold of you. I didn't have your cell, I could only call your work number."

"Yeah, I realized that as I was waiting for you. Everything okay?"

"Yeah, thanks."

Julie fidgeted as Patrick leaned against the counter and seemingly got comfortable. It didn't look as though he was planning on going anywhere anytime soon.

"You lose my number?"

Uh-oh. "No?" The word came out more as a question than the statement Julie wanted it to be.

"Hmm. I haven't heard from you in two weeks."

"I know...I've been busy."

"Julie, I know about you running into Fiona and her friends."

Julie's head came up at that. "You do?"

"Uh-huh. I do. I also know that's why you canceled our date."

"Okay, well. Yeah, good. That *is* why. I just realized it was a stupid thing to want to talk to the guys who rescued me. I mean, it was just a job for them. They don't care, and—"

Patrick interrupted her. "How do you know they don't care?"

"Patrick," Julie said desperately, wanting the conversation to end. "They just don't. Once again, I'm being selfish. I wanted to talk to them for myself, not for them. It's just me thinking of myself again. It's fine. Seriously, can we just drop it?"

Julie couldn't meet his eye as he stood there watching her. "I'll drop it..."

She sighed in relief.

"...for now."

"Well, hell," she muttered before thinking twice about it.

Patrick chuckled. "Now that that's out the way. When are you going to let me take you out?"

"You still want to?" Julie looked up at him in disbelief.

"I still want to. And if you ask me why, I'm going to have to do something drastic."

Julie smiled for what seemed like the first time in a long time. "Well, we wouldn't want that. Okay, I'll go out with you."

"Now."

"What?"

"Now. I'm taking you out now."

"But, I'm the only one here, and I have to—"

"There's no one here. It's three. The store is only supposed to be open for another hour. Put a sign up that says you had an emergency or something."

"But I'd be lying."

Julie didn't understand the broad grin that came over Patrick's face.

"What are you smiling at?"

"You. You can't even lie about taking an hour off to do something for yourself."

When he put it that way, it sounded ridiculous. It wasn't as if she had hordes of people knocking down her door wanting to get in. "Okay, but...where are we going?"

"I thought we'd go casual today. I'd like to take you back to the beach. It's one of my favorite beaches in the area. There's good surf, good sand, and there are a couple of really good food trucks that come down to that area each night."

"Food and an evening walk on the beach. You sure do know how to treat a woman," Julie teased.

"Come on, do what you need to do before closing up. I'll wait."

Julie closed out the cash register and made a sign apologizing for the early closure and attached it to the front door of the store. "I need to run by the bank and deposit this," she told Patrick.

"You don't keep it in a safe here on site?"

Julie shook her head. "No, my dad advised against it. There are too many people desperate for even twenty bucks to risk it. I'd rather be inconvenienced and take the cash to the bank each night than to chance someone knowing I had a safe and robbing me to get at it."

"Smart."

Julie shrugged. "It was my dad's idea."

Patrick didn't say anything, but took her hand as they walked down a few businesses to the drop box at the bank. He walked them to his car and they headed off toward the beach.

Patrick lucked out and found a place to park in the first public lot he pulled into. They grabbed some burritos at a food truck that Patrick insisted were "fucking awesome," then walked along the sand, much as they had the first time they'd met, eating their dinner and talking about nothing important.

There were a lot of families enjoying the balmy evening. Kids played in the surf, floating on boogie boards, waiting for the next wave to come and propel them toward the sand. Finally, after an hour or so of walking and chatting, Patrick said he had to be getting back.

"I've got training in the morning."

"I can't picture you standing there blowing a whistle, yelling at grown men to run faster," Julie teased.

"That's because I don't stand there. I'm right there running with them."

"You are?"

"Yeah. I am."

"I figured you worked out, because you're definitely in shape, but I didn't think you worked out with the SEALs."

Patrick chuckled. "And why not? Because I'm old?"

"Oh lord, no," Julie said and blushed. "I didn't mean it like that. And I still have no idea how old you really are. Fifty-three?"

"Ouch, woman. I think I liked your other guess of thirty-five better. And how *did* you mean it, if you didn't mean I was old?"

She put her face in her hands and shook her head. "Never mind. So...you have training in the morning?"

Patrick laughed and pulled her hands away from her face. "You're so cute. And yes. Around 0-four-hundred in the morning. We're meeting on the beach to run through some exercises with the SEAL wannabes."

Julie caught the evil look in his eye. "And you love torturing them, don't you?"

"Of course."

"Well, come on then. Can't have Cinderella changing into a pumpkin before she has to get home from the ball."

They walked back to the parking lot and Patrick opened the passenger-side door for her and patiently waited until she was settled to close it. He drove them back to her store and when he pulled up to her car, he said, "Wait here."

Julie watched as he got out and surveyed the area carefully, before coming around to her side and opening her door. He helped her out and at her curious look, simply said, "Just making sure it was safe."

Goosebumps rose on Julie's arms at his words. *Just making sure it was safe*. Six words that were quite possibly the most romantic thing she'd ever heard. He was either really good at knowing what to say, or he was the real deal. Julie wasn't sure yet.

She clicked the locks on her door and stood in the open driver's side. "Thanks for dinner, and for the nice night."

"You're welcome. And before I forget, here's my contact numbers. Now you don't have an excuse not to call me again."

Julie took the business card Patrick held out to her. He'd written his cell phone number on the bottom, along with another number that she recognized as being from Virginia. She raised her eyebrows at him.

"It's Tex's number."

"Ah, the mysterious Tex again," Julie said in confusion.

"Yeah. If you ever need anything and can't get ahold of me, you can call Tex. He'll find me."

"I'm not going to call Tex. I don't know him."

"It doesn't matter if you know him or not. There's no one I trust more than him. And if you need me, and can't get ahold of me, he will most definitely be able to get me to you."

Julie shook her head in exasperation and barely resisted rolling her eyes, instinctively knowing Patrick wouldn't appreciate it. "Yeah, okay. Have fun at training in the morning."

"You gonna give me your number?"

"Oh, yeah." Julie rattled off the numbers to him. When he didn't move to write them down, she asked him about it.

"I've got it. I don't need to write it down."

"Prove it," she challenged.

"What do I get if I'm right?"

"What do you want?"

"A kiss."

Julie was surprised, but not upset. "Okay. A kiss."

Patrick recited her number back seemingly without even thinking about it. Before the last number had left his lips, he'd taken a step toward her, crowding her against the frame of her car. He put both hands around the sides of her head and rested his thumbs on her jawbone. Julie grabbed hold of his wrists and looked up.

"I'm going to kiss you now, Julie."

"Okay," she whispered in agreement.

His lips came down on hers and Julie went up on tiptoe to try to get closer to him. She didn't think to let go of his wrists and wrap her arms around him, because she was too busy trying to memorize the feel of his lips on hers.

Patrick ran his tongue along the seam of Julie's mouth, as if he was asking permission to enter. She opened gratefully and sighed when Patrick's tongue swept inside. It felt as if he was branding her. He was hard where she was soft. He was tall to her short. He was über masculine to her feminine frame.

Unfortunately, Patrick didn't linger long. The kiss wasn't passionate, but completely appropriate for a good-night kiss after a first date. He lifted his head from hers, but didn't move his hands. He gazed down at her for a long moment before saying, "I liked that."

Julie smiled. "Me too."

"Okay then. I'll call you."

"Good."

Finally, he dropped his hands, forcing her to let go of him, and he turned her gently toward the car. "In you go. I'll talk to you soon."

Julie sat and started the engine. Seeing he was still standing there watching her, she rolled her window down and told him, "I had a good time tonight. Thanks."

"You're welcome. Drive safe."

"You too." Feeling proud that she only looked back once, Julie smiled all the way to her small apartment.

CHAPTER 9

Julie sat in the circle of Patrick's arms on his couch as they watched *World War Z*. They'd spent time together almost every day since their first "date" a month ago. As far as their physical relationship went, they were taking it slowly, which was fine with Julie.

Yes, she'd had a horrible experience when she'd been kidnapped, but she'd mostly dealt with it. Her dad had immediately gotten her into therapy. She'd also seen a couple of doctors and found out she'd been incredibly lucky and hadn't picked up any diseases from her experience, thank God for something going her way after the hell she'd been through. All in all, Julie knew it could've been a hell of a lot worse, and she chose to focus on the positives rather than losing herself in the negatives of the entire experience.

Dealing with the physical aspects of having a boyfriend, Julie was realizing, was actually much easier than the mental ones. She thought it'd be easy to open up to Patrick and let him know how she was feeling about herself, and about the nightmares she continued to have, especially after their first walk on the beach when she'd tried to explain how important it was to her to be able to thank the SEALs who had rescued her.

But after the cold reception she'd received from Fiona and her friends, and realizing that saying "sorry" wasn't going to suddenly make her feel better about the person she used to be, the urge to open up to Patrick had waned. Hell, it hadn't just waned, it had disappeared altogether.

Julie knew Patrick was trying to ease her into a physical relationship, and she appreciated it. As much as she might have projected a party-girl image back home, she'd never been the type of girl to fall into bed with men on the first date…or even the second or third. She liked to be friends with someone before getting naked with them.

She was certainly ready to get physical with Patrick though. She liked him. He was funny, good-looking, and seemed sincerely interested in her. She'd even told him last week she was ready, but he'd only kissed her on the forehead as if she was twelve, and said *she* might be, but *he* wasn't. Julie would've thought it was a blow off if he hadn't kissed the hell out of her, almost brought her to orgasm with his mouth on her nipples, and if she hadn't seen him every day since then.

Patrick leaned over and muted the television. Julie watched as the zombies silently began to swarm over the wall built around Israel on the screen. She had a feeling whatever Patrick had been wanting to talk to her about before moving them to the next level, now was the time.

"I know you told me you didn't care anymore, but I spoke with the SEALs who rescued you, and they're willing to meet with you."

Julie froze. Oh God. She'd known this would be coming sooner or later. She tried to play it off. "It's okay. I've changed my mind. I've made peace with it." Which was a total lie, but she didn't want to have to deal with their rejection of her apology and thanks as she had with Fiona.

Patrick turned Julie in his arms and pulled her over his lap until she was straddling him and he could look her in the eye, her arms wrapped around his neck.

"Julie. I think you need this. I heard what you told me that first day on the beach."

"Really, Patrick, I'm good. I just needed—"

"You're not good."

"I am," Julie insisted, not very convincingly, even to her own ears.

"You fell asleep on the couch over here last week." Patrick's words were low and earnest. "The second you were down, you started dreaming. I watched you do it. You whimpered in your sleep and called out 'I'm sorry,' over and over. You only stopped when I sat next to you and took you in my arms. You never even woke up until later, when I purposely shook you awake so I could take you home."

Julie stared at Patrick in dismay.

"It's eating you up inside. You need this."

She looked down, sucked her bottom lip into her mouth and stayed silent, not knowing what to say.

"What's holding you back?"

Julie didn't want to tell him, but he was a good guy. He'd been nothing but decent. He'd encouraged her when she doubted both herself and what she was doing with the store, he supported her, he laughed with her, he was a good kisser, and he never, not once, made her feel like the bitch she'd been in what seemed like a previous life.

Most importantly, Julie liked Patrick. If she wanted any kind of real relationship with him, she knew they had to get past this. He was the SEALs' Commander, for Christ's sake. She'd have to see them sooner or later if she and Patrick stayed together. It was a miracle they hadn't already, but she knew that was probably all Patrick's doing.

"What if they don't accept my apology?"

"They will," Patrick said immediately, knowing exactly who she was talking about.

"Fiona didn't," she admitted in a small voice. "Why would they?"

"What do you mean, Fiona didn't?" Patrick asked with concern. He put his finger under her chin and lifted her head. "I know you saw her that one time, and I know there was some shit said."

Patrick had talked to the guys about the incident, and while he knew it wasn't a sunshine-and-roses meeting, he hadn't been aware any of the girls had said anything over-the-top mean. He didn't think it was in them, not after everything they'd been through.

Julie shook her head, lying. "Not really. Look, I don't blame her friends. I was mean to Fiona in the jungle, and she and her friends have the right to not want to talk to me."

"Julie, I talked to the guys. I don't think you know this, you might suspect it, but Fiona is married to the SEAL who got you through the forest. I talked to him. Cookie knows you saw Fee and that you apologized. He would've told me if she was still harboring ill will toward you."

"I figured they were married," Julie said softly, feeling the pit in her stomach grow bigger and bigger, "But I guess I didn't realize it until I saw her that she was married to the SEAL that saved us."

"Yeah," Patrick confirmed.

"I'm not talking to him, or any of the others," Julie stated resolutely.

"Julie, you—"

"No!" She struggled to get off Patrick's lap, relieved when he let her go. "I can't. She was upset to see me. I know her husband has to be pissed at me." Julie paced as she continued. "I can't face him. I thought I could...before. But knowing they got together? That they bonded so completely while we were in that fucking jungle that they fell in love and got married?" She spared a glance at Patrick, not knowing how to put into words what she was thinking.

Julie didn't *really* think if she'd been less of a bitch, *she* might have ended up with the handsome SEAL instead of Fiona, but the thought wouldn't leave her brain. "I'm assuming that's what happened, right?" she finished somewhat lamely.

"Basically, yeah."

"Yeah. So I'm not doing it."

"They're my men," Patrick said in a low, sad voice. "I want you to be there when we have company picnics. I want you to be a part of my Navy life. If you won't see them, you can't be."

Julie felt her heart breaking. She was losing one of the best things to happen to her before she'd even truly had it. But she really was a coward. She couldn't face Fiona again. Couldn't face the censure she saw in all of her friends' faces. Could *not* face the man who loved Fiona, who'd been there in Mexico to see her at her worst. She couldn't do it.

"I can't."

"I'll take you home then. Give you some time to think about it. We'll talk later."

Julie nodded, numb inside. She never should have come to California. She hadn't known at the time this was where the SEALs were stationed who had rescued her, but she should've remembered the Naval base nearby was the home of the SEALs and it was a likely possibility.

Patrick helped her with her coat and led her outside to his car. He opened her door as he always did and waited until she was comfortable before shutting it. He got in without a word and they drove to her apartment in silence.

He pulled into a visitor's parking space and turned to her. "I like you, Julie. I want to be with you. I'm forty-three years old." He watched as she turned to stare at him in disbelief. "I know, I've never told you my age, but there it is. I'm old enough to know what I want in a partner. I've never been married for a reason, because I've never found someone who I can imagine being with for the rest of my life… until you. I know there's a fifteen-year age difference between us, but I don't care."

"Patrick…" Julie started, having no idea what she was going to say, but she didn't have to think of anything, because he continued.

"I know you have demons, we all do. You think after spending most of my time in the Navy as a SEAL, I don't? I've seen some of the worst things you can imagine, and even some you can't. But you have to fight your demons, otherwise they'll take control of you. And sweetheart, they're taking you over. I've seen it the last month or so. When you first called me I didn't want to meet you, but you wouldn't take no for an answer. You were so sure about what you needed to do to move on. But at the first sign of adversity, you gave up. And I know that isn't you."

"It *is* me. You weren't there, you didn't—"

"I wasn't there," Patrick interrupted without a qualm, "but I've been in similar situations. I've gone into various countries and rescued kidnap victims. Some were easygoing, some were scared, some were combative and hostile. I've *seen* it. But, Julie, you told me yourself that you were a different person now than you were then. I *like* the Julie that's sitting in front of me right now. Is everyone in this world going to like you and want to be your best friend? No. I have enemies. I can be a real hard ass and there are SEALs all over this country that I know wouldn't mourn me if they learned I'd suddenly passed away. But Julie, that's *their* issue, not mine.

"I have friends, good friends. I'm happy with my life. If I could do it all again, would I do everything the same? Of course not, but that's a part of life. Learning from your mistakes and moving on. I want you to move on with me. But if that's going to happen, you're going to have to do what you came out here to do—apologize and thank my men. Whatever they do with that is on *them*, not you."

"But they're your men."

"They are. And I know them. You think I'd be giving you this advice if I thought they'd hurt you? No way in hell. But you have to trust me, and them. More importantly, you have to do what *you* need to in order to move on. And God, Julie, I want you to be able to move on with me. I'd like nothing more than instead of waking you up and taking you home, to wake you up with kisses and carry you into our bedroom, where I could make sure you'd sleep like a log every night. I want nothing more than to learn your sweet little body inside and out, to taste you, to hear what you sound like when I'm buried deep inside you—but I can't until I know you're with me. Until I know this can go somewhere."

"Patrick," Julie almost moaned.

"I know I'm not playing fair, but I need to lay it on the line. I like you. I want you. But you need to forgive yourself, and then let my men forgive you. There's a company picnic at La Jolla this weekend. They're usually over at Coronado, but everyone wanted a change. I'd love to get the apology out of the way beforehand, so you can join me there and we can move on, together."

He waited a beat, then said in a low, urgent voice, "I have a feeling you're it for me, Julie. I know we didn't meet under normal circumstances, but I thank God every day that you knew someone who knew a Navy SEAL there in Virginia. I'd say it's amazing he knew Tex, but Tex knows everyone. Tex is a very important part of my men's lives, and has had a hand in saving every single one of their women. He wouldn't have given you my number if he thought what you wanted to do would hurt Cookie or Fiona or any of the other men and the women they love. Please, sweetheart. Be there on Saturday. Let's do this so we can start the rest of our life together."

He stared at Julie for a moment, then turned and climbed out of the driver's seat. He held her open door for her after she got out, leaned down and kissed her on the forehead. There was no making out, no getting to second base and thinking about stealing third.

"Sleep well, and I mean that, Julie. Hopefully I'll see you in a couple of days." Patrick squeezed her shoulders once and then he was done.

Julie headed to her apartment in a trance. Every single word Patrick said was seared on her brain.

He was right. She knew he was, but she understood if she showed up to talk to his men on Saturday, it'd be one of the most difficult things she'd ever done in her life, and she wasn't sure she had it in her, not even for Patrick. Not only would she be opening herself up to his men, and possibly have them treat her with indifference at best and censure at worst, but she'd be letting Patrick know in no uncertain terms that she wanted to be with him too.

She honestly didn't know if she could do it.

CHAPTER 10

The next day, Julie pulled herself out of bed, knowing she wouldn't be able to sleep any more than the three hours she'd somehow snuck in between nightmares. She put on her bathing suit and a pair of shorts and a T-shirt. She threw on a pair of pink flip-flops and grabbed sunscreen, a towel and her phone. She jumped in her car and went to *My Sister's Closet* and put up a "closed for sickness" sign for the first time since she'd moved to California. She needed a day to herself to think about what she wanted to do with her life.

That done, she headed for the beach. She'd always loved swimming, and was actually very good at it. Back in Virginia, she'd gone to the pool and done laps for exercise almost every day. She was in southern California, she needed sun and sand. That was supposed to cure all ailments.

Julie parked at the popular La Jolla beach, knowing she chose it partly because it was the beach she met Patrick at, and walked toward a section where a lot of others were sunbathing and hanging out. She didn't want to be alone and being in the middle of families and others enjoying their day at the beach seemed like a place she wanted to be.

She spread her towel on the sand and stripped off her clothes. She lay back on the sand and tried to relax. Julie closed her eyes and ran through different scenarios in her head. She thought back to the scene in her shop with Fiona and her friends. If she was honest with herself, she didn't blame any of them for acting as they did.

She'd been blindsided with coming face-to-face with Fiona, but if *she'd* been treated as badly as Fiona had been, and then come face-to-face with her tormenter, Julie knew she would've acted the same way Fiona and her friends had. And to be fair, Fiona hadn't thrown her apology back into her face, she just kind of looked at her, shell-shocked.

Julie wondered for the first time since that horrific day if maybe, just maybe if she tried again, she could get Fiona to listen to her. She knew they'd probably never be best friends, and that was okay. But if Julie wanted to be with Patrick, *really* with him, they'd see each other every now and then.

Julie didn't know if the Commander hung out with the SEALs or not; she figured maybe not on a social basis. If he had to send them on dangerous missions and make decisions that affected their lives, he was probably more of a professional friend than a personal one. However, he had hinted that the SEALs were like family to him. She could probably handle seeing Fiona and her friends every now and then, especially if she didn't have to worry about fitting into what was obviously their close circle, but she wasn't sure about having to see them and hang out with them on a social basis. It'd probably be too painful for Fiona, and would definitely be awkward for Julie.

Then there were the SEALs themselves. She definitely hadn't put her best foot forward with them, but men were typically better at not holding grudges and moving on. Fiona's husband notwithstanding, maybe the others would be able to forgive her for being a bitch. She'd have to work harder to show Cookie she'd changed, and wasn't that horrible person he'd had to deal with in the jungle, but maybe she could do it.

Julie was aware that sometime between last night and today her attitude had shifted, but she'd thought long and hard about what

Patrick had said the night before. She'd come to the conclusion that he was right. And more than that, she wanted to be with him too. And if that meant she had to put on her big girl panties and apologize and take whatever the SEALs wanted to dish out to her, she'd do it. Patrick was that important to her. How that had happened so quickly, Julie had no idea, but it had.

And besides, she needed to move on with her life, it's why she'd moved out to California in the first place. The nightmares had increased since she'd seen Fiona, and it was obvious she needed closure. Whether or not any of them forgave her was almost secondary at that point. She'd do the best she could, and that would have to be good enough for her psyche.

Julie was feeling mellow, enjoying the warmth of the sun and the breeze off the water and satisfied with her plans for her future, when she heard the first shout. She ignored it, figuring it was kids goofing off in the surf.

When more shouts came, they sounded more panicked than the first. Julie sat up and opened her eyes, shielding them from the sun with one hand. There were about twenty teenagers in the water, yelling and frantically waving their hands, yelling for help.

Julie looked around. There were three lifeguards running toward the ocean. She knew there was no way the three of them would be able to help all of the people in the water. They needed more help.

Julie reached for her phone almost without thinking. She swiped it to open it and pushed the contact button. She pushed Patrick's name and watched the horror unfolding in front of her with a sinking feeling in her stomach.

The kids were caught in a massive rip current. They were quickly being swept farther and farther out to sea. Julie had learned all about rip currents last year before she'd been kidnapped. She'd taken a trip to Florida with some friends and had seen a small one down there. The lifeguard quickly leaped into action and had made sure the man caught in it made it back to shore. He'd then held an impromptu lesson on rip currents with the awestruck crowd; what caused them and, most importantly, what to do if you were ever caught in one.

And what you should never do was what the kids in the water were now doing. They were panicking and trying to swim directly back to shore. There was no way they were strong enough to fight the current and get back to the shallow water. The only thing they were doing was exhausting themselves and making the likelihood of drowning more like a probability.

Finally, when Julie didn't think Patrick was going to pick up and she'd have to call the mysterious Tex, she heard, "Commander Hurt here."

"Oh thank God! Patrick, it's Julie."

"What's wrong?"

She was thankful he got right down to it. "I'm at La Jolla beach and there's a rip current. A big one. There are about twenty kids caught in it and only three lifeguards. I don't know what you can do all the way from down there, but I thought maybe—"

"I'm on it. Stay out of the water. You hear me?"

"Uh huh, hurry Patrick. It's not looking good."

"I will. I'll talk to you later."

"Bye." Julie hung up the phone and stood, fidgeting from foot to foot. She chewed her nail, hoping to God she wouldn't have to watch the kids disappear forever. Their heads were getting smaller and smaller as they were swept farther and farther out to sea.

"Johnnie!"

Julie turned at the sharp cry. A woman was rushing to the water trying frantically to grab her child, who'd wandered out just a bit too far. Julie wanted to rail at the mother for not watching her child more carefully. Who let their kid get in the ocean when it was obvious what was happening?

Acting without thinking, Julie dropped her cell phone on her towel and ran toward the little boy. Maybe she could get to him before he got sucked out into the ocean. She ran past the hysterical woman, yelling at her, "I'll get him!" before diving into the water and swimming as hard as she could toward the panicking little boy.

Blocking out her own fear, not thinking about the danger she was putting herself in, Julie stroked hard through the water. Before long, she could feel herself being dragged along with the rip current. It actually helped propel her faster toward the child. He was bobbing up and down in the water, clearly panicking. The small waves were washing over his head every now and then and he'd inhale sea water. She finally got near enough that she could grab hold of his flailing arm. As most drowning people do, he latched onto her neck with both arms and tried to climb upward, toward the precious oxygen his body was craving, almost pulling her under in the process.

Julie tucked her head as she'd been taught in a lifeguarding class a long time ago and ducked under the water, making sure to keep hold of the boy. He immediately let go in order to stay near the surface of the water and Julie was able to turn him until his back was to her. She crawled back up his body until her head broke the surface. She put one arm around him and pulled him into her, holding him to her chest as she treaded water with her legs and her free arm.

"I've got you, you're okay. Relax. Don't fight me. Stop struggling." Finally, her words seemed to sink in, and the boy calmed. He still held onto the arm that was around his chest with both hands, his little fingernails digging in, but he'd stopped thrashing. Julie ignored the pain of her arms, and scrutinized her surroundings for the first time since she'd entered the water.

Her heart sank; they were way far away from the shore.

Resolutely, she looked around. Julie knew the best way to get out of a rip current was to swim parallel to the shoreline. Eventually they would break free of the strong current trying to carry them out to sea, but she had no idea how far she'd have to swim, or how far they'd be washed out before they were able to separate themselves from the grip of the water.

Julie wasn't thinking about herself, or her dad, or her situation with Fiona and the SEALs, not even thinking about the horrible things that had happened to her when she was kidnapped. She was wholly focused on the little boy in her arms and getting them both back to the beach.

"What's your name?" she asked him. She knew it was Johnnie, but wanted to keep him engaged with her, rather than on what was happening around him.

"J-J-Johnnie."

"Mine is Julie. Hey, both our names start with the letter J. Cool right?"

"Yeah," Johnnie said uncertainly.

"How old are you?"

"Five."

"Five? You're probably in kindergarten aren't you?"

"Uh-huh."

"Have you ever taken swimming lessons?"

"Yeah." He perked up for the first time since Julie started talking with him. "I'm a good swimmer. Even my teacher says so."

"So you know how to float?"

"Floating's for babies."

Julie couldn't help but smile. "Okay then, here's what we're gonna do. I'm going to let go and—"

"Don't let go!" Johnnie screamed and dug his nails into her arm again, harder this time.

"Johnnie, listen! I'm not going to let you get away from me. I'm only going to take my arm from around your chest so you can lie on your back. I need you to float on your back for me. I'm not going to leave you out here. Okay?"

"Promise?" His voice was wobbly and Julie could tell he was on the verge of tears.

"I promise, Johnnie. You can touch me the entire time. Okay?"

"Okay. Just don't let go."

"I won't. Now, release my arm and lay back. I'm still right here with you." Relieved when he did as she asked and tentatively put his head back until he was looking up at the sky. Julie kicked harder and put both hands under him, one at his shoulder blades and the other at the small of his back. She knew she couldn't tread water next to him like this forever, but she needed to get him comfortable first. Julie tried to strategize her next course of action. Johnnie's little body was rigid and he wasn't exactly floating, but Julie figured she could work with it.

"Good job. You're a very good floater, Johnnie. I'm proud of you. Now, I need one of the hands that's under your back to help me swim, so you'll only feel one of them, but I'm right here, I won't let you out of my grasp."

"Okay, Julie. I trust you."

Julie breathed a sigh of relief. Thank God, she needed a hand to help her swim. She kicked her legs and took an experimental stroke with her arm. So far so good. She was moving sideways. She had no idea how long it would take for them to get out of the rip current, but any progress sideways rather than out to the vast never-ending ocean was good.

Slowly but surely, Julie moved them sideways, watching as the shore got smaller and smaller. Dear God, she had no idea rip currents could go on for so long. She thought once they got a certain distance away from the shore, they simply stopped. She'd obviously been wrong.

Just when she thought they'd never break free of the grip the ocean seemed to have on them, Julie felt the tension of the water decrease. She kept kicking and pulling with her arm until she was sure she was no longer pulling against the strong current. Thank God.

"Guess what, Johnnie?"

"What?"

"We're going to start back in for the beach again. That sound okay to you?"

"Uh-huh. I want my mommy."

"I know, and you're being very brave."

Julie realized that for the moment she wasn't scared at all. It was amazing how, when you were trying to save someone else, you weren't afraid for yourself. She vaguely wondered if that was how it was for the SEALs when they were on a mission.

Another thought struck her. As scared as Johnnie was, and he'd hurt her when he'd been scared, it didn't matter to her. She was going to do the best she could for him anyway.

It was an epiphany, but she didn't have time to dwell on it.

"Do you want to try treading water for a moment, Johnnie?" Julie needed a break. She had a long way to swim back to shore and as much as she wanted to get to it, she knew if she didn't rest for a second, she'd be in trouble.

She helped Johnnie upright and kept her hand on his elbow as she scissor-kicked her legs.

"I'm tired."

"I know you are, baby, and we're gonna get you back as soon as possible."

"But I wanna be back nooooow," Johnnie complained petulantly.

Julie figured rest time was over. It hadn't been long enough, but the little boy was obviously too scared and tired to handle treading water for long.

"Okay, Johnnie. Lie back down and kick your legs, I'll get us back to shore lickety-split."

The little boy continued to complain while Julie towed him next to her and slowly made her way back to safety.

"Are we there yet? I want my mommy!" Julie felt helpless as the tears fell down his little face and disappeared into the blue water of the ocean.

She picked up her head at the sound of a motor in the distance. Thank God! The Calvary had arrived! There were four boats headed her way. They were flying across the water. If they'd been on dry land, they surely would've been breaking the law with how fast they were going. At the moment, however, Julie knew she'd never seen a better sight.

Julie turned to estimate where she'd escaped the rip current and was surprised to see heads bobbing quite a distance away from her. The boats zoomed past her and Johnnie's location and toward the teenagers who'd originally gotten swept away.

"Why'd they go past us? Are we gonna die? I want my mommy!" Johnnie cried. Julie saw he'd turned his head and was watching as the rescue boats raced into the distance.

"They'll be back for us. There are people worse off than us. People who can't float as well as you can, buddy. Just stay floating, they'll be back."

Julie hoped like hell she wasn't lying. The beach looked a long way away and she knew her strength was flagging. She honestly didn't know if she'd be able to get them both all the way back to the shore.

CHAPTER 11

Patrick kept his eyes glued to the water in front of them as Cookie raced through the waves. As soon as he'd hung up with Julie, he'd mobilized his crew. They had all happened to be down at the SEAL training beach, showing some of the recruits some maneuvers.

Patrick had raced to them, barking orders as he ran. "This is not a drill! Rip current at La Jolla beach. At least twenty people caught."

The team was moving before he'd finished speaking. Patrick was the only one not wearing the proper gear, but no one said a word. His battle dress uniform, blue and gray camouflage, was appropriate for everyday wear in the office, but on a mission on the ocean, not so much. Not caring, he leaped into a boat with Cookie and Wolf and the others got into the other two boats. Two other instructors on the beach jumped into the last boat and they were all on their way without knowing exactly what the situation was, only that if the Commander came racing down the beach yelling about a rip current, it was serious.

Patrick filled Cookie and Wolf in on what he knew as they raced across the water, their legs bending with the movement of the boat and the waves as if second nature.

"How'd you find out so quickly?" Wolf questioned.

"Julie called me. She was there as it happened."

"Smart of her," Wolf complimented.

They arrived at La Jolla beach and could see a couple of the life-guards on jet skis in the general area where they needed to go, towing some of the teenagers back to shore.

The SEAL team immediately began to assist, pulling as many people into the boats as they could find. The surfers were all scared and mildly dehydrated from swallowing the salty water and being out in the sun for as long as they'd been, but generally all right. They'd been lucky.

Wolf, Cookie, and Hurt were the first back to shore with their boatload of rescued swimmers. They were greeted by a huge crowd of worried, scared, and curious onlookers. As the kids exited the SEAL boat, a panicked voice rung out over the other general chaos surrounding them.

"Where's my baby? Did you find him?"

Thinking the lady shrieking at them was looking for her teenager, Cookie tried to calm her down. "The other boats are picking up the others. I'm sure he'll be here soon."

"But he's just a baby. He can swim, but not that well. He's only five!"

"Five?" Patrick questioned sharply.

"Yes! I was watching what was happening and didn't realize he'd gone into the water. He's always been curious about the lifeguards and he's been going to swimming lessons. He must've either wanted a closer look or he thought he could help in some way. The current took him away from me before I could get to him. A lady ran in after him, but I haven't seen her come in on any of the boats yet either. You have to find him! He's my only child! Please!"

Patrick looked around uneasily and didn't see Julie anywhere. "A woman went after him? Who?"

"I don't know who, she just told me to stay put and she'd get him for me."

Patrick turned to his men. "I have a bad feeling about this."

Wolf didn't say a word, but after helping the last swimmer out, immediately climbed back into the boat, with Patrick following along behind him. Cookie pushed the inflatable raft with the powerful engine backwards until it had enough depth to turn around, then he leaped inside. Wolf took off, headed back out to sea.

Patrick and Cookie scanned the ocean surface with their binoculars. They didn't see anyone else in the area where all the surfers and boogie boarders had been located.

"Widen the search," Patrick ordered. "I don't know what she knows about rips, but if she knew anything at all, she'd try to swim parallel to get out of it. It has to be why they weren't in the general area with the others. They could be anywhere either right or left of the main current area."

Nobody wanted to mention the possibility that she, and the missing little boy, could have drowned, but each of the men were thinking it.

Wolf cut the engine and grabbed a pair of binoculars. Cookie looked to the right, and Wolf and Patrick looked left. They scanned the surface of the ocean for anything that might look out of place. Spotting a person's head bobbing in the waves was almost impossible. They all knew it, but none of them said a word.

Finally, Wolf said calmly, "I might have something." Cookie immediately dropped his binoculars and grabbed hold of the wheel, turning it to the left and heading to the area Wolf and Patrick had been scanning.

"Turn to your eleven o'clock," Wolf ordered Cookie. "Yeah, right there. Straight ahead, we'll run right into whatever it was I saw."

Patrick dropped the binoculars he'd been squinting into, preferring to see with his own eyes whatever it was Wolf had spotted and praying it was Julie.

The boat slowly made its way to the dark spot in the ocean. As they got closer and closer, they could all make out a dark-haired head bobbing up and down. Then an arm raised and waved at them.

Thank God.

* * *

"HEY JOHNNIE, LOOK!" Julie said excitedly. "A boat!"

"A boat? Where?" Johnnie asked, immediately sitting up in his excitement. Julie sucked in a mouthful of sea water as she struggled to keep the boy's head above the surface.

"Move your legs, Johnnie," she begged. "Tread water."

"I'm too tired," he whined, clinging to Julie's neck.

Julie's legs moved faster to keep both of their heads above water. She was holding Johnnie like she would if they were standing on firm ground. She had her hand under his bottom and he had both legs wrapped around her waist and both arms around her neck. Julie used her free hand to try to help keep them afloat.

Thinking back to Johnnie's complaint, Julie agreed. She was also tired. Exhausted, but she could hang on for another minute or so until the boat reached them. It would suck to be so close to rescue to fail the little boy now.

Finally, after what seemed like hours but was only seconds, the boat was there.

It looked so much bigger now that it was right next to her than it did from far away. Earlier, she'd watched as the boat headed away from the shore and had stopped dead in the water. She'd wondered what they were doing, but hoped they were scanning the area for more people. She'd waved her hand over her head, praying they'd see her. She'd breathed a sigh of relief when it seemed they had.

Julie looked up and was shocked to see Patrick's face peering down at her and Johnnie.

"Hi."

If she had the energy and the free hand to smack herself in the forehead, she would've. "Hi?" That's what she said to the man she thought she wanted to spend the rest of her life with after he kind of broke up with her and after she'd just spent what seemed like an hour treading water in the ocean not knowing if she'd ever put her feet on dry land again? Good lord, she was a dork.

"What's his name?" Patrick was all business.

"Johnnie."

"Hi, Johnnie. I'm Hurt. The guys with me are Cookie and Wolf. How about getting out of the ocean, huh?"

"I want my mommy."

"I know, buddy. And we'll get you to her in just a minute. Can you lift your arms so we can help you in the boat?"

"No! Don't wanna let go of Julie."

Julie turned her attention away from Patrick and Cookie. Shit. It *had* to be Cookie, didn't it? It looked as if she was going to have to face him sooner rather than later. The choice had just been taken out of her hands. But first things first.

"Johnnie, it's okay. I won't let go until you're safe in the boat. Okay? You've been such a brave boy this entire time. But let Cookie and Hurt help now. Yeah? They're Navy SEALs...the best of the best. They're almost like superheroes. They aren't going to let anything bad happen to us."

"Promise?"

Julie smiled at Johnnie. "Promise."

Even though she'd promised, Johnnie still was reluctant to let go of what he obviously knew was the only thing keeping him alive. Finally, he lifted his arms up just enough for Wolf to grab both of his wrists and easily lift him up and out of the water and into the boat. Julie breathed a sigh of relief. Even though the boy hadn't been terribly heavy, she was exhausted and the burden of knowing he was relying on her to keep him alive had been a heavy one. She looked up at Patrick.

"Your turn, Julie. Lift your arms."

She treaded water and looked at the boat dubiously. It was a rubber raft, the kind she saw on documentaries about SEAL training. There was no way she'd be able to climb over the sides without help. She wanted out of the ocean more than anything, but wasn't sure how to accomplish it.

"Uh, you guys wouldn't happen to have a ladder would you?"

Patrick smiled down at her for the first time since he'd arrived, as if she was a shining ray of sun in the rising morning fog. "Nope. Give me your hand."

Julie sighed. He was smiling, but his words were obviously an order. Still not meeting Cookie's eyes, Julie lifted one hand toward Patrick. He immediately grabbed hold of her wrist in a grip she knew she wouldn't slip out of. He had her. She was safe.

"Give Cookie your other hand. We'll lift you over the edge. No problem."

Julie looked at the other man for the first time since the boat pulled up next to her. She bit her cracked lip. Hell. He was holding his hand out toward her.

When their eyes met, he said simply, "It's okay. Trust me."

Shit. She raised her other hand and felt it, too, grasped in a secure grip. Before Julie could even think about how they were going to get her into the boat, she was there. The two men had lifted her as if she weighed five pounds instead of over a hundred. Then she was in Patrick's arms.

They'd set her on her feet on the bottom of the boat, but her knees had immediately given out. She would've crumpled to the floor, but Patrick was there. He wrapped his arms around her and eased her down, still holding her tight. Julie could feel the boat moving, but didn't lift her head. She was exhausted. She felt as if she could sleep for days.

Knowing she had to do it before she either lost her nerve or passed out, she raised her head to look for Cookie. She found him driving the boat, but alternating between watching where he was going, and looking down at her and his Commander.

"Thank you," Julie said without breaking eye contact with Cookie. "Thank you for coming to get me, for being patient with me. I know I was a bitch, and probably the worst rescued person you ever had to deal with. I was a selfish cow and I'm sorry. You probably don't believe me, but I'm working on being a better person. I swear, I'm not the same woman you met in Mexico."

"I know, and you're welcome."

"You know?" Julie asked, surprised and confused.

"Yeah. Hurt wouldn't put up with the bitch I met in Mexico. And since he likes you a heck of a lot, I figure you must've used what happened to you to better yourself."

"You're not pissed at me? I was horrible. And I also heard that you married Fiona...I don't—"

"Julie. Stop. Do I think you and Fee are ever gonna be best friends? No. Are we suddenly gonna go out and get manis and pedis together? Hell no. But I can appreciate that you were under a lot of stress while we were in that hellhole. Don't screw Hurt over, and we're cool. All right?"

Julie nodded and buried her head back in Patrick's neck. "I'm not going to screw you over," she told Patrick in a low voice, "but I can't promise to never be a bitch again. I think I have the gene. It's buried deep, but it's still there."

Patrick chuckled. "I can handle your bitch gene."

"Okay. Patrick?"

"Yeah, sweetheart?"

"Thank you for finding me. I was so scared."

"You did good, Julie. Except for the part where you dove into the middle of a rip current when I specifically told you to stay out of the water. We'll have to talk about that later."

Julie lifted her head and looked at Patrick. She spoke softly so Johnnie wouldn't hear. "There's no way he would've survived. The lifeguards were already all in the water trying to help others. There wasn't anyone else around to go after him."

Patrick didn't respond, but put his hand on the back of her head and returned it to his neck. He held her against him the entire way back to the beach. When they arrived, Cookie pulled the boat as close to shore as he could and Wolf carried the little boy out of the boat. The mother was there and grabbed hold of her child, who immediately started crying now that he was back in his mother's sympathetic arms.

"Where's your stuff?" Patrick asked Julie.

She lifted her head and looked toward where she'd left her stuff. She could see it over the edge of the boat and between the people milling around the crowded beach. "It's over there, next to the three police officers."

Wolf set off toward the men and Julie watched as he gathered up her stuff and headed back to the boat. Without a word, he climbed in and Cookie once again shoved the boat back into the water. The guys who were in the other boats followed behind. They'd been speaking with the lifeguards and the local police. Amazingly, everyone had been accounted for. Between the lifeguards and the SEALs, everyone was back on shore, safe and sound.

They took off back toward Coronado at a much slower pace than they'd left. Patrick still hadn't moved from the bottom of the boat, and thus Julie hadn't either.

The trip back was relatively silent until Wolf said, suddenly and somewhat bizarrely, "Does Johnnie know who you are, Julie?"

She raised her head and looked at Wolf. "What do you mean? He knows my name is Julie, but if you're asking if I gave my phone number to a five-year-old when we were treading water in the middle of the ocean, the answer is no."

"So his mom won't be able to find you to thank you."

"Probably not, unless she really digs. But so what? I didn't jump my ass into the ocean to get accolades. I did it to save Johnnie. He's what mattered He's a five-year-old kid who let his curiosity get the better of him. He made a mistake. He didn't do it on purpose." Julie was slightly miffed that Wolf would think she'd demand thanks from Johnnie's mother, until she saw the smile on his face. She looked over at Cookie who was driving, and he too was smiling.

She turned to Patrick, only to see a smile as big as she'd ever seen creep across his face as well. "What the hell are you all smiling about?"

"You didn't do it for thanks. You did it to save a life. Was it worth it?" Cookie asked.

Slowly Julie understood. "Yeah," she breathed, "it was worth it."

"So, you're welcome, Julie. You now know firsthand that we don't do what we do for thanks. We do it because it needs to be done. Just as you did today."

Cookie's words sank in, but Julie couldn't let it go completely.

Almost, but not quite yet. "But sometimes, the person you saved *needs* to say thanks."

"Then say it so we can be done with it and we can all move on."

Julie smiled. She couldn't be pissed. "Then thank you, Cookie. And Wolf, thank you for getting my ass out of that hellhole."

"Again, you're welcome. Now we're done with that, yeah?" Wolf asked with mock impatience.

"We're done."

"Good."

"Relax, sweetheart," Patrick said into her ear as he pulled her into him again. "You've had a hard day, let me take care of you."

"I can do that." She smiled into Patrick's neck and let him take her weight. It felt right, being in his arms. She was where she was meant to be, and it was a pretty damn good place to end up.

CHAPTER 12

Julie tried not to hyperventilate. The company picnic had been postponed; there was no way Patrick wanted to put any of the people under his command in danger. The rip current was gone, but no one wanted to take a chance on another while their families were enjoying a day at the beach.

After the boats had arrived at the training area at Coronado, Patrick had helped her to his office, sat her on a chair, and told her he'd be back in two minutes to take her home. He'd been true to his word. He'd returned and, without a word, picked her up, even though she'd insisted she could walk, and taken her back to his place.

She'd showered and put on a pair of his sweats, which were huge on her, and a SEAL T-shirt. Patrick had made her drink a full bottle of water to replace some of the fluids she'd lost out in the ocean, and they'd both crawled onto his bed even though it was only five o'clock in the afternoon.

Julie sighed, remembering how safe she'd felt wrapped in Patrick's arms, under his covers, wearing his clothes, snug as a bug in a rug. She'd fallen asleep and hadn't woken up until the next morning, when Patrick kissed her forehead before he'd gotten out of bed.

Apparently her conversation in the boat with Cookie and Wolf had indicated to Patrick that she was ready to talk to the rest of the team—and Fiona. He'd informed her, after another shower and while they were eating yogurt and bagels for breakfast that he'd arranged a team meeting that morning.

Julie had tried to protest, but Patrick had stopped her by asking two questions.

"Do you want to be with me? To see where this can go between us?"

Her answer was immediate. "Yes."

"Then we need to be there at ten. The guys will meet us there, and Fiona is coming over at ten-thirty."

So now it was time. Julie was sitting in a surprisingly comfortable chair in a large meeting room at Patrick's building. The leather chair squeaked a bit as she shifted nervously and tried not to freak out and run screaming from the room. But she wanted this. She did. It was why she'd spoken to Stacey and Diesel back in Virginia in the first place. Why she'd wanted to track down the SEALs. She wanted to move on.

Patrick was sitting next to her, looking amazing in his battle dress uniform. Julie hadn't gotten to fully appreciate it the day before in the middle of her rescue. He was there to support her, to make sure his men didn't say or do anything that would hurt her further. He'd told her they wouldn't, but he was still there, having her back.

The door opened, and Julie watched as Cookie, Wolf, and four other men entered. Four sat in various chairs around the table in the room, while Cookie and one other man stayed standing, leaning against one of the walls.

Julie didn't beat around the bush; she started right in, deciding that drawing it out wasn't the best course of action for her rapidly beating heart and her psyche.

"Thank you for coming down to Mexico to rescue me. I know you did it because of my dad, but I appreciate it nonetheless. I've already had this talk with Cookie and Wolf, and I realize you probably don't need or want my thanks, but you have it anyway. I know it was your job, and you've done it before and you'll probably do it again, but please know that even though I looked unimpressed and acted like a selfish child, I appreciate it more than you'll know."

Julie then turned to Cookie. "And I said it to you yesterday, and I'll say it again today in front of your teammates. I'm sorry about how I acted. I was scared and hurting. That's no excuse, because I know Fiona was too and she didn't act like me. The thing I'm most ashamed of is trying to get you to leave that stupid hut without telling you someone else was there too." Julie looked down at her hands, clasped in her lap under the table. She dug her fingernails into her palms, trying to gather the courage to say what she needed to say. Patrick put his hand over hers and squeezed, letting her know he was there for her.

She looked up into Cookie's eyes. "It doesn't change anything that happened or anything I said or did, but I'm trying to be a better person."

Cookie put her out of her misery. "As I told you yesterday, Julie, you're welcome. I can't lie; you weren't the most enjoyable person to be with in the jungle, and I did have a hard time forgiving you for almost allowing me to leave Fiona there. But, she didn't get left. She's here, alive, and she's doing great. I don't need your thanks or your apology, but they're appreciated all the same."

Julie sagged in relief. Again, though they'd kind of already had this conversation yesterday in the boat, him accepting her apology and her thanks in front of his comrades somehow made it different. More official. She nodded at him, grateful.

The other man standing against the wall spoke up as well. "I'm Dude, and you're right, Julie. No thanks are necessary, but to be honest, it's nice to hear every once in a while." He came over to where she was sitting and held out his hand. Julie put hers into it and was surprised when he pulled her out of her chair and into his arms for a big bear hug. "I'm glad you're changing your life around."

The other men in the room also came over and hugged her, each accepting her thanks in a personal way. Afterwards, they filed out of the room. Finally, it was Cookie's turn. He put his hands on her shoulders and looked her in the eye. "You ready?"

Julie knew what he meant. She nodded.

He walked to the door and looked out and gestured to someone. Fiona came into view and Julie watched as Cookie took hold of her hand and held it as she entered the room. Cookie closed the door behind them.

Again, knowing she had to jump right in, Julie immediately apologized. "I'm sorry I was a bitch, Fiona. You did nothing but try to help me out there. You were gracious and even though you were suffering, you still tried to comfort me. I threw it in your face, making fun of your counting and even being greedy with the food. I played into your insecurities about not being the one they were there to rescue. It was inexcusable and I'm sorrier than you'll ever know." Julie's words were rushed, as if she thought Fiona would butt in and cut her off before she could get them out.

"Apology accepted," Fiona said easily.

Julie's eyes welled with tears and she bit her lip, trying to control herself. She felt Patrick's hand on her back, caressing and reassuring her.

Fiona went on. "I didn't expect to see you in your store. It was a shock and I didn't know what to think or feel. I think I owe *you* an apology for the way my friends handled the situation."

Julie began to interrupt her, but Fiona held up her hand. "Let me finish. In Caroline and Alabama's defense, I'd had a flashback when I got home after Mexico, and I took off. I thought I was back there, and there were men chasing me. No one knew where I was and I totally freaked my friends out. I know they thought seeing you would bring on another flashback and they only wanted to make sure I was safe. It wasn't really about you, Julie."

Julie shook her head sadly. "But they know about me."

Fiona nodded slowly. "Yeah. I told them some of what happened down there. It's what friends do."

It was Julie who nodded this time. "I know. I'll apologize to them too. I'll apologize to anyone you want me to, Fiona. I admire the hell out of you. You survived so much more than me. I wouldn't have been able to do it."

"Yes, you would. I was just like you, Julie. Exactly like you. At first I was ready and willing to do whatever they said so they'd stop hurting me and hopefully let me go. But slowly I realized they weren't going to let me go, so I started fighting them. You would've gotten to that point too. I know it. Look at you now. You have a will of steel. You not only braved Hunter and the other guys, but me too."

The two women smiled at each other. Julie knew they'd never be besties, but maybe, just maybe, they could be comfortable enough that seeing each other wouldn't cause old wounds to open and fester.

"Would it be all right if I stopped by your store sometime soon? I never did get to see all the awesome things you've got there, and I heard all about how great it was from Caroline after she went the first time."

"Of course. Anytime you want to come by, I'll be there. Just let me know, even if it's after hours."

"And you really do donate clothes to women's shelters and to teenagers who need a dress for a school dance and can't afford it?" Fiona asked, sounding somewhat impressed.

Julie nodded. "Uh-huh. I love the looks on their faces when they come out of the dressing room wearing a Vera Wang or Gucci dress and it's obvious they feel fabulous."

"I'd say you've come a long way since that bitch in the jungle."

Julie laughed, not offended in the least. "I hope so. I'm trying."

"You're succeeding."

"Thanks for giving me the chance to apologize, Fiona. Seriously."

"You're welcome."

"See you tomorrow, Hurt?" Cookie asked, shaking his Commander's hand.

"O-five-hundred for PT," Patrick confirmed.

Cookie nodded and he and Fiona left the room.

Julie felt herself being pulled back into Patrick's arms. He wrapped his arms around her from behind and held her cradled against his chest. "You okay?"

"Yeah. That was…" Her voice trailed off, unsure of the word she was looking for.

"Cathartic?"

It was as good a word as any to try to explain how she was feeling. She nodded and nuzzled her cheek against Patrick's shoulder. "Thank you for setting it up for me."

"You're welcome. It's what Tex sent you to me to do, after all."

Julie laughed. "Only a few months later than he expected it to happen though."

"True. You ready to go?"

"Yeah, I have some stuff I need to do at the store. I've been neglecting it too long. The people that work with me are good, but they hate the sales stuff. Daddy hired them because they're good at marketing and accounting. I need to set up a meeting with the director of a women's clinic and see who has interviews coming up and what I can do to help."

"In case I haven't told you already, you're amazing,"

Julie turned in Patrick's grasp, happy he kept his arms around her, and looked up. "It feels good to help people, rather than belittle them or make fun of them for what they don't have. It's what I've done in the past, and I'm ashamed of it."

Instead of responding to her words, Patrick said, "You're coming over tonight, right?"

Julie thought the change of subject was a bit bizarre, but she answered affirmatively anyway.

"Good. I enjoyed holding you in my arms last night. But I think it's time to move our relationship to the next level…if you're ready."

Julie knew exactly what Patrick was saying. She grinned up at him. "I'm definitely ready, and I'd like that."

"I have a meeting at four today, but I'm headed home right after. When can you get there?"

"Anxious, are you?" Julie teased.

"Hell yes. You have no idea what's in store for you tonight, sweetheart. I've dreamed about your body under mine. I've thought about how you'll sound when you come apart for me. All of it. I can't wait. And, as you heard me tell Cookie, I have PT in the morning, so you need to get to my place as soon as possible. I'm not planning on either of us getting much sleep."

Julie knew she had a stupid grin on her face, but she couldn't help it. "I'll make sure I'm there by five. That work?"

"Perfectly. And as much as I want to kiss the hell out of you right now, it's not exactly appropriate for the Commander of a Navy SEAL team to be sucking face at work. So for my professional reputation's sake, get going. I'll see you tonight."

Julie nodded and pulled back reluctantly. "Thank you for being you, Patrick."

He nodded. "Go on. Be safe."

Julie smiled at him and walked backward to the door, not turning around until she'd exited and couldn't see him anymore. The goofy grin on her face stayed there for most of the day.

CHAPTER 13

Dinner was delicious. The dishes were in the dishwasher and Julie was drying her hands on the dishtowel hanging off of the handle on the refrigerator. She'd turned to ask Patrick what else she could do when she found herself being lifted through the air. She screeched and grabbed on to Patrick's shoulders as she was spun around and her butt landed on the table they'd finished eating their meal on not ten minutes earlier.

"Patrick, what the—"

Her words were cut off when his mouth came down on hers and his tongue swept inside, making her lose whatever it was she was saying. She wrapped her legs around his hips and her hands went to his shoulders as she hung on for the ride.

Patrick couldn't wait anymore. He'd controlled himself throughout their pre-dinner small-talk and as they'd eaten. But watching her chew, and laugh, and generally just be the wonderful person she was, had pushed him over the edge.

When he'd watched Julie in his kitchen, happily helping him clean up the mess he'd made preparing the lasagna they'd eaten, something snapped inside.

He needed her. Now.

His hands wandered up her sides, wondering anew about how delicate she seemed. She was tiny compared to him, but her personality more than made up for her small stature. She felt as if she was made to be in his arms. Patrick picked his head up to look her in the eyes. "You ready for this? For me?" He wanted her to be one hundred percent sure. He knew what she'd been through, and they'd had a talk about this once. She'd reassured him that she didn't have any hang-ups about sex, but he needed to be certain. The last thing he wanted to do was traumatize her any more than she'd already been.

"Take me, Patrick. I want you."

It was all he needed to hear. His hands went to the bottom of the shirt she was wearing. It had buttons down the front, but they would take too long to bother with. He drew it upward and Julie lifted her arms to assist him as he pulled it over her head. Patrick threw it behind him without looking. He'd had his lips on her tits in the past, and couldn't wait to suck on them again, but for now he needed more. He needed to be inside her.

His hands went to the button on her pants, but her hands were already there.

"I'll get this. You do yours." Julie's voice was breathy and urgent.

Patrick liked the way she thought. He grabbed his wallet out of his pocket and quickly pulled the condom out. He'd put it there earlier, so it was handy. Holding the packet between his teeth, he quickly undid the button on his jeans and lowered the zipper, never taking his eyes off of Julie's fingers as she did the same to her own pants.

Patrick quickly rolled the condom over his erection and helped Julie pull one leg out of her jeans and panties. He didn't give her a chance to remove them completely. He put his hand over her folds and sighed at the wetness he found there. He put his other hand on her belly, amazed how his entire hand could almost span her from hip bone to hip bone.

"God, you're small," he said, for the first time worrying about her size compared to his.

"You'll fit, Patrick," Julie reassured him, putting her hands over her head and arched her back.

Her wanton pose made him groan. He held her still as his fingers caressed and teased her bundle of nerves and her soaking-wet folds. Never giving her what she was so greedily asking for. "All I could think of while you were eating tonight was laying you out on this table and fucking you so hard you'd feel me for days."

"Then what are you waiting for? Do it!" Julie demanded in exasperation.

"Because now that I have you right here where I'd fantasized about, I've decided I want to go slow, to take my time. I realize I should carry you into my bedroom and take you on my bed, you deserve that and more. But if I have to wait another second to make you mine, I don't know what I'll do."

"Fuck me, Patrick," Julie moaned. "Please, for the love of God, stop teasing me and take me."

Before the last word was out of her mouth, Patrick put one hand next to her hip on the table and guided the tip of his condom-covered cock to her opening with the other.

They both groaned as he entered her for the first time.

"Oh lord, Julie. You're so hot and slick."

"More, give me more!"

Patrick pulled back then pushed in a little farther than he'd been in before. "Slowly, Julie. I want this to be slow. I don't want to hurt you, but I also want to savor it." He put one hand on the back of her neck, making sure she was looking at him. Both of her hands latched on to his waist and she whimpered passionately under him, gazing up at him and breathing hard.

He pulled out and eased inside her a bit farther and held still. "I love you, Julie Lytle. I want to be the only man you let in here for the rest of your life. I want to protect you from anyone who tries to hurt you and be there when you need me. I want to fuck you on my table, on the couch, on the counter, in my shower and in my bed. I don't think I'll ever get enough of you."

Without giving her time to respond, Patrick pushed the rest of the way inside. He ground his hips against hers, loving how she immediately lifted her legs and wrapped them around him, her actions showing him more than words ever could that she was over what had happened to her all those months ago. He could feel her jeans dangling off of one of her legs and his own pants were hanging off his ass. He hadn't even taken the time to take off his shirt.

But even with both of them still half-dressed, Patrick still felt more naked than he had in his entire life as he waited for Julie's reaction to his words.

"Yes, Patrick. I love you too. I have no idea how I got lucky enough to be here, with you, with everything I've done and who I've been in the past, but I'll fight and die to keep it now. To keep *you*."

Patrick groaned, pulled back and thrust back inside Julie, hard. His hands slapped on the table next to her, balancing him over her. He'd wanted to keep this soft and light. To slowly bring them both to an orgasm, but it didn't look as if that was going to happen. Oh, the orgasm would happen, but instead of being a gentle, loving thing, it was going to be hard and explosive. Patrick could already feel the stirrings of it moving over him.

He stood upright abruptly, holding onto Julie's hips and pulling her into him, angling her so that her hips were tilted upward to take his cock but her back was still on the table. He slammed into her once, then twice.

"Oh yeah, that feels amazing," Julie moaned, grabbing hold of both sides of the small square table with her hands, bracing herself for his thrusts. "Again, do it again, Patrick."

Patrick shifted one hand so his thumb could press against her clit as he pistoned in and out of her small body. He felt her body grip him harder as he drew back, as if she didn't want to let him go. Then he pushed through her quaking muscles back inside to heaven.

He'd had plenty of sex in his life, but Patrick didn't remember any of those encounters being like this. He flicked his thumb faster over Julie's bundle of nerves. "Come on, sweetheart. I wanna see you explode for me. That's it…right there. Oh yeah."

Patrick watched as Julie's back arched off the table, her mouth opened with only a groan escaping, and she jerked in his grasp. She humped her hips against his own as her orgasm washed over her. He felt her muscles fluttering around his cock and the rush of wetness against his balls as she thrashed in ecstasy.

He waited until she pulled away from his thumb, which he'd kept on her clit, prolonging her orgasm. She'd reached the point where it wasn't pleasurable anymore because of how sensitive her clit was. Patrick put both hands on the table and leaned over her.

"That was beautiful. Abso-fucking-lutely beautiful. Hold on to me. Watch as you take me over too."

Patrick felt Julie's hands slide under his shirt and latch onto his hips.

"I'm gonna take you hard. You ready?"

"Oh yeah. Do it. Fuck me, Patrick."

It was if her words flicked a switch inside of him. He couldn't hold back any longer. He looked down and watched as his cock disappeared into her body, then reappeared, then disappeared again as he sank into her warm body. "I'm coming...oh God, Julie!" Patrick thrust two more times, hard, and held himself deep as he came. The world narrowed to Julie and the feel of her under him as he emptied himself deep inside her.

He came back to himself and opened his eyes, not realizing at some point he'd closed them, to see Julie smiling up at him. She was running her hands over his sides soothingly, patiently waiting for him to come back to his senses.

"Holy shit," Patrick whispered reverently.

"I think that's my line," Julie teased.

Patrick leaned over and grabbed Julie with one hand around her waist and the other behind her back. She squealed in surprise as he once again easily picked her up.

"Hold on tight."

She did as he asked and Patrick shuffled through his house to his bedroom, trying not to trip over his pants, which had slid down to his knees. He heard Julie giggle as he almost tripped. He made it to his bedroom and stopped by the bed.

"Drop your legs, sweetheart."

"I don't want to lose you."

Her words made his heart swell. "Unfortunately, as much as I might want it, I can't spend the rest of our lives with my cock inside you, as good as it feels. I have to deal with this condom and we have to get these fucking clothes off. I promise, Julie, as soon as I'm up and ready again, I'll be right back in there. But in the meantime, I have time to learn every inch of your body, to taste you, to lick you, to make you mine."

"I *am* yours, Patrick. As long as you want me."

"That's good then, because I want you forever."

She eased her grip on his hips and he pulled back, allowing her to drop her legs to the ground. "Strip."

Within minutes, he'd taken care of the used condom, removed his clothes, and joined Julie in his bed, both of them naked.

"I'm sorry our first time wasn't romantic," Patrick apologized ruefully. "I meant for it to be, but as I told you out there—"

Julie cut off his words. "It was perfect. I rather like that you wanted me so badly you couldn't wait."

"It's a good thing. I have a feeling it's going to be that way a lot."

Julie only grinned up at him and said, "Now...about those other things you said you were going to do...you better get to work...five o'clock is going to come awfully early in the morning."

Patrick mock saluted her and scooted down her body, easing her legs apart and settling in. "Yes, ma'am. Anything you say."

* * *

If you haven't read *Protecting Fiona,* where Julie was first introduced, you should do that. :) You'll have a much better appreciation for what Julie had to apologize for.

JOIN my Newsletter and find out about sales, free books, contests and new releases before anyone else!! Click HERE

Want to know when my books go on sale? Follow me on Bookbub HERE!

Would you like Susan's Book Protecting Caroline for FREE? Click HERE

Also by Susan Stoker

SEAL of Protection Series

Protecting Caroline
Protecting Alabama
Protecting Fiona
Marrying Caroline (novella)
Protecting Summer
Protecting Cheyenne
Protecting Jessyka
Protecting Julie (novella)
Protecting Melody
Protecting the Future
Protecting Kiera (novella)
Protecting Dakota

SEAL of Protection: Legacy Series

Securing Caite (Jan 2019)
Securing Sidney (May 2019)
Securing Piper (Sept 2019)
Securing Zoey (TBA)
Securing Avery (TBA)
Securing Kalee (TBA)

Delta Force Heroes Series

Rescuing Rayne
Rescuing Aimee (novella)
Rescuing Emily
Rescuing Harley
Marrying Emily
Rescuing Kassie
Rescuing Bryn
Rescuing Casey
Rescuing Sadie

Rescuing Wendy
Rescuing Mary (Oct 2018)
Rescuing Macie (April 2019

Badge of Honor: Texas Heroes Series

Justice for Mackenzie
Justice for Mickie
Justice for Corrie
Justice for Laine (novella)
Shelter for Elizabeth
Justice for Boone
Shelter for Adeline
Shelter for Sophie
Justice for Erin
Justice for Milena
Shelter for Blythe
Justice for Hope (Sept 2018)
Shelter for Quinn (Feb 2019)
Shelter for Koren (June 2019)
Shelter for Penelope (Oct 2019)

Ace Security Series

Claiming Grace
Claiming Alexis
Claiming Bailey
Claiming Felicity

Mountain Mercenaries Series

Defending Allye
Defending Chloe (Dec 2018)
Defending Morgan (Mar 2019)
Defending Harlow (July 2019)
Defending Everly (TBA)
Defending Zara (TBA)
Defending Raven (TBA)

Stand Alone

The Guardian Mist

Nature's Rift

A Princess for Cale

A Moment in Time- A Collection of Short Stories

Lambert's Lady

Special Operations Fan Fiction

http://www.AcesPress.com

Beyond Reality Series

Outback Hearts

Flaming Hearts

Frozen Hearts

Writing as Annie George:

Stepbrother Virgin (erotic novella)

ABOUT THE AUTHOR

New York Times, USA Today and *Wall Street Journal* Bestselling Author Susan Stoker has a heart as big as the state of Tennessee where she lives, but this all American girl has also spent the last fourteen years living in Missouri, California, Colorado, Indiana, and Texas. She's married to a retired Army military man who now gets to follow *her* around the country.

She debuted her first series in 2014 and quickly followed that up with the SEAL of Protection Series, which solidified her love of writing and creating stories readers can get lost in.

If you enjoyed this book, or any book, please consider leaving a review. It's appreciated by authors more than you'll know.

www.stokeraces.com
susan@stokeraces.com

facebook.com/authorsusanstoker
twitter.com/Susan_Stoker
instagram.com/authorsusanstoker
goodreads.com/SusanStoker
bookbub.com/authors/susan-stoker
amazon.com/author/susanstoker

Made in the USA
Columbia, SC
16 January 2021

31124036R00348